PENGUIN BOOKS

THE FIRST RUMPOLE OMNIBUS

John Mortimer is a playwright, novelist and former practising barrister. During the war he worked with the Crown Film Unit and published a number of novels before turning to the theatre with such plays as *The Dock Brief*, *The Wrong Side of the Park* and *A Voyage Round My Father*. He has written many film scripts, radio and television plays including six plays on the life of Shakespeare, the Rumpole plays, which won him the British Academy Writer of the Year Award, and the adaptation of Evelyn Waugh's *Brideshead Revisited*. His translations of Feydeau have been performed at the National Theatre and are published in Penguin as *Three Boulevard Farces*.

Penguin publish his collections of stories: *Rumpole of the Bailey*, *The Trials of Rumpole*, *Rumpole's Return*, *Rumpole for the Defence*, *Rumpole and the Golden Thread*, *Rumpole's Last Case*, *Rumpole and the Age of Miracles*, *Rumpole à la Carte* and *Rumpole on Trial*, as well as *The First Rumpole Omnibus*, *The Second Rumpole Omnibus* and *The Best of Rumpole*. Penguin also publish two volumes of John Mortimer's plays, his acclaimed autobiography *Clinging to the Wreckage*, which won the *Yorkshire Post* Book of the Year Award, *In Character* and *Character Parts*, which contain interviews with some of the most famous men and women of our time, and his bestselling novels, *Charade*, *Like Men Betrayed*, *The Narrowing Stream*, *Paradise Postponed*, its sequel *Titmuss Regained*, which together have been published as *The Rapstone Chronicles*, *Summer's Lease* and *Dunster*. *Paradise Postponed*, *Summer's Lease*, *Titmuss Regained* and all the Rumpole books have been made into successful television series. John Mortimer lives with his wife and their two daughters in what was once his father's house in the Chilterns.

John Mortimer

THE FIRST

Rumpole

OMNIBUS

Rumpole of the Bailey

The Trials of Rumpole

Rumpole's Return

PENGUIN BOOKS

PENGUIN BOOKS

Published by the Penguin Group
Penguin Books Ltd, 27 Wrights Lane, London W8 5TZ, England
Penguin Books USA Inc., 375 Hudson Street, New York, New York 10014, USA
Penguin Books Australia Ltd, Ringwood, Victoria, Australia
Penguin Books Canada Ltd, 10 Alcorn Avenue, Toronto, Ontario, Canada M4V 3B2
Penguin Books (NZ) Ltd, 182–190 Wairau Road, Auckland 10, New Zealand

Penguin Books Ltd, Registered Offices: Harmondsworth, Middlesex, England

Rumpole of the Bailey first published 1978
Copyright © Advanpress Ltd, 1978

The Trials of Rumpole first published 1979
Copyright © Advanpress Ltd, 1979

Rumpole's Return first published 1980
Copyright © Advanpress Ltd, 1980

This collection first published 1983
20

Printed in England by Clays Ltd, St Ives plc
Set in Sabon

Contents

Rumpole
of the Bailey

For Irene Shubik

Rumpole and the Younger Generation

I, Horace Rumpole, barrister at law, 68 next birthday, Old
Bailey Hack, husband to Mrs Hilda Rumpole (known to me
only as She Who Must Be Obeyed) and father to Nicholas Rumpole (lecturer in social studies at the University of Baltimore, I
have always been extremely proud of Nick); I, who have a mind
full of old murders, legal anecdotes and memorable fragments
of the *Oxford Book of English Verse* (Sir Arthur Quiller-Couch's
edition) together with a dependable knowledge of bloodstains,
blood groups, fingerprints, and forgery by typewriter; I, who
am now the oldest member of my Chambers, take up my pen at
this advanced age during a lull in business (there's not much
crime about, all the best villains seem to be off on holiday in the
Costa Brava), in order to write my reconstructions of some of
my recent triumphs (including a number of recent disasters) in
the Courts of Law, hoping thereby to turn a bob or two which
won't be immediately grabbed by the taxman, or my clerk
Henry, or by She Who Must Be Obeyed, and perhaps give some
sort of entertainment to those who, like myself, have found in
British justice a life-long subject of harmless fun.

When I first considered putting pen to paper in this matter of
my life, I thought I must begin with the great cases of my
comparative youth, the 'Penge Bungalow Murder', where I
gained an acquittal alone and without a leader, or the 'Great
Brighton Benefit Club Forgery', which I contrived to win by
reason of my exhaustive study of typewriters. In these cases I
was, for a brief moment, in the Public Eye, or at least my name
seemed almost a permanent feature of the *News of the World*,
but when I come to look back on that period of my life at the
Bar it all seems to have happened to another Rumpole, an eager

young barrister whom I can scarcely recognize and whom I am not at all sure I would like, at least not enough to spend a whole book with him.

I am not a public figure now, so much has to be admitted; but some of the cases I shall describe, the wretched business of the Honourable Member, for instance, or the charge of murder brought against the youngest, and barmiest, of the appalling Delgardo brothers, did put me back on the front page of the *News of the World* (and even got me a few inches in *The Times*). But I suppose I have become pretty well known, if not something of a legend, round the Old Bailey, in Pommeroy's Wine Bar in Fleet Street, in the robing room at London Sessions and in the cells at Brixton Prison. They know me there for never pleading guilty, for chain-smoking small cigars, and for quoting Wordsworth when they least expect it. Such notoriety will not long survive my not-to-be-delayed trip to Golders Green Crematorium. Barristers' speeches vanish quicker than Chinese dinners, and even the greatest victory in Court rarely survives longer than the next Sunday's papers.

To understand the full effect on my family life, however, of that case which I have called 'Rumpole and the Younger Generation', it is necessary to know a little of my past and the long years that led up to my successful defence of Jim Timson, the 16-year-old sprig, the young hopeful, and apple of the eye of the Timsons, a huge and industrious family of South London villains. As this case was, by and large, a family matter, it is important that you should understand my family.

My father, the Reverend Wilfred Rumpole, was a Church of England clergyman who, in early middle age, came reluctantly to the conclusion that he no longer believed any one of the 39 Articles. As he was not fitted by character or training for any other profession, however, he had to soldier on in his living in Croydon and by a good deal of scraping and saving he was able to send me as a boarder to a minor public school on the Norfolk coast. I later went to Keble College, Oxford, where I achieved a dubious third in law – you will discover during the course of these memoirs that, although I only feel truly alive and happy in

Law Courts, I have a singular distaste for the law. My father's example, and the number of theological students I met at Keble, gave me an early mistrust of clergymen whom I have always found to be most unsatisfactory witnesses. If you call a clergyman in mitigation, the old darling can be guaranteed to add at least a year to the sentence.

When I first went to the Bar, I entered the Chambers of C. H. Wystan. Wystan had a moderate practice, acquired rather by industry than talent, and a strong disinclination to look at the photographs in murder cases, being particularly squeamish on the fascinating subject of blood. He also had a daughter, Hilda Wystan as was, now Mrs Hilda Rumpole and She Who Must Be Obeyed. I was ambitious in those days. I did my best to cultivate Wystan's clerk Albert, and I started to get a good deal of criminal work. I did what was expected of me and spent happy hours round the Bailey and Sessions and my fame grew in criminal circles; at the end of the day I would take Albert for a drink in Pommeroy's Wine Bar. We got on extremely well and he would always recommend 'his Mr Rumpole' if a solicitor rang up with a particularly tricky indecent assault or a nasty case of receiving stolen property.

There is no point in writing your memoirs unless you are prepared to be completely candid, and I must confess that, in the course of a long life, I have been in love on several occasions. I am sure that I loved Miss Porter, the shy and nervous, but at times liberated daughter of Septimus Porter, my Oxford tutor in Roman Law. In fact we were engaged to be married, but the engagement had to be broken off because of Miss Porter's early death. I often think about her, and of the different course my home life might have taken, for Miss Porter was in no way a girl born to command, or expect, implicit obedience. During my service with the ground staff of the R.A.F. I undoubtedly became helplessly smitten with the charms of an extremely warmhearted and gallant officer in the W.A.A.F.s by the name of Miss Bobby O'Keefe, but I was no match for the wings of a Pilot Officer, as appeared on the chest of a certain Sam 'Three-Fingers' Dogherty. During my conduct of a case, which I shall describe in a later chapter which I have called 'Rumpole and the Alternative

Society', I once again felt a hopeless and almost feverish stirring of passion for a young woman who was determined to talk her way into Holloway Prison. My relationship with Hilda Wystan was rather different.

To begin with, she seemed part of life in Chambers. She was always interested in the law and ambitious, first for her widowed father, and then, when he proved himself unlikely Lord Chancellor material, for me. She often dropped in for tea on her way home from shopping, and Wystan used to invite me in for a cup. One year I was detailed off to be her partner at an Inns of Court ball. There it became clear to me that I was expected to marry Hilda; it seemed a step in my career like getting a brief in the Court of Appeal, or doing a murder. When she proposed to me, as she did over a glass of claret cup after an energetic waltz, Hilda made it clear that, when old Wystan finally retired, she expected to see me Head of Chambers. I, who have never felt at a loss for a word in Court, found absolutely nothing to say. In that silence the matter was concluded.

So now you must picture Hilda and me twenty-five years later, with a son at that same east coast public school which I just managed to afford from the fruits of crime, in our matrimonial home at 25B Froxbury Court, Gloucester Road. (A mansion flat is a misleading description of that cavernous and underheated area which Hilda devotes so much of her energy to keeping shipshape, not to say Bristol fashion.) We were having breakfast, and, between bites of toast, I was reading my brief for that day, an Old Bailey trial of the 16-year-old Jim Timson charged with robbery with violence, he having allegedly taken part in a wage snatch on a couple of elderly butchers: an escapade planned in the playground of the local Comprehensive. As so often happens, the poet Wordsworth, that old sheep of the Lake District, sprang immediately to mind, and I gave tongue to his lines, well knowing that they must only serve to irritate She Who Must Be Obeyed.

'*Trailing clouds of glory do we come   From God, who is our home;   Heaven lies about us in our infancy!*'

I looked at Hilda. She was impassively demolishing a boiled

egg. I also noticed that she was wearing a hat, as if prepared to
set out upon some expedition. I decided to give her a little more
Wordsworth, prompted by my reading the story of the boy
Timson.

'*Shades of the prison house begin to close   Upon the growing
boy.*'

Hilda spoke at last.

'Rumpole, you're not talking about your son, I hope. You're
never referring to Nick . . .'

'*Shades of the prison house begin to close?* Not round our
son, of course. Not round Nick. Shades of the public school
have grown round him, the thousand-quid-a-year remand
home.'

Hilda always thought it indelicate to refer to the subject of
school fees, as if being at Mulstead were a kind of unsolicited
honour for Nick. She became increasingly business-like.

'He's breaking up this morning.'

'Shades of the prison house begin to open up for the holidays.'

'Nick has to be met at 11.15 at Liverpool Street and given
lunch. When he went back to school you promised him a show.
You haven't forgotten?'

Hilda was clearing away the plates rapidly. To tell the truth I
had forgotten the date of Nick's holidays; but I let her assume I
had a long-planned treat laid on for him.

'Of course I haven't forgotten. The only show I can offer him
is a robbery with violence in Number 2 Court at the Old Bailey.
I wish I could lay on a murder. Nick's always so enjoyed my
murders.'

It was true. On one distant half term Nick had sat in on the
'Peckham Billiard Hall Stabbing', and enjoyed it a great deal
more than *Treasure Island*.

'I must fly! Daddy gets so crotchety if anyone's late. And he
does love his visits.'

Hilda removed my half-empty coffee cup.

'Our father which art in Horsham. Give my respects to the
old sweetheart.'

It had also slipped my mind that old C. H. Wystan was laid

up with a dicky ticker in Horsham General Hospital. The hat was, no doubt, a clue I should have followed. Hilda usually goes shopping in a headscarf. By now she was at the door, and looking disapproving.

' "Old sweetheart" is hardly how you used to talk of the Head of your Chambers.'

'Somehow I can never remember to call the Head of my Chambers "Daddy".'

The door was open. Hilda was making a slow and effective exit.

'Tell Nick I'll be back in good time to get his supper.'

'Your wish is my command!' I muttered in my best imitation of a slave out of Chou Chin Chow. She chose to ignore it.

'And try not to leave the kitchen looking as though it's been hit by a bomb.'

'I hear, oh Master of the Blue Horizons.' I said this with a little more confidence, as she had by now started off on her errand of mercy, and I added, for good measure, 'She Who Must Be Obeyed'.

I had finished my breakfast, and was already thinking how much easier life with the Old Bailey judge was than marriage.

Soon after I finished my breakfast with Hilda, and made plans to meet my son at the start of his holidays from school, Fred Timson, star of a dozen Court appearances, was seeing *his* son in the cells under the Old Bailey as the result of a specially arranged visit. I know he brought the boy his best jacket, which his mother had taken specially to the cleaners, and insisted on his putting on a tie. I imagine he told him that they had the best 'brief' in the business to defend him, Mr Rumpole having always done wonders for the Timson family. I know that Fred told young Jim to stand up straight in the witness box and remember to call the judge 'my Lord' and not show his ignorance by coming out with any gaffe such as 'Your Honour', or 'Sir'. The world, that day, was full of fathers showing appropriate and paternal concern.

The robbery with which Jim Timson was charged was an exceedingly simple one. At about 7 p.m. one Friday evening, the date being 16 September, the two elder Brixton butchers, Mr Cadwallader and Mr Lewis Stein, closed their shop in Bombay Road and walked with their week's takings round the corner to a narrow alley-way known as Green's Passage, where their grey Austin van was parked. When they got to the van they found that the front tyres had been deflated. They stooped to inspect the wheels and, as they did so they were attacked by a number of boys, some armed with knives and one flourishing a cricket stump. Luckily, neither of the butchers was hurt, but the attaché case containing their money was snatched.

Chief Inspector 'Persil' White, the old darling in whose territory this outrage had been committed, arrested Jim Timson. All the other boys got clean away, but no doubt because he came from a family well known, indeed almost embarrassingly familiar, to the Chief Inspector, and because of certain rumours in the school playground, he was charged and put on an identity parade. The butchers totally failed to identify him; but, when he was in the Remand Centre, young Jim, according to the evidence, had boasted to another boy of having 'done the butchers'.

As I thought about this case on my way to the Temple that morning, it occurred to me that Jim Timson was a year younger than my son, but that he had got a step further than Nick in following his father's profession. I had always hoped Nick would go into the law, and, as I say, he seemed to thoroughly enjoy my murders.

In the clerk's room in Chambers Albert was handing out the work for the day: rather as a trainer sends his string of horses out on the gallops. I looked round the familiar faces, my friend George Frobisher, who is an old sweetheart but an absolutely hopeless advocate (he can't ask for costs without writing down what he's going to say), was being fobbed off with a nuisance at Kingston County Court. Young Erskine-Brown, who wears striped shirts and what I believe are known as 'Chelsea Boots', was turning up his well-bred nose at an indecent assault at Lambeth (a job I'd have bought Albert a double claret in Pommeroy's for at his age) and saying he would prefer a little civil work, adding that he was so sick to death of crime.

I have very little patience with Erskine-Brown.

'A person who is tired of crime,' I told him quite candidly, 'is tired of life.'

'Your Dangerous and Careless at Clerkenwell is on the mantelpiece, Mr Hoskins,' Albert said.

Hoskins is a gloomy fellow with four daughters; he's always lurking about our clerk's room looking for cheques. As I've told him often enough crime doesn't pay, or at any rate not for a very long time.

When a young man called MacLay had asked in vain for a brief I invited him to take a note for me down at the Old Bailey. At least he'd get a wig on and not spend a miserable day unemployed in Chambers. Our oldest member, Uncle Tom (very few of us remember that his name is T. C. Rowley) also asked Albert if there were any briefs for him, not in the least expecting to find one. To my certain knowledge, Uncle Tom hasn't appeared in Court for fifteen years, when he managed to lose an undefended divorce case, but, as he lives with a widowed sister, a lady of such reputed ferocity that she makes She Who Must Be Obeyed sound like Mrs Tiggywinkle, he spends most of his time in Chambers. He looked remarkably well for 78.

'You aren't actually *expecting* a brief, Uncle Tom, are you?' Erskine-Brown asked. I can't like Erskine-Brown.

'Time was,' Uncle Tom started one of his reminiscences of life in our Chambers. 'Time was when I had more briefs in my corner of the mantelpiece, Erskine-Brown, than you've seen in the whole of your short career at the Bar. Now,' he was opening a brown envelope, 'I only get invitations to insure my life. It's a little late for that.'

Albert told me that the robbery was not before 11.30 before Mr Justice Everglade in Number 1 Court. He also told me who was prosecuting, none other than the tall, elegant figure with the silk handkerchief and gold wristwatch, leaning against the mantelpiece and negligently reading a large cheque from the Director of Public Prosecutions, Guthrie Featherstone, M.P. He removed the silk handkerchief, dabbed the end of his nose and his small moustache and asked in that voice which comes over so charmingly, saying nothing much about any important topic of the day in 'World at One',

'Agin me Rumpole? Are you agin me?' He covered a slight yawn with the handkerchief before returning it to his breast-pocket. 'Just come from an all-night sitting down at the House. I don't suppose your robbery'll be much of a worry.'

'Only, possibly, to young Jim Timson,' I told him, and then gave Albert his orders for the day. 'Mrs Rumpole's gone down to see her father in Horsham.'

'How is Wystan? No better, is he?' Uncle Tom sounded as gently pleased as all old men do when they hear news of illness in others.

'Much the same, Uncle Tom, thank you. And Young Nick. My son . . .'

'Master Nick?' Albert had always been fond of Nick, and looked forward to putting him through his paces when the time came for him to join our stable in Chambers.

'He's breaking up today. So he'll need meeting at Liverpool Street. Then he can watch a bit of the robbery.'

'We're going to have your son in the audience? I'd better be brilliant.' Guthrie Featherstone now moved from the fireplace.

'You needn't bother, old darling. It's his Dad he comes to see.'

'Oh, *touché*, Rumpole! *Distinctement touché!*'

Featherstone talks like that. Then he invited me to walk down to the Bailey with him. Apparently he was still capable of movement and didn't need a stretcher, even after a sleepless night with the Gas Mains Enabling Bill, or whatever it was.

We walked together down Fleet Street and into Ludgate Circus, Featherstone wearing his overcoat with the velvet collar and little round bowler hat, I puffing a small cigar and with my old mac flapping in the wind; I discovered that the gentleman beside me was quietly quizzing me about my career at the Bar.

'You've been at this game a long while, Rumpole,' Feather-stone announced. I didn't disagree with him, and then he went on.

'You never thought of taking silk?'

'Rumpole, Q.C.?' I almost burst out laughing. 'Not on your

Nelly. Rumpole "Queer Customer". That's what they'd be bound to call me.'

'I'm sure you could, with your seniority.' I had no idea then, of exactly what this Featherstone was after. I gave him my view of Q.C.s in general.

'Perhaps, if I played golf with the right judges, or put up for Parliament, they might make me an artificial silk, or, at any rate, a nylon.' It was at that point I realized I had put up a bit of a black. 'Sorry. I forgot. You *did* put up for Parliament.'

'Yes. You never thought of Rumpole, Q.C.?' Featherstone had apparently taken no offence.

'Never,' I told him. 'I have the honour to be an Old Bailey Hack! That's quite enough for me.'

At which point we turned up into Newgate Street and there it was in all its glory, touched by a hint of early spring sunshine, the Old Bailey, a stately Law Court, decreed by the City Fathers, an Edwardian palace, with an extensive modern extension to deal with the increase in human fallibility. There was the Dome and the Blindfold Lady. Well, it's much better she doesn't see *all* that's going on. That, in fact, was our English version of the Palais de Justice, complete with murals, marble statues and underground accommodation for some of the choicest villains in London.

Terrible things go on down the Bailey – horrifying things. Why is it I never go in the revolving door without a thrill of pleasure, a slight tremble of excitement? Why does it seem a much *jollier* place than my flat in Gloucester Road under the strict rule of She Who Must Be Obeyed? These are questions which may only be partly answered in the course of these memoirs.

At the time when I was waving a cheerful umbrella at Harry, the policeman in the revolving door of the Old Bailey extension, my wife Hilda was at her Daddy's bedside at the Horsham General arranging her dozen early daffs and gently probing, so she told me that evening, on the subject of his future, and mine.

'I'll have to give up, you know. I can't go on forever. Crocked up, I'm afraid,' said Wystan.

'Nonsense, Daddy. You'll go on for years.'

I imagine Hilda did her best to sound bracing, whilst putting the daffs firmly in their place.

'No, Hilda. No. They'll have to start looking for another Head of Chambers.'

This gave Hilda her opportunity. 'Rumpole's the senior man. Apart from Uncle Tom and he doesn't really practise now-adays.'

'Your husband the senior man.' Wystan looked back on a singularly uneventful life. 'How time flies! I recall when he was the junior man. My pupil.'

'You said he was the best youngster on bloodstains you'd ever known.' Hilda was doing her best for me.

'Rumpole! Yes, your husband was pretty good on bloodstains. Shaky, though, on the law of landlord and tenant. What sort of practice has Rumpole now?'

'I believe . . . Today it's the Old Bailey.' Hilda was plumping pillows, doing her best to sound casual. And her father showed no particular enthusiasm for my place of work.

'It's always the Old Bailey, isn't it?'

'Most of the time. Yes. I suppose so.'

'Not a frightfully good *address*, the Old Bailey. Not exactly the S.W.1 of the legal profession.'

Sensing that Daddy would have thought better of me if I'd been in the Court of Appeal or the Chancery Division, Hilda told me she thought of a master stroke.

'Oh, Rumpole only went down to the Bailey because it's a family he knows. It seems they've got a young boy in trouble.'

This appealed to Daddy, he gave one of his bleak smiles which amount to no more than a brief withdrawal of lips from the dentures.

'Son gone wrong?' he said. 'Very sad that. Especially if he comes of a really good family.'

That really good family, the Timsons, was out in force and waiting outside Number 1 Court by the time I had got on the fancy dress, yellowing horse-hair wig, gown become more than a trifle tattered over the years, and bands round the neck that

Albert ought to have sent to the laundry after last week's death by dangerous driving. As I looked at the Timson clan assembled, I thought the best thing about them was the amount of work of a criminal nature they had brought into Chambers. They were all dressed for the occasion, the men in dark blazers, suede shoes and grey flannels; the ladies in tight-fitting suits, high heels and elaborately piled hairdos. I had never seen so many ex-clients together at one time.

'Mr Rumpole.'

'Ah, Bernard! You're instructing me.'

Mr Bernard, the solicitor, was a thirtyish, perpetually smiling man in a pinstriped suit. He regarded criminals with something of the naïve fervour with which young girls think of popular entertainers. Had I known the expression at the time, I would have called him a grafters' 'groupie'.

'I'm always your instructing solicitor in a Timson case, Mr Rumpole.' Mr Bernard beamed and Fred Timson, a kindly man and most innocent robber, stepped out of the ranks to do the honours.

'Nothing but the best for the Timsons, best solicitor and best barrister going. You know my wife Vi?'

Young Jim's mother seemed full of confidence. As I took her hand, I remembered I had got Vi off on a handling charge after the Croydon bank raid. Well, there was really no evidence.

'Uncle Cyril.' Fred introduced the plumpish uncle with the small moustache whom I was sure I remembered. What was *his* last outing exactly? Carrying house-breaking instruments by night?

'Uncle Dennis. You remember Den, surely, Mr Rumpole?'

I did. Den's last little matter was an alleged conspiracy to forge log books.

'And Den's Doris.'

Aunty Doris came at me in a blur of henna-ed hair and darkish perfume. What was Doris's last indiscretion? Could it have been receiving a vast quantity of stolen scampi? Acquitted by a majority, at least I was sure of that.

'And yours truly. Frederick Timson. The boy's father.'

Regrettable, but we had a slip-up with Fred's last spot of

bother. I was away with flu, George Frobisher took it over and he got three years. He must've only just got out.

'So, Mr Rumpole. You know the whole family.'

A family to breed from, the Timsons. Must almost keep the Old Bailey going single-handed.

'You're going to do your best for our young Jim, I'm sure, Mr Rumpole.'

I didn't find the simple faith of the Timsons that I could secure acquittals in the most unlikely circumstances especially encouraging. But then Jim's mother said something which I was to long remember.

'He's a good boy. He was ever so good to me while Dad was away.'

So that was Jimbo's life. Head of the family at fourteen, when Dad was off on one of his regular visits to Her Majesty.

'It's young Jim's first appearance, like. At the Old Bailey.' Fred couldn't conceal a note of pride. It was Jim boy's Bar Mitzvah, his first Communion.

So we chatted a little about how all the other boys got clean away, which I told them was a bit of luck as none of them would go into the witness box and implicate Jim, and Bernard pointed out that the identification by the butchers was pretty hopeless. Well, what did he expect? Would you have a photographic impression of the young hopeful who struck you a smart blow on the back of the head with a cricket stump? We talked with that curious suppressed excitement there always is before a trial, however disastrous the outcome may be, and I told them the only thing we had to worry about, as if that were not enough, was Jim's confession to the boy in the Remand Centre, a youth who rejoiced in the name of Peanuts Molloy.

'Peanuts Molloy! Little grass.' Fred Timson spoke with a deep contempt.

'Old "Persil" White fitted him up with that one, didn't he?' Uncle Cyril said it as if it were the most natural thing in the world, and only to be expected.

'Chief Detective Inspector White,' Bernard explained.

'Why should the Chief Inspector want to fit up your Jimbo?'

It was a question to which I should have known what their answer would be.

'Because he's a Timson, that's why!' said Fred.

'Because he's the apple of our eye, like,' Uncle Den told me, and the boy's mother added:

'Being as he's the baby of the family.'

'Old Persil'd fit up his mother if it'd get him a smile from his Super.' As Fred said this the Chief Inspector himself, grey-haired and avuncular, walked by in plain clothes, with a plain-clothes sergeant.

'Morning, Chief Inspector,' Fred carried on without drawing breath.

'Morning, Fred. Morning, Mrs Timson.' The Chief Inspector greeted the family with casual politeness, after all they were part of his daily work, and Vi sniffed back a 'Good morning, Chief Inspector.'

'Mr Timson. We'll shift our ground. Remove good friends.'

Like Hamlet, after seeing the ghost, I thought it was better to continue our conference in private. So we went and sat round a table in the canteen, and, when we had sorted out who took how many lumps, and which of them could do with a choc roll or a cheese sandwich, the family gave me the lowdown on the chief prosecution witness.

'The Chief Inspector put that little grass Peanuts Molloy into Jim's painting class at the Remand Centre.' Fred had no doubt about it.

'Jim apparently poured out his soul to Peanuts.' The evidence sounded, to my old ears, completely convincing, and Bernard read us a snatch from his file.

'We planned to do the old blokes from the butcher's and grab the wages . . .'

'That,' I reminded the assembled company, 'is what Peanuts will say Jim told him.'

'You think I'd bring Jim up to talk in the Nick like that? The Timsons ain't stupid!' Fred was outraged, and Vi, pursing her lips in a sour gesture of wounded respectability added, 'His Dad always told him. Never say a word to anyone you're banged up with – bound to be a grass.'

One by one, Aunty Doris, Uncle Den and Uncle Cyril added their support.

'That's right. Fred's always brought the boy up proper. Like the way he should be. He'd never speak about the crime, not to anyone he was banged up with.'

'Specially not to one of the Molloys!'

'The Molloys!' Vi spoke for the Timsons, and with deep hatred. 'Noted grasses. That family always has been.'

'The Molloys is beyond the pale. Well known for it.' Aunty Doris nodded her henna-ed topknot wisely.

'Peanuts's Grandad shopped my old father in the "Streatham Co-op Robbery". Pre-war, that was.'

I had a vague memory then of what Fred Timson was talking about. The Streatham Co-op case, one of my better briefs – a long case with not much honour shown among thieves, as far as I could remember.

'Then you can understand, Mr Rumpole. No Timson would ever speak to a Molloy.'

'So you're sure Jimbo never said anything to Peanuts?' I was wondering exactly how I could explain the deep, but not particularly creditable, origins of this family hostility to the jury.

'I give you my word, Mr Rumpole. Ain't that enough for you? No Timson would ever speak to a Molloy. Not under any circumstances.'

There were not many matters on which I would take Fred Timson's word, but the history of the Streatham Co-op case came back to me, and this was one of them.

It's part of the life of an Old Bailey Hack to spend a good deal of his time down in the cells, in the basement area, where they keep the old door of Newgate, kicked and scarred, through which generations of villains were sent to the treadmill, the gallows or the whip. You pass this venerable door and ring a bell, you're let in and your name's taken by one of the warders who bring the prisoners from Brixton. There's a perpetual smell of cooking and the warders are snatching odd snacks of six inches of cheese butties and a gallon of tea. Lunch is being got ready, and the cells under the Bailey have a high reputation as

one of the best caffs in London. By the door the screws have
their pinups and comic cartoons of judges. You are taken to a
waiting-room, three steel chairs and a table, and you meet the
client. Perhaps he is a novice, making his first appearance, like
Jim Timson. Perhaps he's an old hand asking anxiously which
judge he's got, knowing their form as accurately as a betting-
shop proprietor. Whoever he is, the client will be nervously
excited, keyed up for his great day, full of absurd hope.

The worst part of a barrister's life at the Old Bailey is going
back to the cells after a guilty verdict to say 'good-bye'. There's
no purpose in it, but, as a point of honour, it has to be done.
Even then the barrister probably gets the best reaction, and
almost never any blame. The client is stunned, knocked out by
his sentence. Only in a couple of weeks' time, when the reality
of being banged up with the sour smell of stone walls and his
own chamber pot for company becomes apparent, does the
convict start to weep. He is then drugged with sedatives, and
Agatha Christies from the prison library.

When I saw the youngest Timson before his trial that morning,
I couldn't help noticing how much smaller, and how much more
experienced, he looked than my Nick. In his clean sports jacket
and carefully knotted tie he was well dressed for the dock, and
he showed all the carefully suppressed excitement of a young
lad about to step into the limelight of Number 1 with an old
judge, twelve jurors and a mixed bag of lawyers waiting to give
him their undivided attention.

'Me speak to Peanuts? No Timson don't ever speak to a
Molloy. It's a point of honour, like,' Jim added his voice to the
family chorus.

'Since the raid on the Streatham Co-op. Your grandfather?'

'Dad told you about that, did he?'

'Yes. Dad told me.'

'Well, Dad wouldn't let me speak to no Molloy. He wouldn't
put up with it, like.'

I stood up, grinding out the stub end of my small cigar in the
old Oxo tin thoughtfully provided by H.M.'s government. It
was, I thought, about time I called the meeting to order.

'So Jim,' I asked him, 'what's the defence?'

Little Jim knitted his brows and came out with his contribution. 'Well. I didn't do it.'

'That's an interesting defence. Somewhat novel – so far as the Timsons are concerned.'

'I've got my alibi, ain't I?'

Jim looked at me accusingly, as at an insensitive visitor to a garden who has failed to notice the remarkable display of gladioli.

'Oh, yes. Your alibi.' I'm afraid I didn't sound overwhelmed with enthusiasm.

'Dad reckoned it was pretty good.'

Mr Bernard had his invaluable file open and was reading from that less-than-inspiring document, our Notice of Alibi.

'Straight from school on that Friday September 2nd, I went up to tea at my Aunt Doris's and arrived there at exactly 5.30. At 6 p.m. my Uncle Den came home from work accompanied by my Uncle Cyril. At 7 p.m. when this alleged crime was taking place I was sat round the television with my Aunty and two Uncles. I well remember we was watching "The Newcomers".'

All very neat and workmanlike. Well, that was it. The family gave young Jim an alibi, clubbed together for it, like a new bicycle. However, I had to disappoint Mr Bernard about the bright shining alibi and we went through the swing doors on our way into Court.

'We can't use that alibi.'

'We can't?' Mr Bernard looked wounded, as if I'd just insulted his favourite child.

'Think about it Bernard. Don't be blinded by the glamour of the criminal classes. Call the Uncles and the Aunties? Let them all be cross-examined about their records? The jury'll realize our Jimbo comes from a family of villains who keep a cupboard full of alibis for all occasions.'

Mr Bernard was forced to agree, but I went into my old place in Court (nearest to the jury, furthest from the witness box) thinking that the devilish thing about that impossible alibi was that it might even be true.

So there I was, sitting in my favourite seat in Court, down in the firing line, and there was Jim boy, undersized for a prisoner, just peeping over the edge of the dock, guarded in case he ran amok and started attacking the judge, by a huge Dock Officer. There was the jury, solid and grey, listening impassionately as Guthrie Featherstone spread out his glittering mass of incriminating facts before them. I don't know why it is that juries all look the same; take twelve good men and women off the street and they all look middle-aged, anonymous, slightly stunned, an average jury, of average people trying an average case. Perhaps being a jury has become a special profession for specially average people. 'What do you want to do when you grow up my boy?' 'Be a jury man, Daddy.' 'Well done my boy. You can work a five-hour day for reasonable expenses and occasionally send people to chokey.'

So, as the carefully chosen words of Guthrie Featherstone passed over our heads like expensive hair oil, and as the enthusiastic young MacLay noted it all down, and the Rumpole Supporters Club, the Timsons, sat and pursed their lips and now and then whispered, 'Lies. All lies' to each other, I sat watching the judge rather as a noted toreador watches the bull from the barrier during the preliminary stages of the corrida, and remembered what I knew of Mr Justice Everglade, known to his few friends as 'Florrie'. Everglade's father was Lord Chancellor about the time when Jim's grandfather was doing over the Streatham Co-op. Educated at Winchester and Balliol, he always cracked *The Times* crossword in the opening of an egg. He was most happy with International Trust companies suing each other on nice points of law, and was only there for a fortnight's slumming down the Old Bailey. I wondered exactly what he was going to make of Peanuts Molloy.

'Members of the jury, it's right that you should know that it is alleged that Timson took part in this attack with a number of other youths, none of whom have been arrested,' Featherstone was purring to a halt.

'*The boy stood on the burning deck whence all but he had fled,*' I muttered, but the judge was busy congratulating learned counsel for Her Majesty the Queen who was engaged that morning in prosecuting the pride of the Timsons.

'It is quite right you should tell the jury that, Mr Featherstone. Perfectly right and proper.'

'If your Lordship pleases.' Featherstone was now bowing slightly, and my hackles began to rise. What was this? The old chums' league? Fellow members of the Athenaeum?

'I am most grateful to your Lordship for that indication.' Featherstone did his well-known butler passing the sherry act again. I wondered why the old darling didn't crawl up on the bench with Mr Justice Everglade and black his boots for him.

'So I imagine this young man's defence is – he wasn't *ejusdem generis* with the other lads?' The judge was now holding a private conversation, a mutual admiration society with my learned friend. I decided to break it up, and levered myself to my feet.

'I'm sorry. Your Lordship was asking about the defence?'

The judge turned an unfriendly eye on me and fumbled for my name. I told you he was a stranger to the Old Bailey, where the name of Rumpole is, I think, tolerably well known.

'Yes, Mr . . . er . . .' The clerk of the Court handed him up a note on which the defender's name was inscribed. 'Rumpole.'

'I am reluctant to intrude on your Lordship's confidential conversation with my learned friend. But your Lordship was asking about the defence.'

'You are appearing for the young man . . . Timson?'

'I have that honour.'

At which point the doors of the Court swung open and Albert came in with Nick, a boy in a blazer and a school-tie who passed the boy in the dock with only a glance of curiosity. I always thank God, when I consider the remote politeness with which I was treated by the Reverend Wilfred Rumpole, that I get on extremely well with Nick. We understand each other, my boy and I, and have, when he's at home, formed a strong but silent alliance against the almost invincible rule of She Who Must Be Obeyed. He is as fond as I am of the Sherlock Holmes tales, and when we walked together in Hyde Park and Kensington Gardens, young Nick often played the part of Holmes whilst I trudged beside him as Watson, trying to deduce the secret lives of those we passed by the way they shined their shoes, or kept their handkerchiefs in their sleeves. So I gave a particularly welcoming smile to Nick before I gave my attention back to Florrie.

'And, as Jim Timson's counsel,' I told his Lordship, 'I might know a little more about his case than counsel for the prosecution.'

To which Mr Justice Everglade trotted out his favourite bit of Latin. 'I imagine,' he said loftily, 'your client says he was not *ejusdem generis* with the other lads.'

'*Ejusdem generis*? Oh yes, my Lord. He's always saying that. *Ejusdem generis* is a phrase in constant use in his particular part of Brixton.'

I had hit a minor jackpot, and was rewarded with a tinkle of laughter from the Timsons, and a smile of genuine congratulation from Nick.

Mr Justice Everglade was inexperienced down the Bailey, he gave us a bare hour for lunch and Nick and I had it in the canteen. There is one thing you can say against crime, the catering facilities aren't up to much. Nick told me about school, and freely confessed, as I'm sure he wouldn't have done to his mother, that he'd been in some sort of trouble that term. There was an old deserted vicarage opposite Schoolhouse (my old House and Nick's) and he and his friends had apparently broken in the scullery window and assembled there for poker parties and the consumption of Cherry Brandy. I was horrified as I drew up the indictment which seemed to me to contain charges of burglary at common law, house breaking under the Forcible Entries Act, contravening the Betting, Gaming, Lotteries Act and Serving Alcohol on Unlicensed Premises.

'Crabtree actually invited a couple of girls from the village,' Nick continued his confession. 'But Bagnold never got to hear of that.'

Bagnold was Nick's headmaster, the school equivalent of 'Persil' White. I cheered up a little at the last piece of information.

'Then there's no evidence of girls. As far as your case goes there's no reason to suppose the girls ever existed. As for the other charges, which are serious . . .'

'Yes, yes, I suppose they are rather.'

'I imagine you were walking past the house on Sunday evening and, attracted by the noise . . . You went to investigate?'

'Dad. Bagnold came in and found us – playing poker.'

Nick wasn't exactly being helpful. I tried another line.

'I know, "My Lord. My client was only playing poker in order not to look too pious whilst he lectured his fellow sixth formers on the evils of gambling and Cherry Brandy".'

'Dad. Be serious.'

'I am serious. Don't you want me to defend you?'

'No. Bagnold's not going to tell the police or anything like that.'

I was amazed. 'He isn't? What's he going to do?'

'Well . . . I'll miss next term's exeat. Do extra work. I thought I should tell you before you got a letter.'

'Thank you, Nick. Thank you. I'm glad you told me. So there's no question of . . . the police?'

'The police?' Nick was laughing. 'Of course not. Bagnold doesn't want any trouble. After all, we're still at school.'

I watched Nick as he finished his fish and chips, and then turned my thoughts to Jim Timson, who had also been at school; but with no kindly Bagnold to protect him.

Back in Court I was cross-examining that notable grass, Peanuts Molloy, a skinnier, more furtive edition of Jim Timson. The cross-examination was being greatly enjoyed by the Timsons and Nick, but not much by Featherstone or Chief Detective Inspector 'Persil' White who sat at the table in front of me. I also thought that Mr Justice 'Florrie' Everglade was thinking that he would have been happier snoozing in the Athenaeum, or working on his grosse-point in Egerton Terrace, than listening to me bowling fast in-swingers at the juvenile chief witness for the prosecution.

'You don't speak. The Molloys and the Timsons are like the Montagues and the Capulets,' I put it to Peanuts.

'What did you say they were?' The judge had, of course, given me my opportunity. I smacked him through the slips for a crafty single. 'Not *ejusdem generis*, my Lord,' I said.

Nick joined in the laughter and even the ranks of Featherstone had to stifle a smile. The usher called 'Silence'. We were back to the business in hand.

'Tell me, Peanuts . . . How would you describe yourself?'

'Is that a proper question?' Featherstone uncoiled himself gracefully. I ignored the interruption.

'I mean artistically. Are you a latter-day Impressionist? Do all your oils in little dots, do you? Abstract painter? White squares on a white background? Do you indulge in watches melting in the desert like dear old Salvador Dali?'

'I don't know what you're talking about.' Peanuts played a blocking shot and Featherstone tried a weary smile to the judge.

'My Lord, neither, I must confess, do I.'

'Sit quietly, Featherstone,' I muttered to him. 'All will be revealed to you.' I turned my attention back to Peanuts. 'Are you a dedicated artist? The Rembrandt of the Remand Centre?'

'I hadn't done no art before.' Peanuts confirmed my suspicions.

'So we are to understand that this occasion, when Jim poured out his heart to you, was the first painting lesson you'd ever been to?'

Peanuts admitted it.

'You'd been at the Remand Centre how long?'

'Couple of months. I was done for a bit of an affray.'

'I didn't ask you that. And I'm sure the reason you were on remand was entirely creditable. What I want to know is, what inspired you with this sudden fascination for the arts?'

'Well, the chief screw. He suggested it.'

Now we were beginning to get to the truth of the matter. Like his old grandfather in the Streatham Co-op days, Jim had been banged up with a notable grass.

'You were suddenly told to join the painting class, weren't you . . . and put yourself next to Jim?'

'Something like that, yeah.'

'What did he say?' Florrie frowned. It was all very strange to him and yet he was starting to get the hint of something that wasn't quite cricket.

'Something like that, my Lord,' I repeated slowly, giving the judge a chance to make a note. 'And you were sent there, not in the pursuit of art, Peanuts, but in the pursuit of evidence! You knew that and you supplied your masters with just what they wanted to hear – even though Jim Timson didn't say a word to you!'

Everyone in Court, including Nick, looked impressed. D.I. White bit hard on a polo mint and Featherstone oozed to his feet in a rescue bid.

'That's great, Dad!'

'Thanks, Nick. Sorry it's not a murder.'

'I don't know quite what my learned friend is saying. Is he suggesting that the police . . .'

'Oh, it's an old trick,' I said, staring hard at the Chief Inspector. 'Bang the suspect up with a notable grass when you're really pushed for evidence. They do it with grown-ups often enough. Now they're trying it with children!'

'Mr Rumpole,' the judge sighed, 'you are speaking a language which is totally foreign to me.'

'Let me try and make myself clear, my Lord. I was suggesting that Peanuts was put there as a deliberate trap.'

By now, even the judge had the point. 'You are suggesting that Mr Molloy was not a genuine "amateur painter"?'

'No, my Lord. Merely an amateur witness.'

'Yes.' I actually got a faint smile. 'I see. Please go on, Mr Rumpole.'

Another day or so of this, I felt, and I'd get invited to tea at the Athenaeum.

'What did you say first to Jim? As you drew your easel alongside?'

'Don't remember.'

'Don't you?'

'I think we was speaking about the Stones.'

'What "stones" are these?' The judge's ignorance of the life around him seemed to be causing him some sort of wild panic. Remember this was 1965, and I was in a similar state of confusion until Nick, whispering from behind me, gave me the clue.

'The Rolling Stones, my Lord.' The information meant nothing to him.

'I'm afraid a great deal of this case seems to be taking place in a foreign tongue, Mr Rumpole.'

'Jazz musicians, as I understand it, my Lord, of some notoriety.' By courtesy of Nick, I filled his Lordship in on 'the scene'.

'Well, the notoriety hasn't reached me!' said the judge, providing the obedient Featherstone with the laugh of the year, if
not the century. When the learned prosecuting counsel had recovered his solemnity, Peanuts went rambling on.

'We was talking about the Stones concert at the Hammersmith
Odeon. We'd both been to it, like. And, well . . . we talked
about that. And then he said . . . Jim said . . . Well, he said as
how he and the other blokes had done the butchers.'

The conversation had now taken a nasty turn. I saw that the
judge was writing industriously. 'Jim said . . . that he and the
other blokes . . . had done the butchers.' Florrie was plying his
pencil. Then he looked up at me, 'Well, Mr Rumpole, is that a
convenient moment to adjourn?'

It was a very convenient moment for the prosecution, as the
evidence against us would be the last thing the jury heard before
sloping off to their homes and loved ones. It was also a convenient moment for Peanuts. He would have his second wind by
the morning. So there was nothing for it but to take Nick for a
cup of tea and a pile of crumpets in the ABC, and so home to
She Who Must Be Obeyed.

So picture us three that evening, finishing dinner and a bottle
of claret, celebrating the return of the Young Master at Hack
Hall, Counsel's Castle, Rumpole Manor, or 25B Froxbury
Court, Gloucester Road. Hilda had told Nick that his grandpa
had sent his love and expected a letter, and also dropped me the
encouraging news that old C. H. Wystan was retiring and quite
appreciated that I was the senior man. Nick asked me if I was
really going to be Head of Chambers, seeming to look at me
with a new respect, and we drank a glass of claret to the future,
whatever it might be. Then Nick asked me if I really thought
Peanuts Molloy was lying.

'If he's not, he's giving a damn good imitation.' Then I told
Hilda as she started to clear away, 'Nick enjoyed the case. Even
though it was only a robbery. Oh, Nick . . . I wish you'd been
there to hear me cross-examine about the bloodstains in the
"Penge Bungalow Murder".'

'Nick wasn't born, when you did the "Penge Bungalow Murder".'

My wife is always something of a wet blanket. I commiserated with my son. 'Bad luck, old boy.'

'You were great with that judge!'

I think Nick had really enjoyed himself.

'There was this extraordinary judge who was always talking Latin and Dad was teasing him.'

'You want to be careful,' Hilda was imposing her will on the pudding plates. 'How you tease judges. If you're to be Head of Chambers.' On which line she departed, leaving Nick and I to our claret and conversation. I began to discuss with Nick the horrifying adventure of *The Speckled Band*.

'You're still reading those tales, are you?' I asked Nick.

'Well . . . not lately.'

'But you remember. I used to read them to you, didn't I? After She had ordered you to bed.'

'When you weren't too busy. Noting up your murders.'

'And remember we were Holmes and Watson? When we went for walks in Hyde Park.'

'I remember *one* walk.'

That was odd, as I recall it had been our custom ever at a weekend, before Nick went away to boarding school. I lit a small cigar and looked at the Great Detective through the smoke.

'Tell me, Holmes. What did you think was the most remarkable piece of evidence given by the witness Peanuts Molloy?'

'When he said they talked about the Rolling Stones.'

'Holmes, you astonish me.'

'You see, Watson. We were led to believe they were such enemies I mean, the families were. They'd never spoken.'

'I see what you're driving at. Have another glass of claret – stimulates the detective ability.' I opened another bottle, a clatter from the kitchen telling me that the lady was not about to join us.

'And there they were chatting about a pop concert. Didn't that strike you as strange, my dear Watson?'

'It struck me as bloody rum, if you want to know the truth, Holmes.' I was delighted to see Nick taking over the case.

'They'd both been to the concert . . . Well, that doesn't mean anything. Not necessarily . . . I mean, *I* was at that concert.'

'Were you indeed?'

'It was at the end of the summer holidays.'

'I don't remember you mentioning it.'

'I said I was going to the Festival Hall.'

I found this confidence pleasing, knowing that it wasn't to be shared with Hilda.

'Very wise. Your mother no doubt feels that at the Hammersmith Odeon they re-enact some of the worst excesses of the Roman Empire. You didn't catch sight of Peanuts and young Jimbo, did you?'

'There were about two thousand fans – all screaming.'

'I don't know if it helps . . .'

'No.'

'If they were old mates, I mean. Jim might really have confided in him. All the same, Peanuts is lying. And *you* noticed it! You've got the instinct, Nick. You've got a nose for the evidence! Your career at the Bar is bound to be brilliant.' I raised my glass to Nick. 'When are you taking silk?'

Shortly after this She entered with news that Nick had a dentist's appointment the next day, which would prevent his re-appearance down the Bailey. All the same, he had given me a great deal of help and before I went to bed I telephoned Bernard the solicitor, tore him away from his fireside and instructed him to undertake some pretty immediate research.

Next morning, Albert told me that he'd had a letter from old C. H. Wystan, Hilda's Daddy, mentioning his decision to retire.

'I think we'll manage pretty well, with you, Mr Rumpole, as Head of Chambers,' Albert told me. 'There's not much you and I won't be able to sort out, sir, over a glass or two in Pommeroy's Wine Bar . . . And soon we'll be welcoming Master Nick in Chambers?'

'Nick? Well, yes.' I had to admit it. 'He is showing a certain legal aptitude.'

'It'll be a real family affair, Mr Rumpole . . . Like father, like son, if you want my opinion.'

I remembered Albert's words when I saw Fred Timson waiting for me outside the Court. But before I had time to brood on family tradition, Bernard came up with the rolled-up poster for a pop concert. I grabbed it from him and carried it as unobtrusively as possible into Court.

'When Jim told you he'd done up the butchers . . . He didn't tell you the date that that had happened?' Peanuts was back, facing the bowling, and Featherstone was up to his usual tricks, rising to interrupt.

'My Lord, the date is set out quite clearly in the indictment.'

The time had come, quite obviously, for a burst of righteous indignation.

'My Lord, I am cross-examining on behalf of a 16-year-old boy on an extremely serious charge. I'd be grateful if my learned friend didn't supply information which all of us in Court know – except for the witness.'

'Very well. Do carry on, Mr Rumpole.' I was almost beginning to like Mr Justice Everglade.

'No. He never told me when, like. I thought it was sometime in the summer.' Peanuts tried to sound co-operative.

'Sometime in the summer? Are you a fan of the Rolling Stones, Peanuts?'

'Yes.'

'Remind me . . . they were . . .' Still vaguely puzzled the judge was hunting back through his notes.

Sleek as a butler with a dish of peas, Featherstone supplied the information. 'The musicians, my Lord.'

'And so was Jim a fan?' I ploughed on, ignoring the gentleman's gentleman.

'He was. Yes.'

'You had discussed music, before you met in the Remand Centre?'

'Before the nick. Oh yes.' Peanuts was following me obediently down the garden path.

'You used to talk about it at school?'

'Yes.'

'In quite a friendly way?' I was conscious of a startled Fred Timson looking at his son, and of Jim in the dock looking, for the first time, ashamed.

'We was all right. Yes.'

'Did you ever go to a concert with Jimbo? Please think carefully.'

'We went to one or two concerts together.' Peanuts conceded.

'In the evening?'

'Yes.'

'What would you do? . . . Call at his home and collect him?'

'You're joking!'

'Oh no, Peanuts. In this case I'm not joking at all!' No harm, I thought, at that stage, in underlining the seriousness of the occasion.

'Course I wouldn't call at his home!'

'Your families don't speak. You wouldn't be welcomed in each other's houses?'

'The Montagues and the Capulets, Mr Rumpole?' The old sweetheart on the bench had finally got the message. I gave him a bow, to show my true love and affection.

'If your Lordship pleases . . . Your Lordship puts it extremely aptly.' I turned back to Peanuts. 'So what would you do, if you were going to a concert?'

'We'd leave school together, like – and then hang around the caffs.'

'Hang around the caffs?'

'Caf*ays*, Mr Rumpole?' Mr Justice Everglade was enjoying himself, translating the answer.

'Yes, of course, the caf*ays*. Until it was time to go up West? If my Lord would allow me, up to the "West End of London" together?'

'Yes.'

'So you wouldn't be separated on these evenings you went to concerts together?' It was one of those questions after which you hold your breath. There can be so many wrong answers.

'No. We hung around together.'

Rumpole breathed a little more easily, but still had the final question, the great gamble, with all Jim Timson's chips firmly piled on the red. *Fait vos jeux, m'sieurs et mesdames* of the Old Bailey jury. I spun the wheel.

'And did that happen ... When you went to the Rolling Stones at the Hammersmith Odeon?'

A nasty silence. Then the ball rattled into the hole.

Peanuts said, 'Yes.'

'That was this summer, wasn't it?' We were into the straight now, cantering home.

'In the summer, Yeah.'

'You left school together?'

'And hung around the caffs, like. Then we went up the Odeon.'

'Together ... All the time?'

'I told you – didn't I?' Peanuts looked bored, and then amazed as I unrolled the poster Bernard had brought, rushed by taxi from Hammersmith, with the date clearly printed across the bottom.

'My Lord. My learned friend might be interested to know the date of the only Rolling Stones concert at the Hammersmith Odeon this year.' I gave Featherstone an unwelcome eyeful of the poster.

'He might like to compare it with the date so conveniently set out in the indictment.'

When the subsequent formalities were over, I went down to the cells. This was not a visit of commiseration, no time for a 'sorry old sweetheart, but ...' and a deep consciousness of having asked one too many questions. All the same, I was in no gentle mood, in fact, it would be fair to say that I was bloody angry with Jimbo.

'You had an alibi! You had a proper, reasonable, truthful alibi, and, joy of joys, it came from the prosecution! Why the hell didn't you tell me?'

Jim, who seemed to have little notion of the peril he had passed, answered me quite calmly, 'Dad wouldn't've liked it.'

'Dad! What's Dad got to do with it?' I was astonished.

'He wouldn't've liked it, Mr Rumpole. Not me going out with Peanuts.'

'So you were quite ready to be found guilty, to be convicted of robbery, just because your Dad wouldn't like you going out with Peanuts Molloy?'

'Dad got the family to alibi me.' Jim clearly felt that the Timsons had done their best for him.

'Keep it in the family!' Though it was heavily laid on, the irony was lost on Jim. He smiled politely and stood up, eager to join the clan upstairs.

'Well, anyway. Thanks a lot, Mr Rumpole. Dad said I could rely on you. To win the day, like. I'd better collect me things.'

If Jim thought I was going to let him get away as easily as that, he was mistaken. Rumpole rose in his crumpled gown, doing his best to represent the majesty of the law. 'No! Wait a minute. I didn't win the day. It was luck. The purest fluke. It won't happen again!'

'You're joking, Mr Rumpole.' Jim thought I was being modest. 'Dad told me about you . . . He says you never let the Timsons down.'

I had a sudden vision of my role in life, from young Jim's point of view and I gave him the voice of outrage which I use frequently in Court. I had a message of importance for Jim Timson.

'Do you think that's what I'm here for? To help you along in a career like your Dad's?' Jim was still smiling, maddeningly. 'My God! I shouldn't have asked those questions! I shouldn't have found out the date of the concert! Then you'd really be happy, wouldn't you? You could follow in Dad's footsteps all your life! Sharp spell of Borstal training to teach you the mysteries of housebreaking, and then a steady life in the nick. You might really do well! You might end up in Parkhurst, Maximum Security Wing, doing a glamorous twenty years and a hero to the screws.'

At which the door opened and a happy screw entered, for the purpose of springing young Jim – until the inevitable next time.

'We've got his things at the gate, Mr Rumpole. Come on Jim. You can't stay here all night.'

'I've got to go,' Jim agreed. 'I don't know how to face Dad, really. Me being so friendly with Peanuts.'

RUMPOLE AND THE YOUNGER GENERATION 39

'Jim,' I tried a last appeal. 'If you're at all grateful for what I did . . .'

'Oh I am, Mr Rumpole, I'm quite satisfied.' Generous of him.

'Then you can perhaps repay me.'

'Why – aren't you on Legal Aid?'

'It's not that! Leave him! Leave your Dad.'

Jim frowned, for a moment he seemed to think it over. Then he said, 'I don't know as how I can.'

'You don't know?'

'Mum depends on me, you see. Like when Dad goes away. She depends on me then, as head of the family.'

So he left me, and went up to temporary freedom and his new responsibilities.

My mouth was dry and I felt about 90 years old, so I took the lift up to that luxurious eatery, the Old Bailey canteen, for a cup of tea and a Penguin biscuit. And, pushing his tray along past the urns, I met a philosophic Chief Inspector 'Persil' White. He noticed my somewhat lugubrious expression and tried a cheering 'Don't look so miserable, Mr Rumpole. You won didn't you?'

'Nobody won, the truth emerges sometimes, Inspector, even down the Old Bailey.' I must have sounded less than gracious. The wily old copper smiled tolerantly.

'He's a Timson. It runs in the family. We'll get him sooner or later!'

'Yes. Yes. I suppose you will.'

At a table in a corner, I found certain members of my Chambers, George Frobisher, Percy Hoskins, and young Tony MacLay, now resting from their labours, their wigs lying among cups of Old Bailey tea, buns and choccy bics. I joined them. Wordsworth entered my head, and I gave him an airing . . . *'Trailing clouds of glory do we come.'*

'Marvellous win, that. I was telling them.' Young MacLay thought I was announcing my triumph.

'Yes, Rumpole. I hear you've had a splendid win.' Old George, ever generous, smiled, genuinely pleased.

'It'll be *years* before you get the cheque,' Hoskins grumbled.

'Not in entire forgetfulness and not in utter nakedness,   But

trailing clouds of glory do we come   From God who is our home . . .' I was thinking of Jim, trying to sort out his situation with the help of Wordsworth.

'You don't get paid for years at the Old Bailey. I try to tell my grocer that. If you had to wait as long to be paid for a pound of sugar, I tell him, as we do for an armed robbery . . .' Hoskins was warming to a well-loved theme, but George, dear old George was smiling at me.

'Albert tells me he's had a letter from Wystan. I just wanted to say, I'm sure we'd all like to say, you'll make a splendid Head of Chambers, Rumpole.'

'Heaven lies about us in our infancy,   Shades of the prison house begin to close   Upon the growing boy . . . But he beholds the light, and whence it flows,   He sees it in his joy.' I gave them another brief glimpse of immortality. George looked quite proud of me and told MacLay, 'Rumpole quotes poetry. He does it quite often.'

'But does the growing boy behold the light?' I wondered. 'Or was the old sheep of the Lake District being unduly optimistic?'

'It'll be refreshing for us all, to have a Head of Chambers who quotes poetry,' George went on, at which point Percy Hoskins produced a newspaper which turned out to contain an item of news for us all.

'Have you seen *The Times*, Rumpole?'

'No, I haven't had time for the crossword.'

'Guthrie Featherstone. He's taken silk.'

It was the apotheosis, the great day for the Labour-Conservative Member for wherever it was, one time unsuccessful prosecutor of Jim Timson and now one of Her Majesty's counsel, called within the Bar, and he went down to the House of Lords tailored out in his new silk gown, a lace jabot, knee breeches with diamanté buckles, patent shoes, black silk stockings, lace cuffs and a full-bottomed wig that made him look like a pedigree, but not over-bright, spaniel. However, Guthrie Featherstone was a tall man, with a good calf in a silk stocking, and he took with him Marigold, his lady wife, who was young enough, and I

suppose pretty enough, for Henry our junior clerk to eye wist-
fully, although she had the sort of voice that puts me instantly in
mind of headscarves and gymkhanas, that high pitched nasal
whining which a girl learns from too much contact with the
saddle when young, and too little with the Timsons of this
world in later life. The couple were escorted by Albert, who'd
raided Moss Bros for a top hat and morning coat for the occasion
and when the Lord Chancellor had welcomed Guthrie to that
special club of Queen's Counsel (on whose advice the Queen,
luckily for her, never has to rely for a moment) they came back
to Chambers where champagne (the N.V. cooking variety, bulk
bought from Pommeroy's Wine Bar) was served by Henry and
old Miss Patterson our typist, in Wystan's big room looking out
over Temple Gardens. C. H. Wystan, our retiring Head, was
not among those present as the party began, and I took an early
opportunity to get stuck into the beaded bubbles.

After the fourth glass I felt able to relax a bit and wandered to
where Featherstone, in all his finery, was holding forth to
Erskine-Brown about the problems of appearing *en travestie*.
I arrived just as he was saying, 'It's the stockings that're the
problem.'

'Oh yes. They would be.' I did my best to sound interested.

'Keeping them up.'

'I do understand.'

'Well, Marigold. My wife Marigold ...' I looked across to
where Mrs Q.C. was tinkling with laughter at some old legal
anecdote of Uncle Tom's. It was a laugh that seemed in some
slight danger of breaking the wine glasses.

'*That* Marigold?'

'Her sister's a nurse, you know ... and she put me in touch
with this shop which supplies suspender belts to nurses ...
among other things.'

'Really?' This conversation seemed to arouse some dormant
sexual interest in Erskine-Brown.

'Yards of elastic, for the larger ward sister. But it works
miraculously.'

'You're wearing a suspender belt?' Erskine-Brown was frankly
fascinated. 'You sexy devil!'

'I hadn't realized the full implications,' I told the Q.C., 'of rising to the heights of the legal profession.'

I wandered off to where Uncle Tom was giving Marigold a brief history of life in our Chambers over the last half-century. Percy Hoskins was in attendance, and George.

'It's some time since we had champagne in Chambers.' Uncle Tom accepted a refill from Albert.

'It's some time since we had a silk in Chambers,' Hoskins smiled at Marigold who flashed a row of well-groomed teeth back at him.

'I recall we had a man in Chambers once called Drinkwater – oh, before you were born, Hoskins. And some fellow came and paid Drinkwater a hundred guineas – for six months' pupillage. And you know what this Drinkwater fellow did? Bought us all champagne – and the next day he ran off to Calais with his junior clerk. We never saw hide nor hair of either of them again.' He paused. Marigold looked puzzled, not quite sure if this was the punch line.

'Of course, you could get a lot further in those days – on a hundred guineas,' Uncle Tom ended on a sad note, and Marigold laughed heartily.

'Your husband's star has risen so quickly, Mrs Featherstone. Only ten years call and he's an M.P. *and* leading counsel.' Hoskins was clearly so excited by the whole business he had stopped worrying about his cheques for half an hour.

'Oh, it's the P.R. you know. Guthrie's frightfully good at the P.R.'

I felt like Everglade. Marigold was speaking a strange and incomprehensible language.

'Guthrie always says the most important thing at the Bar is to be polite to your instructing solicitor. Don't you find that, Mr Rumpole?'

'Polite to solicitors? It's never occurred to me.'

'Guthrie admires you so, Mr Rumpole. He admires your style of advocacy.'

I had just sunk another glass of the beaded bubbles as passed by Albert, and I felt a joyous release from my usual strong sense of tact and discretion.

'I suppose it makes a change from bowing three times and offering to black the judge's boots for him.'

Marigold's smile didn't waver. 'He says you're most amusing out of Court, too. Don't you quote poetry?'

'Only in moments of great sadness, Madam. Or extreme elation.'

'Guthrie's so looking forward to leading you. In his next big case.'

This was an eventuality which I should have taken into account as soon as I saw Guthrie in silk stockings; as a matter of fact it had never occurred to me.

'Leading *me*? Did you say, *leading* me?'

'Well, he has to have a junior now ... doesn't he? Naturally he wants the best junior available.'

'Now he's a leader?'

'Now he's left the Junior Bar.'

I raised my glass and gave Marigold a version of Browning. 'Just for a pair of knee breeches he left us ... Just for an elastic suspender belt, as supplied to the Nursing profession ...' At which the Q.C. himself bore down on us in a rustle of silk and drew me into a corner.

'I just wanted to say, I don't see why recent events should make the slightest difference to the situation in Chambers. You *are* the senior man in practice, Rumpole.'

Henry was passing with the fizzing bottle. I held out my glass and the tide ran foaming in it.

'*You wrong me, Brutus*,' I told Featherstone. '*You said an older soldier, not a better.*'

'A quotation! *Touché*, very apt.'

'Is it?'

'I mean, all this will make absolutely no difference. I'll still support you Rumpole, as the right candidate for Head of Chambers.'

I didn't know about being a candidate, having thought of the matter as settled and not being much of a political animal. But before I had time to reflect on whatever the Honourable Member was up to, the door opened letting in a formidable draught and the Head of Chambers. C. H. Wystan, She's Daddy, wearing a

tweed suit, extremely pale, supported by Albert on one side and
a stick on the other, made the sort of formidable entrance that
the ghost of Banquo stages at dinner with the Macbeths. Wystan
was installed in an armchair, from which he gave us all the sort
of wintry smile which seemed designed to indicate that all flesh
is as the grass, or something to that effect.

'Albert wrote to me about this little celebration. I was determined to be with you. And the doctor has given permission, for
no more than one glass of champagne.' Wystan held out a transparent hand into which Albert inserted a glass of non vintage.
Wystan lifted this with some apparent effort, and gave us a
toast.

'To the great change in Chambers! Now we have a silk.
Guthrie Featherstone, Q.C., M.P.!'

I had a large refill to that. Wystan absorbed a few bubbles,
wiped his mouth on a clean, folded handkerchief, and proceeded
to the oration. Wystan was never a great speech maker, but I
claimed another refill and gave him my ears.

'You, Featherstone, have brought a great distinction to
Chambers.'

'Isn't that nice, Guthrie?' Marigold proprietorially squeezed
her master's fingers.

'You know, when I was a young man. You remember when
we were young men, Uncle Tom? We used to hang around in
Chambers for weeks on end.' Wystan had gone on about these
distant hard times at every Chambers meeting. 'I well recall we
used to occupy ourselves with an old golf ball and mashie niblick,
trying to get chip shots into the waste-paper baskets. Albert was
a boy then.'

'A mere child, Mr Wystan,' Albert looked suitably demure.

'And we used to pray for work. *Any* sort of work, didn't we,
Uncle Tom?'

'We were tempted to crime. Only way we could get into
Court,' Uncle Tom took the feed line like a professional.
Moderate laughter, except for Rumpole who was busy drinking.
And then I heard Wystan rambling on.

'But as you grow older at the Bar you discover it's not having
any work that matters. It's the *quality* that counts!'

'Here, here! I'm always saying we ought to do more civil.'
This was the dutiful Erskine-Brown, inserting his oar.

'Now Guthrie Featherstone, Q.C., M.P. will, of course, command briefs in all divisions – planning, contract,' Wystan's voice sank to a note of awe, 'even Chancery! I was so afraid, after I've gone, that this Chambers might become known as merely a criminal set.' Wystan's voice now sank in a sort of horror. 'And, of course, there's no doubt about it, too much criminal work does rather lower the standing of a Chambers.'

'Couldn't you install pithead baths?' I hadn't actually meant to say it aloud, but it came out very loud indeed.

'Ah, Horace.' Wystan turned his pale eyes on me for the first time.

'So we could have a good scrub down after we get back from the Old Bailey?'

'Now, Horace Rumpole. And I mean no disrespect whatever to my son-in-law.' Wystan returned to the oration. From far away I heard myself say, 'Daddy!' as I raised the hard-working glass. 'Horace does practise almost exclusively in the Criminal Courts!'

'One doesn't get the really fascinating points of *law*. Not in criminal work,' Erskine-Brown was adding unwanted support to the motion. 'I've often thought we should try and attract some really lucrative tax cases into Chambers.'

That, I'm afraid, did it. Just as if I were in Court I moved slightly to the centre and began my speech.

'Tax cases?' I saw them all smiling encouragement at me. 'Marvellous! Tax cases make the world go round. Compared to the wonderful world of tax, crime is totally trivial. What does it matter? If some boy loses a year, a couple of years, of his life? It's totally unimportant! Anyway, he'll grow up to be banged up for a good five, shut up with his own chamber pot in some convenient hole we all prefer not to think about.' There was a deafening silence, which came loudest from Marigold Featherstone. Then Wystan tried to reach a settlement.

'Now then, Horace. Your practice no doubt requires a good deal of skill.'

'Skill? Who said "skill"?' I glared round at the learned friends.

'Any fool could do it! It's only a matter of life and death. That's all it is. Crime? It's a sort of a game. How can you compare it to the real world of Off Shore Securities. And Deductible Expenses?'

'All you young men in Chambers can learn an enormous amount from Horace Rumpole, when it comes to crime.' Wystan now seemed to be the only one who was still smiling. I turned on him.

'You make me sound just like Fred Timson!'

'Really? Whoever's Fred Timson?' I told you Wystan never had much of a practice at the Bar, consequently he had never met the Timsons. Erskine-Brown supplied the information.

'The Timsons are Rumpole's favourite family.'

'An industrious clan of South London criminals, aren't they, Rumpole,' Hoskins added.

Wystan looked particularly pained. 'South London criminals?'

'I mean, do we want people like the Timsons forever hanging about in our waiting room? I merely ask the question.' He was not bad, this Erskine-Brown, with a big future in the nastier sort of Breach of Trust cases.

'Do you? Do you merely ask it?' I heard the pained bellow of a distant Rumpole.

'The Timsons . . . and their like, are no doubt grist to Rumpole's mill,' Wystan was starting on the summing up. 'But it's the balance that *counts*. Now, you'll be looking for a new Head of Chambers.'

'Are we still looking?' My friend George Frobisher had the decency to ask. And Wystan told him, 'I'd like you all to think it over carefully. And put your views to me in writing. We should all try and remember. It's the good of the Chambers that matters. Not the feelings, however deep they may be, of any particular person.'

He then called on Albert's assistance to raise him to his feet, lifted his glass with an effort of pure will and offered us a toast to the good of Chambers. I joined in, and drank deep, it having been a good thirty seconds since I had had a glass to my lips. As the bubbles exploded against the tongue I noticed that the

Featherstones were holding hands, and the brand new artificial silk was looking particularly delighted. Something, and perhaps not only his suspender belt, seemed to be giving him special pleasure.

Some weeks later, when I gave Hilda the news, she was deeply shocked.

'*Guthrie Featherstone!* Head of Chambers!' We were at breakfast. In fact Nick was due back at school that day. He was neglecting his cornflakes and reading a book.

'By general acclaim.'

'I'm sorry.' Hilda looked at me, as if she'd just discovered that I'd contracted an incurable disease.

'He can have the headaches – working out Albert's extraordinary book-keeping system.' I thought for a moment, yes, I'd like to have been Head of Chambers, and then put the thought from me.

'If only you could have become a Q.C.' She was now pouring me an unsolicited cup of coffee.

'Q.C.? C.T. That's enough to keep me busy.'

'C.T.? Whatever's C.T.?'

'Counsel for the Timsons!' I tried to say it as proudly as I could. Then I reminded Nick that I'd promised to see him off at Liverpool Street, finished my cooling coffee, stood up and took a glance at the book that was absorbing him, expecting it to be, perhaps, that spine-chilling adventure relating to the Footprints of an Enormous Hound. To my amazement the shocker in question was entitled simply *Studies in Sociology.*

'It's interesting,' Nick sounded apologetic.

'You astonish me.'

'Old Bagnold was talking about what I should read if I get into Oxford.'

'Of course you're going to read law, Nick. We're going to keep it in the family.' Hilda the barrister's daughter was clearing away deafeningly.

'I thought perhaps P.P.E. and then go on to Sociology.' Nick sounded curiously confident. Before Hilda could get in another word I made my position clear.

'P.P.E., that's very good, Nick! That's very good indeed! For God's sake. Let's stop keeping things in the family!'

Later, as we walked across the barren stretches of Liverpool Street Station, with my son in his school uniform and me in my old striped trousers and black jacket, I tried to explain what I meant.

'That's what's wrong, Nick. That's the devil of it! They're being born around us all the time. Little Mr Justice Everglades ... Little Timsons ... Little Guthrie Featherstones. All being set off ... to follow in father's footsteps.' We were at the barrier, shaking hands awkwardly. 'Let's have no more of that! No more following in father's footsteps. No more.'

Nick smiled, although I have no idea if he understood what I was trying to say. I'm not totally sure that I understood it either. Then the train removed him from me. I waved for a little, but he didn't wave back. That sort of thing is embarrassing for a boy. I lit a small cigar and went by tube to the Bailey. I was doing a long firm fraud then; a particularly nasty business, out of which I got a certain amount of harmless fun.

Rumpole and the Alternative Society

In some ways the coppers, the Fuzz, Old Bill, whatever you may care to call them, are a very conservative body. When they verbal up the criminal classes, and report their alleged confessions in the nick, they still use the sort of Cockney argot that went out at the turn of the century, and perfectly well-educated bank robbers, who go to the ballet at Covent Garden and holidays in Corfu, are still reported as having cried, 'It's a fair cop, guv,' or 'You got me bang to rights,' at the moment they're apprehended. In the early 1970s however, when Flower Power flooded the country with a mass of long hair, long dresses and the sweet smell of the old quarter of Marrakesh, the Fuzz showed itself remarkably open to new ideas. Provincial drug squads were issued with beads, Afghan waistcoats, headbands and guitars along with their size eleven boots, and took lessons in a new language, learning to say, 'Cool it man,' or 'Make love not war,' instead of 'You got me bang to rights.'

It was also a time when the figures of the establishment fell into disrepute and to be a barrister, however close to the criminal fraternity, was to be regarded by the young as a sort of undesirable cross between Judge Jeffries and Mr Nixon, as I knew from the sullen looks of the young ladies Nick, who was then at Oxford and reading P.P.E., brought home in the holidays. I have never felt so clearly the number of different countries, all speaking private languages and with no diplomatic relations, into which England is divided. I cannot think for instance of a world more remote from the Temple or the Inns of Court than that tumble-down Victorian house in the west country (No. 34 Balaclava Road, Coldsands) which the community who inhabited it had christened 'Nirvana', and which contained a tortoise who looked to me heavily drugged, a number of babies, some surprisingly clean young men and women, a pain-in-the-neck named Dave, and a girl called Kathy Trelawny whom I never met until she came to be indicted in the Coldsands Crown Court on a charge of handling a phenomenal amount of cannabis resin, valued at about ten thousand pounds.

Coldsands is a rather unpopular resort in the west of England with a high rainfall, a few Regency terraces, a large number of old people's homes, and a string quartet at tea-time in the Winter Gardens; on the face of it an unlikely place for crime to flourish. But a number of young people did form a community there at 'Nirvana', a place which the local inhabitants regarded as the scene of numerous orgies. To this house came a dealer named Jack, resplendent in his hippie attire, to place a large order for cannabis which Kathy Trelawny set about fulfilling, with the aid of a couple of Persian law students with whom she had made contact at Bristol University. Very soon after the deal was done, and a large quantity of money handed over, Jack the Hippie was revealed as Detective Sergeant Jack Smedley of the local force, the strong arm of the law descended on 'Nirvana', the Persian law students decamped to an unknown address in Morocco, and Rumpole, who had had a few notable successes with dangerous drugs, was dug out of Old Bailey and placed upon the 12.15 from Paddington to Coldsands, enjoying the rare luxury of a quiet corner seat in the first-class luncheon car, by courtesy of the Legal Aid Fund of Great Britain.

I could afford the first-class luncheon, and spread myself the more readily, as I was staying in a little pub on the coast not five miles from Coldsands kept by my old mates and companions in arms (if my three years in the R.A.F. ground staff can be dignified by so military a title), ex-Pilot Officer 'Three-Fingers' Dogherty and his wife Bobby, ex-W.A.A.F., unchallenged beauty queen of the station at Dungeness, who was well known to look like Betty Grable from behind and Phyllis Dixey from the front and to have a charm, a refreshing impertinence and a contempt for danger unrivalled, I am sure, by either of those famous pin-ups from *Reveille*. I have spoken of Bobby already in these reminiscences and I am not ashamed to say that, although I was already married to Hilda when we met, she captured my heart, and continued to hold it fast long after the handsome Pilot Officer captured hers. I was therefore keenly looking forward to renewing my acquaintance with Bobby; we had had a desultory correspondence but we hadn't met for many years. I was also looking forward to a holiday at the seaside, for which Miss Trelawny's little trouble seemed merely to provide the excuse and the financial assistance.

So I was, as you can imagine, in a good mood as we rattled past Reading and cows began to be visible, standing in fields, chewing the cud, as though there were no law courts or judges in the world. You very rarely see a cow down the Bailey, which is one of the reasons I enjoy an occasional case on circuit. Circuit takes you away from Chambers, away from the bene-volent despotism of Albert the clerk, above all, away from the constant surveillance of She Who Must Be Obeyed (Mrs Hilda Rumpole). I began to look forward to a good, old-fashioned railway lunch. I thought of a touch of Brown Windsor soup, rapidly followed by steamed cod, castle pudding, mouse-trap, cream crackers and celery, all to be washed down with a vintage bottle of Château Great Western as we charged past Didcot.

A furtive-looking man, in a short off-white jacket which showed his braces and a mournful expression, looked down at me.

'Ah waiter. Brown Windsor soup, I fancy, to start with.'

'We're just doing the Grilled Platter, sir.' I detected, in the man's voice, a certain gloomy satisfaction.

'Grilled – what?'

'Fried egg and brunch-burger, served with chips and a nice tomato.'

'A nice tomato! Oh, very well.' Perhaps with a suitable an-aesthetic the brunch-burger could be taken. 'And to drink. A reasonable railway claret?'

'No wines on this journey, sir. We got gin in miniatures.'

'I don't care for gin, at lunchtime, especially in miniatures.' Regretfully I came to the conclusion that circuit life had de-teriorated and wondered what the devil they had done with all the Brown Windsor soup.

*

At Coldsands Station a middle-aged man in a neat suit and rimless glasses was there to meet me. He spoke with a distinct and reassuring west-country accent.

'Mr Horace Rumpole? I'm Friendly.'

'Thank God someone is!'

'I was warned you liked your little joke, Mr Rumpole, by London agents. They recommended you as a learned counsel who has had some success with drugs.'

'Oh, I have had considerable success with drugs. And a bit of luck with murder, rape and other offences against the person.'

'I'm afraid we don't do much crime at Friendly, Sanderson and Friendly. We're mainly conveyancing. By the way, I think there's a couple of typing errors in the instructions to counsel.' Mr Friendly looked deeply apologetic.

I hastened to reassure him. 'Fear not, Friendly. I never read the instructions to counsel. I find they blur the judgement and confuse the mind.'

We were outside the station now, and a battered taxi rattled into view.

'You'll want to see the client?' Friendly sounded resigned.

'She might expect it.'

'You're going to "Nirvana"?'

'Eventually. Aren't we all? No, Friendly. I shall steer clear of the lotus eaters of No. 34 Balaclava Road. A land, I rather imagine, in which it seems always afternoon. Bring the client for a con at my hotel. After dinner. Nine o'clock suit you?'

'You'll be at the George? That's where the Bar put up.'

'Then if it's where the Bar put up, I shall avoid it. I'm staying with old mates, from my days in the R.A.F. They run a stately pleasure-dome known as the Crooked Billet.'

'The little pub place out on the bay?' I noticed Friendly smiled when he spoke of the Dogherty's delight, a place, I had no doubt, of a high reputation. The taxi had stopped now, and I was wrestling with the door. When I had it open, I was in a high and holiday mood.

'Out on the bay indeed! With no sound but the sea sighing and the muted love call of the lobster. Know what I say, Friendly?

When you get a bit of decent crime at the seaside . . . Relax and enjoy it!'

Friendly was staring after me, perhaps understandably bewildered, as I drove away.

The taxi took me out to the Crooked Billet and back about twenty-five years. The pub was on the top of some cliffs, above a sandy beach and a leaden sea. From the outside it seemed an ordinary enough building, off-white, battered, with a neglected patch of garden; but inside it was almost a museum to the great days of World War Two. Behind the bar were Sam's trophies, a Nazi helmet, a plaster Mr Churchill which could actually puff a cigar, a model Spitfire dangled from the ceiling, there were framed photographs of ex-Pilot Officer Dogherty in his flying jacket, standing by his beloved Lancaster and a signed portrait of Vera Lynn at the height of her career. Even the pin-table appeared to be an antique, looted from some N.A.A.F.I. There was also an old piano, a string of fairy lights round the bottles and a comforting smell of stale booze. Someone was clanking bottles behind the bar, but I could see no more than a comfortable bottom in old blue slacks. I put out a red alert.

'Calling all air crew! Calling all air crew! Parade immediately.'

At which Bobby Dogherty turned, straightened up and smiled.

Age had not actually withered her, but it had added to the generosity of her curves. Her blonde hair looked more metallic than of old, and the lines of laughter round her mouth and eyes had settled into permanent scars. She had a tipped cigarette in her mouth and her head was tilted to keep the smoke out of her eyes. She looked, as always, irrepressibly cheerful, as if middle age, like the War, was a sort of joke, and there to be enjoyed.

'Rumpole. You old devil!'

'You look beautiful,' I said, as I had often done in the past, and meant it just as much.

'Liar! Drop of rum?' I didn't see why not and perched myself on a bar stool while she milked the rum bottle. Soon Rumpole was in reminiscent mood.

'Takes me right back to the NAAFI hop. New Year's Eve, 1943. Sam was out bombing something and I had you entirely to myself – for a couple of hours of the Boomps-a-Daisy . . . Not to mention the Lambeth Walk.' I raised my glass and gave our old salutation, 'Here's to the good old duke!'

'The good old duke.' Bobby was on her second gin and tonic, and she remembered. 'You never took advantage.'

I lit a small cigar. It caught me in the back of the throat. 'Something I shall regret till the day I cough myself into extinction. How's old Sam? How's ex-Pilot Officer "Three-Fingers" Dogherty?'

'Bloody doctor!' For the first time, Bobby looked less than contented.

'Doctor?'

'Doctor Mackay. Came here with a face like an undertaker.' She gave a passable imitation of a gloomy Scottish medico. '"Mrs Dogherty, your husband's got to get out of the licensing trade or I'll not give him more than another year. Get him into a small bungalow and on to soft drinks." Can you imagine Sam in a bungalow?'

'Or on soft drinks! The mind boggles!'

'He'll find lime juice and soda has a pleasant little kick to it. That's what the doctor told me.'

'The kick of a mouse, I should imagine. In carpet slippers.'

'I told the quack, Sam's not scared. Sam used to go out every night to kill himself. He misses the war dreadfully.'

'I expect he does.'

'Saturday night in the Crooked Billet and a bloody good piss-up. It's the nearest he gets to the old days in the R.A.F.'

'You want to be careful . . . he doesn't rush out and bomb Torquay,' I warned her, and was delighted to see her laugh.

'You're not joking! The point is . . . should I tell Sam?'

'Won't your Doctor Mackay tell him?'

'You know how Sam is. He won't see hide nor hair of the doctor. So what should I do?'

'Why ask me?' I looked at her, having no advice to give.

'You're the bloody lawyer, darling. You're meant to know everything!'

At which point I was aware that, behind us, a man had come into the bar. I turned and saw him scowling at us. He was wearing a blazer, an R.A.F. scarf in an open shirt and scuffed suede shoes. I saw a good-looking face, grey hair and a grey moustache, all gone slightly to seed. It was none other than ex-Pilot Officer Sam 'Three-Fingers' Dogherty.

'We're not open yet!' He seemed to have not yet completely awakened from a deep afternoon kip, as he advanced on us, blinking at the lights round the bar.

'Sam! Can't you see who it is?' Bobby said, and her husband, who had at last identified the invasion, roared at me.

'My God, it's old grounded Rumpole! Rumpole of the ops room!' He moved rapidly to behind the bar and treated himself to a large Teachers which he downed rapidly. 'What the hell brings you to this neck of the woods?'

'He wrote us a letter.'

'Never read letters. Here's to the good old duke!' He was on his second whisky, and considerably more relaxed.

'What brings me? A lady ... you might say, a damsel in bloody great distress.'

'You're not still after Bobby, are you?' Sam was only pretend-ing to be suspicious.

'Of course. Till the day I die. But your wife's not in distress exactly.'

'Aren't I?' Bobby looked down into the depths of her gin and tonic, and I filled them in on the nature of my mission.

'The lady in question is a certain Miss Kathy Trelawny. One of the lotus eaters of "Nirvana", 34 Balaclava Road. Done for the possession of a suitcase full of cannabis resin.'

I had put up, as we used to say in the old days, a Black. If I had asked the Reverend Ian Paisley to pray for the Pope, I couldn't have invited an icier gaze of disapproval than Sam gave me as he said, 'You're *defending* her?'

'Against your crafty constabulary. Come in here, does she?'

'Not bloody likely! That crowd from Balaclava Road wouldn't get past the door. Anyway, they don't drink.' The glass of Teachers was recharged to banish the vision of the lotus eaters invading the Crooked Billet.

'Dear me. Is there no end to their decadence? But you know my client?'

'Never clapped eyes on her, thank God! No doubt she's about as glamorous as an unmade bed.'

'Oh, no doubt at all.' Gloomily, I thought he was almost certainly right, something peering through glasses, I thought, out of a mop of unwashed hair. Sam came out from behind the bar and started to bang about, straightening chairs and tables, switching on more lights.

'How can you defend that creature?'

'Easy! Prop myself to my feet in Court and do my best.'

'But you know damn well she's guilty!'

It's the one great error everyone makes about my learned profession; they think we defend people who have told us they did the deed. This legend doesn't add to the esteem in which barristers are held, and I sighed a little as I exploded the myth for the thousandth time.

'Ah, there you're wrong. I don't know that at all.'

'Pull the other one!' Sam shared the usual public view of legal eagles.

'I don't know. And if she ever admitted it to me, I'd have to make her surrender and plead "Guilty". We've got a few rules, old sweetheart. We don't deceive Courts, not on purpose.'

'You mean, you think she's innocent?' Sam made it clear that no one who lived in a commune called 'Nirvana' could possibly be innocent of anything.

'He told you, Sam! He's got rules about it.' Bobby was polishing glasses and coming to the rescue of an old friend.

'At the moment I think she's the victim of a trick by the police. That's what I'll have to go on thinking, until she tells me otherwise.'

'That's ridiculous! The police don't trick people. Not in England.' Sam clearly felt he'd not delivered us from the Nazi hordes for nothing.

'Never had a plain clothes copper come in here and order a large Scotch after closing time?' I asked him.

'The bastards! But that's entirely different.'

'Yes, of course.'

'Anyway, who's paying you to defend Miss Slag-Heap? That's what I'd like to know.' Sam was triumphant. It hurt me, but I had to tell him.

'Fasten your seat belt, old darling. You are! Miss Kathy Trelawny is on legal aid. And I am here by courtesy of the ratepayers of Coldsands.' I lifted my rum in Sam's direction. 'Thank you, "Three-Fingers". Thank you for your hospitality.'

'Bloody hell.' Sam sounded more sorrowful than angry, and it gave him an excuse to turn the handle once more on the Teachers.

'We don't mind, do we, Sam?' As always Bobby's was the voice of tolerance. 'We don't mind buying Horace the odd drink occasionally.'

Later I sat in the residents' lounge, a small room which opened off the bar, and tried to shut out the considerable noise made by Sam's regular customers, middle-aged men mostly, in a sort of uniform of cavalry twill trousers and hacking jackets. I was working on my brief and already I had a plan of campaign. When the Detective Sergeant went to buy Miss Trelawny's cannabis he was disguised as a hippie and acting, I was quite prepared to argue, as an *agent provocateur*. If I could establish that my client would never have committed any sort of crime unless the police had invited her to I might, given a fair wind and a sympathetic judge, have the whole of the police evidence excluded which would lead to the collapse of the prosecution, a Zen service of thanksgiving at 'Nirvana', and Rumpole triumphant. I had brought a number of law reports on the question of *agent provocateur* and was interested to discover that it was the old hanging judges who regarded these beasts with particular disfavour; it's odd how gentler days have somehow dimmed our passion for liberty.

I had worked out an argument that might appeal to a judge who still had some of the old spark left in him when the door from the bar opened to admit Mr Friendly and my client.

I had, I felt, known Miss Kathy Trelawny for a long time. She had floated before my eyes from my early days with the old *Oxford Book of English Verse*, as Herrick's Julia, or Lovelace's

Lucasta, or 'La Belle Dame Sans Merci', or the 'Lady of Shallot'. As she smiled, she reminded me strongly of Rosalind in the forest of Arden, or Viola comforting the love-sick Duke. She had a long, slender neck, a mass of copper-coloured hair, friendly blue eyes and she was exceedingly clean. As soon as I saw her I decided that my one ambition in life was to keep her out of Holloway. I had to take a quick gulp from the glass beside me before I could steady my nerve to read out a passage from the depositions. Miss Trelawny was sitting quietly looking at me as if I was the one man in the world she had always wanted to meet, and she hoped we would soon be finished with the boring case so we could talk about something interesting, and deeply personal.

'"Real cool house, man,"' I was reading out the Detective Sergeant's evidence with disgust. '"You can't score nothing in this hick town. You don't get no trouble from the Fuzz". Just from the way the old darling talked, didn't you twig he was a Sergeant from the local Drug Squad?'

Miss Trelawny showed no particular reaction, and Friendly quickly filled the silence. 'My client has never come up against the police before.'

'We'll have a bit of fun with this case,' I told them.

'What sort of fun exactly?' Friendly sounded doubtful, as if he didn't exactly look on the coming trial as the annual dinner dance of the Coldsands Rotary.

'A preliminary point! In the absence of the jury we will ask the judge to rule the whole of Detective Sergeant Jack Smedley, alias Jack the Hippie's evidence inadmissible. On the sole ground . . .'

'On what sole ground?'

'That it was obtained contrary to natural justice, in that it constituted a trick. That it is the testimony of an *agent provocateur*.'

'We don't get many of those in conveyancing.' Friendly looked distinctly out of his depth.

'A nasty foreign expression, for a nasty foreign thing. Spies and infiltrators! Policemen in disguise who worm their way into an Englishman's home and trap him into crime!'

'Why should they do that, Mr Rumpole?' I stood up and directed my answer at my client. Her warm and all-embracing smile, and her total silence, were beginning to unnerve me. 'So they can clap innocent citizens into chokey and notch up another conviction on their collective braces! Bloody unBritish – like bidets and eating your pud after the cheese! Now, I mean your average circuit judge ... Circus judges ... we call them down the Bailey.'

Friendly consulted a note. 'It's his Honour James Crispin-Rice tomorrow.'

We were in luck. I knew old Rice Crispies well at the Bar. He was a thoroughly decent chap, who had once stood as a Liberal candidate. He was the product of the Navy and a minor public school. No doubt he'd had it firmly implanted in him in the fourth form – never trust a sneak.

They had left the door slightly open, and through it I could hear the old familiar sound of Bobby thumping the piano.

'You think he might rule out the evidence?'

I got up and shut the door, blotting out some remarkable tuneless rendering of the Golden Oldies which had started up à côté de Chez Dogherty.

'If we can implant a strong dislike of Sergeant Smedley in the old darling,' I told them. 'Disgusting behaviour, your Honour. The police are there to detect crime, not manufacture it. What's the country coming to? Constables tricked out in beads and singing to a small guitar conning an innocent girl into making huge collections of cannabis resin from some Persian pushers she met at Bristol University. She'd never have done it if the policeman hadn't asked her!'

'Wouldn't you, Miss Trelawny?' Friendly gave her the cue to speak. She ignored it, so on I went showing her my quality.

'Withdraw the evidence from the jury, your Honour! It's un-English, unethical and clearly shows that this crime was deliber-ately created by the police. The whole business is a vile outrage to our age-old liberties.' Wordsworth crept into my mind and I didn't send him about his business. *'It is not to be thought of that the Flood of British freedom, which to the open sea ...'* I paused, insecure on the words and then, very quietly and for the first time, Miss Kathy Trelawny spoke, with words appropriately supplied by the old sheep of the Lake District.

'Of the world's praise, from dark antiquity   Hath flowed,
"with pomp of waters unwithstood," . . . Should perish.'

She looked at me, I took over.

'We must be free or die, who speak the tongue   That Shakespeare spake . . .' I decided I'd had enough of Wordsworth, and asked her, surprised, 'You know it?'

'Wordsworth? A little.'

'I thought no one did nowadays. Whenever I come out with him in the Bar Mess they look amazed. Unusual, for a client to know Wordsworth.'

'I teach kids English.'

'Oh yes. Of course you do.' I had learned from the brief that all the inhabitants of 'Nirvana' were in work.

'There's one thing I wanted to ask you.' Now she had broken the ice, there seemed to be no holding her, but Friendly stood up, as if anxious to bring the conference to an end.

'Well, we shouldn't keep Mr Rumpole any longer.'

'Ask me, Miss Trelawny?'

'Yes.' Her smile was unwavering. 'What do you want me to say exactly?'

'Say? Say nothing! Look . . . rely on me, with a little help from Wordsworth. And keep your mouth firmly closed.'

I opened the door. Great gusts of singing blew in on us from the bar. Bobby's voice was leading, 'We'll meet again   Don't know where   Don't know when,   But we're bound to meet again   Some sunny day.'

I remembered my craven cowardice in not speaking to Bobby on the occasion of the N.A.A.F.I. hop, and I asked Miss Trelawny to join me for a drink. Fortunately, Friendly remembered that his wife would be waiting up for him, and I took my client alone into the bar.

As we sat at the counter, Sam came up to us swaying only slightly, like a captain on the deck of his well-loved ship. He looked at Kathy Trelawny with amazed approval.

'Where did you get this popsy, Rumpole?' He leant across the bar to chat to my client intimately. 'You shouldn't be with the ground staff, my dear. You're definitely officer material. What's it to be?'

'I'll have a coke. I don't drink really.' She was smiling at him, the smile I thought, uncomfortably, of universal love bestowed on everyone, regardless of age or sex.

'Oh, don't you? You don't drink!' Sam took offence. 'There's nothing else you don't do, is there?'

'Quite a lot of things.' Sam ignored this and recalled the Good Old Days as he passed me a rum.

'Remember, Rumpole? We used to divide the popsies into beer W.A.A.F.s and gin W.A.A.F.s.' He winked at Kathy Trelawny. 'In my opinion you're a large pink gin.'

'She told you, Sam. She doesn't drink,' I reminded Sam. He was getting impatient.

'Did you pick up this beautiful bit of crackling in a bloody Baptist Chapel?' He poured Miss Trelawny a Coca-Cola.

'Take no notice of him, my dear. You can be teetotal with Rumpole. But let's launch *our* friendship on a sea of sparkling shampoo!'

'I'd probably sink,' Kathy Trelawny smiled at him.

'Not with me you wouldn't. Let me introduce myself. Pilot Officer "Three-Fingers" Dogherty. "Three-Fingers" refers to the measures of my whisky. My hands are in perfect order.' To demonstrate this he put a hand on hers across the bar.

'I haven't met many pilot officers.'

Kathy, I feel I know her well enough to call her Kathy for the rest of this narrative, withdrew her hand. She was still smiling.

'Well, you've met *me*, my dear!' Sam rambled on undiscouraged. 'One of the glamour boys. One of the Brylcreem brigade. One of the very, very few.' He stood himself another Teachers. 'And if I had a crate available, I'd bloody well smuggle you up in the sky for a couple of victory rolls. You see him . . . You see "Groundstaff Rumpole"? Well, we'd leave him far below us! Grounded!'

'I don't think we should do that,' Kathy protested. The only time she stopped smiling was when Sam made a joke.

'Why ever not?' Sam frowned.

'I think I'm going to need him.' As she said this I felt ridiculously honoured.

'Rumpole? Why ever should you *need* Rumpole? What did you say your name was?'

'I didn't.'

Now my time had come. I had great pleasure in performing the introduction.

'This is Miss Kathy Trelawny. Of "Nirvana", 34 Balaclava Road.' And I added, in a whisper to Sam, 'the well-known unmade bed'.

Sam looked like a man who has just lifted what he imagined was a glass of vintage champagne and discovered it contained nothing but Seven Up. He looked at Kathy with pronounced distaste and said, 'No bloody wonder you don't drink.'

'It's just something I don't like doing.' She smiled back at him.

'Naturally. Naturally you won't have a pink gin like a normal girl. Excuse me.' He moved away from us, shouting, 'Drink up please. Haven't any of you lot got homes?'

The piano stopped, people started to drift out into the night.

'Was that meant to be a joke ... All that "pilot officer" business?' Kathy asked me.

'No joke at all. Sam was a great man on bombers. He could find any target you'd care to mention, in the pitch dark, on three fingers of whisky ... He was good, Sam. Extremely good.'

'You mean good at killing people?' When she put it like that, I supposed that was what I did mean. Kathy turned to look at Bobby, who was sitting on the piano stool, lighting a cigarette. She asked me and I told her that was Sam's wife and I used to think she was gorgeous.

'Gorgeous for the war time, anyway. Things were a bit utility then.'

'And now?'

I looked at her. 'Children seem to grow up more beautiful. It must be the orange juice.'

'Or the peace?'

Sam gave us a crescendo version of 'Time Please' and I walked my client to the bus shelter. It was a still, rather warm September night. The sea murmured perpetually, and the moonlight lit up the headland and whitened the strip of beach. There were only very few words for it, and I recited them to Kathy as we moved away from the cars starting up round the Crooked Billet.

'*It is a beauteous evening, calm and free,   The holy time is quiet as a Nun   Breathless with adoration . . .*'

'We read poetry. At the house,' Kathy told me. 'It's a good way to end the day. Someone reads a poem. Anything.' And then she shivered on that warm night, and said, 'They won't lock me up will they?'

'I told you. We'll knock out the evidence! Put your trust in Rumpole!' I tried to sound as cheerful as possible, but she stood still, trembling slightly, her hand on my arm.

'My brother Pete's locked up in Turkey . . . twelve years. He was always such a scared kid. He couldn't sleep with the door shut. Neither of us could.'

'What on earth did your brother do in Turkey?'

'Drugs,' she said, and I wondered what sort of an idiot her brother must be. Then she asked me, 'Will it be over soon?'

'It'll be over.'

There were lights coming up the hill, to take her away from me.

'That's my bus . . . why don't you come and see me in "Nirvana"?'

Then the most strange thing happened, she leant forward and kissed me, quite carefully on the cheek. Then she was gone, and I was saying to myself, ' "Nirvana"? Why ever not?' I walked back to the Crooked Billet in a state of ridiculous happiness. Flower power that year was exceedingly potent.

I was up early the next morning, sinking a boiled egg in the residents' lounge as the sun sparkled on the sea and Bobby fussed around me, pouring tea. Sam was still asleep, God was in his heaven and with old Rice Crispies on the bench I could find nothing particularly wrong with the world. After breakfast I put a drop of eau-de-cologne on the handkerchief, ran a comb through the remaining hair and set off for the Coldsands seat of justice.

When I got down to the Shire Hall, and into the wig and gown, I had my first view of the inhabitants of 'Nirvana', the lotus eaters of 34 Balaclava Road. They were out in force, clean jeans, Mexican-looking shawls, the statutory baby. One tall coloured boy whom I later discovered to be called 'Oswald' was carrying a small flute. I just hoped they weren't going to mistake the whole business for a bit of harmless fun round the South African Embassy.

'Morning. You must be Rumpole. Welcome to the Western Circuit.' I was being addressed by a tall fellow with a rustic tan beneath his wig, a gentleman farmer and gentleman barrister. I looked down to discover if he had jodhpur boots on under the pinstripes.

'Tooke. Vernon Tooke's my name. I'm prosecuting you.'

'Awfully decent of you.' I smiled at him.

Tooke glanced disapprovingly at my supporters club.

'I say, Rumpole. Where did you get that shower from? Rent-a-hippie. What a life, eh . . . Gang-bangs on the National Assistance?'

Did I detect in Farmer Tooke's voice – a note of envy?

'Used to be a decent area,' he continued, 'Balaclava Road. Until that lot got their foot in the door. Squatters, are they?'

'They've got a nine-year lease. And they've all got jobs. The only fellows scrounging off the State, Tooke, are you and I!'

'Really Rumpole?' Tooke looked pained.

'Well, they're paying you on the rates, aren't they?'

'Most amusing!' He looked as if I'd pointed out a bad case of foot and mouth in the herd, but he offered me a cigarette from a gold case. I refused and produced the remains of a small cigar from the waistcoat pocket. Tooke ignited it with a gold lighter.

'Is this going to take long?' he asked anxiously. 'Coldsands gymkhana tomorrow. We tend to make it rather a day out.'

'Take long? I don't suppose so. It's quite a simple point of law.'

'Law, Rumpole . . . Did you say law?' The casually dropped word seemed to fill Tooke with a certain amount of dread.

'That's right. You do have law, I suppose, down on the Western Circuit?'

I left Tooke and moved towards the commune. A young man with dark hair and a permanent frown who seemed to be their leader greeted me, as I thought, in an unfriendly fashion.

'You her lawyer?'

I admitted it. Kathy, smiling as ever, introduced him to me as a friend of hers, named Dave Hawkins. I speculated, with a ridiculous stab of regret, that the friendship was a close one.

'This is Dave.'

'Oh yes?'

'Will she be going in today?' Dave wanted to be put in the picture.

'In?'

'Into the witness box. I mean, there's something I want her to say. It's pretty important.'

I was accustomed to being the sole person in charge of my cases. I put Dave right patiently. 'Dave. May I call you Mr Hawkins? If I were a doctor taking out your appendix, old darling, you wouldn't want Kathy, would you, telling me where to put the knife?' At this point the usher came out of court and called,

'Katherine Trelawny.'

'You'd better answer your bail.' As I said this Kathy gave a little shiver and asked me. 'Will they lock me up now?'

'Of course not. Trust me.'

The usher called her again. I dropped the remnants of the small cigar on the marble floor of the Shire Hall and ground it underfoot. The lance was in the rest, Sir Galahad Rumpole was about to do battle for the damsel in distress, or words to that effect.

Half-way through the afternoon things were going pretty well. Rice Crispies, doing his job in a very decent fashion, was decidedly interested in the point of *agent provocateur*. Kathy was smiling in the dock, the commune were gripped by the spectacle, and outside the Court room the baby, unaware of the solemnity of the occasion, was yelling lustily. In the witness box, Detective Sergeant Jack Smedley was looking extremely square, clean shaven and in his natty Old Bill uniform.

'I see Detective Sergeant,' I had the pleasure to put to him, 'you are no longer wearing your beads.'

'Beads? What beads are those?' The judge was puzzled.

'I was wearing beads, your Honour – on the occasion of my visits to 34 Balaclava Road.'

'*Beads!* With the uniform?' His Honour couldn't believe his ears. No one had sported beads in the Navy.

'Not with the uniform! With the embroidered jeans, and the waistcoat of Afghan goat, and the purple silk drapery knotted round your neck.' I pursued my advantage.

'I was in plain clothes, your Honour.'

'Plain clothes, Sergeant? You were in fancy dress!' I rode over a titter from the commune. 'Now perhaps you'll tell the Court. What's happened to your gaucho moustache?'

'I . . . I shaved it off.'

'Why?'

'In view of certain comments, your Honour, passed in the Station. It wasn't a gaucho. More a Viva Zapata, actually.'

'A Viva, *what* was that, Mr Rumpole?' The judge seemed to feel the world slipping away from him.

'The officer was affecting the moustache, your Honour, of a well-known South American revolutionary.' This news worried the old darling on the bench deeply.

'A South American! Can you tell me, officer, what was the purpose of this elaborate disguise?' The witness paused. I filled the gap with my humble submission.

'May I suggest an answer, Sergeant? You took it into your head to pose as a drug dealer in order to trap this quite innocent young woman . . .' I had the pleasure of pointing out Kathy in the dock . . . 'into taking part in a filthy trade she wouldn't otherwise have dreamed of.'

'Well yes, but . . .'

'What did he say?' Rice Crispies pounced on the grudging admission.

'Your Honour.' The witness tried to start again.

'Shorthand writer, just read me that answer.'

There was a long pause while the elderly lady shuffled through her notes, but at last the passage was reproduced.

'. . . in order to trap this quite innocent young woman into taking part in a filthy trade.' 'Well yes, but . . .'

The judge made a note of that. I could have kissed the old darling. However, I pressed on.

'But what, Sergeant?'

'She wasn't so innocent.'

'What reason had you to suppose that?'

'Her way of life, your Honour.'

'What I want you to tell me, officer, is this.' The judge weighed in in support of Rumpole. 'Did you have any reason to believe that this young woman was dealing in drugs before you went there in your Viva ... What?'

'Zapata, your Honour,' I helped him along.

'Thank you, Mr Rumpole. I'm much obliged.'

'We had received certain information.' The sergeant did his best to make it sound sinister.

'And will you let us into the secret, officer. What was this information?'

'That Miss Trelawny was the type to get involved.'

'Involved by you?'

'Involved already.'

Tooke, who seemed to feel the case was eluding his grasp, rose to his feet. 'I shall be calling the evidence, your Honour, of the neighbour, Miss Tigwell.'

'Very well, Mr Tooke.'

'But if the evidence shows no previous attempt to deal in drugs, then you would agree the whole of this crime was a result of your fertile imagination.' I fired a final salvo at the witness but the judge interrupted me, perfectly fairly.

'Doesn't that rather depend, Mr Rumpole, on the effect of Miss Tigwell's evidence? When we hear it?'

'If your Honour pleases. Of course, as always, your Honour is perfectly right!' I rewarded that upright fellow Rice Crispies with a low bow and sat down in a mood of quiet self-congratulation. I hadn't been sitting long before the man, Dave, was at my side whispering furiously, 'Is that *all* you're going to ask?'

'You want to have a go?' I whispered back. 'Do borrow the wig, old darling.'

The evidence of Kathy's previous malpractices was offered to us in the person of Miss Tigwell who lived opposite at No. 33 Balaclava Road, and whose idea of entertainment appeared to be gazing into the windows of 'Nirvana' in the daily hope of moral indignation.

'I could tell exactly what they were.'

'What were they, Miss Tigwell?'

'Perverted. All living higgledy-piggledy. Men and women, black and white.'

'Did your supervision include the bedrooms?'

'Well . . . No. But they all sat together in the front room.'

'Sat together? What did they talk about?'

'I couldn't hear that.'

'They were a community, that's what it comes to. They might well have been Trappist monks for all you knew.'

'I don't know if Mr Rumpole is suggesting his client is a Trappist monk.' Tooke made a mistake, he should have left the jokes to me. Rice Crispies didn't smile.

'Now, Miss Tigwell, apart from the fact that persons of different sex, *sat* together . . . Did you ever observe anything suspicious from your post in the crow's nest?'

'I saw a man giving her money.' Miss Tigwell was playing her King. 'Quite a lot of money. It was in ten pound notes.'

'Was this the first time you had ever seen money passing or any sort of dealing going on in "Nirvana"?'

'The first time, yes.'

The judge was making a note. I decided to play my Ace and prayed that I wouldn't be trumped by the prosecution.

'Can you describe to his Honour the man you saw passing the money?'

'Dreadful-looking person. A clear criminal type. Looked as if he'd been dragged through a hedge backwards.'

'Long hair?'

'And the horrible sort of moustache.'

'Beads? Embroidered jeans? Afghan goat's hair and purple silk fancy for the neck?' I saw Detective Sergeant ex-hippie Smedley bow his head in shame, and I knew I was home and dry.

'Disgusting! I saw it all quite distinctly!' Miss Tigwell ended in triumph.

'Congratulations, madam. You have now given us a perfectly accurate description of Detective Smedley of the local force.'

As I took off the wig in the robing room, Farmer Tooke was looking distinctly worried. I did my best to cheer him up. 'Ah, Tooke . . . I have good news for you. Hope to get you all off in time for the gymkhana tomorrow. Got a daughter, have you, in the potato race?'

'Do you think the judge is agin me?' Tooke felt all was not well with the prosecution.

'Not you, personally. But I know what he's thinking.'

'Do you?'

'Encourage that sort of police officer and he'll be out in a frock on the Prom tomorrow – soliciting the chairman of the bench.'

Tooke saw the point. 'I say. I suppose that sort of thing is worrying.'

'Not English, if you want my opinion.'

At which Tooke, climbing into his Burberry, put the law behind him and extended an invitation.

'What are you doing tonight, Rumpole? I mean, there'll be a few of us dining at the Bar hotel . . . With the leader of the Circuit.'

'Roast lamb, sea shanties and old jokes from Quarter Sessions? No. Not tonight, Tooke.'

'Oh well. I'm sorry. We like to give our visitors a little hospitality.'

'Tonight, I am dropping out.'

Dinner at 'Nirvana' was a distinct surprise. I'd expected nut cutlets and carrot juice. I got an excellent steak and kidney pud and a very drinkable claret. Oswald had told me he was something of a 'wine freak'. The house was clean and the big cushions and old sofas remarkably comfortable. The babies were good enough to withdraw from the company, the record-player gave us unobtrusive flute music from the Andes and Kathy tended to all my needs, filling my glass and lighting my cigar, and remained a perpetual pleasure to the eye. I began to think that I'd rather live at 34 Balaclava Road than at the Gloucester Road mansion flat with She Who Must Be Obeyed; I'd rather sit back on the scatter cushions at 'Nirvana' and let my mind go a complete blank than drag myself down to the Bailey on a wet Monday morning to defend some over-excited Pakistani accused of raping his social worker. In fact I thought that for tuppence, for a packet of small cigars, I'd give up the law and spend the rest of my life in a pair of old plimsolls and grey flannel bags, shrimping on the beach at Coldsands.

The only fly in this soothing ointment was the fellow Dave. When I told Kathy she wouldn't even have to go into the witness box if we won our *agent provocateur* argument, Dave said, 'I'm not sure I agree with that.' I told him firmly that I wasn't sure he had to.

'When we brought you here I thought you'd understand . . . It's not just another case,' Dave protested. Protesting seemed to be his main occupation.

'Every case is just another case,' I told him.

'To you, all right! To us it's a chance to say what we have to. Can't we put the law straight – on the drug scene?'

'I mean, this isn't a den of thieves, is it? You've seen "Nirvana"!' Oswald put the point more gently. He was right, of course, I had seen 'Nirvana'.

'Now's our only chance to get *through* to the law,' Dave told me. I decided to instruct him on the facts of life.

'The law? You know where the law is now? Down in the George Hotel drinking the Circuit port and singing "What Shall We Do with the Drunken Sailor". The law is talking about the comical way the old Lord Chief passed a death sentence. The law is in another world; but it thinks it's the *whole* world. Just as you lot think the world's nothing but poetry, and perhaps the occasional puff of a dangerous cigarette.'

'That's what we've got you for. To put our point of view across.' Dave had mistaken my function.

'You've got me to get you out of trouble. That's what you've got me for. I'm not going to get up tomorrow and teach old Rice Crispies to sing protest songs . . . to a small guitar.'

'You're just not taking this case seriously!' Dave was totally wrong, and I told him so.

'Oh yes I am. I am seriously determined to keep Kathy out of prison.'

At which Miss Trelawny said it was time for their nightly poem. She found a book and gave it to me open.

'Me?'

'You like this. Read it to us . . .'

So I read to the lotus eaters, quietly at first and then with more emphasis, enjoying the sound of my own voice. *'It is a beauteous evening, calm and free, The holy time is quiet as a Nun Breathless with adoration; the broad sun Is sinking down in its tranquillity.'*

They were all listening as though they actually enjoyed it. except for Dave who was whispering to Kathy.

'Dear Child! dear Girl! that walkest with me here, If thou appear untouched by solemn thought . . .'

Kathy was shushing Dave, making him listen to the old sheep. I looked at her as I read the last lines.

'Thy nature is not therefore less divine: Thou liest in Abraham's bosom all the year; And worshipp'st at the Temple's inner shrine, God being with thee when we know it not.'

I slammed the book shut. I needed to sleep before Court in the morning.

'The Officer was only doing his duty. Active, your Honour, in the pursuit of crime!' Tooke was making his final speech on the point of evidence, to an unenthusiastic audience.

'Or in the manufacture of a crime? That's what troubles me.' The judge was really troubled, bless him. He went on. 'If I thought this young woman only collected drugs . . . only got in touch with any sort of supplier because of the trap set for her – then would you concede, Mr Tooke, I would have to reject the evidence?'

'I think your Honour would.'

Tooke was a lovely prosecutor. Everything was going extremely well when Rice Crispies adjourned for lunch. So I was in festive mood when I set off for a crab sandwich and a nourishing stout in the pub opposite the Shire Hall, looking forward to wetting my whistle and putting the final touch on my clinching argument. But I was stopped by Friendly who said the client wanted to see me as a matter of urgency. He led me into a small room, decorated with old framed leases and eighteenth-century maps of Coldsands, and there, clearly bursting with news to impart, were Miss Kathy Trelawny and her friend Dave.

'We want to tell the truth.' I closed the door carefully and looked at her Dave without encouragement.

'What truth?'

'It's the only way I can get Peter's case across,' Kathy said. She was smiling no longer.

'Peter?'

'My brother. I told you. He was busted.'

'In Turkey. I remember. Well, this isn't Turkey. And it's not Peter's case or anyone else's.' I looked at Kathy. 'It's yours.'

'Kathy wants you to know why she did it.'

She was about to speak, and I almost shouted at her, hoping it still wasn't too late.

'Shut up!'

'You see I had . . .'

'The conference is over! Got to get a bite of lunch. Come on, Friendly.' I moved to the door.

'It appears we have new instructions, Mr Rumpole.' Friendly looked concerned, not half so concerned as I was.

'The old instructions are doing very nicely, thank you. Don't say a word until this evening. When it's all over tell me what you like.'

'She wants everyone to know. How else can we get Pete's case into the papers?'

Dave, like an idiot, had moved between me and the door. I had no way of escaping the fusillade of truth which Kathy then let fly.

'I got the stuff last year after Pete got busted in Istanbul. I was going to sell it anyway. It was going to cost ten thousand pounds to get him out in lawyers' fees and . . .' she looked at me almost accusingly, 'bribes, I suppose . . . He got twelve years. We've got to get people to care about Peter!'

So it was quite clear, she was telling me that she hadn't committed her crime as the result of a request from an *agent provocateur*. She had the stuff before Detective Sergeant Smedley of the west country Drug Squad first came to 'Nirvana'. That was the truth, the last thing in the world I wanted to know. I looked at my watch, and turned to Friendly.

'What is there – a 2.25 back to London? Friendly, run outside, for God's sake, and see if you can't whistle me up a taxi. I'm retiring from this case.'

Friendly, totally puzzled by the turn of events, left us.

'Running out on us?' Dave never made an unexpected remark.

'Why, for God's sake?' Kathy asked me, and I had to tell her. 'Let me try and explain. My existence is bound by a small blue volume handed down like the Tablets on the day of my Call to the Bar by a Master of my Inn in a haze of port and general excitement.'

'What the hell's he talking about!' Dave couldn't resist interrupting, but Kathy told him to listen. I went on with such calm as I could muster.

'Barristers down the ages have killed. They have certainly committed adultery. Although that sort of thing doesn't appeal to me some may well have coveted their neighbours' camels and no doubt worshipped graven images. But I don't believe there's one of us who has ever gone on to fight a case after our client has told us, in clear crystal ringing tones, that they actually did the deed.'

'You mean – you won't help me?' Kathy looked as if it had never occurred to her.

'I can't now.'

'But Kathy wants to tell the judge the pot law's ridiculous. And about Pete.'

'It's my duty to preside over your acquittal, not your martyrdom to the dubious cause of intoxication,' I told her. 'I'll see the judge and tell him I can't act for you any longer . . . personal reasons.'

'The old fool'll think you fancy her.' I can't imagine where Dave got that far-fetched idea, and I went on ignoring him.

'You'll get another barrister. What you tell him is your business. I'll ask the judge to adjourn for a week or two . . . You'll still be on bail.'

'What's the matter? Afraid to stick your neck out? Or would

you starve to death if they made pot legal?' Dave was about to start on another of his political speeches, but Kathy silenced him. She asked him to leave us alone, and I told him to go and find Friendly and my taxi. He went. He had smashed my defence and I was alone with Kathy, looking at the pieces.

'I thought ... We got along together.' Kathy was smiling again. I couldn't help admiring her courage. 'I mean, you keep talking about clients. I didn't think I was a client. I thought I was more of a friend, actually.'

'Never have friends for clients. That really ought to be one of the Ten Commandments.'

'I don't suppose you could forget what I told you?'

'Of course I could. I'd like nothing more than to forget it. I'd forget it at once if I wasn't a bloody barrister!'

'And there's nothing more important than that in your life? Being a barrister.'

I thought about this very carefully. Unfortunately, there was only one answer.

'No.'

'Poetry doesn't mean a damn thing to you! Friendship doesn't mean anything. You're just an old man with a heart full of a book about legal etiquette!' Kathy was angry now, she'd stopped smiling.

'You're saying just what I have long suspected,' I had to agree with her.

'Why don't you do something about it?'

'What do you suggest?' She moved away from me, and went and looked out of the window, at the sunshine and the municipal begonias. At last she said, 'I might leave Coldsands and come up to London. Do a language course.'

'And Dave? Would Dave be coming with you?'

'Dave's stuck here organizing the house. I want to get away. Have a bit of a rest from home-made muesli and debates about the geyser. I thought. Well. I'd get a flat in London. I could come and have lunch with you sometimes. When you're in the Old Bailey.'

'Every man has his price. Is that mine? A lunch down the Old Bailey?'

'Not enough?'

'More than enough. Probably, much more. Something to think about, in the long cold nights with She Who Must Be Obeyed.'

She suddenly turned on me, she was holding on to my arm, as if afraid of falling.

'I'm not going to prison! You won't let them send me to prison!'

There was only one way, now Dave had done his damnedest.

'I can go and see the judge. He might agree to a suspended sentence. I don't know. I can go and see him.'

'That's right! He likes you. I could see you get along. Go and see him. Please go and see him.' She was smiling again, eager. I had to tell her the facts of life.

'You know what it means. If I go and see the judge for you?'

'I . . . I plead guilty.' She knew. I left her then and went to the door. We still had our trump card. Dear old Rice Crispies was simply aching to get away to the gymkhana.

His Honour Judge Crispin-Rice was delighted to see Rumpole and the prosecuting Tooke. He made us Nescafé with the electric kettle in his room. He looked younger with his wig off, and, when we had settled such vital matters as how much milk and no sugar thank you, he and Tooke tried to make me envious of their previous night's revelry in the Bar Mess.

'We had a good evening. You should have been with us, Rumpole. Didn't we have a splendid evening, Vernon?'

'The leader gave us "The Floral Dance".' Tooke relived the great moment.

'Old Pascoe is wonderful for 75. He entertained us in song.' The judge offered us a Senior Service. 'You'd have enjoyed it.'

'A splendid evening! We fined little Moreton a dozen bottles of claret for talking shop at dinner.' Tooke was bubbling at the memory.

'We then started hacking away at the penalty! How many bottles were left?'

'None, Judge. As far as I remember.'

I thought the time had come to return their thoughts to the business in hand.

'Look here, Judge,' I said. 'At the risk of being fined for

talking shop. If . . . If it so happened I could persuade my client to plead guilty . . .' His Honour was stirring his cup, giving me no great assistance. 'You might be grateful for a short afternoon.' Even this didn't hook him. I went on, a little desperately. 'She's a remarkable girl.'

'So I can see.' Old Rice Crispies smiled then. Perhaps, I thought, I could rope him into 'Nirvana'.

'Knows a good deal about Wordsworth.' I didn't know if this would sway the judicial mind.

'Wordsworth? Is he a mitigating factor?'

'Poor old sheep of the Lake District. He can't afford to lose admirers.'

'No. Well. She'd get the full benefit of pleading guilty.' He was using his judge's voice. I stood up, like a barrister.

'Can't you tell me any more than that?'

'There *are* rules.'

'I thought you might indicate . . .'

'The tariff? You know the tariff. How much was it? Twenty pounds weight. A fair wallop!'

'It was only cannabis.' I tried to make it sound like broken biscuits. 'They use the stuff just like whisky. It doesn't occur to them . . .'

'But it isn't whisky, is it?' The judge's voice again. 'It's a Class B drug as defined by the Dangerous Drugs Act.'

'But what do we *know* about it?'

'That it's illegal. Isn't that all we need to know?' He looked at me then, and gave me a charming smile. 'My God, Rumpole. Are we going to see *you* turning up in Court in beads?'

'She's got a good character.' I played my last card.

The judge drained his Nescafé. 'Well, you know about a "good character". Everyone had a "good character" once . . . I mean, if we let everyone out because of their "good character" no one would ever go inside.'

'That'd be a scandal. All those empty prisons.' I said it with too much feeling. Rice Crispies looked at me as if I were coming out in a rash.

'I say, Rumpole. You're not getting *involved* in this case, are you?'

'Involved? Of course not. No, naturally. But I was thinking possibly a suspended sentence?' At which his Honour Judge Crispin-Rice put his wig back on and said something which was no help at all.

'You've got your job to do, Rumpole, and I've got mine.'

I sweated my guts out in my speech in mitigation, and the judge listened to me with perfect courtesy. He then gave Kathy Trelawny three years in the nicest possible way, and she was taken down to the cells. Vernon Tooke came up to me in the robing room. He was on his way to the gymkhana.

'Well. Ended nice and quick.'

'Yes, Tooke, very quickly.'

'Going back to London?'

'Tomorrow. I'll be going back tomorrow.'

'Quite an attractive sort of person, your client.'

'Yes, Tooke.'

'All the same. To prison she had to go.'

When I came out into the main hall the commune was standing in a little group. Oswald was playing a lament on his flute and the baby was silent. None of them spoke to me, but I heard a voice at my elbow say, 'It seems a shame, sir. A girl like that.' It was Detective Sergeant Jack the Hippie Smedley. And he added what we both knew, 'It's an evil place, Holloway.'

Out in the street I was nearly run over by a police car. Miss Kathy Trelawny was sitting in the back and saw me. She was still smiling.

Joviality was at its height in the Crooked Billet that night. Sam told all his old stories, and Bobby played the piano. I stood beside her, my glass of rum on the piano top, and in a pause she looked across at her husband.

'Look at Sam,' she said. 'He's happy as a tick! What's he want with a slow death on lime juice in a bungalow? I made up my mind. I'm not going to tell him. Are you in favour of that?'

'People not telling people things? People not scattering information like bombs? Oh yes,' I told her. 'I'm all in favour of that.'

Then she played 'Roll out the Barrel' and we all joined in, our voices floating out over the sea until Sam called 'Time Please'. I never saw the people from 'Nirvana' again.

Rumpole and the Honourable Member

'You're giving me a rape?'

My clerk, Albert, had just handed me a brief. He then returned to the complicated business of working out the petty cash account; his desk was covered with slips of paper, a cash box and odd bits of currency. I never inquired into Albert's system of book-keeping, nor did anyone else in Chambers.

'Don't you want it, Mr Rumpole?' I turned to look at Henry, our second clerk. Henry had joined as an office boy, a small tousled figure who scarcely seemed able to read or write. Albert used him mainly to run errands and make instant coffee, and told him he would only be allowed to take a barrister into Court when he'd learnt to shine his shoes and clean his fingernails. Henry had changed over the years. His shoes were now gleaming, he wore a neat pinstriped suit with a waistcoat, and was particularly assiduous in his attentions to Guthrie Featherstone, Q.C., M.P., our Head of Chambers. Albert, as head clerk, got ten per cent of our earnings, but Henry was on a salary. I had thought for a long time that Henry thought Albert past it, and had his eye on a head clerk's position. I should add, so you can get the complete picture of life in our clerk's room, that our old lady typist had left us and we had a new girl called Dianne who read quite extraordinarily lurid novels when she wasn't typing, spent a great deal of the day titivating in the loo, and joined Henry in looking pityingly at Albert as he struggled to adjust the petty cash.

'You don't ask whether you want a rape,' I told Henry sharply. 'Rape comes uninvited.' I was gathering my post from the mantelpiece and looked at it with disgust. 'Like little brown envelopes from the Inland Revenue.'

'Morning Rumpole.' I became aware of the presence of young Erskine-Brown who was standing by the mantelpiece, also watching Albert in his struggle to balance the budget. He was holding some sort of legal document and wearing a shirt with broad stripes, elastic-sided boots and an expression of amused contempt at Albert's business methods. As I have made clear earlier in these reminiscences, I don't like Erskine-Brown. I greeted him civilly, however, and asked him if he'd ever done a rape.

'As you know, Rumpole, I prefer the civil side. I really find crime moderately distasteful.'

At this point Erskine-Brown started to complain to Albert about the typing of the distasteful document, some mortgage or other act of oppression, he was carrying, and Albert said if he was interrupted he'd have to start again on his column of figures. I happened to glance down at the pound notes on Albert's desk and noticed one marked with a small red cross in the corner; but I thought no more of it at the time. I then turned my attention to my brief, which I immediately noticed was a paying one and not Legal Aided. I carried it into my room with increased respect.

The first thing I discovered was that my client was a Labour M.P. named Ken Aspen. The next was that he was accused of no less a crime than the rape of one of his loyal party workers, a girl called Bridget Evans, in his committee room late on the night before the election. I couldn't help feeling pleased, and slightly flattered, that such a case had come my way; the press box at the Bailey was bound to be full and the words of the Rumpole might once again decorate the *News of the World*. Then I unfolded an election poster and saw the face of Aspen, the workers' friend, a reasonably good-looking man in his early forties, frowning slightly with the concentrated effort of bringing us all a new heaven and a new earth which would still be acceptable to the Gnomes of Zurich. The poster I had was scrawled over and defaced, apparently by the hand of the complainant, Miss Bridget Evans, at the time of the alleged crime.

I lit a small cigar and read on in my instructions, and, as I read, the wonder grew that an Honourable Member, with a wife and family and a house in Hampstead Garden Suburb, should put it all at risk for a moment of unwelcomed pleasure on the floor of his committee room by night. I had heard of political suicide, but this was ridiculous, and I believed that any jury would find it incredible too. Of course at that time I hadn't had the pleasure of meeting Mrs Kenneth Aspen.

'So Bumble Whitelock, when they made him Chief Justice of the Seaward Isles, I don't know, some God-forsaken hole, had this man in the dock before him, found guilty of living on immoral earnings, and he was puzzled about the sentence. So he sent a runner down to the Docks where the old Chief Justice was boarding a P. & O. steamer home with the urgent message, "How much do you give a ponce?" Look, I'll do this . . .'

It was my practice to retire with my old clerk Albert to Pommeroy's Wine Bar in Fleet Street at the end of a day's work to strengthen myself with a glass or two of claret before braving the tube and She Who Must Be Obeyed. During such sessions I seek to divert Albert with a joke or two, usually of a legal nature. I was in full swing when one of the girls who works at Pommeroy's interrupted us with the full glasses of Château Fleet Street. Albert had his wallet out and was paying for the treat.

'No, sir. Quite honestly.' I happened to see the note as Albert handed it over. It was marked with a small red cross in the corner.

'All right. My turn next. "So the message was," I returned to my story, "How much do you give a ponce?" and the answer came back immediately from the old Chief Justice by very fast rickshaw – "Never more than two and six!" Cheers.'

I don't know why but that story always makes me laugh. Albert was laughing politely also.

'Never more than two and six! You like that one, do you Albert?'

'I've always liked it, sir.'

'It's like a bloody marriage, Albert. We've got to know each other's anecdotes.'

'Perhaps you'd like a divorce, sir. Let young Henry do your clerking for you?'

I looked over to the bar. Erskine-Brown was having a drink with Henry and Dianne, they were drinking Vermouth and Henry seemed to be showing some photographs.

'Henry? We'd sit in here over a Cinzano Bianco, and he'd show me the colour snaps of his holiday in Majorca ... No, Albert. We'll rub along for a few more years. Who got me this brief, for instance?'

'The solicitors, sir. They like the cut of your jib.'

I ventured to contradict my old clerk. 'Privately paid rapes don't fall from the sky, like apples in a high wind – however my jib is cut.'

Then Albert told me how the job had been done, proving once again his true value as a clerk. 'I have the odd drink in here, with Mr Myers of your instructing solicitors. Their managing clerk. Remember old Myersy, he grows prize tomatoes? Likes to be asked about them, sir. If I may suggest it.'

'Fellow with glasses. Overcoat pockets stuffed with writs. Smokes a mixture of old bed socks?' I remember Myersy.

'That's him, Mr Rumpole. He thinks our only chance is to crucify the girl.'

'Seems a bit extreme.'

Now Albert started to reminisce, recalling my old triumphs. 'I remember you, sir. When you cross-examined the complainant in that indecent assault in the old Kilburn Alhambra. You brought out as he'd touched her up during the Movietone News.'

'And she admitted she'd sat through the whole of *Rosemarie* and a half-hour documentary about wild life on the River Dee before she complained to the manager!'

'As I recollect, she fainted during your questioning.'

'Got her on the wing around the tenth question.' It was true. The witness had plummeted like a partridge. Right out of the witness box!

'I told old Myersy that,' said Albert proudly. ' "Will Rumpole be afraid of attacking her?" he said. I told him, "There's not a woman in the world my Mr Rumpole's afraid of." '

I was, I suppose, a little late in returning to the mansion flat in Gloucester Road. As I hung up the coat and hat I was greeted by a great cry from the kitchen of 'Rumpole!' It was my wife Hilda, She Who Must Be Obeyed, and I moved towards the source of the shout, muttering, *'Being your slave, what should I do but tend,   Upon the hours and times of your desire?'*

In the kitchen, Mrs Rumpole was to be seen dimly as through a mist of feathers. She was plucking a bird.

'I have no precious time at all to spend,   Nor services to do till you require . . .'

'I was watching the clock,' Hilda told me, ignoring Shakespeare.

'I've been watching it since half past six!'

'Something blew up. A rape. I bought a bottle of plonk.' I put my peace-offering down on the table. Hilda told me that wouldn't be enough for the feast planned for the morrow, for which she was denuding a guinea-fowl. Our son Nick, back from his year at an American university, was bringing his intended, a Miss Erica Freyburg, to dinner with the family.

'If he's bringing Erica,' I said, 'I'll slip down to the health food centre and get a magnum of carrot juice.' I had already met my potential daughter-in-law, a young lady with strong views on dietary matters, and indeed on every other subject under the sun, whom Nick had met in Baltimore.

'Sometimes I think you're just jealous of Erica.'

'Jealous? About Nicky?' I had got the bottle of plonk open and was sitting at the kitchen table, the snow of feathers settling gently.

'You want your son to be happy, don't you?'

'Of course. Of course I want him to be happy.' Then I put my problem to Hilda. 'Can you understand why an M.P., an Honourable Member, with a wife and a couple of kids should suddenly take it into his head to rape anyone?'

'An M.P.? What side's he on?'

'Labour.'

'Oh well then.' Hilda had no doubt about it. 'It doesn't surprise me in the least.'

The next day the Honourable Member, Ken Aspen, was sitting in my Chambers, flanked by his solicitor's clerk Myers and a calm, competent, handsome woman who was introduced to me as his wife, Anna. I suggested that she might find it less embarrassing to slip out while we discussed the intimate details, perhaps to buy a hat. Well, some judges still like hats on women in Court, but Mrs Aspen, Anna, told me that she intended to stay with her husband every moment that she could. A dutiful wife, you see, and the loyalty shone out of her.

Aspen spoke in a slightly modified public-school accent, and I thought the 'Ken' and the just flattened vowels were a concession to the workers, like a cloth cap on a Labour Member. Being a politician, he started off by looking for a compromise, couldn't I perhaps have a word with Miss Bridget Evans? No, I couldn't, nor could I form a coalition with the judge to defeat her on a vote of no confidence. I received 'Ken's' permission to call him 'Mr Aspen' and then I asked him to tell his story.

It seemed that it was late at night in the committee room and both Janice Crowshott, the secretary, and Paul Etherington, the agent, had gone home. Bridget Evans asked Aspen into her office, saying the duplicating machine was stuck. When he got in she closed the door, and started to talk about politics.

'You're going to tell me that the door of the duplicating room was locked so you could have a good old chat about Home Rule for Wales?'

'Of course not.'

'Or that it was during a few strong words about the export figures that her clothes got torn?'

'She started to accuse me of being unfaithful.'

'To her?' I was puzzled.

'To my principles.'

'Oh. Those.' I wanted to hear his defence, not his platitudes.

'She said I'd betrayed her, and all the Party workers. I'd betrayed Socialism.'

'Well, you were used to hearing that,' I supposed. 'That must be part of the wear and tear of life in the dear old Labour Party.'

'Then she started talking about Anna.'

'She wanted Ken to leave me.' Mrs Aspen was leaning forward, half smiling at me.

'It was the whole set-up she objected to. The house in Hampstead Garden Suburb. The kids' schools.'

'Where do they go exactly?'

'Sarah's at the convent and Edward's down for Westminster.'

'And the loyal voters are down for the Comprehensive.' I couldn't resist it, but it earned me a distinctly unfriendly look from Mrs Aspen.

'I think after that, she started screaming at me. All sorts of abuse. Obscenities. I can't remember. Righteous indignation! And then she started clawing at me. Telling me I didn't even have the courage to . . .'

'The courage. To what?'

'To make love to her. That's what Ken believed,' Mrs Aspen supplied the answer. She'd have made an excellent witness, and I began to regret she wasn't on trial.

'Thank you. Is that true?'

'Of course it's true. Ken made love to her. As she wanted. On the floor.' Again Mrs Aspen provided the answer.

'You believed that was what she wanted?'

At last my client spoke up for himself. 'Yes. Yes. That's what I believed.'

I lit a small cigar, and began to get a sniff of a defence. The House of Lords has decided it's a man's belief that matters in a rape case; there are very few women among the judges of the House of Lords. Meanwhile the Honourable Member carried on with the good work.

'She was goading me. Shouting and screaming. And then, when I saw what she'd done to my face on the poster!'

I found the election poster, scored over with a pen and torn.

'You saw that *then*?'

'Yes. Yes. I think so.'

'You'd better be sure about this. You saw this poster scrawled on before anything happened?'

'Yes. I'm almost sure.'

'Not *almost* sure, Mr Aspen. *Quite*, quite sure?'

'Well. Yes.'

'She didn't do it when you were there?'

'No.'

'So she must have done it before she called you into the room?'

'That would seem to follow,' Mr Myers took his pipe out of his mouth for the first time.

'Oh yes, Mr Myers. You see the point?' I congratulated him.

'Is it important?' the Member asked innocently.

'Oh, no. A triviality. It only means she hated your guts before anyone suggests you might have raped her. You know, Mr Aspen, if you're applying the same degree of thought to the economy as you are to this case, no wonder the pound's dickie.' I have been politer to clients, but Aspen took it very well. He stood up, smiling, and said,

'You're right. The case is yours, Mr Rumpole. I'll go back to worrying about the pound.'

Mrs Aspen also stood and looked at me as though I was a regrettable necessity in their important lives, like drains.

I said nothing cheering, 'Case?' I told them. 'We haven't got a case. Yet. Because at the moment, Mr Myers doesn't know a damn thing about Miss Bridget Evans.'

That evening the fatted guinea-fowl was consumed. I brought home three very decent bottles of claret from Pommeroy's and we entertained Nick and his intended. It was always a treat to have Nick at home with us, even though he'd given up reading Sherlock Holmes and taken to sociology, a subject which might, for me, be entirely written in the hieroglyphics of some remote civilization. I can think of no social theory which could possibly account for such sports as Rumpole and She Who Must Be Obeyed, and I honestly don't believe we're exceptions, being surrounded by a sea of most peculiar, and unclassifiable individuals.

Dinner was over, but we still sat round the table and I was giving the company one of my blue-chip legal anecdotes, guaranteed to raise a laugh. It was the one about the retiring Chief Justice of the Seaward Isles.

'How much do you give a ponce!' I was laughing myself now, in joyful anticipation of the punch line, 'And the answer came

back by very fast rickshaw, "Never more than two and six."'
Nick joined me in a burst of hilarity.

Hilda said, 'Well! Thank goodness that's over,' and Erica
looked totally mystified. Then she told us that Nick had been
offered a vacancy in the department of social studies in the
University of Baltimore, which came as something of a surprise
to us as we both thought Nick had settled on the job he'd been
offered at Warwick.

'So it's not decided,' Hilda said, voicing the general anxiety.

'From our point of view I suppose Warwick would have certain advantages over Baltimore,' I told Nick.

'I doubt the academic standards are any higher,' Erica was
defensive.

'No. But it is a great deal nearer Gloucester Road. Another
glass of water?' I rose and poured for Erica. She was a good-
looking girl and seemed healthy enough, although I regretted
her habit of drinking water, as I told her. 'Scientific research has
conclusively proved that water causes the hair to drop out,
fallen arches and ingrowing toe nails. They should pass a law
against it.' At this point Erica did her best to raise the level of
the conversation, by saying, 'Nicky's told me all about your
work. I think it's just great the way you stand up in Court for
the underprivileged!'

'I will stand up in Court for absolutely any underprivileged
person in the world. Provided they've got Legal Aid!'

'What's your motivation – in taking on these sort of cases?'
Erica asked me seriously, and I told her, 'My motivation is the
money.'

'I think you're just rationalizing.'

'He does it because he can't resist the sound of his own voice,'
Nick, who knows most about me, told her; but I would allow
no illusions.

'Money! If it wasn't for the Legal Aid cheque, I tell you,
Rumpole would be silent as the tomb! The Old Bailey would no
longer echo with my pleas for acquittal and the voice of the
Rumpole would not be heard in the Strand. But, as it is, the
poor and the underprivileged can rely on me.'

'I'm sure they can,' Erica sounded consoling.

'And the Legal Aid brings us a quite drinkable claret.' I refilled my glass. 'From Jack Pommeroy's Wine Bar. As a matter of fact I get privately paid sometimes. Sometimes I get a plum!'

'Erica wants to come and hear you in Court,' Nick told me and she smiled.

'How could I miss it?'

'Well, I'm not exactly a tourist attraction.'

'If I'm going to live in England I want to know all I can about your mores,' Erica explained. Well, if she wanted to see the natives at their primitive crafts who was I to stop her?

'Come next week. Down the Bailey. Nick'll bring you for lunch. We'll have steak and kidney pud. Like the old days. Nick used to drop in at the Bailey when he came back from school. He enjoyed the occasional murder, didn't you Nick? That's settled then. We'll have a bit of fun!'

'Fun? What sort of fun?' Erica sounded doubtful, and I told her, 'Rape.'

Mr Myers, of my instructing solicitors, went to the Honourable Member's constituency and discovered gold. Miss Bridget Evans was not greatly liked in the local party, being held to be a left-wing activist, and a bloody nuisance. More important than her adherence to the late Leon Trotsky was her affair with Paul Etherington, the Labour Party agent. I was gloating over this, and other and more glorious goodies provided by the industrious Myers, when there was a knock on my door in Chambers and in filtered Erskine-Brown, glowing with some mysterious triumph.

'Rumpole. One doesn't want to bother the Head of Chambers . . .'

'Why not bother him? He's got very little on his mind, except settling a nice fat planning case and losing at golf to the Lord Chancellor. Guthrie Featherstone, Q.C., old sweetheart, is ripe for bothering!' I turned my attention back to the past of Miss Bridget Evans.

'It's our head clerk,' Erskine-Brown went on mysteriously.

'Albert? You want to go and bother him?'

Erskine-Brown could restrain himself no longer. 'He's a criminal! Our head clerk is a criminal, Rumpole.'

I looked at the man with considerable disapproval. 'As an ornament of the civil side, don't you find that sort of word a little distasteful?'

'I have proof.' And Erskine-Brown fished a pound note out of his pocket. I examined it curiously.

'Looks like a fairly conventional portrait of Her Majesty.'

'There's a red cross in the corner,' he announced proudly. 'I put it there. I marked the money in the petty cash!'

I looked at my fellow barrister in astonishment.

'I've suspected Albert for a long time. Well, I saw him in Pommeroy's Wine Bar and I got the note he'd paid with off one of the girls. Perhaps it's difficult for you to believe.'

'Extremely!' I stood up and fixed him with an unfriendly gaze. 'A private eye. Taking up the Bar as a profession!'

'What do you mean, Rumpole?'

'I mean, in my day they used to be nasty little men in macs, sniffing round the registers in cheap hotels. They used to spy into bedrooms with field-glasses, in the ever-present hope of seeing male and female clothing scattered around. It's the first time I ever heard of a private Dick being called to the Bar, and becoming an expert on the law of contract.'

I handed the marked pound back to Erskine-Brown, the well-known Dick. He looked displeased.

'It's obvious that I will have to go straight to the Head of Chambers.' As he made for the door I stopped him.

'Why not?' I said. 'Oh just one thing that may have escaped your attention, my dear Watson.'

'What's that?'

'Yesterday afternoon, I borrowed five pound notes from petty cash – no doubt notes decorated by you. And I paid for all of Albert's drinks in Pommeroys.'

'Rumpole. Are you sure?' I could see he felt his case crumbling.

'I would really advise you, Erskine-Brown, as a learned friend, not to go round Chambers making these sort of wild allegations against our clerk. A man who's been here, old darling, since you were in nappies!'

'Very well, Rumpole. I'm sorry I interrupted your rape.' Erskine-Brown had the door open, he was about to slink away.

'Say no more, old sweetheart. Not one word more. Oh, convey my condolences to the unfortunate Henry. The position of second clerk must be continually frustrating.'

When I was alone I was well pleased. Albert and I had been together now for forty years and I was anxious not to cross my old Dutch. And the evidence little Myersy had uncovered put me in mind of Lewis Caroll.

'*Oh, hast thou slain the Jabberwock? Come to my arms! Thou beamish boy . . .*' 'Not yet father', I said to myself. 'But I will. Oh yes. I certainly will . . .'

'Tomatoes doing well, Mr Myers, are they?'

'I apply a great deal of artificial, you see, Mr Rumpole. And they're just coming up to the fourth truss.'

'Fourth truss, are they? Lively little blighters, then!'

We were waiting outside Court. Mr and Mrs Aspen were sitting on a bench, he looking curiously relaxed, she glaring across at Miss Bridget Evans who was looking young and demure on a bench some distance away. Meanwhile I was going through the old legal gambit of chatting up the instructing solicitor. I showed concern for his tomatoes, he asked after my son whom he remembered as a visitor to the Courts of Law.

'Nick? Oh, he's the brains of the family. Sociology. They've offered him a lectureship at Warwick University! And he's engaged to be married. Met her in America and now he's bringing the lady to live in England.'

'I never had a family,' Mr Myers told me, and added, 'I do find having young kids about plays merry hell with your tomatoes.'

At which point Mrs Anna Aspen drew me aside for a conference. The first thing she said surprised me a little.

'I just hope you're not going to let me down.'

'Let *you* down, Mrs Aspen? So far as I can see you're in no danger of the Nick.'

'I'm in danger of losing everything I ever worked for.'

'I understand.'

'No. You don't understand, Mr Rumpole. It's been hard work, but I made Ken fight. I made him go for the nomination. I made him fight for the Seat. When he got in he wanted . . . I don't know, to relax on the back benches. He said he'd throw in ideas. But I told him to fight for the P.P.S.'s job and he's got it!' She looked across to where her husband was actually trying the ghost of a smile in Bridget's direction. 'He can't see it's either him or her now. Ken can't see that! You're right about him looking for compromises. Sometimes it makes me so angry!'

'Angrier than the idea of your husband and Miss Bridget Evans. On the floor of the office?'

'Oh that! Why should I worry about that?'

Before I could answer her question, an usher came out to invite the Honourable Member to step into the dock, and we were away.

When you go into Court in a rape case it's like stepping into a refrigerator with the light off. All the men on the jury are thinking of their daughters, and all the women are sitting with their knees jammed together. I found a sympathetic-looking, moderately tarty, middle-aged lady juror, the sort that might have smiled at the Honourable Member and thought, 'Why didn't you ring me, dearie. I'd have saved you all this trouble.' But her lips snapped shut during the opening by Mr Twentyman, Q.C. for the prosecution, and I despaired of her.

Even the judge, old Sam Parkin, an amiable old darling, perfectly capable of giving a conditional discharge for manslaughter or putting an old lag on probation, even old Sam looked, when the case opened, as if he'd just heard the clerk say, 'Put up Jack the Ripper.' Now he seemed to be warming to Miss Bridget Evans who was telling her hair-raising story with effective modesty. As I tottered to my feet old Sam gave me an icy look. When you start to cross-examine in a rape case you open the flap of the tent, and you're out in the blizzard.

'Miss Bridget Evans. This . . . this incident involving Mr Aspen occurred at 11.30 on Wednesday night?'

'I don't know. I wasn't watching the clock.'

The door of the Court opened, to admit the Rumpole fan club, my son Nick and Erica his intended. She was wearing an ethnic skirt and gave me a warm smile, as though to encourage my efforts on behalf of the underprivileged and the oppressed.

'After all the witnesses had conveniently departed. When there was no one there, to establish my client's innocence. After it was all over, what did you do?'

'I went home.'

'A serious and terrible crime had been committed and you went home, tucked yourself up in bed and went to sleep! And you said not one word to the police about it until 6.30 the following day?'

Albert, also of the fan club, was sitting in front of me next to Mr Myers. I heard his penetrating whisper, 'He's doing the old Alhambra cinema technique.' It was nice to feel that dear old Albert was proud of me.

'When you went to bed. Did you go alone?'

'I don't see what that's got to do with it.' Her answer had a hint of sharpness and, for the first time, there was a centimetre up in some of the juror's eyebrows.

'Did you go alone?'

'I told you. I went to bed.'

'Miss Evans. I shall ask my question again and I shall go on asking it all night if it's necessary in the interests of my client. Did you go to bed alone?'

'Do I have to answer that sort of question, my Lord?'

'Yes you do. And my Lord will so direct.' I got in before Sam could draw breath.

'Perhaps if you answer Mr Rumpole's questions shortly you will be out of the box quite quickly, and your painful experience will be over.' Sam Parkin meant well, but I intended to keep her there a little while longer.

'Yes. I went to bed alone.'

'How long had that been going on?'

'How long had what been going on, Mr Rumpole?' Sam asked.

'That the witness had taken to sleeping alone, my Lord. You were no longer friendly with Mr Etherington?'

'Paul and I? We split about two years ago. If you're interested in the truth.' I began to hear what a barrister longs for when he's cross-examining, the note of anger.

'Yes, Miss Evans. I am interested in the truth, and I expect the ladies and gentlemen of the jury are also.'

The tarty lady nodded perceptibly. She and I were beginning to reach an understanding.

'Mr Rumpole. Is it going to help us to know about this young lady and Paul . . .' Sam was doing his best.

'Paul Etherington, my Lord. He was the Parliamentary agent.'

'I'm anxious not to keep this witness longer than is necessary.'

'I understand, my Lord. It must be most unpleasant.' Almost as unpleasant, I thought, as five years in the nick, which was what the Honourable Member might expect if I didn't demolish Miss Evans. 'But I have my duty to do.'

'And a couple of refreshers to earn,' Mr Twentyman, Q.C., whispered, a thought bitchily, to his junior.

'You had been living with Paul Etherington for two years before you parted?'

'Yes.'

'So you were eighteen when you started living together.'

'Just . . . nearly eighteen.'

'And before that?'

'I was at school.'

'You had lovers before Paul?'

'Yes.'

'How many?'

'One or two.'

'Or three or four? How many? or didn't they stay long enough to be counted?'

My dear friend the lady juror gave a little disapproving sigh. I had misjudged her. The old darling was less a *fille de joie* than a member of the festival of light, but I saw Erica whisper to Nick, and he held her hand, shushing her.

'Mr Rumpole!' Sam had flushed beneath his wig. I took a swift move to lower his blood pressure.

'I apologize my Lord. Pure, unnecessary comment. I withdraw it at once.'

'Your Mr Rumpole is doing us proud,' I heard Mr Myers whisper to Albert who replied complacently, 'His old hand has lost none of its cunning, Myersy.'

After a dramatic pause, I played the ace. 'How old were you when you had the abortion?'

I looked round the Court and met Erica's look; not exactly a gaze of enraptured congratulation.

'I was nineteen . . . It was perfectly legal.' Miss Evans was now on the defensive. 'I got a certificate. From the psychiatrist.'

'Saying you were unfit for childbirth?'

'I suppose so.'

'And the psychiatrist certified . . . you were emotionally unstable?' It was a shot in the bloody dark, but I imagine that's what trick cyclists always say, to prevent any unwanted increase in the population.

'Something like that . . . yes.' I gave Ken Aspen a cheering glance. He was busy writing a note, containing, I hoped, more ammunition for Rumpole in the firing line.

'So the jury have to rely, in this case, on the evidence of a young woman who has been certified emotionally unstable.'

The jury were looking delightfully doubtful as the usher brought me the note from the dock. No ammunition, not even any congratulation, but just one line scrawled, 'Leave her alone now, please! K. A.' I crumpled the note with visible irritation; in such a mood, no doubt, did Nelson put the glass to his blind eye when reading the signal to retreat.

'Just three months ago, you were rushed into hospital. You'd taken a number of sleeping tablets. By accident?' I continued to attack.

'No.'

'Why?'

'Well, it was . . . I told you. I'd just parted from Paul.'

'Come now, Miss Evans. Just think. You'd parted from Paul over a year ago.'

'I was . . . I was confused.'

'Was it then you first met Mr Aspen?'

'Just . . . Just about that time.'

'And fell in love with him?'

'No!'

She was really angry now, but she managed to smile at the jury who didn't smile back. If I could have dropped dead of a coronary at that moment, I thought, Miss Bridget Evans might be dancing for joy.

'Became so obsessed with him that you were determined to pursue him at any cost to him, or to his family?'

'Shall I tell you the truth? I didn't even like him!'

'And that night after you and Mr Aspen had made love . . .'

'Love! Is that what you call it?'

'He refused to leave his wife and children.'

'We never discussed his wife and children!'

'And it was in rage, because he wouldn't leave his family, that you made up this charge to ruin him. You hate him so much.'

'I don't hate him.'

'Oh. Can it be you are still in love with him?'

'I never hated him, I tell you. I was indifferent to him.'

It was the answer I wanted, and just the moment to hold up the poster of Ken's face, scrawled on by Miss Evans in her fury.

'So indifferent that you did that. To his face on the wall?'

'Perhaps. After.'

'Before! Because you had done that early in the evening, hadn't you? In one of your crazy fits of rage and jealousy?'

Now Bridget Evans was crying, her face in her hands, but whether in fury or grief, or simply to stop the questions, not I but the jury would have to judge.

'Will that poster be Exhibit 24, Mr Rumpole?' Sam spoke in his best matter-of-fact judge's voice, and I gave him a bow of deep satisfaction and said, 'If your Lordship pleases.'

'Is *that* your work?' I was entertaining Nick and Erica to an *après*-Court drink in Pommeroy's Wine Bar. A group from Chambers, Guthrie Featherstone, Erskine-Brown, my friend George Frobisher and old Uncle Tom were at the bar. The Rumpole family occupied a table in that part of Pommeroy's where ladies are allowed to assemble. I felt as if I'd spent a day digging the roads, in a muck sweat and exhausted after the cross-examination. I was, of course, moderately well pleased with the way it had gone and I had asked Joan the waitress to bring us a bottle of Pommeroy's cooking champagne, and Erica's special, a Coca-Cola. When it came I took a quick glassful and answered her question.

'When it goes well. We made a bit of headway, this afternoon.'

'You sure did.'

'Erica was a bit upset,' Nick looked from one to the other of us, embarrassed.

'Is that the way you make your living?' Erica repeated.

'A humble living. With an occasional glass of cooking champagne, with paying briefs.'

'Attacking women?' I must confess I hadn't thought of Bridget Evans as a woman, but as a witness. I tried to explain.

'Not women in particular. I attack anyone, regardless of age or sex, who chooses to attack my client.'

'God knows which is the criminal. Him or her.'

'But, old darling. That's what we're rather trying to find out.'

'What worries Ricky is,' Nick was doing his best to explain, 'the girl has to go through all that. I mean, it's not only the rape.'

'Not *only* the rape?'

'Well, it's like *she's* getting punished, isn't it?'

'Aren't you rather rushing things? I mean, who's saying a rape took place?'

'Well, isn't she?'

'Oh, I see. You think it's enough if she *says* it? It's a different sort of crime, is it? I mean, not like murder or shoplifting, or forging cheques. They still have to be proved in the old-fashioned way. But rape . . . Some dotty girl only has to *say* you did it and you trot off to chokey without asking embarrassing questions . . . Look, you don't want to discuss a boring old case. What've you been doing Nick? Getting ready for Warwick?'

But Erica wasn't to be deterred.

'Of course we should discuss the case.' She'd have made an advocate, this Erica, she was dogged. 'I mean, it's the greatest act of aggression that any human being can inflict!'

'Ricky! Dad's just doing his job. I'm sorry we came.' Nicky looked at his watch, no doubt hoping they had an appointment.

'I'm glad! Oh sure I'm glad,' Erica was smiling, quite mirthlessly. 'He's a field study in archaic attitudes!'

'Look, old sweetheart. Is it archaic to believe in some sort of equality of the sexes?'

She looked taken aback at that. 'Equality! You're into equality?'

'For God's sake, yes! Give you equal pay, certainly. Let you be all-in wrestlers and Lord Chancellor. By all means! I'll even make the supreme sacrifice and give up giving my seat in the bus ... But you're asking for women witnesses to be more equal than any other witnesses!'

'But in that sort of case,' Erica wasn't to be won over by any sort of irony, 'a man forcing his masculinity . . .'

'Or a woman getting her revenge?' I suggested. 'I mean, I don't suppose I'll ever have to actually choose between being raped and being put in the cooler for five years, banged up with a bar of soap and a chamber pot, but if I ever had . . .'

'You're being defensive again!' Erica smiled at me, quite tolerantly.

'Am I?'

'The argument's kind of painful so you make a little joke.'

'Perhaps. But it's not exactly a joke. I mean, have you considered the possibility of my client being innocent?'

'Well, he'd better be. That's all I can say. After what you did to that girl this afternoon, he'd better be!'

Then Nick remembered they were due at the pictures and they left me, Erica with the warm feeling of having struck a blow for her sex, Nick perhaps a little torn between us, but holding Erica's arm as he steered her out. I went over to the bar for a packet of small cigars and there were the learned friends poring over a pink slip of paper which Jack Pommeroy was showing them. As soon as I drew up beside the bar, Jack showed me the cheque; it was made out to me from a firm of solicitors called Sprout and Pennyweather and had my name scrawled on the back. It was for the princely sum of nine pounds fifty, my remuneration for a conference. I looked at my purported signature and felt unaccountably depressed.

'No need to tell us, Rumpole,' said Guthrie Featherstone, Q.C., M.P. 'It's Albert's signature.'

'It's peaceful down here. Extraordinarily peaceful.'

The Honourable Member was eating spaghetti rings and

drinking hot, sweet tea down in the cells; Sam Parkin had declined bail in the lunch hour. He seemed extraordinarily contented, a fact which worried me not a little.

'I'm afraid it's hardly a three rosettes in the Michelin, as far as the grub's concerned,' I apologized to Aspen.

'It's tasteless stodge. Like nursery tea. Sort of comforting.'

'Really there are only two important things to remember. One. You saw the poster scribbled on as soon as you came into the room.' I tried to wrench his attention back to the case. 'And you believed she wanted it. That's all! You just believed it.'

'Did you *have* to ask her those questions?' Aspen looked at me, more in sorrow than in anger.

'Yes.'

'Dragging out her life, for the vultures in the press box.'

'I want you to win.' This bizarre ambition of mine made the Honourable Member smile.

'You sound like my wife. She wants me to win. Always. I'm so tired. It's peaceful down here, isn't it? Very peaceful.'

'Look out, old darling. You're not falling love with the Nick, are you?' I had seen it before, that terrible look of resignation.

'For years, oh, as long as I can remember, Anna's worked so hard. On me winning.' He seemed to be talking to himself; I felt strangely superfluous. 'Sitting on platforms. Chatting up ministers. Keeping in with the press. Trying to convince the faithful that it all still meant something. My wife . . . Anna, you know. She wanted me in the cabinet. She'd like to have been – a minister's wife.'

'And what did you want?' It was a long time before he answered me, and then he said, 'I wanted it to stop!'

Calling your own client is the worst part of a trial. You can't attack him, or lead him, or do anything but stand with your palms sweating and hope to God the old nitwit tells the right story. Mrs Aspen was staring at her husband, as if to transfer to him a little of her indomitable will. He stood in the witness box, smiling gently, as though someone else was on trial and he was a not very interested spectator. I showed him the defaced poster and asked the five thousand dollar question, 'Did you see that had been done when you went into the room?'

He looked at me almost as if I was the one to be pitied, and said, after a pause, 'I can't remember.'

I smiled as if I'd got exactly the answer I wanted, a bit of a sickly smile. 'Did Miss Evans start talking about your wife?'

'About Anna. Yes.'

'Did she want you to leave your wife?'

'Did she?' Sam Parkin was helping me out in the silence.

'I can't . . . I can't exactly remember. She went on and on, goading me.'

'What happened then?'

It was then the Honourable Member showed his first sign of passion. 'She'd been asking for it! All that clap-trap about betraying the Party. All those clichés about power corrupting. I suddenly got angry. It was then I . . .'

'Then you what?'

'Made . . . Made love to her.'

'In anger?' Sam Parkin was frowning.

'I suppose so. Yes.'

I saw Anna's look of fear, and then the judge leaned forward to ask, 'Just tell us this, Mr Aspen. Did you believe that was what she wanted?'

So the old darling on the bench had chucked Ken Aspen a lifebelt. I hoped to God the drowning man wasn't going to push it away. It seemed about a year before he answered. 'I don't know, what I believed then. Exactly.'

'It wasn't your fault, if I may say sir.' When I got back to the clerk's room, Albert was, as ever, consoling. 'It was the client.'

'That's right, Albert. These things are always so much easier without clients.'

I saw that Henry, our second clerk, was smiling as he told me that there was a Chambers meeting and I was to go up to our learned leader's room. When Albert offered to take me up, Henry said that Featherstone had said that it was a meeting for members of Chambers only, and our head clerk wasn't invited. Albert looked at me and I could see he was worried.

'Cheer up Albert,' I told him. 'See you at Pommeroy's later.'

Featherstone was pouring us all Earl Grey out of his fine bone china tea service.

'It seems that Albert has been pursing a long career of embezzlement,' hec said as he handed round sugar.

'That seems a very long word for nine pounds fifty,' I told them. 'I'd say the correct legal expression was fiddling.'

'I don't see how we can excuse crime. Whatever you call it.' Erskine-Brown was clearly appearing for the prosecution.

'Anyway, it was my nine pounds fifty. It seems to me I can call it what I like. I can call it a Christmas present.'

At which Uncle Tom, who was dozing in the corner said, 'I suppose it will be Christmas again soon. How depressing.'

'Apparently, it's not just *your* money, Rumpole.' Featherstone sat judicially behind his desk.

'Isn't it? Is there the slightest evidence that anyone else suffered?' I asked the assembled company.

'The petty cash!' Erskine-Brown was the only one to answer.

'I told you about the petty cash.' I was too tired to argue with Erskine-Brown.

'You told me *you'd* borrowed from Albert's float.'

'Yes. And paid for the drinks in Pommeroy's.'

'You were lying, weren't you, Rumpole?' Now even Featherstone realized Erskine-Brown had gone too far. 'Erskine-Brown,' he said. 'That's not the sort of language we use to another member of Chambers. If Rumpole says he borrowed the money then I for one am prepared to accept his word as a gentleman.'

Suddenly I grew impatient with the learned friends. I pushed myself to my feet. 'Then you're a fool, that's all I can say as a gentleman. Of course I was lying.'

'What does Rumpole say he was doing?' Uncle Tom asked George for information.

'Lying.'

'Dear me, how extraordinary.'

'I lied because I don't like people being condemned,' I explained. 'It goes against my natural instincts.'

'That's very true. He never prosecutes. You don't prosecute, do you, Rumpole?' George gave me a friendly smile. I liked old George.

'No. I don't prosecute.'

'All right. Now we'll hear Rumpole's defence of Albert.' Erskine-Brown leant back in Featherstone's big leather chair, trying to look like a juvenile judge.

'It doesn't seem to me that it's Albert that's in trouble.'

'Not in trouble?'

'It's us! Legal gentlemen. Learned friends. So friendly and so gentlemanly that we never check his books, or ask to see his accounts. Of course he cheats us, little small bits of cheating, nine pounds fifty, to buy a solicitor a drink or two in Pommeroy's. He feels it's a mark of respect. Due to a gent. Like calling you "Sir" when you go wittering on about the typing errors in your statement of claim.'

'Rather an odd mark of respect, wouldn't you say, Rumpole?' Featherstone stopped me, and called the meeting to order. 'I move we vote on this.'

'It's a matter for the police,' Erskine-Brown said predictably.

'Rumpole. You wouldn't agree?' The learned leader was asking for my vote.

'You'd hardly expect him to.' Erskine-Brown could never let a sleeping Rumpole lie.

'Well . . . Albert's part of my life . . . He always has been.'

'I remember when Albert first came to us. As a boy. He was always whistling out of tune.' Uncle Tom was reminiscing. And I added my tuppence worth. 'He's like the worn-out lino in the Chambers loo and the cells under the Old Bailey. I feel comfortable with Albert. He's like home. And he goes out and grubs for briefs in a way we're too gentlemanly to consider.'

'He's cheated us. There's no getting away from that.' George interrupted me, quite gently.

'Well, we've got to be cheated occasionally. That's what it's all about, isn't it?' I looked round at their blank faces. 'Otherwise you'd spend your whole life counting your change and adding up bills, and chucking grown men into chokey because they didn't live up to the high ideals of the Chambers, or the Party, or some bloody nonsense.'

'I don't know that I exactly follow.' George was doing his best.

'Neither do I. I've done a rather bloody case. I'm sorry.' I sat down beside our oldest member. 'How are you, Uncle Tom?'

'I never expected Christmas to come again so quickly!' This was Uncle Tom's contribution. Now Featherstone was summing up. 'Personally, speaking quite personally, and without in any way condoning the seriousness of Albert's conduct . . .'

'Rape's bloody tiring,' I told them. 'Specially when you lose.'

'I would be against calling in the police.' This was Featherstone's judgement.

'Not very gentlemanly having Old Bill in Chambers. Stamping with his great feet all over the petty cash vouchers.' I lit my last small cigar.

'On the other hand, Albert, in my view, must be asked to leave immediately. All those in favour?' At Featherstone's request all the other hands went up.

'Well, Rumpole,' said Erskine-Brown, teller for the 'Ayes'. 'Have you anything to say?'

'Have you anything to say why sentence of death should not be passed against you?' I blew out smoke as I told them an old chestnut. 'They say Mr Justice Snaggs once asked a murderer that. "Bugger all", came a mutter from the dock. So Snaggs J. says to the murderer's counsel, "Did your client *say* something?" "Bugger all, my Lord," the counsel replied. "Funny thing," says Mr Justice Snaggs. "I thought I heard him *say* something."' My story ended in a hoot of silence. It was one that my old clerk Albert laughed at quite often, in Pommeroy's Wine Bar.

A couple of nights later I was sitting alone in Pommeroy's, telling myself a few old legal anecdotes, when to my surprise and delight Nick walked in alone. He sat down and I ordered a bottle of the best Château Fleet Street.

'I dropped into Chambers. Albert wasn't there.'

'No. We have a new clerk, Henry.'

'I'm sorry about the case.'

'Yes. The Honourable Member got five years.' I took a mouthful of claret to wash away the taste of prisons, and saw

Nick looking at me. 'He had a strong desire to be found guilty. I don't know why exactly.'

'So really you needn't have asked all those questions?'

'Well, yes, Nick. Yes. I had to ask them. Now, are we going to see you both on Sunday?'

There was a pause. Nick looked at me. He obviously had something far more difficult to communicate than the old confessions of poker games in the deserted vicarage during his schooldays.

'I wanted to tell you first. You see. Well, I've decided to take the job in Baltimore. Ricky wants to go back. I mean, we can get a house there . . . and . . . well, her family'd miss her if she were stuck with me in England.'

'*Her* family?'

'They're very close.'

'Yes. Yes, I suppose they are.'

'Apparently her mother hates the idea of Ricky being in England.' He smiled 'She's the sort of woman that'd start sending us food parcels.'

I could think of nothing to say, except, 'It was good of you, Nick. Good of you to spare the time to drop into Chambers.'

'We'll be back quite often. Ricky and I. We'll be back for visits.'

'You and Ricky, of course. Well then, Cheers.'

We had one for our respective roads and I gave my son a bit of advice. 'There's one thing you'll have to be careful of, you know, living in America.'

'What's that?'

'The hygiene! It can be most awfully dangerous. The purity! The terrible determination not to adulterate anything! You will be very careful of it, won't you, Nick?'

Some weeks later, as I was packing the bulging briefcase after breakfast for a day down the Bailey with a rather objectionable fraud, She Who Must Be Obeyed came in with a postcard from our son and his intended, written in mid-air, with a handsome picture of a jet and a blue sky on the front and kisses from Nick and Ricky on the back. I handed it back to her and she gave it an attentive re-read as she sat down for another cup of tea. Then she said, 'You know why Erica went back home, don't you?'

I confessed total ignorance.

'She didn't like it when she came to see you in Court. She didn't like the way you asked all those questions. She made that quite clear, when they were here for lunch last Sunday. When they came to say "Good-bye". She thought the questions you asked that girl were tasteless.'

'Distasteful.' I was on my way to the door. 'That's the word. Distasteful.'

'There's a picture of their jet on the front of this postcard.'

'I saw it. Very handsome.' I opened the kitchen door as dramatically as possible. '*Fare thee well! and if forever still forever, fare thee well.*' It takes a bad moment to make me fall back on Lord Byron.

'Don't be silly.' Hilda frowned. 'What're you going to do today, Rumpole?'

It was a day, like all the others, and I said. 'I suppose. Go on asking distasteful questions.'

Rumpole and the Married Lady

Life at the Bar has its ups and downs, and there are times when there is an appalling decrease in crime, when all the decent villains seem to have gone on holiday to the Costa Brava, and lawfulness breaks out. At such times, Rumpole is unemployed, as I was one morning when I got up late and sat in the kitchen dawdling over breakfast in my dressing gown and slippers, much to the annoyance of She Who Must Be Obeyed who was getting the coffee cups shipshape so that they could be piped on board to do duty as teacups later in the day. I was winning my daily battle with the tormented mind who writes *The Times* crossword, when Hilda, not for the first time in our joint lives, compared me unfavourably with her late father.

'Daddy got to Chambers dead at nine every day of his life!'

'Your old dad, old C. H. Wystan, got to Chambers dead on nine and spent the morning on *The Times* crossword. I do it at home, that's the difference between us. You should be grateful.'

'Grateful?' Hilda frowned.

'For the companionship,' I suggested.

'I want you out of the house, Rumpole. Don't you understand that? So I can clear up the kitchen!'

'*O woman! in our hours of ease   Uncertain, coy and hard to please.*' Hilda doesn't like poetry. I could tell by her heavy sigh.

'Just a little peace. So I can be alone. To get on with things.'

'And when I come home a little late in the evenings. When I stop for a moment in Pommeroy's Wine Bar, to give myself strength to face the Inner Circle. You never seem particularly grateful to have been left alone in the house. To get on with things!'

'You've been wasting time. That's what I resent.'

'*I wasted Time — and now doth Time waste me.*' I switched

from Scott to Shakespeare. The reaction of my life-mate was no better.

'Chattering to that idiot George Frobisher! I really don't know why you bother to come home at all. Now Nick's gone it seems quite unnecessary.'

'Nick?' It was a year since Nick had gone to America and we hadn't had a letter since Christmas.

'You know what I mean! We used to be a family. We had to try at least, for Nick's sake. Oh, why don't you go to work?'

'Nick'll be back.' I moved from the table and put an arm on her shoulder. She shook it off.

'Do you believe that? When he's got married? When he's got his job at the University of Baltimore? Why on earth should he want to come back to Gloucester Road?'

'He'll want to come back sometime. To see us. He'll want to hear all our news. What I've been doing in Court,' I said, giving Hilda her opening.

'What you've been doing in Court? You haven't been doing anything in Court apparently!'

At which moment the phone rang in our living-room and Hilda, who loves activity, dashed to answer it. I heard her telling the most appalling lies through the open door.

'No, it's *Mrs* Rumpole. I'll see if I can catch him. He's just rushing out of the door on his way to work.'

I joined her in my dressing gown; it was my new clerk, the energetic Henry. He wanted me to come into Chambers for a conference, and I asked him if the world had come to its senses and crime was back in its proper place in society. No, he told me, as a matter of fact it wasn't crime at all.

'You haven't even shaved!' Hilda rebuked me. 'Daddy'd never have spoken to his clerk on the telephone before he'd had a shave!'

I put down the telephone and gave Mrs Rumpole a look which I hoped was enigmatic. 'It's a divorce,' I told her.

As I walked through the Temple, puffing a small cigar on the way to the factory, I considered the question of divorce. Well, you've got to take what you can nowadays, and I suppose divorce is in a fairly healthy state. Divorce figures are rising. What's harder to understand is the enormous popularity of marriage! I remembered the scene at breakfast that morning, and I really began to wonder how marriage ever became so popular. I mean, was it 'Home Life' with She Who Must Be Obeyed? Gloucester Road seemed to be my place of work, of hard, back-breaking toil. It was a relief to get down to the Temple, for relaxation. By that time I had reached my Chambers, No. 1 Equity Court, a place of peace and quiet. It felt like home.

When I got into the hallway I opened the door of the clerk's room, and was greeted by an extraordinary sight. A small boy, I judged him to be about ten years old, was seated on a chair beside Dianne our typist. He was holding a large, lit-up model of a jet aeroplane and zooming it through the air at a noise level which would have been quite unacceptable to the New York Port authority.

I shut the door and beat a hasty retreat to the privacy of my sanctum. But when I opened my own door I was astounded to see a youngish female seated in my chair, wearing horn-rimmed specs and apparently interviewing a respectable middle-aged lady and a man who gave every appearance of being an instructing solicitor. I shut that door also and turned to find the zealous Henry crossing the hall towards me, bearing the most welcome object in my small world, a brief.

'Henry,' I said in some panic. 'There's a woman, seated in my chair!'

'Miss Phillida Trant, sir. She's been with us for the last few months. Ex-pupil of Mr Erskine-Brown. You haven't met her?'

I searched my memory. 'I've met the occasional whiff of French perfume on the stairs.'

'Miss Trant's anxious to widen her experience.'

'Hence the French perfume?'

'She wants to know if she could sit in on your divorce case. I've got the brief here. "Thripp v. Thripp." You're the wife, Mr Rumpole.'

'Am I? Jolly good.' I took the brief and life improved considerably at the sight of the figure written on it. 'Marked a hundred and fifty guineas! These Thripps are the sort to breed

from! Oh, and I don't know if you're aware of *this*, Henry.
There seems to be a child in the clerk's room, with an aeroplane!'

'He's here for the conference.'

I didn't follow his drift. 'What's the child done? It doesn't
want a divorce too?'

'It's the child of the family in "Thripp *v.* Thripp", Henry
explained patiently, 'and I rather gather the chief bone of con-
tention. So long now, Mr Rumpole.' He moved away towards
the clerk's room. 'Sorry to have interrupted your day at home.'

'You can interrupt my day at home any time you like, for a
brief marked a hundred and fifty guineas! Miss Phillida *Trant*,
did you say?'

'Yes sir. You don't mind her sitting in, do you?'

'Couldn't you put her off, Henry? Tell her a divorce case is
sacrosanct. It'd be like a priest inviting a few lady friends to join
in the confessional.'

'I told her you'd have no objection. Miss Trant's very keen to
practise.'

'Then couldn't she practise at home?'

'We're about the only Chambers without a woman, Mr Rumpole. It's not good for our image.' He seemed determined, so I
gave him a final thought on my way into the conference. 'Our
old clerk Albert never wanted a woman in Chambers. He said
there wasn't the lavatory accommodation.'

So there I was at the desk having a conference in a divorce
case with Miss Phillida Trant 'sitting in', Mr Perfect the solicitor
looking grave, and the client, Mrs Thripp, leaning forward and
regarding me with gentle trusting eyes. As I say, she seemed an
extremely nice and respectable woman, and I wasn't to know
that she was to cause me more trouble than all the murderers I
have ever defended.

'As soon as you came into the room I felt *safe* somehow, Mr
Rumpole. I knew Norman and I would be safe with you.'

'Norman?'

'The child of the family.' Miss Trant supplied the information.

'Thank you, Miss Trant. The little aviator in the clerk's room. Quite. But if I'm to help you, you'll have to do your best to help me too.'

'Anything! What is it you want exactly?' Mrs Thripp seemed entirely co-operative.

'Well, dear lady, a couple of black eyes would come in extremely handy,' I said hopefully. Mrs Thripp looked at Miss Trant, puzzled.

'Mr Rumpole means, has your husband ever used physical violence?' Miss Trant explained.

'Well, no . . . Not actual violence.'

'Pity.' I commiserated with her. 'Mr Thripp doesn't show a very helpful attitude. You see, if we're going to prove "cruelty" . . .'

'We don't have to, do we?' I noticed then that Miss Trant was sitting in front of a pile of legal text books. 'Intolerable conduct. Since the Divorce Law Reform Act 1969.'

I thought then that it's not the frivolity that makes women intolerable, it's the ghastly enthusiasm, the mustard keeness to get into the lacrosse team, the relentless drive to learn the Divorce Law Reform Act by heart: that *and* the French perfume. I could have managed that conference quite nicely without Miss Trant. I said to her, however, as politely as possible, 'The Divorce Law Reform Act, which year did you say?'

'1969.'

'Yes,' I smiled at Mrs Thripp. 'Well, you know how it is. Go down the Old Bailey five minutes and you've found they've passed another Divorce Reform Act. Thank you, Miss Trant, for reminding me. Now then what's this intolerable conduct, exactly?'

'He doesn't speak,' Mrs Thripp told me.

'Well, a little silence can come as something of a relief. In the wear and tear of married life.'

'I don't think you understand,' Mrs Thripp smiled patiently. 'He hasn't spoken a word to me for three years.'

'*Three* years? Good God! How does he communicate?' The instructing solicitor laid a number of little bits of paper on my desk.

'By means of notes.'

I then discovered that the man Thripp, who I was not in the least surprised to learn was a chartered accountant, used his matrimonial home as a sort of Post Office. When he wished to communicate with his wife he typed out brusque and business-like notes, documents which threw a blinding light, in my opinion, on the man's character.

'To my so-called wife,' one note read, 'if you and your so-called son want to swim in hot water you can go to the Public Baths. From your so-called husband.' This was fixed, it seemed, to a padlocked geyser. Another billet doux was found in the biscuit tin in the larder, 'To my so-called wife. I have removed what you left of the assorted tea biscuits to the office for safe keeping. Are you determined to eat me into bankruptcy? Your so-called husband.' 'To my so-called wife. I'm going out to my Masonic Ladies' Night tomorrow (Wednesday). It's a pity I haven't got a lady to take with me. Don't bother to wait up for me. Your so-called husband, F. Thripp.'

I made two observations about this correspondence, one was that it revealed a depth of human misery which no reasonable woman would tolerate, and the other was that all the accountant Thripp's notes were written on an Italian portable, about ten years old.

'My husband's got an old Olivetti. He can't really type,' Mrs Thripp told me.

Many years ago I scored a notable victory in the 'Great Brighton Benefit Club Forgery' case, and it was during those proceedings I acquired my vast knowledge of typewriters. Having solved the question of the type, however, got me no nearer the heart of the mystery.

'Let me understand,' I said to Mrs Thripp. 'Are you interested in someone else?'

'Someone else?' Mrs Thripp looked pained.

'You're clearly an intelligent, obviously still a reasonably attractive woman.'

'Thank you, Mr Rumpole,' Mrs Thripp smiled modestly.

'Are there not other fish in your particular sea?'

'One man's quite enough for me, thank you.'

'I see. Apparently you're still *living* with your husband.'

'Living with him? Of course I'm living with him. The flat's in our joint names.' Mrs Thripp said this as though it explained everything. I was still bewildered.

'Wouldn't you, and the young hopeful outside, be better off somewhere else? *Anywhere* else?'

'There's your mother in Ruislip.' Mr Perfect supplied the information.

'Thank you Mr Perfect.' I turned back to Mrs Thripp. 'As your solicitor points out. Anyone's mother in Ruislip must surely be better than life with a chartered accountant who locks up the geyser! And removes the tea biscuits to his office.'

'I move out?' Apparently the thought had never occurred to her.

'Unless you're a glutton for punishment.'

'Move out? And let *him* get away with it?'

I rose to my feet, and tried to put the point more clearly. 'Your flat in Muswell Hill, scene of historic events though it may well be, is not the field of Waterloo, Mrs Thripp, if you withdraw to happier pastures there would be no defeat, no national disaster.'

'Mrs Thripp is anxious about the furniture,' Mr Perfect offered an explanation.

'The furniture?'

'She's afraid her husband would dispose of the lounge suite if she left the flat.'

'How much human suffering can be extracted by a *lounge suite*?' I asked the rhetorical question. 'I can't believe it's the furniture.'

There was a brief silence and then Mrs Thripp asked quietly, 'Won't you take me on, Mr Rumpole?'

I thought of the rent and the enormous amounts of money Sho Who Must Be Obeyed spends on luxuries like Vim. I also remembered the fact that crime seemed remarkably thin on the ground and said I, 'Of course, dear lady. Of course I'll take you on! That's what I'm here for. Like an old taxi cab waiting in the rank. Been waiting quite a little time, if you want to know the truth. You snap your fingers and I'll drive you almost anywhere you want to go. Only it'd be a help if we knew exactly what destination you had in mind.'

'I've told Mr Perfect what I want.'

'You want a divorce. Those are my instructions,' Mr Perfect told me, but his client put it a little differently.

'I want my husband taken to Court. Those are *my* instructions, Mr Rumpole.'

I have spoken in these reminiscences of my old friend George Frobisher. George is a bachelor who has lived in an hotel in Kensington since his sister died. He is a gentle soul, unfitted by temperament for a knock-about career at the Bar, but he is a pleasant companion for a drink at Pommeroy's after the heat and labour of the day. That evening I bought the first round, two large clarets, flushed with the remunerative collapse of the Thripp marriage.

'Things are looking up, George,' I raised my glass to my old friend and he, in turn, toasted me.

'A little.'

'There's light at the end of the tunnel. Today I got a hundred and fifty pound brief. For a divorce.'

'That's funny. So did I.' George sounded puzzled.

'Sure to last at least six days. Six refreshers at fifty pounds a day. Think of that, George! Well, there's that much to be said. For the institution of marriage?'

'I never felt the need of marriage somehow,' George told me.

'*With one chained friend, perhaps a jealous deadly foe,   The longest and the dreariest journey go.*' I gave George a snatch of Shelley and a refill.

'I've had a bit of an insight into marriage. Since reading that divorce brief.' George was in a thoughtful mood.

'If we were married we couldn't sit pleasantly together,' I told him. 'You'd be worrying what time I got home. And when I did get home you wouldn't be pleased to see me!'

'I really can't see why a person puts up with marriage,' George went on. 'When a woman starts conversing with her husband by means of little notes!'

I looked at him curiously. 'Got one of those, have you?' There seemed to be an epidemic of matrimonial note-leaving.

'*And* she cut the ends off his trousers.' George seemed deeply shocked.

'Sounds a sordid sort of case. Cheers!' We refreshed ourselves with Pommeroy's claret and George went on to tell me about his divorce.

'He was going to an evening at his Lodge. You know what this Jezebel did? Only snipped off the ends of his evening trousers. With nail scissors.'

'Intolerable conduct that, you know. Under the 1969 Act.' I kept George abreast of the law.

'Moss Bros was closed. The wretched fellow had to turn up at the Café Royal with bags that looked as if they'd been gnawed by rats. Well! That's marriage for you. Thank God I live by myself, in the Royal Borough Hotel.'

'Snug as a bug in there, are you George?'

'We have television in the Residents' Lounge now. Coloured television. Look here, you must dine with me there one night, Rumpole. Bring Hilda if you'd care to.'

'We'd like to George. Coloured television? Well, I say. That'll be a treat.'

'Quiet life, of course. But the point of it is. A man can keep his trousers more or less safe from destruction in the Royal Borough Hotel.'

I must admit that George Frobisher and I loitered a little in Pommeroy's that night and, when I got home, Hilda had apparently gone up to bed; she often had an early night with a glass of milk and a library book. I went into the kitchen and switched on the light. All was quiet on the Western front, but I saw it on the table – a note from my lady wife.

'If you condescend to come home, your dinner's in the oven.' I took the hint and was removing a red-hot plate of congealed stew from the bowels of our ancient cooker when the telephone rang in the living-room. I went to answer it and heard a woman's voice.

'I just *had* to ring you. I feel so alone in the world, so terribly lonely.'

'Look it's not terribly convenient. Just now.' It was my client in the case of Thripp *v*. Thripp.

'Don't say that! It's my life. How can you say it's not convenient?'

'All right. A quick word.' I supposed the ancient stew could wait a little longer.

'He's going to say the most terrible things about me. I've got to see you.'

'Shall we say tomorrow, four o'clock. But not here!' I told her firmly.

'I don't know how I can wait.'

'You've waited for three years haven't you? Look forward to seeing you then. Goodnight now, beloved lady.' I said that, I suppose, to cheer up Mrs Thripp and to soften the blow as I put down the receiver. Just before I did so I heard a little click, and remembered that Hilda had insisted on an extension in our bedroom.

The next day our clerk's room was buzzing. Henry was on the telephone dispatching barristers to far-flung Magistrates Courts. That smooth young barrister, Erskine-Brown, was opening his post and collecting papers, and Uncle Tom, old T. C. Rowley, was starting his day of leisure in Chambers by standing by the mantelpiece and greeting the workers. The ops room was even graced by the presence of our Head of Chambers, Guthrie Featherstone, Q.C., M.P., who was taking time off from such vital affairs of state as the Poultry Marketing Act to supervise Dianne who was beating out one of his learned opinions on our old standard Imperial.

Henry told me that my divorce conference was waiting in my room, and Erskine-Brown gave his most condescending smile. 'Divorcing now, Rumpole?' he asked me. I told him I was and asked him if he was still foreclosing on mortgages. 'I'm all for a bit of divorce in Chambers,' Featherstone smiled tolerantly. 'Widens our repertoire. You were getting into a bit of a rut with all that crime, Horace.'

'Crime! It seems a better world. A cleaner world. Down at the Old Bailey,' I told him.

'Don't you find criminal clients a little – depressing?'

'Criminal clients? They behave so well.'

'Really Rumpole?' Erskine-Brown sounded quite shocked.

'What do they do?' I asked him. 'Knock people on the head, rob banks, cause, at the worst, a temporary inconvenience. They don't converse by means of notes. They don't lock up the geyser. They don't indulge in three years silence to celebrate the passage of love.'

'Love? Have you become an expert on that, Rumpole?' Erskine-Brown seemed amused. '*Rumpole in Love*. Should sell a bomb at the Solicitors' Law Stationers.'

'And I'll tell you another great advantage of criminal customers.' I went on. 'They're locked up, mostly, pending trial! They can't ring you up at all hours of the day and night. Now you get involved in a divorce and your life's taken over!'

'We used to have all the facts of divorce cases printed out in detail in *The Times*,' Uncle Tom remembered.

'Oh, hello, Uncle Tom.'

'It used to make amusing reading! Better than all this rubbish they print now, about the Common Market. Far more entertaining.'

Erskine-Brown left to go about his business, not before I had told him that divorce, for all its drawbacks, was a great deal less sordid than foreclosing on mortgages and then Henry presented me with another brief, a mere twenty-five guineas this time, to be heard by old Archie McFee, the Dock Street magistrate.

'You're an old girl called Mrs Wainscott, sir,' Henry told me. 'Charged with keeping a disorderly house.'

'An old Pro? Is this what I've sunk to now, Henry? Plodding the pavements! Flogging my aged charms round the Dock Street Magistrates Court!' I checked the figure on the front of the brief. 'Twenty-five smackers! Not bad, I suppose. For a short time in Dock Street. Makes you wonder what I could earn round the West End.'

I left Henry then; he seemed not to be amused.

*

The other side, that is to say Mr F. Thripp and his legal advisers, had supplied his wife, married in some far-off and rash moment in a haze of champagne and orange blossom, with the evidence to be used against her. I was somewhat dismayed when I discovered that this evidence included an equal number of notes, typed on the same old Olivetti as that used by the husband, but travelling in the opposite direction. I picked out at random, 'To my so-called husband. If you want your shirts washed, take them down to the office and let *her* do them. She does everything else for you doesn't she? Your so-called wife.'

'Oh dear, Mrs Thripp. I wish you hadn't written this.' I put down the note which I had been viewing through a magnifying glass to check the type. 'By the way, whom did you suspect of doing his washing for him?'

I looked at the client, so did Miss Trant who was 'sitting in' in pursuit of knowledge of Rumpole's methods, so did Mr Perfect. Master Norman Thripp, who had joined us, sat in a corner pointing a toy sub-machine gun at me in a way I did my best to ignore.

'Who?'

'We had him watched Mr Rumpole,' Mr Perfect told me.

'He has an elderly secretary. Apparently she's a grandmother. There doesn't seem to be anyone else.'

'There doesn't seem to be anyone else for either of you.' I picked up the husband's answer. 'He alleges you assaulted his trousers.'

'No. No I didn't do that, Mr Rumpole.'

'His evening trousers were damaged apparently.'

'Probably at the cleaners. You remember, he refused to take me to his Ladies' Night – he went on his own, so his trousers can't have been all that bad can they?'

'Did you *mind* him going?' I was finding the Thripp marriage more and more mysterious.

'Mind? Of course I minded.'

'Why?'

'Because I wanted to go with him, of course.'

'You wanted to go with the man who hasn't spoken to you for three years, who communicates by wretched little notes, who locked up your bath water?'

At this point Mrs Thripp brought out a small lace handker-chief and started to sob.

'I don't know. I don't *know* why I wanted to go with him.'

The sobs increased in volume. I looked at Mrs Thripp with deep approval.

'All right, Mrs Thripp. I'm simply asking the questions your husband's barrister will ask unless we're extremely lucky.'

'You think my case is hopeless?' Mrs Thripp was mopping up noisily.

'Mr Rumpole's afraid you may not make a good witness.' It was Miss Phillida Trant, giving her learned opinion uninvited.

'Miss Trant!' I'm afraid I was somewhat sharp with her. 'You may know all about Divorce Law Reform Acts. But I know all about witnesses. Mrs Thripp will be excellent in the box.' I patted the still slightly heaving Thripp shoulder. 'Well done, Mrs Thripp! You broke down at exactly the right stage of the cross-examination.'

I picked up the first of the wretched chartered accountant's notes; I was by now looking forward to blasting him out of the witness box, and saw, 'I am going to my Masonic Ladies' Night. It's a pity I haven't got a lady to take with me.' 'There's not a man sitting as a judge in the Family Division,' I promised her, 'who won't find that note from your husband absolutely intolerable.'

When the Thripps, *mère et fils*, had been shepherded out by their solicitor, Perfect, Miss Trant loitered and said she wanted my advice. I expressed some surprise that she didn't know it all; but I lit a small cigar and, in the best tradition of the Bar, prepared to have my brains picked. It seemed that Miss Trant had been entrusted with a brief for the prosecution, before that great tribunal, old Archibald McFee at the Dock Street Magistrates Court.

'It's a disorderly house. I mean it's an open and shut case. I can't think why Mrs Wainscott's defending.'

'The old trout's probably got a weird taste for keeping out of Holloway.' I blew out smoke, savouring a bit of fun in the offing. Fate had decreed that I should be prosecuted by Miss Phyllida Trant. I kept cunningly quiet about my interest in the case of the Police *v.* Wainscott and Erskine-Brown's former pupil proceeded to deliver herself into my hands.

'What I wanted to ask you was how much law should I . . .'

'Yes?'

'Take? I mean, how many books will this magistrate want, on the prosecution case?'

Miss Trant had asked for it. I stood and gave her my learned opinion.

'My dear Miss Trant. Old Archie McFee is a legal beaver. Double First in Jurisprudence. Reads Russel on Crime in bed and the Appeal Cases on holiday. You want to pot the old bawdy-house keeper? Quote every case you can think of. Archie'll love you for it. How many books do you need? My advice to you is, fill the taxi!'

So we all gathered at Dock Street Magistrates Court. There was old Mother Wainscott, sitting beneath a pile of henna-ed hair in the dock, and there was old Archie McFee, looking desperately bored and gazing yearningly at the clock as Miss Trant with a huge pile of dusty law books in front of her and her glasses on the end of her nose, lectured him endlessly on the law relating to disorderly houses.

'Section 8 of the 1751 Statute, sir. "Any person who acts or behaves him- or herself as Master or Mistress or as the person having the care, government, or managements of any bawdy house or other disorderly house shall be deemed to be the keeper thereof." Now, if I might refer you to Singleton and Ellison, 1895, 1, Q.B. page 607 . . .'

'Do you *have* to refer me to it, Miss Trant?' the learned magistrate sighed heavily.

'Oh yes, sir. I'm sure you'll find it most helpful.'

I sat smiling quietly, like a happy spider as Miss Trant walked into the web. She had looked shocked when she discovered that I was defending. Now she would discover that I had deceived her. Archie McFee couldn't *stand* law: his sole interests were rose growing, amateur dramatics and catching the 3.45 back to Esher. I was amazed she couldn't see the fury rising to the level of his stiff collar as he watched the clock and longed for Victoria.

'It is interesting to observe that in R. *v.* Jones it was held that all women under 21 years of age are "girls" although females may be "women" at the age of eighteen.' Miss Trant was un-stoppable.

'I suppose it interests you, Miss Trant.'

'Oh yes, indeed, sir. Turning now, if you please, sir, to the Sexual Offences Act, 1896 . . .'

A very long time later, when it came to my turn, and the prosecution had sunk under the dead weight of the law, I made a speech guaranteed to get old Archie off to the station in three minutes flat.

'Sir. My learned friend has referred you to many books. I would only remind you of one: a well-known book in which it is written "Thou shalt not bear false witness."' I glared at the young officer in charge of the case. 'And I would apply that remark to the alleged observations of the police officer.'

'Yes. I'm not satisfied this charge is made out. Summons dismissed.' As Archie went, he fired his parting shot. 'With costs, Miss Trant.'

Mrs Thripp rang me at home again that evening and told me that her solicitor, Perfect, had fixed up a hearing in ten days' time. She wondered how she could live until then and told me I was her only friend in the world. I was comforting her as best I could and stemming the threatened flow of tears over the wire by saying. 'You'll be free in a couple of weeks. Think of that old darling,' when I noticed that Hilda had come into the room and was viewing me with a look of disapproval. I put down the phone: I suppose to a hostile observer the movement may have looked guilty. However, She Who Must Be Obeyed affected to ignore it and said casually, 'I'm having tea with Dodo tomorrow.'

'Dodo?'

'Dodo Perkins and I were tremendously close at Wycombe Abbey,' said Hilda coldly.

'Oh, Dodo! Yes, of course. The live one.'

'She's living in Devon nowadays. She's running her own tea shop.'

'Well. Nice part, Devon. You won't have seen her for some years.'

'We correspond. I sent her a postcard and said, let's meet

when you're next up in London.' She gave me a look I can only describe as meaningful. 'I want to ask her advice about something. We may do some shopping – and have tea at Harrods.'

'Well, go easy on the chocolate gateaux.'

'What?'

'I know how much these teas at Harrods cost. I don't want to see all my profit on the disorderly house vanishing down Dodo's little red lane.'

Hilda ignored this and merely gave me some quite gratuitous information. 'Dodo never liked you. You know that, Rumpole?'

She went, leaving me only vaguely disconcerted. When I went to the gin bottle, however, to prepare an evening Booths and tonic, I was astonished to notice a pencil mark on the label, apparently intended to record the drinking habits of Rumpole. I sloshed out the spirit, well past the plimsoll line. Our existence in Froxbury Court, I thought, was beginning to bear an uncomfortable resemblance to the way life was lived in Maison Thripp.

My life in those days seemed inseparable from women and their troubles. When I got to Chambers the next morning I found Miss Phillida Trant in my room, her glasses off, her eyes red and her voice exceedingly doleful. She announced that, after careful thought, she had decided, in view of her disastrous appearance at the Dock Street Magistrates Court, to give up the Bar and take up some less demanding profession.

'And after you'd been so helpful!' Miss Trant's undeserved gratitude gave me an unusual twinge of guilt.

'Please! Don't mention it.' I wanted to get her off the subject of my unhelpful advice.

'I know I'll never make it! I mean, I know the law. I was top student of my year and . . .'

I interrupted her and said, 'Being a lawyer's got almost nothing to do with knowing the law.'

'An open and shut case! I had all the police observations! And I went and lost it.'

'That wasn't because you didn't know all about the law. It

was because you didn't know enough about Archie McFee.'

'You just made rings round me!'

'Never underestimate the craftiness of Rumpole.' Now I was giving her genuinely helpful advice.

'It seems ungrateful. After you'd been so kind to me.'

'I wish you wouldn't go on saying that, Miss Trant.'

'But I'll have to give it up!'

'You can't! Once you're a lawyer you're addicted. It's like smoking, or any other habit-forming drug. You get hooked on cross-examination, you get a taste for great gulps of fresh air from the cells. You'll find out.'

'No! No, I won't ever.'

I lit a small cigar and sat down at the desk opposite her. She looked surprisingly young and confused and I found myself warming to Miss Trant. For some reason I wanted her to continue her struggle against magistrates and judges and cunning opponents: even her appearance at Dock Street had shown some misguided courage.

'You know, we all have our disappointments. I do.'

'*You?*' She looked incredulous.

'One year I did the "Penge Bungalow Murder". Without a leader. *And* the "Great Brighton Benefit Club Forgery" case, which is where I got my vast knowledge of typewriters. And what am I doing now? Playing around with disorderly houses. I have even sunk to a divorce!' I looked at her, and saw a solution. 'You know what your mistake is, in Court, I mean?'

Miss Trant shook her head, she still had no idea of where she'd gone wrong.

'I would suggest a little more of the feminine qualities. Ask anyone in the Temple. How does Rumpole carry on in Court? Answer. Rumpole woos, Rumpole insinuates, Rumpole winds his loving fingers round the jury box, or lies on his back purring, "If your Lordship pleases," like old mother Wainscott from Dock Street.'

I was rewarded with a small smile as she said, 'That's ridiculous!'

'Lawyers and tarts,' I told her, and I meant it, 'are the two oldest professions in the world. And we always aim to please.'

*

If I had managed to cheer up Miss Trant, and even return her small nose to the legal grindstone, I had no luck with She Who Must Be Obeyed. Relations, as they say, deteriorated and I got up one morning to find her suitcase packed and standing in the hall. Hilda was in the living-room, hatted, coated and ready for travel.

'You can come home as late as you like now, Rumpole. And you can spend all the time you like with *her*.'

'Her?' Whoever could she be talking about?

'I've heard her! Time and time again. On the telephone.'

'Don't be ridiculous.' I tried a light laugh. 'That's a client.'

'Rumpole! I've lived with you for a good many years.'

'Man and boy.'

'And I've never known you to be telephoned by a client. At home!'

'I usually have quiet, undemanding clients. Murderers don't fuss. Robbers can usually guess the outcome, so that they're calm and resigned. Divorcing ladies are different. They're inclined to telephone constantly.'

'So I've noticed!'

'Also they're always on bail. They're not kept locked up in Brixton, pending the hearing.'

'More's the pity! I'm going to stay with Dodo. I'm going to stay with Dodo and help her out with her business.'

'The tea shop?' I tried hard to remember this Dodo, who was coming to play a major part in our lives.

'It's far better I leave you, Rumpole! To enjoy your harem!'

'Listen, Hilda.' I did my best to remain calm. 'I have a client whose unhappy marriage may well provide you and Dodo with another tea in Harrods. That can't be why you're leaving.'

There was one of those silences that had become so frequent between us, and then she said, 'No. No, it isn't.'

'Then why?'

'You've changed, Rumpole. You don't go to work in the mornings. And as for the gin bottle!'

'You marked it! That was unforgivable.'

'Then don't forgive me.'

'An Englishman's gin bottle is his castle.'

At which point the phone rang. Hilda picked it up, apparently thinking it was a taxi she had ordered; but it was, of course, Mrs Thripp, the well-known married lady, who seemed to depend entirely on Rumpole. Hilda handed me the phone as though her worst suspicions were now thoroughly justified.

Hilda went while I was still pacifying the client. In the days that followed, I stayed later at Pommeroy's, got my own breakfast, had a poached egg in the evenings, and turned up alone and unaccompanied to have dinner with George Frobisher at the Royal Borough Hotel in Kensington. We sat in a draughty dining-room, surrounded by lonely persons whose tables were littered with their personal possessions, their own bottles of sauce, their half bottles of wine, their pills, their saccharin, and their medicines. It was the sort of place that encourages talking in whispers, so George and I muttered over the coffee, getting such warmth as we could from our thimblefuls of port.

'I'm sorry it's not Thursday,' George told me sadly. 'They give us the chicken on Thursday. Tonight it was the veal so it must be Monday. Soup of the day is exactly the same all through the week. Enjoy your *pommes de terre à l'anglaise*, did you?'

'Boiled spuds? Excellent! Hilda'll be sorry she missed this.'

'Hilda cares for veal, does she? We always get veal on Mondays. So we know where we are.' George suddenly remembered something. 'Monday! Good God! I've got this divorce case tomorrow. The other side stole a march on us. They expedited the hearing!'

'George.'

'Yes, Rumpole?'

'What's your divorce about, exactly?'

'I told you. I'm a husband tomorrow.'

'It's just that; well. I've got one too, you know,' I confessed. 'I'm a wife.'

'Horrible case! I think I told you. We allege this monstrous female savaged my trousers. Furthermore, she hasn't spoken to me for three years.'

'*She* hasn't spoken to *you*?'

'She started it!'

'That's a damned lie, George!' I felt a sense of outrage on behalf of Mrs Thripp and raised my voice. A nearby diner looked up from his soup of the day.

'Oh really? And is it a damned lie about the bath water?'

'What about the bath water?'

'You ran off all the hot water deliberately. You put a note on the geyser, "Out of Bounds".'

'I haven't had a bath there for the last month. I have to go all the way to Ruislip, to my mother's.'

'Rumpole! You're against me?'

'Of course I'm against you. I'm the wife! You want to turn me out of the house – and my child!'

'Your child! You've alienated Norman's affections.'

'What?'

'You've turned him against me!'

It's no doubt a strange habit of barristers to identify themselves so closely with their clients. But by now we had both raised our voices, and the other diners were listening but looking studiously away, as though they were overhearing a domestic quarrel.

'That is the most pernicious rubbish I ever heard and if you dare to put that forward in Court I shall cut you in small pieces, George, and give you to the usher. I've behaved like a saint.'

'Oh yes, you. Joan of Arc!' George was becoming quite spirited.

'And I suppose you're Job himself.'

'I'd have to be. To put up with you.'

'You are nothing but a great big bully, George. Oh, you're all very fine and brave when you've got someone weaker than yourself.'

'You! Weaker than me! I told you ... You're a Jezebel!'

'Bluebeard!'

'Lady Macbeth!'

'Let's just see how you stand up in Court, George. Let's just see how you stand up to cross-examination.'

'Don't rely on cross-examination. It's the evidence that matters. By the way, I'm making my evening trousers an exhibit!'

At this startling news the other diners had given up all pretence of not listening and were gazing at each other with a wild surmise. I wasn't taking these allegations against my wronged client lying down.

'Anyone, George, can lacerate their own evening trousers with a pair of nail scissors. It's been done before! Thank you for the dinner!'

'Rumpole!'

'Perhaps in the long watches of the night, George. Perhaps as you are watching Match of the Day on your colour T.V. it may occur to you to do the decent thing and let this case go undefended. Hasn't an unhappy woman suffered enough?'

I left the dining-room then, with all the diners staring at me. When I got home, and poured myself an unlimited gin, I began to wonder exactly what they had thought of my relationship with my old friend George Frobisher.

When I had rashly advised Mrs Thripp that there wasn't a man sitting as a judge who wouldn't be appalled at hearing of her treatment at the hands of Thripp, I had made a serious miscalculation. I had forgotten that Mrs Justice Appelby sat in the Family Division of the High Court of Justice, and her Ladyship was known as the only genuine male chauvinist pig in the building. They used to say that when she went out on circuit, to try murders, she used to put on a thin line of lipstick before summing up to the jury. That was the nearest Mrs Justice Appelby ever got to the art of seduction.

If the judge was an unpleasant surprise, Mr F. Thripp was a disappointment. He was hardly ideal casting for the part of Bluebeard; in fact he looked decidedly meek and mild, a small man in rimless glasses and a nervous smile; we could have hoped for something about twice the size.

The clerk called the case and we were off. I rose to open a tale whose lightest word would harrow up the soul and freeze the young blood. I weighed in on a high note.

'This is one of the strangest cases this Court may ever have heard. The case of a Bluebeard who kept his wife a virtual prisoner in their flat in Muswell Hill. Who denied her the simple comforts of biscuits and bath water. Who never gave her the comfort of his conversation and communicated with her by means of brusque and insulting little notes.'

'Mr Rumpole.' Mrs Justice Appelby's blood was no doubt frozen already. She looked unimpressed. 'May I remind you of something? The jury box is empty. This is a trial by judge alone. I don't require to be swayed by your oratory which no doubt is enormously effective in criminal cases. Just give me the relevant dates, will you?'

I gave her the dates and then I called my client. She had dressed in black with a hat, an excellent costume for funerals or divorces. After a gentle introduction, I put her husband's notes to her.

'You and your so-called son can be off to your mother's in Ruislip. Let her pay for the light you leave blazing in the toilet.'

'That was pinned up on my kitchen cupboard.'

'And what was the effect on you, Mrs Thripp, of that heart-breaking notice to quit?'

'She stayed for more, apparently.' It was Mrs Justice Appelby answering my question. She turned to the witness box with that cold disapproval women reserve especially for each other. 'Well, you didn't go, did you? Why not?'

'I didn't know *what* he would do if I left him.' Mrs Thripp was looking at her husband. I was puzzled to see that the look wasn't entirely hostile. But the judge was after her, like a terrier.

'Mrs . . . Thripp. You put up with this intolerable conduct from your husband for three years. Why exactly?'

'I suppose I was sorry for him.'

'Sorry for him. Why?'

'I thought he'd never manage on his own.'

When we came out for lunch I saw Norman waiting outside the Court. He had a brand new armoured car with flashing lights, a mounted machine gun and detachable soldiers in battle dress. Someone was doing well from this case; apart from Rumpole and George Frobisher.

In the afternoon I cross-examined the respondent, Thripp. Miss Trant, sitting beside me in her virginal wig, waited with baited breath for my first question.

'Mr Thripp. Is there anything in your conduct to your wife of which you are thoroughly ashamed?' In the pause while Thripp examined this poser I whispered to Miss Trant, my eager apprentice, 'Good question that. If he says "yes" he's made a damaging admission. If he says "no", he's a self-satisfied idiot.'

At which point Thripp said 'No', proving himself a self-satisfied idiot.

'Really, Mr Thripp. You have behaved absolutely perfectly?' Her Ladyship had the point. I made that fifteen love to Rumpole, in the second set.

'"I'm going out to my Masonic Ladies' Night. It's a pity I haven't got a lady to take with me."' I was quoting from the Thripp correspondence. 'Is that the way a perfect husband writes to his wife?'

'Perhaps not, *but* . . . I was . . . annoyed with her, you see. I *had* asked her to the Ladies' Night.'

'Asked her?'

'I left a note for her, naturally. She didn't reply.'

'Tell me, Mr Thripp, did you actually *want* your wife to accompany you to your Masonic Ladies' Night?'

'Oh yes, indeed.'

'This inhuman monster who drains away your bath water and refuses to wash your shirts . . . you were looking forward to spending a pleasant evening with *her*?'

'I had no one else to go with.'

'And would rather go with her than no one?'

'Of course I would. She's my wife, isn't she?'

'Mr Thripp, I suggest all your charges against her are quite untrue.'

'They're not untrue.'

'But you wanted her with you! You wanted to flaunt her on your arm, at the Café Royal. Why? Come, Mr Thripp. Will you answer that question? It can hardly have been because you love her.'

There was a long pause, and I began to have an uneasy suspicion that I had asked one question too many. Then I knew I had because Mr Thripp said in the sort of matter-of-fact tone he might have used to announce the annual audit, 'Yes I do. I love her.'

I looked across at Mrs Thripp. She was sighing with a sort of satisfaction, as if she had achieved her object at last.

'Mr Rumpole,' Mrs Justice Appelby's voice, like a cold shower, woke me from my reverie. 'Is it really too late for commonsense to prevail?'

'Commonsense, my Lady?'

'Could there not be one final attempt at a reconciliation?'

I felt a sinking in the pit of the stomach. Could it be that even divorce was slipping away from us, and George and I would both have to go back to the crossword puzzle?

'I have no power to order this.' The judge did her best to look pleasant, it was not a wild success. 'But it does seem to me that Mr and Mrs Thripp might meet perhaps in counsel's Chambers? Simply to explore the possibilities of a reconciliation. There is one very important consideration, of course, and I refer to young Norman Thripp. The child of the family. I shall adjourn now until tomorrow morning.'

At which her Ladyship rose smartly and we were all upstanding in Court. Obedient to Mrs Justice Appelby's orders, the Thripps met in my room that afternoon. George Frobisher and I, our differences now sunk in the face of the new menace from the judge, shared my small cigars and our anxieties.

'They've been there a long time,' George was looking nervously at my closed door. 'I'm afraid it doesn't look too healthy.'

Just then the clerk's room door opened for Henry to come out about some business. I had a brief glimpse of Norman Thripp, the child of the family, seated at Dianne's desk. He was banging the keys of our old standard Imperial, no doubt playing at 'secretaries'.

'In my opinion,' George was still grumbling, 'they shouldn't allow women on the bench. That Mrs Justice Appelby! What does she think she's doing, depriving us of our refreshers?'

Before I could agree wholeheartedly, the door of my room opened to let out a beaming Thripp.

'Well, gentlemen,' he said. 'I think we'll be withdrawing the case tomorrow. We still have one or two things to talk over.'

'Talk over! Well, that'll be a change,' said Mrs Thripp following him out. Then they collected Norman, who was still
happily playing with Dianne's typewriter, and took him home,
leaving George and I in a state of gloomy suspense.

The next morning I got to the Law Courts early, climbed into
the fancy dress and found Mrs Thripp and young Norman waiting for me outside Mrs Justice Appelby's forum in the Family
Division.

'Well, Mrs Thripp. I suppose we come to bury Caesar, not to
praise him.'

'What do you mean Mr Rumpole?'

'You're dropping the case?'

Mrs Thripp, to my surprise, was shaking her head and opening her handbag. She brought out a piece of paper and handed it
to me, her voice tremulous with indignation. 'No, Mr Rumpole,'
she said. 'I'm going on with the case. I got *this* this morning.
Leaning up against the cornflakes packet at breakfast.'

I took the note from her.

'The old barrister you dug up's going to lose this case. I'll
have you and your so-called son out of here in a week. Your so-
called husband.' I read the typewritten document, and then
studied it with more care.

'He's mad! That's what he is. I can't live with a maniac, Mr
Rumpole!' As far as my client was concerned, the reconciliation
was clearly off.

'Mrs Thripp.'

'We've got to beat him! I've got to think of Norman – caged
up with a man like that!'

'Yes. Norman.' I pulled out my watch. 'We've got a quarter
of an hour. I feel the need of a coffee. Do you think Norman
would like a doughnut?'

'I'm sure we'd be glad to.'

'Not "we", Mrs Thripp. In this instance I'd like to see young
Norman on his own.'

So I took Norman down to the café in the crypt of the Law
Courts, and, as he tucked into a doughnut and fizzy orangeade,

I brought the conversation round to the business in hand.

'Rum business marriage . . . You've never been married, have you Norman?' I lit a small cigar and gazed at the young hopeful through the smoke.

'Of course not.' Norman found the idea amusing.

'No seriously. Married people have odd ways of showing their love and affection.'

'Have they?'

'Some whisper endearments. Some send each other abusive notes. Some even have to get as far as the Divorce Court to prove they can't do without each other. A rum business! Care for another doughnut?'

'No. No, I'm all right, thanks.'

He was eating industriously with sugar on the end of his nose as I moved in to the attack.

'All right? You were all right, weren't you, Norman? When they really looked like separating?'

'I don't know what you mean.'

'When they were both trying to win you over to their side. When you got a present a week from Mum and a rival present from Dad? Tanks, planes, guns, it's been a sort of arms race between them, hasn't it, Norman?'

'I don't know what you're talking about, Mr Rumpole,' Norman repeated, with rather less conviction.

'This mad impulse of your parents to get together again doesn't show much consideration for you, or for me either, come to that.'

'I don't mind if they get together. It's their business, isn't it?'

'Yes, Norman. Their business.'

'I'm not stopping them.'

I ordered the child another doughnut, he was going to need it.

'Really?'

'Course I'm not!'

The second doughnut came and I gave Norman a fragment of my autobiography. 'I don't do much divorce, you know. Crime mainly. I was in the "Great Brighton Benefit Club Forgery".'

'What's forgery?' The child was round-eyed with innocence. You had to admire the act.

'Oh, you're good Norman! You'll come out wonderfully in your interviews with the police! The genuine voice of innocence. What's forgery?' I whipped out the latest item in the Thripp correspondence. 'This is! Inspect it carefully, Norman! All the other notes were typewritten.'

'So's this.' Norman kept his head.

'The others were done on the old Olivetti your parents keep in Muswell Hill. This morning's note was typed on a standard Imperial with a small gap in the capital "S".'

I got out my folding pocket glass and offered it to him.

'Here. Borrow my glass.'

Norman dared to do so and examined the evidence.

'Typed on the Imperial on which Dianne in my Chambers hammers out my so-called learned opinions. The typewriter *you* were playing with so innocently yesterday in the clerk's room. I put it to you, Norman – you typed that last note! In a desperate effort to keep this highly profitable divorce case going.'

Norman looked up from my magnifying glass and said, 'I didn't see any gap in the capital "S".'

'Didn't you, Norman? The judge will.'

'What judge?' For the first time he sounded rattled.

'The judge who tries you for forgery, a word you understand perfectly. I'll take the evidence now.' I retrieved the last in-criminating note. 'Four years they gave the chief villain in the Brighton case.'

'They *wouldn't*?' Norman looked at me. I felt almost sorry for him, as if he were my client.

'As your lawyer, Norman, I can only see one way out for you. A full confession to your Mum and Dad.'

He bit hard into the second doughnut, seriously considering the possibility.

'And one more word of advice, Norman. Settle for being a chartered accountant. You've got absolutely no talent for crime.'

My old friend George was extremely angry with me when Norman confessed and the Thripps were re-united. We lost all our refreshers, he told me, just because I had to behave like a

damned detective. I explained to him that I couldn't resist using
the skills I had learnt in the great Brighton fraud case, and he
told me to stick to crime in the future.

'You Rumpole,' said George severely, 'have absolutely
buggered up the work in the Family Division.'

Further surprises were in store. When I got back to the mansions in search of the poached egg and the lonely bed, I found
Hilda's case in the hall and She, apparently just arrived and still
in her overcoat, installed wearily in her chair by the simulated
coals of our electric fire.

'Rumpole!'

'What's the matter? Fallen out with Dodo? Had a bit of a
scene over a drop scone?'

'You're home early. Daddy was never back home at three
o'clock in the afternoon. He always stayed in Chambers till six
o'clock. Regular as clockwork. Every day of his life.'

'My divorce collapsed under me.' I lit a small cigar. Hilda
rose and started to make the room shipshape, a long-neglected
task.

'You're going to seed, Rumpole. You hang about at home in
the mornings.'

'And you know why my divorce collapsed?' I thought I should
tell her.

'If I'm not here to keep an eye on you, you'll go to seed
completely.'

I blew out smoke, and warmed my knees at the electric fire.

'The clients were reconciled. Because, however awful it is,
however silent and unendurable, however much they may hate
each other's guts and quarrel over the use of the geyser, they
don't want to be alone! Isn't that strange, Hilda? They'd rather
have war together than a lonely peace.'

'If I'd stayed away any longer you'd have gone to seed completely.' She was throwing away *The Times* for a couple of
weeks.

'*O Woman! in our hours of ease.*' I got to my feet and gave
her the snatch of Walter Scott again. '*Uncertain, coy and hard
to please!*'

'You'd have stayed home from Chambers all day. Doing the crossword and delving into the gin bottle.'

'*And variable as the shade   By the light of quivering aspens made.*' I moved to the door.

'If you're going to the loo, Rumpole, try to remember to switch the light off.'

'*When pain and anguish ring the brow,   A ministering angel thou.*'

I was half way down the passage when I heard She calling after me.

'It's for your own good, Rumpole. I'm telling you for your own good!'

Rumpole and the Learned Friends

'Now more than ever seems it rich to die, To cease upon the
midnight with no pain.'

'Doctor Hanson told you, Rumpole. You're not dying.
You've got flu.'

I was lying on my back, in a pair of flannel pyjamas, my brow
with anguish moist and fever dew, and Hilda, most efficiently
playing the part of Matey, or Ward Sister, was pouring out the
linctus into a spoon and keeping my mind from wandering.
Whatever Doctor Hanson, who in my humble opinion would be
quite unable to recognize a case of death when he saw it, might
say, I felt a curious and trance-like sense of detachment, not at
all unpleasant, and seriously wondered if Rumpole were not
about to drop off the twig.

'Fade far away, dissolve and quite forget What thou among
the leaves hast never known, The weariness, the fever and the
fret.'

As I recited to her Hilda took advantage of the open mouth to
slide in the spoonful of linctus. I didn't relish the taste of artifi-
cially sweetened hair oil. All the same little Johnny Keats, Lord
Byron's piss-a-bed poet, had put the matter rather well. Then
more than ever, seemed it rich to get away from it all. No more
judges. No more bowing and saying 'If your Lordship pleases.'
No more hopelessly challenging the verbals. No more listening
to endless turgid speeches from my learned friends for the prosecution. 'To cease upon the midnight. With no pain.' From my
position between two worlds I heard the telephone beside the
bed ringing distantly. Hilda picked it up and told whoever it
was that they couldn't speak to Mr Rumpole.

'Who? Who can't speak to me?'

'Well, he's busy at the moment.' Hilda lied to the telephone. In fact I had done absolutely nothing for the last three days.

'Busy? I'm not busy.'

'Busy dying.' Hilda laughed, I thought a trifle flippantly. 'That's what he says anyway. No, Henry. Well, not this week, certainly . . .'

'It's my clerk. My clerk Henry!' I returned to earth and grabbed the telephone from She.

'I'm sorry to hear you're dying, sir.' Henry, as always, sounded perfectly serious, and not tremendously interested.

'Dying, Henry? Well, that's a bit of an exaggeration.'

'There was a con for you, sir. At Brixton Prison. 2.30. The "Dartford Post Office Robbery". Mr Bernard's got the safe blower . . .'

A safe blowing in Dartford! I felt my head clear and swung my legs out of bed and feet to the floor. There's nothing like the prospect of the Old Bailey for curing all other diseases.

'I'll tell Mr Bernard you can't be there.'

'Tell him nothing of the sort, Henry. I'll be there. No trouble at all. I'll just fling on a few togs.'

As I made for the wardrobe Hilda looked at me as if my recent flirtation with the Unknown had been some sort of a charade.

'I thought you were dying,' she said.

Dying, as I explained to her, would have to be postponed. Safe blowing came first.

When I was dressed, wrapped in a muffler and buttoned into an overcoat by Matey, I set out for Chambers. And there I made two unpleasant discoveries, the first being that there were those who would not have regretted Rumpole's continued absence from Chambers by reason of death. At that time we were suffering from a good deal of overcrowding and Erskine-Brown's small room, which opened into the entrance hall, had to accommodate not only Erskine-Brown himself, but his ex-pupil Miss Phyllida Trant, and his two new pupils who sometimes dived into my room to borrow books and then shot out again like frightened rabbits. Also my old friend George Frobisher took refuge there whenever *his* old friend Hoskins, with whom George shared a room, was having an intimate conference with a divorcée.

As I passed Erskine-Brown's open door I could see his room was bursting at the seams, and, as I hung up my hat and coat in the hallway, I heard the voice of the Erskine-Brown say he supposed they'd have to hang on in that Black Hole of Calcutta a little longer. 'But,' he added, 'At least *he* can't be with us forever.'

'Who can't be with us forever?' It was Miss Trant's voice.

'Rumpole, of course. I mean, he's bound to retire sometime. He's a good age and Henry's been telling me he's not all that well.'

I chose that moment to stick my nose into the Black Hole.

'Morning, Erskine-Brown. Nose to the grindstone, Miss Trant?'

Miss Trant looked up from the brief she was reading and gave me a smile. She really has decidedly pretty teeth; ever since I deceived her so heartlessly I have become almost fond of Miss Trant.

'Oh, hello, Rumpole. I thought you were off sick.' Erskine-Brown was trying to move George's particulars of nuisance off his statement of claim.

'Recovered now.' I sneezed loudly. 'Rumpole Resurrected. Sorry to disappoint you.'

'That's a nasty cold you've got. Oughtn't you to be in bed?' Miss Trant was solicitous. I looked at her brief, neatly underlined in red and green, points for and against.

'Women are such industrious creatures! Who's your client?'

'Oh, just a thief. He'll have to plead guilty. He's said such ridiculous things to the police.'

'You twist his arm, Philly. Judges don't like you wasting the Court's time with hopeless cases.' Erskine-Brown was one of nature's pleaders. I decided that the stage of her career had come when Miss Trant might benefit from some proper advice.

'Never plead guilty!' I told her. 'That should be written up in letters a foot high. In every room in Chambers.'

'A foot high! We haven't got the room for it.' Erskine-Brown was still sulking, and George looked up from the corner of the desk he was occupying as though he'd just noticed me.

'Hello, Rumpole. Haven't seen you about lately.'

'I've been dying.'

'I say, don't do that. I should miss your help with the crossword.'

Thinking uneasily that the sole justification of my existence seemed to be helping George Frobisher with the crossword, I went into the clerk's room and Henry presented me with the brief in the 'Dartford Post Office Robbery'.

'You've got plenty of time, Mr Rumpole. They don't want the two of you down there till three o'clock now.'

'The *two* of us?' I was puzzled.

'The defendant Wheeler's got a certificate for two counsel.'

'Excellent! Giving me a junior, are they? Someone to take a note?'

'Well, not exactly, Mr Rumpole.' Henry had the grace to look embarrassed. 'You're being led. They're briefing a silk. You can take it easy for once.'

I was being led! I was a junior barrister, in the 67th year of my life.

'Easy! I don't want to take it easy!' I'm afraid I exploded at Henry. 'Haven't they heard? I'm out of rompers! I'm off the bloody leading rein. I managed the "Penge Bungalow Murder" alone and without a leader.'

I came out of the clerk's room clutching my junior brief and was met with a whiff of after-shave as the tall, elegant figure of Guthrie Featherstone, Q.C., appeared through the front door in his gent's natty velvet-collared overcoat and bowler hat, slumming down in Chambers after a triumph in the House.

'Hullo, Rumpole.' He greeted me affably. 'I'm afraid you're going to see a lot of my back this week.'

'Your back? What do you mean, your *back*?'

'I'm leading you. In the "Dartford Post Office Robbery".' He smiled in a damnably friendly fashion and went into the clerk's room.

'*You're* leading *me*, Featherstone?' I called after him, but he affected not to hear. I went on towards my room but, as I passed

her open door, I looked in once more on that tireless worker
Miss Phyllida Trant.

'You were perfectly right, Miss Trant. I ought to have stayed
in bed.'

I don't expect you've noticed Brixton Prison as you've driven
down to Brighton on a sunny Sunday morning. The prison gates
are down a long, extremely dreary street off the main road; you
pass little knots of visitors, girl friends, black mums with their
babies, and large screws going or coming from their time off.
Being a screw has become something of a growth industry; I met
one who gave up school teaching for wardering, the pay's so
much better and you get free golf. No matter what the weather
is like in other parts of London, a fine rain always seems to be
falling on the long walk down to Brixton. That day Featherstone
had parked his well-manicured Rover up in the main road and
leader and junior walked together up to the gates of the prison
house.

Our client was a well-known minor South London villain
named Charlie Wheeler, a professional safe blower with a string
of convictions going back to his childhood days, when Charlie
forced the Dr Barnardo's box in the local church, and which
included many notable exploits with safes. The evidence against
him wasn't much, just Charlie's fingerprints found on a fragment
of gelignite left beside the blown safe in the post office. It wasn't
much; but it was quite satisfactory evidence provided you were
appearing for the prosecution. If you were for the defence, well,
you'd have to improvise. I explained this to Featherstone, but he
looked gloomy and said,

'If you ask me this case is as dead as a doornail.'

'So are we all, eventually.' I tried to cheer him up.

'Two men in stocking masks hold up the post office, one has
a shotgun and our friend Wheeler's fingerprints are on a lump
of explosive!'

'I know. I know.'

We'd reached the prison doors and rang the visitors' bell.
Featherstone smiled faintly.

'I wonder why he didn't leave his visiting card?'

'I'll tell you, old sweetheart.' I was serious. 'Old cons like Charlie Wheeler don't have visiting cards.'

The small hole in the huge wooden doors rattled open. I waved Featherstone in.

'After you, my learned friend. Leaders always go into prison first.'

As soon as I get into a prison I become moody and depressed and have a strong desire to scream and fight my way out. If this is how a visitor feels, treated with respect, even deference, by the screws, I don't know how I could stand a five-year sentence, and yet I've had clients who greet five years rather like a pound from the poor box. I have also been entirely convinced, since my seventh year, that I would land up in the nick sooner or later, for some trivial reason or other, and fear it constantly. That wet afternoon in the inner courtyard at Brixton, with the killer Airedales sniffing around at the end of their leads, and the trusty boys planting out chrysanths in the sooty flower beds, the feeling came over me more strongly than ever, stronger than the fear of death. When they put me inside, I said to myself, I'll volunteer to be one of those trusties that plant out the chrysanths, at least I'll get to learn about horticulture. But before I could plan further we were in the neat, glass-panelled interview room. You could see through the walls to where, in a succession of similar rooms, cons were having meetings with their briefs. In the centre of the complex the screws sat by a table on which cacti grew in pots, among stones, providing half a dozen elegant and miniature Japanese gardens. I can tell you, it's really very cosy in Brixton.

So we all sat round, Charlie Wheeler's advisers, Featherstone the Q.C., Rumpole the junior, Bernard the solicitor and Joyce, his secretary, a jolly, fair-haired girl in jeans and a mac, dressed more for a wet weekend in Haslemere than the Nick, who clutched the file and was inclined to giggle disconcertingly during serious passages of the evidence. I once had her in Court in a murder, and she laughed so audibly at the pathologist's report that she had to be led out. Well, we were both younger then; now she seemed moderately composed as Charlie Wheeler held out his hand to me, as though we were alone in the room.

'I'm glad to see you, Mr Rumpole. It'd amaze you. The reputation you got in E Wing.'

I felt a dry cough coming on, and my head still swam a little. 'They can inscribe that on my tombstone. "He had an amazing reputation round E Wing".'

'You're not going to *die*, are you, Mr Rumpole?' Charlie seemed genuinely concerned.

'I was considering the possibility.'

'I'm that glad you're doing my case.'

'I'm not exactly doing your case, Charlie.' I hated to disappoint him. 'Your case is being conducted by Mr Guthrie Featherstone, Q.C., M.P. His name is constantly mentioned, Charlie, in the corridors of power!'

'I haven't heard much of you,' Charlie looked doubtfully at the Q.C., M.P. 'Not from the blokes in E Wing.'

'Rumpole. If I may . . .' Featherstone was apparently about to gather up the reins.

'Of course, of course, my learned leader. You want to conduct this conference? Well, it's your right.'

'Now then, Wheeler.'

'He means you, Charlie,' I translated.

'Rumpole . . . please!'

'I shall make a note of all your words of wisdom from now on.' I got out a note book and pen. Featherstone went on with admirable calm.

'What I wanted to say, Wheeler, was . . .'

'Not too fast, if you don't mind.' I was putting him down at dictation speed.

'We're here to fight this case. We're going to leave no stone unturned to fight it. To the best of my poor ability!'

'My poor ability.' I repeated what seemed to me to be a key phrase as I wrote.

'But Mr Bernard's no doubt told you who our judge is,' Featherstone went on, ignoring the interruption.

'I know.' Charlie sounded deeply depressed. 'Judge Bullingham.'

'So any sort of attack on the honesty of the police . . .' Featherstone went on, and Bernard raised a voice in warning:

'I told you, Charlie!'

'Would act like a red rag to a Bullingham. I suppose you told him that?' I supplied the thought for Charlie to chew over.

'Look, Mr Bernard's explained it to me. I don't want to lay into "Dirty" Dickerson.'

'Who's that?' Featherstone looked puzzled and I enlightened him from my memory of the brief.

'I imagine that is a reference to Detective Inspector Dickerson, the officer in charge of the case.'

'I mean, there ain't a whole lot of point . . .' Charlie seemed resigned, for which Featherstone was extremely grateful.

'Well, exactly! The evidence against you is undisputable. So what's the point of annoying the judge with a whole lot of questions?'

'I told you, Charlie.' Bernard nodded wisely.

'I mean, if I don't say nothing against Dickerson. If I keep quiet, like. Well . . . How much, Mr Rumpole? I were hoping for . . . an eight.'

'Hope springs eternal in the human breast!' I could tell him no more.

'In my experience . . .'

'Listen. To the wise words of the learned leader!'

When they came the leader's words were by no means filled with original thought. 'Any sort of attack on the police, in a case like this, will add considerably to your sentence. So let's be sensible. I must warn you, Wheeler, the time may very well come when I have to throw in my hand.'

'You mean Charlie's hand, don't you?' I said and Featherstone looked at me as if he wished he'd been lumbered with any other junior counsel in the Temple, however old and near to death.

As we walked back to the main road and the parked Rover, Featherstone put his problem in a nutshell.

'I can't make bricks without straw, Rumpole.'

'Down the Bailey you have to make bricks without bricks. You never get the luxury of straw . . .'

'Of course I'll mitigate,' Featherstone said sportingly.

I tried to point out the hopelessness of this course. 'What could you say in mitigation? "My client only called in for a 7p

stamp, my Lord, but as he was kept waiting behind ten old
ladies with pension books, and a lunatic arguing over a dog
licence, he lost his patience and blew the safe"?'

'Well, Rumpole. Hardly.'

We were standing on each side of the Rover, eyeing each
other in an unfriendly fashion across the polished roof, as
Featherstone unlocked the driver's door.

'Forget mitigation for a moment!' I told him. 'What's the use
of spending your life in an attitude of perpetual apology? Do
you think Charlie Wheeler's going to blow a safe without gloves
– even in a sub post office in Dartford? Do you think he's going
to leave a bit of spare gelignite around – with his trade mark on
it? Is that the mark of a professional?'

Featherstone slid into the driver's seat and opened the passenger door.

'Think about it, Featherstone.' I bundled myself into the car
beside him. 'It would be like you standing up in Court and
mitigating in your pyjamas!'

I decided that evening to drown all uneasy thoughts as to the
conduct of Wheeler's defence in three or four glasses of Château
Fleet Street in Pommeroy's Wine Bar. I went there with my old
friend George Frobisher and saw that the watering hole was
well filled, barristers at one end of the bar, including Erskine-
Brown, Miss Trant and Guthrie Featherstone going walkabout
among his loyal subjects, journalists at the other, and myself
and George at one of the crowded tables in the snug.

'They say Uncle Tom's not too well,' George told me about
our oldest, no longer practising, member of Chambers.

'Who is nowadays?'

'They say old T. C. Rowley is distinctly seedy. Well, he's a
good age. He's over 80.'

'What's good about being over 80?'

I really would have liked an answer to this question. Does the
pain of hopeless frustration in which we all live become, at such
an age, a dull and bearable ache of resignation? Is the loss of
hearing and eyesight compensated for by a palate more than
ever sensible to the thin warmth of Château Fleet Street? Before

I could press George further on the subject, however, a young man in a tweed suit with horn-rimmed glasses and a falling lock of fair hair, detached himself from the journalists' group and approached our table.

'Mr Rumpole?'

I admitted it.

'Philbeam. I write the "In Depth" column, in the *Sunday* . . .'

George stood. I don't believe he trusts journalists. 'Forgive me, Rumpole. I thought I'd call in on old Tom, on my way back to the hotel. Any messages?'

'Give him my love. Oh, and tell him we'll all be joining him eventually.'

'Really Rumpole!' George sounded shocked and he went, whereupon Philbeam sat opposite me and fixed me with his glittering horn-rims.

I made him welcome and ordered further clarets. 'A gentleman of the press! I'll always be grateful for the space you gave me, during the "Penge Bungalow Murder"!'

'I think that was before my time.'

'I rather think it was. Probably reported by your grandfather.' Philbeam, I could see by looking at him, had a point.

'I was in Court when you defended Ken Aspen. The rape case with the Member of Parliament.'

'Hardly one of my major triumphs.'

'Admired the way you cross-examined that girl.' I was just wondering where all this chat with the smooth-talking Philbeam was getting us, when he leaned forward and said, 'What I wanted to ask you, Mr Rumpole, was . . .'

'Yes?'

'Have you ever run up against a Detective Inspector Dickerson round Dartford somewhere?'

' "Dirty" Dickerson?' I was interested.

'Have you heard that too?' Philbeam smiled. 'You know how he got his name?'

'No,' I said, 'I've no idea.'

So he started to tell me. Up by the bar I heard Featherstone say 'Santé' as he raised his glass to Erskine-Brown. I discovered later that Erskine-Brown had been picked to make one of his comparatively rare appearances at the Bailey in the role of prosecuting counsel in the Dartford post office case, and that Featherstone was drinking to what promised to be a most civilized occasion, with both sides being of the greatest possible assistance to each other, and prosecution and defence collaborating in seeing Charlie Wheeler put gently away for a very long time indeed. Whilst this was going on Philbeam was telling me of an investigation his paper was carrying out on Dickerson. There were the usual sort of allegations, villains verballed unless they paid up, money taken for not opposing bail and such like police procedure.

'I once did an interview with a man called Harris,' Philbeam told me. 'Minor sort of South London villain. Loads of convictions . . .'

'Sounds like my kind of criminal.'

'Never printed it, of course. But Harry Harris told me D.I. Dickerson once handed him a stolen cigarette case. Got his finger-prints all over it. Then he made Harris pay him 300 quid not to be prosecuted for the theft.'

'Glory Hallelujah!' I had my first hint then of how dangerously Charlie Wheeler might be defended. 'You are a blessing, Philbeam, in an excellent disguise. I trust this is not an isolated incident?'

'I've got a whole file on Dickerson. Of course, I can't use it. Yet. The Leading Lady likes to win his libel actions.'

'Leading Lady?'

'That's what we call our editor.'

I let that pass. I had an urgent mission for Philbeam. 'Can you find us Harris?'

'I know the pubs he goes to. Shouldn't be difficult.'

'Oh, please, I beg you, Philbeam. Find him! Leave no pub unturned! He sounds like a small straw, we might just make a brick or two with him.'

Until Harris was found I had really nothing to go on, nothing that I could make Featherstone use as ammunition in a fight. Even if I had Harris and a pile of similar cannon-balls I was beginning to doubt if I could ever get Guthrie to fire a shot. I looked across to my learned leader at the bar, and saw him get out a large silk handkerchief and sneeze. It was not, I feared, a signal to charge, rather a trumpet call to retreat.

Lacking Harris, or any other tangible defence, I had to fall back on the flu as ammunition for my learned leader. Accordingly I brought to Court a throat spray, a pile of clean handkerchiefs, and a packet of cough drops which could be opened and noisily consumed during vital parts of the prosecution evidence. I ranged these weapons out in front of me on the first, remarkably uneventful, day in Court.

It was so uneventful, in fact, and so little was said on behalf of the defence, that his Honour Judge Bullingham became positively benign. One of the unsolved mysteries of the universe, and a matter I find it harder to speculate upon than such relatively straightforward problems as Free Will or Life after Death, is why on earth Ronnie Bullingham was ever made an Old Bailey judge. It's not his fault that he has a thick, heavily veined neck and the complexion of a beetroot past it first youth; his personal habits such as picking his teeth and searching in his ear with his little finger while on the bench I can forgive, and his unreasoning prejudice against all black persons, defence lawyers and probation officers I can mercifully attribute to some deep psychological cause. Perhaps the Bull's mother, if such a person can be imagined, was assaulted by a black probation officer who was on his way to give evidence for the defence. What I cannot forgive is his Honour's appalling treatment of the English language. His summing-ups have to be translated by the Court of Appeal like pages of Urdu, and all the jury get is a vague impression of a man so shaken with rage that some dreadful crime *must* have caused it. The only kind of sentence in which Bullingham never falters is one of seven years and up.

So there we were before this appalling tribunal, Charlie Wheeler resigned, Bernard tremendously anxious, his nice secretary blushing as the judge stared with undisguised hostility at her trousers, and Erskine-Brown taking Mr Fingleton, the fingerprint expert, through his predictably damaging evidence. It was a rare occasion, peace and tranquillity in Bullingham's Court.

'Mr Fingleton,' said Erskine-Brown. 'Do you produce enlarged photographs of the first, second and third fingers of the defendant, Wheeler?'

'Yes.'

I carefully unfolded the first of my pile of hankies and loudly blew the Rumpole nose, diverting the attention of some of the jury.

'Does the defence admit them?' The Bull glared towards us. Featherstone rose and bowed as if he'd been addressing the House of Lords.

'Those are admitted, my Lord.'

'Well, thank you,' said the judge in an unprecedented burst of good manners. 'I'm very much obliged to you, Mr Feather-stone.'

'I bet you are, old darling!' I muttered as Featherstone sank gracefully back into his seat.

'And do you also produce enlarged photographs of the finger-prints on the small piece of gelignite taken by Detective Inspector Dickerson from the scene of the crime?'

'Yes.'

I could see it was time to use the throat spray. I lifted it to the open mouth.

'Now what do you say about those two sets of fingerprints?'

I puffed the throat spray, regrettably I couldn't drown the answer.

'I have found 32 distinct points of similarity.'

'And by points of similarity you mean . . .?' The Bull wanted it spelt out for the jury.

'The break in the first whorl on the index finger, for instance, my Lord, is exactly the same in both cases.'

The photographs were handed round twelve good jury-persons, who were flattered into becoming experts.

'Yes, I think the members of the jury can see that *quite* clearly. You can, *can't* you?' Bullingham's manner to the jury was a nice mixture of a creep and a crow.

'And so, Mr Fingleton, what is your conclusion? Just tell the jury.' Erskine-Brown's approach was more subtle, he simply wanted the witness to tell us his views, provided, of course, they were the views of the prosecution.

'My conclusion is . . .' Fingleton was an experienced witness. He turned politely to the jury. But Rumpole was an experienced defender. He worked at the throat spray producing a cloud of medicated mist and created a genuine diversion. Even Fingleton paused and turned to look.

'This is *not* a hospital!' The judge's remark seemed painfully obvious. 'I would stress that. For the benefit of *junior* counsel for the defence. Yes, Mr Fingleton?'

In the enforced silence that followed Fingleton struck. 'The fingerprints are identical, my Lord.'

'Thank you very much, Mr Fingleton.' Erskine-Brown sat down with great pleasure. I don't know what I expected of the rustling silk in front of me. An attack on the whole theory of the fingerprint as first promulgated by Professor Purkinje of the University of Breslau? The classification into whorls, loops, arches and composites pioneered by Sir E. R. Henry of the Bengal Police? Something, anything, to puzzle the jury and infuriate the Bull. As it was the Q.C. rose in all his glory to deliver himself of his single *bon mot*:

'No questions, my Lord.' 'I can't do anything with this evidence,' Featherstone whispered to me as he sat down.

'No. *You* can't,' I told him. I gave out a final fusillade of coughs, the only effect of which was to drown the judge as he thanked my leader, with every appearance of delight, for his brilliant contribution to the trial.

That evening I was re-reading my brief in the living-room at Froxbury Court with a still slightly feverish eye. I came again to something in Charlie Wheeler's proof of evidence that had always puzzled me, a conversation he had had with D.I. Dickerson at about two in the morning in a police cell. Charlie's recollection of the event hadn't been particularly clear but it seemed there had been an offer of bail in exchange for a confession and it had ended in some sort of temporary agreement, because the officer had shaken Charlie's hand before leaving him for the rest of the night. I read the short, unilluminating paragraph through several times before something which could hardly be called an idea, more a vague hint of the possibility of some future thought, floated into my mind. I lit a small cigar, which considerably improved the quality of my cough, and gazed at the rising smoke.

Then the telephone rang, a most unexpected caller, none other than Mrs Marigold Featherstone speaking directly from the sick bed. She was heart-broken to tell me, but poor Guthrie had a temperature of 102. It had come at the worst possible time, what with the Foreign Office dinner next week and his speech on Devolution. She really couldn't let Guthrie risk all that by coming down to the Old Bailey . . .

'Of course not! Don't dream of it! You keep the old darling tucked up in bed.' Rumpole was extremely solicitous. 'And keep the hot-water-bottles going, and beef tea constantly simmering on the hob. The Old Bailey's a nasty draughty place.'

Marigold sounded grateful and passed the phone to her husband who croaked an apology and said did I mind holding the fort, and he was sure I agreed there was nothing to do but to mitigate in view of the evidence we had heard.

'Quite right, Guthrie,' I assured him. 'Of course we'll have to plead. No, I won't attack the officer in charge of the case. I'll adopt your technique. I admired it so much. "No questions, my Lord." That really endeared you to the old Bull. You had the old sweetheart purring. Now you stay in bed, Guthrie. Twenty-four hours at least. Don't you dream of moving.'

I was putting down the phone with a grin of pure pleasure when Hilda came in, flushed from the washing up, and asked who was on the phone. I stood and greeted her with words of delight.

'*Oh frabjous day!*, Hilda,' I said. '*Callooh! Callay! He chortled in his joy!*'

'What on earth's the matter with you, Rumpole?'

'The matter? Nothing's the matter! It's an occasion for rejoicing. I've given my learned leader the flu!'

Then I phoned the night editor of that prestigious Sunday paper which examines our lives in depth, and left a message for the industrious Philbeam.

I got up early the next morning and was down at Ludgate

Circus, as the all-night printers came off work, and indulged myself in the treat of breakfast in Jock's Cafe opposite the Old Bailey, a place patronized by the discerning coppers, reporters, and meat porters of Smithfield, where the two eggs, rashers and fried slice are the best in London, and where I have roughed out, over a third cup of coffee, some of my most devastating cross-examinations and most moving speeches for the defence. I was joined at breakfast by Philbeam, to whom I gave the glad tidings that the world's greatest mitigator was docked in bed for the remainder of the trial. My spirits were only a little dashed by the fact that Philbeam had, so far, failed in his search for Harris.

'I've been round twenty pubs,' he told me. 'No joy. But I've got a number to phone. Place where his sister works.' He looked at his watch. 'They won't be open till 9.30.'

'Oh, find him, Philbeam, old darling. We may be all set for the unmasking of "Dirty" Dickerson.'

I sent Philbeam about his business and went over to the Palais de Justice. The dear old place was as I liked it best, quiet and peaceful with only a few tired cleaning ladies and sleepy attendants to greet me. I got changed into my working clobber, wig, gown and so on, at my leisure and went down to the lower ground floor. I had rung Bernard the night before and asked him to meet me for an early conference with the client. But when I got to the old battered Newgate door, which divides the safe sheep from the imperilled goats, I found only the secretary Joyce, looking harassed and with her arms full of files.

'Oh, Mr Rumpole,' she panted at me, 'Mr Bernard won't be with you this morning. A funeral.'

'Not his?'

'A client's.'

'That's all right then. I'm just going down the cells to see Charlie.'

'Oh. Oh, well. I'm with Mr Hoskins on a fraud in the West Court. We've got a conference over there and . . .'

'You run along, my dear,' I reassured her. 'I believe I can cope with a conference alone and without a leader.'

At which she went off gratefully and I went up to the iron gate to do what no sensible barrister ever does, see a client alone before a trial. Perhaps I was too full of my sudden freedom from the leading rein to be sensible at that moment, and I was still in a cheerful mood when the screw left his mug of tea and jam sandwich to open the door to me.

'Got Wheeler, have you?' I asked him. 'Charlie Wheeler?'

'Well, I don't think he's gone out anywhere.' This screw was a wit. 'He don't get many invitations.'

'Not many invitations! That's rich, that is. Exceeding rich!' I laughed appreciatively.

You know what being an Old Bailey Hack over the years blunts? It blunts the sensitivity. The sensitivity comes out like hair on the comb, and when you go down the cells you're prepared to laugh at anything.

'You ever paid Dickerson money, Charlie?' Wheeler and I were *à deux* in the interview room, both smoking away at my small cigars.

'I'd never entertain it! Oh, I know some as paid him.'

'Including Harry Harris?'

'You knows a lot, don't you?' Charlie looked at me with some admiration.

'I try to keep abreast of the underworld. So you were known to the Detective Inspector as a dedicated non-payer?'

'You could say that.' There was a pause as I searched for Charlie's statement in the brief. Then he said, 'Mr Featherstone not here today?'

'We had a bit of luck with the flu. It says somewhere here that the D.I. was on the point of offering you bail . . .'

'That seemed funny to me, like.'

'Very funny. With your record.'

'Of course, he wanted something for it. He was asking me to put my hands up, like.'

'Sign a confession? You weren't going to?'

'I never done that, Mr Rumpole. It's not the way I work. All the same . . .'

'Yes?'

'I strung him along a bit. I let him think we might do a deal. We even shook hands on it like.'

'Yes. Tell me more about that.'

'Shook hands on the deal, like. Well, he put out his hand, like . . . and took mine.'

'You ever had your hand taken by a police officer before?' This was the part that interested me.

'No! Only me collar.'

'Show me, how he shook hands with you. You be the Detective Inspector.'

Charlie took my hand, but only for a moment. 'It was all over in a second. And I never made no statement. It ain't in me character.'

'How did Dickerson look when he shook hands with you? Did he look pleased – triumphant?'

'I couldn't hardly see him.'

'What?'

'It was in my cell. In the Dartford Nick. I don't know . . . about two o'clock of a morning. I was half asleep . . . well, he was in the dark, like. He did seem that little bit nervous.'

'Nervous?'

'Well. You know what you expect from a man of his build. Good firm grip. Well, that hand of his felt a bit clammy and soft.'

I stood up, the vague thought had not only become an idea but a plan of attack, a series of questions for cross-examination.

'How do you feel about this case, Mr Rumpole?' Charlie looked up at me doubtfully.

'Feel? Like stout Cortez.'

'Who?'

'*When with the eagle eyes   He stared at the Pacific – and all his men   Looked at each other with a wild surmise.*'

'You got me there, Mr Rumpole.'

'Keats! It's been an autumn of Keats. "*To cease upon the midnight with no pain.*" Quite enough of that! We're recovered now. Rumpole resurrected!'

'You reckon we've got a chance, Mr Rumpole?'

'A tiny chance perhaps. Like a small electric light bulb in a dark cell. More chance than mitigating.'

I sat down again at the table and started to explain the position as clearly as I could to Charlie. 'I can't tell you, understand that? I can't put you in the box and let the jury have your excellent record as a safe blower read out to them. But I want your express instructions . . .'

'You 'ave them, Mr Rumpole. What you got in mind?'

'I think I ought to ask Inspector "Dirty" Dickerson a few impertinent questions. So this is what I'm going to ask him, with your kind permission . . .'

It was then that I got Charlie Wheeler's instructions to do exactly as I did in his trial. I think, in view of the following disastrous happenings, I should make that perfectly clear.

D.I. Dickerson was a large, smiling man with greying hair which covered the top of his ears and a bright and expensive silk tie and matching handkerchief. He looked the sort of man who would be the life and soul of the office party, or the man on the package holiday to Ibiza you would be most careful to move away from. He was holding his prized possession, a small plastic bag containing a minute quantity of gelignite, labelled 'Exhibit 1', as Erskine-Brown came to the end of his questions.

'We have heard from the expert that Wheeler's fingerprints are on that small piece of gelignite. Where did you find it?'

'Beside the safe at the scene of the crime, my Lord,' Dickerson said respectfully.

'In the Dartford post office?' the Bull weighed in.

'Yes, my Lord.'

'Thank you, Detective Inspector.' Erskine-Brown sat down, his duty done.

'Have you any questions to ask the Detective Inspector?' the judge dared me.

'Just a few, my Lord.' Rumpole rose slowly to his feet.

'Well then, get on with it.' The judge was treating the defence with his usual courtesy.

'Do you know a man named Harris, Harry Harris?'

There are two ways to cross-examine, depending on the witness and your mood. You either start off politely, asking a series of questions to which the answer will be 'Yes', gaining the subject's confidence and agreement, leading him gently up the garden path to a carefully planned booby trap, or you go in like an old warship, with all guns blazing. I had decided that the Bull's Court at the Bailey was no place for subtlety and I went in for the broadside approach. The D.I. looked somewhat taken aback, but answered with his usual bonhomie.

'I know a Harry Harris.'

'A friend of Charlie Wheeler's?'

'Yes.'

'How would you describe him?'

'You want me to describe him?'

'Mr Rumpole has asked the questions. The risk is on his head.' The Bull's image was imprecise but his knowing leer at the jury made his meaning plain.

'Harris is a minor villain, sir. Round the Dartford area.'

'You asked for it, Mr Rumpole,' the judge was delighted and the jury smiled. I battled on, ignoring the barracking from the bench.

'Have you had any financial dealings with Harris?'

'My Lord.' As if I hadn't got enough opponents, Erskine-Brown rose to interrupt.

'Erskine-Brown,' I muttered, 'Will you not interrupt my cross-examination!'

'Can I ask how questions about this man Harris are in any way relevant to the case of Wheeler?' Erskine-Brown persisted, with a glare of judicial encouragement.

'Quite right,' the judge challenged me. 'What's this man Harris got to do with this case?'

'Not *this case*, my Lord, but . . .'

'Then your question is entirely irrelevant.' A simple mind, that of the Bull.

'My Lord, when the character of this officer is called into question . . .'

'Oh, really? Are you attacking this officer's character?' The judge tried a voice of dangerous courtesy, but only succeeded in sounding ordinarily rude.

'I wasn't offering him a gold medal.' At this the jury laughed. Bullingham let that one go and then said:

'I can only assume you're making this attack on instructions.'

'I take full responsibility, my Lord.'

'I see your learned leader isn't in Court.'

'Unfortunately, my Lord, he is struck down by the flu.' I tried to sound depressed. Bullingham came insultingly to my aid:

'Perhaps you'd like me to adjourn this cross-examination. So it can be done properly. By learned leading counsel?'

'Thank you, my Lord. I am quite happy to proceed.' I had no time to lose, for God's sake! Guthrie's flu might be better by the next day. The judge tried a last attack.

'I hope you are not making this suggestion without being in a position to call Harris?'

I looked round the Court, and, at this moment my good angel Philbeam came bursting in through the swing doors. I put my stake on an even chance and said, 'Certainly I can call him.'

At this point the witness nobly volunteered to answer my questions, however objectionable they might be, and I beckoned Philbeam to my side. The news was not good. Harris's sister had been contacted, but hadn't heard of her brother for two years. Philbeam whispered:

'Shall I keep trying?'

'For God's sake!' I whispered back, and then straightened to hear D.I. Dickerson tell the judge that he never had any financial dealings of any sort with Harris. The Bull wrote this down carefully and said:

'Very well. Mr Rumpole has his answer, although it probably wasn't the one he wanted.' With this judge the rapier was always replaced by the bludgeon. 'Do you want to try your luck with any *more* questions, Mr Rumpole?'

'Just one or two, my Lord. Detective Inspector. When Charlie Wheeler was in the Dartford Nick . . .'

'Where?' the judge frowned.

'In the police cells. At Dartford Police Station,' I translated politely.

'There is such a thing as plain English, Mr Rumpole. Just as well to use it.' *Bullingham* said that to me. I had no time to lose my temper with him and I was off in pursuit of the D.I.

'Did you ever on any occasion at Dartford Police Station shake hands with Charlie Wheeler?'

There was a moment's hesitation, and the witness put his big hands in his jacket pockets.

'Is my English plain enough for you?'

'Shake his hand? I may have done.'

'Have you ever shaken a prisoner's hand before?'

'Not that I can remember.'

'So why should you have shaken hands with Charlie Wheeler?'

Suddenly the Court was quiet, the jury were paying attention. Dickerson took a long ten seconds to think of his answer.

'Your client told me he was about to make a confession statement. I was congratulating him on showing a bit of sense.'

The silence was broken by a general giggle, led by the judge.

'Is that the answer you wanted, Mr Rumpole?' The Bull was positively beaming.

'Yes, my Lord, it is. I wished to establish that this officer took my client by the hand.'

'*As* he was prepared to make a confession,' the jury were reminded from the bench.

Once again I ignored the interruption and asked the witness, 'Did you discuss bail with him on that occasion?'

'Bail? No, sir. There was no discussion of bail whatsoever.' Dickerson looked pained at the suggestion.

'Did you say you wouldn't oppose bail if he made a confession?'

'I said nothing of the sort, my Lord.'

Bullingham sighed heavily, threw down his pencil and turned on me. 'Mr Rumpole, are there any *further* allegations of a serious nature to be made against this officer?'

'Only one, my Lord. May I have Exhibit 1, please?'

The usher brought me the little lump of gelignite in its plastic bag.

'That is the small piece of gelignite,' the judge took great pleasure in reminding the jury. 'With your client's fingerprints on it.'

'Exactly, my Lord. Who found this piece of gelignite, Detective Inspector?'

'I did. At the scene of the crime.'

'Did you show it to any other officer?'

'When I got back to the station.'

'When you got back to the station! So the jury must rely on your evidence and your evidence alone to satisfy them that this small piece of gelignite was ever at the scene of the crime.'

'If my evidence isn't good enough . . .'

'If your evidence isn't good enough, Detective Inspector, Charlie Wheeler is entitled to be acquitted.' I felt the quietness in Court again, the jury were listening. I leant forward and spoke to the witness as though we were alone in the room. 'Have you ever in your long experience known a safe blower to leave his gelignite with his fingerprints on it at the scene of a crime?'

At which, of course, the judge had to comment to the jury. 'If criminals never made mistakes, we would have no trials at the Old Bailey.'

However, I felt they were becoming more interested in the witness than the judge and I went on quickly, 'You see, there is another possibility the jury may have to consider . . .'

'Is there?' Dickerson smiled, politely interested.

'We have no idea when the fingerprints got on the gelignite.'

'Haven't we?'

'Or where. Is it just possible, Detective Inspector, that Charlie Wheeler only touched the gelignite in the Dartford Police Station?'

There was another, minute pause before he answered. 'I don't know what you mean.'

It was time to tell the jury exactly what I meant, and bring Charlie's defence out into the open. 'In that dark cell, at two o'clock in the morning, do you think *you* had the gelignite, this little piece of gelignite, concealed in your palm when you held your hand out to him. And shook hands. As you had never shaken hands with any prisoner in your life before? Is *that* the only explanation of how Charlie Wheeler's fingerprints got on to Exhibit 1?'

I hadn't expected Dickerson to crumble and apologize, but I had hoped for a bluster, an outraged denial which might have said more than he intended. But he was too experienced a witness for that; he only smiled tolerantly and said, 'If that's what

Wheeler told you. I mean *if* . . . Then it's a load of nonsense. You know that, Mr Rumpole.'

'Is it all lies, Detective Inspector?' Bullingham asked.

'All lies, my Lord.'

The judge wrote that last answer down, in case he forgot it. Then he gave the jury one of his least lovable grins. 'It's always painful to watch an officer of this sort of length of service under attack, members of the jury. I expect we'd all be glad of a break. Back at ten past two, Mr Erskine-Brown.'

So, ignoring Rumpole, he bundled himself out of Court.

'Mr Featherstone heard from the doctor, sir,' Henry was waiting for me as I came out of Court. 'He's to stay in bed for the rest of the week. He was asking, is it all over?'

'Tell him it's all going according to plan. Nothing to send his temperature up.'

In the lift, on my way up to the robing room, I met Miss Phillida Trant. She seemed in a mood of strange elation and told me that everything was going wonderfully.

'Everything?'

'I took your advice and I didn't plead.' She was positively glowing, the light of battle burning behind her specs. 'Now it seems that there's no note of some of the verbals and most of it was after he was charged anyway and . . .'

'Good news from somewhere!'

'You were right, of course. When you said, always fight everything.'

Fight everything; what else had we left to do? I called the Sunday paper again from the robing room. Philbeam had gone out again and left no message.

'Wheeler. You're a coward as well as a thief. You tied up this helpless sub Post Mistress and you robbed. What makes it all a great deal more grave. You deliberately chose, through your counsel, to attack the honesty and good name of someone of twenty-five years standing in the police force. I mean Detective Inspector Dickerson. I've had the misfortune to sit here and hear that fine officer subjected to a number of questions . . .'

We were at the last gasp of the Wheeler trial, a proceeding marked by the continued absence of any man called Harris . . . Even so the jury had taken three hours to find Charlie guilty by a majority, a fact which had clearly displeased the judge. I waited for the Bull to finish the ill-phrased lecture and come to announce a figure, when, to the surprise of everyone in Court, there was a voice of protest from the dock.

'I never!'

'Silence!' The usher shouted, but Charlie battled on.

'I never wanted my barrister to ask them questions! I told him to keep quiet!'

I sat quite still. I couldn't blame Charlie; but I began to feel that we were at the start of something that could prove deeply embarrassing for Rumpole. Ignoring the interruption the judge went on.

'You have the most appalling record and it is clearly time that society was protected from you for a considerably long period. The least sentence I can pass is one of twelve years' imprisonment. Take him down.'

Charlie was removed from the dock. I levered myself to my feet and started to move out of counsel's row when Bullingham stopped me.

'Just one moment. I have something to add, Mr Rumpole.'

I stopped, rooted to the spot. The judge proceeded to sentence once more.

'Your attack on the integrity of Detective Inspector Dickerson was not only not backed up by the evidence. It's now clear it was an adventure of your own. Without instructions. I take a very serious view of it. Very serious indeed.'

Fourteen years, I wondered? But the judge contented himself with saying ominously:

'I intend to report the matter in the proper quarter.'

'If your Lordship pleases.'

I gave him my politest bow, a much-needed lesson in Courtroom manners and, perhaps, Rumpole's last genuflection in front of the bench. What had I to look forward to now, except the end of life as I knew it? As I took off the wig and looked in the robing room mirror I seemed to see a new Rumpole, a man who might just possibly not be a barrister any more.

Featherstone, back in the land of the living, was pacing his room, I thought somewhat nervously, while I sat in his big leather armchair and smoked a small cigar.

'Reported to the Benchers of your Inn. A disciplinary hearing. Before the Senate! My dear Horace. I don't want to worry you . . .'

'On the contrary, you're having a most calming effect,' I reassured him. 'I've thought about retiring from the Bar for a long time. Perhaps I shall start a small market garden, behind Gloucester Road tube station?'

'I've had to write to the Senate myself about the case,' Guthrie looked embarrassed.

'To tell them that the attack on "Dirty" Dickerson was an escapade dreamt up by your learned junior. Yes, I'm sure you had to write and tell them that.'

'You'll confirm that, of course?'

'Don't worry, old sweetheart. You've got a perfect alibi.' I stood as if in Court. 'My Lord, I call Mrs Marigold Featherstone. She will prove conclusively that my client was flat on his back having his chest rubbed with Vick and chewing aspirin at the time of the dark deeds down the Bailey.'

'Rumpole, don't you wish . . .'

'He is entirely innocent of the attempted rape of D.I. "Clean Fingers" Dickerson.'

'Don't you wish you'd been laid up with flu? During R. *v.* Wheeler?'

I looked at him, astonished at his lack of understanding. 'You want to know the truth, Guvnor? All right. I'll come clean. You've got me bang to rights.'

'Rumpole!'

'I loved that cross-examination. I enjoyed every minute of it, and, what's more, I swear by Almighty God, I was onto something. If I'd only had a tiny bit of straw to make a brick with . . .'

'I hope you're not going to say *that*, in front of the Senate!'

Featherstone looked so worried that I comforted him by asking his advice.

'What would you suggest I said . . . As my brief?'

He took me quite seriously and gave my hopeless case his most learned opinion. 'I think,' he said at last, 'I'd put it in *this* way. In your enthusiasm, understandable enthusiasm, for your client's interests, you were carried away, Rumpole. In the heat of the moment you made an attack on the honesty of a senior police officer which you now deeply regret . . .'

'What do you think I might get? Probation?'

'The worst aspect of your case, in my opinion . . .' Featherstone was giving the matter judicial consideration now.

'In your *learned* opinion?'

'Is that you proceeded entirely without instructions.'

I looked at him with astonishment. 'Do you think I'm totally insane?'

'I must say I was beginning to wonder.'

'Of course I had instructions.'

'But at the conference in Brixton we clearly decided . . .'

'I had another conference. Whilst you were tucked up with your hot-water-bottle.'

'Charlie Wheeler gave you instructions to put to this officer . . .?'

'That he handed him the gelignite! Yes, of course I got instructions.'

Of course Featherstone asked the question which they'd be bound to ask in the Senate. 'You made a note of them at the time?'

'A note! I've got too old for making notes, in or out of Court. I carry things in my head.' There's no fool like an old fool, of course I should have made a note.

'Our solicitor! Bernard will have a note of the conference. Or at any rate a recollection.' Featherstone was doing his best.

'Bernard was off enjoying himself at some funeral or other. He left me to the tender mercies of Joyce.'

'Then Joyce will remember. We'll get hold of Joyce.' He saw another ray of light and reached for the phone.

'Joyce wasn't there. Oh, she had some sort of fraud on with Hoskins in the West Court.'

'You mean you actually saw the client alone?' Featherstone was reduced to the unalterable fact.

'Oh, we live dangerously,' I told him, 'down the Old Bailey.'

'The trouble is . . .'

'More trouble?'

'Wheeler denied he'd given you instructions. He told the judge as much.'

'Wouldn't you have done that in his place, old darling?'

'As a matter of fact, Rumpole, I've never been on trial for safe blowing.'

I did my best to help Featherstone's imagination. 'You've just waited three hours for the jury to find you guilty. You've been told by learned leading counsel, no less, in Brixton Prison, that it's a few extra years for asking the "Dirty" D.I. certain rude questions. Wouldn't you deny you'd given any instructions? I'm too old to expect honour among safe blowers.'

'It's a problem!' Featherstone sat at his desk, temporarily bankrupt of ideas. I felt sorry for him.

'To me it seems perfectly simple.'

'I'll have to give it a good deal of thought.'

'Give what a good deal of thought?' I was on my way to the door. It was only then I realized that the old darling had actually briefed himself for my defence.

'Exactly what I'm going to say. On your behalf to the Senate.'

'*Say?* I don't want you to *say* anything. You'd only mitigate.'

Featherstone wasn't the only one who had been giving thought to the nature of Rumpole's defence. A few days later Hilda rang up Chambers and invited my old friend George Frobisher to dinner. She put on a very passable meal for us, and, as we sat over our apple pie and cream, gave me some words of wisdom, apparently learned at her father's knee.

'Daddy always said, a man should stand up and admit he's in the wrong. He said that was by far the best way.'

'Hilda. What are you talking about?' I was puzzled by the relevance of the thoughts of Daddy.

'He always told his clients, "An apology costs nothing, but it can earn you untold gold in sympathy from the judge." ' Hilda finished triumphantly.

'Old C. H. Wystan, your Daddy, was hardly one of the nation's fighters, was he, George?'

'A man with a good deal of wisdom, for all that.' George and Hilda seemed to be in agreement.

'I'll go and make some coffee.'

'All right. Quite all right.'

'I'll leave you two gentlemen to your wine.'

Hilda left us and I poured port for George. I meant to pluck out the heart of his mystery.

'George,' I said, 'How long is it since Hilda last asked you to dinner with us?'

'It must be a good few years now.'

'A good few years. Yes, it must be. So why do you think my wife felt this sudden longing to have you share our cutlets?'

'You know perfectly well Hilda's worried, Rumpole. And so am I. Very worried by the stand you're taking.'

'Stand, George? What sort of stand is that?'

'This wretched man, this Wheeler. How can he be worth risking your career over, Rumpole? Your wife can't understand that and I must say I have considerable difficulty . . .'

'He was worth defending. Everyone's worth defending. That's what we're for, isn't it? Do we have any other function?'

'But Hilda says that you admitted to her that the man was a professional safe blower.' George looked at me, distinctly puzzled, but he had put his finger on the exact point.

'Professional? Of course! So he wouldn't have left finger-prints . . .'

'Do you honestly believe, can you put your hand on your heart, Rumpole, and tell me you really *believe* that this man Wheeler was innocent?'

'Oh, come now, George. How many of your clients can you swear were innocent?'

'So you don't believe he was innocent?'

'If you ask my view of the matter – and you know my view is strictly irrelevant . . .'

'All the same, Rumpole. I'd like you to answer my questions.'

I admired him then, a new George, quiet but firm and not to be put off. I told him he'd make a cross-examiner yet, and poured him another glass of port. Then I gave him his answer. 'No. No, I don't believe he was innocent. In fact I think Charlie Wheeler probably blew the safe in the Dartford post office.'

'So no injustice was done.'

'Probably not . . .'

George stood up then. He was beaming at me, apparently hugely relieved. 'So that *is* good news, Rumpole. You've seen sense at last.'

Hilda came in with the coffee tray and George gave her the glad tidings. 'I believe your husband's seen sense at last.'

'I knew you'd be able to talk to him.' Hilda smiled as she poured the coffee. 'You've always told me, Rumpole, "George is so sensible." Rumpole's always had a tremendous amount of respect for you, George.'

'Guthrie Featherstone agrees it can all be dealt with by way of an apology – and now you admit it was unnecessary to attack the officer!' George took his coffee and smiled at me. I hated to disappoint him.

'Unnecessary? Did you say unnecessary?'

'You said yourself, Wheeler was probably guilty.' George seemed to think that was an end of the matter.

'Guilty or innocent. What's it matter? What matters is – he may have been convicted on faked evidence.'

'But, Rumpole, if he'd done it anyway . . .' Hilda was as puzzled as George. I did my best to explain it to them both.

'We can't decide guilt or innocence. That's not for us, *you* know that, George. That's for twelve puzzled old darlings pulled off the street for three boring days with a safe blower. But we can make sure they're not lied to, not deceived, not tricked by some smiling copper who wants to take away their decision from them by a few conjuring tricks in a dark cell. Oh, for God's sake, have another glass of port.'

I felt he needed it, for he sat looking quite despondent and asked what on earth I thought I was going to do.

'Grow vegetables. We'll probably have to go to the country to do it.'

'Rumpole. They won't disbar you . . .' George did his best to sound comforting. I went over to the old desk in the corner and found a packet of small cigars.

'Suspend me, disbar me, I don't care. I shan't apologize for what I did for Wheeler.'

'Talk to him, George. Please talk to him.' Hilda sounded desperate. George did his best.

'Rumpole. Forget Wheeler for a moment. You've got yourself to think about.'

I found my cigars and lit one. I was still searching for something I had concealed in a drawer of the desk. 'Oh, I am thinking of myself. You see, Hilda, with the insurance policy and what we'd get for this flat, we could get quite a decent cottage and a small-holding.'

'A small-holding! Oh, George. Has he gone quite mad? You wouldn't know what to do with a small-holding, Rumpole!'

'Dig it and dung it! That's what I'd do. And grow the stuff I'm rather keen on. Artichokes and marrows and parsnips and, after a few years, perhaps asparagus . . .' I had found what I wanted, a seed catalogue, full of fine colour photographs of prize vegetables. 'Look, Hilda. Do look at this. Please look at it.'

I took the catalogue over to Hilda and held it open at a particularly succulent row of runner beans. 'Don't you think it all looks rather splendid?'

She shook her head. Hilda Rumpole is incredibly urban, all her life has revolved round Law Courts and barristers' Chambers; she could only see a row of runners, or even a picking of early peas, through a haze of tears.

A man, under our system, is innocent until he's proved guilty, and in the time that elapsed before my case was due to be heard in the Senate, by the tribunal that decides matters of discipline at the Bar, I continued business as usual, although the briefs didn't exactly fall like summer rain onto the fertile soil of Rumpole's Chambers. However, I left home earlier than usual, largely to escape the sorrowful and rebuking eyes of She Who Must Be Obeyed, often had breakfast on my own with *The Times* crossword at Jock's Café, and lingered late in Pommeroy's Wine Bar. I was sitting there at a lonely table with my head deep in the *Evening Standard* when I heard Erskine-Brown's voice ringing from the bar.

'Vegetables! Did you say Rumpole was going to grow vegetables?'

'He actually bought a catalogue. A list of seeds. With illustrations.' George sounded like a doctor, announcing the symptoms of a fatal disease.

'How *old* is Rumpole? Do you think he might be going a bit screwy?'

'Of course not!' The female voice was quite positive. 'The first thing I learned at the Bar was, never underestimate the cunning of Rumpole.' It was the clear and dulcet tone of Miss Trant.

For a while their voices were drowned in the general clatter of legal anecdotes, journalists' attempted seductions and cries for claret, which make up the full orchestra of the sound of Pommeroy's, and then I heard my old friend George booming sadly.

'Obstinate! Rumpole's incredibly obstinate. You know what he's saying now? Even if they just suspend him – for a little while. Even if they censure him – he'll leave the Bar, and he won't apologize!'

'Then surely one thing's perfectly clear, George.' It was Erskine-Brown again.

'What's that?'

'Rumpole has absolutely no one to blame but himself. I'm going back to Chambers. Come on, Philly. I've got to pick up a brief, and then we're off to the Festival Hall!'

'I'll catch you up.'

I sank my head deeper in the 'Londoner's Diary' and then looked up as Miss Trant's voice came again, from about three feet away. 'You going to send us up some nice fresh vegetables?'

As I lowered the paper Miss Trant sat down and joined me uninvited; it was amazing, the confidence she had developed since her baptism of fire in Dock Street. 'Peas and carrots. New potatoes! Sounds delicious.'

'I have been having doubts.' I suppose I needed someone to

talk to at that moment, life with Hilda being then on the silent side. 'Looking back at my past life, hanging round Law Courts, I found absolutely no evidence for the proposition that I have green fingers.'

'Neither have I.'

'What?'

'My pot plants all go yellow.'

'It's only that, whenever I visit prisons and see the trusties planting out straight rows of chrysanths in the sooty soil, I think, yes. That's the job I'll choose when I'm in the Nick.'

Then an extraordinary thing happened. Miss Trant actually seemed to lose her temper with me. 'Really! You're not going to the Nick. You told me never to underestimate your cunning – like the time when I was prosecuting you and you got me to bore the magistrate with a load of law – and you won the case!'

'Finally tumbled to that, did you?' I smiled, remembering the occasion.

'Well, if you can think of that in the Dock Street Mag's Court can't you deal with this little case of yours in the Senate?'

'I shan't apologize!' I told her that quite firmly, and another surprise: she didn't argue.

'Of course you won't. Why? Were you thinking of it?'

'Was I?'

'Creeping off to the country. To grow vegetables! It's like pleading guilty. Well, stuff that for a lark!' This slip of a girl had the spirit which was lacking in Featherstone, or Hilda, or even George; the courage of an advocate.

'Miss Trant,' I told her, 'I remember when you first came to the Chambers, you were a somewhat straight-laced young woman, only interested in law reports.'

'I've learned a lot since then.'

'From your pupil master, Erskine-Brown?'

'No, from you! What do you say we ought to have written up in Chambers, in letters a foot high? *Never plead guilty!*'

'Bricks without bricks, Miss Trant ... Bricks without the bloody shadow of a brick. Unless ...'

'Well, go on. Unless?'

'Someone could lay their hands on a man called Harry Harris.'

When she had gone I sat for a while alone. I thought of my hearing before the Senate of the Inns of Court. What would that august body do to me? Change me utterly? I might leave their presence as someone quite new, perhaps even as myself. It seemed to me that I had spent my whole life being other people, safe blowers, fraudsmen, a few rather gentle murderers. I'd had remarkably little time to be Rumpole. Would I have time now; and if I had time, hanging heavy on my hands forever, should I enjoy the experience of being my own, genuine, unadulterated Rumpole at last?

Jack Pommeroy broke in on this uncomfortable reverie. There was a phone call for me, from Philbeam. He wanted me to stay where I was, he was bringing a man round for a drink, a man called Harry Harris.

A few nights later Detective Inspector Dickerson was sitting in the corner of his favourite Chinese restaurant (The Garden of Delights, in Bromley) waiting. His eyes lit up when a tall, very thin man with grey hair came in, for had this man not arrived the Detective Inspector was in great danger of having to pay his own bill.

'Harris!' Dickerson waved a large hand at the empty chair at his table. 'Where you been keeping yourself, Harry?'

'I got word you wanted to see me, Dickerson.'

'You want to buy me a Chinese, do you? The A1 combination with the sweet and sour lobster.'

'I'd be glad to.' Harris smiled patiently.

'I thought you would. You been a bit late on your instalments, Harris.'

'Sorry, Dickerson. I've been travelling.' At this point Harris took a bulky envelope out of his breast pocket and handed it to the Detective Inspector, whose manner became, if possible, even more affable.

'Well, leave a forwarding address then. We'll get on much more nicely if I can bleed you regular. I think,' Dickerson consulted the wine list, 'a nice bottle of Chablis'd go well with the sweet and sour.'

When Harris had ordered the Chablis from the Chinese waiter

he broached an awkward subject. 'Can we forget it now?' he asked, and his voice had, for the first time, a whining tone.

'Forget what, Harris?'

'A couple of fingerprints on a gold case.'

There was a long silence and then Dickerson said, 'You're so careless, Harris, where you put your fingers. You're as bad as your friend Charlie Wheeler.'

'I heard you fitted Charlie up nicely too.'

'Fitted him up? Who told you I fitted Charlie up? The jury convicted him, didn't they?' Dickerson sounded cautious, but Harris was laughing.

'Such a nice friendly lad, Charlie. He'd shake hands with anyone!'

It was a little while before Dickerson joined in the joke, but apparently he found it irresistible. 'All right, Harris,' he said through chuckles, 'Very funny. Very funny indeed. But let it be a lesson to you ... If you don't bleed regular I'll have your fingers round a lump of jelly. Just the way I did with Charlie.'

There was an interruption then, when the waiter brought the Chablis. Dickerson turned his attention to the temperature of the bottle. If he hadn't done so he might have noticed the tip of a small metallic object, hidden in the breast pocket of Harris's jacket. The reason for that, and for my having a verbatim account of this conversation, is that it was being taken down for posterity, and the subsequent police inquiry, on a small but efficient tape recorder which was later delivered to Philbeam's car, parked outside the Garden of Delights.

Whilst I was explaining matters to the Senate the learned friends of No. 1 Equity Court were holding a Chambers meeting. I am grateful to George Frobisher for supplying me with a note of what was said during my enforced absence. The first item on the agenda was the question of accommodation in Chambers, and was raised by Erskine-Brown.

'It seems likely,' he began, 'that we shall soon be having a vacancy in Chambers.'

'What do you mean exactly?' Miss Trant asked the question.

'Well, Philly. After today's hearing, Rumpole's made it quite clear. He intends to leave the Bar and grow vegetables.'

'Vegetables? I hadn't heard about the vegetables.' Featherstone was understandably puzzled.

'Shouldn't we perhaps wait?' George suggested, but Erskine-Brown was not to be stopped.

'I think it's important,' he said, 'that we should decide what the policy is. As you know, my own room is impossibly overcrowded. George Frobisher is sharing with Hoskins, which isn't always convenient when it comes to conferences. I mean, do we take in another young man who could make himself useful and do a bit of paper work and so on?'

The door was behind him and he didn't stop immediately when I opened it. 'Or do we use Rumpole's room to relieve our acute accommodation problem?'

'Do you want to take over my room, Erskine-Brown?' I was back from my hearing, from Erskine-Brown's point of view like bloody Banquo at the dinner party. He stopped in full flow and George said:

'Rumpole! It can't be over?'

'Ah, Horace.' Featherstone pulled up a chair for the ghost of Rumpole. 'You can help us. We've just been discussing the possible future.'

'So have I, old darling, and I'll tell you what. The possible future is rather interesting.' I lit a small cigar. 'Remember Detective Inspector Dickerson? He's suspended, a full inquiry. When he heard that in the Nick, Charlie suddenly remembered giving me instructions. So, we're applying to the Court of Appeal, with fresh evidence. I was rather thinking of doing it alone – without a leader. I'm sorry, Erskine-Brown. The vegetables have been postponed indefinitely . . .'

I left them then, the learned and astonished friends, to sort out their accommodation problems knowing that Rumpole's room would not be available in the foreseeable future.

When I got home to the mansions I found Hilda sitting inert by one bar of a sullen electric fire. She looked up as I came into the living room and said, 'Rumpole. Is it over?'

'I'm afraid so.'

'Oh, Rumpole. It's over!'

'I know, my dear. No peace. No quiet. No just being Rumpole. Above all, no vegetables. I'm doing rather a larky manslaughter tomorrow. At Chelmsford.'

'They let you off?' I couldn't imagine why she sounded so surprised. I filled in the details.

'Acquitted. By unanimous verdict. Left the dock without a stain on my character. In fact, I was commended for picking out one of the few rotten apples in that sweet-smelling barrow-load, the Metropolitan Police.'

'Oh, Rumpole!' It was an astonishing moment. She Who Must Be Obeyed actually had her arms round me, she was holding me tightly, rather as though I were some rare and precious object and not the old White Elephant that continually got in her way.

'Hilda. Hilda, you're not . . .?' I looked down at her agitated head. 'You weren't worried, were you?'

'Worried? Well, of course I was worried!' She broke away and resumed the Royal Manner. 'Having you at home all day would have been impossible!'

'Yes. Yes. I suppose it would.'

'Now we can go on. Just as before.'

'Just as before. I suppose . . . it calls for a celebration.' I went to the drinks table and poured two Booths, taking care not to ruin them with too much tonic.

'Well, just a tiny one. I've got dinner to get and . . .'

'I'm sorry to have to tell you this, Hilda. You know your old Daddy, old C. H. Wystan, was quite wrong.' I handed her a steadying G. and T.

'Wrong? Why was Daddy wrong?'

'Never plead guilty! Come on, old thing, bottoms up.'

I raised my glass. Hilda raised hers and we drank to a future which was going to be, thanks to the wonders of tape recording and the fallibility of human nature, as indistinguishable as possible from our past.

Rumpole and the Heavy Brigade

The story of my most recent murder, and my defence of Petey Delgardo, the youngest, and perhaps the most appalling of the disagreeable Delgardo brothers, raises several matters which are painful, not to say embarrassing for me to recall. The tale begins with Rumpole's reputation at its lowest, and although it has now risen somewhat, it has done so for rather curious and not entirely creditable reasons, as you shall hear.

After the case of the 'Dartford Post Office Robbery', which I have recounted in the previous chapter, I noticed a distinct slump in the Rumpole practice. I had emerged, as I thought, triumphant from that encounter with the disciplinary authority; but I suppose I was marked, for a while, as a barrister who had been reported for professional misconduct. The quality of briefs which landed on the Rumpole corner of the mantelpiece in our clerk's room were deteriorating and I spent a great deal more time pottering round Magistrates Courts or down at Sessions than I did in full flood round the marble halls of the Old Bailey.

So last winter picture Rumpole in the November of his days, walking in the mists, under the black branches of bare trees to Chambers, and remembering Thomas Hood.

'No *warmth, no cheerfulness, no healthful ease,* No *comfortable feel in any member. No shade, no shine, no butterflies, no bees, No fruits, no flowers, no leaves, no birds, – November!'*

As I walked, I hoped there might be some sort of trivial little brief waiting for me in Chambers. In November an old man's fancy lightly turned to thoughts of indecent assault, which might bring briefs at London Sessions and before the Uxbridge Justices. (Oh God! Oh, Uxbridge Justices!) I had started forty years ago, defending a charge of unsolicited grope on the Northern Line. And that's what I was back to. In my end is my beginning.

I pushed open the door of my Chambers and went into the clerk's room. There was a buzz of activity, very little of it, I was afraid, centring round the works of Rumpole, but Henry was actually smiling as he sat in his shirt-sleeves at his desk and called out, 'Mr Rumpole.'

'Stern daughter of the Voice of God! Oh, duty! Oh my learned clerk, what are the orders for today, Henry? Mine not to reason why. Mine but to do or die, before some Court of Summary Jurisdiction.'

'There's a con. Waiting for you, sir. In a new matter, from Maurice Nooks and Parsley.'

Henry had mentioned one of the busiest firms of criminal solicitors, who had a reputation of being not too distant from some of their heavily villainous clients. In fact the most active partner was privately known to me as 'Shady' Nooks.

'New matter?'

' "The Stepney Road Stabbing". Mr Nooks says you'll have read about it in the papers.'

In fact I had read about it in that great source of legal knowledge, the *News of the World*. The Delgardo brothers, Leslie and Basil, were a legend in the East End; they gave copiously to charity, they had friends in 'show business' and went on holiday with a certain Police Superintendent and a well-known Member of Parliament. They hadn't been convicted of any offence, although their young brother, Peter Delgardo, had occasionally been in trouble. They ran a club known as the Paradise Rooms, a number of protection rackets, and a seaside home for orphans. They were a devoted family and Leslie and Basil were said to be particularly concerned when their brother Peter was seen by several witnesses kneeling in the street outside a pub called the Old Justice beside the blood-stained body of an East End character known as Tosher MacBride. Later a knife, liberally smeared with blood of MacBride's group, was found beside the driver's seat of Peter Delgardo's elderly Daimler. He was arrested in the Paradise Rooms to which he had apparently fled for protection after the death of Tosher. The case seemed hopeless but the name 'Delgardo' made sure it would hit the headlines. I greeted the news that it was coming Rumpole's way with a low whistle of delight. I took the brief from Henry.

' "*My heart leaps up when I behold . . . a rainbow in the sky.*" Or a murder in the offing. I have to admit it.'

I suddenly thought of the fly in the ointment.

'I suppose they're giving me a leader – in a murder?'

'They haven't mentioned a leader,' Henry seemed puzzled.

'I suppose it'll be Featherstone. Well, at least it'll get me back to the Bailey. My proper stamping ground.'

I moved towards the door, and it was then my clerk Henry mentioned a topic which, as you will see, has a vital part to play in this particular narrative, my hat. Now I am not particularly self-conscious as far as headgear is concerned and the old black Anthony Eden has seen, it must be admitted, a good many years' service. It has travelled to many far-flung courts in fair weather and foul, it once had a small glowing cigar end dropped in it as it lay under Rumpole's seat in Pommeroy's, it once blew off on a windy day in Newington Causeway and was run over by a bicycle. The hat is therefore, it must be admitted, like its owner, scarred and battered by life, no longer in its first youth and in a somewhat collapsed condition. All the same it fits me comfortably and keeps the rain out most of the time. I have grown used to my hat and, in view of our long association, I have a certain affection for it. I was therefore astonished when Henry followed me to the door and, in a lowered tone as if he were warning me that the coppers had called to arrest me, he said,

'The other clerks were discussing your hat, sir. Over coffee.'

'My God! They must be hard up for conversation, to fill in a couple of hours round the ABC.'

'And they were passing the comment, it's a subject of a good many jokes in the Temple.'

'Well, it's seen some service.' I took the offending article and looked at it. 'And it shows it.'

'Quite frankly, Mr Rumpole, I can't send you down the Bailey, not on a top-class murder, in a hat like it.'

'You mean the jury might get a peep at the titfer, and convict without leaving the box?' I couldn't believe my ears.

'Mr Featherstone wears a nice bowler, Mr Rumpole.'

'I am not leading counsel, Henry,' I told him firmly. 'I am not the Conservative-Labour M.P. for somewhere or other, and I don't like nice bowlers. Our old clerk Albert managed to live with this hat for a good many years.'

'There's been some changes made since Albert's time, Mr Rumpole.'

Henry had laid himself open, and I'm afraid I made the unworthy comment.

'Oh, yes! I got some decent briefs in Albert's time. The "Penge Bungalow Murder", the Brighton forgery. I wasn't put out to grass in the Uxbridge Magistrates Court.'

The chairs in my room in Chambers have become a little wobbly over the years and my first thought was that the two large men sitting on them might be in some danger of collapse. They both wore blue suits made of some lightweight material, and both had gold wrist watches and identity bracelets dangling at their wrists. They had diamond rings, pink faces and brushed back black hair. Leslie Delgardo was the eldest and most affable, his brother Basil had an almost permanent look of discontent and his voice easily became querulous. In attendance, balanced on my insecure furniture, were 'Shady' Nooks, a silver haired and suntanned person who also sported a large gold wristwatch, and his articled clerk, Miss Stebbings, a nice-looking girl fresh from law school, who had clearly no idea what area of the law she had got into.

I lit a small cigar, looked round the assembled company, and said, 'Our client is not with us, of course.'

'Hardly, Mr Rumpole,' said Nooks. 'Mr Peter Delgardo has been moved to the prison hospital.'

'He's never been a well boy, our Petey.' Leslie Delgardo sounded sorrowful.

'Our client's health has always been an anxiety to his brothers,' Nooks explained.

'I see.' I hastily consulted the brief. 'The victim of the murder was a gentleman called Tosher MacBride. Know anything about him?'

'I believe he was a rent collector.' Nooks sounded vague.

'Not a bad start. The jury'll be against murder but if someone has to go it may as well be the rent collector.' I flipped through the depositions until I got to the place where I felt most at home, the forensic report on the blood.

'Bloodstains on your brother's sleeve.'

'Group consistent with ten per cent of the population,' said Nooks.

'Including Tosher MacBride? And Exhibit 1, a sheath knife. Mr MacBride's blood on that, or, of course, ten per cent of the population. Knife found in your brother's ancient Daimler. Fallen down by the driver's seat. Bloodstains on his coat sleeve? Bloodstained sheath knife in his car?'

'I know it looks black for young Peter.' Leslie shook his head sadly.

I looked up at him sharply. 'Let's say it's evidence, Mr Delgardo, on which the prosecution might expect to get a conviction, unless the judge has just joined the Fulham Road Anarchists – or the jury's drunk.'

'You'll pull it off for Petey.' It was the first time Basil Delgardo had spoken and his words showed, I thought, a touching faith in Rumpole.

'Pull it off? I shall sit behind my learned leader. I presume you're going to Guthrie Featherstone, Q.C., in these Chambers?'

Then Nooks uttered words which were, I must confess, music to my ears.

'Well, actually, Mr Rumpole. On this one. No.'

'Mr Rumpole. My brothers and I, we've heard of your wonderful reputation,' said Basil.

'I did the "Penge Bungalow Murder" without a leader,' I admitted. 'But that was thirty years ago. They let me loose on that.'

'We've heard golden opinions of you, Mr Rumpole. Golden opinions!' Leslie Delgardo made an expansive gesture, rattling his identity bracelet. I got up and looked out of the window.

'No one mentioned the hat?'

'Pardon me?' Leslie sounded puzzled, and Nooks added his voice to the vote of confidence.

'Mr Delgardo's brothers are perfectly satisfied, Mr Rumpole, to leave this one entirely to you.'

'Now is the Winter of my Discontent, Made Glorious Summer by a first-class murder.' I turned back to the group, apologetic. 'I'm sorry, gentlemen. Insensitive, I'm afraid. All these months round the Uxbridge Magistrates Court have blunted my sensitivity. To your brother it can hardly seem such a sign of summer.'

'We're perfectly confident, Mr Rumpole, you can handle it.' Basil lit a cigarette with a gold lighter and I went back to the desk.

'Handle it? Of course I can handle it. As I always say, murder is nothing more than common assault, with unfortunate consequences.'

'We'll arrange it for you to see the doctor.' Nooks was businesslike.

'I'm perfectly well, thank you.'

'Doctor Lewis Bleen,' said Leslie, and Nooks explained patiently, 'The well-known psychiatrist. On the subject of Mr Peter Delgardo's mental capacity.'

'Poor Petey. He's never been right, Mr Rumpole. We've always had to look after him,' Leslie explained his responsibilities, as head of the family.

'You could call him Peter Pan,' Basil made an unexpected literary reference. 'The little boy that never grew up.'

I doubted the accuracy of this analogy. 'I don't know whether Peter Pan was actually responsible for many stabbings down Stepney High Street.'

'But that's it, Mr Rumpole!' Leslie shook his head sadly. 'Peter's not responsible, you see. Not poor old Petey. No more responsible than a child.'

Doctor Lewis Bleen, Diploma of Psychological Medicine from the University of Edinburgh, Head-Shrinker Extraordinaire, Resident Guru of 'What's Bugging You' answers to listeners' problems, had one of those accents which remind you of the tinkle of cups and the thud of dropped scones in Edinburgh tea-rooms. He sat and sucked his pipe in the interview room at

Brixton and looked in a motherly fashion at the youngest of the Delgardos who was slumped in front of us, staring moodily at nothing in particular.

'Remember me, do you?'

'Doctor B . . . Bleen.' Petey had his brothers' features, but the sharpness of their eyes was blurred in his, his big hands were folded in his lap and he wore a perpetual puzzled frown. He also spoke with a stammer. His answer hadn't pleased the good doctor, who tried again.

'Do you know the time, Petey?'

'N . . . N . . . No.'

'Disorientated . . . as to time!' Better pleased, the doctor made a note.

'That might just be because he's not wearing a watch,' I was unkind enough to suggest.

The doctor ignored me. 'Where are you, Peter?'

'In the n . . . n . . .'

'Nick?' I suggested.

'Hospital wing.' Peter confirmed my suggestion.

'Orientated as to place!' was my diagnosis. Doctor Bleen gave me a sour look, as though I'd just spat out the shortcake.

'Possibly.' He turned back to our patient. 'When we last met, Peter, you told me you couldn't remember how MacBride got stabbed.'

'N . . . No.'

'There appears to be a complete blotting out of all the facts,' the doctor announced with quiet satisfaction.

'Mightn't it be worth asking him whether he was *there* when Tosher got stabbed?' I was bold enough to ask, at which Nooks chipped in.

'Mr Rumpole. As a solicitor of some little experience, may I interject here?'

'If you have to.' I sighed and fished for a small cigar.

'Doctor Bleen will correct me if I'm wrong but, as I understand, he's prepared to give evidence that at the relevant moment . . .'

'So far I have no idea when the relevant moment was.' I lit the cigar, Nooks carried on regardless.

'Mr Delgardo's mind was so affected that he didn't know the

nature and quality of his act, nor did he know that what he was doing was wrong.'

'You mean he thought he was giving Tosher a warm hand-shake, and welcome to the Rent Collectors' Union?'

'That's not exactly how I suggest we put it to the learned judge.' Nooks smiled at me as though at a wayward child.

'Then how do you suggest we tell it to the old sweetheart?'

'Guilty but insane, Mr Rumpole. We rather anticipated your advice would be that, guilty but insane in law.'

'And have you anticipated what the prosecution might say?'

'Peter has been examined by a Doctor Stotter from the Home Office. I don't think you'll find him unhelpful,' said Doctor Bleen. 'Charles Stotter and I play golf together. We've had a word about this case.'

'Rum things you get up to playing golf. It always struck me as a good game to avoid.' I turned and drew Peter Delgardo into the conversation. 'Well, Peter. You'll want to be getting back to the telly.'

Peter stood up. I was surprised by his height and his apparent strength, a big pale man in an old dressing gown and pyjamas.

'Just one question before you go. Did you stab Tosher Mac-Bride?'

The doctor smiled at me tolerantly. 'Oh I don't think the answer to *that* will be particularly reliable.'

'Even the question may strike you as unreliable, doctor. All the same, I'm asking it.' I moved closer to Peter. 'Because if you did, Peter, we can call the good shrink here, and Doctor Stotter fresh from the golf course, and they'll let you off lightly! You'll go to Broadmoor at Her Majesty's Pleasure, and of course Her Majesty will be thinking of you constantly. You'll get a lot more telly, and some exciting basket-weaving, and a handful of pills every night to keep you quiet, Petey, and if you're very good they might let you weed the doctors' garden or play cricket against the second eleven of male warders . . . but I can't offer you these delights until I know. Did you stab Tosher?'

'I think my patient's tired.'

I turned on the trick cyclist at last, and said, 'He's not your patient at the moment. He's my client.'

'Doctor Bleen has joined us at great personal inconvenience.' Nooks was distressed.

'Then I wouldn't dream of detaining him a moment longer.' At which point Doctor Lewis Bleen D.P.M. (Edinburgh) left in what might mildly be described as a huff. When he'd been seen off the premises by a helpful trusty, I repeated my question.

'Did you do it, Peter?'

'I c . . . c . . . c . . .' The answer, whatever it was, was a long time in coming.

Nooks supplied a word. 'Killed him?' but Peter shook his head.

'Couldn't of. He was already c . . . cut. When I saw him, like.'

'You see, I can't let you get sent to hospital unless you did it,' I explained as though to a child. 'If you didn't, well . . . just have to fight the case.'

'I wants you to f . . . f . . . fight it. I'm not going into any nut house.' Peter Delgardo's instructions were perfectly clear.

'And if we fight we might very well lose. You understand that?'

'My b . . . b . . . brothers have told me . . . You're hot stuff, they told me . . . Tip top l . . . awyer.'

Once again I was puzzled by the height of my reputation with the Delgardos. But I wasn't going to argue. 'Tip top? Really? Well, let's say I've got to know a trick or two, over the years . . . a few wrinkles . . . Sit down, Peter.'

Peter sat down slowly, and I sat opposite him, ignoring the restive Nooks and his articled clerk.

'Now, hadn't you better tell me exactly what happened, the night Tosher MacBride got stabbed?'

I was working overtime a few days later when my door opened and in walked no less a person than Guthrie Featherstone, Q.C., M.P., our Head of Chambers. My relations with Featherstone, ever since he pipped me at the post for the position of Head, have always been somewhat uneasy, and were not exactly improved when I seized command of the ship when he was leading me in the matter of the 'Dartford Post Office Robbery'.

We have little enough in common. Featherstone, as Henry pointed out, wears a nice bowler and a black velvet collar on his overcoat; his nails are well manicured, his voice is carefully controlled, as are his politics. He gets on very well with judges and solicitors and not so well with the criminal clientele. He has never been less than polite to me, even at my most mutinous moments, and now he smiled with considerable bonhomie.

'Rumpole! You're a late bird!'

'Just trying to feather my nest. With a rather juicy little murder.'

Featherstone dropped into my tattered leather armchair, reserved for clients, and carefully examined his well-polished black brogues.

'Maurice Nooks told me, he's not taking in a leader.'

'That's right.'

'I know the last time I led you wasn't *succès fou*.'

'I'm a bit of a back seat driver, I'm afraid.'

'Of course, you're an old hand at crime,' Featherstone conceded.

'An old lag you might say.'

'But it's a question of tactics in this case. Maurice said, if I appeared, it might look as if they'd rather over-egged the pudding.'

'You think the jury might prefer – a bit of good plain cooking?' I looked at him and he smiled delightfully.

'You put things rather well, sometimes.'

There was a pause, and then the learned leader got down to what was, I suppose, the nub and the purpose of his visit.

'Horace. I'm anxious to put an end to any sort of rift between the two senior men in Chambers. It doesn't make for a happy ship.'

'Aye aye sir.' I gave him a brief nautical salute from my position at the desk.

'I'm glad you agree. *Sérieusement*, Horace, we don't see enough of each other socially.' He paused again, but I could find nothing to say. 'I've got a couple of tickets for the Scales of Justice ball at the Savoy. Would you join me and Marigold?'

To say I was taken aback would be an understatement. I was astonished. 'Let's get this quite clear, Featherstone.'

'Oh "Guthrie", please,'

'Very well Guthrie. You're asking me to trip the light fantastic toe . . . with your wife?'

'And if you'd like to bring *your* good lady.'

I looked at Featherstone in total amazement. 'My . . .'

'Your missus.'

'Are you referring, at all, to my wife? She Who Must Be Obeyed? Do I take it you actually want to spend an evening out with She!'

'It'll be great fun.'

'Do you really think so?' He had lost me now. I went to the door and unhooked the mac and the old hat, preparatory to calling it a day. However, Featherstone had some urgent matter to communicate, apparently of an embarrassing nature.

'Oh, and Horace . . . this is rather embarrassing. It's just that . . . It's well . . . your name came up on the bench at our Inn only last week. I was lunching with Mr Justice Prestcold.'

'That must have been a jolly occasion,' I told him. 'Like dinner with the Macbeths.' I knew Mr Justice Prestcold of old, and he and I had never hit it off, or seen eye to eye. In fact you might say there was always a cold wind blowing in court between counsel and the bench whenever Rumpole rose to his feet before Prestcold J. He could be guaranteed to ruin my cross-examination, interrupt my speech, fail to sum up the defence and send any Rumpole client down for a hefty six if he could find the slightest excuse for it. Prestcold was an extraordinarily clean man, his cuffs and bands were whiter than white, he was forever polishing his rimless glasses on a succession of snowy handkerchiefs. They say, and God knows what truth there is in it, that Prestcold travels on circuit with a portable loo seat wrapped in plastic. His clerk has the unenviable job of seeing that it is screwed in at the lodgings, so his Lordship may not sit where less fastidious judges have sat before.

'He was asking who we had in Chambers and I was able to tell him Horace Rumpole, *inter alia*.'

'I can't imagine Frank Prestcold eating. I suppose he might just be brought to sniff the bouquet of a grated carrot.'

'And he said, "You mean the fellow with the disgraceful hat?"'

'Mr Justice Prestcold was talking about my *hat*?' I couldn't believe my ears.

'He seemed to think, forgive me for raising this, that your hat set the worst possible example to younger men at the Bar.'

With enormous self-control I kept my temper. 'Well, you can tell Mr Justice Prestcold – the next time you're sharing the Benchers' Vegetarian Platter ... That when I was last before him I took strong exception to his cuff links. They looked to me just as cheap and glassy as his eyes!'

'Don't take offence, Horace. It's just not worth it, you know, taking offence at Her Majesty's judges. We'll look forward to the Savoy. Best to your good lady.'

I crammed on the hat, gave him a farewell wave and left him. I felt, that evening, that I was falling out of love with the law. I really couldn't believe that Mr Justice Prestcold had been discussing my hat. I mean, wasn't the crime rate rising? Wasn't the State encroaching on our liberties? Wasn't Magna Carta tottering? Whither Habeus Corpus? What was to be done about the number of 12-year-old girls who are making advances to old men in cinemas? What I thought was, hadn't judges of England got enough on their plates without worrying about my hat! I gave the matter mature consideration on my way home on the Inner Circle, and decided that they probably hadn't.

A few mornings later I picked up the collection of demands, final demands and positively final demands which constitutes our post and among the hostile brown envelopes I found a gilded and embossed invitation card. I took the whole lot into the kitchen to file away in the tidy bin when She Who Must Be Obeyed entered and caught me at it.

'Horace,' She said severely. 'Whatever are you doing with the post?'

'Just throwing it away. Always throw bills away the first time they come in. Otherwise you only encourage them.'

'If you had a few decent cases, Rumpole, if you weren't always slumming round the Magistrates Courts, you might not be throwing away bills all the time.' At which she pedalled open the tidy bin and spotted the fatal invitation.

'What's that?'

'I think it's the gas.' It was too late, She had picked the card out from among the potato peelings.

'I never saw a gas bill with a gold embossed crest before. It's an invitation! To the Savoy Hotel!' She started to read the thing. 'Horace Rumpole and Lady.'

'You wouldn't enjoy it,' I hastened to assure her.

'Why wouldn't I enjoy it?' She wiped the odd fragment of potato off the card, carried it into the living-room in state, and gave it pride of place on the mantelpiece. I followed her, protesting.

'You know what it is. Boiled shirts. Prawn cocktail. Watching a lot of judges pushing their wives round the parquet to selections from *Oklahoma*.'

'It'll do you good Rumpole. That's the sort of place you ought to be seen in: the Scales of Justice ball.'

'It's quite impossible.' The situation was becoming desperate.

'I don't see why.'

I had an inspiration, and assumed an expression of disgust. 'We're invited by Marigold Featherstone.'

'The wife of your Head of Chambers?'

'An old boot! A domestic tyrant. You know what the wretched Guthrie calls her? She Who Must Be Obeyed. No. The ball is out, Hilda. You and Marigold wouldn't hit it off at all.'

Well, I thought, She and sweet Marigold would never meet, so I was risking nothing. I seized the hat and prepared to retreat. 'Got to leave you now. Murder calls.'

'Why didn't you tell me we were back to murder? This *is* good news.' Hilda was remarkably cheerful that morning.

'Murder,' I told her, 'is certainly better than dancing.' And I was gone about my business. Little did I know that the moment my back was turned Hilda looked up the Featherstone's number in the telephone book.

'You can't do it to Peter! I tell you, you can't do it! Fight the case? How can he fight the case?' Leslie Delgardo had quite lost the cool and knowing air of a successful East End businessman. His face was flushed and he thumped his fist on my table, jangling his identity bracelet and disturbing the notice of additional evidence I was reading, that of Bernard Whelpton, known as 'Four Eyes'.

'Whelpton's evidence doesn't help. I'm sure you'll agree, Mr Rumpole,' Nooks said gloomily.

'You read that! You read what "Four Eyes" has to say.' Leslie collapsed breathless into my client's chair. I read the document which ran roughly as follows. 'Tosher MacBride used to take the mick out of Peter on account he stammered and didn't have no girl friends. One night I saw Peter try to speak to a girl in the Paradise Rooms. He was asking the girl to have a drink but his stutter was so terrible. Tosher said to her, "Come on, darling ... It'll be breakfast time before the silly git finishes asking for a light ale." After I heard Peter Delgardo say as he'd get Tosher. He said he'd like to cut him one night.'

'He's not a well boy,' Leslie was wiping his forehead with a mauve silk handkerchief.

'When I came out of the Old Justice pub that night I see Tosher on the pavement and Petey Delgardo was kneeling beside him. There was blood all over.' I looked up at Nooks. 'You know it's odd. No one actually *saw* the stabbing.'

'But Petey was there wasn't he?' Leslie was returning the handkerchief to his breast pocket. 'And what's the answer about the knife?'

'In my humble opinion,' Nooks's opinions were often humble, 'the knife in the car is completely damning.'

'Oh completely.' I got up, lit a small cigar, and told Leslie my own far from humble opinion. 'You know, I'd have had no doubts about this case if you hadn't just proved your brother innocent.'

'I did?' The big man in the chair looked at me in a wild surmise.

'When you sent Doctor Lewis Bleen, the world-famous trick cyclist, the head shrinker extraordinaire, down to see Petey in Brixton. If you'd done a stabbing, and you were offered a nice quiet trip to hospital, wouldn't you take it? If the evidence was dead against you?'

'You mean *Peter* turned it down?' Leslie Delgardo clearly couldn't believe his ears.

'Of course he did!' I told him cheerfully. 'Petey may not be all that bright, poor old darling, but he knows he didn't kill Tosher MacBride.'

The committal was at Stepney Magistrates Court and Henry told me that there was a good deal of interest and that the vultures of the press might be there.

'I thought I should warn you sir. Just in case you wanted to buy . . .'

'I know, I know,' I interrupted him. 'Perhaps, Henry, there's a certain amount of force in your argument. "Vanity of vanities, all is vanity," said the preacher.' Here was I a barrister of a certain standing, doing a notable murder alone and without a leader, the type of person whose picture might appear in the *Evening Standard*, and I came to the reluctant conclusion that my present headgear was regrettably unphotogenic. I took a taxi to St James' Street and invested in a bowler, which clamped itself to the head like a vice but which caused Henry, when he saw it, to give me a smile of genuine gratitude.

That evening I had forgotten the whole subject of hats and was concerned with a matter that interests me far more deeply: blood. I had soaked the rubber sponge that helps with the washing up and, standing at the kitchen sink, stabbed violently down into it with a table knife. It produced, as I had suspected, a spray of water, leaving small spots all over my shirt and waistcoat.

'Horace! Horace, you look quite different.' Hilda was looking at the evening paper in which there was a picture of Pete Delgardo's heroic defender arriving at Court. 'I know what it is, Horace! You went out. And bought a new hat. Without me.'

I stabbed again, having re-soaked the sponge.

'A bowler. Daddy used to wear a bowler. It's an improvement.' Hilda was positively purring at my dapper appearance in the paper.

'Little splashes. All over the place,' I observed, committing further mayhem on the sponge.

'Horace. Whatever are you doing to the washing up?'

'All over. In little drops. Not one great stain. Little drops. Like a fine rain. And plenty on the cuff.'

'Your cuff's soaking. Oh, why couldn't you roll up your sleeve?'

I felt the crook of my arm, and was delighted to discover that it was completely dry.

'Now I know why you didn't want to take me to the Scales of Justice annual ball.' Hilda looked at the *Evening Standard* with less pleasure. 'You're too grand now, aren't you Rumpole? New hat! Picture in the paper! Big case! "Horace Rumpole. Defender of the Stepney Road Stabber". Big noise at the Bar. I suppose you didn't think I'd do you credit.'

'That's nonsense, Hilda.' I mopped up some of the mess round the sink, and dried my hands.

'Then why?'

I went and sat beside her, and tried to comfort her with Keats. 'Look. We're in the Autumn of our years. "*Season of mists and mellow fruitfulness,   Close bosom-friend of the maturing sun . . .*"'

'I really can't understand *why*!'

'"*Where are the songs of Spring? Ay, where are they?   Think not on them, thou hast thy music too.*" But not jigging about like a couple of Punk Rockers. At a dance!'

'I very much doubt if they have Punk Rockers at the Savoy. Doesn't it occur to you, Rumpole? We never go out!'

'I'm perfectly happy. I'm not longing to go to the ball, like bloody Cinderella.'

'Well, I am!'

I thought Hilda was being most unreasonable, and I decided to point out the fatal flaw in the entire scheme concerning the Scales of Justice ball.

'Hilda. I can't dance.'

'You can't what?'

'Dance. I can't do it.'

'You're lying, Rumpole!'

The accusation was so unexpected that I looked at her in a wild surmise. And then she said,

'Would you mind casting your mind back to the 14th of August 1938?'

'What happened then?'

'You proposed to me, Rumpole. As a matter of fact, it was when you proposed. I shouldn't expect you to remember.'

'1938. Of course! The year I did the "Euston Bank Robbery". Led by your father.'

'Led by Daddy. You were young, Rumpole. Comparatively young. And where did you propose, exactly? Can't you try and remember that?'

As I have said, I have no actual memory of proposing to Hilda at all. It seemed to me that I slid into the lifetime contract unconsciously, as a weary man drifts off into sleep. Any words, I felt sure, were spoken by her. I also had temporarily forgotten where the incident took place and hazarded a guess.

'At a bus stop?'

'Of course it wasn't at a bus stop.'

'It's just that your father always seemed to be detaining me at bus stops. I thought you might have been with him at the time.'

'You proposed to me in a tent.' Hilda came to my aid at last. 'There was a band. And champagne. And some sort of cold collation. Daddy had taken me to the Inns of Court ball to meet some of the bright young men in Chambers. He told me then, you'd been very helpful to him on blood groups.'

'It was the year before I did the "Penge Bungalow Murder",' I remembered vaguely. 'Hopeless on blood, your father, he could never bring himself to look at the photographs.'

'And we danced together. We actually waltzed together.'

'That's simple! That's just a matter of circling round and round. None of your bloody jigging about concerned with it!'

It was then that Hilda stood up and took my breath away. 'Well, we can waltz again. Rumpole. You'd better get into training for it. I rang up Marigold Featherstone and I told her we'd be delighted to accept the invitation.' She gave me a little smile of victory. 'And I tell you what. She didn't sound like an old boot at all.'

I was speechless, filled with mute resentment. I'd been double-crossed.

My toilette for the Delgardo murder case went no further than the acquisition of a new hat. As I sat in Court listening to the evidence for the prosecution of Bernard 'Four Eyes' Whelpton, I was vaguely conscious of the collapsed state of the wig (bought secondhand from an ex Chief Justice of Tonga in the early thirties), the traces of small cigar and breakfast egg on the waistcoat, and the fact that the bands had lost their pristine crispness and were forever sagging to reveal the glitter of the brass collar-stud.

I looked up and saw the judge staring at me with bleak disapproval and felt desperately to ensure that the fly buttons were safely fastened. Fate span her bloody wheel, and I had drawn Mr Justice Prestcold; Frank Prestcold, who took such grave exception to my hat, and who now looked without any apparent enthusiasm at the rest of my appearance. Well, I couldn't help him, I couldn't even hold up the bowler to prove I'd tried. I did my best to ignore the judge and concentrate on the evidence. Mr Hilary Painswick, Q.C., the perfectly decent old darling who led for the prosecution, was just concreting in 'Four Eyes' story.

'Mr Whelpton. I take it you haven't given this evidence in any spirit of enmity against the man in the dock?'

The man in the dock looked, as usual, as if he'd just been struck between the eyes with a heavy weight. Bernie Whelpton smiled charmingly, and said indiscreetly, 'No. I'm Petey's friend. We was at university together.'

At which Rumpole rose up like thunder and, to Prestcold J.'s intense displeasure, asked for the jury to be removed so that he could lodge an objection. When the jury had gone out the judge forced himself to look at me.

'What is the basis of your objection, Mr Rumpole? On the face of it the evidence that this gentleman was at university with your client seems fairly harmless.'

'This may come as a surprise to your Lordship.'

'May it, Mr Rumpole?'

'My client is not an old King's man. He didn't meet Mr "Four

Eyes" Whelpton at a May Ball during Eights Week. The university referred to is, in fact, Parkhurst Prison.'

The judge applied his razor-sharp mind and saw a way of over-ruling my objection.

'Mr Rumpole! I very much doubt whether the average jury-man has your intimate knowledge of the argot of the underworld.'

'Your Lordship is too complimentary.' I gave him a bow and a brassy flash of the collar-stud.

'I think no harm has been done. I appreciate your anxiety to keep your client's past record out of the case. Shall we have the jury back?'

Before the jury came back I got a note from Leslie Delgardo telling me, as I knew very well, that Whelpton had a conviction for perjury. I ignored this information, and did my best to make a friend of the little Cockney who gazed at me through spectacles thick as ginger beer bottles.

'Mr Whelpton, when you saw my client, Peter Delgardo, kneeling beside Tosher MacBride, did he have his arm round Mr MacBride's neck?'

'Yes, sir.'

'Supporting his head from behind?'

'I suppose so.'

'Rather in the attitude of a nurse or a doctor who was trying to bring help to the wounded man?'

'I didn't know your client had any medical qualifications!' Mr Justice Prestcold was trying one of his glacial jokes. I pretended I hadn't heard it, and concentrated on Bernie Whelpton.

'Were you able to see Peter Delgardo's hands when he was holding Tosher?'

'Yes.'

'Anything in them, was there?'

'Not as I saw.'

'He wasn't holding this knife, for instance?' I had the murder weapon on the desk in front of me and held it up for the jury to see.

'I tell you. I didn't see no knife.'

'I don't know whether my learned friend remembers.' Hilary

Painswick uncoiled himself beside me. 'The knife was found in the car.'

'Exactly!' I smiled gratefully at Painswick. 'So my client stabbed Tosher. Ran to his car. Dropped the murder weapon in by the driver's seat and then came back across the pavement to hold Tosher in his arms and comfort his dying moments.' I turned back to the witness. 'Is *that* what you're saying?'

'He might have slipped the knife in his pocket.'

'Mr Rumpole!' Prestcold J. had something to communicate.

'Yes, my Lord?'

'This is not the time for arguing your case. This is the time for asking questions. If you think this point has any substance you will no doubt remind the jury of it when you come to make up your final address; at some time in the no doubt distant future.'

'I'm grateful. And no doubt your Lordship will also remind the jury of it in your summing up, should it slip my memory. It really is *such* an unanswerable point for the defence.'

I saw the Prestcold mouth open for another piece of snappy repartee, and forestalled him by rapidly re-starting the cross-examination.

'Mr Whelpton. You didn't see Tosher stabbed?'

'I was in the Old Justice wasn't I?'

'You tell us. And when you came out, Tosher . . .'

'Might it not be more respectful to call that good man, the deceased, "Mr MacBride"?' the judge interrupted wearily.

'If you like. "That good man Mr MacBride" was bleeding in my client's arms?'

'That was the first I saw of him. Yes.'

'And when he saw you Mr Delgardo let go of Tosher, of that good man Mr MacBride, ran to his car and got into it?'

'And then he drove away.'

'Exactly. You saw him get into his car. How did he do it?'

'Just turned the handle and pulled the door open.'

'So the car was unlocked?'

'I suppose it was. I didn't really think.'

'You suppose the door was unlocked.' I looked at the judge who appeared to have gone into some sort of a trance. 'Don't go too fast, Mr Whelpton. My Lord wants an opportunity to make a note.' At which the judge returned to earth and was forced to take up his pencil. As he wrote, Leslie Delgardo leaned forward from the seat behind me and said,

'Here, Mr Rumpole. What do you think you're doing?'

'Having a bit of fun. You don't grudge it to me, do you?'

The next item on the agenda was the officer in charge of the case, a perfectly reasonable fellow with a grey suit, who looked like the better type of bank manager.

'Detective Inspector. You photographed Mr Delgardo's antique Daimler when you got it back to the station?'

'Yes.' The officer leafed through a bundle of photographs.

'Was it then exactly as you found it outside the Old Justice?'

'Exactly.'

'Unlocked? With the driver's window open?'

'Yes. We found the car unlocked.'

'Then it would have been easy for anyone to have thrown something in through the driver's window, or even put something in through the door?'

'I don't follow you, sir. Something?'

I found my prop and held it up. Exhibit 1, a flick knife. 'Something like this knife could have been dropped into Peter Delgardo's car, in a matter of moments?'

I saw the judge actually writing.

'I suppose it could, sir.'

'By the true murderer, whoever it was, when he was running away?'

The usher was beside me, handing me the fruit of Mr Justice Prestcold's labours; a note to counsel which read, 'Dear Rumpole. Your bands are falling down and showing your collar-stud. No doubt you would wish to adjust accordingly.' What was this, a murder trial, or a bloody fashion parade? I crumpled the note, gave the bands a quick shove in a northerly direction, and went back to work.

'Detective Inspector. We've heard Tosher MacBride described as a rent collector.'

'Is there to be an attack on the dead man's character, Mr Rumpole?'

'I don't know, my Lord. I suppose there are charming rent collectors, just as there are absolute darlings from the Income Tax.'

Laughter in Court, from which the judge remained aloof.

'Where did he collect rents?'

'Business premises.' The officer was non-committal.

'What sort of business premises?'

'Cafés, my Lord. Pubs. Minicab offices.'

'And if the rent wasn't paid, do you know what remedies were taken?'

'I assume proceedings were taken in the County Court.' The judge sounded totally bored by this line of cross-examination.

'Alas, my Lord, some people have no legal training. If the rents weren't paid, sometimes those minicab offices caught on fire, didn't they Detective Inspector?'

'Sometimes they did.' I told you, he was a very fair officer.

'To put it bluntly, that "good man" Tosher MacBride was a collector for a protection racket.'

'Well, officer, was he?' said Prestcold, more in sorrow than in anger.

'Yes, my Lord. I think he was.'

For the first time I felt I was forcing the judge to look in a different direction, and see the case from a new angle. I rubbed in the point. 'And if he'd been sticking to the money he'd collected, that might have provided a strong motive for murder by someone other than my client? Stronger than a few unkind words about an impediment in his speech?'

'Mr Rumpole, isn't that a question for the jury?' I looked at the jury then, they were all alive and even listening, and I congratulated the old darling on the bench.

'You're right! It is, my Lord. *And for no one else in this Court!*'

I thought it was effective, perhaps too effective for Leslie Delgardo, who stood up and left Court with a clatter. The swing doors banged to after him.

By precipitously leaving Court, Leslie Delgardo had missed the best turn on the bill, my double act with Mr Entwhistle, the forensic expert, an old friend and a foeman worthy of my steel.

'Mr Entwhistle, as a scientific officer I think you've lived with bloodstains as long as I have?'

'Almost.'

The jury smiled, they were warming to Rumpole.

'And you have all the clothes my client was wearing that night. Have you examined the pockets?'

'I have, my Lord.' Entwhistle bowed to the judge over a heap of Petey's clothing.

'And there are no bloodstains in any of the pockets?'

'There are none.'

'So there can be no question of a bloodstained knife having been hidden in a pocket whilst my client cradled the deceased in his arms?'

'Of course not.' Entwhistle smiled discreetly.

'You find that a funny suggestion?'

'Yes I do. The idea's ridiculous.'

'You may be interested to know that it's on that ridiculous idea the prosecution are basing their case.'

Painswick was on his feet with a well-justified moan. 'My Lord . . .'

'Yes. That was a quite improper observation, Mr Rumpole.'

'Then I pass from it rapidly, my Lord.' No point in wasting time with him, my business was with Entwhistle. 'Had Mr Delgardo stabbed the deceased, you would expect a spray of blood over a wide area of clothing?'

'You might have found that.'

'With small drops spattered from a forceful blow?'

'I should have expected so.'

'But you found nothing like it?'

'No.'

'And you might have expected blood near the area of the cuff of the coat or the shirt?'

'Most probably.'

'In fact, all we have is a smear or soaked patch in the crook of the arm.'

Mr Entwhistle picked up the overcoat, looked and, of course, admitted it.

'Yes.'

'Totally consistent with my client having merely put an arm round the deceased when he lay bleeding on the pavement.'

'Not inconsistent.'

'A double negative! The last refuge of an expert witness who doesn't want to commit himself. Does "not inconsistent" translated into plain English mean consistent, Mr Entwhistle?'

I could have kissed old Entwhistle on the rimless specs when he turned to the jury and said, 'Yes, it does.'

So when I got outside and saw Leslie Delgardo sitting on a bench chewing the end of a cigar, I thought he would wish to congratulate me. I didn't think of a gold watch, or a crinkly fiver, but at least a few warm words of encouragement. So I was surprised when he said, in a tone of deep hostility, 'What're you playing at, Mr Rumpole? Why didn't you use Bernie's conviction?'

'You really want to know?' Other members of the family were thronging about us, Basil and a matronly person in a mink coat, dabbing her eye make-up with a minute lace hanky.

'We all want to know,' said Basil, 'all the family.'

'I know I'm only the boy's mother,' sobbed the lady in mink.

'Don't underestimate yourself madam,' I reassured her. 'You've bred three sons who have given employment to the legal profession.' Then I started to explain. 'Point one. I spent all this trial trying to keep your brother's record out. If I put in the convictions of a prosecution witness the jury'll get to know about Peter's stretch for unlawful wounding, back in 1970. You want that?'

'We thought it was helpful,' Basil grumbled.

'Did you?' I looked at him. 'I'm sure you did. Well, point two, the perjury was forging a passport application. I've already checked it. And point three.'

'Point three, Mr Rumpole. You're sacked.' Leslie's voice was high with anger. I felt grateful we weren't in a turning off Stepney High Street on a dark night.

'May I ask why?'

'You got that judge's back up proper. He'll do for Petey. Good afternoon, Mr Rumpole. I'm taking you off the case.'

'I don't think you can do that.' He'd started to walk away, but now turned back with a look of extreme hostility.

'Oh don't you?'

'The only person who can take me off this case is my client, Mr Peter Delgardo. Come along Nooks, we'd better go down to the cells.'

'Your brother wants to sack me.'

Petey looked at me with his usual lack of understanding. Nooks acted as a smooth interpreter.

'The position is, Mr Leslie Delgardo is a little perturbed at the course this case is taking.'

'Mr Leslie Delgardo isn't my client,' I reminded Peter.

'He thinks we've got on the wrong side of the judge.'

I was growing impatient. 'Would he like to point out to me, strictly for my information, the *right* side of Mr Justice Prestcold? What *does* that judge imagine he is? Court correspondent for *The Tailor and Cutter*?' I stamped out my small cigar. 'Look, Peter, dear old sweetheart. I've abandoned the judge. He'll sum up dead against you. That's obvious. So let the jury think he's nothing but a personal anti-pollution programme who shoves air-wick up his nostrils every time he so much as smells a human being and we might have *got* somewhere.'

'Mr Leslie Delgardo is definitely dissatisfied. This puts me in a very embarrassing position.' Nooks looked suitably embarrassed.

'Cheer up, Nooks!' I smiled at him. 'Your position's nothing like so embarrassing as Peter's.' Then I concentrated on my client. 'Well. What's it going to be? Do I go or stay?'

Peter began to stammer an answer. It took a long time to come but, when it did, it meant that just one week later, on the day of the Scales of Justice ball, I was making a final speech to the jury in the case of the Queen against Delgardo. I may say that I never saw Leslie, or Basil, or their dear old Mum again.

'Members of the jury, may I call your attention to a man we haven't seen. He isn't in the dock. He has never gone into that witness box. I don't know where he is now. Perhaps he's tasting the delights of the Costa Brava. Perhaps he's very near this Court waiting for news. I'll call him Mr X. Did Mr X employ that "good man" Tosher MacBride to collect money in one of his protection rackets? Had Tosher MacBride betrayed his trust and was he to die for it? So that rainy night, outside the Old Justice pub in Stepney, Mr X waited for Tosher, waited with this knife and, when he saw his unfaithful servant come out of the shadows, he stabbed. Not once. Not twice. But you have heard the evidence. Three times in the neck.'

The jury was listening enrapt to my final speech; I was stabbing violently downwards with my prop when Prestcold cleared his throat and pointed to his own collar meaningfully. No doubt my stud was winking at him malevolently, so he said, 'Hm! . . . Mr Rumpole.'

I ignored this, no judge alive was going to spoil the climax of my speech, and I could tell that the jury were flattered, not to say delighted, to hear me tell them,

'Of course you are the *only* judges of fact in this case. But if you find Peter Delgardo guilty, then Mr X will smile, and order up champagne. Because, wherever he is, he will know . . . he's safe at last!'

Frank Prestcold summed up, as I knew he would, dead against Petey. He called the prosecution evidence 'overwhelming' and the jury listened politely. They went out just after lunch, and were still out at 6.30 when I telephoned Hilda and told her that I'd change in Chambers, and meet her at the Savoy, and I wanted it clearly understood that I wasn't dancing. I was just saying this when the usher came out and told me that the jury were back with a verdict.

After it was all over, I looked round in vain for Nooks. He had apparently gone to join the rest of the Delgardos in the great unknown. So I went down to say 'good-bye' to Peter in the cells. He was sitting inert, and staring into the middle distance.

'Cheer up, Peter.' I sat down beside him. 'Don't look so bloody miserable. My God. I don't know how you'd take it if you'd lost.'

Peter shook his head, and then said something I didn't wholly understand. 'I was . . . meant to l . . . l . . . lose.'

'Who meant you to? The prosecution? Of course. Mr Justice Prestcold? Undoubtedly, Fate. Destiny. The Spirit of the Universe? Not as it turned out. It was written in the stars. "Not Guilty of Murder. And is that the verdict of you all?".'

'That's why they ch . . . chose you. I was meant to lose.'

What the man said puzzled me. I admit it I found enigmatic. I said, 'I don't follow.'

'Bloke in the cell while I was w . . . w . . . waiting. Used to be a mate of Bernie "Four-Eyes". He told me why me brothers chose you to defend me.'

Well I thought I knew why I had been chosen for this important case. I stood up and paced the room.

'No doubt I have a certain reputation around the Temple, although my crown may be a little tarnished; done rather too much indecent assault lately.'

'He heard them round the P . . . P . . . Paradise Rooms. Talking about this old feller Rumpole.' Peter seemed to be pursuing another line of thought.

'The "Penge Bungalow Murder" is in *Notable British Trials*. I may have become a bit of a household name, at least in criminal circles.'

'They was l . . . looking for a barrister who'd be sure to lose.'

'After this, I suppose, I may get back to better quality crime.' The full force of what Peter had said struck me. I looked at him and checked carefully. '*What* did you say?'

'They wanted me defended by someone they could c . . . count on for a guilty verdict. That's why they p . . . p . . . picked you for it.'

It was, appallingly, what I thought he'd said.

'They wanted to fit me up with doing Tosher,' Peter Delgardo went on remorselessly.

'Let me get this clear. Your brothers selected *me* to nobble your defence?'

'That's it! You w . . . was to be the jockey like.' That pulled me back.

'How did they light on me exactly? Me . . . Rumpole of the Bailey?'

My entire life, Sherlock Holmes stories, Law degree, knock-about apprenticeship at Bow Street and Hackney, days of triumph in murder and forgery, down to that day's swayed jury and notable victory, seemed to be blown away like autumn leaves by what he said. Then, the words came quickly now, tumbling out of him, 'They heard of an old bloke. Got p . . . past it. Down to little bits of cases . . . round the M . . . M . . . Magistrates Courts. Bit of a muddler, they heard. With a funny old broken-down hat on him.'

'The hat! Again.' At least I had bought a bowler.

'So they r . . . reckoned. You was just the bloke to lose this murder, like.'

'And dear old Nooks. "Shady" Nooks. Did he help them to choose me?' I suspected it.

'I d . . . don't know. I'm n . . . n . . . not saying he didn't.'

'So that's my reputation!' I tried to take stock of the situation, and failed abysmally.

'I shouldn't've told you.' He sounded genuinely apologetic.

'Get Rumpole for the defence – and be sure of a conviction.'

'Perhaps it's all lies.' Was he trying to cheer me up? He went on. 'You hear lots of s . . . s . . . stories. In the cells under the Bailey.'

'And in the Bar Mess too. They rubbish your reputation. Small cigar?' I found a packet and offered him one.

'All right.'

We lit up. After all, one had to think of the future.

'So where does this leave you, Peter?' I asked him.

'I'd say, Mr Rumpole, none too s . . . safe. What about you?'

I blew out smoke, wondering exactly what I had left.

'Perhaps not all that safe either.'

I had brought my old dinner jacket up to Chambers and I changed into it there. I had a bottle of rum in the cupboard, and I gave myself a strong drink out of a dusty glass. As I shut the cupboard door, I noticed my old hat, it was on a shelf, gathering dust and seemed to have about it a look of mild reproach. I put it on, and noticed how comfortably it fitted. I dropped the new, hard bowler into the wastepaper basket and went on to the Savoy.

'You look charming, my dear.' Hilda, resplendent in a long dress, her shoulders dusted with powder, smiled delightedly at Mrs Marigold Featherstone, who was nibbling delicately at an after-dinner mint.

'Really, Rumpole.' Hilda looked at me, gently rebuking. 'She!'

'She?' Marigold was mystified, but anxious to join in any joke that might be going.

'Oh "She",' I said casually. 'A woman of fabulous beauty. Written up by H. Rider Haggard.' A waiter passed and I created a diversion by calling his attention to the fact that the tide had gone out in my glass. Around us prominent members of the legal profession pushed their bulky wives about the parquet like a number of fresh-faced gardeners executing elaborate manoeuvres with wheelbarrows. There were some young persons among them, and I noticed Erskine-Brown, jigging about in solitary rapture somewhere in the vicinity of Miss Phillida Trant. She saw me and gave a quick smile and then she was off circling Erskine-Brown like an obedient planet, which I didn't consider a fitting occupation for any girl of Miss Trant's undoubted abilities.

'Your husband's had a good win.' Guthrie Featherstone was chatting to Hilda.

'He hasn't had a "good win", Guthrie.' She put the man right. 'He's had a triumph!'

'Entirely thanks...to my old hat.' I raised my glass. 'Here's to it!'

'What?' Little of what Rumpole said made much sense to Marigold.

'My triumph, indeed, my great opportunity, is to be attributed solely to my hat!' I explained to her, but She couldn't agree.

'Nonsense!'

'What?'

'You're talking nonsense,' She explained to our hosts. 'He does, you know, from time to time. Rumpole won because he knows so much about blood.'

'Really?' Featherstone looked at the dancers, no doubt wondering how soon he could steer his beautiful wife off into the throng. But Hilda fixed him with her glittering eye, and went on, much like the ancient mariner.

'You remember Daddy, of course. He used to be *your* Head of Chambers. Daddy told me. "Rumpole," Daddy told me. In fact, he told me that on the occasion of the Inns of Court summer ball, which is practically the last dance we went to.'

'Hilda!' I tried, unsuccessfully, to stem the flow.

'No. I'm going to say this, Horace. Don't interrupt! "Horace Rumpole," Daddy told me, "knows more about bloodstains than anyone we've got in Chambers."'

I noticed that Marigold had gone a little pale.

'Do stop it, Hilda. You're putting Marigold off.'

'Don't you find it,' Marigold turned to me, 'well, sordid sometimes?'

'What?'

'Crime. Don't you find it terribly sordid?'

There was a silence. The music had stopped, and the legal fraternity on the floor clapped sporadically. I saw Erskine-Brown take Miss Trant's hand.

'Oh, do be careful, Marigold!' I said. 'Don't knock it.'

'I think it must be sordid.' Marigold patted her lips with her table napkin, removing the last possible trace of after-dinner mint.

'Abolish crime,' I warned her, 'and you abolish the very basis of our existence!'

'Oh, come now, Horace!' Featherstone was smiling at me tolerantly.

'He's right,' Hilda told him. 'Rumpole knows about bloodstains.'

'Abolish crime and we should all vanish.' I felt a rush of words to the head. 'All the barristers and solicitors and dock officers and the dear old matron down the Old Bailey who gives aspirins away with sentences of life imprisonment. There'd be no judges, no Lord Chancellor. The Commissioner of the Metropolitan Police would have to go out selling encyclopaedias.' I leant back, grabbed the wine from the bucket, and started to refill all our glasses. 'Why are we here? Why've we got prawn cocktail and *duck à l'orange* and selections from dear old *Oklahoma*? All because a few villains down the East End are kind enough to keep us in a regular supply of crime.'

A slightly hurt waiter took the bottle from me and continued my work.

'Don't *you* help them?' Marigold looked at me, doubtfully.

'Don't I *what*?'

'Help them. Doing all these crimes. After all. You get them off.'

'Today,' I said, not without a certain pride. 'Today, let me tell you, Marigold, I was no help to them at all. I showed them ... no gratitude!'

'You got him off!'

'What?'

'You got Peter Delgardo off.'

'Just for one reason.'

'What was that?'

'He happened to be innocent.'

'Come on, Horace. How can you be sure of that?' Featherstone was smiling tolerantly but I leant forward and gave him the truth of the matter.

'You know, it's a terrifying thing, my learned friend. We go through all that mumbo jumbo. We put on our wigs and gowns and mutter the ritual prayers. "My Lord, I humbly submit." "Ladies and gentlemen of the jury, you have listened with admirable patience ..." Abracadabra. Fee Fo Fi Bloody Fum. And just when everyone thinks you're going to produce the most ludicrously faked bit of cheese-cloth ectoplasm, or a phoney rap on the table, it comes. Clear as a bell. Quite unexpected. The voice of truth!'

I was vaguely aware of a worried figure in a dinner jacket coming towards us across the floor.

'Have you ever found that, Featherstone? Bloody scaring sometimes. All the trouble we take to cloud the issues and divert the attention. Suddenly we've done it. There it is! Naked and embarrassing. The truth!'

I looked up as the figure joined us. It was my late instructing solicitor.

'Nooks. "Shady" Nooks!' I greeted him, but he seemed in no mood to notice me. He pulled up a chair and sat down beside Featherstone.

'Apparently it was on the nine o'clock news. They've just arrested Leslie Delgardo. Charged him with the murder of Tosher MacBride. I'll want a con with you in the morning.'

I was left out of this conversation, but I didn't mind. Music started again, playing a tune which I found vaguely familiar. Nooks was muttering on; it seemed that the police now knew Tosher worked for Leslie, and that some member of the rival Watson family may have spotted him at the scene of the crime. An extraordinary sensation overcame me, something I hadn't felt for a long time, which could only be described as happiness.

'I don't know whether you'll want to brief me for Leslie, Nooks,' I raised a glass to old 'Shady'. 'Or would that be rather over-egging the pudding?'

And then an even more extraordinary sensation, a totally irrational impulse for which I can find no logical explanation, overcame me. I put out a hand and touched She Who Must Be Obeyed on the powdered shoulder.

'Hilda.'

'Oh yes, Rumpole?' It seemed I was interrupting some confidential chat with Marigold. 'What do you want now?'

'I honestly think,' I could find no coherent explanation, 'I think I want to dance with you.'

I suppose it was a waltz. As I steered Hilda out onto the great open spaces it seemed quite easy to go round and round, vaguely in time to the music. I heard a strange sound, as if from a long way off.

'*I'll have the last waltz with you,   Two sleepy people together* . . .' Or words to that effect. I was in fact singing. Singing and dancing to celebrate a great victory in a case I was never meant to win.

The Trials
of Rumpole

For Leo McKern

Rumpole and the Man of God

As I take up my pen during a brief and unfortunate lull in Crime (taking their cue from the car-workers, the villains of this city appear to have downed tools causing a regrettable series of lay-offs, redundancies and slow-time workings down the Old Bailey), I wonder which of my most recent Trials to chronicle. Sitting in Chambers on a quiet Sunday morning (I never write these memories at home for fear that She Who Must Be Obeyed, my wife Hilda, should glance over my shoulder and take exception to the manner in which I have felt it right, in the strict interests of truth and accuracy, to describe domestic life *à coté de* Chez Rumpole); seated, as I say, in my Chambers I thought of going to the archives and consulting the mementoes of some of my more notorious victories. However when I opened the cupboard it was bare, and I remembered that it was during my defence of a South London clergyman on a shoplifting rap that I had felt bound to expunge all traces of my past, and destroy my souvenirs. It is the curse, as well as the fascination of the law, that lawyers get to know more than is good for them about their fellow human beings, and this truth was driven home to me during the time that I was engaged in the affair that I have called 'Rumpole and the Man of God'.

When I was called to the Bar, too long ago now for me to remember with any degree of comfort, I may have had high-flown ideas of a general practice of a more or less lush variety, divorcing duchesses, defending stars of stage and screen from imputations of unchastity, getting shipping companies out of scrapes. But I soon found that it's crime which not only pays moderately well, but which is also by far the greatest fun. Give me a murder on a spring morning with a decent run and a tolerably sympathetic jury, and Rumpole's happiness is complete. Like most decent advocates, I have no great taste for the law; but I flatter myself I can cross-examine a copper on his notebook, or charm the Uxbridge Magistrates off their Bench, or have the old darling sitting number four in the jury-box sighing with pity for an embezzler with two wives and six starving children. I am also, and I say it with absolutely no desire to boast, about the best man in the Temple on the subject of bloodstains. There is really nothing you can tell Rumpole about blood, particularly when its out of the body and on to the clothing in the forensic laboratory.

The old Head of my Chambers, C. H. Wystan, now deceased (also known reluctantly to me as 'Daddy', being the father of Hilda Wystan, whom I married after an absent-minded proposal at an Inns of Court Ball. Hilda now rules the Rumpole household and rejoices in the dread title of 'She Who Must Be Obeyed'), old C. H. Wystan simply couldn't stand bloodstains. He even felt queasy looking at the photographs, so I started by helping him out with his criminal work and soon won my spurs round the London Sessions, Bow Street and the Old Bailey.

By the time I was called on to defend this particular cleric, I was so well-known in the Ludgate Circus Palais de Justice that many people, to my certain knowledge, called Horace Rumpole an Old Bailey Hack. I am now famous for chain-smoking small cigars, and for the resulting avalanche of ash which falls down the waistcoat and smothers the watch chain, for my habit of frequently quoting from the *Oxford Book of English Verse*, and for my fearlessness in front of the more savage type of Circuit Judge (I fix the old darlings with my glittering eye and whisper 'Down Fido' when they grow over-excited).

Picture me then in my late sixties, well-nourished on a diet consisting largely of pub lunches, steak-and-kidney pud, and the cooking claret from Pommeroy's Wine Bar in Fleet Street, which keeps me astonishingly regular. My reputation stands very high in the remand wing of Brixton Nick, where many of my regular clients, fraudsmen, safe-blowers, breakers-in and carriers of offensive weapons, smile with everlasting hope when their solicitors breathe the magic words, 'We're taking in Horace Rumpole'.

I remember walking through the Temple Gardens to my Chambers one late-September morning, with the pale sun on the roses and the first golden leaves floating down on the young solicitors' clerks and their girlfriends, and I was in a moderately expansive mood. Morning was at seven, or rather around 9.45, the hillside was undoubtedly dew-pearled, God was in his heaven, and with a little luck there was a small crime or two going on somewhere in the world. As soon as I got into the clerk's department of my Chambers at Number 3 Equity Court Erskine-Brown said 'Rumpole. I saw a priest going into your room.'

Our clerk's room was as busy as Paddington Station with our young and energetic clerk Henry sending barristers rushing off to distant destinations. Erskine-Brown, in striped shirt, double-breasted waistcoat and what I believe are known as 'Chelsea Boots', was propped up against the mantelpiece reading the particulars of some building claim Henry had just given him.

'That's your con, Mr Rumpole,' said Henry, explaining the curious manifestation of a Holy Man.

'Your *conversion*? Have you seen the light, Rumpole? Is Number 3 Equity Court your Road to Damascus?'

I cannot care for Erskine-Brown, especially when he makes jokes. I chose to ignore this and go to the mantelpiece to collect my brief, where I found old Uncle Tom (T. C. Rowley), the oldest member of our Chambers, who looks in because almost anything is preferable to life with his married sister in Croydon.

'Oh dear,' said Uncle Tom. 'A vicar in trouble. I suppose it's the choirboys again. I always think the Church runs a terrible risk having choirboys. They'd be far safer with a lot of middle-aged lady sopranos.'

I had slid the pink tape off the brief and was getting the gist of the clerical slip-up when Miss Trant, the bright young Portia of Equity Court (if Portias now have rimmed specs and speak with a Roedean accent) said that she didn't think vicars were exactly my line of country.

'Of course they're my line of country,' I told her with delight. 'Anyone accused of nicking half a dozen shirts is my line of country.' I had gone through the brief instructions by this time.

It seems that the cleric in question was called by the somewhat Arthurian name of the Reverend Mordred Skinner. He had gone to the summer sales in Oxford Street (a scene of carnage and rapine in which no amount of gold would have persuaded Rumpole to participate), been let off the leash in the gents' haberdashery, and later apprehended in the Hall of Food with a pile of moderately garish shirtings for which he hadn't paid.

Having spent a tough ten minutes digesting the facts of this far from complex matter (well, it showed no signs of becoming a State trial or House of Lords material) I set off in the general direction of my room, but on the way I was met by my old friend George Frobisher exuding an almost audible smell of 'bay rum' or some similar unguent.

I am not myself against a little *Eau de Cologne* on the handkerchief, but the idea of any sort of cosmetic on my friend George was like finding a Bishop '*en travestie*', or saucy seaside postcards on sale in the vestry. George is an old friend and a dear good fellow, a gentle soul who stands up in Court with all the confidence of a sacrificial virgin waiting for the sunrise over Stonehenge, but a dab hand at *The Times* crossword and a companionable fellow for a drink after Court in Pommeroy's Wine Bar off Fleet Street. I was surprised to see he appeared to have a new suit on, a silvery tie, and a silk bandana peeping from his top pocket.

'You haven't forgotten about tonight, have you?' George asked anxiously.

'We're going off for a bottle of Château Fleet Street in Pommeroy's?'

'No . . . I'm bringing a friend to dinner. With you and Hilda.'

I had to confess that this social engagement had slipped my mind. In any event it seemed unlikely that anyone would wish to spend an evening with She Who Must Be Obeyed unless they were tied to her by bonds of matrimony, but it seemed that George had invited himself some weeks before and that he was keenly looking forward to the occasion.

'No Pommeroy's then?' I felt cheated of the conviviality.

'No, but . . . We might bring a bottle with us! I have a little news. And I'd like you and Hilda to be the first to know.' He stopped then, enigmatically, and I gave a pointed sniff at the perfume-laden haze about him.

'George . . . You haven't taken to brilliantine by any chance?'

'We'll be there for seven-thirty.' George smiled in a sheepish sort of fashion and went off whistling something that someone might have mistaken for the 'Tennessee Waltz' if he happened to be tone deaf. I passed on to keep my rendezvous with the Reverend Mordred Skinner.

The Man of God came with a sister, Miss Evelyn Skinner, a brisk woman in sensible shoes who had foolishly let him out of her sight in the haberdashery, and Mr Morse, a grey-haired solicitor who did a lot of work for the Church Commissioners and whose idea of a thrilling trial was a gentle dispute about how many candles you can put over the High Altar on the third Sunday in Lent. My client himself was a pale, timid individual who looked, with watery eyes and a pinkish tinge to his nostrils, as if he had caught a severe cold during his childhood and had never quite got over it. He also seemed puzzled by the mysteries of the Universe, the greatest of which was the arrival of six shirts in the shopping-bag he was carrying through the Hall of Food. I suggested that the whole thing might be explained by absent-mindedness.

'Those sales,' I said, 'would induce panic in the hardiest housewife.'

'Would they?' Mordred stared at me. His eyes behind steel-rimmed glasses seemed strangely amused. 'I must say I found the scene lively and quite entertaining.'

'No doubt you took the shirts to the cash desk, meaning to pay for them.'

'There were two assistants behind the counter. Two young ladies, to take money from customers,' he said discouragingly. 'I mean there was no need for me to take the shirts to any cash desk at all, Mr Rumpole.'

I looked at the Reverend Mordred Skinner and re-lit the dying cheroot with some irritation. I am used to grateful clients, co-operative clients, clients who are willing to pull their weight and put their backs to the wheel in the great cause of Victory for

Rumpole. The many murderers I have known, for instance, have all been touchingly eager to help, and although one draws the line at simulated madness or futile and misleading alibis, at least such efforts show that the customer has a will to win. The cleric in my armchair seemed, by contrast, determined to put every possible obstacle in my way.

'I don't suppose you realized that,' I told him firmly. 'You're hardly an *habitué* of the sales, are you? I expect you wandered off looking for a cash desk, and then your mind filled with next week's sermon, or whose turn it was to do the flowers in the chancel, and the whole mundane business of shopping simply slipped your memory.'

'It is true,' the Reverend Mordred admitted, 'that I was thinking a great deal, at the time, of the Problem of Evil.'

'Oh really?'

With the best will in the world I didn't see how the Problem of Evil was going to help the defence.

'What puzzles the ordinary fellow is,' he frowned in bewilderment, 'if God is all-wise and perfectly good – why on earth did he put evil in the world?'

'May I suggest an answer?' I wanted to gain the poor cleric's confidence by showing that I had no objection to a spot of theology. 'So that an ordinary fellow like me can get plenty of briefs round the Old Bailey and London Sessions.'

Mordred considered the matter carefully and then expressed his doubts.

'No . . . No, I can't think *that*'s what He had in mind.'

'It may seem a very trivial little case to you Mr Rumpole . . .' Evelyn Skinner dragged us back from pure thought, 'but it's life and death to Mordred.' At which I stood and gave them all a bit of the Rumpole mind.

'A man's reputation is never trivial,' I told them. 'I must beg you both to take it extremely seriously. Mr Skinner, may I ask you to address your mind to one vital question? Given the fact that there were six shirts in the shopping-basket you were carrying, how the hell did they get there?'

Mordred looked hopeless and said, 'I can't tell you. I've prayed about it.'

'You think they might have leapt off the counter, by the power of prayer? I mean, something like the loaves and fishes?'

'Mr Rumpole.' Mordred smiled at me. 'Yours would seem to be an extremely literal faith.'

I thought that was a little rich coming from a man of such painful simplicity, so I lit another small cigar, and found myself gazing into the hostile and somewhat fishy eyes of the sister.

'Are you suggesting, Mr Rumpole, that my brother is guilty?'

'Of course not,' I assured her. 'Your brother's innocent. And he'll be so until twelve commonsensical old darlings picked at random off Newington Causeway find him otherwise.'

'I rather thought – a quick hearing before the Magistrates. With the least possible publicity.' Mr Morse showed his sad lack of experience in crime.

'A quick hearing before the Magistrates is as good as pleading guilty.'

'You think you might win this case, with a jury?' I thought there was a faint flicker of interest in Mordred's pink-rimmed eyes.

'Juries are like Almighty God, Mr Skinner. Totally unpredictable.'

So the conference wound to an end without divulging any particular answer to the charge, and I asked Mordred to apply through the usual channels for some sort of defence when he was next at prayer. He rewarded this suggestion with a wintry smile and my visitors left me just as She Who Must Be Obeyed came through on the blower to remind me that George was coming to dinner and bringing a friend, and would I buy two pounds of cooking apples at the tube station, and would I also remember not to loiter in Pommeroy's Wine Bar taking any sort of pleasure.

As I put the phone down I noticed that Miss Evelyn Skinner had filtered back into my room, apparently desiring a word with Rumpole alone. She started in a tone of pity.

'I don't think you quite understand my brother . . .'

'Oh. Miss Skinner. Yes, well . . . I never felt totally at home with vicars.' I felt some sort of apology was in order.

'He's like a child in many ways.'

'The Peter Pan of the Pulpit?'

'In a way. I'm two years older than Mordred. I've always had to look after him. He wouldn't have got anywhere without me, Mr Rumpole, simply nowhere, if I hadn't been there to deal with the Parish Council, and say the right things to the Bishop. Mordred just never thinks about himself, or what he's doing half the time.'

'You should have kept a better eye on him, in the sales.'

'Of course I should! I should have been watching him like a hawk, every minute. I blame myself entirely.'

She stood there, busily blaming herself, and then her brother could be heard calling her plaintively from the passage.

'Coming, dear. I'm coming at once,' Evelyn said briskly, and was gone. I stood looking after her, smoking a small cigar and remembering Hilaire Belloc's sound advice to helpless children:

> Always keep tight hold of nurse,
> For fear of finding something worse.

George Frobisher brought a friend to dinner, and, as I had rather suspected when I got a whiff of George's perfume in the passage, the friend was a lady, or, as I think Hilda would have preferred to call her, a woman. Now I must make it absolutely clear that this type of conduct was totally out of character in my friend George. He had an absolutely clean record so far as women were concerned. Oh I imagine he had a mother, and I have heard him occasionally mutter about sisters; but George had been a bachelor as long as I had known him, returning from our convivial claret in Pommeroy's to the Royal Borough Hotel, Kensington, where he had a small room, reasonable *en pension* terms and coloured television after dinner in the residents' lounge, seated in front of which device George would read his briefs, occasionally taking a furtive glance at some long-running serial of Hospital Life.

Judge of my surprise, therefore, when George turned up to dinner at Casa Rumpole with a very feminine, albeit middle-aged, lady indeed. Mrs Ida Tempest, as George introduced her, came with some species of furry animal wreathed about her neck, whose eyes regarded me with a glassy stare, as I prepared to help Mrs Tempest partially disrobe.

The lady's own eyes were far from glassy, being twinkling, and roguish in their expression. Mrs Tempest had reddish hair (rather the colour of falsely glowing artificial coals on an electric fire) piled on her head, what I believe is known as a 'Cupid's Bow' mouth in the trade, and the sort of complexion which makes you think that if you caught its owner a brisk slap you would choke in the resulting cloud of white powder. Her skirt seemed too tight, and her heels too high, for total comfort; but it could not be denied that Mrs Ida Tempest was a cheerful and even a pleasant-looking person. George gazed at her throughout the evening with mingled admiration and pride.

It soon became apparent that in addition to his lady friend, George had brought a plastic bag from some off-licence containing a bottle of non-vintage Moët. Such things are more often than not the harbinger of alarming news, and sure enough as soon as the pud was on the table George handed me the bottle, to cope with an announcement that he and Mrs Ida Tempest were engaged to be married, clearly taking the view that this news should be a matter for congratulation.

'We wanted you to be the first to know,' George said proudly.

Hilda smiled in a way that can only be described as 'brave' and further comment was postponed by the explosion of the warm Möet. I filled everyone's glasses and Mrs Tempest reached with enthusiasm for the booze.

'Oh, I do love bubbly,' she said. 'I love the way it goes all tickly up the nose, don't you Hilda?'

'We hardly get it often enough to notice.' She Who Must Be Obeyed was in no celebratory mood that evening. I had noticed, during the feast, that she clearly was not hitting it off with Mrs Tempest. I therefore felt it incumbent on me to address the Court.

'Well then. If we're all filled up, I suppose it falls to me. Accustomed as I am to public speaking . . .' I began the speech.

'Usually on behalf of the criminal classes!' Hilda grumbled.

'Yes. Well . . . I think I know what is expected on these occasions.'

'You mean you're like the film star's fifth husband? You know what's expected of you, but you don't know how to make it new.' It appeared from her giggles and George's proud smile that Mrs Tempest had made a joke. Hilda was not amused.

'Well then!' I came to the peroration. 'Here's to the happy couple.'

'Here's to us, George!' George and Mrs Tempest clinked glasses and twinkled at each other. We all took a mouthful of warmish gas. After which Hilda courteously pushed the food in George's *fiancée*'s direction.

'Would you care for a little more Charlotte Russe, Mrs Tempest?'

'Oh, Ida. Please call me Ida. Well, just a teeny-weeny scraping. I don't want to lose my sylph-like figure, do I Georgie? Otherwise you might not fancy me any more.'

'There's no danger of that.' The appalling thing was that George was looking roguish also.

'Of you not fancying me? Oh, I know ...' La Tempest simpered.

'Of losing your figure, my dear. She's slim as a bluebell. Isn't she slim as a bluebell, Rumpole?' George turned to me for corroboration. I answered cautiously.

'I suppose that depends rather on the size of the bluebell.'

'Oh, Horace! You are terrible! Why've you been keeping this terrible man from me, George?' Mrs Tempest seemed delighted with my enigmatic reply.

'I hope we're all going to see a lot of each other after we're married.' George smiled round the table, and got a small tightening of the lips from Hilda.

'Oh yes, George. I'm sure that'll be very nice.'

The tide had gone down in Mrs Tempest's glass, and after I had topped it up she held it to the light and said admiringly. 'Lovely glasses. So tasteful. Just look at that, George. Isn't that a lovely tasteful glass?'

'They're rejects actually,' Hilda told her. 'From the Army and Navy Stores.'

'What whim of providence was it that led you across the path of my old friend George Frobisher?' I felt I had to keep the conversation going.

'Mrs Tempest, that is Ida, came as a guest to the Royal Borough Hotel.' George started to talk shyly of romance.

'You noticed me, didn't you dear?' Mrs Tempest was clearly cast in the position of prompter.

'I must admit I did.'

'And I noticed him noticing me. You know how it is with men, don't you, Hilda?'

'Sometimes I wonder if Rumpole notices me at all.' Hilda struck, I thought, an unnecessarily gloomy note.

'Of course I notice you,' I assured her. 'I come home in the evenings – and there you are. I notice you all the time.'

'As a matter of fact we first spoke in the Manageress's Office,' George continued with the narration, 'where we had both gone to register a complaint, on the question of the bath water.'

'There's not enough hot to fill the valleys, I told her, let alone cover the hills!' Mrs Tempest explained gleefully to Hilda, who felt, apparently, that no such explanation was necessary.

'George agreed with me. Didn't you, George?'

'Shall I say, we formed an alliance?'

'Oh, we hit it off at once. We've so many interests in common.'

'Really.' I looked at Mrs Tempest in some amazement. Apart from the basic business of keeping alive I couldn't imagine what interests she had in common with my old friend George Frobisher. She gave me a surprising answer.

'Ballroom dancing.'

'Mrs Tempest,' said George proudly, 'that is Ida, has cups for it.'

'George! You're a secret ballroom dancer?' I wanted Further and Better Particulars of this Offence.

'We're going for lessons together, at Miss McKay's *École de Dance* in Rutland Gate.'

I confess I found the prospect shocking, and I said as much to George. 'Is your life going to be devoted entirely to pleasure?'

'Does *Horace* tango at all, Hilda?' Mrs Tempest asked a foolish question.

'He's never been known to.' Hilda sniffed slightly and I tried to make the reply lightly ironic.

'I'm afraid crime is cutting seriously down on my time for the tango.'

'Such a pity, dear.' Mrs Tempest was looking at me with genuine concern. 'You don't know what you're missing.'

At which point Hilda rose firmly and asked George's intended if she wanted to powder her nose, which innocent question provoked a burst of giggles.

'You mean, do I want to spend a penny?'

'It is customary,' said Hilda with some *hauteur*, 'at this stage, to leave the gentlemen.'

'Oh, you mean you want a hand with the washing-up,' Mrs Tempest followed Hilda out, delivering her parting line to me.

'Not too many naughty stories now, Horace. I don't want you leading my Georgie astray.' At which I swear she winked.

When we were left alone with a bottle of the Old Tawney George was still gazing foolishly after the vanishing Ida. 'Charming,' he said, 'isn't she charming?'

Now at this point I became distinctly uneasy. I had been looking at La Belle Tempest with a feeling of *déjà vue*. I felt sure that I had met her before, and not in some previous existence. And, of course, I was painfully aware of the fact that the vast majority of my social contacts are made in cells, courtrooms and other places of not too good repute. I therefore answered cautiously. 'Your Mrs Tempest ... seems to have a certain amount of vivacity.'

'She's a very able business-woman, too.'

'Is she now?'

'She used to run an hotel with her first husband. Highly successful business apparently. Somewhere in Kent ...'

I frowned. The word 'hotel' rang a distant, but distinctly audible, bell.

'So I thought, when we're married, of course, she might take up a small hotel again, in the West Country perhaps.'

'And what about you, George? Would you give up your work at the Bar and devote all your time to the veleta?' I rather wanted to point out to him the difficulties of the situation.

'Well. I don't want to boast, but I thought I might go for a Circuit Judgeship.' George said this shyly, as though disclosing another astonishing sexual conquest. 'In fact I *have* applied. In some rural area ...'

'*You* a judge, George? A *judge*? Well, come to think of it, it might suit you. You were never much good in Court, were you, old darling?' George looked slightly puzzled at this, but I blundered on. 'It wasn't in Ramsgate, by any chance? Where your *inamorata* kept a small hotel?'

'Why do you ask?' George was lapping up the port in a sort of golden reverie.

'Don't do it George!' I said, loudly enough, I hoped, to blast him out of his complacency.

'Don't be a judge?'

'Don't get married! Look, George. Your Honour. If your Lordship pleases. Have a little consideration, my dear boy.' I tried to appeal to his better nature. 'I mean – where would you be leaving me?'

'Very much as you are now, I should imagine.'

'Those peaceful moments of the day. Those hours we spend with a bottle of Château Fleet Street from 5.30 on in Pommeroy's Wine Bar. That wonderful oasis of peace that lies between the battle of the Bailey and the horrors of Home Life. You mean they'll be denied me from now on? You mean you'll be bolting like a rabbit down the Temple Underground back to Mrs Tempest and leaving me without a companion?'

George looked at me, thoughtfully, and then gave judgement with, I thought, a certain lack of feeling.

'I am, of course, extremely fond of you, Rumpole. But you're not exactly ... Well, not someone who one can share *all* one's interests with.'

'I'm not a dab hand at the two-step?' I'm afraid I sounded bitter.

'I didn't *say* that, Rumpole.'

'Don't do it, George! Marriage is like pleading guilty, for an indefinite sentence. Without parole.' I poured more port.

'You're exaggerating!'

'I'm not, George. I swear by Almighty God. I'm not.' I gave

him the facts. 'Do you know what happens on Saturday mornings? When free men are lying in bed, or wandering contentedly towards a glass of breakfast Chablis and a slow read of the Obituaries? You'll both set out with a list, and your lady wife will spend your hard-earned money on things you have no desire to own, like Vim, and saucepan scourers, and J-cloths ... and Mansion polish! And on your way home, you'll be asked to carry the shopping-basket ... I beg of you, don't do it!'

This plea to the jury might have had some effect, but the door then opened to admit La Belle Tempest, George's eyes glazed over and he clearly became deaf to reason. And then Hilda entered and gave me a brisk order to bring in the coffee tray.

'She Who Must Be Obeyed!' I whispered to George on my way out. 'You see what I mean?' I might as well have saved my breath. He wasn't listening.

Saturday morning saw self and She at the check-out point in the local Tesco's, with the substantial fee for the Portsmouth Rape Trial being frittered away on such frivolous luxuries as sliced bread, Vim, cleaning materials and so on, and as the cash register clicked merrily up Hilda passed judgement on George's *fiancée*.

'Of course she won't do for George.'

I had an uneasy suspicion that she might be correct, but I asked for further and better particulars.

'You think not? Why exactly?'

'Noticing our glasses! It's such bad form noticing people's things. I thought she was going to ask how much they cost.'

Which, so far as She was concerned, seemed to adequately sum up the case of Mrs Ida Tempest. At which point, having loaded up and checked that the saucepan scourers were all present and correct, Hilda handed me the shopping-basket, which seemed to be filled with lead weights, and strode off unimpeded to the bus stop with Rumpole groaning in her wake.

'What we do with all that Vim, I can never understand.' I questioned our whole way of life. 'Do we *eat* Vim?'

'You'd miss it, Rumpole, if it wasn't there.'

*

On the following Monday I went down to Dockside Magistrates Court to defend young Jim Timson on a charge of taking and driving away a Ford Cortina. I have acted for various members of the clan Timson, a noted breed of South London villain, for many years. They know the law, and their courtroom behaviour, I mean the way they stand to attention and call the magistrate 'Sir', is impeccable. I went into battle fiercely that afternoon, and it was a famous victory. We got the summons dismissed with costs against the police. I hoped I'd achieve the same happy result in the notable trial of the Reverend Mordred Skinner, but I very much doubted it.

As soon as I was back in Chambers I opened a cupboard, sneezed in the resulting cloud of dust and burrowed in the archives. I resisted the temptation to linger among my memories and pushed aside the Penge Bungalow photographs, the revolver that was used in the killing at the East Grimble Rep, and old Charles Monti's will written on a blown ostrich egg. I only glanced at the drawing an elderly R.A. did, to while away his trial for soliciting in the Super Loo at Euston Station, of the Recorder of London. I lingered briefly on my book of old press cuttings from the *News of the World* (that fine Legal Text Book in the Criminal Jurisdiction), and merely glanced at the analysis of bloodstains from the old Brick Lane Billiard Hall Murder when I was locked in single-handed combat with a former Lord Chief Justice of England and secured an acquittal, and came at last on what I was seeking.

The blue folder of photographs was nestling under an old wig tin and an outdated work on forensic medicine. As I dug out my treasure and carried it to the light on my desk, I muttered a few lines of old William Wordsworth's, the Sheep of the Lake District,

> Perhaps the plaintive numbers flow
> For old, unhappy, far-off things,
> And battles long ago.

On the cover of the photographs I had stuck a yellowing cutting from the *Ramsgate Times*. 'Couple Charged in Local Arson Case' I read again. 'The Unexplained Destruction of the

Saracen's Head Hotel!' I opened the folder. There was a picture of a building on the sea front, and a number of people standing round. I took the strong glass off my desk to examine the figures in the photograph and saw the younger, but still roguishly smiling, face of Mrs Ida Tempest, my friend George's intended.

Having tucked the photographs back in the archive, I went straight to Pommeroy's Wine Bar, nothing unusual about that, I rarely go anywhere else at six o'clock, after the day's work is done; but George wasn't in Chambers and I hoped he might drop in there for a strengthener before a night of dalliance with his *inamorata* in the Royal Borough Hotel. However when I got to Pommeroy's the only recognizable figure, apart from a few mournful-looking journalists and the opera critic in residence, was our Portia, Miss Phillida Trant, drinking a lonely Cinzano Bianco with ice and lemon. She told me that she hadn't seen George and said, rather enigmatically, that she was waiting for a person called Claude, who, on further inquiry, turned out to be none other than our elegant expert on the Civil side, my learned antagonist Erskine-Brown.

'Good God, is he Claude? Makes me feel quite fond of him. Why ever are you waiting for him? Do you want to pick his brains on the law of mortgages?'

'We *are* by way of being engaged,' Miss Trant said somewhat sharply.

The infection seemed to be spreading in our Chambers, like gippy tummy. I looked at Miss Trant and asked, simply for information, 'You're sure you know enough about him?'

'I'm afraid I do.' She sounded resigned.

'I mean, you'd naturally want to *know* everything, wouldn't you – about anyone you're going to commit matrimony with?' I wanted her confirmation.

'Go on, surprise me!' Miss Trant, I had the feeling, was not being entirely serious. 'He married a middle-aged Persian contortionist when he was up at Keble? I'd love to know that – and it'd make him *far* more exciting.'

At which point the beloved Claude actually made his appearance in a bowler and overcoat with a velvet collar, and

announced he had some treat in store for Miss Trant, such as
Verdi's *Requiem* in the Festival Hall, whilst she looked at him
as though disappointed at the un-murkiness of the Erskine-
Brown past. Then I saw George at the counter making a small
purchase from Jack Pommeroy and I bore down on him. I had
no doubt, at that stage, that my simple duty to my old friend
was immediate disclosure. However when I reached George I
found that he was investing in a bottle far removed from our
usual Château Fleet Street.

'1967. Pichon-Longueville? Celebrating, George?'

'In a way. We have a glass or two in the room now. Can't get
anything decent in the restaurant.' George was storing the nectar
away in his brief-case with the air of a practised *boulevardier*.

'George. Look. My dear fellow. Look ... will you have a
drink?'

'It's really much more comfortable, up in the room,' George
babbled on regardless. 'And we listen to the BBC Overseas
Service, old Victor Sylvester records requested from Nigeria.
They only seem to *care* for ballroom dancing in the Third World
nowadays.' My old friend was moving away from me, although
I did all I could to stop him.

'Please, George. It'll only take a minute. Something ... you
really ought to know.'

'Sorry to desert you, Rumpole. It would never do to keep Ida
waiting.'

He was gone, as Jack Pommeroy with his purple face and the
rose-bud in his buttonhole asked what was my pleasure.

'Red plonk,' I told him. 'Château Fleet Street. A large glass.
I've got nothing to celebrate.'

After that I found it increasingly difficult to break the news to
George, although I knew I had to do so.

The Reverend Mordred Skinner was duly sent for trial at the
Inner London Sessions, Newington Causeway in the South East
corner of London. Wherever civilization ends it is, I have always
felt, somewhere just north of the Inner London Sessions. It is a
strange thing but I always look forward with a certain eagerness
to an appearance at the Old Bailey. I walk down Newgate

Street, as often as not, with a spring in my stride and there it is, in all its glory, a stately law court, decreed by the City Fathers, an Edwardian palace with a modern extension to deal with the increase in human fallibility. Terrible things go on down the Bailey, horrifying things. Why is it I never go through its revolving door without a thrill of pleasure, a slight tremble of excitement? Why does it seem a much jollier place than my flat in Gloucester Road under the strict rule of She Who Must Be Obeyed?

Such pleasurable sensations, I must confess, are never connected with my visits to the Inner London Sessions. While a hint of spring sunshine often touches the figure of Justice on the dome of the Bailey it always seems to be a wet Monday in November at Inner London. The Sessions House is stuck in a sort of urban desert down the Old Kent Road, with nowhere to go for a decent bit of steak-and-kidney pud during the lunch hour. It is a sad sort of Court, with all the cheeky Cockney sparrows turned into silent figures waiting for the burglary to come on in Court 2, and the juries there look as if they relied on the work to eke out their social security.

I met the Reverend gentleman after I had donned the formal dress (yellowing wig bought second-hand from an ex-Attorney General of Tonga in 1932, somewhat frayed gown, collar like a blunt extension). He seemed unconcerned and was even smiling a little, although his sister Evelyn looked like one about to attend a burning at the stake; Mr Morse looked thoroughly uncomfortable and as if he'd like to get back to a nice discussion of the Almshouse charity in Chipping Sodbury.

I tried to instil a suitable sense of the solemnity of the occasion in my clerical customer by telling him that God, with that wonderful talent for practical joking which has shown itself throughout recorded history, had dealt us His Honour Judge Bullingham.

'Is he very dreadful?' Mr Skinner asked almost hopefully.

'Why he was ever made a judge is one of the unsolved mysteries of the universe.' I was determined not to sound reassuring. 'I can only suppose that his unreasoning prejudice against all black persons, defence lawyers and probation officers, comes from some deep psychological cause. Perhaps his mother, if such a person can be imagined, was once assaulted by a black probation officer who was on his way to give evidence for the defence.'

'I wonder how he feels about parsons.' My client seemed not at all put out.

'God knows. I rather doubt if he's ever met one. The Bull's leisure taste runs to strong drink and all-in wrestling. Come along, we might as well enter the *corrida*.'

A couple of hours later, His Honour Judge Bullingham, with his thick neck and complexion of a beetroot past its first youth, was calmly exploring his inner ear with his little finger and tolerantly allowing me to cross-examine a large gentleman named Pratt, resident flatfoot at the Oxford Street Bazaar.

'Mr Pratt? How long have you been a detective in this particular store?'

'Ten years, sir.'

'And before that?'

'I was with the Metropolitan Police.'

'Why did you leave?'

'Pay and conditions, sir, were hardly satisfactory.'

'Oh, really? You found it more profitable to keep your beady eye on the ladies' lingerie counter than do battle in the streets with serious crime?'

'Are you suggesting that this isn't a serious crime, Mr Rumpole?' The learned judge, who pots villains with all the subtlety of his namesake animal charging a gate, growled this question at me with his face going a darker purple than ever, and his jowls trembling.

'For many people, my Lord,' I turned to the jury and gave them the message, 'six shirts might be a mere triviality. For the Reverend Mordred Skinner, they represent the possibility of total ruin, disgrace and disaster. In this case my client's whole life hangs in the balance.' I turned a flattering gaze on the twelve honest citizens who had been chosen to pronounce on the sanctity or otherwise of the Reverend Mordred. 'That is why we must cling to our most cherished institution, trial by jury. It is not the value of the property stolen, it is the priceless matter of a man's good reputation.'

'Mister Rumpole,' the Bull lifted his head as if for the charge. 'You should know your business by now. This is not the time for making speeches, you will have an opportunity at the end of the case.'

'And as your Honour will have an opportunity *after* me to make a speech, I thought it as well to make clear who the judges of *fact* in this matter are.' I continued to look at the jury with an expression of flattering devotion.

'Yes. Very well. Let's get on with it.' The Bull retreated momentarily. I rubbed in the victory.

'Certainly. That is what I was attempting to do.' I turned to the witness. 'Mr Pratt. When you were in the gents' haberdashery . . .'

'Yes, sir?'

'You didn't see my client remove the shirts from the counter and make off with them?'

'No, sir.'

'If he had, no doubt he would have told us about it,' Bullingham could not resist growling. I gave him a little bow.

'Your Honour is always so quick to notice points in favour of the defence.' I went back to work on the store detective. 'So why did you follow my client?'

'The Supervisor noticed a pile of shirts missing. She said there was a Reverend been turning them over, your Honour.'

This tit-bit delighted the Bull, he snatched at it greedily. 'He might not have told us that, if you hadn't asked the wrong question, Mr Rumpole.'

'No question is wrong, if it reveals the truth,' I informed the jury, and then turned to Pratt. I had an idea, an uncomfortable feeling that I might just have guessed the truth of this peculiar case. 'So you don't know if he was carrying the basket when he left the shirt department?'

'No.'

'Was he carrying it when you first spotted him, on the moving staircase?'

'I only saw his head and shoulders . . .'

The pieces were fitting together. I would have to face my client with my growing notion of a defence as soon as possible. 'So you first saw him with the basket in the Hall of Food?'

'That's right, sir.'

At which point Bullingham stirred dangerously and raised the curtain of his top lip on some large yellowing teeth. He was about to make a joke. 'Are you suggesting, Mr Rumpole, that a basket full of shirts mysteriously materialized in your client's hand in the Tinned Meat Department?'

At which the jury laughed obsequiously. Rumpole silenced them in a voice of enormous gravity.

'Might I remind your Honour of what he said. This is a serious case.'

'As you cross-examined, Mr Rumpole, I was beginning to wonder.' Bullingham was still grinning.

'The art of cross-examination, your Honour, is a little like walking a tight-rope.'

'Oh is it?'

'One gets on so much better if one isn't continually interrupted.'

At which Bullingham relapsed into a sullen silence and I got on with the work in hand.

'It would have been quite impossible for Mr Skinner to have paid at the shirt counter, wouldn't it?'

'No, sir. There were two assistants behind the counter.'

'Young ladies?'

'Yes, sir.'

'When you saw them, what were they doing?'

'I . . . I can't exactly recall.'

'Well then, let me jog your memory.' Here I made an informed guess at what any two young lady assistants would be doing at the height of business during the summer sales. 'Were they not huddled together in an act of total recall of last night in the disco or Palais de Hop? Were they not blind and deaf to the cries of shirt-buying clerics? Were they not utterly oblivious to the life around them?'

The jury was looking at me and smiling, and some of the ladies nodded understandingly. I could feel that the old darlings knew all about young lady non-assistants in Oxford Street.

'Well, Mr Pratt. Isn't that exactly what they were doing?'

'It may have been, your Honour.'

'So is it surprising that my client took his purchase and went off in search of some more attentive assistance?'

'But I followed him downstairs, to the Hall of Food.'

'Have you any reason to suppose he wouldn't have paid for his shirts there, given the slightest opportunity?'

'I saw no sign of his attempting to do so.'

'Just as you saw no sign of the sales-ladies attempting to take his money?'

'No but . . .'

'It's a risky business entering your store, isn't it, Pratt?' I put it to him. 'You can't get served and no one speaks to you except to tell you that you're under arrest.'

I sat down to some smiles from the jury and a glance from the Bull. An eager young man named Ken Rydal was prosecuting. I had run up against this Rydal, a ginger-haired, spectacled wonder who might once have been a senior scout, and won the Duke of Edinburgh award for being left out on the mountainside for a week. 'Ken' felt a strong sense of team spirit and loyalty to the Metropolitan Police, and he was keen as mustard to add the Reverend Mordred Skinner to the notches on his woggle.

'Did you see Mr Skinner make any attempt to pay for his shirts in the Hall of Food?' Ken asked Pratt.

I read a note from my client that had finally arrived by way of the usher.

'No. No, I didn't,' said Pratt.

Ken was smiling, about to make a little scout-like funny. 'He didn't ask for them to be wrapped up with a pound of ham, for instance?'

'No, sir.' Pratt laughed and looked round the Court, to see that no one was laughing. And the Bull was glaring at Ken.

'This is not a music hall, Mr Rydal. As Mr Rumpole has reminded us, this is an extremely serious case. The whole of the Reverend gentleman's future is at stake.' The judge glanced at the clock, as if daring it not to be time for lunch. The clock cooperated, and the Bull rose, muttering 'Ten past two, members of the jury.'

I crumpled my client's note with some disgust and threw it on the floor as I stood to bow to the Bull. The Reverend Mordred had just told me he wasn't prepared to give evidence in his own defence. I would have to get him on his own and twist his arm a little.

'I simply couldn't take the oath.'

'What's the matter with you? Have you no religion?'

The cleric smiled politely and said, less as a question than a statement of fact, 'You don't like me very much, do you?'

We were sitting in one of the brighter hostelries in Newington Causeway. The bleak and sour-smelling saloon bar was sparsely populated by two ailing cleaning-ladies drinking stout, another senior citizen who was smoking the dog ends he kept in an old Oxo tin and exercising his talents as a Cougher for England, and a large drunk in a woolly bobble-hat who kept banging in and out the Gents with an expression of increasing euphoria. I had entrusted to Mr Morse the solicitor the tricky task of taking Miss Evelyn Skinner to lunch in the public canteen at the Sessions House. I imagined he'd get the full blast of her anxiety over the grey, unidentifiable meat and two veg. Meanwhile I had whisked the Reverend out to the pub where he sat with the intolerably matey expression vicars always assume in licensed premises.

'I felt you might tell me the truth. You of all people. Having your collar on back to front must mean something.'

'Truth is often dangerous. It must be approached cautiously, don't you think?' My client bit nervously into a singularly unattractive sausage. I tried to approach the matter cautiously.

'I've noticed with women,' I told him, 'with my wife, for instance, when we go out on our dreaded Saturday morning shopping expeditions, that She Who Must Be Obeyed is in charge of the shopping-basket. She makes the big decisions. How much Vim goes in it and so forth. When the shopping's bought, I get the job of carrying the damn thing home.'

'Simple faith is far more important than the constant scramble after unimportant facts.' Mordred was back on the old theology. 'I believe that's what the lives of the Saints tell us.'

Enough of this Cathedral gossip. We were due back in Court in half an hour and I let him have it between the eyes. 'Well, my simple faith tells me that your sister had the basket in the shirt department.'

'Does it?' He blinked most of the time, but not then.

'When Pratt saw you in the Hall of Food you were carrying the shopping-basket, which she'd handed you on the escalator.'

'Perhaps.'

'Because she'd taken the shirts and put them in the bag when you were too busy composing your sermon on the Problem of Evil to notice.' I lit a small cigar at that point, and Mordred took a sip of sour bitter. He was still smiling as he started to talk, almost shyly at first, then with increasing confidence.

'She was a pretty child. It's difficult to believe it now. She was attracted to bright things, boiled sweets, red apples, jewellery in Woolworth's. As she grew older it became worse. She would take things she couldn't possibly need ... Spectacles, bead handbags, cigarette cases although she never smoked. She was like a magpie. I thought she'd improved. I try to watch her as much as I can, although you're right, on that day I was involved with my sermon. As a matter of fact, I had no need of such shirts. I may be old-fashioned but I always wear a dog collar. Always.'

'Even on rambles with the Lads' Brigade?'

'All the same,' my client said firmly, 'I believe she did it out of love.'

Well, now we had a defence: althought he didn't seem to be totally aware of it.

'Those are the facts?'

'They seem to be of no interest to anyone – except my immediate family. But that's what I'm bound to say, if I take my oath on the Bible.'

'But you were prepared to lie to me,' I reminded him. He smiled again, that small, maddening smile.

'Mr Rumpole. I have the greatest respect for your skill as an advocate, but I have never been in danger of mistaking you for Almighty God.'

'Tell the truth *now*. She'll only get a fine. Nothing!'

He seemed to consider the possibility, then he shook his head.

'To her it would be everything. She couldn't bear it.'

'What about you? You'd give up your whole life?'

'It seems the least I can do for her.' He was smiling again, hanging that patient little grin out like an advertisement for his humility and his deep sense of spiritual superiority to a worldly Old Bailey Hack.

I ground out my small cigar in the overflowing ashtray and almost shouted. 'Good God! I don't know how I keep my temper.'

'I do sympathize. He found His ideas irritated people dreadfully. Particularly lawyers.' He was almost laughing now. 'But you do understand? I am quite unable to give evidence on oath to the jury.'

As every criminal lawyer knows it's very difficult to get a client off unless he's prepared to take the trouble of going into the witness-box, to face up to the prosecution, and to demonstrate his innocence or at least his credentials as a fairly likeable character who might buy you a pint after work and whom you would not really want to see festering in the nick. After all fair's fair, the jury have just seen the prosecution witnesses put through it, so why should the prisoner at the Bar sit in solemn silence in the dock? I knew that if the Reverend told his story, with suitable modesty and regret, I could get him off and Evelyn would merely get a well-earned talking to. When he refused to give evidence I could almost hear the rustle of unfrocking in the distance.

Short of having my client dragged to the Bible by a sturdy usher, when he would no doubt stand mute of malice, there was nothing I could do other than address the jury in the unlikely hope of persuading them that there was no reliable evidence on which they could possibly convict the silent vicar. I was warming to my work as Bullingham sat inert, breathing hoarsely, apparently about to erupt.

'Members of the jury,' I told them. 'There is a Golden Thread that runs throughout British justice. The prosecution must prove its case. The defence has to prove nothing.'

'*Mr* Rumpole . . .' A sound came from the judge like the first rumble they once heard from Mount Vesuvius.

I soldiered on. 'The Reverend Mordred Skinner need not trouble to move four yards from that dock to the witness-box unless the prosecution has produced evidence that he *intended* to steal – and not to pay in another department.'

'Mr *Rumpole*.' The earth tremor grew louder. I raised my voice a semitone.

'Never let it be said that a man is forced to prove his innocence! Our fathers have defied kings for that principle, members of the jury. They forced King John to sign Magna Carta and sent King Charles to the scaffold and it has been handed down even to the Inner London Sessions, Newington Causeway.'

'If you let me get a word in edgeways . . .'

'And now it is in your trust!'

I'm not, as this narrative may have made clear, a religious man; but what happened next made me realize how the Israelites felt when the waters divided, and understand the incredulous reaction of the disciples when an uninteresting glass of water flushed darkly and smelt of the grape. I can recall the exact words of the indubitable miracle. Bullingham said, 'Mr Rumpole. I entirely agree with everything you say. And,' he added glowering threateningly at the Scout for the prosecution, 'I shall direct the jury accordingly.'

The natural malice of the Bull had been quelled by his instinctive respect for the law. He found there was no case to answer.

I met my liberated client in the Gents, a place where his sister was unable to follow him. As we stood side by side at the porcelain I congratulated him.

'I was quite reconciled to losing. I don't think my sister would have stood by me somehow. The disgrace you see. I think,' he looked almost wistful, 'I think I should have been alone.'

'You'd have been unfrocked.'

'It might have been extremely restful. Not to have to pretend to any sort of sanctity. Not to pretend to be different. To be exactly the same as everybody else.'

I looked at him standing there in the London Sessions loo, his mac over his arm, his thin neck half-strangled by a dog collar. He longed for the relaxed life of an ordinary sinner, but he had no right to it.

'Don't long for a life of crime, old darling,' I told him. 'You've obviously got no talent for it.'

Upstairs we met Evelyn and Mr Morse. The sister gave me a flicker of something which might have been a smile of gratitude.

'It was a miracle,' I told her.

'Really? I thought the judge was exceedingly fair. Come along, Mordred. He's somewhere else you know, Mr Rumpole. He can't even realize it's all over.' She attacked her brother again. 'Better put your mac on, dear. It's raining outside.'

'Yes, Evelyn. Yes. I'll put it on.' He did so, obediently.

'You must come to tea in the Rectory, Mr Rumpole.' I had a final chilly smile from Evelyn.

'Alas, dear lady. The pressure of work. These days I have so little time for pleasure.'

'Say goodbye to Mr Rumpole, Mordred.'

The cleric shook my hand, and gave me a confidential aside. 'Goodbye, Mr Rumpole. You see it was entirely a family matter. There was no need for anyone to know anything about it.'

And so he went, in his sister's charge, back to the isolation of the Rectory.

> Will no one tell me what she sings?
> Perhaps the plaintive numbers flow
> For old, unhappy, far-off things
> And murders long ago.

Had I, against all the odds, learned something from the Reverend? Was I now more conscious of the value of secrecy, of not dropping bombs of information which might cause ruin and havoc on the family front? It seems unlikely, but I do not know why else I was busily destroying the archive, pushing the photographs into the unused fireplace in my Chambers and applying a match, and dropping the durable articles, including the ostrich egg, into the waste-paper basket. As the flames licked across the paper and set Mrs Tempest the arsonist curling into ashy oblivion the door opened to admit Miss Trant.

'Rumpole! What on earth are you doing?'

I turned from the smoking relics.

'You keep things, Miss Trant? Mementoes? Locks of hair? Old letters, tied up in ribbon? "Memories",' I started to sing tunelessly, ' "were made of this." '

'Not really.'

'Good.'

'I've got my first brief. From when I prosecuted you in Dock Street.' This was the occasion when I tricked Miss Trant into boring the wretched Beak with a huge pile of law, and so defeated her.* It was not an incident of which I am particularly proud.

'Destroy it. Forget the past, eh? Miss Trant. Look to the future!'

'All right. Aren't you coming up to Guthrie Featherstone's room? We're laying on a few drinks for George.'

'George? Yes, of course. He'll have a lot to celebrate.'

Guthrie Featherstone, Q.C., M.P., the suave and elegant Conservative-Labour M.P. for somewhere or another who, when he is not passing the 'Gas Mains Enabling Bill' or losing politely at golf to various of Her Majesty's judges, condescends to exercise his duties as Head of Chambers (a post to which I was due to succeed by order of seniority of barristers in practice, when I was pipped at the post by young Guthrie taking silk. Well, I didn't want it anyway†); Guthrie Featherstone occupied the best room in Chambers (first floor, high windows, overlooking Temple Gardens) and he was engaged in making a speech to our assembled members. In a corner of the room I saw our clerk Henry and Dianne the typist in charge of a table decorated by several bottles of Jack Pommeroy's cooking champagne. I made straight for the booze, and at first Featherstone's speech seemed but a background noise, like Radio Four.

'It's well known among lawyers that the finest advocates never make the best judges. The glory of the advocate is to be opinionated, brash, fearless, partisan, hectoring, rude, cunning and unfair.'

'Well done, Rumpole!' This, of course, was Erskine-Brown.

*See 'Rumpole and the Married Lady', pp. 105–33.
†See 'Rumpole and the Younger Generation', pp. 9–48.

'Thank you very much, Claude.' I raised my glass to him.

'The ideal judge, however,' Featherstone babbled on, 'is detached, courteous, patient, painstaking and above all, quiet. These qualities are to be found personified in the latest addition to our Bench of Circuit Judges.'

' "Circus" Judges, Rumpole calls them,' Uncle Tom said loudly, to no one in particular.

'Ladies and gentlemen,' the Q.C., M.P. concluded, 'please raise your glasses to His Honour Judge George Frobisher.'

Everyone was smiling and drinking. So the news had broken. George was a Circuit Judge. No doubt the crowds were dancing in Fleet Street. I moved to my old friend to add my word of congratulation.

'Your health George. Coupled with the name of Mrs Ida Tempest?'

'No, Rumpole. No.' George shook his head, I thought sadly.

'What do you mean, "No"? Mrs Tempest should be here. To share in your triumph. Celebrating back at the Royal Borough Hotel, is she? She'll have the Moët on ice by the time you get back.'

'Mrs Tempest left the Royal Borough last week, Rumpole. I have no means of knowing where to find her.'

At which point we were rudely interrupted by Guthrie Featherstone calling on George to make a speech. Other members joined in and Henry filled up George's glass in preparation for the great oration.

'I'm totally unprepared to *say* anything on this occasion,' George said, taking a bit of paper from his pocket to general laughter. Poor old George could never do anything off the cuff.

'Ladies and gentlemen,' George started. 'I have long felt the need to retire from the hurly-burly of practice at the Bar.'

'Comes as news to me that George Frobisher had a practice at the Bar,' Uncle Tom said to no one much in a deafening whisper.

'To escape from the benevolent despotism of Henry, now our senior clerk.' George twinkled.

'Can you do a Careless Driving at Croydon tomorrow, your Honour?' Henry called out in the cheeky manner he had adopted since he was an office boy.

Laughter.

'No, Henry, I can't. So I have long considered applying for a Circuit Judgeship in a Rural Area . . .'

'Where are you going to, George? Glorious Devon?' Featherstone interrupted.

'I think they're starting me off in Luton. And I hope, very soon, I'll have the pleasure of you all appearing before me!'

'Where did George say they were sending him?' Uncle Tom asked.

'I think he said Luton, Uncle Tom,' I told him.

'Luton, glorious Luton!' Henry sometimes goes too far, for a clerk. I was glad to see that Dianne sssshed him firmly.

'Naturally as a judge, as one, however humble, of Her Majesty's judges, certain standards will be expected of me,' George went on, I thought in a tone of some regret.

'No more carousing in Pommeroy's with Horace Rumpole!' Uncle Tom was still barracking.

'And I mean to try, to do my best, to live up to those standards. That's really all I have to say. Thank you. Thank you all very much.'

There was tumultuous applause, increased in volume by the cooking champagne, and George joined me in a corner of the room. Uncle Tom was induced to make his speech, traditional and always the same on all Chambers' occasions, and George and I talked quietly together.

'George. I'm sorry. About Mrs Tempest . . .'

'It was your fault, Rumpole.' George looked at me with an air of severe rebuke.

'My fault!' I stood amazed. 'But I said nothing. Not a word. You know me, George. Discretion is Rumpole's middle name. I was silent. As the tomb.'

'When I brought her to dinner with you and Hilda. She recognized you at once.'

'She didn't show it!'

'She's a remarkable woman.'

'I was junior Counsel, for her former husband. I'm sure he led her on. She made an excellent impression. In the witness-box.' I tried to sound comforting.

'She made an excellent impression on me, Rumpole. She thought you'd be bound to tell me.'

'She thought that?'

'So she decided to tell me first.'

I stood looking at George, feeling unreasonably guilty. Somewhere in the distance Uncle Tom was going through the usual form of words.

'As the oldest member of Chambers, I can remember this set before C. H. Wystan, Rumpole's revered father-in-law, took over. It was in old Barnaby Hawks' time and the young men were myself, Everett Longbarrow, and old Willoughby Grime, who became Lord Chief Justice of Basutoland . . . He went on Circuit, I understand, wearing a battered opera hat and dispensed rough justice . . .'

The other barristers joined in the well-known chorus 'Under a Bong Tree'.

'As I remember, Ida Tempest got three years.'

'Yes,' said George.

'Her former husband got seven.' I was trying to cheer him up. 'I don't believe Ida actually applied the match.'

'All the same, it was a risk I didn't feel able to take.'

'You didn't notice the smell of burning, George? Any night in the Royal Borough Hotel . . .?'

'Of course not! But the Lord Chancellor's secretary had just told me of my appointment. It doesn't do for a judge's wife to have done three years, even with full remission.'

I looked at George. Was the sacrifice, I wondered, really necessary? 'Did you *have* to be a judge, George?'

'I thought of that, of course. But I had the appointment. You know, at my age, Rumpole, it's difficult to learn any new sort of trade.'

'We had no work in those days,' Uncle Tom continued his trip down memory lane. 'We had no briefs of any kind. We spent our days practising chip shots, trying to get an old golf ball into the waste-paper basket with . . .'

'A mashie niblick!' the other barristers sang.

'Well, that was as good as training as any for life at the Bar,' Uncle Tom told them.

I filled George's glass. 'Drink up, George. There may be other ladies . . . turning up at the Royal Borough Hotel.'

'I very much doubt it. Every night when I sit at the table for one, I shall think – if only I'd never taken her to dinner at Rumpole's! Then I might never have known, don't you see? We could have been perfectly happy together.'

'Of course. C. H. Wystan never ever took silk. But now we have a Q.C., M.P. and dear old George Frobisher, a Circus, beg his pardon, a Circuit Judge!' Uncle Tom was raising his glass to George, his hand was trembling and he was spilling a good deal on his cuff.

'Sometimes I feel it will be difficult to forgive you, Rumpole,' George said, very quietly.

'But I do recall when dear old Willoughby Grime was appointed to Basutoland, we celebrated the matter in song.'

'George, what did I do?' I protested. 'I didn't say anything.' But it wasn't true. My mere existence had been enough to deny George his happiness.

At which point the other barristers raised their glasses to George and started to sing 'For He's a Jolly Good Fellow'. I left them, and went out into the silence of the Temple, where I could still hear them singing.

Next Saturday morning I was acting the part of the native bearer with the Vim basket, following She Who Must Be Obeyed on our ritual shopping expedition.

'They've never made George Frobisher a judge!' My wife seemed to feel it an occasion for ridicule and contempt.

'In my view an excellent appointment. I shall expect to have a good record of acquittals. In the Luton Crown Court.'

'When are they going to make you a judge, Rumpole?'

'Don't ask silly questions . . . I'd start every Sentence with, "There but for the Grace of God goes Horace Rumpole".'

'I can imagine what *she's* feeling like.' Hilda sniffed.

'She . . .?'

'The cat-that-swallowed-the-cream! Her Honour Mrs Judge. Mrs Ida Tempest'll think she's quite the thing, I'll be bound.'

'No. She's gone.'

'Gone, Rumpole? What did George say about that?'

> 'Cried, and the world cried too, "Our's the Treasure".
> Suddenly, as rare things will, she vanished.'

We climbed on a bus, heavily laden, back to Casa Rumpole.
'George is well out of it, if he wants my opinion.'

'I don't think he does.'

'What?'

'Want your opinion.'

Later, in our kitchen, as she stored the Vim away under the sink and I prepared our Saturday morning G and T, a thought occurred to me. 'Do you know? I'm not sure I should've taken up as a lawyer.'

'Whatever do you mean?'

'Perhaps I should have taken up as a vicar.'

'Rumpole. Have you been getting at the gin already?'

'Faith not facts, is what we need, do you think?'

Hilda was busy unpacking the saucepan scourers. Perhaps she didn't quite get my drift.

'George Frobisher has always been a bad influence, keeping you out drinking,' she said. 'Let's hope I'll be seeing more of you, now he's been made a judge.'

'I'd never have to know all these *facts* about people if I hadn't set up as a lawyer.'

'Of course you should have been a lawyer, Rumpole!'

'Why exactly?'

'If you hadn't set up as a lawyer, if you hadn't gone into Daddy's Chambers, you'd never have met me, Rumpole!'

I looked at her, suddenly seeing great vistas of what my life might have been.

'That's true,' I said. 'Dammit, that's very true.'

'Put the Gumption away for me, will you, Rumpole?'

She Who Must Be Obeyed. Of course I did.

Rumpole and the Showfolk

I have written elsewhere of my old clerk Albert Handyside who served me very well for a long term of years, being adept at flattering solicitors' clerks, buying them glasses of Guinness and inquiring tenderly after their tomato plants, with the result that the old darlings were inclined to come across with the odd Dangerous and Careless, Indecent Assault, or Take and Drive Away which Albert was inclined to slip in Rumpole's direction. All this led to higher things such as Robbery, Unlawful Wounding and even Murder; and in general for that body of assorted crimes on which my reputation is founded. I first knew Albert when he was a nervous office boy in the Chambers of C. H. Wystan, my learned father-in-law; and when he grew to be a head clerk of magisterial dimensions we remained firm friends and often had a jar together in Pommeroy's Wine Bar in the evenings, on which relaxed occasions I would tell Albert my celebrated anecdotes of Bench and Bar and, unlike She Who Must Be Obeyed, he was always kind enough to laugh no matter how often he had heard them before.

Dear old Albert had one slight failing, a weakness which occurs among the healthiest of constitutions. He was apt to get into a terrible flurry over the petty cash. I never inquired into his book-keeping system; but I believe it might have been improved by the invention of the Abacus, or a monthly check-up by a Primary School child well versed in simple addition. It is also indubitably true that you can't pour drink down the throats of solicitors' managing clerks without some form of subsidy, and I'm sure Albert dipped liberally into the petty cash for this purpose as well as to keep himself in the large Bells and sodas, two or three of which sufficed for his simple lunch. Personally I never begrudged Albert any of this grant in aid, but ugly words such as embezzlement were uttered by Erskine-Brown and others, and, spurred on by our second clerk Harry who clearly thirsted for promotion, my learned friends were induced to part with Albert Handyside. I missed him very much. Our new clerk Henry goes to Pommeroy's with our typist Dianne, and tells her about his exploits when on holiday with the *Club Méditerranée* in Corfu. I do not think either of them would laugh at my legal anecdotes.

After he left us Albert shook the dust of London from his shoes and went up North, to some God-lost place called Grimble, and there joined a firm of solicitors as managing clerk. No doubt Northerly barristers' clerks bought him Guinness and either he had no control of the petty cash or the matter was not subjected to too close an inspection. From time to time he sent me a Christmas card on which was inscribed among the bells and holly 'Compliments of the Season, Mr Rumpole, sir. And I'm going to bring you up here for a nice little murder just as soon as I get the opportunity. Yours respectfully, A. Handyside.' At long last a brief did arrive. Mr Rumpole was asked to appear at the Grimble Assizes, to be held before Mr Justice Skelton in the Law Courts, Grimble: the title of the piece being the Queen (she does keep enormously busy prosecuting people) *versus* Margaret Hartley. The only item on the programme was 'Wilful Murder'.

Now you may have noticed that certain theatrical phrases have crept into the foregoing paragraphs. This is not as inappropriate as it may sound, for the brief I was going up to Grimble for on the Inter-City train (a journey about as costly as a trip across the Atlantic) concerned a murder which took place in the Theatre Royal, East Grimble, a place of entertainment leased by the 'Frere-Hartley Players': the victim was one G. P. Frere, the leading actor, and my client was his wife known as 'Maggie Hartley', co-star and joint director of the company. And as I read on into R. *v.* Hartley it became clear that the case was like too many of Rumpole's, a born loser: that is to say that unless we drew a drunken prosecutor or a jury of anarchists there seemed no reasonable way in which it might be won.

One night after the performance, Albert's instructions told me, the stage-door keeper, a Mr Croft, heard the sound of raised voices and quarrelling from the dressing-room shared by G. P. Frere and his wife Maggie Hartley. Mr Croft was having a late cup of tea in his cubby-hole with a Miss Catherine Hope, a young actress in the company, and they heard two shots fired in quick succession. Mr Croft went along the passage to investigate and opened the dressing-room door. The scene that met his eyes was, to say the least, dramatic.

It appeared from Mr Croft's evidence that the dressing-room was in a state of considerable confusion. Clothes were scattered round the room, and chairs overturned. The long mirror which ran down the length of the wall was shattered at the end furthest from the door. Near the door Mr G. P. Frere, wearing a silk dressing-gown, was sitting slumped in a chair, bleeding profusely and already dead. My client was standing half-way down the room still wearing the long white evening-dress she had worn on the stage that night. Her make-up was smudged and in her right hand she held a well-oiled service revolver. A bullet had left this weapon and entered Mr Frere's body between the third and fourth metacarpal. In order to make quite sure that her learned Counsel didn't have things too easy, Maggie Hartley had then opened her mouth and spoken, so said Croft, the following unforgettable words, here transcribed without punctuation.

'I killed him what could I do with him help me.'

In all subsequent interviews the actress said that she remembered nothing about the quarrel in the dressing-room, the dreadful climax had been blotted from her mind. She was no doubt, and still remained, in a state of shock.

I was brooding on this hopeless defence when an elderly guard acting the part of an air hostess whispered excitedly into the intercom. 'We are now arriving at Grimble Central. Grimble Central. Please collect your hand baggage.' I merged into a place which seemed to be nestling somewhere within the Arctic Circle, the air bit sharply, it was bloody cold, and a blue-nosed Albert was there to meet me.

*

'After I left your Chambers in disgrace, Mr Rumpole . . .'

'After a misunderstanding, shall we say.'

'My then wife told me she was disgusted with me. She packed her bags and went to live with her married sister in Enfield.'

Albert was smiling contentedly, and that was something I could understand. I had just had, *à coté de* Chez Albert Handyside, a meal which his handsome, still youngish second wife referred to as tea, but which had all the appurtenances of an excellent cold luncheon with the addition of hot scones, Dundee cake and strawberry jam.

'Bit of luck then really, you getting the petty cash so "confused".'

'All the same. I do miss the old days clerking for you in the Temple, sir. How are things down South, Mr Rumpole?'

'Down South? Much as usual. Barristers lounging about in the sun. Munching grapes to the lazy sounds of plucked guitars.'

Mrs Handyside the Second returned to the room with another huge pot of dark brown Indian tea. She replenished the Rumpole cup and Albert and I fell to discussing the tea-table subject of murder and sudden death.

'Of course it's not the Penge Bungalow Job.' Albert was referring to my most notable murder and greatest triumph, a case I did at Lewes Assizes alone and without the so-called aid of leading Counsel. 'But it's quite a decent little case, sir, in its way. A murder among the showfolk, as they terms them.'

'The showfolk, yes. Definitely worth the detour. There is, of course, one little fly in the otherwise interesting ointment.'

Albert, knowing me as he did, knew quite well what manner of insect I was referring to. I have never taken silk. I remain, at my advanced age, a 'junior' barrister. The brief in R. *v*. Hartley had only one drawback, it announced that I was to be 'led' by a local silk, Mr Jarvis Allen, Q.C. I hated the prospect of this obscure North Country Queen's Counsel getting all the fun.

'I told my senior partner, sir. I told him straight. Mr Rumpole's quite capable of doing this one on his own.' Albert was suitably apologetic.

'Reminded him, did you? I did the Penge Bungalow Murders alone and without a leader.'

'The senior partner did seem to feel . . .'

'I know. I'm not on the Lord Chancellor's guest list. I never get invited to breakfast in knee breeches. It's not Rumpole, Q.C. Just Rumpole, Queer Customer . . .'

'Oo I'm sure you're not,' Mrs Handyside the Second poured me another comforting cup of concentrated tannin.

'It's a murder, sir. That's attracted quite a lot of local attention.'

'And silks go with murder like steak goes with kidney! This Jarvis Allen, Q.C. . . . Pretty competent sort of man, is he?'

'I've only seen him on the Bench . . .'

'On the what?'

The Bench seemed no sort of a place to see dedicated defenders.

'Sits as Recorder here. Gave a young tearaway in our office three years for a punch-up at the Grimble United Ground.'

'There's no particular *art* involved in getting people into prison, Albert,' I said severely. 'How is he at keeping them out?'

After tea we had a conference fixed up with my leader and client in prison. There was no women's prison at Grimble, so our client was lodged in a room converted from an unused dispensary in the Hospital Wing of the masculine nick. She seemed older than I had expected as she sat looking composed, almost detached, surrounded by her legal advisers. It was, at that first conference, as though the case concerned someone else, and had not yet engaged her full attention.

'Mrs Frere.' Jarvis Allen, the learned Q.C. started off. He was a thin, methodical man with rimless glasses and a general rimless appearance. He had made a voluminous note in red, green and blue Biro: it didn't seem to have given him much cause for hope.

'Our client is known as Maggie Hartley, sir,' Albert reminded him. 'In the profession.'

'I think she'd better be known as Mrs Frere. In Court,' Allen said firmly. 'Now, Mrs Frere. Tommy Pierce is prosecuting and of course I know him well . . . and if we went to see the judge, Skelton's a perfectly reasonable fellow. I think there's a sporting chance . . . I'm making no promises, mind you, there's a sporting chance they might let us plead to manslaughter!'

He brought the last sentence out triumphantly, like a Christmas present. Jarvis Allen was exercising his remarkable talent for getting people locked up. I lit a small cigar, and said nothing.

'Of course, we'd have to accept manslaughter. I'm sure Mr Rumpole agrees. You agree, don't you, Rumpole?' My leader turned to me for support. I gave him little comfort.

'Much more agreeable doing ten years for manslaughter than ten years for murder,' I said. 'Is that the choice you're offering?'

'I don't know if you've read the evidence ... Our client was found with the gun in her hand.' Allen was beginning to get tetchy.

I thought this over and said, 'Stupid place to have it. If she'd actually *planned* a murder.'

'All the same. It leaves us without a defence.'

'Really? Do you think so? I was looking at the statement of Alan Copeland. He is ...' I ferreted among the depositions.

'What they call the "juvenile", I believe, Mr Rumpole,' Albert reminded me.

'The "juvenile", yes.' I read from Mr Copeland's statement. 'I've worked with G. P. Frere for three seasons ... G.P. drank a good deal. Always interested in some girl in the cast. A new one every year ...'

'Jealousy might be a powerful motive, for our client. That's a two-edged sword, Rumpole.' Allen was determined to look on the dreary side.

'Two-edged, yes. Most swords are.' I went on reading. 'He quarrelled violently with his wife, Maggie Hartley. On one occasion, after the dress rehearsal of *The Master Builder*, he threw a glass of milk stout in her face in front of the entire company ...'

'She had a good deal of provocation, we can put that to the judge. That merely reduces it to manslaughter.' I was getting bored with my leader's chatter of manslaughter.

I gave my bundle of depositions to Albert and stood up, looking at our client to see if she would fit the part I had in mind.

'What you need in a murder is an unlikeable corpse ... Then if you can find a likeable defendant ... you're off to the races! Who knows? We might even reduce the crime to innocence.'

'Rumpole.' Allen had clearly had enough of my hopeless optimism. 'As I've had to tell Mrs Frere very frankly. There is a clear admission of guilt – which is not disputed.'

'What she said to the stage-door man, Mr . . .'

'Croft.' Albert supplied the name.

'I killed him, what could I do with him? Help me.' Allen repeated the most damning evidence with great satisfaction. 'You've read that, at least?'

'Yes, I've read it. That's the trouble.'

'What *do* you mean?'

'I mean, the trouble is, I read it. I didn't *hear* it. None of us did. And I don't suppose Mr Croft had it spelled out to him, with all the punctuation.'

'Really, Rumpole. I suppose they make jokes about murder cases in London.'

I ignored this bit of impertinence and went on to give the Q.C. some unmerited assistance. 'Suppose she said . . . Suppose our client said, "I killed him" and then,' I paused for breath, '"What could I do with him? Help me!"?'

I saw our client look at me, for the first time. When she spoke her voice, like Cordelia's, was ever soft, gentle and low, an excellent thing in woman.

'That's the reading,' she said. I must admit I was puzzled, and asked for an explanation.

'What?'

'The reading of the line. You can tell them. That's exactly how I said it.'

At last, it seemed, we had found *something* she remembered. I thought it an encouraging sign; but it wasn't really my business.

'I'm afraid, dear lady,' I gave her a small bow, 'I shan't be able to tell them anything. Who am I, after all, but the ageing juvenile? The reading of the line, as you call it, will have to come from your Q.C., Mr Jarvis Allen, who is playing the lead at the moment.'

After the conference I gave Albert strict instructions as to how our client was to dress for her starring appearance in the Grimble Assize Court (plain black suit, white blouse, no make-

THE THEATRE ROYAL, EAST GRIMBLE

The Frere-Hartley Players
present
G. P. Frere and Maggie Hartley

in

'PRIVATE LIVES'

by

NOËL COWARD

with

**Alan Copeland
Catherine Hope**

Directed by Daniel Derwent

Stalls £1.50 and £1. Circle £1 and 75p.
Matinées and Senior Citizens 50p.

up, hair neat, voice gentle but audible to any O.A.P. with a
National Health deaf-aid sitting in the back row of the jury,
absolutely no reaction during the prosecution case except for a
well-controlled sigh of grief at the mention of her deceased
husband) and then I suggested we met later for a visit to the
scene of the crime. Her Majesty's Counsel for the defence had to
rush home to write an urgent, and no doubt profitable, opinion
on the planning of the new Grimble Gas Works and so was
unfortunately unable to join us.

'You go if you like, Rumpole,' he said as he vanished into a
funereal Austin Princess. 'I can't see how it's going to be of the
slightest assistance.'

The Theatre Royal, an ornate but crumbling Edwardian
Music Hall, which might once have housed George Formby and
Rob Wilton, was bolted and barred. Albert and I stood in the
rain and read a torn poster.

A cat was rubbing itself against the poster. We heard the
North Country voice of an elderly man calling 'Puss . . . Puss . . .
Bedtime, pussy.'

The cat went and we followed, round to the corner where the
stage-door man, Mr Croft, no doubt, was opening his door and
offering a saucer of milk. We made ourselves known as a couple
of lawyers and asked for a look at the scene.

'Mr Derwent's round the front of the house. First door on the
right.'

I moved up the corridor to a door and, opening it, had the
unnerving experience of standing on a dimly lit stage. Behind
me flapped a canvas balcony, and a view of the Mediterranean.
As I wandered forward a voice called me out of the gloom.

'Who is it? Down here, I'm in the Stalls Bar.'

There was a light somewhere, a long way off. I went down
some steps that led to the stalls and felt my way towards the
light with Albert blundering after me. At last we reached the
open glass door of a small bar, its dark-red walls hung with
photographs of the company, and we were in the presence of a
little gnome-like man, wearing a bow tie and a double-breasted
suit, and that cheerily smiling but really quite expressionless
apple-cheeked sort of face you see on some ventriloquist's dolls.

His boot-black hair looked as if it had been dyed. He admitted to Albert that he was Daniel Derwent and at the moment in charge of the Frere-Hartley Players.

'Or what's left of them. Decimated, that's what we've been! If you've come with a two-hander for a couple of rather untalented juveniles, I'd be delighted to put it on. I suppose you *are* in the business.'

'The business?' I wondered what business he meant. But I didn't wonder long.

'Show business. The profession.'

'No ... Another ... profession altogether.'

I saw he had been working at a table in the empty bar, which was smothered with papers, bills and receipts.

'Our old manager left us in a state of total confusion,' Derwent said. 'And my ear's out to *here* answering the telephone.'

'The vultures can't hear of an actor shot in East Grimble but half the Character Men in *Spotlight* are after me for the job. Well, I've told everyone. Nothing's going to be decided till after Maggie's trial. We're not re-opening till then. It wouldn't seem right, somehow. *What* other profession?'

'We're lawyers, Mr Derwent,' Albert told him. 'Defending.'

'Maggie's case?' Derwent didn't stop smiling.

'My name's Handyside of Instructing Solicitors. This is Mr Rumpole from London, junior Counsel for the defence.'

'A London barrister. In the Sticks!' The little Thespian seemed to find it amusing. 'Well, Grimble's hardly a number-one touring date. All the same, I suppose murder's a draw. Anywhere ... Care for a tiny rum?'

'That's very kind.' It was bitter cold, the unused theatre seemed to be saving on central heating and I was somewhat sick at heart at the prospect of our defence. A rum would do me no harm at all.

'Drop of orange in it? Or as she comes?'

'As she comes, thank you.'

'I always take a tiny rum, for the chords. Well, we depend on the chords, don't we, in our professions.'

Apart from a taste for rum, I didn't see then what I had in common, professionally or otherwise, with Mr Derwent. I wandered off with my drink in my hand to look at the photographs of the Frere-Hartley Players. As I did so I could hear the theatre-manager chattering to Albert.

'We could have done a bomb tonight. The money we've turned away. You couldn't buy publicity like it.' Derwent was saying.

'No ... No, I don't suppose you could.'

'Week after week all we get in the *Grimble Argus* is a little para. "Maggie Hartley took her part well." And now we're all over the front page. And we can't play. It breaks your heart. It does really.' I heard him freshen his rum with another slug from the bottle. 'Poor old G.P. could have drawn more money dead than he ever could when he was alive. Well, at least he's sober tonight, wherever he is.'

'The late Mr G. P. Frere was fond of a drink occasionally?' Albert made use of the probing understatement.

'Not that his performance suffered. He didn't act any worse when he was drunk.'

I was looking at a glossy photograph of the late Mr G. P. Frere, taken about ten years ago I should imagine: it showed a man with grey sideburns and an open-necked shirt with a silk scarf round his neck and eyes that were self-consciously quizzical. A man who, despite the passage of the years, was still determined to go on saying 'Who's for tennis?'

'What I admired about old G.P.,' I heard Derwent say, 'was his selfless concern for others! Never left you with the sole responsibility of entertaining the audience. He'd try to help by upstaging you. Or moving on your laugh line. He once tore up a newspaper all through my long speech in *Waiting for Godot* ... Now you wouldn't do that, would you, Mr Rumpole? Not in anyone's long speech. Well, of course not.'

He had moved, for his last remarks, to a point rather below, but still too close to, my left ear. I was looking at the photographs of a moderately pretty young girl, wearing a seafaring sweater, whose lips were parted as if to suck in a quick draft of ozone when out for a day with the local dinghy club.

'Miss Christine Hope?' I asked.

'Miss Christine Hopeless I called her.' This Derwent didn't seem to have a particularly high opinion of his troupe. 'God

knows what G.P. saw in her. She did that audition speech from
St Joan. All breathless and excited . . . as if she'd just run up
four flights of stairs because the angel voices were calling her
about a little part in *Crossroads*. "We could *do* something with
her," G.P. said. "I know what," I told him. "Burn her at the
stake."'

I had come to a wall on which there were big photographs of
various characters, a comic charlady, a beautiful woman in a
white evening-dress, a Duchess in a tiara, a neat secretary in
glasses, and a tattered siren who might have been Sadie Thomp-
son in *Rain* if my theatrical memory served me right. All the
faces were different, and they were all the faces of Maggie Hartley.

'Your client. My leading lady. I suppose *both* our shows
depend on her.' Derwent was looking at the photographs with a
rapt smile of appreciation. 'No doubt about it. She's good.
Maggie's good.'

I turned to look at him, found him much too close and retreated
a step. 'What do you mean,' I asked him, 'by good exactly?'

'There is a quality. Of perfect truthfulness. Absolute reality.'

'Truthfulness?' This was about the first encouraging thing
we'd heard about Maggie Hartley.

'It's very rare.'

'Excuse me, sir. Would you be prepared to say that in Court?'
Albert seemed to be about to take a statement. I moved tactfully
away.

'Is that what you came here for?' Derwent asked me nervously.

I thought it over, and decided there was no point in turning a
friendly source of information into a hostile witness.

'No. We wanted to see . . . the scene of the crime.'

At which Mr Derwent, apparently reassured, smiled again.
'The Last Act,' he said and led us to the dressing-room, typical
of a provincial rep. 'I'll unlock it for you.'

The dressing-room had been tidied up, the cupboards and
drawers were empty. Otherwise it looked like the sort of room
that would have been condemned as unfit for human habitation
by any decent local authority. I stood in the doorway, and made

sure that the mirror which went all along one side of the room was shattered in the corner furthest away from me.

'Any help to you, is it?'

'It might be. It's what we lawyers call the *locus in quo*.'

Mr Derwent was positively giggling then.

'Do you? How frightfully camp of you. It's what we actors call a dressing-room.'

So I went back to the Majestic Hotel, a building which seemed rather less welcoming than Her Majesty's Prison, Grimble. And when I was breaking my fast on their mixed grill consisting of cold greasy bacon, a stunted tomato and a sausage that would have looked ungenerous on a cocktail stick, Albert rang me with the unexpected news that at one bound put the Theatre Royal Killing up beside the Penge Bungalow Murders in the Pantheon of Rumpole's forensic triumphs. I was laughing when I came back from the telephone, and I was still laughing when I returned to spread, on a slice of blackened toast, that pat of margarine which the management of the Majestic were apparently unable to tell from butter.

Two hours later we were in the judges' room at the Law Courts discussing, in the hushed tones of relatives after a funeral, the unfortunate event which had occurred. Those present were Tommy Pierce, Q.C., Counsel for the prosecution, and his junior Roach, the learned judge, my learned leader and my learned self.

'Of course these people don't really live in the real world at all,' Jarvis Allen, Q.C., was saying. 'It's all make-believe for them. Dressing up in fancy costumes . . .'

He himself was wearing a wig, a tailed coat with braided cuffs and a silk gown. His opponent, also bewigged, had a huge stomach from which a gold watch-chain and seal dangled. He also took snuff and blew his nose in a red spotted handkerchief. That kind and, on the whole, gentle figure Skelton J. was fishing in the folds of his scarlet gown for a bitten pipe and an old leather pouch. I didn't think we were exactly the ones to talk about dressing up.

'You don't think she appreciates the seriousness,' the judge was clearly worried.

'I'm afraid not, Judge. Still, if she wants to sack me . . . Of course it puts Rumpole in an embarrassing position.'

'Are you embarrassed, Rumpole?' His Lordship asked me.

As a matter of fact I was filled with a deeper inner joy, for Albert's call at breakfast had been to the effect that our client had chosen to dismiss her leading Counsel and put her future entirely in the hands of Horace Rumpole, B.A., that timeless member of the Junior Bar.

'Oh yes. Dreadfully embarrassed, Judge.' I did my best to look suitably modest. 'But it seems that the lady's mind is quite made up.'

'Very embarrassing for you. For you both.' The judge was understanding. 'Does she give any reason for dispensing with her leading Counsel, Jarvis?'

'She said . . .' I turned a grin into a cough. I too remembered what Albert had told us. 'She said she thought Rumpole was "better casting".'

' "Better casting"? Whatever can she mean by that?'

'Better in the part, Judge,' I translated.

'Oh dear.' The judge looked distressed. 'Is she very actressy?'

'She's an actress,' I admitted, but would go no further.

'Yes. Yes, I suppose she is.' The judge lit his pipe. 'Do you have any views about this, Tommy?'

'No, Judge. When Jarvis was instructed we were going to ask your views on a plea to manslaughter.'

The portly Pierce twinkled a lot and talked in a rich North Country accent. I could see we were in for a prosecution of homely fun, like one of the comic plays of J. B. Priestley.

'Manslaughter, eh? Do you want to discuss manslaughter, Rumpole?' I appeared to give the matter some courteous consideration.

'No, Judge, I don't believe I do.'

'If you'd like an adjournment you shall certainly have it. Your client may want to think about manslaughter . . . Or consider another leader. She should have leading Counsel. In a case of this . . .' the judge puffed out smoke . . . 'seriousness.'

'Oh, I don't think there's much point in considering another leader.'

'You don't?'

'You see,' I was doing my best not to look at Allen, 'I don't honestly think anyone else would get the part.'

When we got out of the judges' room, and were crossing the imposing Victorian Gothic hallway that led to the Court, my learned ex-leader, who had preserved an expression of amused detachment up to that point, turned on me with considerable hurt.

'I must say I take an extremely dim view of that.'

'Really?'

'An extremely dim view. On this Circuit we have a tradition of loyalty to our leaders.'

'It's a local custom?'

'Certainly it is.' Allen stood still and pronounced solemnly. 'I can't imagine anyone on this Circuit carrying on with a case after his leader has been sacked. It's not in the best traditions of the Bar.'

'Loyalty to one's leader. Yes, of course, that is extremely important ...' I thought about it. 'But we must consider the other great legal maxim, mustn't we?'

'Legal maxim? What legal maxim?'

'"The show must go on." Excuse me. I see Albert. Nice chatting to you but ... Things to do, old darling. Quite a number of things to do ...' So I hurried away from the fired legal eagle to where my old clerk was standing, looking distinctly anxious, at the entrance of the Court. He asked me hopefully if the judge had seen fit to grant an adjournment, so that he could persuade our client to try another silk, a course on which Albert's senior partner was particularly keen.

'Oh dear,' I had to disappoint him. 'I begged the judge, Albert. I almost went down on my knees to him. But would he grant me an adjournment? I'm afraid not. No, Rumpole, he told me, the show must go on.' I put a comforting hand on Albert's shoulder. 'Cheer up, old darling. There's only one thing you need say to your senior partner.'

'What's that, sir?'

'The Penge Bungalow Murders.'

I sounded supremely confident of course; but as I went into Court I suddenly remembered that without a leader I would have absolutely no one to blame but myself when things went wrong.

'I don't know if any of you ladies and gentlemen have actually attended *performances* at the Theatre Royal . . .' Tommy Pierce, Q.C., opening the case for the prosecution, chuckled as though to say 'Most of us got better things to do, haven't we, members of the jury?' 'But we all have passed it going up the Makins Road in a trolley-bus on the way to Grimble Football Ground. You'll know where it is, members of the jury. Past the Snellsham Roundabout, on the corner opposite the Old Britannia Hotel, where we've all celebrated many a win by Grimble United . . .'

I didn't know why he didn't just tell them: 'The prisoner's represented by Rumpole of the Bailey, a smart-alecky lawyer from London, who's never ever heard of Grimble United, let alone the Old Britannia Hotel.' I shut my eyes and looked un-interested as Tommy rumbled on, switching, now, to portentous seriousness.

'In this case, members of the jury, we enter an alien world. The world of the showfolk! They live a strange life, you may think. A life of make-believe. On the surface everyone loves each other. "You were wonderful, darling!" said to men and women alike . . .'

I seriously considered heaving myself to my hind legs to pro-test against this rubbish, but decided to sit still and continue the look of bored indifference.

'But underneath all the good companionship,' Pierce was now trying to make the flesh creep, 'run deep tides of jealousy and passion which welled up, in this particular case, members of the jury, into brutal and, say the Crown, quite cold-blooded murder . . .'

As he went on I thought that Derwent, the little gnome from the theatre, whom I could now see in the back of the Pit, some-where near the dock, was perfectly right. Murder *is* a draw. All the local nobs were in Court including the judge's wife Lady Skelton, in the front row of the Stalls, wearing her special matinée hat. I also saw the Sheriff of the County, in his fancy dress, wearing lace ruffles and a sword which stuck rather inconveniently between his legs, and Mrs Sheriff of the County, searching in her handbag for something which might well have been her opera glasses. And then, behind me, the star of the show, my client, looking as I told her to look. Ordinary.

'This is not a case which depends on complicated evidence, members of the jury, or points of law. Let me tell you the facts.'

The facts were not such that I wanted the jury to hear them too clearly, at least not in my learned friend's version. I slowly, and quite noisily, took a page out of my notebook. I was grateful to see that some of the members of the jury glanced in my direction.

'It simply amounts to this. The murder weapon, a Smith and Wesson revolver, was found in the defendant's hand as she stood over her husband's dead body. A bullet from the very weapon had entered between the third and fourth metacarpal!'

I didn't like Pierce's note of triumph as he said this. Accordingly I began to tear my piece of paper into very small strips. More members of the jury looked in my direction.

'Ladies and gentlemen. The defendant, as you will see on your abstract of indictment, was charged as "Maggie Hartley". It seems she prefers to be known by her maiden name, and that may give you some idea of the woman's attitude to her husband of some twenty years, the deceased in this case, the late Gerald Patrick Frere...'

At which point, gazing round the Court, I saw Daniel Derwent. He actually winked, and I realized that he thought he recognized my paper-tearing as an old ham actor's trick. I stopped doing it immediately.

'It were a mess. A right mess. Glass broken, blood. He was sprawled in the chair. I thought he were drunk for a moment, but he weren't. And she had this pistol, like, in her hand.' Mr Croft, the stage-doorman was standing in the witness-box in his best blue suit. The jury clearly liked him, just as they disliked the picture he was painting.

'Can you remember what she said?' The learned prosecutor prompted him gently.

'Not too fast ...' Mr Justice Skelton was, worse luck, preparing himself to write it all down.

'Just follow His Lordship's pencil ...' said Pierce, and the judicial pencil prepared to follow Mr Croft.

'She said, "I killed him, what could I do with him?"'

'What did you understand that to mean?'

I did hoist myself to my hind legs then, and registered a determined objection. 'It isn't what this witness understood it to mean. It's what the jury understands it to mean ...'

'My learned friend's quite wrong. The witness was there. He could form his own conclusion ...'

'Please, gentlemen. Let's try and have no disagreements, at least not before luncheon,' said the judge sweetly, and added, less charmingly, 'I think Mr Croft may answer the question.'

'I understood her to say she was so fed up with him, she didn't know what else to do ...'

'But to kill him ...?' Only the judge could have supplied that and he did it with another charming smile.

'Yes, my Lord.'

'Did she say anything else? That you remember?'

'I think she said, "Help me."'

'Yes. Just wait there, will you? In case Mr Rumpole has some questions.'

'Just a few ...' I rose to my feet. Here was an extremely dangerous witness whom the jury liked. It was no good making a head-on attack. The only way was to lure Mr Croft politely into my parlour. I gave the matter some thought and then tried a line on which I thought we might reach agreement.

'When you saw the deceased, Frere, slumped in the chair, your first thought was that he was drunk?'

'Yes.'

'Had you seen him slumped in a chair drunk in his dressing-room on many occasions?'

'A few.' Mr Croft answered with a knowing smile, and I felt encouraged.

'On most nights?'

'Some nights.'

'Were there some nights when he *wasn't* the worse for drink? Did he ever celebrate, with an evening of sobriety?'

I got my first smile from the jury, and the Joker for the prosecution arose in full solemnity.

'My Lord . . .'

Before Tommy Pierce could interrupt the proceedings with a speech I bowled the next question.

'Mr Croft. When you came into the dressing-room, the deceased Frere was nearest the door . . .'

'Yes. Only a couple of feet from me . . . I saw . . .'

'You saw my client was standing half-way down the room?' I asked, putting a stop to further painful details. 'Holding the gun.'

Pierce gave the jury a meaningful stare, emphasizing the evidence.

'The dressing-room mirror stretches all the way along the wall. And it was broken at the far end, away from the door?'

'Yes.'

'So to have fired the bullet that broke that end of the glass, my client would have had to turn away from the deceased and shoot behind her back . . .' I swung round, by way of demonstration, and made a gesture, firing behind me. Of course I couldn't do that without bringing the full might of the prosecution to its feet.

'Surely that's a question for the jury to decide.'

'The witness was there. He can form his own conclusions.' I quoted the wisdom of my learned friend. 'What's the answer?'

'I suppose she would,' Croft said thoughtfully and the jury looked interested.

The judge cleared his throat and leaned forward, smiling politely, and being as it turned out, surprisingly unhelpful.

'Wouldn't that depend, Mr Rumpole, on where the deceased was at the time that particular shot was fired . . .?'

Pierce glowed in triumph and muttered 'Exactly!' I did a polite bow and went quickly on to the next question.

'Perhaps we could turn now to the little matter of what she said when you went into the room.'

'I can remember that perfectly.'

'The words, yes. It's the reading that matters.'

'The *what*, Mr Rumpole?' said the judge, betraying theatrical ignorance.

'The stress, my Lord. The intonation . . . It's an expression used in show business.'

'Perhaps we should confine ourselves to expressions used in Law Courts, Mr Rumpole.'

'Certainly, my Lord.' I re-addressed the witness. 'She said she'd killed him. And then, after a pause, "What could I do with him. Help me."'

Mr Croft frowned. 'I . . . That is, yes.'

'Meaning. What could I do with his dead body, and asking for your help . . .?'

'My Lord. That's surely . . .' Tommy Pierce was on his hind legs, and I gave him another quotation from himself.

'He was there!' I leant forward and smiled at Croft trying to make him feel that I was a friend he could trust.

'She never meant that she had killed him because she didn't know what to do with him?'

There was a long silence. Counsel for the prosecution let out a deep breath and subsided like a balloon slowly settling. The judge nudged the witness gently. 'Well. What's the answer, Mr Croft? Did she . . .?'

'I . . . I can't be sure how she said it, my Lord.'

And there, on a happy note of reasonable doubt, I left it. As I came out of Court and crossed the entrance hall on my way to the cells I was accosted by the beaming Mr Daniel Derwent, who was, it seemed, anxious to congratulate me.

'What a performance, Mr Rumpole. Knock-out! You were wonderful? What I admired so was the timing. The pause, before you started the cross-examination.'

'Pause?'

'You took a beat of nine seconds. I counted.'

'Did I really?'

'Built-up tension, of course. I could see what you were after.' He put a hand on my sleeve, a red hand with big rings and polished fingernails. 'You really must let me know. If ever you want a job in Rep.'

I dislodged my fan club and went down the narrow staircase to the cells. The time had clearly come for my client to start remembering.

Maggie Hartley smiled at me over her untouched tray of vegetable pie. She even asked me how I was; but I had no time for small talk. It was zero hour, the last moment I had to get some reasonable instructions.

'Listen to me. Whatever you do or don't remember ... it's just impossible for you to have stood there and fired the first shot.'

'The first shot?' She frowned, as if at some distant memory.

'The one that *didn't* kill him. The one that went behind you. He must have fired that. He *must* ...'

'Yes.' She nodded her head. That was encouraging. So far as it went.

'Why the hell ... why in the name of sanity didn't you tell us that before?'

'I waited. Until there was someone I could trust.'

'Me?'

'Yes. You, Mr Rumpole.'

There's nothing more flattering than to be trusted, even by a confirmed and hopeless villain (which is why I find it hard to dislike a client), and I was convinced Maggie Hartley wasn't that. I sat down beside her in the cell and, with Albert taking notes, she started to talk. What she said was disjointed, sometimes incoherent, and God knows how it was going to sound in the witness-box, but given a few more breaks in the prosecution case, and a following wind I was beginning to get the sniff of a defence.

One, two, three, four ...

Mr Alan Copeland, the juvenile lead, had just given his evidence-in-chief for the prosecution. He seemed a pleasant enough young man, wearing a tie and a dark suit (good witness-box clothing) and his evidence hadn't done us any particular harm. All the same I was trying what the director Derwent had admired as the devastating pause.

Seven . . . eight . . . nine . . .

'Have you any questions, Mr Rumpole?' The judge sounded as if he was getting a little impatient with 'the timing'. I launched the cross-examination.

'Mr Alan . . . Copeland. You know the deceased man owned a Smith and Wesson revolver? Do you know where he got it?'

'He was in a spy film and it was one of the props. He bought it.'

'But it was more than a bit of scenery. It was a real revolver.'

'Unfortunately, yes.'

'And he had a licence for it . . .?'

'Oh yes. He joined the Grimble Rifle and Pistol Club and used to shoot at targets. I think he fancied himself as James Bond or something.'

'As James who . . .?' I knew that Mr Justice Skelton wouldn't be able to resist playing the part of a mystified judge, so I explained carefully.

'A character in fiction, my Lord. A person licensed to kill. He also spends a great deal of his time sleeping with air hostesses.' To Tommy Pierce's irritation I got a little giggle out of the ladies and gentlemen of the jury.

'Mr Rumpole. We have quite enough to do in this case dealing with questions of *fact*. I suggest we leave the world of fiction . . . outside the Court, with our overcoats.'

The jury subsided into serious attention, and I addressed myself to the work in hand. 'Where did Mr Frere keep his revolver?'

'Usually in a locker. At the Rifle Club.'

'Usually?'

'A few weeks ago he asked me to bring it back to the theatre for him.'

'He asked *you*?'

'I'm a member of the Club myself.'

'Really, Mr Copeland.' The judge was interested. 'And what's your weapon?'

'A shot gun, my Lord. I do some clay pigeon shooting.'

'Did Frere say *why* he wanted his gun brought back to the theatre?' I gave the jury a puzzled look.

'There'd been some burglaries. I imagine he wanted to scare any intruder . . .'

I had established that it was Frere's gun, and certainly not brought to the scene of the crime by Maggie. I broached another topic. 'Now you have spoken of some quarrels between Frere and his wife.'

'Yes, sir. He once threw a drink in her face.'

'During their quarrels, did you see my client retaliate in any way?'

'No. No, I never did. May I say something, my Lord . . .'

'Certainly, Mr Copeland.'

I held my breath. I didn't like free-ranging witnesses, but at his answer I sat down gratefully.

'Miss Hartley, as we knew her, was an exceptionally gentle person.'

I saw the jury look at the dock, at the quiet almost motionless woman sitting there.

'Mr Copeland. You've told us you shot clay pigeons at the Rifle Club.' The prosecution was up and beaming.

'Yes, sir.'

'Nothing much to eat on a clay pigeon, I suppose.'

The jury greeted this alleged quip with total silence. The local comic had died the death in Grimble. Pierce went on and didn't improve his case.

'And Frere asked for this pistol to be brought back to the theatre. Did his wife know that, do you think . . .?'

'I certainly didn't tell her.'

'May I ask why not?'

'I think it would have made her very nervous. I certainly was.'

'Nervous of what, exactly?'

Tommy Pierce had broken the first rule of advocacy. Never ask your witness a question unless you're quite sure of the answer.

'Well . . . I was always afraid G.P.'d get drunk and loose it off at someone . . .'

The beauty of that answer was that it came from a witness

for the prosecution, a detached observer who'd only been called to identify the gun as belonging to the late-lamented G. P. Frere. None too soon for the health of his case Tommy Pierce let Mr Copeland leave the box. I saw him cross the Court and sit next to Daniel Derwent, who gave him a little smile, as if of congratulation.

In the course of my legal career I have had occasion to make some study of firearms; not so intensive, of course, as my researches into the subject of blood, but I certainly know more about revolvers than I do about the law of landlord and tenant. I held the fatal weapon in a fairly expert hand as I cross-examined the Inspector who had recovered it from the scene of the crime.

'It's clear, is it not, Inspector, that two chambers had been fired?'

'Yes.'

'One bullet was found in the corner of the mirror, and another in the body of the deceased, Frere?'

'That is so.'

'Now. If the person who fired the shot into the mirror pulled back this hammer,' I pulled it back, 'to fire a second shot . . . the gun is now in a condition to go off with a far lighter pressure on the trigger?'

'That is so. Yes.'

'Thank you.'

I put down the gun and as I did so allowed my thumb to accidentally press the trigger. I looked at it, surprised, as it clicked. It was a moderately effective move, and I thought the score was fifteen-love to Rumpole. Tommy Pierce rose to serve.

'Inspector. Whether the hammer was pulled back or not, a woman would have no difficulty in firing the pistol?'

'Certainly not, my Lord.'

'Yes. Thank *you*, Inspector.' The prosecution sat down smiling. Fifteen-all.

The last witness of the day was Miss Christine Hope who turned her large *ingénue* eyes on the jury and whispered her evidence at a sound level which must have made her

unintelligible to the audiences at the Theatre Royal. I had
decided to cross-examine her more in sorrow than in anger.

'Miss Hope. Why were you waiting at the stage door?'

'Somehow I can never bear to leave. After the show's over . . .
I can never bear to go.' She gave the jury a 'silly me' look of
girlish enthusiasm. 'I suppose I'm just in love with The
Theatre.'

'And I suppose you were also "just in love with G. P. Frere"?'

At which Miss Hope looked helplessly at the rail of the witness-box, and fiddled with the Holy Bible.

'You waited for him every night, didn't you? He left his wife
at the stage door and took you home.'

'Sometimes . . .'

'You're dropping your voice, Miss Hope.' The judge was
leaning forward, straining to hear.

'Sometimes, my Lord,' she repeated a decibel louder.

'Every night?'

'Most nights. Yes.'

'Thank you, Miss Hope.'

Pierce, wisely, didn't re-examine and La Belle Christine left
the box to looks of disapproval from certain ladies on the jury.

I didn't sleep well that night. Whether it was the Majestic
mattress, which appeared to be stuffed with firewood, or the
sounds, as of a giant suffering from indigestion, which reverber-
ated from the central heating, or mere anxiety about the case, I
don't know. At any rate Albert and I were down in the cells as
soon as they opened, taking a critical look at the client I was
about to expose to the perils of the witness-box. As I had instructed her she was wearing no make-up, and a simple dark
dress which struck exactly the right note.

'I'm glad you like it,' Maggie said. 'I wore it in *Time and the
Conways*.'

'Listen to the questions, answer them as shortly as you can.' I
gave her her final orders. 'Every word to the North Country
comedian is giving him a present. Just stick to the facts. Not a
word of criticism of the dear departed.'

'You want *them* to like me?'

'They shouldn't find it too difficult.' I looked at her, and lit a small cigar.

'Do I have to swear on . . . the Bible?'

'It's customary.'

'I'd rather affirm.'

'You don't believe in God?' I didn't want an obscure point of theology adding unnecessary difficulties to our case.

'I suppose He's a possibility. He just doesn't seem to be a very frequent visitor to the East Grimble Rep.'

'I know a Grimble jury,' Albert clearly shared my fears. 'If you *could* swear on the Bible?'

'The audience might like it?' Maggie smiled gently.

'The jury,' I corrected her firmly.

'They're not too keen on agnostic actresses. Is that your opinion?'

'I suppose that puts it in a nutshell.'

'All right for the West End, is that it? No good in Grimble.'

'Of course I want you to be *yourself* . . .' I really hoped she wasn't going to be difficult about the oath.

'No you don't. You don't want me to be myself at all. You want me to be an ordinary North Country housewife. Spending just another ordinary day on trial for murder.' For a moment her voice had hardened. I looked at her and tried to sound as calm as possible as I pulled out my watch. It was nearly time for the curtain to go up on the evidence for the defence.

'Naturally you're nervous. Time to go.'

'Bloody sick to the stomach. Every time I go on.' Her voice was gentle again, and she was smiling ruefully.

'Good luck.'

'We never say "good luck". It's bad luck to say "good luck". We say "break a leg" . . .'

'Break a leg!' I smiled back at her and went upstairs to make my entrance.

Calling your client, I always think, is the worst part of any case. When you're cross-examining, or making a final speech, you're in control. Put your client in the witness-box and there the old darling is, exposed to the world, out of your protection, and all you can do is ask the questions and hope to God the answers don't blow up in your face.

With Maggie everything was going well. We were like a couple of ballroom dancers, expertly gyrating to Victor Sylvester and certain to walk away with the cup. She seemed to sense my next question, and had her answer ready, but not too fast. She looked at the jury, made herself audible to the judge, and gave an impression, a small, dark figure in the witness-box, of courage in the face of adversity. The Court was so quiet and attentive that, as she started to describe that final quarrel, I felt we were alone, two old friends, talking intimately of some dreadful event that took place a long time ago.

'He told me . . . he was very much in love with Christine.'

'With Miss Hope?'

'Yes. With Christine Hope. That he wanted her to play Amanda.'

'That is . . . the leading lady? And what was to happen to you?'

'He wanted me to leave the company. To go to London. He never wanted to see me again.'

'What did you say to that?'

'I said I was terribly unhappy about Christine, naturally.'

'Just tell the ladies and gentlemen of the jury what happened next.'

'He said it didn't matter what I said. He was going to get rid of me. He opened the drawer of the dressing-table.'

'Was he standing then?'

'I would say, staggering.'

'Yes, and then . . .?'

'He took out the . . . the revolver.'

'This one . . .?'

I handed the gun to the usher, who took it to Maggie. She glanced at it and shuddered.

'I . . . I think so.'

'What effect did it have on you when you first saw it?'

'I was terrified.'

'Did you know it was there?'

'No. I had no idea.'

'And then . . .?'

'Then. He seemed to be getting ready to fire the gun.'

'You mean he pulled back the hammer . . .?'

'My Lord . . .' Pierce stirred his vast bulk and the judge was inclined to agree. He said:

'Yes. Please don't lead, Mr Rumpole.'

'I think that's what he did,' Maggie continued without assistance. 'I didn't look carefully. Naturally I was terrified. He was waving the gun. He didn't seem to be able to hold it straight. Then there was a terrible explosion. I remember glass, and dust, everywhere.'

'Who fired that shot, Mrs Frere?'

'My husband. I think . . .'

'Yes?'

'I think he was trying to kill me.' She said it very quietly, but the jury heard, and remembered. She gave it a marked pause and then went on. 'After that first shot. I saw him getting ready to fire again.'

'Was he pulling . . .?'

'Please don't lead, Mr Rumpole.' The trouble with the great comedian was that he couldn't sit still in anyone else's act.

'He was pulling back . . . That thing.' Maggie went on without any help.

Then I asked the judge if we could have a demonstration and the usher went up into the witness-box to play the scene with Maggie. At my suggestion he took the revolver.

'We are all quite sure that thing isn't loaded?' The judge sounded nervous.

'Quite sure, my Lord. Of course, we don't want *another* fatal *accident*!'

'Really, my Lord. That was quite improper!' Pierce rose furiously. 'My learned friend called it an accident.'

I apologized profusely, the point having been made. Then Maggie quietly positioned the usher. He raised the gun as she asked him. It was pointed murderously at her. And then Maggie grabbed at the gun in his hand, and forced it back, struggling desperately, against the usher's chest.

'I was trying to stop him. I got hold of his hand to push the gun away . . . I pushed it back . . . I think . . . I think I must have forced back his finger on the trigger.' We heard the hammer click, and now Maggie was struggling to hold back her tears. 'There was another terrible noise . . . I never meant . . .'

'Yes. Thank you, Usher.'

The usher went back to the well of the Court. Maggie was calm again when I asked her:

'When Mr Croft came you said you had killed your husband?'

'Yes . . . I had . . . By accident.'

'What else did you say?'

'I think I said . . . What could I do with him? I meant, how could I help him, of course.'

'And you asked Mr Croft to help you?'

'Yes.'

It was time for the curtain line.

'Mrs Frere. Did you ever at any time have any intention of killing your husband?'

'Never . . .! Never . . .! Never . . .!' Now my questions were finished she was crying, her face and shoulders shaking. The judge leaned forward kindly.

'Don't distress yourself. Usher, a glass of water?'

Her cheeks hot with genuine tears, Maggie looked up bravely.

'Thank you, my Lord.'

'Bloody play-acting!' I heard the cynical Tommy Pierce mutter ungraciously to his junior, Roach.

If she was good in chief Maggie was superb in cross-examination. She answered the questions courteously, shortly, but as if she were genuinely trying to help Tommy clear up any doubt about her innocence that may have lingered in his mind. At the end he lost his nerve and almost shouted at her:

'So according to you, you did nothing wrong?'

'Oh yes,' she said. 'I did something terribly wrong.'

'Tell us. What?'

'I loved him too much. Otherwise I should have left him. Before he tried to kill me.'

During Tommy's final speech there was some coughing from the jury. He tried a joke or two about actors, lost heart and sat down upon reminding the jury that they must not let sympathy for my client affect their judgement.

'I agree entirely with my learned friend,' I started my speech. 'Put all sympathy out of your mind. The mere fact that my client clung faithfully to a drunken, adulterous husband, hoping vainly for the love he denied her; the terrible circumstance that she escaped death at his hands only to face the terrible ordeal of a trial for murder; none of these things should influence you in the least . . .' and I ended with my well-tried peroration. 'In an hour or two this case will be over. You will go home and put the kettle on and forget all about this little theatre, and the angry, drunken actor and his wretched infidelities. This case has only been a few days out of your lives. But for this lady I have the honour to represent . . .' I pointed to the dock, '*all* her life hangs in the balance. Is that life to be broken and is she to go down in darkness and disgrace, or can she go back into the glowing light of her world, to bring us all joy and entertainment and laughter once again? Ask yourselves that question, members of the jury. And when you ask it, you know there can only be one answer.'

I sank back into my seat exhausted, pushing back my wig and mopping my brow with a large silk handkerchief. Looking round the Court I saw Derwent. He seemed about to applaud, until he was restrained by Mr Alan Copeland.

There is nothing I hate more than waiting for a jury to come back. You smoke too much and drink too many cups of coffee, your hands sweat and you can't do or think of anything else. All you can do is to pay a courtesy visit to the cells to prepare for the worst. Albert Handyside had to go off and do a touch of Dangerous Driving in the Court next door, so I was alone when I went to call on the waiting Maggie.

She was standing in her cell, totally calm.

'This is the bad part, isn't it? Like waiting for the notices.'

I sat down at the table with my notebook, unscrewed my fountain pen.

'I had better think of what to say if they find you guilty of manslaughter. I think I've got the facts for mitigation, but I'd just like to get the history clear. You'd started this theatrical company together?'

'It was my money. Every bloody penny of it.' I looked up in

some surprise. The hard, tough note was there in her voice; her face was set in a look which was something like hatred.

'I don't think we need go into the financial side.' I tried to stop her, but she went on:

'Do you know what that idiotic manager we had then did? He gave G.P. a contract worth fifty per cent of the profits: for an investment of nothing and a talent which stopped short of being able to pour out a drink and say a line at the same time. Anyway I never paid his percentage.' She smiled then, it was quite humourless. 'Won't need to say that, will we?'

'No.' I said firmly.

'Fifty per cent of ten years' work! He reckoned he was owed around twenty thousand pounds. He was going to sue us and bankrupt the company . . .'

'I don't think you need to tell me any more.' I screwed the top back on my fountain pen. Perhaps she had told me too much already.

'So don't feel too badly, will you? If we're not a hit.'

I stood up and pulled out my watch. Suddenly I felt an urgent need to get out of the cell.

'They should be back soon now.'

'It's all a game to you, isn't it?' She sounded unaccountably bitter. 'All a wonderful game of "let's pretend". The costume. The bows. The little jokes. The onion at the end.'

'The onion?'

'An old music-hall expression. For what makes the audience cry. Oh, I was quite prepared to go along with it. To wear the make-up.'

'You didn't wear any make-up.'

'I know, that was brilliant of you. You're a marvellous performer, Mr Rumpole. Don't let anyone tell you different.'

'It's not a question of performance.' I couldn't have that.

'Isn't it?'

'Of course it isn't! The jury are now weighing the facts. Doing their best to discover where the truth lies.' I looked at her. Her face gave nothing away.

'Or at least deciding if the prosecution has proved its case.'

Suddenly, quite unexpectedly, she yawned, she moved away from me, as though I bored her.

'Oh, I'm tired. Worn out. With so much *acting*. I tell you, in the theatre we haven't got time for all that. We've got our livings to get.'

The woman prison officer came in.

'I think they want you upstairs now. Ready, dear?'

When Maggie spoke again her voice was low, gentle and wonderfully polite.

'Yes thanks, Elsie. I'm quite ready now.'

'Will your foreman please stand? Mr Foreman. Have you reached a verdict on which you are all agreed?'

'Not guilty, my Lord.'

Four words that usually set the Rumpole ears tingling with delight and the chest to swell with pleasure. Why was it, that at the end of what was no doubt a remarkable win, a famous victory even, I felt such doubt and depression? I told myself that I was not the judge of fact, that the jury had clearly not been satisfied and that the prosecution had not proved its case. I did the well-known shift of responsibility which is the advocate's perpetual comfort, but I went out of Court unelated. In the entrance hall I saw Maggie leaving, she didn't turn back to speak to me, and I saw that she was holding the hand of Mr Alan Copeland. Such congratulations as I received came from the diminutive Derwent.

'Triumph. My dear, a total triumph.'

'You told me she was truthful . . .' I looked at him.

'I meant her acting. That's quite truthful. Not to be faulted. That's all I meant.'

At which he made his exit and my Learned Friend for the Prosecution came sailing up, beaming with the joy of reconciliation.

'Well. Congratulations, Rumpole. That was a bloody good win!'

'Was it? I hope so.'

'Coming to the Circuit dinner tonight?'

'Tonight?'

'You'll enjoy it! We've got some pretty decent claret in the mess.'

If my judgement hadn't been weakened by exhaustion I would never have agreed to the Circuit dinner which took place, as I feared, in a private room at the Majestic Hotel. All the gang were there, Skelton J., Pierce, Roach and my one-time leader Jarvis Allen, Q.C. The food was indifferent, the claret was bad, and when the port was passed an elderly silk who they called 'Mr Senior' in deference to his position as Leader of the Circuit, banged the table with the handle of his knife and addressed young Roach at the other end of the table.

'Mr Junior, in the matter of Rumpole.'

'Mr Senior,' Roach produced a scribble on a menu. 'I will read the indictment.'

I realized then that I had been tricked, ambushed, made to give myself up to the tender mercies of this savage Northerly Circuit. Rumpole was on trial, there was nothing to do but drink all the available port and put up with it.

'Count One,' Roach read it out. 'Deserting his learned leader in his hour of need. That is to say on the occasion of his leader having been given the sack. Particulars of Offence . . .'

'Mr Senior. Have five minutes elapsed?' Allen asked.

'Five minutes having elapsed since the loyal toast, you may now smoke.'

Tommy Pierce lit a large cigar. I lit a small one. Mr Junior Roach continued to intone.

'The said Rumpole did add considerably to the seriousness of the offence by proceeding to win in the absence of his learned leader.'

'Mr Junior. Has Rumpole anything to say by way of mitigation?'

'Rumpole.' Roach took out his watch, clearly there was a time limit in speeches. I rose to express my deepest thoughts, loosened by the gentle action of the port.

'The show had to go on!'

'What? What did Rumpole say?' Mr Justice Skelton seemed to have some difficulty in hearing.

'Sometimes. I must admit, sometimes . . . I wonder why.' I went on, 'What sort of show is it exactly? Have you considered what we are *doing* to our clients?'

'Has that port got stuck to the table?' Allen sounded plaintive and the port moved towards him.

'What are we *doing* to them?' I warmed to my work. 'Seeing they wear ties, and hats, keep their hands out of their pockets, keep their voices up, call the judge "my Lord". Generally behave like grocers at a funeral. Whoever they may be.'

'One minute,' said Roach, the time-keeper.

'What do we tell them? Look respectable! Look suitably serious! Swear on the Bible! Say nothing which might upset a jury of lay-preachers, look enormously grateful for the trouble everyone's taking before they bang you up in the nick! What do we find out about our clients in all these trials, do we ever get a fleeting glimpse of the truth? Do we . . .? Or do we put a hat on the truth. And a tie. And a serious expression. To please the jury and My Lord the Judge?' I looked round the table. 'Do you ever worry about that at all? Do you *ever*?'

'Time's up!' said Roach, and I sat down heavily.

'All right. Quite all right. The performance is over.'

Mr Senior swigged down port and proceeded to judgement.

'Rumpole's mitigation has, of course, merely added to the gravity of the offence. Rumpole, at your age and with your experience at the Bar you should have been proud to get the sack, and your further conduct in winning shows a total disregard for the feelings of an extremely sensitive silk. The least sentence I can pass is a fine of twelve bottles of claret. Have you a chequebook on you?'

So I had no choice but to pull out a chequebook and start to write. The penalty, apparently, was worth thirty-six quid.

'Members of the Mess will now entertain the company in song,' Roach announced to a rattle of applause.

'Tommy!' Allen shouted.

'No. Really . . .' The learned prosecutor was modest but was prevailed upon by cries of 'Come along, Tommy! Let's have it. "The Road to Mandalay" . . . etc. etc.'

'I'm looking forward to this,' said Mr Justice Skelton, who was apparently easily entertained. As I gave my cheque to young Roach, the stout leading Counsel for the Crown rose and started in a light baritone.

> 'On the Road to Mandalay . . .
> Where the old Flotilla lay . . .
> And the dawn came up like thunder
> Out of China 'cross the Bay!'

Or words to the like effect. I was not really listening. I'd had quite enough of show business.

Rumpole and the Fascist Beast

'This is where I came in,' I said. 'I've seen it all before.'

I was sitting one Sunday in front of the gas fire at Casa Rumpole (25B Froxbury Court, Gloucester Road). I was wearing a comfortable old cardigan and carpet slippers, and sipping a G and T but the news in the paper wasn't comforting, moreover it was unpleasantly familiar to anyone who made a tentative entrance into life before the First World War, and was therefore in time to hear Hitler screeching on the wireless and see newsreels of jackboots marching into Czechoslovakia in preparation for the next.

' "BRITAIN FIRST" Rally in Brixton. Clashes with New Socialist Party. Candidate arrested.' As I said to She Who Must Be Obeyed as she came in through the front door with her mackintosh and shopping string-bag weighed down with a few unappetizing-looking goodies, it was all exactly like the bad old days.

'Rumpole! It's good news,' said Hilda. 'I've got a tin of mulligatawny soup.'

'Congratulations.' I went on reading the paper. 'Fascist marches in London. I know exactly what happens next.'

My wife took her string-bag into the kitchen, and left the door open as she unpacked her shopping. I shouted my predictions through to her.

'Next comes gas masks. Call-up. The R.A.F. groundstaff.' Surely I was getting a bit old for the R.A.F. groundstaff.

'And I managed to find some frozen beefburgers!' She seemed very proud of her Sunday shopping.

'Then they'll give us dried eggs. Whale steak. J. B. Priestley on the wireless. Songs by Dame Vera Lynn.' It was an appalling prospect. I dropped the paper and wandered into the kitchen to search out another bottle of gin.

'I had to go all the way down to the tube station.' Hilda was pouring tinned mulligatawny soup into a saucepan. I lit a paper spill in the gas and applied it to the end of a small cigar.

'I couldn't stand the whole damn programme round again.' I puffed out smoke. 'I suppose they've got a gramophone record of Churchill's speeches.'

'Hardly a white face to be seen. Down by the tube station.' Oh dear. 'She' does come out with these embarrassing remarks occasionally.

'Were you looking for one? I thought you were looking for mulligatawny soup.'

'My Aunt Fran would turn in her grave if she could see London nowadays.' My wife accepted a large G and T to help her through stirring the tin of soup.

'As I recall it, your Aunt Fran was married to your Uncle Percy Wystan, late Deputy Controller of the Punjabi Railway,' I reminded her.

'That is exactly what I mean!'

'She spent her life running up curries and kedgerees, supervising the punka-wallah, organizing tea parties on the backs of elephants. Your Aunt Fran would have been totally at home round our tube station.' I looked at Hilda and started to cross-examine her, a daring thing to do to She Who Must Be Obeyed. 'You didn't get the supper at Chatterjee's General Stores by any chance?'

'Everywhere else was shut.' The witness was on the defensive.

'You don't grudge Mr Chatterjee a little hospitality, do you? I mean in return for a couple of centuries, putting up with your Aunt Fran?'

Cornered, the witness had to resort to 'Don't be so silly Rumpole', a sure sign of defeat. I reckoned the score was fifteen-love to me in the first set of the evening.

I had for some time considered taking a pupil, someone to look up law whenever that commodity was needed, or to run round and adjourn things. Perhaps I felt the need of someone to

talk to since my old friend George Frobisher had accepted a
minor judgeship, and gone off to a Circus Bench somewhere in
the general direction of Luton. Our Inn sent us round a list of
names of those anxious to secure a pupillage, together with their
life stories (Grimsby Grammar, Captain of Debates, or Eton and
Oriel, doesn't wish to be connected with divorce or crime,
warmly recommended by the Master of the Rolls). I passed by
various candidates until I came to the name of Mr Lutaf Ali
Khan. I rang the Inn and we arranged an appointment at my
Chambers for 9.30 one morning. If Mr Ali Khan was to turn out
to be anything like Mr Chatterjee, Hilda's useful grocer, he
would be inclined, I thought, to work industriously, Sunday
afternoons included.

When Mr Khan duly arrived at Chambers I was in conference.
He went into the clerk's room and found the usual scene of
chaos and overcrowding. Erskine-Brown was collecting papers
and grumbling to our clerk Henry about the slow arrival of his
fees, and Hoskins, the middle-aged father of four hungry daughters, was having a quick look at a 'break and enter' before
rushing off to Inner London. Uncle Tom was looking through
the obituaries in the *Daily Telegraph*. Dianne and Angela, our
new assistant typist, were clattering away and Miss Trant, our
budding Portia, was having a glance at a matrimonial. I rely on
her account for the reception of Mr Khan in our clerk's room.
He announced himself as Mr Lutaf Ali Khan and said he had an
urgent appointment with my learned self. When Henry promised
to ring through to my room Mr Khan beamed at them. He was
eager and rather young.

'Thrilling! This is thrilling to have a chance of pupillage in
the Chambers of Horace Rumpole, the legend of the Criminal
Bar of England.' Uncle Tom caught his eye.

'And you, of course, sir. I will have a lot to learn from a
person of your age and seniority. I expect to pick up hundreds
of red-hot tips, from the whole lot of you!'

'We'll do our best to help.' Miss Trant didn't notice a particularly warm welcome from the rest of Chambers, so she
advanced on him with a compensating smile.

'Thank you. You are on the secretarial side?'

'Miss Trant is a very rising young barrister,' Uncle Tom told him.

'The great fraternity of the Bar! Truly it embraces all sorts and conditions of men ... and women also,' Mr Khan said enthusiastically and then Henry rose from his desk to lead him into the presence. When he had gone Uncle Tom spoke to Miss Trant in a tone of some bewilderment.

'I don't see very clearly. It gets dark in the morning, but was that fellow some sort of Babu?'

'Indian, I'd say.' Hoskins gave his expert opinion.

'I suppose he'll pick our brains here and then go out and become Prime Minister of somewhere. Do very nicely out of it.' Uncle Tom sniffed behind the *Daily Telegraph*.

'What on *earth* does Rumpole think he's up to?' Erskine-Brown wondered, and Miss Trant gave him a look of stern disapproval.

'My old Uncle Jarvis had that fellow Gandhi in his Chambers as a pupil.' Uncle Tom was off on one of his reminiscences. 'He wore a bowler hat in those days apparently, not a loin cloth. I mean Gandhi didn't wear a loin cloth, not my Uncle Jarvis, of course.'

'What do you mean? What's Rumpole up to?' Miss Trant asked Erskine-Brown in a challenging manner.

'Taking a pupil without going through the pupillage committee in Chambers.'

'You mean taking *that* pupil, don't you?'

At which moment, Miss Trant told me, she slammed out of the clerk's room and started off down the passage. Erskine-Brown set off in pursuit, he was after all, as you may remember, her *fiancé*.

'For all I know whatever-his-name-is Khan may be a perfectly sound fellow ... but ...'

'But! But?'

'I mean ...'

'I know perfectly well what you mean,' said Miss Trant, with an anger that did her the greatest credit.

'Don't forget *Un Ballo In Maschera*.' Claude Erskine-Brown

was an Opera Buff who intended, that night, to take his *inamorata* to Covent Garden. 'It's curtain-up at 7.30.'

'Stuff *Un Ballo In Maschera*!' said the admirable Miss Trant and slammed into her room.

All this while I was in conference on a matter which was new to me, an alleged offence under the Race Relations Act, arising out of those very political events which had, on Sunday afternoon, made me feel that they were winding back the film of history so that we should find ourselves, in the fullness of time, reliving World War Two. My client, Captain Rex Parkin, late of the Pay Corps, was a prospective 'Britain First' parliamentary candidate, one, I profoundly hoped, whose deposit was no way safe. He had appeared at his party's rally in Brixton and made a regrettable speech in which, so ran the police evidence, he had recommended repatriation of all migrants ('We want our tinted brothers to be thoroughly *at home*. In their homes, my friends, not in ours') and he ended his speech with the gnomic utterance, 'The answer, my friends, is ... Blood.'

Someone at the meeting broke the window of an Indian grocer's shop and the gallant Captain was arrested before he, in his turn, was attacked by the New Socialists, who had armed themselves with chairs, sticks and other mementoes from a nearby building site for the occasion.

Captain Parkin was a middle-aged humourless man who wore a neat blue suit, a Pay Corps tie, a sparse sandy moustache and the expression of someone prepared to die for his cause. He sat bolt upright on a hard chair whilst young Simmonds, an articled clerk from Parkin's solicitors' office, wallowed in my client's armchair, looked puzzled and lost documents. When Mr Lutaf Ali Khan was shown into the room by Henry there was such a sharp disapproving intake of breath from Captain Parkin that I couldn't resist taking the eager young Pakistani there and then.

'Khan! My dear fellow. You come warmly recommended from the Inn. An apt pupil ... Ready to start work, are you?'

'As soon as you say so, Mr Horace Rumpole. I am mustard keen, I must say.'

'That's the ticket! This is the client Mr . . . No, sorry, *Captain*. Captain Rex Parkin.'

'And young Simmonds. Our instructing solicitor. My new pupil . . .'

'Lutaf Ali Khan. At your service, Captain.'

The Captain avoided Khan's eager eye. There was an awkward silence.

'Yes. Well, why not sit down here, dear boy. Learn to take notes, I never have.'

Khan sat on the other side of Rumpole's desk, his pen poised. Captain Parkin cleared his throat.

'I would like to stress, Mr Rumpole. This is a *confidential* matter.'

'Oh, don't mind Khan. It's the only thing to do with pupils. Throw them in at the deep end. You know what we have here, Khan? A rather nasty charge under the Race Relations Act.'

'Let's see what I know about our client, the Captain. You are ex-Pay Corps.' I flicked through my brief for Khan's benefit.

'Served. Overseas . . .?'

'I served my country as best I could. Given my medical condition.' The Captain looked dignified.

'Flat feet . . .' I read it in the brief, and comforted the client. 'Don't worry. I was in the R.A.F. groundstaff. We both avoided the temptations of heroism.'

'Worked after demobilization selling . . . *World Wide Encyclopedia*. Married for twenty-five years to Mavis Parkin. Owns his own bungalow "Mandalay", Durbar Lane, Bexley Heath. Employed since 1958 as a clerk in the South-East Area Gas Board . . .' It sounded like a life full of incident and romance.

'Captain Parkin wishes it to be known that he's absolutely sincere.' This was young Simmonds's contribution.

'Unfortunately that isn't a defence in law. I've known quite a number of very genuine robbers. They sincerely wanted to be rich.' I continued to read. 'The answer is . . . Blood.'

'Mr Rumpole. On the question of sentence . . .' The Captain raised a delicate question.

'Sorry. You want to know what you might be in for?'

'The maximum. If you please, sir.'

'Two years' imprisonment. Or a fine. Or both. Section 6 of the 1978 Act.' The admirable Khan had the answer at his fingertips.

> 'And still they gazed, and still the wonder grew,
> That one small head could carry all he knew . . .

You see what a huge advantage a pupil is, Captain. Well, now you know the worst.'

And then Captain Parkin said something so unexpected, so unknown in a client, that I was left staring at him in amazement.

'I want you, sir, to ask for the maximum penalty.'

'Now Captain Perkins . . . Parkin. Now listen to me a moment, my old darling . . . Regard me,' I told him, 'as your professional attendant. Who cares for your health. Now if I were treating you for a nasty go of 'flu, Captain Perkins, I couldn't allow you to dance naked in the East wind at midnight, on a damp lawn, could I?'

'I intend, in the trial, sir, to behave as Ghandi did before the District Magistrate in Ahmedobad. I intend to argue for the maximum sentence.' Captain Parkin had risen to his feet and seemed to be standing to attention.

'Excuse me, Captain, but wasn't the Mahatma of foreign extraction?'

'One can learn at times, sir, from the enemy. Mr Ghandi asked for life imprisonment. It was the best way he could serve his cause – as a martyr.'

'Well, I suppose I have a cause too, of a sort,' I told him. 'I defend people. I don't think I could ask a judge to send a client of mine to prison. It'd be against my religion.'

'Then, sir. I am wasting your time.' Captain Parkin moved to the door. 'I'll conduct my own case. I presume I'm entitled to do that?'

'It's a free world . . . For the moment.' Before I'd got the words out the door slammed, my client had gone off on his own.

'He's a fool, Mr Rumpole. If he won't take your advice.' Young Simmonds looked intensely embarrassed.

'It's his affair entirely,' I comforted him, 'our prison system's open to all, old darling. Regardless of creed or colour.'

When I told Hilda I had a pupil, she was pleased. She remembered that her 'Daddy', old C. H. Wystan, had had a pupil, namely me. She told me to bring my pupil home to dinner one night and promised to make him a nice roast. Remembering the nonsense she had talked about the old days of the British Raj I agreed to do so.

A couple of weeks later Khan and I received another visit from Captain Rex Parkin and his distraught solicitor. It seemed that the central committee for the South-Eastern Region of the 'Britain First' Party had met at my client's bungalow 'Mandalay'. Prominent members, a Mr 'Cliff' Worseley, a local garage-owner and a Mr Sidney Cox, a quantity surveyor and local party chairman, had persuaded the Captain that it was in the party's interests that the case should be fought. The Captain had told them I was an ageing junior barrister with a Pakistani pupil whereupon 'Cliff' Worseley had said that was an excellent thing as it would prove to the jury that 'Britain First' was not a racialist party. During this account Khan smiled politely, and I promised to fight the good fight and forget the Captain's former ambition to be convicted.

There were those, of course, who didn't approve of my having taken on Captain Parkin's defence. When I went into Pommeroy's Wine Bar for an evening jar I met the most distinguished member of our Chambers, Guthrie Featherstone, Q.C., M.P., who looked at me from his considerable height and in his most distinguished manner.

'Rumpole. I'm prosecuting you in the Race Relations case. Phillida Trant's my junior.'

'Sounds a formidable combination.'

'You know, Rumpole,' Featherstone went on, 'I was talking to old Keith from the Lord Chancellor's office the other day. He was suprised at you of all people. . . defending a wretched Fascist beast.'

'I defend murderers. Doesn't mean I approve of murder.'

'No, but politically. I was thinking. The time may come, Rumpole, when you might think of subsiding gently on the Circuit Bench.'

'Rumpole a Circus Judge?' It was a fate which has always seemed to me considerably worse than death.

'It's not a job the Lord Chancellor's office hands out, to fellows who stand up for Fascists.'

'Oh, really?' I sank a large glass of Château Fleet Street and began to negotiate with Jack Pommeroy for more.

'Afraid so, Rumpole. I mean, you're not getting much younger. I don't know what your pension scheme is . . .'

My pension, as he well knew, consisted of my growing overdraft and the dwindling lease on my flat at Froxbury Court, Gloucester Road. However, I was rapidly losing patience with Guthrie Featherstone, Q.C., M.P.

'My pension scheme is about as non-existent as your friend old Keith's knowledge of Voltaire.'

'Voltaire?' The Q.C., M.P. looked puzzled.

'M. Arouet,' I explained. 'Remember what he said, "I disagree with what you say, but I will defend to the death your right to say it"? You might read that to the jury, when you're opening the little matter of the Queen against Captain Rex Parkin . . .'

The evening came when I took Mr Khan home to meet my wife Hilda and her roast. She Who Must Be Obeyed didn't actually scream or send for the police when she clapped eyes on my pupil, but she looked severely shaken, and matters were so tense round the festive board that I was constrained to tell one of my best stories as I carved the beef. I chose the beauty about two men charged with an act of buggery under Waterloo Bridge and tried by dear old Judge Darcy at the Bailey.

'These two men were caught misbehaving themselves under Waterloo Bridge and when he was passing sentence that exquisite old Judge Hubert Darcy said, "You two men have done an abominable act. A most disgusting and horrible act . . . And what makes it worse – you chose to do it under one of the most *beautiful* bridges in London." '

I laughed loudly at this *conte*, as I always do. Khan smiled politely, Hilda was appalled. She looked even more anxious as she pushed a laden plate of roast to Khan.

'Oh dear. I didn't realize. Can you eat beef?'

'Of course he can, Hilda. What do you think? He'd be afraid it was a reincarnation of his grandmother?' I looked at Khan reassuringly. 'Don't worry, dear boy. We got it at Sainsbury's.'

'Roast beef of old England. Perfectly fine. Suits me down to the ground.' Khan sounded enthusiastic. I tried to pour claret into his glass, but the young Pakistani put his hand over it.

'Oh, come along. If you're starting a career at the Bar, we've got to introduce you to the delights of Pommeroy's claret.'

'Well then, just a snifter.' I was glad to see him lap up the claret. I went to turn off one bar of the electric fire.

'What are you doing, Hilda, turning the place into the hothouse at Kew?'

'Don't you find England very cold, Mr Khan?' Hilda asked nervously.

'No. No, I assure you. It is much much colder in the Punjab in the winter.'

'Wasn't your Aunt Fran in the Punjab, Hilda?'

'Oh, that was in the old days. The British Raj, you know.'

'All gone now, eh Khan? Much to the regret of our client Captain Parkin.' I gave them a bit of Kipling.

> 'Far-call'd our navies melt away
> On dune and headland sinks the fire . . .
> Lo, all our pomp of yesterday
> Is one with Nineveh, and Tyre . . .'

'My uncle was District Railway Officer Percy Wystan. I don't know if you ever met him?' Hilda asked, a singularly stupid question.

'Rather before my time, I'm afraid, Mrs Rumpole. All the same. We had some sensible fellows in the government then. Not these silly asses we get today.'

'Do you really think so?' She Who Must Be Obeyed seemed to be thawing slightly.

'All the same, they are your own silly asses. Isn't that the point?' I put it to Khan.

'Oh yes. But they make us blush sometimes.'

At which Hilda actually smiled and I raised a beaker to young Khan's future at the Bar.

'How can I go wrong,' Khan said, 'with such a distinguished teacher as Mr Horace Rumpole?'

'You think he's a distinguished teacher?' She was incredulous.

'Oh gosh, yes, Mrs Rumpole. Your husband's bound to end up seated on the Bench, at least at Circuit Judge level.'

'Rumpole! Do you hear that?' She was delighted.

'Never. Never in a million years . . .'

'I always thought, if you would take a bit of prosecution work, Mr Rumpole. That seems to be the path to the Bench nowadays.' Khan said, and Hilda agreed.

'Mr Khan. That's exactly what I'm always telling him.'

'I don't fancy the idea of people locked up with their own chamber-pots. Not for years on end, anyway. I wouldn't like to cross-examine them into it . . . And I don't want to sentence them to it either.'

'Someone has to do it, Mr Rumpole,' Khan said, winning more of Hilda's approval.

'Someone has to clean out the sewers. Just so long as it isn't me.'

'You know, Mrs Rumpole. I don't entirely agree with my learned pupilmaster. There are two dreadful Pakistani students in my digs and I can swear they stole my transistor radio. I'd send them inside, double-quick pronto.'

At which Hilda smiled at him sweetly. I could see that life at the Bar would hold no further terrors for Khan. The Lord Chief. The Court of Appeal. The House of Lords. The Uxbridge Magistrates. They'd all be child's play to him now. Like shooting fish in a water butt. Now he'd dealt in so masterly a fashion with She Who Must Be Obeyed.

Meanwhile Mr Khan was looking at me with serious concern.

'I honestly think Mrs Rumpole has a point though, sir. You should think in terms of a judgeship, in the years to come.'

Judge 'Jimmie' Jamieson was a thin, ferret-faced Scotsman of about my age. He had his wig off and was offering a silver cigarette box round to me, Guthrie Featherstone, Q.C., M.P. and Miss Trant in the privacy of his room before we started on the case of R. *v.* Parkin.

'You are an O.L., aren't you, Rumpole?' The judge asked me and I wondered if his Honour was gratuitously insulting. 'You were at Linklater's, weren't you?'

Linklater's! My old school. A wind-blasted penal colony on the Norfolk coast, where thirteen-year-olds fought for the radiators and tried to hide the lumpy porridge in letters from home.

'I haven't seen you at the O.L. dinners recently,' the judge went on.

'No.' He hadn't seen me at the Embalmers' Annual Ball, either.

'They put on a very good show for us last year, at the Connaught Rooms. – This case going to last long, is it?'

'Three days, Judge. Three or four days at the most.' Guthrie Featherstone had the time-table. Now I remembered the judge. A small trembling child from Scotland. He wore a chest protector and was incredibly mean about his tuck.

'I'm hoping to get a week's fishing in starting on Monday,' Jamieson said. 'I just wanted to get the timing from you fellows. Remember our last case, Rumpole?'

'The Paddington affray.'

'Crowds of piccaninnies scraping with knives on Paddington Station.' The judge smiled as if at a happy memory.

'Only real worry was . . . some passing white might have got hurt.'

Oh dear! Oh my ears and whiskers! We could hardly hope for a trial in the spirit of Voltaire. Miss Trant, I thought, looked especially disgusted.

Shortly thereafter the case was underway in one of the New Courts at the Bailey, and I was cross-examining the officer in charge.

'This broken window, of the grocer's shop, Inspector. You have no way of knowing if the perpetrator of that act had heard my client's oration, had you?'

'No, sir.'

'Let us hope he was not at Linklater's, Rumpole!' said the judge, and seemed to find it amusing.

'Now, you say my client said something ... about blood?' I carried on, killing the laugh.

'He said. "The answer is ... blood!" ' The Inspector consulted his notebook. 'I couldn't hear all that clearly.'

'Exactly! The rival factions were yelling their heads off. So he might have said "The answer is *in* the blood"?'

'Really. If my learned friend thinks there is any difference ...' Guthrie Featherstone rose wearily.

'Let me instruct my learned friend. If he said, "The answer *is* blood", it might well be an incitement to violence.'

'I am glad my learned friend at least appreciates the point of the prosecution case ...'

'But if he said, "The answer is *in* the blood", he was merely referring to some supposed difference in racial characteristics, and the remark was quite innocuous.'

'There is a clear distinction, is there not, Mr Featherstone?' I was half-ashamed to discover that the judge was on my side.

'If your Lordship pleases.' Featherstone subsided, and I gave the jury a friendly smile as I said:

'I am glad that my learned friend has at last grasped the nature of the defence.'

'Straight up, Mr Rumpole. He's got the Union Jack flying on his bungalow.'

I was in the pub opposite the Bailey to which I had inveigled my pupil Khan, who was taking a note for me in the case, for a quick shepherd's pie and a pint of draught Guinness (Khan had become quite a healthy drinker under my tuition, and a good companion both in the pub at lunchtime and in Pommeroy's after the battle of the day was done) and I had been approached by a tall, overweight individual, with a blotchy pink face, whose long tow-coloured hair hung over the rabbit-fur collar of his 'car coat'. It appeared that this unpromising individual was 'Cliff' Worseley, garage-owner of Purley and committee member of the South-Eastern section of the 'Britain First' movement. 'Cliff' had been giving me a number of details of the character and way of life of my client, Captain Parkin, including a description of the decor of his bungalow 'Mandalay', his relationship with his wife Mavis, and his addiction to home-made curries and homing pigeons.

'Union Jack on his bungalow? I don't suppose,' I asked hopefully, 'he lowers it at sunset by any chance?'

'He does Mr Rumpole! I swear to you he does,' 'Cliff' laughed delightedly. 'Is that sort of stuff any use to you?'

'I would say extremely useful.'

'Cliff' disappeared into the crowd, and I went over to the bar to find Miss Trant in sympathetic conversation with my pupil. As I arrived she went off to join her learned leader, Guthrie Featherstone, who was on the point of returning to Court.

'That woman!' Khan said looking after her. 'Is she of immoral character or what is she?'

'Why? Whatever did she say?'

'She said that she and I had the same problems. She wanted us to be friends and allies.'

'Oh, Khan . . .'

'I told her that my father, who is Chief of Police in the Punjab, had gone to financial sacrifices to send me to England, and I was in no position to form any alliance with her even if I wanted to. In my country we would call that an immoral woman.'

Poor Miss Trant. The way of the liberal is extremely hard, as I found out when I came to address the jury at the end of the proceedings of R. *v.* Parkin.

I had worked carefully on my final speech and I joyfully incorporated all the information about my client that 'Cliff' had given me. As a matter of fact I thought it went rather well.

'Ladies and gentlemen of the jury,' I said, 'let me introduce you to a dreamer! He doesn't dream of money, or women – he dreams of the ancient days of the British Raj. Captain Rex Parkin. It's true. He's an ex-Captain of the Pay Corps. True that he's never been further East, as far as I know, than a day trip to Boulogne.'

One jury woman smiled, gradually others started to smile.

'The closest he's got to India is the weekly night out he has with his Memsahib, Mrs Mavis Parkin, in the "Star of India Curry House" in Bexley Heath.'

Someone in the jury started to laugh. I caught a glimpse of Captain Parkin's furious face in the dock and bashed on regardless.

'But Captain Rex Parkin, dreaming away amongst his pigeons and his old bound copies of the *Boys' Own Paper*, fancies himself an officer of the British Raj. The Union Jack flies daily over his bungalow "Mandalay", number 12B Durbar Lane, and is solemnly lowered every evening at sunset. Hardly appropriate dreams, are they, for the world of today? When you can hardly call out the Bengal Lancers to subdue a spot of trouble on the Ealing frontier.'

Now I was getting continuous snuffles of laughter from the jury, and behind me the prisoner at the bar was becoming increasingly restless.

'Or ride out by elephant to accept the surrender of the Maharajah of Muswell Hill?'

Captain Parkin struggled to his feet, but the Dock Officer put a hand on his arm and he subsided. He sat more or less quiet for my peroration.

'Is this a free country, members of the jury? Is this a country where Captain Parkin and other eccentrics can flourish in all their dottiness? I may not agree with what Captain Parkin said ... It's very easy to believe in free speech for those who agree with ... But someone, a wise French man, once gave us the answer ... "I disagree with everything you say, but I will defend to the death your right to say it." '

'I wish to say ...' My client was standing rigidly to attention, apparently about to make another speech repudiating the charge of dottiness made against him by his learned Counsel.

'Sit down, Rex!' The words were only whispered but they came quite clearly from 'Cliff' in the back of the Court.

'I wish to say. I obey orders,' said Captain Parkin, and sat down and kept his mouth shut from then on.

Judge Jimmie Jamieson's summing-up came in for a good deal of criticism in the press and on telly, so I'll just give you the final, ill-considered, passage:

'What the defendant is alleged to have said, members of the

jury, is that most of us are happier in our own homes. You may have heard the old saying, "My heart's in the Highlands, my heart isn't here". I myself am a native of another country, members of the jury. I was born in Kirkcudbrightshire. Often amid the bustle of London's traffic I long for the peace of the little village I came from and where, I hope, in my retirement, to return. I don't suppose I'd be in the least upset if anyone said that about me. Nor would I take offence if he said I have different blood in my veins. The blood of Clan Jamieson of the Glen! I don't think I can help you any further, ladies and gentlemen. You will go out and consider your verdict.'

As I have written elsewhere I regard the time when the jury is out as the worst part of a barrister's life. Your mouth is dry, your hands sweat, and, whatever the case, all your life's work seems to be on trial and waiting for a verdict. I went up to the Bar Mess on the top floor of the Old Bailey, and barristers in similar circumstances were playing draughts, or drinking coffee, or reading the *Sun*. I lit a small cigar and Miss Trant came up to me, clearly enraged.

'What did you think of that jury?'

'I thought they seemed moderately sympathetic.' In fact they seemed to be a middle-aged lot of solid citizens from the New Cross area. I saw them nod several times at the judge's summing-up.

'Oh, did you really? Charmed, do you think they were, by your call to free speech?'

'I think they saw the point,' I told her. 'In fairness.'

'And Jimmie Jamieson wanted to pay his glowing tribute to Voltaire, too. For the first time in his life?'

'Miss Trant. You're becoming eloquent!' I looked at her with approval. No doubt she had learned her art from me, but she might turn out to be a credit to our Chambers.

'I'll tell you about that jury,' she went on remorselessly. 'I was watching their faces. They just wanted the faintest excuse to let the Fascist beast off. That's all they want.'

'Don't be ridiculous, Miss Trant. They'll decide the whole thing perfectly fairly. If they acquit it'll be because they believe in free speech.'

'Or because they're a bunch of Paki-bashers?'

I wished she wouldn't say such things. I was beginning to find them curiously unsettling. I was further unsettled when the jury came back half an hour later with a unanimous verdict 'Not Guilty'. I went over to congratulate my client, who was being 'sprung' from the dock. He looked at me with his strangely colourless eyes, standing like a ram-rod, in his parody of a military bearing, and said something to me which I shall not quickly forget.

'May God forgive you, Mr Rumpole,' he said. 'I certainly shan't.'

It was some months later that I learned the end of the Captain Rex Parkin story. A plump, grey-haired lady came to see me with young Simmonds, it seemed she wanted to sue certain members of the South-Eastern Committee of the 'Britain First' Party for damages for the way they had treated her husband. She asked me if she had a case, and described a meeting of the committee which took place in the living-room of their bungalow 'Mandalay' soon after I had secured her husband's acquittal. 'Cliff' Worseley was there, and Sydney Cox as chairman. I pictured the scene, the sullen faces seated round among the souvenirs of the Empire, the silent Captain Parkin sitting to attention on an upright chair, Mavis Parkin pouring coffee for the group and staying to listen to the debate. I can even imagine the offensive pomposity with which 'Cliff' put the motion.

'In a pitiful attempt to save his own skin, Rex Parkin showed the yellow streak, gentlemen. He allowed his barrister, in a so-called Court of Law, to pour scorn on the party. To make us a laughing stock! At the Old Bailey and in the National Press! Therefore I beg to move, Sydney, as deputy-chairman, and gentlemen, that Rex Parkin having proved himself unworthy of the high office we have entrusted to him, be removed as a prospective candidate of the 'Britain First' Party.

'Have you anything to say, Rex?' the chairman asked him.

'No. No. Nothing to say.'

The motion it seemed was carried and 'Cliff' Worseley was

chosen as the new candidate. He stood and made a short opening address.

'Gentlemen, the need of the party is for more positive, dynamic leadership. The days of the British Raj are over. The gorgeous "Empah" on which the sun never set . . . is gone. We have work to do, gentlemen, more suited to the desperate needs of this particular moment in time . . . And in that work we must not be afraid of dirtying our hands in the interests of the party.'

Mavis watched as her husband got up, stood to attention and left the room. It seemed that he kept his pigeons in an old shed at the bottom of the garden. What his wife didn't know was that he also kept there an old army revolver and a certain amount of ammunition. She was washing up the coffee cups when she heard a shot, and saw the pigeons fly up in a white cloud. Captain Parkin, having been responsible, as he thought, for my ridiculing his party, had shot himself.

'They always wanted to get rid of him, you see. So they used that as an excuse. And it was Rex's whole life, his whole life entirely.'

I had to advise her that, so far as I could see, she had no legal remedy.

We were having one of our regular Chambers meetings, drinking tea out of Guthrie Featherstone's bone china tea set in Guthrie Featherstone's big room, and we were discussing the question of new tenants.

'The departure of George Frobisher to the Circuit Court Bench has left something of a gap in Chambers. Clearly we need a new tenant,' said the Q.C., M.P. 'Erskine-Brown will remind us of the candidates. There seem to be two main contenders.'

'Well, we have had an application from Owen Glendour-Owen. He wants to move up to London. He has a very sound practice in Wales. Apparently he'll bring us a large number of Welsh solicitors.'

'That's what I'm afraid of,' I grumbled.

'Really, Rumpole!' I was rebuked.

'I'm sorry. I forgot about the Race Relations Act.'

'I have seen Glendour-Owen. He seems to me to be an admirable candidate,' Featherstone told us.

'I do miss George. I can't see myself revelling in Pommeroy's Wine Bar with Glendour whatever-you-call-him.'

'The other candidate is Rumpole's pupil, Lutaf Ali Khan . . .'

'Now Khan does represent something of a special case . . .' Featherstone started innocently, but the eloquent Miss Trant was on her feet at once.

'Oh yes! I was a special case, wasn't I?'

'Now Philly . . .' Erskine-Brown tried vainly to calm her down.

'No. No, I'm going to say this. I was a special case when I joined Chambers. No one wanted a woman. I had this extraordinary difficulty getting hold of the key to the loo. And Albert had to go through the embarrassment of explaining that the barrister he was sending out to the Hendon Court might turn out to be a woman . . . Now he'll have to explain that he's a . . . a . . . what do you want me to say . . . Gentleman from Pakistan . . .? It doesn't matter how good we are. We start out with a built-in handicap. That's what you mean by a special case, isn't it?'

'As a matter of fact what I meant was,' Featherstone explained patiently, 'we're under a good deal of pressure from the Bar Council. I also happen to know the views of the Lord Chancellor's office. Keith's tremendously keen on places being found in Chambers for . . . overseas applicants.'

'I wouldn't, speaking for myself, be influenced by the wishes of the Bar Council, or even of the Chancellor's department.' Claude Erskine-Brown adopted his most judicial manner and Miss Trant barked at him.

'I'm sure you wouldn't.'

'I have given a certain amount of paper-work to Khan,' Erskine-Brown went on, 'and I happened to be in Bow Street, waiting when I heard him do a prosecution, standing in for Hoskins.'

'You were waiting in Bow Street?' I was surprised.

'I had a licensing application,' Erskine-Brown said with dignity.

'Don't worry, old sweetheart. No one's accusing you of having been nabbed for soliciting.'

'In my opinion Lutaf Khan would make a useful and

hard-working member of Chambers.' Ignoring me Erskine-Brown concluded his judgement and Miss Trant looked at him, surprised and grateful.

'He also has genuine if not particularly formed musical tastes. He can feel his way round Donizetti but I hope to help him towards Wagner. I've promised him an evening at Covent Garden, Philly.'

'He'd probably rather have another afternoon at Bow Street,' I told him.

'Thank you, Erskine-Brown,' Featherstone said. 'Thanks for your contribution. Well now, suppose we take a vote. All those in favour of the candidacy of Owen Glendour-Jones?'

'Is that the darkie?' Uncle Tom whispered deafeningly.

In the end we voted to invite my pupil to occupy a permanent seat in Chambers, and I went off to tell the news which I had no doubt, with the present shortage of places in decent sets, would overjoy him.

When I got to my room, I found Khan working hard and a letter on my desk from the Lord Chancellor's department. I opened it with somewhat mystified fingers to discover that old Keith Hopner, Guthrie's friend, wanted to see me as soon as possible at the House of Lords. Was Rumpole tipped for High Office? I put the thought aside and turned to Khan.

'We just had a discussion of your candidacy up at the Chambers meeting and I'm delighted to tell you . . . You're in.'

'No? . . .' As I thought, the man was overwhelmed.

'Difficult to believe? Not at all. There was just a short discussion . . . and of course you can go on sharing my room. Keep your desk over there and . . .'

'This is terribly embarrassing.'

'Not at all. Be glad to have you. Look, if you'd like to start making a note of the deps in this nice little murder . . .' I offered him a pile of papers that had just come in.

'The truth is . . . Oh gosh. I don't want to offend Mr Featherstone and I *have* enjoyed it here. But no. No, I don't want to stay in these Chambers.'

'You don't *what*?' I couldn't believe my ears.

'I am more interested in prosecuting, Mr Rumpole. As you

know, I am most keen that some of those terrible fellows get their come-uppance.'

'Yes, but Khan ... You can get prosecution briefs here. I don't do them but ...'

'Careless driving, Mr Rumpole. Take and drive away. Small potatoes. I am after the bigger fish.'

By now I must admit I was feeling ever so slightly miffed.

'Oh yes. And where exactly are you going to put down your nets?'

'I am offered a place in a Treasury Counsel's Chambers. We have a direct line there, to the Director of Public Prosecutions. With a great respect, it doesn't seem to me that you fellows have too much contact ... with the Powers That Be.'

I looked at Khan amazed.

'I am sorry, Mr Rumpole. I have admired your way of doing cases ... It's your technique to laugh at them, isn't it? I suppose that's what Captain Rex Parkin found a bit too much to bear.'

'I wouldn't have thought you'd feel Captain Parkin was a great loss to society!'

'It is what is coming after him. That's what makes me more nervous.'

I let that one go, and returned to the business of his future, rather than this country's.

'It's your decision, Khan,' I told him. 'You must do exactly what you think best. But you're quite wrong if you think this Chambers has no connection with the Powers That Be.' I picked up the letter from my desk. 'I have a letter here. An invitation to the Lord Chancellor's office ... for a little chat.'

Walking down the Embankment towards the House of Lords, on a sunny day with the seagulls shrieking round Boadicea's statue, I asked myself who on earth wanted to be a Circus Judge? Poor old George Frobisher did. I pitied him. I really pitied him. Working every day. Ten till four. Paying as you earn. Might as well be a bank manager. Besides which it was a lonely job, being a judge. No friends. No real mates. No companionable jars, at the end of the day, in Pommeroy's Wine Bar. I also wondered who in hell wanted to judge people. I mean what would I say to them? 'Mr Bloggs, you will go to prison for two years, and there, but for the Grace of God, Horace Rumpole goes with you'?

But when I was being led down the red-carpeted corridors of that dream palace, the House of Lords, past the portraits of old Dukes and Marquesses, my thoughts, I must confess, took a somewhat different turn. On the other hand, well, on the other hand ... It's an easy life. I mean, you sit there, without any strain or worry. I mean, you don't give a damn who *wins*. And of course there's a bit of pension attached. Once you get your bottom on the Bench you're in for a pension. Hilda and I would be glad of a pension, I thought.

And I might even be able to do a bit of good, as a judge. Show appropriate mercy. 'Madam, you are more sinned against than sinning. The sentence will be half an hour's imprisonment which you have already served. You are free to go.' Look of cold fury on the officer in charge of the case. Being a judge might even provide Rumpole with a certain amount of harmless fun ...

At which point I was shown into the presence of Sir Keith Hopner, o.b.e., a large pink vision in a black jacket and pin-striped trousers, who sat in a leather chair and looked at me smiling.

'I have been thinking it over most carefully, Keith,' I told him, 'and I'm not totally opposed to the suggestion.'

'Good. That's very good. Judge Jamieson said you might be interested ...'

'*He* said that?' I was surprised he had been discussing my elevation with the primitive Scot.

'Yes. Pity about Jimmie. Pity he put his foot in it.'

'Well, one does have to be rather careful,' I sounded circum-spect, 'what one says on the Bench.'

'I'm so glad you agree.'

'I've thought a lot about it,' I told him. 'But the fact is, I get rather tired these days. Not quite so young as I was, of course. Slogging from the Sessions to the Bailey and out to Chelmsford ... Plays hell with the back.'

'I hope you'll have *time* for this job,' Sir Keith was concerned.

'Well, of course. Ten till four. No home-work! Wonderful.'

'Well, it shouldn't take as long as *that*.'

'What won't?' I was puzzled.

'The little job I have in mind ... Let me explain.'

'Well. Of course I can get used to it.'

'I'm sure you can. After all, you were at "Linklater's" weren't you?'

I couldn't see what my old school had to do with it.

'Yes. But is that a qualification?'

'Didn't Jimmy Jamieson make it clear?' Sir Keith explained carefully. 'We wanted you to take on as Secretary of the "Old Linklater's" at the Bar society. The O.L.B.S. We dine once a year, you know. In the Connaught Rooms. Come on Rumpole! We old members of school have got to stick together!'

My look of amazement turned suddenly to laughter. In fact I was still laughing as I walked back to the Temple, along the Embankment. It sounded as if the seagulls were laughing with me.

Rumpole and the Case of Identity

'Was this the face that launched a thousand ships
And did the stabbing in the Wandsworth Off-Licence?'

These lines passed through my mind as I sat working late in
Chambers. My wife Mrs Hilda Rumpole, known to me as She
Who Must Be Obeyed, had joined some dubious club called
the Bar Choral Society and was out in the evenings at this
time, indulging her fantasies in rehearsing Handel's *Messiah*
as Christmas was growing remorselessly near. On my desk
was a police identikit photograph of a long-faced young man
with bristling sideburns wearing, just in case no one noticed
him, a loudly checked red-and-yellow tartan cap. This was the
face, unreliably created from snatches of memory and a police
artist's pencil, of the man who entered an off-licence in
Wandsworth and stabbed the licensee, a small Irishman named
Tosher O'Neil, in the face and arm, making it necessary for
repair work to be carried out to the tune of twenty-seven
stitches. Also on my desk was a photograph of my client, a
young man in his twenties named David Anstey, a driver in
the well-known South London mini-cab firm 'Allbright's Cars'.
Friends and fellow drivers had told the police that David's
sartorial taste ran to an unfortunate red-and-yellow tartan cap
(I wondered how many thousand lunatics went to football
matches each weekend in such headgear). If the prosecution
could prove that this was the face Tosher remembered behind
the descending knife, then David was due for a substantial
visit to Her Majesty for Grievous Bodily Harm: which would
be a pity as he had an excellent work record, was just married
to a young wife, and his previous slips ran to driving off other

people's Ford Cortinas, so that knifing his fellow citizens would seem to be something of a new departure.

I was also wondering, as I read the papers in R. *v.* Anstey, how many seconds Tosher had really had to see his attacker's face; and I was brooding on the horrible difficulty, and total unreliability, of trials decided on identification evidence. Do all the middle-aged ladies who write to 'Any Answers' calling for the return of hanging understand that the fallibility of human memory would ensure that we hanged at least a few of the wrong people, or is that a risk we are bound to take in the pursuit of their favourite sport? I was thinking of all these things, and of the greater difficulty in our case: Tosher O'Neil had picked David Anstey out at an identification parade when my unfortunate client wasn't wearing a cap at all. As I turned back to compare the identikit picture with the undoubted face of the said Anstey there was a brisk knock at my door and the anxious face of Claude Erskine-Brown peered into my room.

'Rumpole . . . you're burning the midnight oil?'

'Ah, Erskine-Brown, Claude.' I decided to use him as a test for man's power of identification. 'How would you describe me, exactly?'

'You? Why on earth . . .?'

'Let's say I'm getting unsure of my own identity. Describe Rumpole as you saw him go into Chambers this morning. Are you sure you *did* see me go into Chambers this morning? Can you swear you're not mistaken?'

'Of course I saw you coming into Chambers. Look, Rumpole . . .'

'Yes, but how *did* you know it was me?' I pressed him.

'Well, it looked like you,' he answered rudely, 'short and fat.'

'You mean well filled out. Generously proportioned. Comfortable?'

'No. Fat. Look. There's something going on down the passage and I don't like the look of it . . .' He moved closer to me in a conspiratorial fashion.

'Are you *sure* it was me?' I returned to the subject which was starting to become an obsession.

'Of course it was you. It had your muffler. And your dreadful old hat on!'

'My old hat on! Exactly. You recognized the hat!' I felt that I had hit on a vital clue to David Anstey's defence.

'Rumpole. Will you come and look at this? It's a question of Chambers security!'

Erskine-Brown had become so insistent that I had to humour him. So off we set to the room of our learned Head of Chambers, Guthrie Featherstone, Q.C., M.P. There was a light on, showing a bright streak under the door, so that it seemed that he too was burning the midnight oil. However, Claude Erskine-Brown assured me, the door was locked, and by way of evidence he turned the handle and failed to gain admittance. There did seem to be a small sound, only a whisper like the intake of breath, or perhaps my old ears deceived me and it was the sigh of some building sinking into the ground or the distant thunder of traffic on the Embankment.

'Well, what's wrong?' I asked him, for some reason we both seemed to be whispering. 'Featherstone always locks his door. He's afraid people'll come in and read his "All England Reports", and pinch his paper clips.'

At which I thought I heard another sound from behind the door, less a distant whisper than a suppressed giggle.

'What on earth's that?' Erskine-Brown looked seriously alarmed.

'Mice!' I reassured him. 'These old places are overrun by mice.'

'It was a sound . . . more like giggling.'

'Even mice – can enjoy a joke occasionally.' I put a comforting hand on Claude's shoulder. 'You're working too hard.'

'I have been snowed under lately,' the distraught man admitted.

'Pack it in, Erskine-Brown. Abandon the affidavits . . . Come and have a nightcap at Pommeroy's Wine Bar.' I steered him away down the passage. 'You ought to watch out you know. A man's got to be very careful when he starts to hear mice giggling in the night.'

It was some weeks prior to this night of adventure that a second typist had joined our clerk's room staff, a fairly personable brown-haired young lady named Angela who wore jeans and an American combat shirt of the sort that might have been bought secondhand from some Vietnam veteran. I can't imagine that this apparition would have produced in old C. H. Wystan (my late father-in-law and our one-time Head of Chambers) any result less dramatic than a heart attack, but Guthrie Featherstone made no protest, Henry appeared to tolerate her and Uncle Tom seemed positively charmed by her; although I did catch in Erskine-Brown's eye, when he noticed her, the gleam of an early New England settler who's brought face to face with a young, attractive and particularly burnable witch. I came into the clerk's room one lunch-time, the jury at London Sessions having convicted three cannabis dealers of mine, and told the bad news to Henry. My clients had got three years apiece.

'I suppose the judge went off and drank his large whisky and soda!' Angela spoke indignantly from behind her typewriter.

'Yes. I suppose he did.' The judge had in fact been old Bullingham, so the young lady's instinct was undoubtedly correct.

'Still, it wasn't your fault. You did your best. You were defending, weren't you?' She gave me a warm smile of approval, at which point Erskine-Brown came in with some document and asked Angela to type it. She ran a quick eye over the pleading and gave us a quotation. ' "The Plaintiffs, the Gargantua Trust Property Company Ltd, are landlords of the said premises." '

'Brilliant! You *can* read it,' Erskine-Brown said with more than a hint of irony.

' "And the defendant, Mrs Parfitt, is in default of rent to the extent of £208.13. Notice to quit having been given." ' Angela read with considerable disapproval and then exploded, 'Whose side are we on?'

'We are on the side, Angela, that sends us the work,' Erskine-Brown told her coldly.

'She got notice to quit. For a measly £208.13! Gargantua Trust Property Company Ltd! Well, I don't imagine they're short of a bob or two . . .'

I was observing this scene, which I was starting to enjoy as Erskine-Brown became irate.

'Angela! You're not required to judge the case. That can be

left in the safe hands of the judge of the Marylebone County Court.'

'I bet Mrs Parfitt's an elderly widow,' said Angela with some considerable satisfaction.

'Of course. With twenty-three starving children. It doesn't matter what she is, Angela. Just you type it out.'

I had thought nothing of the mysterious incident of the light in the locked room (it's easy enough to forget to switch the light off when you lock a door) but I was a little worried, at this time, by the appearance and behaviour of our Head of Chambers, Guthrie Featherstone, Q.C., M.P. He came into Chambers very late, he looked pale and somewhat seedy, and he showed a marked lack of enthusiasm for his practice at the Bar. I put all this down to the burden of governing England, seeing us through inflation, settling Rhodesia etc. which he had assumed; but, as I sat over an early evening claret with him and Erskine-Brown in Pommeroy's Wine Bar I couldn't help feeling that Claude's incessant complaints were adding considerably to the burdens of office. When the matter of the petty cash and Dianne's salary had been brought up the Head of Chambers gave a world-weary sigh.

'All-night sitting,' he said. 'I don't know how long the old frame'll stand it.'

'Really. What great affair of State were you discussing?' I asked.

'Some earth-shaking measure for the protection of cod in Scottish waters . . .' Guthrie told us.

'I want to raise the matter of security in Chambers.' Poor Featherstone groaned slightly. Erskine-Brown went on remorselessly. 'The other night there were lights left on. After you'd locked up . . .'

'I must have forgotten . . .'

'And we distinctly heard a sound. Coming from your room!'

'How extraordinarily odd!' Featherstone seemed puzzled.

'Rumpole thought it might have been mice.'

'Oh, really?' The Q.C., M.P. looked at me, I thought, gratefully.

'And there's another matter I wanted to raise.'

'Another?' Here was a camel, I felt, whose back was about to be broken.

'That new girl, Angela. The one who does the typing now . . .'

'Henry says she's a bit of an asset. I know nothing about her, of course.' Featherstone sounded casual. 'But it seems that Dianne just couldn't cope single-handed . . .'

'The girl objects to typing a landlord's statement of claim. She only wants to type on behalf of the tenant. It really adds a new horror to life at the Bar, if one is going to have all one's cases decided in the typing pool.' Erskine-Brown completed the indictment and Featherstone gave him another uneasy smile.

'I really don't see how you can dignify those two girls, Dianne and "Angela", did you say her name was? with the title of "typing pool". Anyway, Henry tells me she's extremely good. It seems she's pretty well indispensable. But perhaps you'll head a small committee, Claude, to deal with the question of mice in Chambers.'

Shortly after this Erskine-Brown went off to some musical evening with Miss Phillida Trant, and Henry called in for a quick Cinzano Bianco and a complaint to his Head of Chambers.

'It's that new girl, Angela, Mr Featherstone. Quite frankly she's getting on my wick.'

At which I was amazed to hear Guthrie Featherstone say,

'Really, Henry? Mr Erskine-Brown was just saying what an enormous help she is, typing his pleadings.'

Henry turned to me for support.

'She wants to turn our clerk's room into a co-operative, sir. She thinks the girls should chip in to my percentage of Chambers' fees.'

'Workers' participation, Henry,' Featherstone closed his eyes wearily, 'it's bound to come.'

At which Henry gave me a look which said more clearly than words, 'not in these Chambers it bloody isn't', and I was left to brood on the strange duplicity of Guthrie Featherstone, Q.C., M.P.

'Would I wear me cap, Squire? Would I? Not if I was going to cut up some geezer in an off-licence. That'd be like leaving me visiting card.' I was with my client, young David Anstey, and Jennifer, a pleasant and hard-working solicitor's clerk, in the interview room at Brixton Prison.

'Mr Anstey,' I told him. 'If I ever get you out of this hotel, you might consider reading for the Bar. Because, old darling, you have put your finger on the bull point of the defence! Why would anyone wear a comical cap when out on an errand of mayhem and malicious wounding? Unless . . .'

'Unless they wanted to be recognized!' Jennifer suggested.

'Unless they wanted *someone* to be recognized . . .' I lit a small cigar. Outside the glass box of the interview room I could see other barristers interviewing other clients in other glass boxes, until the series ended in the screws' office, with its pleasant collection of cacti in pots. Outside in the yard other screws were exercising malignant Airedales.

'I'm not worried, Squire,' Dave Anstey sounded unhealthily optimistic. 'I'm just not worried at all. I'm in the clear.'

'No one in Brixton's in the clear, old darling,' I told him. 'Not till they hear the magical words "Not Guilty".' I sat down, for the purpose of reading my brief. 'Now, this little alibi of yours . . . It entirely depends on the evidence of your guv'nor?'

'He's very good to me, Mr Rumpole. And to the wife, since we got married. He bought all our home for us. Very generous-minded individual. "Freddy Allbright will see you right." That's his motto. Biggest mini-cab owner in London.'

'You were with him all the evening of Tuesday, March the fourth?' The stabbing in the off-licence had taken place at about a quarter to nine.

'I come back from a trip to Wembley at 8. Then Freddy took me for a curry. We was together until 10.30. Then I went home to the wife.'

Alibis always sound so delightfully healthy, but they crack up dreadfully easily. I asked Dave how his kindly employer could possibly fix the date of one out of a long line of curries.

'It was the evening before his wife's birthday. He'd got Mrs Allbright a gift.'

'What exactly?'

'It was an evening bag. Highly tasteful. For his Ladies' Night down at the Masons. He even showed it to me. Look, Mr Rumpole, it's cast iron, my alibi.'

Whatever the truth about his defence, Dave Anstey it seemed had total faith in it. As for me, I'm not sure that I like cast iron alibis. They're the sort that sink quickest, to the bottom of the sea.

To wash away the sour taste of Brixton Nick I went for a glass of Château Fleet Street (as a matter of fact the metallic flavour of this particular claret gives it a slight prison flavour, as if the grape had been grown on the sunless side of Wormwood Scrubs: I exaggerate, of course; this is a libel on Pommeroy's Wine Bar, whose budget Bordeaux has elevated my evenings and kept me astonishingly regular for years). As I arrived in the bar I was greeted by Erskine-Brown who was waving a crumpled copy of *The Times* newspaper, and by Miss Phillida Trant, who had been booked as junior to 'Soapy Joe' Truscott of Treasury Council, to appear on behalf of Her Majesty the Queen in the case of David Anstey. No sooner had I drawn up a stool and ordered a bottle of the cooking claret and three glasses than Erskine-Brown shoved his newspaper under my nose, open at the uninspiring account of yesterday's debates in Parliament.

'Just take a look at the end. I've marked it in red.' Erskine-Brown was almost too excited for coherent speech.

'After the defeat of the motion to Preserve the Ancient Grasslands, the House rose at 10.30,' I read aloud. 'Earth-shattering news, is it, Claude? What, am I meant to flee the country? Put myself out to pasture in some newly preserved grasslands?'

'Guthrie Featherstone clearly told me that last night he was at an *all-night sitting* on the Cod Fisheries (Scotland) Bill.' Erskine-Brown had apparently reached the punch-line.

'Well, I don't see what's peculiar about that . . .' I gave him a blankish look.

'It sounds to me like the collapse of an alibi.' Miss Trant, our Portia, seemed to have sniffed a *prima facie* case.

'Exactly!' Erskine-Brown chimed in. I did my best to give their excitement a douche of cold water.

'Not at all. My God, I can see where you're headed, Miss Trant. The Portia of the Prosecution! Suspicious of everyone.' The claret arrived, I gave them each a glass and some soothing words. 'It's perfectly natural for Q.C., M.P.s to forget which day it is. Poor devils, they must be constantly under the delusion that they've been discussing cod in Scotland until the small hours. If you take my advice, Miss Trant, you'll keep your mind on the off-licence stabbing. I was meaning to ask the prosecution. Who owns that off-licence, by the way?' I was looking for a motive for the Wandsworth stabbing, so I casually asked the question which was almost fatal to the defence.

'Who *owns* it?' Miss Trant frowned. 'I don't know. I could find out for you.'

'Oh, do do that, Miss Trant. It might be so much more important than the busy life of our learned Head of Chambers.'

That evening an event of unearthly, not to say spooky significance occurred in Casa Rumpole, 25B Froxbury Court in the Gloucester Road. I was sitting by the electric fire, reading the depositions in a promising little indecent assault and taking a bedtime bracer of the old and Tawney, when the house was riven by the sound of a rich contralto voice raised in what seemed to be some devout ditty.

> 'The Lord God Omnipotent . . .
> The Lord God Omnipotent . . .
> The Lord God Omnipotent . . .

sang what I first took for the ghost of some member of the Bach Choir, justifiably murdered long ago in Froxbury Court. Then I remembered that my wife was in the kitchen, the apparent source of the sound. Had She Who Must Be Obeyed taken leave of her senses?

'*Hilda*! What on *earth*'s going on?'

'I'm doing the *Messiah*,' Hilda said enigmatically, making a non-singing entrance with two cups of steaming Nescafé.

'What the hell for?'

'The Bar Choral Society.' She put down the coffee as though I should have known all about it. 'Marigold Featherstone rang me up and asked if I'd be interested. They take on wives.'

'An assembly of barrister's wives. Giving tongue. How perfectly ghastly!' I lapped up port, this was no moment for coffee.

'In praise of God, Rumpole. It is going to be Christmas.' Hilda installed herself on the other side of the electric fire.

'Sometimes I wonder if God enjoys Christmas all that much.'

At which Hilda put down her cup and saucer and leant forward to say, extremely seriously, 'Marigold Featherstone's not a happy woman.'

'Perhaps it's the *Messiah* getting her down. It's been known to have that effect on people.'

'It's Guthrie Featherstone.' Hilda shook her head sadly. 'If you ask my opinion, that marriage is dying for lack of attention.'

'Hilda! You shock me. You don't stand there at choir practice when you should be giving praise to the Lord, gossiping away about Featherstone's marriage?'

'It's not gossip, Rumpole. I told you. She's not a happy woman. Of course, it's enormously difficult being married to a politician . . .'

Or a part-time contralto . . . That was what I felt like saying. Actually I remained mute of malice.

'Their marriage is cracking up, Rumpole. And it's all *your* fault.'

'My fault?' I was astonished. I had only met Marigold Featherstone occasionally at a Chambers 'do'. An ex-nurse who had once played tennis for Roedean, she was not exactly Rumpole's bottle of claret.

'Guthrie's out late. Of course he has his all-night sittings. But even when he hasn't . . . it seems you keep him in Pommeroy's Wine Bar for hours. Boozing.'

'I do?' I only rarely took a glass with Guthrie, and, whenever I did, he was in and out of the bar like a rabbit in a hurry.

'Marigold asks him where he's been and he says, "Old

Rumpole kept me talking about Chambers business in Pommeroy's. I simply couldn't get away from him.'''

'*Old* Rumpole? Is that what he calls me?' If our learned Head of Chambers was going to use me as an alibi he might at least have been polite about me.

'I suppose that's what you were getting up to tonight.'

I had, it was true, whiled away a couple of hours in Pommeroy's, a place notable for the absence of Guthrie Featherstone, Q.C., M.P.

'Well, there wouldn't have been much point in coming back here, would there? Not while you were hitting high notes with Marigold Featherstone.'

'You want to be very careful, Rumpole. You want to be careful you don't break up *two* marriages.' On which line She returned to the kitchen to keep an urgent appointment with the washing-up. As the plates clattered I heard her, over again, carolling:

> 'The Lord God Omnipotent . . .
> The Lord God Omnipotent . . .
> The Lord God Omnipotent . . . e . . . e . . . e . . . ent
> *Reigneth!*'

Oh well, I thought, thank God He's doing something at last.

In due course we assembled, myself, 'Soapy Joe' leading for the prosecution, Miss Trant, junior for the prosecution, Dave Anstey and Jennifer my solicitors' managing clerk, before Mr Justice Vosper, a pale and sarcastic judge who has never learnt to sit quietly, but always wants to take part in the proceedings, usually as a super-leader for the prosecution. Tosher O'Neil, scarred down one side of his face, a living piece of evidence for the sympathetic jury, was in the witness-box, concluding his examination-in-chief by Miss Trant.

'Can you describe the man who attacked you?'

'He had this red cap on . . .'

'Apart from the red cap?'

'Yes. Apart from the red cap. Come on, Portia,' I muttered at her. It didn't put her off.

'Well, he was tall. Big-built.' The witness gave the man in the dock a meaningful look.

'Like about twenty million others,' I muttered, and found the judge staring in my direction, with some distaste.

'Did you say something, Mr Rumpole?' his Lordship asked.

'Nothing at all, my Lord.'

'What about his hair? What you could see of it.' Miss Trant asked.

'He had long sideburns. Sort of brown colour. What I could see of it.'

Miss Trant whispered to her leader to check she had asked all the relevant questions, and I heaved myself to my hind legs to cross-examine.

'If you look at my client, Mr O'Neil, you can see quite clearly. He has no sideburns at all.'

'No. No, he hasn't.'

'Mr Rumpole. I'm sure you don't need reminding. We live in the age of the electric razor.' Mr Justice Vosper was really the worst sort of judge; the judge who makes jokes.

'My Lord?'

'Sideburns can be shaved off. If it's convenient to do so.' Vosper J. didn't actually wink at the jury, but they gave him a conspiratorial smile.

I re-attacked the witness O'Neil.

'You told us his sideburns were sort of brown. Sort of ginger-brown? Greyish-brown? Blackish-brown? Or just brown-brown?'

Tosher didn't answer, so I pressed on.

'You know, we have heard the evidence of Mr Smith who was waiting for a bus outside the off-licence. He told us about a man with a red tartan cap and *black* sideburns.'

'I . . . didn't have a lot of time to notice him. It was that quick.'

'That quick! You only saw him, didn't you, for a matter of seconds?'

'Yes.'

'So my client stands on trial for a couple of seconds . . .'

'It will no doubt be considerably longer, by the time *you're* finished, Mr Rumpole.' Vosper could never resist that sort of remark; the jury gave him an obedient titter, and I said, 'if your Lordship pleases' as coldly as possible, then I asked the witness,

'You've never met Dave Anstey?'

'Never in my life.'

'So far as you knew he had absolutely no motive for attacking you?'

'Not as far as I know.'

'Mr Rumpole. As you know perfectly well, motive is quite irrelevant in a criminal prosecution.' Mr Justice Vosper was giving me a rough ride. I began to long for a 'Not Guilty' verdict, if only to see his Lordship's look of bemused disappointment.

Outside the Court, when we broke for lunch, a large man smelling of Havana cigars, wearing a camel-hair overcoat and several obtrusive rings came to me smiling cheerfully. He was accompanied by a blonde and extremely personable young woman, lapped in an expensive fur coat.

'How're we doing, Mr Rumpole?' the man asked, and the lady announced herself as 'Dave's wife. Betty Anstey'.

'Betty's only been married to Dave six months,' the man said. 'Lovely girl, isn't she, Mr Rumpole? Particularly lovely girl . . .'

'You are . . .?'

'Freddie Allbright. "Allbright will see you right." That's my motto, Mr Rumpole. In mini-cars as in everything else.'

'Our alibi witness?' I asked Jennifer.

'I've got the alibi ready, Mr Rumpole. Ready to go whenever you want it.' Freddie Allbright smiled, ready, it seemed, to see us right at any time.

'Can't talk to witnesses, you know.' It silenced him. 'I expect we'll call you on Monday.' I asked Mrs Anstey if she'd been in Court. She shook her head tearfully.

'I can't go in there, Mr Rumpole. I really can't. Not to have everyone staring at me because of David. Dave's all right, is he?'

'As well as can be expected,' I told her. 'I'm sure he'd appreciate a visit, down the cells.'

'I promised the young lady a lunch, Mr Rumpole,' Freddie told me. 'Better get our skates on, Betty love. Don't want some lawyer snitching our table at the Savoy, do we, Mr Rumpole?'

'No. No, I'm sure you don't.'

I watched Betty put her arm in Freddie's and they walked away. I was trying to think of the implications of this vision when Miss Trant came alongside with some rather odd news.

'I've got that information for you,' she said helpfully. 'The landlord of the off-licence. It's a company called "Allbright Motors".'

'Thank you, Miss Trant.' I wished I hadn't asked.

I didn't myself have lunch in the Savoy that day. In fact I didn't even have a slice of cold pie in the pub opposite. I went straight down to the cells with Jennifer and voiced my anxieties to our client Dave Anstey.

'If an alibi comes unstuck, everything comes unstuck.' I looked at him thoughtfully and lit a small cigar. 'They may not believe *you*, just because they don't believe your alibi . . .'

'They'll believe Freddie, Squire. Freddie's got no axe to grind.' Dave seemed imperturbably cheerful.

'Hasn't he?'

'Has he, Mr Rumpole?' Jennifer frowned.

'Freddie Allbright owns the off-licence where Tosher was cut.'

'Never!' Dave seemed genuinely surprised to hear it.

'You didn't know that?'

'Straight up, Squire, I didn't . . . Does it make any difference?'

'I don't know. Tosher picked you out at the I.D. parade. You'd never seen him before.'

'Never in my life. Straight up.'

'*Someone* must have told him . . . about you and your remarkable head-gear. You trust Freddie Allbright?' Dave's answer was so enthusiastic that I almost began to doubt my own doubts.

'You must be joking. The things the Guvnor's done for me! Big bonus when we married. Canteen of cutlery, must have cost him two hundred nicker . . .'

'And a fur coat?' I asked him. But Dave Anstey didn't know anything about his wife's fur coat. And Jennifer seemed worried at my apparent distrust of our case on the alibi.

'If we don't call the alibi evidence,' she wondered, 'won't the prosecution comment? They've got Mr Allbright's statement.' She's a thoughtful girl Jennifer, with more sense of a trial than her employers who were no doubt lunching in the West End at length, setting up launderettes and discos: I gave her the benefit of my learned opinion.

'Let Soapy Joe comment till he's blue in the face. He'll be left with a weak case of identification.'

However any thought of giving our alibi a miss was clearly repugnant to our client.

'I want the Guvnor called,' he said. 'Freddie's been like a father to me.'

'Think about it, Dave. Then I'll need your written instructions before I call Mr Freddie Allbright.' I moved to the door. Dave looked up at me, he was frowning:

'What sort of coat exactly?'

'God knows! No doubt some rare animal gave up its life for it.'

'My Betty works, don't she? She saved up for it.' Dave had apparently convinced himself. 'You got to call the Guvnor, Mr Rumpole.'

'Please. Think about it, Dave.'

I was also thinking about it; and I was starting to get a glimmer of what later turned out to be the truth about the Anstey case as I called into Chambers the next morning to collect my brief, and a fresh supply of small cigars, on my way to the Bailey. When I got into my room I sniffed a female perfume and saw a familiar well-turned-out figure sitting in my client's chair. Although familiar I couldn't place my visitor at first, but the look of a rather attractive horse matched with the brisk tone of a ward sister left me in no doubt.

'I'm Marigold Featherstone. You remember me?'

'Of course. I'm just on my way down to the Bailey,' I dived for the brief and cheroots. 'Guthrie's room's along the passage.'

'He's not in. Whenever I ring up Chambers he's not in.'

'Perhaps, if I could give him some sort of message . . .' I went to the door in a meaningful manner. At which point

Marigold, wife of our Head of Chambers, dropped her bomb-shell.

'Mr Rumpole. Do you handle divorce?'

'Only rarely. And with a strong pair of tongs. Look, I must rush, I'm . . .'

'I want you to act for me. If it should come to that.'

'Come to what, Mrs . . . Marigold?' I paused. somewhat weakly.

'Divorce! Guthrie's behaving extremely oddly. He's never there.'

I could see that the woman was outraged, and I tried to cheer her up.

'Well, that can be an advantage, I suppose. In married life. Speaking for myself, I'm married to someone who's always there. Now, if you'll excuse me . . .'

However Mrs Marigold Featherstone wouldn't let me go until she had given evidence.

'I saw Guthrie in Sloane Square. I saw him from the top of a bus. He was arm-in-arm with a girl. They were looking into Peter Jones's window. When I tackled him, he denied it.'

'Well now. How can you be sure it was Guthrie?' Instinctively I started to test the evidence. 'I mean from a bus what did you see? The top of his head . . . For how long . . . a couple of seconds?'

'I'm *sure* it was Guthrie.' The witness was almost too positive. 'He had his black jacket on, and striped trousers.'

I renewed the cross-examination. 'Ah, Mrs Feather . . . Ah, Marigold. Now that's where mistakes are so easily made. You see, just *because* he had a black jacket on, you thought it was your husband! It's so easy to put a black jacket on, isn't it, or a red-and-yellow tartan cap. Do I make myself clear?'

'Not in the least.' Marigold frowned.

'Anyway. I'm a friend of Guthrie's. We stay out together late, boozing in Pommeroy's Wine Bar. That's where he is, a lot of the time.' I was beginning to feel anxious for the fate of the wretched Q.C., M.P.

'So he tells me.' Marigold did not sound friendly.

'And I'm in his Chambers. So I couldn't possibly act for you if it comes to divorce. It'd be extremely embarrassing,' I assured her.

Marigold's answer sounded like a brisk rebuke to a probationer nurse on the subject of bed-pans.

'If it comes to a divorce, Mr Rumpole,' she said, 'I want it to be as embarrassing as possible.'

Marigold's fell purpose was not, I was later to discover, the only trouble into which our Head of Chambers had been getting himself. It appeared that he had reached the stage of life when men are said to get hot flushes (I can't remember going through it myself) and suffer from the delusion that they embody the least admirable qualities of Don Juan and the late Rudolf Valentino. I heard that when Miss Phillida Trant, who is in fact, beneath a business-like exterior, extremely personable, went into Featherstone's room to borrow a book he invited her to lunch in Soho. When she told him, as was the case, that she was going out with Erskine-Brown (a contemporary phrase which I take to mean 'staying in' with Erskine-Brown) the rogue Guthrie said that Erskine-Brown never took her anywhere interesting, and asked if she had, in fact, ever been taken to 'Fridays', a dark cellar off Covent Garden where he said the B.P.s (Featherstone's appalling phrase, apparently it means Beautiful People) met nightly to jig about to loud music in the dark. This painful interview ended by Guthrie trying to remove Miss Trant's spectacles, in the way he said James Stewart always did, to reveal the full beauty of girl librarians in the films of the thirties.

It is a matter of history that, one night after a prolonged experience of *Rigoletto* at the Royal Opera House, Miss Trant did persuade her escort Erskine-Brown to take her down the inky entrance of 'Fridays'. There they saw, or thought they saw, a disturbing spectacle which was only described to me later. At that time I had no thoughts in my head except for those concerning the defence of Dave Anstey, and the perils we might face when we tried to prove his alibi.

When I got down to the Old Bailey I saw Betty Anstey, proudly wrapped in the fur in which I was beginning to suspect she slept, waiting outside our Court. I drew the usher aside and asked him as a particular favour to call her into Court when I tipped him the wink, and on no account give her the chance of taking off her coat. I then went into the ring and, having had firm instructions from Dave to do so, breathed a silent prayer, fastened my seat belt, and called Freddie Allbright Esq. in support of our alibi. Freddie walked confidently into the witness-box, large and neat in a blue suit, with a spotted blue tie and matching handkerchief, and smiled towards the dock (which smile was returned by Dave with a simple faith in good things to come).

At first we were rolling fairly smoothly. I established a curry dinner sometime in March, and then I asked an apparently helpful Freddie Allbright about the time.

'8.45. 'Course I was with Dave at 8.45. I took him for a meal at 8, and we was together till 9.30.' So far so good, I moved stealthily towards the clincher.

'Now, can you fix the date?'

''Course I can. My wife's birthday . . .' Well, nothing to worry about as yet.

'What's the date of that?'

'March the fifth. Same every year. I'd got her an evening bag, and I told Dave about it when I met him the next day.' Freddie was still smiling as he said it, but I felt as if I'd stepped into a liftshaft some moments after the lift had gone. Was there a chance that we misunderstood each other?

'The *next* day?' I asked, apparently unconcerned.

'Right. The next day when we went for the curry.' There was no chance. Dave was looking stricken and incredulous—and the judge was making a careful note. He looked up, and asked with casual pleasure.

'That would be March the sixth?'

'That's right, my Lord.' Freddie agreed eagerly.

'I wanted to ask you about the day *before* your wife's birthday.' I felt like a surgeon trying to sew up an ever-expanding wound.

'March the fourth? Oh, I don't know what Dave was doing then. No. I tell a lie.'

'Do you, Mr Allbright?' I asked him. I hoped I sounded dangerous. Freddie only asked me an innocent question.

'Was that the Tuesday, March the fourth?'

'Yes.'

'Then Dave had *that* night off.' Freddie hammered the last nail in our coffin. 'I remember he'd been off a couple of nights before we went for the curry.'

Dave seemed about to shout from the dock. Wise Jennifer ssshed him. The judge leant forward to emphasize the hopelessness of our position. He addressed our broken reed of a witness.

'So you don't know what Mr Anstey was doing on the night of the fourth?'

'Haven't a clue, my Lord.' Freddie smiled charmingly.

The judge turned to me and put the boot in, gently but with deadly accuracy.

'You may like to remind the jury, Mr Rumpole, that the stabbing in the off-licence took place on the fourth of March.'

'I leave that to you, old darling. You're obviously loving it,' was what I thought of saying. Instead I asked the usher to present Mr Allbright (of 'Allbright's will see you right', not in Court they won't) with his signed statement in support of our alibi.

'Mr Allbright!' I put it to him. 'Did you not sign that document making it clear that you were with Mr Anstey on the evening of the *fourth* of March?'

'I may have done. Yes.'

At which Soapy Joe arose, his hands clasped together, his voice humble and low, and made a typically Soapy interjection.

'My Lord, is my learned friend entitled to cross-question his own witness?'

'If the witness is hostile. Yes.' I argued the law.

'Does my learned friend suggest that the witness is hostile to *him*?' said his Soapiness.

'No. I suggest that the witness is hostile to the *truth*!' I looked at the jury who were beginning to sense a Scene in Court and stirred with modified excitement.

'If the witness has signed a previous inconsistent statement you may cross-examine him,' said Vosper J. judicially and added

I thought maliciously, 'if you think that's a *wise* course, Mr Rumpole.' The jury smiled at what they felt might have been a joke. Soapy Joe subsided, and I said I was obliged to his Lordship and began to attack the traitor in the witness-box. The time for half-measures was over. Now it was all or nothing.

'Mr Allbright. Is your company the landlord of the off-licence where Tosher was stabbed?'

'It might be.' My first shot had ruffled the Allbright feathers a little.

'What do you mean by that? Is your business empire so vast you can't be sure where your boundaries lie?'

'We've got the lease on the off-licence. Yes.'

'So Tosher was working for *you*.'

'He might have been.'

'And what was he doing? Putting his hand in the till. Not paying his dues? Did you have to send someone to teach him a lesson?'

Now the jury was interested. Freddie played a safe delaying shot. He looked puzzled.

'Someone?'

'Who are you suggesting *someone* might be, Mr Rumpole?' Mr Justice Vosper was weighing in on behalf of the witness. I ignored him and spoke directly to Allbright.

'Someone you sent in a cap like that worn by my client Dave Anstey.'

Even Vosper J. was quiet at that. I saw Dave looking lost in the dock and Freddie Allbright attempting a disarming smile.

'Now why would I do a thing like that, Mr Rumpole?'

I didn't answer him straight away. I was whispering a word of instruction to the usher who left the Court. I then turned again to the witness.

'Mr Allbright. Are you friendly with my client's wife, Betty?'

'I'm like a father to both of them. Yes.' Freddie smiled at the jury. They didn't smile back.

'Whilst my client's been in custody, have you been seeing Betty Anstey regularly?'

'I've tried to take her out of herself, yes,' Freddie admitted after a helpful pause.

'Has taking her out of herself included buying her an expensive fur coat? The one she's wearing now?'

The usher opened the door. Betty came in, nestling in her slaughtered article of wild life. Dave looked at her from the dock. She avoided his eye. Freddie improved the effect of this scene on the jury by saying:

'I may have lent her a bob or two, to tide her over.'

'Yes. Thank you, Mrs Anstey.' I let Betty go with the bob or two of fur on her back, and some nasty looks from the ladies in the jury following her. When the Court was quiet again I unloosened the broadside.

'Mr Allbright,' I thundered. 'Has your object in this case always been to have Dave Anstey convicted?'

Freddie gave another answer which, from his point of view, could only be described as a bad error of judgement. 'No. I wanted to help Dave.'

'Is that why you've gone back on your alibi statement? Because you wanted to *help* him?'

'Or have you gone back on it because you are trying to tell us the truth?' The judge was doing his best in a tricky situation.

'Look. I put March the fourth first because Dave asked me to,' Freddie explained.

'*Mr Anstey* asked you to?' the judge was delighted.

'He said that was the date of the stabbing, like. Look, I'm sorry I can't help you, Mr Rumpole . . .'

'I'm sorry I can't help *you*, Allbright. In your attempt to get your mistress's husband put inside for a long period of years . . .'

'Mr Rumpole. Is there any basis for that suggestion?' Justice Vosper was losing what I believe is known nowadays as 'his cool'.

'If there isn't perhaps my learned friend will call the lady to rebut it. She's still outside Court.' I let the jury notice the lack of enthusiasm from Soapy Joe and went on, 'You sent your hireling, wearing that entirely recognizable cap, to teach Tosher a lesson. So Tosher identified him . . .'

'May I remind you, Mr Rumpole,' the judge sighed wearily, 'when your client was picked out at the identification parade, he wasn't wearing a cap.'

'Of course not, my Lord.' I turned on the witness.

'Perhaps you'd care to tell us, Allbright . . . who was it gave Tosher his instructions?'

Freddie looked in silence at the unsympathetic jury. I went on, more in sorrow than in anger, to pry into this wretched conspiracy.

'Didn't Tosher know who you wanted fitted up with this little enterprise in the off-licence?'

'"Fitted-up" is hardly a legal term, Mr Rumpole,' the judge tried the flippant approach. 'It makes it sound like a cupboard.'

I thought I'd teach Vosper J. to make jokes in Court.

'Then shall we say "framed", Allbright?' I said. 'It sounds like a picture. In this case the wrong picture entirely!'

The cross-examination of a hostile Allbright was, of course, only the beginning of a long and hot struggle with the judge which ended after two more days, with Rumpole suggesting to the jury that they had the alternative explanation of the events in the off-licence and they could not be certain that the case put forward by Soapy Joe on behalf of Her Majesty was certain to be correct.

'If you find Dave Anstey guilty,' I told them, 'the other man, the other man in the tartan cap sent by Freddie Allbright to enforce his dominion over the garages and off-licences of his part of Wandsworth, that "other man" will not go away or disappear, but he will return to haunt our dreams with the terrible possibility of injustice . . . It is your choice, members of the jury. Your choice entirely.'

After a nerve-wracking absence of five hours, and by a majority of ten to two, the jury opted for unhaunted dreams and decided to give Dave the benefit of the doubt and spring him from the dock. When I said 'goodbye' to him he was looking lost.

'Where do I go now, Mr Rumpole?'

'Not to Brixton at least.'

'I got no marriage, Squire. I got no job. I can't believe in anyone no more.'

'You'll get a job, Dave. You'll find another girl.'

'Not in Wandsworth I won't. Freddie'll see to that. He's got Wandsworth sewn up, has Fred Allbright. He's highly respected in this area.'

I was surprised by the tone in which he still spoke of his former employer.

'Cheer up, Dave. There is a world outside Wandsworth.'

Mr Anstey shook his head and went away looking as if he rather doubted that. I knew what I needed then, and went to find it in Pommeroy's Wine Bar, where I also saw the members of our clerk's room, Henry, Dianne and Angela in a corner and, at the bar, Erskine-Brown and Miss Trant. My former prosecutor gave me a smile of congratulation.

'We thought we had you chained up, padlocked into a tin trunk and sunk in the bottom of the sea,' she said. 'But with one leap Houdini was free.'

'Out five hours. It was a damned-close-run thing.'

'It was a smashing cross-examination, a lesson to us all,' Miss Trant told her *fiancé*.

'It's high time,' said Erskine-Brown, 'that a little justice was done to you, Rumpole.'

'Justice?'

'It's a rotten shame. You should have been Head of Chambers long ago. It was yours as the senior man. Everybody thought so.'

It was true that there had been a time when I was expected to be Head of Chambers; but Guthrie Featherstone, the newly arrived Q.C., M.P., put in for knee breeches and pair of silk stockings and so got the blessing of my old Dad-in-law C. H. Wystan as the most desirable successor.*

'I can't remember you voting for me at the time, Erskine-Brown,' I reminded him.

'Well, Guthrie Featherstone arrived. And he took silk and . . .'

'Popped in betwixt the election and my hopes.'

'It was a rotten shame, actually!' Miss Trant agreed.

'Of course, in those days . . . we didn't know the truth about Guthrie Featherstone . . .' Erskine-Brown said darkly.

---

* See 'Rumpole and the Younger Generation', pp. 9–48.

'Oh, no? And what is the truth about Guthrie Featherstone, Q.C., M.P.?' I challenged him.

'Claude quite honestly thinks he's lost his marbles.' Miss Trant shook her head sadly.

'He made a pass at Philly!' Erskine-Brown sounded incredulous.

'Well, actually, he simply asked me out to lunch.'

But Erskine-Brown looked darkly across at Angela and almost whispered. 'And he's quite simply having it off with that female Communist in the typing pool.'

'Young Angela? You astonish me!' I raised an unbelieving eyebrow.

'We must have a reliable Head of Chambers,' Erskine-Brown insisted. 'Not someone who's about to be involved in an unsavoury scandal!' I wondered what a savoury scandal would be: a scandal fried on toast, perhaps, with an anchovy and a dash of Worcester Sauce?

'Everyone's noticed things about Guthrie,' Miss Trant said.

'Things?'

'Definite signs of unreliability. The point is . . . We'll ask Guthrie Featherstone to resign and make way for *you*, Rumpole, as Head of Chambers.' Erskine-Brown the kingmaker was, it seemed, about to make me a definite offer.

'I do think you'd make an absolutely super Head!' Miss Trant seconded the motion with flattering enthusiasm. At which moment Featherstone looked into the bar, waved at us and left immediately for an unknown destination. When he had gone I gave my learned friend Erskine-Brown a warning.

'Guthrie Featherstone, Q.C., M.P. isn't an experienced Labour-Conservative M.P. for nothing. He hogs the middle of the road just in case anyone's trying to pass him. Perhaps he's not the resigning kind.'

'Then we simply move out from under him. To one of the new sets of Chambers in Lincoln's Inn,' Erskine-Brown smiled. 'I've sounded out Henry . . . and Hoskins, and Owen Glendour-Jones.'

'Tell me, Erskine-Brown. Have you had any time for your practice with all this sounding?'

'No one's going to work with a Head of Chambers who's having it off with a revolutionary from the typing pool.'

At which point Miss Angela Trotsky got up and left the bar. Was it at a signal from our Head of Chambers?

'I'd just like to know *why* you're making this extraordinary allegation?' I asked Erskine-Brown for further and better particulars.

'Claude and I saw Guthrie Featherstone dancing. In "Fridays",' Miss Trant came out with a surprising piece of news.

'The Q.C., M.P. dancing? What's your evidence for that?'

'The evidence of my own eyes!' Erskine-Brown said proudly.

'The evidence of people's own eyes can, as Miss Trant knows, be extremely unconvincing. Did you see his face? What about the sideburns?'

'We didn't see his face exactly . . .' Miss Trant said.

'He had his back to us. But *she* was there!' said Erskine-Brown.

'The Communist menace of the clerk's room?'

'And Guthrie was wearing some sort of multi-coloured green-and-yellow shirt. With flowers on it.' Erskine-Brown brought out the full horror of the offence.

'Then it couldn't have been Guthrie Featherstone!' I assured him.

'Of course it was!'

'Mistaken identity. Guthrie Featherstone simply doesn't wear multi-coloured shirts with flowers on them.' I drained the blushing beaker of Château Fleet Street. 'As for the other matter. I'll think about it.' At which point I left Counsel for the prosecution of Guthrie Featherstone.

After Court the next evening I was in Guthrie Featherstone's room, awaiting an interview with our Head of Chambers. A cupboard door was squeaking, swinging open. I got up to shut it and looked into the cupboard. All I saw was Guthrie Featherstone, Q.C.'s gear hanging on hangers. On another hanger I blinked at the sight of a ghastly green-and-yellow shirt, with a floral pattern. I shut the cupboard door quickly as Featherstone entered the presence.

'Henry said you wanted to see me . . .' he started.

'Don't you want to see *me*?'

'Not particularly.' He looked extremely tired.

'I would say, you needed a little help.'

'I'm perfectly all right. Thank you, Rumpole.'

'Are you? They're closing in! Your wife Marigold wants to start a divorce. She consulted me.'

'*You!* Whatever did she consult *you* for?' Featherstone sounded shaken.

'No doubt to cause the maximum havoc. Young Erskine-Brown alleges he saw you dancing.'

The extraordinary thing was that Featherstone then smiled, apparently delighted with the accusation.

'With Angela?'

'Claude Erskine-Brown suspects you of having a Red in the bed, so far as I can gather.'

The accused Featherstone went to sit at his desk. He seemed perfectly relaxed as he made a full verbal confession.

'All right. It's all true. It's all perfectly true, Rumpole.'

'You plead guilty?' I must say I was surprised.

'As a matter of fact it's all terribly innocent,' he rambled on. 'Jumping about in "Fridays" till two o'clock in the morning. Then back for an hour or two in Angela's ridiculously narrow bed in Oakley Street. Then off to breakfast in the House of Commons.'

'That must be the worst part about it!'

'What?'

'Breakfast in the House of Commons.' I gave him a critical look-over. 'You're obviously not cut out for that type of existence.'

'The physical strain *is* exhausting.' Guthrie sighed.

'I imagine so. It must come as a terrible shock to a man only used to somnolent parliamentary debates and a little golf.'

'Golf! It happened when I was playing with Mr Justice Vosper. You know him?'

'Only in Court. Never on the green.'

'He was talking about the Death Penalty.'

'With nostalgia, I assume.'

'I sliced a drive into the rough,' Featherstone reminisced. 'I went behind a patch of low scrub and there were a boy and girl making love, not undressed, you understand. No great white bottoms waving in the air. Just kissing each other, and laughing. I felt there was an entire world I had totally missed. I told the judge I'd been taken ill, and left the course.'

'Taken ill? Of course you had.' I had no illusions about Guthrie's complaint.

'I spent the afternoon just wandering about Richmond. In search of adventure.'

'You drew a blank, I should imagine.'

'Next morning I came into Chambers and saw Angela. She's twenty-one, Rumpole, can you imagine it?'

'With difficulty. Tell me. What is that military uniform she affects?'

'An American combat shirt. It's a sort of joke. To show her pacifist convictions.'

'Most amusing! So you set out, quite deliberately, to destroy your position in Chambers?'

'Deliberately?'

'Of course. Locking yourself in this room. What on earth was that for?'

'We couldn't go back to Oakley Street. Her flatmate was entertaining a man from the B.B.C. World Service . . .'

I remembered, with some humiliation, the night I'd played the unlovely role of eavesdropper with Erskine-Brown.

'Barristers' Chambers have been put to many uses, Featherstone, but only rarely as a setting for French farce! Oh, you were very determined, weren't you? Telling Marigold the most transparent lies. Carefully informing Miss Trant and therefore Erskine-Brown of the disco or Palais de Hop where you are apparently to be found nightly, tripping the light fantastic!' (I went to the cupboard and threw it open, dramatically displaying the incriminating evidence.) 'Keeping your dancing apparel in the cupboard.'

'Angela gave me that for my birthday,' Featherstone looked at the shirt with a tired affection. 'I couldn't take it home to Marigold.'

'What do you intend to do with it?' I asked with some contempt. 'Send Henry round to the launderette?'

'I don't know, Rumpole. What do you suggest?'

'I suggest you give it to the deserving poor. Look, Featherstone. My dear Guthrie.' I tried to bring some common sense to bear on the subject. 'You can't do it!'

'Do what, exactly?'

'Escape! You came to us as the ready-made figure of respectability. Q.C., M.P. Pipped me to the post as I remember it, for Head of Chambers – and remarkably gratified to get it. What are you going to do now? Abandon us, like a lot of ageing wives, leave us to rot on Bingo and National Assistance, while you go prancing off down Oakley Street in a remarkably lurid Paisley blouse! You can't do it. It's quite impossible. Out of the question!'

'Why *can't* I?' Featherstone was sitting behind his desk, smiling up at me.

'Because it was decided differently for you! When your mother gave proud birth to another Featherstone. When you became the youngest prefect at Marlborough. When you humbly asked the Lord Chancellor for a pair of knee breeches and took Marigold's advice on a suspender belt for your silk stockings. And when you got yourself elected Head of Chambers! It's all mapped out for you, Guthrie! The tram-lines are leading to Solicitor General in the next middle-of-the-road Conservative-Labour government, and the High Court Bench, and death of Sir Guthrie Featherstone, a judge of courteous severity, and flags fluttering at halfmast over the Benchers' dining hall . . .'

'I don't *have* to do all that,' Guthrie stood up, defiant.

'What's the alternative? Hanging round the Pier Hotel, waiting for the man from the B.B.C. to go on the night duty. Scratching a living writing "Advice from a Barrister" in the Sunday papers. Come off it, that's someone else entirely. That's not our Guthrie Featherstone.'

He took all this quietly, and stood looking at me. Finally he made the most extraordinary counter-accusation.

'You're jealous!'

'Am I?' I was, I confess, puzzled.

'Just because *you* can't escape . . .'

'Can't I? Of course I can. I am a free soul.' I resented the accusation. 'A free soul entirely.'

'Just because you're tied hand and foot by the Income Tax and the V.A.T.-man and when Henry's going to find you another brief, and "She Who Must Be Obeyed".'

'Featherstone! Is that any way to speak of Mrs Hilda Rumpole?'

'I don't know. You do.'

'That, sir, is a husband's privilege. Anyway. Why do you say I'm jealous?'

'I don't know. Is it because you want to be the only anarchist in Chambers?'

Featherstone moved away and lit a cigarette. I stood and looked at him, thoughtful, and if I'm honest I must say worried. Was there a certain truth in what he said? Had Guthrie Featherstone put his finger on the Achilles Heel of Rumpole? Did I need *him* to make me feel a free, roving spirit. With Guthrie gone should I be reduced to a mere barrister, perhaps a deadly respectable Head of Chambers, calling meetings about the regrettable failure of learned friends to switch the light off in the loo, and their extravagance with the soap? I decided to deny his allegations.

'I don't need your sort of adventure to be a free soul, Featherstone. I can be bounded in the Temple and count myself a king of infinite space.' I went to the door, using that moment to remind him of a case in which he was prosecuting. 'Remember we've got a case on next week. Importation of cannabis. You're against me.'

'Prosecuting?' He sounded doubtful.

'That is . . .' I looked at him accusingly, 'unless you've "Gone Dancing".'

I am not especially proud of what I did then, but the chance of Guthrie Featherstone appearing as the Protector of Society against the insidious attacks of the drug culture seemed too good to miss. Before the Q.C., M.P. rose to open the prosecution, I had phoned Chambers and asked Harry to send Angela straight down to the Old Bailey as I had urgent need of her services as a shorthand note-taker. When I got to Court I was delighted to see our Head of Chambers standing erect as a pillar of the Establishment, saying exactly what I required him to say.

'In this case I appear with my learned friend Mr Owen Glendour-Jones to prosecute and the defence is represented by my learned friend Mr Horace Rumpole. Members of the jury, this case concerns the possession of a dangerous drug – cannabis resin.' Guthrie began promisingly. At which moment the glass door swung open to admit that girlish G.I. Angela. She came to my side and I asked her to sit and take a note of Guthrie's opening speech. Intent on his work he seemed not to have noticed her arrival. As he carried on I could feel Angela's indignation glowing behind me.

'Cannabis, whatever you may have read in the papers, members of the jury, is a dangerous drug. Prohibited by Parliament,' said Featherstone. 'Oh, it may be very fashionable for young people to say that it does less harm than a whisky and soda, or that smoking cannabis in some way makes you a better, purer soul than squares like us, members of the jury, who may prefer an honest pint, or in the case of the ladies of the jury, a small gin and tonic? You will hear a lot in this case about the defendant feeling it his mission to "turn us all on", as if we were electric lights. The fact remains, says the prosecution, that the dealer in cannabis resin is merely a common criminal, engaged in breaking the law for sordid commercial gain . . .'

The Court door banged. The outraged Angela, by now totally disillusioned with her swinging lover, had gone. We never saw her round the Temple or the Bailey again.

Christianity has no doubt brought great benefits to humanity, but in my opinion Christmas is not one of them. With a sickening of the heart I began to notice, as I went quietly about my life of crime, the dreadful signs of the outbreak of Christmas fever. My take-away claret from Pommeroy's was wrapped in paper decorated with reindeer and robins, Henry and Dianne began to put up holly in the clerk's room. Soon we should have to struggle down Oxford Street so that I could buy She the lavender water she never uses, and She could buy me the tie I never wear. Paper streamers went up in the list office at the Bailey, and there was plastic holly in the gate room at Brixton Nick. In time more decorations were hung in Featherstone's room in Chambers, where was held our annual Christmas thrash (wives and girl-friends invited, warm gin and vermouth and Dianne traditionally far from steady on her pins before the end of the evening). I had gone through a drink or two at this gathering when I found myself in the centre of a group which consisted solely of Erskine-Brown and Miss Trant. I took the opportunity of telling them that I would take no part in a Chambers revolution; and that having looked carefully into the allegations against Guthrie Featherstone I found that the prosecution had not made out its case, indeed I believed the unfortunate Guthrie had this in common with Dave Anstey. They were both victims of cases of mistaken identity.

'What're you up to now, Houdini?' Miss Trant asked suspiciously.

'It may be. It may very well be,' I suggested, 'that there has been someone, a totally different someone, masquerading as Guthrie Featherstone!' I looked towards Featherstone, well-turned-out in a grey suit, who had arrived, escorting a smiling Marigold. 'All I can tell you for certain is,' I went on to the plotters, 'our respected Head of Chambers is clearly not the person you saw whooping it up in the disco. Look at him now, graciously escorting his lovely wife to our Christmas celebration. Look at him carefully, Erskine-Brown! Observe him closely, Miss Trant. Is that the man you saw? Certainly not! Do I make myself clear?'

'Not in the least, Rumpole,' Erskine-Brown grumbled and frowned displeased. I moved off. Marigold was enjoying a stimulating sherry. I came up to her. 'Mrs Featherstone. Marigold. I owe you an apology . . .'

'Mr Rumpole?'

'Keeping your husband out late boozing in Pommeroy's. Disgusting behaviour! I have put a complete stop to it.'

'So I've noticed.' Marigold smiled graciously. 'The all-night sittings seem to have dropped off lately, too. I get Guthrie for dinner nowadays.'

'How delicious!' I gave her a small bow and She Who Must Be Obeyed hove into view, clutching a large G and T.

'Rumpole!' She trumpeted.

'You know She . . . you know my wife, of course.' I did my best to introduce her.

'Of course,' Marigold inclined her head. 'We sing together.'

'You're coming to the *Messiah*, Rumpole,' Hilda said.

'Oh yes, Mr Rumpole,' Marigold added her pennyworth. 'Do come. We make a jolly brave stab at the "Hallelujah chorus".'

'Do you really? How very sporting of you. I hate to miss it: but you see, the pressure of work in Chambers . . .'

'You *are* coming to the *Messiah*, Rumpole!' In She's mouth it was an announcement, not an invitation. Further conversation was precluded by Henry calling for silence for our Head of Chambers.

'I'm not going to make a speech . . .' Featherstone began to general applause. 'I just wanted to welcome you all . . . Members and wives and girlfriends who are members also . . .' Here he raised his glass to our Portia, Miss Trant. 'To our annual Christmas "do". We have had a pretty good year, Henry tells me, in Chambers . . .' In fact Henry was wearing a new suit as a small tribute to his ten per cent. Featherstone boomed on, 'And we have managed to stick together throughout this year . . .'

'Except for one departure in the typing department,' I reminded him tactlessly.

Featherstone ignored this and continued, 'Glendour-Jones has joined us, since the departure of George Frobisher for the Circuit Court Bench. I only want to say . . .'

' "That he which hath no stomach to this fight" . . .' I felt it was time to put some force into this oration, so I almost shouted King Harry's call to battle.

'Did you want to say something Horace?' Featherstone smiled and I cantered on, after draining my glass.

> 'Let him depart; his passport shall be made,
> And crowns for convoy put into his purse:
> We would not plead in that man's company
> That fears his fellowship to plead with us.'

'What on earth's your husband talking about?' I heard Marigold whisper to She.

'It's Shakespeare. He does it all the time at home. I wish he wouldn't do it when we're out. So dreadfully embarrassing.'

'When people speak of a split in Chambers or of the possibility of any other head but our distinguished Q.C., M.P. . . .' I turned my eyes on the subversive Erskine-Brown, 'they are making a grave error, and a terrible mistake . . . Like the mistakes in identity which may do such terrible injustice in our Courts. My learned leader, Guthrie Featherstone Q.C., M.P. is a man fashioned by nature to be Head of Chambers. He couldn't possibly be anything else. So we Old Bailey Hacks, we common soldiers at the Bar, will attack a New Year, under his leadership, crying together, "God for Guthrie, Henry and Dianne!" '

I moved to Featherstone, put a hand on his shoulder.

'Sorry, old darling,' I said quietly. 'You're lumbered with it!'

Rumpole and the Course of True Love

Love, although the staple diet of the *Oxford Book of English Verse*, and the subject which seems the concern of the majority of its contributors, has not, so far, much disturbed the even course of these memoirs, which have been mainly concerned with bloodstains, mayhem, murder and other such signs of affection. I cannot help thinking that the time occupied in the course of an average lifetime in the pursuit of love has been greatly exaggerated. Dr Donne and Lord Byron, I am convinced, spent many more of their spare moments asleep, or staring aimlessly into the middle distance, or having a lonely chop and an early night than they would have us believe. The days spent by Rumpole, for instance, in the hectic pursuit of passion during the course of an average lifetime at the Bar, if laid end to end, would hardly fill out a summer holiday.

I was, it is true, extremely fond of Miss Porter, my *fiancée*, the daughter of my old Oxford tutor, but our engagement had to be broken off by reason of her inappropriate and quite unexpected death. She was a docile young woman, with a gentle uncomplaining voice, and had I married her I would no doubt have been spared the more military aspect of home life with She Who Must Be Obeyed, whose tone of voice often seems more suited to the barrack square than to the boudoir. I stumbled, rather than plunged, into marriage with She (Mrs Hilda Rumpole) as the result of a gentle push from her father, old C. H. Wystan, my one-time Head of Chambers, and was rash enough to propose to her when my gills were awash with champagne during a distant Inns of Court Ball (we all make mistakes during our early years at the Bar). It can hardly be said that hectic passion has been the keynote of my married life with She Who

Must Be Obeyed, although I remember a holiday we took around 1949 in Brittany when She showed an unwonted enthusiasm for the stuff (I have always put it down to the shellfish). Although embarrassing at the time this holiday did ultimately produce the enduring benefit of my son Nicholas Rumpole, with whom I found considerable rapport and formed what I sincerely hope is a lasting friendship.

It would be idle, of course, to pretend that the Rumpole heart has been forever chilled and that those lyrical effusions which fill so much of my old *Oxford Book* (Sir Arthur Quiller-Couch edition) have no resonance for me. I was deeply taken with a comrade-in-arms, young 'Bobby' O'Keefe who looked, in those days, as pert and exquisitely rounded as ladies on the cover of *Reveille*. I met 'Bobby' when she was in the W.A.A.F. and I was doing my best to serve my country in the Air Force groundstaff, but her sudden marriage to Pilot Officer Sam 'Three Fingers' Dogherty broke off this potentially inconvenient romance.

I should also add, in the interests of honesty, that there is a girl with copper-coloured hair and an engaging smile behind the urn in a café opposite the Old Bailey who brightens my breakfasts, with whom I enjoy what can only be described as light banter (although my heart sinks unaccountably when she tells me about her boyfriend who is apparently in the weight-lifting business).

So much for love and Rumpole. I must now deal with the disastrous effects of this disease on the learned Head of my Chambers, Guthrie Featherstone, Q.C., M.P. and on a client of mine, Ronald Ransom, teacher of English Language and Literature at the John Keats Comprehensive School in the wilds of Hertfordshire.

The John Keats was, so my client Ransom told me, the very model of a modern comprehensive school: designed to enhance the name of State Education, and to empty the public schools of all but a hard core of sado-masochists and the children of Asiatic bankers. The John Keats was, it seemed, so free and yet so self-disciplined, so well-equipped and yet so 'caring' (unlike my old public school where they certainly didn't care whether you lived or died), and so genuinely 'civilized' that many Labour M.P.s and even some Cabinet Ministers bought homes in that part of Hertfordshire, so that they could enjoy the double advantage of an excellent education for their children, and an easy conscience when presenting themselves as men of the people.

The John Keats Comprehensive was enlightened in its teaching methods. In History, so Ransom told me, the social life of the medieval village, or the economic basis of the Industrial Revolution were taught, rather than the dates of the Kings and Queens of England. The Domestic Science students could run up a reasonable 'moussaka' or 'salade Nicoise'; the Literature classes spent a great deal of time extemporizing short playlets on the hopelessness of life in a comprehensive school; Sex Instruction took place from an early age, and the John Keats pupil graduated from basic intercourse in Junior Three, to 'The Value of Foreplay' and 'The Toleration of Sexual Minorities' in the Sixth.

There's no doubt that my client Ransom enjoyed his life and work at the John Keats Comprehensive. He had been brought up by a strict Methodist family in Scotland and sent to a grimly academic school, where Shakespeare had been reduced to a grammatical exercise and the construing of Virgil was no more exciting than lower mathematics. Neither that, nor his teachers' training college, had led him to hope of an educational establishment where art was held to be more important than exams, where Mahler was thought to be more exciting than football, and where *Romeo and Juliet* was discussed as a poetic and sexual experience and not picked over for familiar quotations. His pleasure in his work was in no way diminished by the fact that there sat in the front row of his classroom, eagerly drinking in his explanation of the convoluted passions of Dr John Donne, and deeply grateful for his soft Scottish reading of Andrew Marvell's impatient verses to his coy mistress, a Miss Francesca Capstick, the moderately bright daughter of a local bank manager. It was to her that he addressed Marvell's dire warning not to hang about until 'worms should try, that long-preserved virginity', and she was, of course, the reason for his ending up in my Chambers one summer morning. Miss Capstick was, at the time relevant to the offence, fifteen years and eleven months old.

I had, later, an opportunity of examining Miss Capstick in some detail. She was by no means the blousy, tarty sort of girl who misleads men as to her age with make-up or hair dye. In fact she wore no make-up, her hair was long, brown and very clean, her eyes were large and gentle, her voice quiet, at times hardly audible. Her face can be seen in a hundred reproductions among the nymphs attendant upon Botticelli's 'Primavera'; she was called 'Frank' by her friends and chewed gum during some part of her evidence.

> 'I wonder by my troth, what thou, and I
> Did, till we loved? were we not weaned till then,
> But sucked on country pleasures, childishly?
> Or snorted we in the seven sleepers' den?'

The Headmaster of the John Keats read out the verses with initial anger and disgust which turned, Ransom told me, to the sincere guttural trill of a Radio Three poetry reader. The Head always produced the school play and fancied himself as some mute inglorious Gielgud who had got lost in the State Education system. He therefore could not read the immortal words, even in a document he felt to be incriminating, without giving them a little rhythm, a touch of projection.

> 'Twas so, but this all pleasures fancies bee
> If any beauty I did see
> Which I desired and got,
> Twas but a dream of thee,'

Ransom supplied helpfully.

'That's not the point.' The Headmaster threw the letter down on his desk and started to pace the room with the nervous rage he had tried to get into his Sixth Formers' rendering of the quarrel scene in *Julius Caesar*. 'The point is that you were writing these amorous ravings to a young girl who has not yet had the maturing experience of attempting O-levels. Francesca Campstick.'

'Her name's Francesca Capstick and I'm teaching her John Donne. So naturally I sent her that quotation.'

'And since the night at the Festival Hall, and the cannelloni and Orvieto at "Luigi's", I realize I love you spiritually and physically more than anyone I've ever loved in my life before.' The Headmaster had now repossessed himself of the letter. 'Is that a quotation from John Donne?'

'No. As a matter of fact, it's a quotation from me.'

'I rather thought it was.' The Headmaster was quick as a bloodhound on the scent, although it was not a difficult deduction to make as the letter was undoubtedly in his English master's handwriting. 'You see, I've got your letter!'

'Yes,' said Ronnie. 'And I rather wonder who gave it to you.'

'A . . . A well-wisher.'

'A well-wisher of yours, or mine?'

'I think, perhaps, a well-wisher of Francesca's. And what exactly does that passage mean?'

'It means we went to the Royal Festival Hall, where we heard a Vivaldi concert conducted by Neville Marriner, and afterwards we went to "Luigi's" in Covent Garden where we had cannelloni and a bottle of Orvieto.'

'Anything else?' By this time, apparently, the Headmaster was playing the sneering role of the minor inquisitor from *St Joan*.

'Anything else? Oh yes.' Ronnie kept his head admirably. 'Francesca had a large cassata ice and I had a cup of black coffee and a Strega.'

By this time, Ransom told me, the Headmaster was trembling. No doubt if he had been running an old-fashioned blood-and-thunder type of academy he might have remained more calm. He might even have torn up Ransom's letter and told him to take girls *en masse* to Vivaldi in the future, rather than give them individual attention. But as the Head of a Progressive school he no doubt feared that he was only a whisper away from anarchy, one false step and he would have a Maoist take-over in the P.E. period, strip-shows in the art classes and group tactile experience during Religious Instruction. Accordingly he pressed Ransom with cross-examination, ever a dangerous weapon in the hands of the amateur.

'And what does this mean?' he asked again, brandishing the letter. ' "I realize I love you physically and spiritually more than anyone I've ever loved in my life before"?'

'It means exactly what it says,' Ransom told him. 'Francesca is an extremely sensitive and intelligent girl as well as being physically beautiful. What is does *not* mean is that I have ever been to bed with her.'

'Well,' the Headmaster said, and Ransom told me the gleam in the old Thespian's eye was undoubtedly salacious. 'We will have to see what Miss Clapstick says about that.'

'I'm sure she'll tell you exactly the same thing,' Ransom answered, as subsequently recorded in the deposition of the Headmaster's evidence. 'And she may even tell you that her name is "Capstick" as well.'

'I'm glad you reminded me of that,' said the old trooper, hogging the curtain line. 'As I also mean to write to her father.'

What Miss Capstick did tell the Headmaster led to a letter from the Headmaster to Capstick *père* regretting that, as there were bad apples in every barrel, so there were black sheep, or persons who took the message of the poets too literally, even among the teaching staff of the John Keats Comprehensive. When Mr Capstick the bank manager received the bad news it led to his visiting the Old Bill. In due course Inspector David Hewitt of the local Constabulary rang up Ronald Ransom and asked him if he might find it convenient to call in at the Station the next morning, that is if he wanted to spare himself the embarrassment of a couple of the local rozzers tramping in to finger his collar just as he was explaining the saucier passages in *Measure for Measure* to a crowded classroom of delighted adolescents.

That particular chain of events led inevitably to a conference in my room in Chambers at Number 3 Equity Court, and to my asking Ransom that unavoidable but always embarrassing question, 'Well, did you do it?'

'I can't fight the case.' Ransom was a pleasant-looking young man, I'd say in his late twenties, a dark-haired, blue-eyed Scot. He wore an old tweed jacket which he'd probably had since he was a student and a tie that might, for all I knew, have been hand-woven by some admirer in evening classes.

'That doesn't sound exactly like an answer to my question.'

'Well, she told the old boy I did, didn't she?'

It was a question and not an answer and seemed to me to show traces of a fighting spirit; so I eagerly prepared for battle.

'Fantasy! That's why she said that. Pure fantasy!'

'You really think so?'

'Well, of course. I mean, children . . .'

'She's almost sixteen.'

It was that 'almost' that had landed him on the windy side of the law. I tried again. 'Young people . . . persons, reading poetry. Well, naturally it stimulates the imagination. I will have to educate the trial judge, who may well consider the All England Law Reports the height of erotic fantasy. I will have to explain to him exactly how poetry affects the mind.'

'How about the body?' As a client this gentle young Scot seemed unlikely to prove helpful.

'We'd better forget about the body. Judges in this class of case don't really like to be reminded that the body exists. "This case," we shall say (I was already framing some of the better phrases for my final speech), "this case, members of the jury," (I stood up and lit, with relish, a small cigar) "this case exists entirely in a young girl's imagination, an imagination overstimulated by indulgence in the love poems of John Donne. When I was a lad, members of the jury, when some of us were lads, we read about brave Horatius, and imagined we were fighting to keep the bridge and defend, single-handed, the City of Rome. Young Fanny Chopstick . . .'

'Capstick.'

'Whatever her name is . . . "reads about being someone's enthusiastic mistress and so she imagines she is *precisely that*!"' I paused for a moment to consider whether this was a proposition sound in law and logic. Given a reasonably educated jury (I'd settle for one member with the *Guardian* sticking out of his pocket) I decided that it was.

'You'd have to cross-examine her?' Ransom asked me.

'Gently. To point out the vividness of her imagination.'

'I couldn't have her put through that in Court, Mr Rumpole.'

I looked at him, at his almost embarrassingly honest eyes, his frayed jacket and homespun tie. 'May I remind you, Mr

Ransom,' I said, 'of the present overcrowded conditions in our prisons. Are you seeking to add to the congestion?'

'I know, but . . .'

'And may I also remind you of the unpopularity with the other inmates of anyone convicted of offences with young girls. It's so easy to spill boiling cocoa on someone's head. I believe it's known as "cocoaing the S.O.s".'

'What's an S.O., Mr Rumpole?' Ransom sounded detached.

'A sexual offender.' I could have also told him that an unpopular prisoner could fairly easily choke to death on a rock-cake.

'The client,' up spoke Mr Grayson, the local Hertfordshire solicitor, an anxious and kindly looking individual who in fact had the *Guardian* not sticking out of his pocket, indeed, but nestling in his pile of papers in the case of the Queen against Ronald Ransom (and it was most definitely *not* the sort of case, in my opinion, in which Her Majesty should have let herself get involved). 'The client wants to keep out of prison.'

'Well,' I smiled. 'How unusual!'

'It wouldn't be prison, would it?' Ransom looked alarmed for the first time. 'I mean, she was nearly sixteen . . .'

'She *is* sixteen now,' Mr Grayson added.

'*Now* is hardly the point,' I told them. 'Whether Mr Ransom goes to prison or not would depend, in my opinion, entirely on the judge concerned. Now, at the Bailey if we drew "Pokey" Peterson, who happens to be paying maintenance to an ageing ex-wife, and who has just married a young lady from the chorus at Churchill's Club, well, you'd probably get a conditional discharge; but if fate span the wheel and sent us Mr Justice Vosper, I'm afraid you'd be into the slammer before you can say "the expense of spirit in a waste of shame". So if it's merely a question of sparing a young girl's feelings . . .'

'It is. It's a question of that,' Ransom answered me.

'Then think of yourself. Your job.'

'I don't care about the job really. I'd like to try and write something. I've never had the time.'

'You may get the time now. Possibly eighteen months.'

Ransom was kind enough to laugh at this pleasantry. 'You're

too ruthless a questioner, Mr Rumpole,' he flattered me. 'And I think too much of Francesca to have her put through the mill by you. I'm definitely pleading guilty. But surely they won't send me to prison, will they?' For the first time his eyes avoided me.

'I told you. It depends entirely on the judge. Now, if you can tell me who we're likely to get . . .'

'Oh, I can tell you *that*,' Mr Grayson announced our incredible, our earth-shattering good fortune just as if it were the date, or the probable length of the hearing. 'It's in our local Circuit Court. We'll have His Honour Judge Frobisher.'

His Honour Judge George Frobisher! His Honour old George. His Honour my oldest, my dearest friend, in whose company I have sunk more bottles of Pommeroy's plonk and solved more knotty clues in *The Times* crossword than with any other person, alive or dead. Old George with whom I spent almost forty years in Chambers until he was elevated, or demoted as I would prefer to call it, to a position on the Circuit, or Circus Bench. Dear old George, who confided in me when he was thinking of committing an unpremeditated act of matrimony with a lady who, I recalled, had a touch of arson in her past.* I had crossed swords with old George in friendly duels in almost every Court in England, from the Uxbridge Magistrates to the Family Division, and from London Sessions to Lewes Assizes; and for the life of me I couldn't remember any occasion when George had emerged victorious. Old George Frobisher, it has to be said, is the dearest of fellows, the kindest of companions and the best of listeners; he is sound on his law and takes a good note of the evidence; but in Court he stands up with all the eager self-confidence of a rabbit with a retiring disposition caught in the headlights of an oncoming car. He was also, at the Bar, frenetically incapable of making up his mind; not only on vital issues, such as whether to put his client into the witness-box, but on minor matters, such as whether to start his final speeches, 'Members of the jury' or 'Ladies and gentlemen of the jury'. (Sometimes he compromised and called them both.) He was also extremely suggestible, and many is the Country Court claim I have been able to settle with

*See 'Rumpole and the Man of God,' pp. 205–37.

old George on extremely favourable terms, and many are the prosecutions charges I have been able to persuade him to drop like a hot potato. In short, I have never had, in Court or out of it, the slightest trouble with old George.

'You don't mean to tell me . . .' I was almost, I swear it, laughing with delight. 'You don't mean to tell me our judge is my old friend George Frobisher?'

'His Honour Judge George Frobisher, yes,' Mr Grayson replied, in a tone of what I thought was quite unnecessary awe.

'Then I promise you more, I give you my word,' I was happy to assure Mr Ronald Ransom, 'your chances of being cocoaed are nil. What is more, you will never be banged up, even in an open prison. Plead guilty if you feel you have to. We shall have absolutely no trouble with old George.'

The good fortunes of my client Ransom seemed to be increasing daily. One early morning in the following weeks I called into my breakfast café opposite the Old Bailey, and was disappointed to find that the attraction by the tea urn was noticeably absent (a chill, perhaps, or exhaustion after a night out with the weight-lifter). Sitting there, however, nursing a cup of coffee, shivering slightly and looking distinctly green about the gills was Miss Phillida Trant, our talented Chambers' token tribute to sexual equality, the Portia of Number 3 Equity Court.

'Hullo, Rumpole,' she said. 'I hear you're going to be agin me out in the wilds of Hertfordshire. Case of R. v. Ransom. Spot of unlawful carnal knowledge.' The trouble with lady barristers, you will have noticed, is that they talk more like men barristers than men barristers do.

'Good heavens,' I said. 'Miss Trant! You don't look in the least bit well. Are you sickening for something?' I wasn't coming straight to the point, you notice, which was my firm determination to keep Ronald Ransom out of the cooler. I was determined to try a little circuitous politeness first.

'Yes,' she said. 'I'm afraid I am.'

'Can I get you something?' I asked solicitously. 'They do a particularly good bacon and egg on a fried slice here.' At which news Miss Trant went, if possible, even greener.

'No, thank you,' she said. 'As a matter of fact, I've just thrown up in the loo at Blackfriars Station.'

'It's gastric flu.' I sat down beside her and lit a small cigar which didn't seem to help matters; Miss Trant coughed and waved her hand in the air. 'There's a lot of it about.'

'It's not gastric flu,' Miss Trant told me. 'I'm up the bloody spout.'

I didn't know whether congratulations or commiseration were in order. Accordingly I took a gulp of coffee, with an expression of deep sympathy and respect.

'I don't know why I'm telling *you*,' she said. 'I haven't even told Claude yet.' Claude, I remembered, was the baptismal name of Erskine-Brown, the pompous young specializer in mortgages and company law, and the member of our Chambers least sympathetic to Rumpole, to whom Miss Trant had been rash enough to get herself engaged. 'I suppose I'm telling you because, well, you've brought me up in the law, haven't you? You're a sort of father figure. Ever since you gave me such a terrible beating in the Dock Street Magistrates Court.'*

I am no longer proud of the way in which I induced Miss Trant, who was prosecuting, to bore the Dock Street Magistrate to such a state of irritation, by quoting law to him by the yard, that he gave judgement for Rumpole. Accordingly I asked with some sympathy, 'The proposed nipper does emanate from Erskine-Brown, I suppose?'

'Oh yes,' Miss Trant nodded vigorously. 'The trouble is, I can't seem to bring myself to tell him. He'll want to marry me or something.'

'You don't want to get married?'

'I've got three new firms of solicitors,' Miss Trant told me, 'and a six-month-long firm fraud starting in Portsmouth in November. Of course I don't want to get married! What would I want to get married for?'

The trouble, as I say, with lady barristers is that they're so much keener on being barristers than barristers are.

'Claude'll want me to stay at home,' Miss Trant went on pathetically, 'and mix up Ostermilk.'

* See 'Rumpole and the Married Lady', pp. 105–33.

'Well,' I told her judicially. 'I see your problem, Miss Trant. But I suppose it'll have to come out in the end.'

'Yes,' she said, 'that's what I'm afraid of.'

The conversation seemed to be weaving unhealthily towards the gynaecological, an area of life I have always strictly avoided. 'Well, yes,' I said. 'Now about this wretched school-teacher, poor old Ronald Ransom . . .'

'It's not going to take long, is it?' Miss Trant put on her glasses again and looked at me anxiously. 'I'm prosecuting a larceny at the Bailey the week after.'

'I thought about three weeks.' Ransom's luck seemed to be holding out marvellously. 'Unless of course I can twist his arm and get him to plead guilty.'

'Is there any hope of that?' Miss Trant sounded eager.

'I suppose anything's possible.' I looked thoughtful. 'Of course, I'd have to be sure he wouldn't get sent to prison.'

'Why on earth should he get sent to prison?' Miss Trant looked at me, surprised. 'She was almost sixteen. Anyway, in my opinion, the bloody girl asked for it.'

Only one thing is certain in the dubious world of the law. No one is harder on a lady than a lady barrister.

Ronald Ransom and Miss Phillida Trant weren't the only ones for whom the course of true love was not running particularly smoothly at that time. I have written already* of the unfortunate time when the learned Head of our Chambers, Guthrie Featherstone, Q.C., M.P., had apparently lost his marbles (in Erskine-Brown's vivid phrase) and taken up with a junior typist in our clerk's room of such pronounced left-wing views that she declined to type a statement of claim on behalf of a landlord in a possession case. She would only type on behalf of tenants, defendants, abandoned wives and other unprivileged persons. It is true that I had managed, with what I can say without boasting was consummate legal skill, to extricate Featherstone from his unfortunate situation. However, with that longing for self-immolation which seizes persons who plead

* See 'Rumpole and the Case of Identity', pp. 296–328.

guilty, or make long statements to the police, Guthrie Feather-stone had, in an intimate moment, over an up till then cheerful dinner at 'L'Étoile', confessed the whole affair to his wife Marigold, who had been predictably furious and left the table with her *poulet à l'estragon* practically untouched.

After the confession Marigold's mood ranged from the martyred to the vindictive in varying degrees of unbearability, so that the unfortunate Guthrie often arrived at Chambers looking less like a suave and successful Q.C. (for undoubtedly he was still successful) than a man who spends his nights watching over a dynamite factory in which all the employees are allowed to smoke.

Now it was about this time that I was defending a rather beguiling young man called Higgins on a long series of safe-breakings and warehouse-enterings. The evidence against him consisted of a swollen bank account for which no particular explanation could be given and a collection of heavy tools and comic masks in his car. It was alleged to appeal to Higgins's sense of comedy to enter enclosed premises wearing a Mickey Mouse or Count Dracula mask to prevent identification.

This case was being prosecuted, competently enough, by my learned Head of Chambers, and as we sat together chattering before the judge came into Court, I happened to remark that Guthrie wasn't looking quite up to snuff. In fact he seemed to be in a mood of deep despondency. He explained, in answer to my solicitous inquiry, that his wife Marigold was still cutting up extremely rough and had what the poor man described as 'a touch of the nervy'.

'She's threatening to divorce me, Rumpole.'

'Not *still*?'

'I just couldn't face the whole stink of a divorce at the moment. I mean, a divorce just plays havoc with your chance of getting your bottom on to the Bench.'

At last all was explained. Since I had put Guthrie Featherstone back on the road of respectability he had gone the whole hog and was hell bent on a scarlet-and-ermine trimmed dressing-gown.

'You want to get your bottom there, of course . . .'

'It's not me so much. It's Marigold.'

'Marigold?'

'My wife, Marigold.'

'Oh, *that* Marigold.'

'She's fired off an ultimatum. Unless I can make the High Court Bench she's going to up sticks and file a petition.'

'Seems a bit desperate.'

'She *is* desperate.'

'But my dear Guthrie. My dear old Featherstone. What are you going to do about it? I mean, you can't just knock on the Lord Chancellor's door and ask . . .'

'Vosper J. has a bit of influence in appointments . . .'

I was sure he had. Mr Justice Vosper was a man who could well be capable of ordering muffins after a death sentence, if muffins and death sentences still existed, but he was a powerful figure in the judicial hierarchy and his influence on appointments, among many other factors, would ensure that there would never be a Mr Justice Rumpole known to history.

'I'm playing golf with Vosper at the weekend, and with old Keith from the Lord Chancellor's office,' Guthrie answered proudly.

It seems that Marigold Featherstone had driven her desperate spouse a long way down the Primrose Path that leads to the eternal isolation in the Judges' Lodgings. However, I wanted to be helpful.

'If you're playing golf with Vosper J.,' I said, 'it might be as well not to win.'

'That thought, Rumpole, had occurred to me.'

Another thought had occurred to me also. It was a wheeze that I thought could be put to some good purpose in the defence of my client Higgins.

'I suppose,' I said casually, 'that if you *really* want the High Court Bench, you have to start doing your cases in a different sort of way.'

'What sort of way do you mean by that exactly, Rumpole?' Guthrie asked anxiously.

'Well. I mean, you have to stop being too much the advocate. Stop trying to win too hard. You'll have to show yourself above the dust of the arena. You have to adopt the *judicial attitude*.'

'The judicial attitude, of course, yes. You think I should adopt it?' Guthrie was swallowing the Rumpole plan, hook, line and sinker.

'I don't think you can start too soon,' I told him.

Shortly after that the judge (who was, of course, given Rumpole's usual run of bad luck, dear old Vosper J.) arrived and put his bottom on its accustomed place on the Bench, and Guthrie Featherstone rose to make his final speech for the prosecution which came out, to my great satisfaction, as a sterling attempt to adopt 'the judicial attitude'.

'Of course, members of the jury,' said Guthrie, 'as prosecuting counsel I adopt an attitude which is quite fair and, I hope, judicial. The prosecution has to prove its case, and if it doesn't do so the defence is entitled to succeed.' I saw my client Higgins look at Guthrie with a wild surmise. It was rather as if a heretic, dragged before the Inquisition, had been told he'd just won a holiday in the Bahamas. 'If you think he might possibly have won the money in his bank account at the races, even if he has forgotten the name of the horse and even the track concerned, then you must acquit him! If you think he may have been taking those various animal masks to a children's party at a Dr Barnardo's Home, or if you think he possibly needed those heavy tools to put up the "Do-It-Yourself Shelving" to accommodate his *Encylopaedia Britannica*, then the prosecution will not have proved its case and the defendant Higgins is entitled to be acquitted. In all things we must be judicial, totally fair and keep a balanced view. We must keep ourselves calm, you know, and above the dust of the arena . . .'

'What on earth was the matter with that brief what prosecuted me?' asked a puzzled Mr Higgins as he later left the Court without a stain on his character. 'Is he ill or something?'

'Not ill,' I assured him. 'Just suffering the terrible consequences of love.'

'The course of true love never did run smooth.' I was talking, in a rare moment of conversational amity, to Mrs Hilda

Rumpole. 'And what's more, there's such a lot of it about these days.'

'A lot of what about, Rumpole?'

'Love. Miss Trant, the Portia of our Chambers, is apparently expecting offspring.'

'She told you *that*? Whatever for?'

'I think she was trying to explain why she couldn't fancy two eggs and a fried slice.'

'I suppose that man Claude Erskine-Brown's responsible.' Hilda referred, of course, to Miss Trant's *fiancé*, not one of Rumpole's greatest fans.

'I imagine so. The poor little thing's probably lying in the womb boning up on the law of landlord and tenant. They'll expect it to get a place in Chambers.'

'Oh. And are they expecting to get married at any time? Or will she be too busy with the baby?' Hilda seemed, most unjustly, to be somehow blaming me for the moments of passion which seemed to have transported Miss Trant and Erskine-Brown after some particularly hectic rendering of *Lohengrin*. I thought I would deflect her displeasure by feeding her another juicy gobbet of Chambers gossip.

'And Marigold wants Featherstone to be a judge. Apparently she means to divorce him if he doesn't get a red dressing-gown.'

'Marigold Featherstone,' said She judicially, 'has had a lot to put up with.'

'Poor Guthrie's looking in a terrible way. He's reduced to having to play golf with Vosper J. and old Keith from the Lord Chancellor's office.'

'Guthrie Featherstone will make a splendid judge.' She came to a firm decision, 'I'll have to have a talk about this with Marigold. We're meeting at choir practice tomorrow. You'll be coming to the *Elijah*, won't you, Rumpole?'

It will be remembered that Hilda and Marigold had joined a dreaded group of lawyers' wives who insisted on adding endless Oratorios to the other horrors of Yuletide. I fielded the invitation by neatly changing the subject.

'And speaking of love . . .'

'Were we, Rumpole?'

'Of course we were. I'm doing an Unlawful Carnal Knowledge in Hertfordshire tomorrow. Before old George Frobisher. Who is now,' I reminded her, 'a Circuit Judge.'

'Oh well, George Frobisher,' Hilda sounded dismissive. 'You'll be able to wrap him round your little finger, won't you, Rumpole?'

Hilda had, with rare discernment, voiced my own opinion as to how a case before His Honour Judge Frobisher would go. As I saw it my client was prepared to plead guilty if there were no question of his being called upon to visit Her Majesty; so when we arrived at the local Court I requested an interview with His Honour, and roped Miss Trant, for the prosecution, into what I hoped would prove a fruitful and friendly meeting. The news came back that the learned judge would be delighted to receive us both, and we proceeded down a passage in the new Hertfordshire Palais de Justice, a place with a lot of glass, light-polished wood and a strong smell of rubber floor-covering, and were shown into the presence of my dear old friend and sweetest of men, George Frobisher, our late stable-mate at Number 3 Equity Court in the Temple.

'George. My dear old friend. Judge George Frobisher,' I greeted him.

'Good to see you, Rumpole. I've been looking forward to the day when you came before me.'

'I'm sure you have, George. I'm sure you have. Of course, I may not be before you today for very long.'

'Oh, really?'

'I have had a word with my learned friend, with the opposition, who happens to be, by a happy coincidence, our old stable-mate. You remember Miss Trant? The Portia of our Chambers?'

'Miss Trant. Glad, of course, to have you before me too.'

'Thank you, Judge,' said Miss Trant. So far all so very amiable.

'And we've been able to put our heads together, well, we had breakfast together as it so happens. They do a pretty good egg and bacon and fried slice in that little café opposite the Old

Bailey . . . And we've been able, Miss Trant and I, to come to a certain view about this case.'

'Have you?' George sounded curiously uninterested. 'Of course, I've come to no sort of view at all. I find it far better in this job not to come to any sort of view before one has heard the evidence.'

'And how do you enjoy it, George?' I was going to play the whole business slowly, and in the friendliest possible way.

'Enjoy what, Rumpole?'

'The job.'

'Lonely. It gets extremely lonely sometimes. Yes. Life is very lonely nowadays. I must say that it is.'

'Give you a decent lunch here, do they?' I tried to sound solicitous.

'Sandwiches!' George said sadly. 'The usher brings in sandwiches. It's usually cheese and tomato, but on Fridays for some reason he always brings one sardine.'

'Probably got a Catholic usher there, George,' I suggested.

'Perhaps he is,' George gave a faint smile. 'You know, that hadn't occurred to me.'

'Well, sandwiches are no good to you, George. No good to you at all. Bring you in a glass of plonk from the off-licence, does he?'

'There's a machine in the front hall that expels some sweet warm liquid in a plastic cup. I'm never quite sure whether my usher pushes the button marked Tea, Cocoa, Coffee, or Oxtail Soup.'

'George. The conditions of your work sound squalid in the extreme.'

'Not squalid, Rumpole. Not squalid really.' George looked extremely depressed. 'Just extremely lonely. Of course, I always led a lonely sort of life in the evenings in my diggings at the Royal Borough Hotel, Kensington. But I had the companionship of you fellows in Chambers during the day.' He looked at Miss Trant. 'Fellows' clearly meant her as well.

'And our drinks together in Pommeroy's Wine Bar when the day's work was done.'

'Of course, Rumpole. I look back on those evenings with considerable nostalgia.'

'The high spot, wouldn't you say, George, of your life at the Bar?' I established all he owed to Rumpole.

'Well . . . Of course I won't say that being awarded a Circuit Judgeship hasn't struck me as something of an achievement,' George said modestly.

'But as nothing compared to those happy pints of plonk we downed at Pommeroy's, eh George? As nothing compared to the bottles of Château Fleet Street we consumed together whilst battling with the powerful and anonymous brain behind *The Times* crossword.'

'They were certainly good times, Rumpole.'

'The best,' I assured him. 'I would certainly say the best. I miss you, George, now that they've fitted you up with a mauve dressing-gown.'

'And of course, Rumpole, I miss you too. That goes without saying. It's good to have you here. You said you didn't expect to be here long?'

'No. No, George. Not long at all.'

'Pity.'

'From my point of view, yes. But for my client . . .'

'Rumpole says it's going to be a plea,' Miss Trant seemed anxious to press on with the meeting.

'Really?' George looked surprised. 'That's not like you, Rumpole.'

'I know.' Miss Trant smiled. 'He always taught me never to plead guilty.'

'I'm not saying it will be a plea. I'm saying it *might* be. Look here, George. My silly old client . . .'

'The young schoolmaster?' George's tone was somewhat cold.

'Yes. The schoolmaster.'

'Of course, he was *in loco parentis* . . .' George started to ramble. I cut him short.

'Let's cut out the Latin, George, and get down to some sort of reality. Ransom doesn't want to put the girl through the ordeal of being cross-examined by me. Which I think is very decent of him. Particularly, as you may remember, as I do have some sort of skill, in the art of cross-examination.'

'Indeed, Rumpole,' George smiled politely, 'we all admired it. Didn't we, Miss Trant?'

'Gosh, yes!' Miss Trant agreed. 'I had a client who once compared Rumpole's cross-examination to being hit by a steam-roller at ninety miles per hour.'

'You're all very kind. Well, my client is quite prepared to spare the girl that, which must earn him a considerably lower tariff.'

'Must it?' To my amazement George sounded unconvinced.

'And bearing in mind that the girl no doubt consented, on her own evidence.'

'Did she?'

'That's perfectly clear, Judge,' Miss Trant supported me. 'In fact, the prosecution will go so far as to say she led the man on. The first letter, you will see from the depositions, was the one she wrote to him and left in his locker in the staff-room. It contains the quotation from *Romeo and Juliet*.'

'I wonder if there isn't really too much poetry taught in schools nowadays,' George frowned unhappily.

'She was inciting him though. That's Miss Trant's point, George,' I tried to point out patiently.

'It's one thing to be tempted, Rumpole. But you don't have to give in to it.'

> ''Tis one thing to be tempted, Escalus,
> Another thing to fall.'

I helped him out. 'Shakespeare's *Measure for Measure*. Is that what you're trying to remember, George?'

'Perhaps it is, Rumpole. Perhaps it is.'

'But those lines were spoken by Angelo in the play. A dreadful judge of whom the author said that his urine was congealed ice. You're not like that, are you, George?' I wanted to shame my old friend into a quick decision.

'I hope not, Rumpole. I sincerely hope not. Mind you, I have been having a little trouble with the water-works lately, pardon me, Miss Trant . . .' He was clearly rambling again. I was determined to put an end to it.

'Well then. Don't let's have this nonsense about "It's one

thing to be tempted". The fact is, this young girl was never for a moment seduced.'

George looked mildly at both of us and spoke most politely. 'You two no doubt have all the law at your fingertips. But that's absolutely no defence, is it?'

'No, it's not a defence. But it must be mitigation.' Miss Trant was doing her best.

'Thank you, Miss Trant,' I smiled at her. 'Of course it is, George. Powerful mitigation!'

'Then no doubt you will raise it, Rumpole. At the proper time?'

'The proper time?' I was giving George the message loud and clear; but he didn't seem to be getting it.

'At the end of the case. If your client's found guilty.'

'George. The proper time is now.' I tried to explain, as if to a child. 'Look, my friend, my dear old friend . . .' Then I lost patience. 'Oh, pull yourself together, George. Look. The girl would have been sixteen in another month. She's over sixteen now!'

'Is that a defence? Remind me. What's your client's age?' The man was being singularly obtuse. I chose an answer from literature.

'Do you know how old Juliet was when she met Romeo?'

'No, I don't. But no doubt you'll be making use of the fact in your speech to the jury.'

'She was under fourteen! You remember her old Nurse?'

'Not personally.' George smiled, I thought foolishly.

> 'Even or odd, of all days of the year
> Come Lammas Eve at night shall she be fourteen,'

I reminded him.

'You remember so much more Shakespeare than I do, Rumpole. I've always admired you for it.'

'That was how old Juliet was, at the time she married Romeo and went to bed with him.'

'And came to a rather unpleasant end, if I remember. What was it, locked up in a tomb and taking poison?' If he was trying to catch me out on Shakespeare I could get the better of him.

'All because of that idiotic monk. We don't want *you* making any mistakes like that, George.'

'I try not to make mistakes in this job, Rumpole. One can only do one's best.'

'When you spoke of locking up, of course nothing of that sort would be appropriate here.' I tried to make the position clear.

'Wouldn't it, Rumpole?'

'Of course it wouldn't.' I was trying to keep my temper.

'The prosecution wouldn't regard this as an offence that warrants a prison sentence.' Miss Trant offered her help. I was grateful for it.

'But then it's really nothing to do with the prosecution, is it?' George was smiling at her.

'Well, not strictly . . .'

'It's *my* job to decide on sentence. I must say, I never find it at all easy. Particularly when it comes to prison.' George was passing from the obtuse to the obnoxious.

'That must come as a great comfort to those you bang up. To know it caused you a little difficulty, George,' I told him.

'But I must say, if your client's found guilty . . .'

I tried to explain the situation for the last time. 'I told you. He's prepared to plead. And face a conditional discharge.' George looked impassive. I went on, 'Or at the most a suspended sentence. Damn it all, he'll lose his job, George!'

'It's his job, I must confess, that's worrying me, Rumpole.' George frowned. 'His job was to look after this girl.'

'This young woman,' I corrected him.

'This minor. Not to fill her up with Vivaldi and cannelloni and take her to bed in some maisonette in Fitzjohn's Avenue, borrowed from friends.'

'They're a couple from the B.B.C. Highly respectable people.'

'They weren't respectable if they knew what was going on.'

'They didn't.'

'Then your client was abusing their hospitality, as well as his position as a school-teacher.'

'George. Abelard was Éloise's tutor.'

'Éloise and Abelard aren't on trial in this Court,' George said firmly. 'If they were I might have something rather unpleasant to say to them.' George stood up unexpectedly. 'Well, I'm sorry

I can't do more for you. And I'm sorry your visit won't be a longer one, Rumpole.'

'It may be longer,' I told him. 'I'm not pleading guilty unless . . .'

'Rumpole,' George interrupted me. 'You know perfectly well I can't come to any sort of bargain.'

'Just tell me, George . . .' I was almost pleading with him, 'George, we know each other well enough!'

'Well enough for me to tell you both this,' George actually interrupted me, 'I can't possibly hold out any promises. If Ransom's found guilty I'll have to consider sentence, very carefully. I couldn't rule out the possibility of prison. I couldn't rule it out at all. Does that help you?'

'You know bloody well it doesn't!' I wanted George to be in no doubt. 'Come along, Miss Trant.' At the door I turned to wish my old friend ill. 'Enjoy your sandwiches!'

'Sandwiches! I hope they choke him! Thank God it's not Friday. He won't even get sardine.' I was reporting to Ransom and Grayson the solicitor in the corridor outside the Court.

'I thought he was a friend of yours, Mr Rumpole.' Ransom frowned.

'He was a friend. I suppose he is one still. The bloody mauve dressing-gown. It's gone to his head!'

'I don't want Francesca to suffer,' Ransom was playing the old gramophone record.

'All right then,' I told him, 'you suffer. Do you want to be away? Maybe for a year? Maybe eighteen months, locked in with a gay mugger, watched over by an underpaid screw with a fifteen-year-old daughter of his own, spending your time slopping out and volunteering for pills to decrease your libido? Because if that's what you want, my friend George is prepared to offer it to you. On a plate!' I paused for my words to take effect, looked at Ransom, and then I said, 'Of course, if you tell me that you actually bedded the young lady.'

'No. No, I don't tell you that,' Ransom answered slowly.

'Then we plead "Not Guilty". We teach old George a lesson he'll never forget. And we win this case!'

'How do we do that, Mr Rumpole?' Grayson seemed to be merely asking for information.

'By having a go at Miss Francesca Capstick.'

'Please, Mr Rumpole. Treat her gently,' Ransom still insisted.

'I shall treat her as gently as if I were a steam-roller, going at ninety miles per hour,' I reassured him. 'How much is known about her?'

'Nothing at all is known about her. By *me*,' Mr Grayson said.

'You mean *someone* might know?'

'Well, Hughie . . . Hughie might know a good deal.'

'Who is this invaluable grass?'

'My son Hughie,' Grayson admitted. 'He goes to John Keats. He knows most of Francesca's friends.'

So we had a dependable source of information for the cross-examination of Francesca. Even then, it seemed, Ransom's luck was holding well.

The proceedings in R. *v.* Ransom were opened kindly and gently by Miss Trent. She told the ladies and gentlemen of the jury that there was no question but that Francesca was a willing party, she was almost sixteen at the time, and they must be careful of accepting her evidence unless it was corroborated in a material particular. She then called the Headmaster who was apparently anxious to get away (no doubt to an urgent meeting of the British Drama League). I thought the most interesting part of his evidence was the fact that a whole bundle of Ransom's letters (poetic effusions which left the issue as to whether he had in fact committed an offence under Section 6 of the Sexual Offences Act 1956 quite unresolved) together with copies, or drafts of Francesca's letters to him, appeared as if by magic, fastened with an elastic band, on the Headmaster's desk, and were waiting for him when he came back from Assembly (a reading from *Lord of the Rings* and a snatch of Joan Baez on the record-player). Who, I wondered, had been kind enough to present the Ransom-Capstick correspondence to the Headmaster, and who had abstracted it from its beautiful recipient?

When the witness went on to describe the interview he had with Miss Capstick on the vital issue, Rumpole pushed himself to his hind legs to protest.

'Your Honour.'

'Yes, Mr Rumpole.' George, my old friend, sounded curiously aloof.

'Any statement made by this young lady is no evidence. I object . . .'

'Very well,' said the co-operative Miss Trant. 'I won't press the matter.' Good old Portia. I sat down, delighted, when George did something totally unexpected.

'The evidence of a complaint is admissible, surely,' he said. 'In a sexual case. To negative consent.'

'But everyone agrees she consented! Consent is not an issue here.' I almost added, 'Come on, George. You never had any instinctive grasp of the rules of evidence.' (He probably found it more convenient to look it all up in a book.)

'It is my responsibility to rule on the evidence and I do so now,' said George pompously. The whole business of becoming a judge seemed to have done absolutely nothing for his personality. 'The evidence of a complaint is admissible. Yes. What was the question, Miss Trant?'

I sat in a fury which I did absolutely nothing to conceal while Miss Trant asked her questions, and the answers revealed that Miss Capstick had 'complained' that she had been taken to a concert, an Italian meal and to bed in a place in Fitzjohn's Avenue where 'the defendant' had borrowed a room. 'Intimacy had also taken place' in Ransom's Ford Capri while parked in a wood near St Albans, at Francesca's house whilst her parents were away for the weekend and, in what must have been a hasty moment of extreme danger and discomfort, in a corner of the art-room during the course of a school dance. All this had happened within two weeks. Ransom and Francesca, it seemed, had taken the advice of Andrew Marvell in the poem they had read together.

> 'Thus, though we cannot make our sun
> Stand still, yet we will make him run . . .'

At the lunch break I saw Francesca leaving Court with her parents and a sixteen-year-old, spotty-faced youth with ginger hair, glasses, a long scarf and a scowl of perpetual bad temper. I was standing with my client as the group passed us; all, including Francesca, looking self-consciously in the opposite direction. However, after they had gone by I saw the youth turn his head to look back at Ransom with a smile which I can only describe as unpleasantly triumphant.

'It's agonizing!' Ransom said. 'Hearing the letters read out. Hers and mine. It was love, that's all it was. Does it have to be dragged out in Court and cheapened?'

'I'm afraid it does,' I told him, and led the way to the bleak pub opposite, where we sat on tartan-covered benches, listened to piped music and consumed Scotch eggs and gassy beer. 'By the way, who was that unpleasant-looking youth with Francesca? Not her brother?'

'Someone in her class,' Ransom told me vaguely. 'His name's Mowersby. C. J. Mowersby.'

'Charlie?'

'I don't know. He always put C.J. on the top of his essays.'

'Any good, are they?'

'What?'

'His essays.'

'Absolutely appalling. C. J. Mowersby can't wait to give up English language and literature and take up computer-programming as his special subject. Why on earth are you interested in him?'

'He looked as if he hated you.'

'Probably because I wrote on one of his essays, "Poetry is emotion recollected in tranquillity; not quotations collected for a quick O-level." I remember writing that.'

'C. J. Mowersby is not an admirer of poetry?'

'As far as I can tell, he's not an admirer of anything. Except computers.'

'And Francesca?'

'She talks to him of course. She talks to everyone. She's such a wonderful, friendly sort of kid.'

'Yes, of course. There's no particular reason why he should be with her family at this trial?'

'None I can think of.'

Ransom returned to his theme of the horrors of having the

tender emotions of a young Juliet such as his pupil dragged out in Court to be coarsely prodded and examined by the hard hands of such as Rumpole; and I asked Grayson to instruct his son Hughie, our undercover-agent at the John Keats Comprehensive, to give us all the dirt on Mowersby, C. J.

As we went back to Court the Mowersby youth was lurking alone on the steps that led up to the public gallery. He gave my client another look of undisguised contempt.

'You must have done more to him,' I suggested, 'than write a snide remark on his Wordsworth essay.'

'Well. I may have suggested to the Headmaster that his attitude was simply bloody-minded in Poetry Appreciation. I remember Mowersby saying in a seminar on the metaphysicals that all my bloody understanding of John Donne didn't mean I could knock up more than four thousand a year. I believe I told the H.M. that Mowersby was quite unsuitable for John Keats and might be asked to continue his education elsewhere.'

'So he's come to sit at your trial,' I said, 'like an old woman knitting by the side of the guillotine.'

After Court that day Mr Grayson drove me to his house where young Hughie Grayson was delighted to knock off his biology prep and give me an hour on the life and loves of Form Five B. By the end of our little chat I felt I had lived through a peculiarly sultry chapter in the History of the Italian Renaissance, around the time when the Borgias were at the height of their sexual potency. I also knew why C. J. Mowersby was so greatly enjoying our trial.

'The bundle of letters left on the Headmaster's desk consisted of letters from Mr Ransom and copies of your letters to him.' I was cross-examining Francesca. She looked pretty and demure, she answered softly, and was unostentatiously chewing gum.

'That's right. I kept them in a bundle together.'

'You kept copies of the letters you wrote to him?'

'Yes.' Her voice sank another few decibels.

'Speak up, please.'

'Yes, I did. I kept copies.'

'Why?'

'I don't know. I suppose I just wanted to.'

'Was it because you were in love with Mr Ransom?'

Francesca removed her chewing-gum delicately, stuck it under the rail of the witness-box, shrugged slightly and answered, 'I just kept copies.'

'And this correspondence started with a letter from you?'

'Did it?'

I fished out the first incriminating document and waved it at her. 'It's the first letter in date order you wrote to Mr Ransom, "And all my fortunes at thy foot I'll lay," you wrote, "And follow thee my Lord throughout the world".'

'It comes from the play we were doing. *Romeo and Juliet.*'

'Exactly! And what did you mean by all your "fortunes"?'

There was a pause. Then she shrugged again. 'I don't know.'

'You weren't offering your teacher your pocket money or your savings certificates?'

'Not exactly.' She smiled politely, as if she thought I had made a joke.

'You were offering your love.'

'That's what I *said*,' she qualified her answer.

'Offering to do *anything* for him.'

After only a second's hesitation she answered, 'Yes.'

'And to follow him wherever he asked you to go?'

'Your client wasn't *bound* to take advantage of that offer, Mr Rumpole,' George put his oar in, as I thought quite unnecessarily.

'Oh no, your Honour. I just wish to establish who made the first approach.' I turned to the witness. 'Miss Capstick. Have you any idea how this bundle of letters got on to the Headmaster's table?'

'No. No idea.' She was starting to look bored, as if I were a particularly dull geography lesson.

'Presumably you kept them safely?'

'Yes.'

'Did you keep them at home?'

A small hesitation, then she said, 'No.'

'Because you didn't want your parents to find them?'

'I didn't keep them at home.'

'So you kept them at school. In your locker, perhaps?'

'No. No, I gave them to a friend of mine to keep for me.'

'May we hear the name of this friend?'

But George put in another unhelpful word. 'Really, Mr Rumpole. Is that relevant?'

'Perhaps not, my Lord. I'll leave it for the moment.' I turned back to Francesca and again attempted, not too successfully, to engage her interest. 'You have a good many friends at school, haven't you?'

'Of course I have.'

'Of course. You're a very popular girl.' She didn't look in the least flattered and I picked up the copy of her first letter again. 'When you wrote this first letter to Mr Ransom, did you have any particular friends at that time?'

'Girlfriends, do you mean?'

'You know I don't mean girlfriends,' I pressed her and she looked slightly more interested.

'You mean anyone I was going out with?'

'Going out with so often means staying in with, doesn't it?'

'Really, Mr Rumpole . . .' George tried to protest.

I ignored him and repeated. 'Doesn't it?'

'You mean Charles?'

'Yes.' Now at last something was cooking. I hoped it was C. J. Mowersby's goose.

'You mean I was going out with Charles . . . Yes, I was. What about it?' She smiled at the jury. They didn't smile back.

'Is Charles Mowersby in Court? Perhaps he'd stand up.' I looked round and saw the sullen, spotty face in the gallery. He didn't move. 'Perhaps he'd stand up,' I repeated. The unappealing youth lumbered to his feet. 'Is that Mr C. J. Mowersby?'

'That's Charles. Yes.' Unsmiling and sullen as ever, Mr Mowersby resumed his seat.

'He's the one you were going out with. When you wrote the letter, swearing to follow your Lord Mr Ransom throughout the world?'

'Yes.'

'Tell me. The school term's still on, isn't it? Do you know why Mr Mowersby is here?'

'I suppose he's interested.'

'Yes. Yes, I suppose he is.' I picked up the letters again. 'Before you wrote your first letter to Mr Ransom had you been on a school holiday in France, camping with Charles Mowersby?'

'With all our class. Yes.'

'Camping. Sleeping under canvas?'

'I was sharing a tent with my girlfriend.'

'Exactly. A girl named Mary Pennington?'

'With Mary. Yes.'

'Did a boy called Hugh Grayson go on that holiday with you?' I was now prepared to divulge the source of my information.

'Hughie did. Yes. He was sharing a tent with Charles.'

'Exactly. And on the first night did you ask Mary Pennington to go into Hughie Grayson's tent so that Charles Mowersby could come into yours?'

There was a long pause. The jury looked at her stonily, but Miss Capstick said, 'I might have done . . .' clearly, almost defiantly.

'Did you spend the night with Charles Mowersby? Did you sleep with him?'

This time the answer was quiet, inaudible. 'What did you say?'

'Mr Rumpole. I'm really wondering what the relevance . . .' Once again George needed ignoring. I kept my eyes on the witness.

'What did you say?'

'I said I might have done.'

'And did you say to Mr C. J. Mowersby of Form Five B of the John Keats Comprehensive "I'll follow thee my Lord throughout the world"?'

'No, I didn't.'

'Why not?'

'Charles doesn't like poetry.'

'Charles doesn't like poetry. And he doesn't like Mr Ransom either, does he?'

'Mr Rumpole . . .' It was George again. I carried on regardless.

'Does he?' I asked, with some determination. 'Because Mr Ransom writes rude remarks on his essays on Wordsworth, and Mr Ransom reported him to the Headmaster, and Mr Ransom thought that Mr C. J. Mowersby might be invited to continue his education elsewhere. So Charles doesn't like your school-teacher?'

'He doesn't like him. No.'

'He hates him.'

'Perhaps.'

By now even George had given up and the jury were clearly interested.

'The friend you gave your bundle of letters to for safe keeping. Was that Mr Mowersby, by any chance?'

The witness-box is an odd sort of place. Sometimes people feel unable to lie in it. Francesca said, 'Yes.'

'And it was Mr Mowersby who gave them to the Headmaster?'

'It might have been.'

'Mr Rumpole. Suppose all this is true . . .' George was burbling on again and I turned on him and almost shouted.

'Suppose all this is true? Then this whole charge is nothing but a pretence, a cruel joke, played on my client by this . . . this young woman who wanted to help her boyfriend get his revenge!' I said to Francesca quietly, 'Your first letter . . . your letter full of Juliet's love. Didn't Charles suggest you write that?'

'He wanted to show Mr Ransom up.' At last, she gave me the answer I wanted.

'For what? For a fool who'd have his head turned by young girls writing poetry?'

'Something like that. Yes.'

'So Charles suggested you write that letter?'

'He found the bit out of the play. Yes.'

'Really! That must have been the first time Mr Mowersby showed an interest in literature.' The jury gave an obedient titter. 'And did you hand my client's replies to Mowersby as you got them?'

'More or less.'

'And I suppose he was delighted with the way things were

going? He had a nice little bundle of trouble for Mr Ransom to drop on the Headmaster's table?'

'I suppose he did. He never wanted me to go to the concert though.' She answered quickly and I stopped to think of the next question.

'You mean the concert at the Festival Hall?'

'Charles never wanted me to go to that.' I felt a sort of danger, but ignored it and pressed on.

'You're not going to say you acted independently for once in your life?' By now Francesca was answering quite confidently, as if she were telling me some not very interesting school gossip. 'I'd found out Charles was taking Mary Pennington out. Hughie Grayson told me he'd seen them together at *Saturday Night Fever.*'

I looked up again at the sullen, spotty face in the gallery, the glasses, the muffler, the ginger hair: I tried to imagine Charles Mowersby in the role of a demon lover and failed utterly.

'So, well . . . I went to the concert.'

'But not to bed with my client?' I said it with all possible determination. She didn't answer, and that encouraged me to go on. 'Not to bed with the man on whom you were playing an elaborate practical joke, just so your boyfriend could get him into trouble with the Headmaster? Your victim! Your poor, wretched gull. You didn't go to bed with *him*, did you?'

There was a pause. Francesca sighed, and then said patiently, as though explaining things to an idiot, 'I told you. I'd heard Charles was taking out Mary Pennington. So that's how it happened.'

'How what happened?'

'How I had it away with Mr Ransom.'

'You mean sexual intercourse?' George asked, showing himself to be unexpectedly up in contemporary English.

'Yes,' said Francesca.

'Because you were annoyed with Charles. You did *that*?' I tried to sound incredulous.

'I wasn't annoyed. I was furious with him.'

'Because of that, you say, you made love to my client?'

'That was the reason. Really.'

'Without love?'

'Yes.'

'Did you enjoy the experience?'

'Not much. He kept on spouting poetry.'

I looked at my client's face. I knew that nothing, no prison sentence that George had it in his power to award, would now hurt him more than the words that his young Juliet, Miss Francesca Capstick, had just spoken. I took a deep breath and began again, 'I put it to you that what you have just told us is a deliberate and wicked lie. You never went to bed with my client.'

'I did. We did it again too . . .'

'Just as your letter to him was a wicked and deliberate lie, aimed to deceive him, your evidence has been completely invented to deceive this jury.' I went on like that for the rest of the afternoon. But my heart was no longer in it.

Guthrie Featherstone played golf with Mr Justice Vosper and Keith from the Lord Chancellor's office, but his luck was out. Vosper got stuck in some sort of sand dune, Keith hit his ball into a river, and Guthrie committed the unpardonable and quite unintentional social blunder of holing out in one on the thirteenth; so for the moment his heavy hints of his willingness to exchange the hectic struggle of the front row for the peace and comfort of the Judicial Bench went unheeded.

Worse still, Hilda told all my gossip to Marigold Featherstone, who told Guthrie. who summoned Erskine-Brown to him and said that the last thing he needed was to be Head of a Chambers in which irregular unions and unsanctified births were a common occurrence. As his own marriage would founder unless he got a judgeship, he begged Erskine-Brown to pop the question to an ever-increasing Miss Phillida Trant.

At first his proposal was received somewhat coldly, but when Erskine-Brown insisted that he was particularly fond of children, Miss Trant asked him if he would be prepared to baby-sit if she were kept late at London Sessions, and when he showed willing Claude was accepted without more ado. The happy couple were married in the Temple Church and we had a reception in a tent in Temple Gardens. Old George Frobisher came and we sank our noses into glasses of non-vintage Pommeroy's Shampoo.

'Sorry to have had to put that fellow Ransom away,' George said. 'I really had no alternative. Was two years too much?'

'Two days would have been too much. You know that, George.'

George ignored this and gulped champagne. 'I heard they're not prosecuting that young boy Mowersby. No doubt that's a wise decision. It's different, isn't it, for the young?'

'You mean they're so much more grown-up, and experienced?'

'But your client was her schoolmaster. He was in charge of her.'

'No, George. She was in charge of him. Totally.'

'Are you angry with me, Rumpole?'

'I was. Exceedingly.'

'It wasn't my fault.'

He was right, of course. It wasn't George's fault. It was the fault of life, the fault of love, the fault of poetry, the fault of youth, the fault of the law. Not George's fault at all. Ronald Ransom had thanked me for all I'd done, but I knew he hated me for it. As for Miss Francesca Capstick, she left the Court arm-in-arm with C. J. Mowersby. It was the only time I ever saw him smile.

Rumpole and the Age for Retirement

'Sir Mathew told the Police Federation that the work of crime detection was becoming more and more frustrating. "And when you catch them," he said, "there's always some clever dick of a bent barrister who earns his living by finding a legal loophole for the crook to wriggle out of."'

The wireless set in the kitchen at Casa Rumpole, where I was moodily chewing a slice of burnt toast and drinking a cup of instant before setting off for the Ludgate Circus Palais de Justice, crackled with indignation as it reported the words of some highly placed copper who was intent, as highly placed coppers are nowadays, on repealing Magna Carta, abolishing Habeas Corpus, reversing the presumption of innocence and substituting a brief hearing before the sergeant in the local Station (from which all lawyers would, of course, be barred) for the antiquated and unsatisfactory system of trial by jury. As I went for the ancient hat and well-used mackintosh I heard that Sir Mathew had regretted 'the recent serious epidemic of acquittals at the Old Bailey, which was a glaring example of the injustice caused by underworld legal vultures'.

Oh dear, and a very big 'oh dear' at that. Rumpole's occupation, that of making sure that citizens of all classes are not randomly convicted of crimes they didn't do just so that the prison statistics may look more impressive, seems to have fallen into disrepute. I felt more than usually unappreciated as I burrowed down the Gloucester Road tube on my mole-like journey to irritate the constabulary and pour sand in the gear-box of justice, and when I emerged, blinking, into the daylight of the Temple Station I was beginning to wonder if it was not time to abandon the up-hill struggle. Was it possible that Rumpole should retire from the Bar?

Of course I have nothing to retire on, except an overdraft at the National Westminster Bank and a dribble of uncollected fees. But now my son Nick has gone off to seek a Newer World, being something pretty high up in the University of Baltimore (Sociology Department) and living with his wife Erica in some luxurious ranch-style edifice, with a swimming-pool in what my daughter-in-law mysteriously refers to as the 'Back Yard' (I always thought of a back yard as a place for dustbins, bicycles and possibly a cage for ferrets), Hilda and I are more or less alone in the world.

'It little profits that an idle king . . .' I quoted to myself as I climbed into the frayed black gown and crowned myself with the antique wig, and poor old Alfred Tennyson's words seemed more than usually apposite:

> 'By this still hearth, among these barren crags,
> Matched with an aged wife, I mete and dole
> Unequal laws unto a savage race,
> That hoard and feed and sleep and know not me . . .'

I recalled the poor old Laureate's words again that day when, delivered of my final speech in a case where I was defending a certain Melvin Glassworth on a well-aimed charge of conspiracy to steal various works of art and valuable antiques, I sat in Number 3 Court at the Old Bailey, listening to the summing-up of that singularly unattractive judge, Mr Justice Vosper. Just as a gambler at Monte Carlo may be bankrupted by a long run on the black when all his savings are staked on the red, so I had suffered the misfortune of facing Vosper J. in three cases running at the Bailey. This judge, who in my considered opinion has a great deal in common with Shakespeare's Angelo (they both urinate congealed ice), suffered all the worst faults of a judge; he was unable to keep quiet, he invariably acted as leading counsel for the prosecution, and he could never resist trying to make a joke instead of leaving the comedy to Rumpole. Anyway there we sat, Counsel for the prosecution relaxed, the jury looking young and serious (they had all no doubt heard the wise words of the Head Copper on the wireless that morning) and Mr Melvin Glassworth, a plumpish, pinkish man who smelt of vari-

ous toilet preparations, sweating slightly in the dock as he saw
the doors of the prison house begin to close. I shut my eyes and
from afar became aware that the words now falling from his
Lordship, might be construed as discouraging Rumpole's continued activity about the Courts of Justice.

'Finally, members of the jury, allow me to remind you,' said
his Lordship, 'you decide this case on the facts and not on the
speeches of Counsel, however eloquently they address you.' In
other words his message was 'Beware of Rumpole, the Old
Bailey Hack'. 'Counsel for the defence in this case,' the judge
went on, 'has chosen to challenge the police evidence as he is
entitled to do. But you are entitled to form your own view of the
evidence, quite independent of the view of learned Counsel,
however long he may have been practising at the Bar.' Why
didn't he just tell them 'Rumpole's past it?' 'We all enjoy Mr
Rumpole's speeches. We always find his little jokes *most amusing*. But you and I have a more serious duty to perform . . .' I
knew he was delighted that I was only there to provide light
relief. Bring on the dancing Rumpole.

'Of course, if by any chance you think there is a reasonable
doubt in this case you will follow Mr Rumpole's advice and
acquit the defendant Glassworth of this serious charge of conspiracy to steal these valuable works of art.' Here his Lordship
smiled tolerantly at the jury, in the full knowledge that they
would agree that this was a truly laughable suggestion. 'But if
you think that the prosecution case is unanswerable . . .' In
other words, Vosper J. was saying, if you have an ounce of
common sense, 'then it is your plain duty, in accordance with
your oath, to find the defendant guilty as charged.' And bugger
Rumpole, he might have added. 'So will you please go now and
consider your verdict. The only question for you is whether
Melvin Glassworth is guilty as charged . . . Mr Jury Bailiff . . .'

Whereupon the usher rose in the well of the Court, held up a
Bible and swore to take the jury to some convenient place to
consider this simple question, and I prayed silently that they
would consider the feelings of an old man and stay out for a
decent interval, or at least more than five minutes. Meanwhile I
went out into the corridor, lit a small cigar with the nervous

hand and the dry mouth I always experience when the jury goes out to consider its verdict, and was immediately accosted by a bulky man of about my own age, wearing a lightweight checked summer sports-jacket, who addressed me in a low, rumbling, transatlantic accent.

'Mr Rumpole,' he said, 'I have heard a lot about you, sir. Your fame has spread to the States.'

'I can't believe it.'

'Oh yes, sir. You know, I practised as an attorney myself. For many years. Of course, I didn't wear the rug.'

I thought he must be referring to some sort of plaid, perhaps for use in cold courts, and I was confused.

'The *what*?'

'The headpiece. The horse-hair peruque.'

'Oh this.' I slapped my antique wig. 'Of course, we're invisible without it. Unless we've got it on the judge can't see us. Sometimes I'm tempted to remove the wig and disappear entirely from view.'

'I can understand, sir. Exactly how you feel.' The gravelly voice was sympathetic. 'The learned judge seemed to regard you as a senior citizen.'

'I'm not all *that* senior.' I was defensive. 'And he's not all that learned!'

'I long ago gave up the dust of conflict for the Groves of Academe. What do you call an academic lawyer here?'

As bad language is not encouraged from members of my learned profession round the Bailey I didn't tell him.

In the ensuing silence he pulled out his wallet and presented me with an embossed card.

'Professor Kramer. Head of the Department of Law', it announced, 'in the University of Baltimore.'

Baltimore! My son's university; but the usher came bustling up to put an end to further inquiry.

'Mr Rumpole,' he said urgently, 'they're coming back, Mr Rumpole.'

'How extremely rude of them.' I turned to Professor Kramer. 'My son Nick's at Baltimore. Teaching Sociology. He's got his own small Department now. And a new house. 1106 East Drive,

Baltimore. You know it? Of course, Nick's the brain of the family.'

'They've got a verdict, Mr Rumpole,' the usher intoned.

'Look, I've got to go now, Professor . . .'

'Kramer, Julius Kramer. I shall be in touch! Back to the dust of battle, Mr Rumpole. I have to tell you. It's just great to be out of it!'

The jury came back and announced their unanimous decision, the judge announced the three-year sentence he'd been planning throughout the trial, and I went down to the cells to say goodbye to Mr Melvin Glassworth. Taking your leave of a convicted client is one of those awkward social occasions which I would give anything to avoid, but which are as mandatory as an invitation to the Palace (not that I have ever had an invitation to the Palace; but I have kept many disappointed engagements down the cells at the Bailey). However disastrous the result or excessive the sentence you rarely get blamed for losing a case; the prisoner may be almost relieved that it wasn't as bad as he feared, and he is always numb; it's only after a week in chokey that the shock wears off, the pain starts, and the customer faces up to the reality of stone walls and banging up and stinking chamber-pots and tears, I have no doubt, start to prick behind his eyes.

As I have said, you rarely get blamed. Mr Melvin Glassworth was, however, the exception that proves the rule. When my solicitor, Mr Bernard, and I went down to the cells he was red-faced, sweating more than ever, and extremely angry. It was no good suggesting that three years for a theft worth at least twenty-thousand nicker was not outrageous, so Rumpole lit a small cigar, and contented himself into looking genuinely grieved. Mr Bernard provided cold comfort by pointing out that it was only two really, with time off for good behaviour.

'Oh, what's two? A long weekend in the country. Is that what you're trying to tell me? I suppose you want me to be grateful.' Mr Glassworth mopped his forehead with a purple silk handkerchief that smelt of old pear drops. 'I'm a man of a certain fastidiousness,' he told us. 'I have to have two shirts a day, me!

Two clean shirts is not an indulgence as far as I'm concerned. It's a necessity! Do they still have slopping out?'

'I'm afraid they do,' I had to tell him. He moved away from us; I was afraid that the tears were coming now.

'I have spent my life in the acquisition of beautiful objects,' Mr Glassworth said. That, of course, was really the problem. 'Slopping out. How can I live through it, me!' He went on, 'And the sickening sexual advances of beefy warders!'

'I shouldn't count on that, old darling,' I said, not quite sufficiently under my breath.

'What did you say?'

'Nothing . . . I'm sorry.'

'*You're* sorry! *You* can go home.' Mr Glassworth's misery exploded in anger. 'Have a bath with a decent tablet of Imperial Leather. Dry on a warm fleecy towel. Use talcum powder and *eau de toilette*, you!'

'I don't actually . . .' But there was no real point in establishing my bathroom habits.

'Attacking the police! That wasn't a smash hit with the jury, was it? And those little jokes in your final speech, they didn't exactly bring the house down!'

'The judge went too far in his summing-up, Melvin. We can think about an appeal.' Mr Bernard was soothing, but Melvin Glassworth turned on me, unappeased.

'You know what you ought to be thinking about, you. Retirement!' he said. 'That's what you ought to do! Bloody retire!'

My next appearance before Mr Justice Vosper took place after old Uncle Percy Timson found Jesus Christ unexpectedly in his lock-up garage.

I have written elsewhere of the Timson family,* that huge clan of South London villains whose selfless devotion to crime has kept the Rumpoles in such luxuries as Vim, Gumption, sliced bread and saucepan scourers over the years, not to mention the bare necessities of life, such as gin, tonic and cooking claret from Pommeroy's Wine Bar. Uncle Percy Timson, who lived with his wife Noreen in a respectable semi-detached

* 'Rumpole and the Younger Generation', pp. 9–48.

somewhere in the general direction of Kent, had practised for many years the profession of a small-time fence or receiver of stolen property. The business was small, personal and regular: it enabled Uncle Percy and Auntie Noreen to run an elderly Cortina, grow prize leeks and go for an annual holiday on the Costa Brava. They had, it seemed, recently been away for such a package adventure, and the morning after their return, as they sat brewing early-morning tea in their kitchen, Auntie Noreen saw something which caused her to throw the fine Georgian silver tea-pot she was using (part of the business stock) straight into the tidy bin. When Percy joined her at the window he said:

'That new one . . . that Detective Inspector Broome's got no bloody manners. When it was old "Persil" White's patch he at least gave you time to finish your breakfast.'

Detective Inspector Broome, known as the new Broome among the disapproving Timsons, was a young zealous officer with horn-rimmed spectacles, a small but aggressive moustache, and views on lawyers which coincided entirely with those which Sir Mathew, the Chief Copper, had been expounding on steam radio. He was at that moment advancing remorselessly on Uncle Percy's garage leading a posse which included Detective Constable Wood, a uniformed officer, and an Alsatian dog. At the garage doors old Uncle Percy came out in his dressing-gown and encountered the D.I. His conscience was easy and his manner relaxed. So far as he knew there was nothing of interest to be found in the garage; the load from the Deptford job went the week before, and a consignment of electric blankets was not due till the following Saturday.

'You're interested in buying my Banger, Mr Broome, are you?' Percy asked. 'One owner, and he was the Vicar of Gravesend and only used it for funerals.'

'Open up, Percy.' D.C. Wood sounded distinctly hostile. 'Or you want us to break the door down?'

'We know what you got there, Percy. We know exactly what you've got,' D.I. Broome said.

'Nothing, I do assure you, Mr Broome, what's not perfectly legitimate.'

At which, with a confidence which turned out to be ill-founded, Percy Timson unlocked his garage. A huge religious picture, which had been leaning against the door, toppled forward, Our Lord and Saviour, his hand raised in gentle Benediction, was descending on the astonished onlookers.

'Jesus ... Ker-ist!' said Percy, he was more surprised than anyone.

So it happened that Percy Timson found himself in the local nick being interviewed by those fearless battlers against crime, D.I. Broome and D.C. Wood. Broome, in the interests of making his case barrister-proof, was after Uncle Percy's autograph on a confession statement, a brief admission of the crime of receiving a religious art-work in his lock-up garage well knowing it to have been stolen.

Meanwhile Mr Bernard the solicitor, who shared with me the honour of being permanent legal adviser to the Timsons, had dropped in on Noreen in answer to her almost hysterical calls, a hysteria brought about by the supernatural quality of the manifestation in the garage rather than by the everyday occurrence of Uncle Percy being taken down to the nick.

'Percy's got too old for it, Mr Bernard!' she told him, over a nice cup of tea from the rescued Georgian silver pot. 'The whole family told him. He's got too old altogether. He ought to retire. Fancy keeping Jesus in his lock-up garage. He's getting that careless!'

'Not sufficiently careless, let's hope Mrs Timson, to give D.I. Broome his autograph.' At which point Bernard managed to get hold of the Detective Inspector on the phone. The answers he got were only to be expected. Mr Broome was unable to say where Percy Timson was being held incommunicado. All he could say was that he was not prepared to let Percy see, or speak to, or have any dealings with a lawyer for the reason, which seemed good to the D.I., that if Percy were guilty he'd only be stopped confessing, and if he were innocent why did he need a lawyer anyway?

Having satisfactorily disposed of the legal profession Broome returned to where Percy was sitting being fed tea and biscuits by

D.C. Wood (playing the sympathetic role) and briskly informed him that his wife Noreen was in the cells below, about to be charged with conspiracy to receive Jesus, unless Percy at once supplied his autograph. The fact that this statement was an outrageous lie was merely one of the sacrifices the eager Inspector was prepared to make in his devoted pursuit of law and order.

'Tell me,' Broome speculated. 'Just how long is it since your old woman saw the inside of Holloway? We want a statement signed in your own words, Percy.' What were his own words, exactly? Constable Wood read out the composition on which he had been working.

'I received the religious art-work in my garage, well knowing it to be stolen by a person whose name I am not prepared to divulge.'

'Which of them was it, Percy? Which of the Timson family was it, exactly?' Broome asked.

'I am not prepared to divulge.' Although prepared to do almost anything to save Noreen, Percy was not, by nature, a grass, any more than he was a signer of confessions.

'No doubt on the advice of his bloody lawyer,' Broome commented.

'I was intending to dispose of this picture at the earliest opportunity,' Wood read on, and Percy interrupted.

'Like when I went up the King's Elm Saturday and met a few of my contacts, I want that in.'

'Like when I went up the King's Elm Saturday and met a few of my contacts.' Wood read on obediently, and then the document, calculated to stop the boldest, bentest barrister dead in his tracks, was put before Uncle Percy for signature. So, when the brief arrived at my Chambers, I was faced with a clearly signed confession of guilt plus an inexplicable picture of Jesus in the garage. Apart from that little difficulty, the defence seemed moderately plain sailing.

As I walked down to the Temple tube station some weeks later, on my way home to Casa Rumpole, I saw a large figure flitting like some bloated white moth through the twilight along the Embankment. It was Julius Kramer, jogging in a track-suit.

'Professor Kramer!' I called out, hoping for news of my son

Nick in Baltimore. Nick and I were extremely close when he was a young lad, in fact we formed some sort of unholy alliance against the constant attacks made by She Who Must Be Obeyed on our peace and privacy. Nick would stop her growing restive if I called in at Pommeroy's for a glass of Château Fleet Street on my way home, and I would do my best to frustrate her attempts to send Nick to the hairdresser or the dentist, or to other unwelcome destinations. We used to enjoy a good walk across Hampstead Heath, during which I would play 'Holmes' and Nick 'Watson', and we would search for clues. Since Nick married an American girl (a young lady who indulged herself on an extremely dangerous diet of organic vegetation and iced water) and since he took up his lectureship in Sociology, I had seen little of Nick, and to be perfectly frank, I missed his company and that instant rapport it seemed to me that we had when he was about ten years of age.

'Professor Kramer!' I called again; but my voice was lost in the shadows, the cry of the seagulls and the roar of the traffic, and the large man trundled out of view.

When I got home I was amazed to find that She Who Must Be Obeyed not only smiled at me in a way which was clearly meant to be welcoming. She sat me down in front of the glowing plastic coal of our electric fire, pushed a footstool towards my legs and actually poured me a generous G and T.

'Are you tired, dear?' She asked, solicitously.

'Are *you* feeling quite well, Hilda?' I was puzzled enough to ask.

'A day in Court is so hard for man of your age. Daddy always said it was such physical labour, standing up in Court.'

'Perhaps that's why your Daddy always sat down so remarkably quickly, particularly if anyone raised the subject of blood-stains. He couldn't stand the mention of blood, your Daddy.'

'Look at the danger to your health, Rumpole,' Hilda continued, unperturbed.

'I know. It's like bloody mountaineering. You take your life in your hands in the law. There's always the risk of falling down the last two steps of the Gents in Pommeroy's Wine Bar.'

'Anyway, Rumpole. You won't want to die in harness. You know poor old Daddy died in harness.'

'Really? I thought he died in the Tonbridge Hospital.'

At which point she produced a bag full of fluffy white knitting-wool and the room was filled with the unusual click of needles.

'Rumpole. You must take things seriously,' warned the gloomy *tricoteuse*. 'You don't want to drop dead in Court.'

I supposed she was right. I didn't fancy the idea of pegging out in the unconcerned presence of Mr Justice Vosper. Harness may be all right, but dying in a wig! To introduce a less depressing topic I asked She what garment she was constructing. Was it, perhaps, bedsocks?

'It's for Mrs Erskine-Brown's baby. Your Miss Phillida Trant as was. That nice girl in your Chambers. She'll have to give up the Bar, now she's got the baby.'

'Birth and death. They silence us all in the end. What are you knitting for it? A dust sheet?'

'No. A matinée jacket. Oh, I forgot. There's a letter for you.'

'Will the baby go to many matinées?' I asked, and didn't get a laugh. Instead She handed me the letter which announced that it came 'From the desk of Prof Julius Kramer, of Baltimore University,' and continued, 'Dear Mr Rumpole. Your name has long been known to us as a legal luminary. We would wish to invite you, and of course your good lady, to visit us on campus during the autumn semester and deliver a series of lectures on the alienation factor in the psychological aspects of owner deprivation . . .'

'What does that mean, Rumpole?'

'Owner deprivation? Presumably nicking things.'

'It's from Baltimore University,' Hilda reminded me, quite unnecessarily, 'Nick's University. What a coincidence!'

There was a further coincidence. Later that evening the phone rang and my son Nick's voice came to me, not frozen by the Atlantic breakers, but clear as a bell. He was flying over to England, it seemed on University business, and he would stay with us. I was, of course, delighted; it was going to be like the old days when he came up for half-term and visited the Old Bailey to listen to one of my murders (always so much more *suitable*, I thought, than the cinema). He could come and watch my performance in Court and I could give him lunch. Life was distinctly improving.

The prosecution of Uncle Percy Timson was in the hands of that recent father and married man, Claude Erskine-Brown. As we gathered outside Court Number 2 in the Old Bailey my heart sank. Once again the wheel of fortune had spun and turned up a disaster for the gambler Rumpole. The case was to be tried by Mr Justice Vosper.

As I stood reeling under this blow Erskine-Brown came bustling up and showed me the photograph of a somewhat elderly-looking baby. In fact it looked even older than I felt.

'It's an extraordinarily talented baby. For its age,' Erskine-Brown boasted. 'It has an amazingly powerful grip!'

'That will be for hanging on to its mother's tail as they spring from bough to bough,' I said, forgetting at the moment that the mother was one of my learned friends. Erskine-Brown put away the photograph reluctantly.

'I think it has a remarkably intelligent look. I can't get Philly to see it.'

'Quite remarkable. Any day now it should be picking up a few briefs in the Chancery Division,' I assured him.

'Rumpole. You're not being serious!'

'Perfectly serious! With an expression like that we might find it a place on the Circuit Bench. I shouldn't be at all surprised.'

Erskine-Brown looked at a bench-load of stolid well-fed and dishonest citizens, the Timson family, who had come to lend comfort and support to their Uncle Percy. I recognized Noreen and such old clients as Fred, Dennis, Cyril and Fred's wife, Vi Timson. The men were smartly dressed in blazers and flannels; the women had elaborate perms.

'Are those all your witnesses?' Erskine-Brown asked as the clan Timson gave me warm smiles of encouragement.

'Oh no. My client's family. They're the sort to breed from, the Timsons. Their activities have kept me in work for years.'

'This isn't a fight, is it?' Erskine-Brown asked as we moved into Court.

'Oh, my dear Erskine-Brown. Claude! Shall we say . . . just a little skirmish?'

'But the picture was in *your* garage. And *you* signed a confession!'

'That means I start with a considerable handicap. Which is probably fair, considering the difference in our form.' I told him that with an optimism I hardly felt. Erskine-Brown looked disappointed.

'I was hoping for a quick plea. You see, I rather like to get back in time for the afternoon feed.'

'Really? You indulge in a high-tea, Erskine-Brown?'

'Oh no. Not *my* feed. The baby's!'

Among the prosecution witnesses Erskine-Brown called a Mr Rowland, a man with a bald, skull-like head, who was, it seemed, an art expert.

'I would say that work is quite priceless,' Rowland told Erskine-Brown, pointing to the picture in the well of the Court.

'But if you had to name a figure . . .'

'*How* can you put a price on beauty?' The death's head appealed to the allegedly learned judge.

'It has been done in the past, Mr Rowland, by some quite well-known ladies.' Oh dear, we were all most amused by his Lordship's little jokes. There was obedient laughter in Court.

'Shall we say, a quarter of a million?' Mr Rowland dropped his bombshell, turning poor old Uncle Percy, the small-time fence, into a major criminal. 'Pounds not dollars.' Uncle Percy looked about to faint dead away, and the rest of the Timsons were still whistling under their breath as I rose to cross-examine.

'Mr Rowland. You say this is an undoubted painting by Taddeo di Bartolo . . .' I waved in a casual manner at Our Lord, who had been made Exhibit One, 'nicknamed "Il Zoppo", the lame one.' I gave him back his learning. 'A Siennese master of the fourteenth century?'

'The Quattrocento.'

'The Quattrocento. I'm obliged. And it is a good example of the master's work?'

'I would say an excellent example,' Mr Rowland gave me what might have been a smile had it appeared on a living face.

'Il Zoppo. "The lame one." Is he a painter well known to the general public?' I asked politely.

'He is extremely well known to connoisseurs.'

'Oh, I'm sure he is. I just wondered, if his work was instantly recognizable by the crowd who get in the King's Elm on a Saturday night?'

'My Lord . . .' Erskine-Brown had risen to his hind legs protesting. I ignored him.

'Well. What's the answer?'

'I should imagine . . . Probably not.'

'And . . .' I went on at increased volume, to drown any interruption. 'Any drinker in the saloon bar who did recognize Il Zoppo's work and wanted to buy it would have to be provided with a half a million pounds in his hip pocket to complete the transaction?'

'My Lord. I really don't know what the relevance of these questions is,' Erskine-Brown bleated, and then sat down exhausted.

I picked up Uncle Percy's signed confession and looked at it with disgust. 'The relevance, my Lord, is that in his so-called voluntary statement Mr Timson said he proposed to flog the art-work up the King's Elm next Saturday night! Even judicial knowledge, my Lord, must encompass the fact that the King's Elm is not Sotheby's.'

The judge, however, gave me a brisk return. 'And even your extensive knowledge of crime, Mr Rumpole,' he said, 'must encompass the possibility that your client himself had no idea of how valuable the painting was.'

So, with the score at fifteen-all, a small diversion was caused by Henry bringing my son Nick Rumpole into Court and finding him a seat behind me. Nick had arrived the night before and gone to bed before we had more than a couple of jars, a short chat and some coloured slides of his lovely home, his wife Erica, the swimming-pool and a number of visiting academics cooking a meal on some sort of open fire (although I assumed the house had a reasonably equipped kitchen). Nick had kept his promise to come down to the Bailey for a morning's entertainment and a spot of lunch, and I thought as I turned to look at him, how extraordinary it was that he was so large: I always think of Nick as a solemn boy in a school blazer sitting in silent fascination in the back row of a murder. However I was resolved to give my son an entertaining day at the Bailey, and I entered with enthusiasm into the *mano e mano* with Detective Inspector Broome.

I was asking the officer about the call he had from Mr Bernard, my instructing solicitor. He smiled tolerantly at the jury, as if to warn them that we were now coming to the suspect evidence of bent lawyers, and lied effectively.

'Mr Bernard did not ring me,' he said.

'Mr Bernard will say that he did.'

'I expect he will.' A nudge-nudge, wink-wink at the jury.

'And that he was denied access to his client.'

'Does he say that?' Broome sounded bored.

'You told him that Percy Timson couldn't see a solicitor.'

'No.'

'Would you have allowed Percy Timson to see a solicitor, at the time this precious document was signed?'

'No, I would not.'

I turned and gave Nick a quick smile, and got his nod of approval. Then I re-attacked the witness.

'So if Mr Bernard had telephoned he would have been refused access?'

'Yes.'

'Why?'

'No doubt you were still making your inquiries, were you not, Inspector?' Mr Justice Vosper supplied the answer.

'That is so, my Lord,' said Broome.

'Or was it because you knew that his solicitor wouldn't have allowed him to make a statement?' I asked, and once more the judge interposed himself between the D.I. and Rumpole's steel.

'I suppose in your experience lawyers don't encourage loquacity in a subject,' he said.

'That is one of their disadvantages, my Lord,' Broome agreed.

'So that this elderly man, with no legal experience, was left absolutely without legal advice?' I did my best to sound outraged, but was somewhat deflated by a dangerous thrust from the judge.

'Are you putting your client forward as a man with no legal experience, Mr Rumpole?' he asked. Well, as Percy had a good fifty years of legal experience in and out of various Courts I could not do that. I decided that it was time for Rumpole to skate off to some thicker ice.

'Well, this elderly man . . .'

'Yes. Clearly he *is* elderly.' Mr Justice Vosper appeared to be enjoying himself. I picked up Percy's admission with renewed distaste.

'Can you explain, Officer, why Mr Percy Timson should have signed this confession, in the absence of his solicitor?'

'I don't know, Mr Rumpole. People sometimes tell the truth.' Broome was delighted by his answer. 'In the *absence* of their solicitor.'

'And people sometimes want to protect their wives, don't they, Inspector?'

'I suppose they may,' the D.I. sounded less happy.

'You know my client has been married to his wife Noreen for almost thirty years?'

'Are you putting your client forward as a perfect husband, Mr Rumpole?' The judge weighed in, no doubt sensing danger.

'No, my Lord. Merely as a loving husband.' This shut his Lordship up for a moment and I turned to the witness.

'Did you tell Percy Timson that you had his wife downstairs in the station?'

'It's possible. I can't remember. I do have other cases, you know, Mr Rumpole.' The witness answered carelessly.

'Did you say she was in the station?' I pressed him.

'I may have done.'

'I have here the station book.' I lifted the ledger which the confident Broome had not bothered to read.

'Have you?'

'There is no record whatsoever of Mrs Noreen Timson being taken into the station on that or any other day.'

'I accept that.'

'Why did you lie to my client, Inspector?'

'I didn't lie to him!' The bizarre suggestion that police officers are ever less than a hundred per cent truthful appeared to have disconcerted the witness.

'Why did you tell him Noreen had been brought into the station and charged?'

'I expect I said it, because I intended to do exactly that,' Broome said, as though that explained everything.

'You intended to charge her?'

'Yes.'

'Why did you change your mind?'

'What?'

'You never did charge her, did you?'

'Well, there was no need to after . . .'

'No need to after Percy had signed his statement. Is that what you mean?'

I saw the jury look at Broome as if some of them were beginning to doubt the doctrine of the infallibility of the Police.

'No need to after that. No.' Broome admitted.

'After he'd fallen into your trap, the bait could be thrown away. You'd got what you wanted, hadn't you?'

'What had I wanted?' The defensive position didn't suit D.I. Broome.

'An untrue confession. Signed in the hope of saving his wife from the unwelcoming gates of Holloway Prison.'

It was clearly the moment for his Lordship to come to the prosecution's rescue, and he did with some skill.

'Mr Rumpole?' The politeness from the Bench was icy.

'Yes, my Lord.'

'Aren't you forgetting something? This admirable example of Italian Renaissance art was actually found in your client's garage! Isn't *that* the point?' At which he gave the jury a meaningful look. 'Yes, members of the jury. Shall we say five past two?'

'Isn't that the point, Dad?' Nick and I were enjoying a sustaining steak pie with boiled cabbage, washed down with a pint of draught Guinness in the pub opposite the Bailey. On a corner table the Timson men were consuming brown ales and buying snowballs for their ladies, and in the middle distance the officers

in charge of the case were scoffing Harp Lagers and cold sausage.

'But I mean if he's guilty *anyway* . . .' Nick continued to cross-examine his father.

'If he's guilty anyway, why bother to squeeze a confession out of him?' I looked across at the Timson table. 'You see, Nick, I know the Timson family. Their activities paid your school fees for years. They never sign confessions.'

'You'll be able to lecture on that,' Nick was laughing.

'Lecture?' I didn't follow his drift.

'You met Julius Kramer?'

'Was that *your* doing, Nick?' For the first time I got a sniff of some kind of plot.

'You must come to Baltimore. Really, there's a lot of room in the new house. Erica'd be thrilled to have you.'

'Well, if I can get away . . .' I was doubtful.

'Of course you can get away. You've really *got* to get away.'

'*Got* to?'

'Ma says, you've been so tired lately.' Nick was looking at me, concerned. At which moment D.I. Broome was passing us on his way back to Court, and he stopped for an unfriendly chat.

'Enjoying the pantomime, Mr Rumpole?' he asked.

'Is that what you call it?'

'Don't you?'

'No. I call it a trial. Based on the quaint, old-fashioned notion that a man's innocent until you prove him guilty. This is my son . . .'

'Oh, really? Following in father's footsteps?' It was clear that the D.I. didn't consider that such a course would provide Nick with a satisfactory or even an honourable career.

'No . . . actually, I'm not.'

The Inspector turned to me, satisfied of Nick's innocence. 'Come on, sir. You know Percy Timson's been a fence for years . . .' D.I. Broome was trying the realistic approach. The Timson family fell silent at their table.

'So what should we do?' I asked politely. 'Convict him on a certificate signed by the Chief Constable?'

'Of course it all makes money for you gentlemen. I suppose you'll still be going through the motions again. This afternoon.'

'Yes. I'll be going through the motions.'

'Man of his age.' The D.I. looked at Nick. 'I really don't know why he bothers.' On which parting shot he left. I finished my Guinness and lit a small cigar.

'Detective Inspector Broome! The new Broome. Trials are just an unnecessary interruption, in his fearless battle against crime.'

'All the same . . .' Nick sounded doubtful.

'All the same what, Nick?'

'Well, it's not as if it was one of the murders you used to take me to. I mean. They were *serious* cases.'

'Yes. You enjoyed those murders, didn't you, Nick?'

'I mean, if Percy Timson really *is* a professional fence . . .'

'Oh, he is. Quite professional.'

Nick looked at me, he was smiling gently. 'Well then, why bother really?' he said.

The Timson case proceeded slowly, we kept having days off due to the fact that Mr Justice Vosper was dividing his time between us and a Government Committee on 'The Treatment of the Young Offender' (they were discussing the possibility of building a number of detention centres where the less friendly features of H.M.S. *Bounty,* Devil's Island and nineteenth-century Eton would be combined for the purpose of delivering 'a short salutary shock' to Jamaican teenagers).

Meanwhile a deep-laid plot was going on involving my wife, Nick, and the mysterious Professor Kramer of which I had no more than an inkling. It's true that, when I was alone in my flat, an unknown woman rang the bell, came in and nosed about, asked impertinent questions about the built-in cupboards and the central heating, and then drifted away. I took her for some busybody from a government department; but I suppose I should have realized then that her visit had one clear meaning. 'This flat has been put up for sale.' I only learned months later that Mrs Erskine-Brown (Miss Phillida Trant in real life) had been invited for tea in Gloucester Road, had gone there, received the

matinée jacket on behalf of the baby, and been involved in the
following conversation concerning the future of Rumpole.

'I really wonder you had time to come over to tea,' Hilda
began obliquely, 'what with the baby.'

'They had a day off Court. So Claude's holding the fort.
Actually he enjoys it.'

'Rumpole's not having a day off. He's gone for a conference
in Wandsworth. Well, he's doing far too much, for a man of his
age.'

'He looks tired,' Nick told Phillida. 'Don't you think so?'

'I think he looks . . . well, just as usual.'

'He is desperately tired! We just can't wait to get him away!'

'Get Rumpole away? Where to exactly?'

'America.'

'I want them both to come and live with us. In Baltimore,'
Nick said.

'You want Rumpole to give up the Bar?' Mrs Erskine-Brown
was astonished.

'Well, to retire. Everyone retires, don't they?'

'Everyone possibly. But Rumpole?' Clearly Chambers had
never considered the possibility.

'He's not immortal, you know! Rumpole's hardly immortal.
Anyway, not a word to him at the moment. We're luring him
across the "Herring Pond" by an offer of lectures in Nick's
University,' Hilda told her.

'I've got him an offer from one of our professors. He's going
to lecture on law.' Nick revealed the full details of the plot.

'Rumpole? On law?' Apparently my learned friend Miss Trant
sounded incredulous.

'Well really, Miss Trant! Surely he knows about the law.' She
bridled a little.

The way Mrs Erskine-Brown answered her wasn't entirely
flattering, but no doubt it contained a certain amount of truth.

'Hardly anything. Oh, he could lecture on how to tear up
paper in the prosecution speech, or how to trick his opponent
into boring the Court with a lot of unnecessary cases. That's the
one he played on me, when I first started. He knows all about
how to cross-examine and which members of the jury to get on

his side, but if you ask my honest opinion, Rumpole doesn't know anything about the *law*.'

'But it's only the bait, for getting him over. And I've put this flat on the market. So we'll have a little money, and living with Nick . . .' Hilda seemed to see no problems.

'I'm sure once he sees the house he'll stay,' Nick said.

'Nick has a swimming-pool, he was telling me. And a sort of camp fire.'

'Barbecue, mother.'

'Is Rumpole tremendously keen on swimming?' Their visitor was doubtful.

'If you ask me, he's bored to tears with the sort of cases he's doing nowadays.' Nick seemed to have no doubt about the matter. 'An obvious receiver! And the defence is, he didn't do it because he's finished the last job and was preparing for the next. Now how could that interest anybody?'

'I'm not sure . . .' Miss Trant as-was knew me, I'm sad to say, perhaps better than my son.

'Dad's in a hopeless position, with the judge and the police dead against him.'

'Are they? Oh well then. I know exactly how he's feeling . . .'

'Pretty depressed, I imagine.' Nick supplied his answer, but the lady lawyer had hers.

'I should think, by now, he's just starting to have fun.'

The conversation at that tea-time was, as I say, unknown to me for many months. And unconscious of my consignment, by my nearest and dearest, to the scrapheap of rusty and worn-out barristers I was, in fact, having a certain amount of quiet pleasure in pursuing a line of inquiry with that well-known expert on stolen art-treasures Mr Melvin Glassworth, whom I had gone to visit in Wandsworth, ostensibly to discuss the matter of his appeal.

'Screws treating you all right, are they?' I asked him as we met among the pot plants of the prison interview-room, and offered him a small cigar.

'*Some* of them are rather sweet. But you've got to get me out of here, Mr Rumpole. Sorry I was a bit irritable last time.'

THE TRIALS OF RUMPOLE

'I'd be a bit irritable, if I'd just got three years,' I assured him.

'*You* can get me out, Mr Rumpole. I know you can.'

'I have been considering your appeal . . .' I started judicially.

'I hope to God you've come up with a few bright ideas.'

'I have found at least ten places in which the judge misdirected the jury as to our defence.'

'Then you'll tell the Court of Appeal for me. You will, won't you, Mr Rumpole?'

'I may not be able to take your case on, Mr Glassworth,' I sounded doubtful. 'Pressure of other work.'

'But if you've found ten good points. He's duty bound, isn't he, Mr Barnard?' The plump man, paler but no thinner since his conviction, looked appealingly at my instructing solicitor.

'I'll have to see.' I paused and then said casually. 'Meanwhile, perhaps you can help me. As an expert in stolen art-works.'

'An expert, me? Well, I suppose I am. What do you want to know?'

'A very valuable painting might be too well-known to dispose of?' I made a guess.

'You get that trouble, yes. It's hopeless trying to flog a Goya for instance.'

'Or a Taddeo di Bartolo. Nicknamed "Il Zoppo"?' I inquired casually.

'They're never charging me with that one, are they, Mr Rumpole? *Me?*' Mr Glassworth was appalled.

'Not as yet.' I looked at him, speculatively. 'What would you do if you had a well-known di Bartolo? "The Benediction", for instance?'

'Well. You'd never sell it. Too well-known . . .'

'No,' I agreed. 'But what would you do?'

'You mean, what would whoever had purloined such an art-work do, Mr Rumpole?' My art expert was cautious.

'Exactly.'

'Dump it!' Melvin Glassworth had no hesitation.

'Really?'

'Only thing to do with it. Of course. It might pay you to let the insurance company know where it got left.'

'Dump it,' I wondered. 'In what sort of place exactly?'

'Somewhere anonymous, I suppose. Somewhere that couldn't be connected with you. The municipal rubbish tip . . .'

'Has that ever been used?'

'It has been known. Look, about this appeal. It's bloody impossible in here. You can't get a decent shampoo. I wash my hair daily, me!'

I promised to deal with his appeal. He had given me a little help with Percy Timson's case, but I got a lot more assistance when I was met at the prison gates by Mrs Vi Timson (on her way to pay a family visit to her brother Charlie who had just got a two for carrying housebreaking implements by night). Vi said she wanted an urgent word in my ear in private, so I sent Barnard walking up the road and withdrew with her to a corner of the prison wall.

'I'll never forget Mr Rumpole,' she started, 'how you got my young Jim out of that nasty robbery of the Butchers.'[*]

'Oh yes. Yes, of course. How *is* Jim?'

'Oh, doing very well Mr Rumpole. Yes, thank you. He's got his own little window-cleaning firm now.'

'Oh dear. I'm sorry to hear it.' Window-cleaning is, of course, the best way to reconnoitre possible breaks and enters.

'The thing is. I wanted to tell you,' Vi burst out, 'I never agreed with what the family done to Uncle Percy!'

'What the *family* did?' I frowned, bewildered.

'Poor old Auntie Noreen. She's up the wall about it. It wasn't all the family exactly. It was Dennis mainly. You know Den was hopping mad when Percy let all that rubber-backed carpet go for twenty pounds . . .' The words were rushing out of her, I put a calming hand on her arm.

'Mrs Timson. Vi . . . Perhaps you'd better tell me all about it.'

The family plot or 'Put-Rumpole-out-to-grass movement' gathered impetus in the next few days. Mrs Erskine-Brown, the baby's mother, told Erskine-Brown, the father, presumably when they met briefly over the Cow-and-Gate tin, that Rumpole was on the verge of retirement. Erskine-Brown told Guthrie Featherstone, Q.C., M.P., and our learned Head of Chambers

[*] See 'Rumpole and the Younger Generation', pp. 9–48.

met Mr Justice Vosper, who was having a drink with his tall, lanky and singularly unattractive son Simon, in their Club, the Sheridan. What had happened then was also something I did not discover till much later.

'Simon's just finished his pupillage,' the judge told Featherstone. 'Naturally he's looking for a seat in Chambers. Aren't you, Simon?'

'Yes, Daddy,' said Master Vosper, whose legal experience consisted in sitting next to his father on the Bench, and industriously sharpening his pencils.

'There might be a vacancy, Judge.' Featherstone was anxious to help. 'Apparently Rumpole's retiring. He's going to live with his son in America.'

'Rumpole retiring!' The judge thought this scheme over and, so Featherstone told me later, approved of it. 'Can't be too soon for me. I've got him before me at the moment. Rumpole simply hogs the limelight. Hopeless case, but you can't stop the fellow fighting.'

Whilst Featherstone was selling my birthright to Master Simon Vosper in the Sheridan Club, I was entertaining the Timson family (all except Noreen who had gone to deliver a clean shirt and an ounce of 'Golden Bar' to Percy in the cells) to tea in the café opposite the Old Bailey. As Vi sorted out beverages I called the meeting to order.

'I wanted to discuss with you, as members of the family,' I said, 'your Uncle Percy Timson's defence.'

'Yes, Mr Rumpole. Has that got two lumps, dear?' Fred was pleasantly co-operative.

'Well. We rely on you, Mr Rumpole.' Cyril smiled.

'The Timson family has always been able to rely on Mr Rumpole,' Dennis assured me.

'Yes. But can Mr Rumpole rely on the Timson family?'

'Mine's the lemon tea, Vi,' Dennis said and asked me. 'What do you mean exactly?'

'As you well know,' I explained, 'half a million nicker and art-works from the Italian Quattrocentro are quite out of Uncle Percy's league. Therefore I shall have to put him into the witness-box to explain exactly what his league is.'

'What do you mean, Mr Rumpole?' For the first time Fred Timson sounded uneasy.

'I mean,' I warned them, 'Percy's going to tell the judge he disposed of four thousand Green Shield stamps for you, Fred. And a couple of lorryloads of nylon tights for you, Cyril. And innumerable canteens of cutlery. And twenty-five yards of rubber-backed carpet from the local Odeon for Dennis. As well as the electric blankets and the three freezer-loads of stolen scampi.'

'I ain't got no convictions,' Dennis protested breaking the appalled silence, and he had the grace to add, 'thanks to you, Mr Rumpole.'

'Oh yes,' I said. 'And I understand you've even got a legitimate job now, Dennis. What is it?'

'Den's a crane-driver,' Cyril said, 'on the municipal muck heap.'

'On the municipal muck heap! Now isn't that a coincidence?' I looked round the embarrassed family.

'What do you mean, Mr Rumpole?'

'I mean that it was on a municipal muck heap that some far more cultivated villain than any of you dumped "The Benediction" by Taddeo di Bartolo. Uncle Percy hasn't been doing too well as a fence lately, has he?'

'Not too brilliant. No.' Freddy admitted.

'Percy's past it.' It was Dennis who said it.

'Getting past it.' I gave it to him then. 'Oh, I know. Letting your hard-won consignment of electric blankets go half-price. Gossiping away in pubs when some minor grass is listening.'

'He got our lad Jim six months, chattering away like that, Mr Rumpole,' Fred was deeply hurt.

'Silly old fool,' said Cyril.

'He's a menace to everyone is Uncle Percy.' Dennis pronounced judgement.

'Is that why you decided he ought to be retired?' I asked them, and was answered by a nasty silence. 'You decided to put Uncle Percy out to grass,' I went on, 'give him his cards. Rusticate him. Put him on the shelf. You all decided Uncle Percy was past it, didn't you? The whole family. So you wanted him to retire, quickly.'

There was another lengthy, and guilty, pause, and then Fred Timson made an admission.

'We couldn't persuade Percy it was time to go, Mr Rumpole.'

'Honest. He wouldn't listen to reason,' Dennis protested.

'The man was bloody dangerous, carrying on at his age,' Cyril told me.

I gave them all a cold look, and told them.

'So Den with the clean record plants a picture on him and rings up D.I. Broome with the information. Hardly a golden handshake, was it? Not even a gold watch from the company. The trouble with you all is you're none of you Bernard Berenson.'

'We're not *what*, Mr Rumpole?' Fred was puzzled.

'You're not even Lord Clark. You never studied civilization even on the telly. You couldn't tell a genuine Fra Angelico from the top of a box of biscuits. And because of your total abysmal ignorance of matters artistic, Uncle Percy's up on a half-million-pound handling and three-quarters of the way to Parkhurst, Isle of Wight!'

'Well. What are you going to do about it, Mr Rumpole?' Dennis asked uncomfortably.

'No. What are *you* going to do about it, Dennis?' I stood up and prepared to leave the assembled Timsons. 'You'd better think a bit quickly,' I told him, 'Uncle Percy's going to give his evidence tomorrow.'

By the time I got back to the flat I was feeling low and somewhat exhausted. I sat by the electric fire, alone in the dark and was roused from a blackish reverie by Nick coming in and switching on the light. It seemed that She Who Must Be Obeyed was out on a visit to the fascinating Erskine-Brown baby. Nick looked at me in the way that relatives look at old people on hospital visits, with a sort of hushed concern.

'A bad day in Court?'

'Detective Inspector Broome wants to reverse the burden of proof, revoke Magna Carta and abolish barristers. Well, that might be all right, if only he could resist gingering up the evidence whenever it suits him. And there's no honour among thieves any more, Nick. I'm ashamed of the Timson family.'

'I've always thought your job must be pretty depressing,' Nick said briskly.

'They wanted to get poor old Uncle Percy to retire, so the family cooked up the most diabolical plot. I don't know . . . I really don't know what things are coming to . . . Drop of G and T?' I shuffled off to the reviving drinks table.

'Thanks.'

'Things have reached a low ebb, Nick. They've even got piped music in Pommeroy's Wine Bar. I have to come home now, to avoid the crooner.'

'How disgusting!'

At which I recalled the good old days, when Nick was about ten.

'Remember when we used to go for walks on the Heath, Nick? I was Holmes and you were Watson, and we used to pick up clues?'

Nick took his G and T, smiled and entered into the spirit of the thing. 'What's the explanation of this half-used box of matches on the path, Holmes?' he said in his Watson voice.

'Someone's either got a hole in his jacket pocket, or he suddenly gave up smoking!'

'You amaze me, Holmes!'

'You can't go for a walk up on the Heath now,' I told him. 'Not a decent Sherlock Holmes voyage of exploration. You keep tripping over the permissive society. I'll never forget those walks. It doesn't matter we don't see so much of each other now, Nick. It doesn't matter in the least. Bound to happen anyway. People growing up and all that sort of thing.'

'Perhaps we can do something about it.'

'Growing up?'

'Not seeing each other. Look, honestly,' Nick protested. 'Haven't you got into a terrible rut?'

> 'Matched with an aged wife, I mete and dole
> Unequal laws unto a savage race . . .'

I started off and my son, God bless him, was on to Alfred Lord Tennyson like a terrier.

'Tis not too late to seek a new world'

said Nick.

'Push off, and sitting well in order smite
The sounding furrows . . .'

'You remember it, Nick!' I was delighted, and stood up in a
determined manner,

'For my purpose holds'

I carried on,

'To sail beyond the sunset and the baths
Of all the western stars until I die . . .'

'You are going to, aren't you?' Nick asked.
'Die?'
'Of course not! Sail beyond the sunset. You're coming to
Baltimore?'
'It's a long way from the Old Bailey!' I suppose I sounded
doubtful.
'Wouldn't that be a relief?'
'Perhaps it might be.'
'It's still on, you know. The lectures.'
'Oh yes, the lectures.'
'I saw Professor Kramer today. The only trouble is, he's no
longer at the Savoy. They've taken him into the Charing Cross
Hospital.' Nick broke the news to me as a matter of some
seriousness. 'He collapsed while jogging.'
'While jogging, eh? Well, I've always avoided exercise.' I
tried to look serious also. 'Exercise is simply an invitation to
death!'

When I turned up at the Bailey next day I saw Guthrie
Featherstone, Q.C., M.P., robed for the Court next door, in earn-
est conversation with my opponent Claude, the family man. As I
drew up alongside Featherstone broke off and looked, I thought,
exceedingly shifty.
'Morning, Erskine-Brown,' I said. 'Ready for the battle? I
think we may have a little surprise for you today.'

'Ah, Horace. Are you free, by any chance, next Thursday evening?' Featherstone asked in a casual sort of manner.

'Free? I don't suppose so. I'll probably be at home with my wife.'

'Oh, we want Hilda to come too. And your son, of course. I believe he's over.'

'Come? Where?' I was puzzled.

'I'm giving a little dinner at my Club,' Featherstone said, 'the Sheridan. Most of Chambers will be there. Pencil it in, now. Like a good chap.' He went, and I turned to Erskine-Brown for clarification.

'What's the matter with our learned Head of Chambers?' I asked him. 'Has he come into money?'

A couple of hours later that doughty advocate, Claude Erskine-Brown, was cross-examining Dennis Timson who had just given evidence on behalf of the defence.

'Let me get this clear,' Erskine-Brown asked with some scorn, 'you found the picture on the municipal rubbish dump?'

'Where I works. Yes.' Dennis smiled at the jury, who were looking, in turn, at the exhibited depiction of Our Saviour giving a half-million-pounds Benediction.

'And you put it in your Uncle Percy's garage?'

'I had a key. Percy lent me his Cortina when they went on holiday,' Dennis explained patiently.

'You put it there at night. Without telling your Uncle what you had done?'

'I did it quietly, like. Not wanting to awaken the old couple.'

'Why store it in Uncle Percy's garage?'

'I didn't have no accommodation. Not for a thing of that size at home.'

'Mr Timson,' asked the exasperated Erskine-Brown, 'can you think of one reason why the members of the jury should believe this extraordinary story?'

'Yes.' Dennis turned to the jury in a business-like way. 'You see, members of the jury. I rang the local nick that night. I said there was this picture, like, and if they was interested they could find it in Uncle Percy's garage. So they was there next morning with the dawn patrol.'

Erskine-Brown sat down on this, and I saw him speaking to Henry who had just come into Court. I rose to re-examine with confidence.

D.I. Broome had clearly been told by someone that there was something interesting in Percy's garage, and that informant was now revealed as Den.

'Who did you speak to, at the local nick?' I asked.

'I spoke to D.I. Broome. He'll tell you that.'

'We shall see,' I said, 'if the prosecution recalls him to deny it.' From the whispers from the officers in charge of the case it seemed unlikely that they would.

'You told the Detective Inspector the picture was in your Uncle's garage?'

''Course I did.'

'But you never told your Uncle. He remained in ignorance?'

'Total ignorance, my Lord,' Dennis told the judge without hesitation.

'Yes, thank you, Mr Timson. Unless your Lordship has any further questions?'

But by now even Mr Justice Vosper was silent. And Erskine-Brown was busy giving a cheque to our clerk Henry, his contribution, as I later discovered, to the Chambers present to mark the retirement of Rumpole; a handsome clock to be presented at the forthcoming dinner organized by Guthrie Featherstone, Q.C., M.P., at the Sheridan Club.

The jury was out for four hours and acquitted Percy Timson by a majority. He went back to work to the great satisfaction of Noreen, and the resigned regret of the rest of the family. On the following Thursday, I duly turned up with my wife and son at feeding-time at the Sheridan. We penetrated the somewhat chilly portals, passed a somnolent and sleepy uniformed figure in a glass case, and went up a staircase to a fire-warmed hall where I was delighted to see my old friend George Frobisher, now a Circuit Judge, and less delighted to see Mr Justice Vosper, and his lanky son Simon. I did my best to ignore the High Court Judge, and greeted the inferior tribunal, His Honour Judge Frobisher.

'George! My old friend. My dear old friend. You've come all the way from Hertfordshire?' I was touched.

'To have dinner in your honour, Rumpole. Of course I have. No hard feelings, about the young schoolmaster?'* George smiled, I thought he was pleased to see me.

'Not at all,' I reassured him, 'and I miss you at Pommeroy's. No friendly jar there when the day's work is over.' I sat down, for a moment, on a nearby and inviting settee.

'That's the drawback of being a Circuit Judge, Rumpole. The work's over at tea-time and you're not even allowed to go to the pub.'

'I say, Rumpole. You're not a member here, are you?' Mr Justice Vosper always had to have his two-pennyworth.

'No, Judge. I don't believe I am.'

'Well. You're sitting on the members' sofa! I suppose you plead ignorance?'

'No, Judge. I plead exhaustion.' But I had to move when an elderly waitress appeared and told us that Mr Featherstone was receiving his guests in the small dining-room. So George and the Rumpole family set off in the direction she indicated, and arrived in a room hung with pictures of old actors, judges and best-selling novelists, and found a table lit by candles and gleaming with old silver, with Guthrie Featherstone and all the other members of Chambers, including Henry and Dianne from the clerk's room, chatting merrily and drinking sherry. I was surprised that my entrance produced a sort of awed silence.

Then Guthrie Featherstone stepped forward with a welcoming 'Rumpole!'

'Here he is. The Guest of Honour!' said Erskine-Brown.

'Rumpole of the Bailey!' his wife chimed in.

'Rumpole, my dear fellow. Mrs Rumpole. And Nick. Delighted you could come.' Featherstone did the honours, and I heard Uncle Tom, our oldest inhabitant and non-practising barrister, whisper to Erskine-Brown.

'Are we feeding the entire Rumpole family?'

'What is this, a wedding or a wake?' I asked the world at

* See 'Rumpole and the Course of True Love', pp. 329–62.

large, and then moved towards the smiling Erskine-Browns. 'The baby left home, has it?'

'It's actually in its carrycot with the lady downstairs,' our Portia told me, and the proud father added,

'One of us'll have to leave early to give it its ten o'clock feed.'

'*One* of us . . .' I thought that his wife was looking at him in a meaningful manner. I also thought it was time to get off the nappy-chat, so I said cheerfully,

'Well, Erskine-Brown. I thoroughly enjoyed our little scrap.'

'I suppose it's nice for you to go out on a win,' Erskine-Brown admitted grudgingly.

'Go out? Go out where?' I was puzzled. 'Oh, you mean go out for dinner?'

'I didn't enjoy our case much,' Erskine-Brown said. 'I find these days I really prefer paper-work at home. It keeps one with the family.'

'And I love Court!' His wife was enthusiastic. 'Of course, now there'll be such a lot of crime going spare in Chambers.'

'Oh, really? Are you expecting a new outbreak of villainy?'

Before I could fully understand Mrs Erskine-Brown's prophecy of extra work in Chambers I heard a well-known and unloved voice say, 'Rumpole!'

'Oh my God!' I turned at the unwelcome sound.

'Only our judge,' Erskine-Brown reassured me. What had happened was all too clear. Featherstone had invited Mr Justice Vosper and his unlikely lad to dinner.

'I think you know my son, Simon. He's endlessly grateful for the favour you're doing him. Aren't you grateful to Rumpole, Simon?'

'Of course I am Daddy.'

I had no idea what particular kindness, if any, I had unintentionally done young Simon Vosper. Before I could ask for further particulars the judge rattled on.

'I say, that was an outrageous win you had today. Your client should have been potted!'

'I'm sorry you mis-cued.'

'Mis-cued!' The judge laughed mirthlessly. 'Funny that. You'll probably have some outrageous wins too, Simon, as soon as you get your bottom on to Rumpole's chair!'

What on earth was he talking about? His son's bottom on my chair? Was Mr Justice Vosper getting past it? Before I could inquire further the antique waitress called us to the trough.

'Come on, Rumpole,' Featherstone called to me. 'I've ordered pheasant. Game chips and all the trimmings. The best that the Sheridan can offer!'

'The last time I remember having pheasant was in old Willoughby Grimes's day. We had a Chambers dinner here and they dished us up pheasant.' Uncle Tom was reminiscing as we moved to the table.

'The occasion was Tiny Banstead's being appointed Recorder of Swindon, which was considered a great honour at the time.'

'Dinner's ready, Uncle Tom,' Mrs Erskine-Brown called from the table. But our oldest inhabitant insisted on finishing his story.

'Well, poor old Tiny got one of those little pheasant bones stuck in his gullet and they rushed him to hospital. Death by suffocation! He never sat as a Recorder. Quite a disappointment to his wife . . .'

A couple of hours later, during which I had been speculating about a mysterious cardboard box in front of Featherstone's place, the learned Head of our Chambers beat on a glass with a spoon and rose to his feet to address the cigar-smoking, port-swilling company who were all still present, save Erskine-Brown who had slipped away mysteriously after the pud.

'Just a few words from me,' said Featherstone. 'Horace Rumpole has become part of our lives in Chambers. Like a valued piece of antique furniture which we see every day, and only notice perhaps, and miss, when it's gone.'

Well, that fell into the category of things which could have been put better, but I let him carry on, seeing that he was about to open the box in front of him.

'But I hope, Horace, I sincerely hope that you and Mrs Rumpole will accept this clock as a token of our affection and respect. May it tell many happy hours in the future.'

As the handsome time-piece was thrust into my hands,

engraved as it was with the names of all the members of Chambers, including Henry and Dianne, and as I fondled their gift, and as their voices were raised in asking for a speech in reply, the pieces of the jigsaw, as they say in detective stories, fell into place. I saw clearly that there had been a plot against me as ruthless and well-planned as the Timson family's scheme to dispose of Uncle Percy. I was being retired, and their clock was my parting gift. I had little time to consider the participation of my wife and son in this conspiracy. My final speech was expected of me, and I gave it.

'If your Lordship pleases. Hilda, Nick, my friends. My old friends. This occasion has cheered me considerably!' I drank port, and my audience smiled pleasantly. 'There have been times lately, during the long hours in your Lordship's Court . . .' I went on, and Vosper J. called out, 'Pretty long for me, Rumpole.' However, I ignored the interruption. 'Listening to the constant attacks on our profession by the police, there have been times, I must confess, when I wondered if I hadn't been getting into some sort of rut.'

'That's exactly what I've been thinking!' I heard Nick whisper to George. And then I gave them the first whiff of Tennyson:

> 'Matched with an aged wife, I mete and dole
> Unequal laws unto a savage race,
> That hoard and sleep and feed and know not me . . .'

Members of Chambers all looked at Hilda in a friendly fashion; and she smiled and said, 'Really Rumpole!'

'In such moods, I must confess, I have been tempted to chuck it all in. To retire. To go out to grass.' Here I paused and looked round at them all gratefully. 'But your support, your affection, and above all this very generous gift, have made me change my mind.'

There was a moment's puzzled silence; but before they could ask a question I had launched into the final great passage of the old Laureate's *Ulysses*.

> 'Tis not too late, to seek a new world . . .'

I told them,

'Push off, and sitting well in order, smite
The sounding furrows: for my purpose holds
To sail beyond the sunset . . .'

'A new world?' George whispered to Nick. 'Perhaps he's going
after all.'
'Of course he is!'

'. . . And the baths
Of all the western stars until I die.'

I went on, and I heard Hilda assure Mrs Erskine-Brown, 'he's
definitely going'.

'It may be that the gulfs will wash us down'

I told them,

'It may be we shall touch the Happy Isles
And see the great Achilles, whom we knew.
Tho' much is taken, much abides; and tho'
We are not now that strength which in the old days
Moved earth and heaven: that which we are, we are . . .'

'What are we?' Uncle Tom was asking.
'What we are, apparently,' George assured him.

'One equal temper of heroic hearts . . .'

'He still makes a good final speech, old Rumpole.' This was
Featherstone muttering to Mr Justice Vosper, to which the judge
replied, 'Goes on a bit long.'

'Made weak by time and fate, but strong in will
To strive, to seek, to find, and not to yield.'

I paused. There was a smatter of applause.
'Well. Is that it?' Uncle Tom asked, but I had the final clear
announcement to make.
'This handsome time-piece will encourage me, my old friends,'
I told them, 'to forget all thought of surrender and retirement,
and not to yield in all my future cases at the Old Bailey, London Sessions, Luton Crown – or even before the Uxbridge

Magistrates! And I shall never be late. This will always get me to the Court on time!'

I was standing, holding the clock proudly whilst the assembled company stared at me with mingled hostility and amazement. At last Uncle Tom spoke, to no one in particular.

'If Rumpole's *not* retiring,' he said, 'does he really mean to hang on to our clock?'

Rumpole's
Return

For Penny

Else I my state should much mistake
   To harbour a divided thought
From all my kind – that, for my sake,
   There should a miracle be wrought.

No, I do know that I was born
   To age, misfortune, sickness, grief:
But I will bear these with that scorn
   As shall not need thy false relief.

Nor for my peace will I go far,
   As wanderers do, that still do roam;
But make my strengths, such as they are,
   Here in my bosom, and at home.

Ben Jonson: 'A Farewell to the World'

Chapter One

One dark, wet and almost arctic night in springtime (in fact it was Thursday, 13 March, and the sort of brutal English weather which ought to have made me profoundly grateful for where I was at the time) a 35-year-old clerk in the Inland Revenue named Percival Simpson left his evening class in Notting Hill Gate and went, as he always did on Thursday nights, into the Delectable Drumstick to buy his take-away supper. The meal in question consisted of a cardboard box in which was stowed a pale and hairy portion of greasy, battery-fed chicken and a number of soggy chips. It was, in short, the sort of mass-produced, Americanized food which tastes at the best of wet blotting-paper and at the worst of very old bicycle tyres: such a dinner as makes me more than ever anxious for the speedy collapse of Civilization As We Know It. Having secured this repellent repast, Simpson paid for it with money from the purse which he always carried about his person and made his way out of the neon-lit splendours of the Delectable Drumstick into the stormy unpleasantness of the street. He was going, as usual, to take the tube to his bed-sitting room in Paddington.

Exactly what followed never became altogether clear. Prosecuting counsel failed to elicit a coherent story from the various witnesses, and the defence was, as usual, only too happy to allow the picture to remain somewhat opaque. As Simpson walked along the broad and fairly well-lit pavement, he passed a large and rather muddy vehicle (it was later shown to be a Volvo estate car with a Hampshire registration) which drew up behind him. A man got out, of no more than Simpson's age but of an entirely different appearance. He was large and burly, a first class Rugby football player, whereas Simpson was on the skinny side and his game, on the rare occasions when he could find a partner, was draughts. The man from the estate car wore a suit made by Huntsman's in Savile Row, a hat from Lock's and made-to-measure shoes from Lobb; Simpson was dressed in a nondescript manner by courtesy of the January sales in the Civil Service Stores. The man from the Volvo was a product of Eton, Sandhurst and the Brigade of Guards; Simpson had acquired his mastery of mathematics at Stanmore Comprehensive and the North London Poly. It would be difficult to think of two more dissimilar young men than Percival Simpson and the Honourable Roderick (known to his many friends as Rory) Canter, younger son of the late Marquess of Freith. And yet they were to be inextricably joined in a famous double act, playing the parts of corpse and defendant in a trial staged before a large public at the Old Bailey.

We can now go conveniently to the evidence of Mr Byron MacDonald, the Jamaican guard of a train which was waiting at the platform of Notting Hill Gate station, bound for Paddington. Mr MacDonald was standing looking out of the open door of his compartment when he saw the fresh-faced Honourable Rory, with his well-cut clothes and general air of a gentleman farmer, come down onto the platform. Mr MacDonald waited for this late passenger to get onto the train, but Rory Canter showed no signs of doing so, and instead moved to a place on the platform where there was a bench set in a kind of small cave of lavatory tiling. He stood in the alcove, as the guard Byron MacDonald shouted, 'Mind the doors please!' and gave the signal for the train to move out of the station.

As the doors shut and the train sighed heavily and lumbered rheumatically forward, Mr MacDonald saw Simpson come onto the platform in his shapeless raincoat, still clutching his plastic dinner-bag, which bore on it the well-known symbol of the Delectable Drumstick. Simpson looked round, and then stepped back towards the alcove where Rory Canter was standing. The last sight that Byron MacDonald saw, as the train carried him off into the darkness of the tunnel, was two apparent strangers struggling together, locked in some inexplicable combat or embrace.

James 'Peanuts' Anderson and Dianna 'Smokey' Revere were part of a group of young people who came down to the platform about four minutes later on pleasure bent. They were variously dressed in black leather, safety-pins and a job lot of Iron Crosses and other emblems of the Wehrmacht. Peanuts' cropped hair was of a light green shade and Dianna's was tinted orange. They both wore heavy eye-shadow and, with their companions, were deriving such innocent pleasure as they could from kicking an empty lager can down the stairs and along the platform. From time to time during their progress, they punched or kicked each other in an affectionate manner.

Dianna Smokey Revere remembered seeing the man in the mackintosh move away from the seat on which the man in the trilby hat and the tweed suit was left sitting. At that moment another train came in, the doors opened and the young people kicked their beer can into an empty compartment. They went into the same compartment and milled around at one end, re-freshing themselves from other tins of lager which they had brought with them. The girl Smokey remembered seeing Simp-son sitting alone at the other end of the carriage, his plastic bag of dinner on the floor between his knees. He was carrying some object, what it was she could not exactly see, but it seemed to her to be about a foot long. She saw him drop it, whatever it was, into the plastic bag, inside which it hit the floor with a metallic clang. Her final view of the platform included the sight of a pale Rory Canter slipping sideways on the seat where he was sitting, so that he hit the lavatory tiles and then slithered to the ground. From the moving train it looked as though he were drunk; and so he seemed not at all out of place on Notting Hill Gate tube station at night.

Smokey, Peanuts and their friends scarcely paid any attention to Simpson when he left the train at Paddington. When he got out of the station, he made a few turnings away from the main thoroughfare into a short cul-de-sac called Alexander Herzen Road. Number 2 was the tall, crumbling, Victorian house which contained his bed-sit. By the stone steps which led up to the front door there was a row of dustbins, round which had gathered the debris left by resentful dustmen who never got a

Christmas box. Percival Simpson opened the lid of one of these dustbins and dropped into it his plastic bag of dinner untasted. When he had done this he seemed somewhat relieved in his mind, and went, as always, up to his room alone.

Although these events might, in the old days, have provided a certain amount of grist to the Rumpole mill, and might have been expected to yield the good things of the earth such as briefs, and money to pay the tax man and my clerk Henry, and the ever-increasing tick at Pommeroy's Wine Bar, and even keep my wife Hilda, known to me in awe as She Who Must Be Obeyed, in Vim for a month or two, they were now as remote from my sphere as the alleged delinquencies of little green men in outer space. At the time when Simpson caught his tube train and left the collapsing Hon. Rory on his bench, I was in a deck chair gently ripening to a roseate hue in the brilliant sunshine of southern Florida, looking out past the golden sand and assorted geriatrics to the Atlantic Ocean. I was in a strange condition which could be described as neither life nor death but something in between; a kind of air-conditioned purgatory. Not to put too fine a point on it, I had retired and gone to live in America.

The summons to this lotus-eating existence had come from my son, Nick, always the brains of the family, who had crowned his academic career by becoming Head of the Department of Social Studies in the University of Miami. He had also acquired a sizeable house with a swimming bath in the garden, a place which his wife Erica mysteriously referred to as the 'back yard'. When I add that Erica was expecting the Rumpole grandchild, and that Nick was constantly arguing that the time had come for me to hang up my old wig, give up the unequal struggle against the forces of law and order and join him and his wife in a sun-blessed haven far from the piercing draughts of our old mansion flat in Gloucester Road, and the cold winds and brutal proceedings of the Uxbridge Magistrates Court, you will understand why my wife Hilda was naturally and persistently in favour of this scheme. However, she would never have persuaded me if it hadn't been for the powerful argument advanced by his Honour Judge Roger Bullingham.

I lost ten cases in a row before Judge Bullingham. Bullingham, or the mad Bull, was, some years ago, elevated from his relative obscurity in the London Sessions to perform in the more popular arena of the Central Criminal Court. Far from maturing into any sort of civilization, the Bull relapsed into a deeper barbarity in his new post. He growled savagely at witnesses, he shouted and reduced young male barristers to stammering jellies and made lady barristers weep (Miss Trant, the Portia of our Chambers, once fled in tears from Bullingham's Court, saying that the cause of justice there would be advanced if they brought back trial by ordeal). He smiled with crawling sycophancy at juries, commiserated with them on the length of defence cross-examinations and told them the Test Match score, hoping to woo them to a conviction. During defence speeches he slept ostentatiously, or explored his ear with his little finger, or industriously picked his nose. When welfare officers suggested probation, he trumpeted with contempt; when police officers gave their evidence of improbable verbal admissions, he passed it on to the jury with the solemnity of Moses relaying the Tablets of the Law. His sentences were invariably greeted with outbursts of hysterical weeping by women in the public gallery.

I have always said that if you could choose your judge you could win most cases, and to avoid this undesirable result the authorities award judges to cases by some mysterious system of chance. The night before a case your clerk tells you which judge you have drawn in the lottery, and when I got his Honour Judge Bullingham for the tenth time I felt like some Monte Carlo gambler who, against all the odds, faces a record run on the black, leading to bankruptcy and a pistol shot on the terrace. All the same, my client was a Post Office worker of hitherto unblemished reputation, his wife was suffering from a long illness and the amount he was alleged to have fiddled was no more than two hundred pounds. The Bull, however, was at his worst. He fawned on the jury, constantly interrupted my cross-examination and forced me to make my final speech on Friday afternoon, so that the jury would have forgotten it by Monday morning when he made the ferocious prosecution plea which he called his summing-up. The jury obediently convicted, and my back and head were aching as I heaved myself to my hind legs in a vain attempt to appeal to the Bull's better nature in the matter of sentence. Eventually I subsided with the familiar Bull phrases ringing in my ears: 'Very serious crime ... Gross breach of trust by a public servant ... It is quite inappropriate for counsel to ask for leniency in this class of case ... Post Office frauds are going to be stamped out as far as this Court is concerned ... The least sentence I can pass is one of four years' imprisonment ...'

My client's daughter sobbed in the public gallery as he was led down to the cells. 'And the least sentence I can pass on you, Bull,' I said, only just under my breath, 'is banishment for life. Avaunt and quit my sight. Let the earth hide thee. Thy bones are marrowless, thy blood is cold. Thou hast no speculation in those eyes that thou dost glare with!' and a good deal more to the like effect. It was clear, of course, that the only way I could really banish Judge Bullingham from my life was to hang up my wig and leave the Old Bailey for ever. So we accepted Nick's invitation and moved to southern Florida.

On our shopping days, after a somewhat insubstantial and teeth-freezing lunch of a mountainous salad (jumbo prawns, inflatable tomatoes, Icelandic lettuce – the stuff to avoid is 'Thousand Island Dressing': so many islands, you might have thought, are hardly needed to provide a mixture of salad cream and tomato ketchup), Hilda and I would take chairs on the beach and go through the back numbers of *The Times* that my old friend George Frobisher posted to us from time to time. Around us 'Senior Citizens', old men wearing long shorts, peaked cotton caps and eye shields, antique ladies whose shrunken arms and necks were loaded with jewellery, sat blinking in the sun or queued for the three dollar blood pressure service which was available to warn of a sudden heart attack as the Dow Jones average plummeted, or the microchip in charge of our destinies mischievously ordered up a nuclear war.

'That *is* nice,' said She Who Must Be Obeyed, clucking approvingly at her copy of *The Times*. 'Queen's Birthday Honours go to Mrs Whitehouse and Margaret Thatcher's milkman.'

There are moments when I scarcely regret my exile from England, and this was one of them. But then I began to read the account of an unsolved London crime: '"Notting Hill Gate Mystery. The Honourable Rory Canter, younger brother of Lord Freith and wealthy Hampshire landowner, stabbed in underground station." My God. It *is* a mystery. What's an Honourable doing down the tube, like a common barrister?'

The smile put on it by the elevation of the Prime Minister's milkman faded from Hilda's face.

'I wish you'd stop worrying about that sort of thing, Rumpole, now I've persuaded you to retire.'

'You didn't persuade me to retire. His Honour Judge Bullingham persuaded me to retire. Anyway, I was losing my touch. I couldn't've shovelled more customers into Wandsworth if I'd joined the Old Bill.' I tried to forget Bullingham by reading the account of a more or less decent crime. '"Mr Canter had abandoned his Volvo estate car and gone down the underground." The Honourable gentleman must have been a tube-spotter.'

'I think Nick and I rescued you from murders just in time, Rumpole. You were looking distinctly seedy.'

'Not half as seedy as my clients. I'd leave the Temple every night, like Napoleon making a quick retreat from Moscow, abandoning the dead and dying to their fate...'

'You should be grateful to Nick. Thanks to him we shall have Christmas in this wonderful climate.'

I looked up at the relentlessly blue sky for signs of rain. 'Excellent climate, I'm sure,' I told Hilda, 'if you happen to be an orange.'

'And Nick's inviting his university friends over for a barbecue tonight. Poolside,' Hilda reminded me. It was true that my son had acquired a strange habit of cooking meals on a sort of camp-fire beside the swimming bath. 'The Professor of Law's coming. You'll have someone to talk to.'

'What can I say? I'm not a lawyer... any more.' I looked back, a little puzzled, at the *Times* account of the Notting Hill Gate murder. 'Now why should a man abandon his Volvo estate car and dive down the tube...? Oh well... Never mind! It can't possibly be my business any more. Rumpole's occupation's gone.'

'What did you say, Rumpole?'

'Nothing, Hilda. Nothing at all.' I closed my eyes and tried to rewrite *Othello*.

> 'Farewell the Ancient Court,
> Farewell the wiggéd troup and the old Judge,
> That made oppression virtue. Oh farewell,
> Pride, pomp and circumstance of glorious London Sessions . . .'

By this time I felt further pangs of nostalgia, even at the mention of that desolate courthouse down past the Elephant and Castle. So I tried to remember the things I missed least about my life in the law: such as Bullingham passing sentence and Chambers meetings, presided over by my learned ex-Head of Chambers, Guthrie Featherstone, Q.C., M.P.

Chapter Two

At about the time that I was reading the prodigiously delayed account of the Notting Hill Underground Murder Mystery, the evening peace of the Temple was shattered by the roar of a powerful motor-bicycle and a figure, hugely helmeted and dressed from neck to ankle in black leather, astride an over-powered Japanese Honda, came thundering in through the Embankment gates, waved a gauntleted greeting at the startled porter on duty and did a racing turn into Kings Bench Walk, narrowly missing a collision with the hearse-like vintage Daimler of a Lord of Appeal in Ordinary. The Dirt Track Rider screamed to a halt, dismounted and unfastened a black briefcase from his pillion. He then proceeded on foot towards Equity Court, where my old Chambers is situated.

Entering Number Two, the Speedway King passed the door on which the list of familiar names was painted. Guthrie Feather-stone, Q.C., M.P., led all the rest, beating by a short head the name Horace Rumpole, which had been crossed out in biro, the Temple sign-painter having never got around to painting it out and moving the other names, Thomas Cartwright (Uncle Tom), Judge George Frobisher, Claude Erskine-Brown, Phillida Trant (who has now, in the make-believe world of married life, adopted the pseudonym of Mrs Erskine-Brown), Clement Hos-kins, Flavius Quint, etc. The motor-bicyclist, who had now removed the huge plastic balloon from his head and emerged as a reasonably good-looking young man of thirty with a tumbling lock of black hair, thick eyebrows and the expression of one who constantly believes that he is about to be insulted and doesn't intend to stand for it, glanced at the list of names, as he had done on many occasions, appeared to notice a glaring omission and continued on into the clerk's room, looking more resentful than ever.

As it was six thirty my ex-clerk Henry, whom I can remember as a barely literate office boy, was just leaving to take our typist Dianne for their customary Cinzano Bianco in Pommeroy's, where they lit each other's cigarettes, occasionally held hands when they thought no one was looking, and tried to delay, for as long as possible, the inevitable journey home to their respective spouses. Henry is now touching forty, his hair no longer covers his ears, his trousers are less flared and his suits more conservative: he is beginning to look like a man with the sort of income a young barrister might aspire to only after years of practice. He watched without expression as the biker undid a multitude of zips, shed his skin of leather and emerged, like a somewhat formal snake, in a grey suit.

'Mind if I hang my gear on your door, Henry? Being a squatter gives you no damn place to put anything.'

He looked at my ex-clerk as if expecting some reactionary opposition to his plan, which he would be able to denounce on a point of democratic principle. He seemed almost disappointed when Henry's reply was, 'That's quite all right, Mr Cracknell. The Chambers meeting's being going on about ten minutes.'

The man addressed as Cracknell raised his eyes to the ceiling above which, in Featherstone's room, the established members of Chambers were discussing matters of great importance, particularly to him.

'This Chambers meeting is the first we have held in the absence of a once familiar figure . . .'

Guthrie Featherstone was in the chair, behaving with his customary mixture of self-assurance and nervousness, as if constantly aware that things might all get terribly out of hand (I owe my knowledge of this meeting to Miss Phillida Trant, the Portia of our Chambers, who described it all to me much, much later).

'Rumpole!' It was my old friend George Frobisher, now a Circuit (or as I prefer to call it, Circus) Judge who guesses that Featherstone, in his somewhat elliptical way, was referring to the Old Bailey Hack, now put out to grass in a distant land.

'I understand a card has been dispatched to carry our joint greetings to Horace Rumpole in his well-deserved retirement,' Featherstone told them and smiled. 'No doubt the cost has been deducted from Chambers' expenses.'

'We thought we'd never get rid of Rumpole. We kept giving him farewell dinners,' Uncle Tom grumbled. No doubt he remembered the clock they all gave me in the hope of putting me out to grass, a suggestion which, on that occasion, I made bold to resist. Then up spoke a diminutive, grey-haired Welshman with an insinuating voice and the look of a man who could apply a good deal of low cunning to running-down cases. He was a practitioner on the Welsh Circuit named Owen Glendour-Owen and a recent addition to Chambers.

'The man's lucky to have a son doing well at a foreign university, from what I can gather. Very comfortable billet he must have there now.'

'All the same, Chambers doesn't seem Chambers without Rumpole.' My old friend George Frobisher put in a word for me.

'Exactly! We seem to have got rid of the stink of cheap, small cigars in the passages.' Claude Erskine-Brown, never one of the Rumpole fan club, had no regrets.

'There do seem to be rather fewer villains loitering about Chambers,' George admitted.

And Uncle Tom, our oldest, and absolutely briefless member of Chambers (he comes in every day to read the law reports, do the *Times* crossword and get away from the unmarried sister who polishes violently round him if he stays at home) came out with one of his interminable reminiscences. 'I seem to recall,' he said, 'that one of Rumpole's clients took up the waiting-room carpet before a conference. And removed it in a hold-all!'

Featherstone smiled round at the conspirators, who seemed to be agreeing that they were better off without Rumpole. 'And I don't have the embarrassment of judges raising the question of Rumpole's hat – as a disgrace to the legal profession! However, I digress.' He got down to business. 'Rumpole's final retirement, much delayed as Uncle Tom reminds us . . .'

'He kept making his positively last appearance,' Uncle Tom suggested, quite unnecessarily, 'like a bloody opera singer!'

'Rumpole's final departure' – Featherstone was now in full flood – 'has left a considerable gap in our ranks. In fact you may say that the loss of one Rumpole has made room for at least two other members of the Bar. We have been fortunate indeed that Owen Glendour-Owen has joined us from Cardiff, with his useful connection with car insurance.'

The addition of this cunning Celt, which might have been greeted with cries of despair in happier days, now seemed an occasion of deep satisfaction to my treacherous ex-colleagues. There were murmurs of approval, cries of 'Welcome, Owen' and 'Hear, hear!', at which the tiny Welshman twinkled complacently and told them proudly, 'They call me "Knock-for-Knock" Owen in the valleys.'

Featherstone called the meeting to order. 'I thought I'd take this opportunity,' he said, 'to raise the question of the other candidate who might share Rumpole's old room with you, Glendour-Owen. As you all know, young Cracknell has been with us during the past year as a squatter . . .'

Here, perhaps, I should explain a legal term. The average young man, hopeful of pursuing a brilliant career at the Bar, may think that he is brought to the 'Off' simply by passing his exams, eating his dinners, getting 'called' by his Inn and doing his six months' pupillage in the Chambers of some established practitioner. If he thinks this, he's in for an unpleasant surprise. Once his pupillage is over, he may well be flung out of the Chambers and left with nowhere to park his backside or put his briefs on the mantelpiece. He is without a clerk to send him rushing out for ten quid to Uxbridge Magistrates Court, and he hasn't even the corner of a room to hold a decent conference. In short, our young hopeful cannot start to practise until he finds some set of Chambers to take him in. Accordingly he clings on to his place of pupillage with the tenacity of a drowning man clutching an overcrowded raft: although he knows he is unwanted, and there is probably not enough ship's biscuits and water to go round, he prefers to hang on rather than brave the dark and hostile waters around him. An ex-pupil in this position is called a 'squatter'; he turns up at Chambers every day like a perpetual rebuke, does his work in some inconvenient corner and will continue to squat on until he's either pushed off to sink or swim somewhere else in the Temple, or accepted (as he devoutly hopes) as a permanent tenant with a right to sit at a desk, be clerked by Henry, typed for by Dianne and raise his voice at Chambers meetings. And since my retirement there had arrived to squat at Number Two Equity Court none other than the Dirt Track Rider himself, young Kenneth Cracknell.

'Cracknell? Is that the fellow that looks as though he's dropped in from Mars?' George sounded disapproving.

'I saw him in the clerk's room the other day. I thought he'd come to deliver a telegram.' Erskine-Brown was scarcely more enthusiastic.

'Oh, I know you're all against Ken.' Phillida Trant looked round at the male members of Chambers in a defensive fashion.

'Ken?' George wondered. 'Is Ken the person from outer space?'

'Cracknell gets a fair amount of work. He's about to do a long fraud with Phillida Trant, and a dirty books case in the north.' Glendour-Owen seemed to have a more intimate acquaintance with the squatter, whom he seemed to see as a potential money-spinner.

'Do we really *want* dirty books in Chambers?' Erskine-Brown sounded unimpressed.

'Probably a good deal more amusing than the Law Reports.' Uncle Tom put the other side of the argument.

Featherstone smiled round at them all; but he smiled most at the lady I shall always remember as Miss Phillida Trant. He thought she was looking particularly beautiful, flushed with opposition to the oppressive anti-Cracknell faction which included her husband. Featherstone had never been entirely able to understand why the proudly beautiful Miss Trant, whose appearance in wig and gown, stiff collar, white bands and horn-rimmed specs was one, to his mind, of flagrant sexuality, had been snatched off and put in pod by Claude Erskine-Brown who, by any sensible board of selectors, would undoubtedly be chosen to bore for England. Featherstone, in spite of his appearance of respectability and his longing for the High Court Bench, was frequently troubled by pangs of ill-directed love, of the sort that had brought him so near to disaster in the case of Angela, our temporary Trotskyite typist.* As he saw Miss Trant glaring with hostility at her husband, Featherstone felt the stimulating tremor of a marriage breaking up and resolved to lose no opportunity in inviting Miss Trant to lunch. He also decided to throw his weight on her side in the Cracknell controversy.

'Interesting fellow, Cracknell,' Featherstone said. 'He tells me that he intends to do cases connected with civil rights.'

'Exactly!' Erskine-Brown sounded as though his worst fears were confirmed. Miss Trant looked at her husband with a hostility that made Featherstone's heart flutter.

'Well, what's wrong with civil rights? Better than civil wrong, wouldn't you say so? Of course, Ken's a radical lawyer. I know that's the sort you don't want to have the key of the lavatory . . . like women and blacks!' She started her usual oration, and her husband looked at her, puzzled.

'Philly, what on earth's come over you?'

'Blacks! That reminds me . . .' Uncle Tom had somewhat lost the thread of the argument. 'They nearly wished a Parsee on us once. I voted for you, old fellow.' He slapped a surprised Glendour-Owen on the shoulder. 'Even though you're Welsh.' †

'Well, I'm not sure Cracknell sounds in the least bit desirable.' Erskine-Brown looked at his wife. 'From what you tell me, Philly, he lives in a commune.'

'I told you, Claude, that he lives in a community. Near King's Cross.' His wife corrected him and went on, flushed with sincerity, 'I've seen Ken once or twice in action. Down at Bow Street. Believe it or not, he's a very attractive advocate.'

At which point the door opened and the squatter entered. The others looked somewhat startled, as if they'd been caught out in some discreditable conspiracy. Miss Phillida Trant was the first to greet him, using that shortened version of his Christian name which he insisted on to show that he was of radical views, a

* See 'Rumpole and the Case of Identity', pp. 296–328.
† See 'Rumpole and the Fascist Beast', pp. 273–95.

man of the people, totally without pretensions, and not a pompous barrister like the rest of us.

'Oh, hello, Ken,' said Miss Trant, almost shyly.

'Well, hullo.' Young Cracknell looked round the room, unsmiling. 'Aren't squatters invited?'

'Of course.' Featherstone was almost too effusive. 'And you
won't be a squatter forever. We're considering the position of
accommodation in Chambers, now that Rumpole's left.'

'Rumpole?' Ken Cracknell seemed genuinely puzzled. 'Everyone's always talking about Rumpole. I've never met the man.'

Chapter Three

'It's a sunshine day.'

'Well, as a matter of fact, it always is.'

I was standing on the 'sidewalk' of a busy shopping street in Miami; around me the population were busily Dunkin' Dough-nuts or chewing Happy Brunchburgers, or pushing overburdened trolleys filled with convenience foods, or merely standing on the street corners of Dade City (it's a little-known fact that the late Colonel Dade was actually defeated by the Red Indians) hoping, in an unconvinced sort of way, for Good Times Just Around The Corner. I had bought a new box of small cigars, Hilda was waiting for me in a battered yellow taxi, and I was confronted with an unusual sight in that bustling city, where the young people looked as if they'd just swum in from Cuba and the old people looked anxiously embalmed, of a young man wearing a quiet tie, a clean white shirt, well-ironed jeans and industriously polished shoes. His hair was short, clean and neatly parted. He was proffering to me, held between finger and thumb, a large yellow flower, which looked, considering the surrounding petrol fumes and the humidity, surprisingly perky.

'A sunshine day for you and me, friend and brother,' the young man repeated. 'Praise to the Eternal Sun!'

I had been thinking for weeks of the soft rain falling round the Temple tube station, but I didn't want to argue. As politeness seemed to demand it, I took his chrysanth. In a tone of voice which sounded quite practical he announced that he had something more to offer.

'Want to take a hand-out?' he said. He had a bunch of pamphlets, in favour of what? Strip shows, life insurance, cut-price burial or the protection of whales?

'Are you selling something?' I asked him.

'Sunlight!' The young man was smiling at me. I thought he might be a salesman for picture windows or patio doors. Whatever sort of sunlight he was dealing in, I imagined it came at a fair old price.

I opened the taxi door and was about to get in beside Hilda when he said, 'Meet and talk?'

'What?'

'We shall meet and talk, friend and brother. As sure as the seeds grow in the sunlight. We shall meet and talk . . .'

'Sorry. Got to get back home now. My son Nick's giving a party. Poolside.'

I shut the taxi door then, but I still saw his pleasant face, framed in the open window. He raised his hand in a sort of cheerful salute and said, 'Sunlight to Children of Sun! Blood to Children of Dark!'

As the taxi moved away I returned the friendliest greeting I could think of. 'And a very Happy Christmas to you too.'

'Rumpole,' said She Who Must Be Obeyed. 'You're holding a flower.'

'Well, so I am.'

'He seemed a very nice young man,' Hilda said. 'He looked so very different from most young people nowadays.'

She was smiling, so I gave her the flower. She sniffed it enthusiastically and then put it on the seat beside her, where it wilted in the long traffic jam going out of the city.

' "Meet and talk." A total stranger came up to me in the city, gave me a chrysanth and said, "Meet and talk." '

'It may seem just crazy to you, Dad,' my daughter-in-law said, giving me that sweet smile of toleration for the Senior Citizen which I find particularly irritating, 'but people around here just like to rap on . . . about life, and God and such like.' Erica was wrapped in some sort of ethnic, handwoven garment which did little to conceal the fact that she was expecting the first Rumpole ever to become a citizen of the United States. 'Maybe now you've given up the rat race you'll learn to rap with strangers, Dad.'

It grated a little, I must confess, to hear all the real world I once inhabited, the cloud-capped Assize Courts, the golden pinnacles of the Old Bailey itself, the Lords of Appeal and the Great Villains, the Circus Judges and the Timson family (notorious crooks of South London), my notable trials including the Penge Bungalow Murders and the Great Grimsby Fish Fraud, all referred to as the rat race. I looked at Nick, my son, who had the brazier going on which he proposed to cook large steaks, which would be served with salad and glasses of Californian wine (not really *much* worse than Pommeroy's plonk) when the guests arrived. I remembered that the last time I had seen him cook out of doors was when he was about eight and we boiled shrimps over a camp-fire on the beach at Lowestoft. And then the chime of bells sounded at Nick's front door and he went in through the house to receive his visitors.

'I guess you'll be able to make your own space now you're retired, Dad.' Erica was often difficult to follow. 'You'll really be able to find yourself.'

'I don't know about that,' I said when I'd thought the matter over. 'I might not like myself after I'd found me.'

At which point Nick came back to the camp-fire with the guests for the evening: Professor Nathan Blowfield, Head of the Legal Faculty (a small, round man in a tartan jacket whose health was in constant danger owing to his indulgence in the habit of jogging), and his wife Betsy Blowfield, both of whom I knew already; and a couple who were strangers to me, a very pretty and smiling black girl in a white silk shirt, clean dungarees and gold glasses, and her attendant male, a supervisor from the English Department. Their names were announced as Paul Gilpin and Tiffany Jones.

'Any time you want to come up to the campus, Mr Rumpole,' Professor Blowfield smiled invitingly, 'I'm sure my students would be honoured to meet a trial lawyer from England.'

'Am I a trial lawyer?' I asked him. 'I used to think I'd passed the test.'

'Tell me,' young Paul Gilpin looked at me with amusement, 'do you guys still wear the rug . . . ?' He patted the top of his head. 'What do you call it, the peruke? In your courtrooms . . .'

'I have hung up my old wig.' I downed a sizeable gulp of the Californian claret-style. 'Rumpole's occupation's gone. But yes. I wore my crown of itchy horsehair for almost half a century.'

'And I'm sure you looked real nice in it.' Tiffany Jones was smiling at me; she seemed a pleasant girl whose serious spectacles and matter-of-fact American voice belied her exotic, African appearance. 'You must have looked like George Washington or something.'

'If that was the old darling who never told a lie,' I had to admit, 'well really, not much.'

'Nick tells us you're retired now,' Paul Gilpin said.

'Yes. I dropped out. I bought this sunshine shirt.' I had, in fact, invested in a Miami shirting which was about as discreet as the eruption of Vesuvius. 'And Hilda and I spend our days bumming round the beach.'

'You've found time to breathe a little?' Paul Gilpin asked me in a meaningful sort of way.

'I used to breathe down the Old Bailey,' I told him, 'strange as it may seem.'

'I guess Paul only meant that you'd found peace of mind, since your retirement.' The others had wandered away in search of food and drink and I was left with Tiffany Jones, whose gentle voice made me feel that I had been unnecessarily rude to the well-meaning Paul.

'I'm not sure peace of mind interests me exactly. You see,' I did my best to explain, 'after a life of crime, I suppose I'm finding it difficult to go straight.' Again she made me feel I was talking too much about myself, and even wallowing in *nostalgie de l'*Old Bailey. She seemed a particularly nice girl, and I wanted to find out more about her. 'What department are you in up at the University, Miss ... Jones?'

'Oh please, "Tiffany".' She put a long-fingered brown hand on my arm as she spoke, and I avoided looking for any reaction from She Who Must Be Obeyed. 'I'm in social economics and statistics.' It had to be admitted that the confession was not romantic, although the manner in which she made it was. 'I've always had a head for figures. Since I was a kid, I guess. I cover the economic statistics for Nick's Department of Sociology.'

'How many one-parent families in inner-city areas take to pinching milk bottles.' I knew what she meant: I once had a twelve-year-old delinquent for a client who told me his trouble was he couldn't 'relate to his mother in a one-to-one supportive relationship'.

'That kind of thing.' Tiffany grinned. 'I like the statistics . . . but the rest of it's a lot of crap, isn't it? I mean, wherever you come from, you can always choose between God and the Devil.' Although she was still looking happy and radiant, her words had a sudden, almost chilling seriousness.

'Can we choose?' I asked her. 'Fate dealt me an old devil called Judge Bullingham for ten cases running.'

'No matter what luck you have, there's always a choice between light and darkness. The choice is yours, as sure as the seed grows in the sunshine.'

I frowned, trying to remember. Her words troubled me, like an unfamiliar quotation; but when she spoke again, of course, I got the source immediately.

'We must meet and talk on this subject, friend and brother,' Tiffany Jones said. 'You and I must meet and talk.'

'Did you hear that, Rumpole?' Hilda interrupted from the middle distance. I looked down and noticed, with mingled regret and relief, that Tiffany's hand had left my arm. 'Erica says it's wonderful to feel that we don't have to rush off back to England. Haven't you got anything to say to that?'

'Have you got anything to say, why sentence of death should not be passed upon you?' Her words had put me in mind of an old legal anecdote, and as Professor Blowfield was then refilling my glass with Château Vieux Frontier, or whatever strange name it went by, I decided to give him the benefit of it. 'I'll tell you a bit of law, Professor. A bit of legal history . . .'

'I sure wish my students could hear it, Mr Rumpole.'

'He was a devil!' I told them. 'The old Lord Chief Justice! When I was first at the Bar. An enormously unlovable character. Used to order muffins for tea at his Club after passing death sentences. Anyway, this old Lord Chief was about to pass sentence in his usual manner . . .'

'I'm going to get your husband to give a seminar to the Law

Faculty,' I heard Professor Blowfield tell Hilda with some pride, to which she answered shortly, 'That's very thoughtful of you, Professor Blowfield. But I do want Rumpole to rest.'

Undeterred I battled on with the anecdote. 'And the clerk of the Court intoned, "Have you anything to say why sentence of death should not be passed upon you?" "Bugger all, my Lord," the murderer muttered. Whereupon the old Lord Chief turned to this murderer's counsel, a nervous sort of individual called Bleaks. "Did your client say something, Mr Bleaks?" "Bugger all, my Lord", Bleaks stammered. "That's distinctly odd," grunted the old Lord Chief. "I could've sworn I heard him *say* something." '

I can't say the Rumpole comic turn brought a standing ova-tion. I laughed, as I have for years at that particular story, and I was flattered to find that Tiffany laughed with me. Nick made an effort and smiled; Hilda also made an effort and didn't. Paul Gilpin, the Blowfields and Erica all looked seriously puzzled.

'Poor old Nick,' I said, feeling sorry for my son. 'He was brought up on that story. That story was "Goldilocks and the Three Bears" to my son Nicholas.'

Professor Blowfield cleared his throat. He had, it seemed, decided to open the seminar. 'Mr Rumpole, in your experience, what was the most important case in Britain during your long career?'

That was an easy one, and I had no doubt at all as to the answer. 'The most important case was undoubtedly the Penge Bungalow Murder.'

'The Penge Bungalow? What did that decide exactly?' The Professor tried in vain to recall his legal textbooks.

'It decided,' I told him, 'that I was able to win a murder, alone and without a leader. It was the start – of the Rumpole career.'

'Did it turn on a nice point of law?' the Professor asked eagerly.

'Law?' I had to disillusion him. 'There was no law about it. It turned on a nice point of blood.'

Chapter Four

Blood, of course, was to prove the undoing of Percival Simpson; blood and the fact that he possessed an extremely observant landlady who had never liked him and had always found his natural shyness and reserve deeply suspicious. As I was giving Professor Blowfield a Golden Oldie from my collection of legal anecdotes, Simpson was coming down the stairs of his lodgings in Alexander Herzen Road with his mackintosh over his arm to meet the inquisitive landlady hoovering in the hall.

'Just slipping out to the cleaners, Mrs O'Dwyer.' Simpson said it in a half-hearted attempt at friendliness, but the unsolicited information immediately attracted her attention to the mackintosh over his arm, and to what seemed to her to be, although faintly, a pinkish stain only half hidden by a fold in the cloth. So, as soon as her lodger was safely out of the house, Mrs O'Dwyer abandoned her Hoover and went up to his room for a good look round. She saw what she had often seen, and disapproved of, on previous visits when she did her minimal cleaning. On Simpson's dressing-table was a crude and amateurish water-colour, cheaply framed, of a naked couple, hands stretched upwards towards a flaming yellow sun in a deep-blue sky. Beside it was, also framed, the coloured portrait photograph of a cleric with crinkly white hair, kindly eyes beaming behind rimless glasses and a deep and healthy suntan. In front of the photograph stood, in a votive position, a half-burned candle in a china holder; beside it lay an ornately handled and curved Moroccan dagger in a bronze sheath, and, carefully folded and kept in place by the handle of the dagger, was a square of white paper through which some scrawled, red lettering was just visible.

Mrs O'Dwyer looked at this collection, the only pool of colour in the drab room, and saw nothing that she had not seen before. She looked at the narrow divan-bed with its porridge-coloured hessian bedspread, and the shelf over it on which were lodged a Bible and several volumes on revenue law, together with a tattered copy of *The House at Pooh Corner*, a relic of Simpson's childhood. Then she opened the wardrobe. There were very few clothes hanging in it: an old jacket, a suit for very best, a few shirts and underclothes; but Mrs O'Dwyer looked down at a pile of dirty washing at the bottom of the cupboard. She picked up a shirt and looked at the cuff, and there she found, to her considerable excitement and enormous satisfaction, a stain that was a deeper pink, in which the attempt at washing had been less successful than the mark on the mackintosh that her secretive lodger had been taking to the cleaners. She went straight down to the hall and lifted the telephone.

The wail of police sirens is not an unknown noise around Alexander Herzen Road near Paddington. The neighbours paid only casual attention to the posse of uniformed officers and to the police dogs nosing round the area's steps. No one saw the treasure that dogs and men recovered from one of the dustbins; a plastic bag from the Delectable Drumstick inside which, beside a box of mouldering chicken, lay an army sheath knife, found, on forensic examination, to be liberally stained with blood of the same group as that which once flowed in the veins of the Honourable Rory Canter. When he returned to the house and found police officers waiting for him, Percival Simpson smiled a little wearily, but did not seem at all surprised.

The officers in charge of the Notting Hill Gate Underground Murder were led by Detective Inspector Wargrave, a friendly and comfortable-looking copper who sang bass-baritone in the Gilbert and Sullivan put on by his local operatic society and always cast himself as the Dutch uncle in interviews. Young Detective Constable Jarwood, on the other hand, was pale, sharp-featured and unsmiling, and conducted interviews as if the responsibility of fighting crime rested on him alone.

'Want a cup of tea, lad, do you?' D.I. Wargrave started the interrogation of Simpson with the soft approach.

'I know,' the arrested man looked at the D.I. as though he hadn't heard, 'I have sinned.'

'You're telling us you're guilty, then?' D.C. Jarwood sounded almost disappointed as he made a note; like an eager huntsman who sees the fox come trotting up to the meet and lie down. Simpson seemed to have fallen into a sort of reverie from which the D.I. sought to awaken him.

'How long have you known him, Percy?'

'How long have you known the Honourable Rory Canter?' Jarwood repeated the question, more insistently. 'The one you cut.'

Simpson shook his head and said, quite gently, 'I didn't know him.'

'Don't lie to us, Simpson,' the Detective Constable came in dead on cue.

'It's true. I'd never seen him before.' Simpson sounded as if he didn't really care whether they believed him or not. 'Of course, I knew he'd come . . . sometime.'

'So you went after him?' Jarwood asked.

'No!' Simpson said it quite positively; but then he sighed and added, 'What's the use? They'll never let me escape now. Never!'

At which point the Detective Inspector took a plastic envelope from a file and carefully withdrew from it the folded sheet of paper he had found on Simpson's dressing-table, on which a curious message had been printed in blotchy and uneven capitals.

'This is your handwriting, Percy?' Simpson nodded his head, making no attempt to deny it.

'Strange sort of letter, isn't it?' Jarvis suggested.

'Perhaps. To you.' Simpson's interest in the proceedings seemed hard to retain.

'It's written in blood, isn't it, Percy?' Wargrave said it as though he were inviting Simpson to another cup of tea. 'We had the forensic on it, you see. You wrote this in the blood of the gentleman you knifed.'

At which Simpson looked up at him surprised, and for the first time since the interview began he seemed to be genuinely afraid. 'No! Not his blood. Unless . . .' He looked at the sheet of paper almost in awe. 'Something miraculous!'

'You're lying to us again, Percy. That's no use to you, you know.' Jarwood's reaction was predictable, but Simpson looked at him without dissent.

'Of course,' he nodded. 'Nothing's any use. They've got the power! I can't fight it.'

'It's just no good. He can't fight it. He tells the police he's guilty. The bloody knife's in the dustbin. He's identified by at least three witnesses at the tube station and he writes some spooky letter in his victim's blood. The case is as dead as mutton.'

'Just the sort of case Rumpole would have enjoyed.'

In due course Percival Simpson had made his first appearance in the Magistrates Court; it was a short and silent appearance as far as he was concerned and he seemed to show little interest in the proceedings. He was, as was inevitable on a murder charge, granted legal aid and his case was passed to an eager young solicitor, Labour councillor and leading light of the local Law Centre called Michael, or Mike, Mowbray. Mike knew Ken Cracknell (they had been fellow students at the London School of Economics) and, as anxious to advance his friend's career as his own, he gave the brief in this desirable murder (the sort of case for which in my early years at the Bar I would have been tempted to go out and do the deed myself) to the ex-squatter, Dirt Track Rider, now tenant of my old room, K. Cracknell, Esq. Cracknell, although naturally excited as he undid the pink tape which bound the important brief, became increasingly depressed as he calculated the odds stacked against the defence. So he was now sitting in Rex's Café, opposite the Old Bailey, eating some of the superb scrambled eggs that they serve there from dawn on, telling his troubles to the Portia of our Chambers, Mrs Phillida Erskine-Brown (née Trant).

As for Miss Trant, she had taken to setting out from home early, leaving the feeding of the Erskine-Brown infant in the hands of her husband and a large and unsmiling au pair from Iceland who would, as Miss Trant feared, give notice if she gave her the opportunity of the briefest conversation. 'Got to read a brief for 10.30,' Miss Trant would call over her shoulder as she fled the domestic scene. 'I'll grab a cup of coffee at Rex's.' And off she would go, leaving the child, her husband Claude and Miss Reykjavik to form a gloomy and abandoned alliance. It may also be said that her step lightened as she put an increasing distance between herself and family life in South Kensington, not only because she loved her work, which she did, but because she had grown agreeably used to breakfast with Ken Cracknell, who looked this morning, with his dark hair and smouldering eyes, like a young Heathcliff of the legal aid system.

'Just my luck!' Cracknell continued to complain. 'I thought I'd do my first murder on my own and score a triumphant victory. Now . . . no way! I'll be a triumphant loser.'

'That letter . . . !' Miss Trant had eagerly and helpfully read her friend Ken Cracknell's brief and had seen the photostat of the strange missive that Percy Simpson appeared to have written in his victim's blood.

'The jury's going to love that!' Cracknell filled his mouth with scrambled egg on a slice and chewed bitterly. 'He doesn't only knife a member of the aristocracy, he uses him as an inkwell to write his correspondence.' Ken looked, if possible, more savagely depressed. 'It's a case that's going to do my career at the Bar no sort of good at all.'

Miss Trant looked at him, smiled and put a hand on his arm. 'I must say, Ken,' she said, 'you're frightfully ambitious. For a radical lawyer.'

'Even radical lawyers are meant to win their cases.' He looked at her, pleased with her obvious concern. 'Why don't we have a hamburger tonight and talk about it. I could show you the commune.'

'I can't, Ken, honestly.' Miss Trant sounded genuinely disappointed. 'My husband'll have dinner all ready. He's started to cook French traditional from the *Observer* colour supplement.'

'Ring him and say you've been kept late in Chambers. A late con.'

'No, I can't. Another time.' She squeezed his arm and let it go, so she could deal better with her marmalade and double toast.

'Another time. You promise?' Ken Cracknell smiled, the effect of which upon Miss Trant was powerful.

'All right. I promise,' she said. She lit a thoughtful, low tar, filter-tipped and quite tasteless cigarette, and added thoughtfully, 'Ken. About that defence of yours . . . There *is* someone who really knows about blood stains.'

'You mean Professor Andrew Ackerman?' Cracknell mentioned the Prince of the Morgues, the best forensic science witness in the business. 'He's giving evidence for the prosecution.'

'No.' And Miss Trant breathed out smoke through elegantly flaring nostrils. 'But someone as good as Ackerman. I could write to him, if you like.'

Chapter Five

'Dear Rumpole. It seems ages since you left us and of course we all miss you.' My correspondent, as an advocate, was more ready to say what she thought the tribunal might like to hear than to stick to the strict truth; but let that pass. 'We have got a new fellow in Chambers though, a rather super bloke called Ken Cracknell (he's always called Ken, which shows that there's simply no side or snobbery about him). He always defends, or appears for, tenants, or Indian teachers in front of the Race Relations Boards, and all that sort of thing. In fact, Ken's a real radical lawyer, just like you used to be.' Wrong. In fact there has never been a moment in my long and chequered career in which I have ever borne the remotest resemblance to Kenneth Cracknell, Esq.; but let that pass also. 'Your old enemy the Mad Bull is now a senior Old Bailey Judge.' As I read this the Florida sun seemed warmer and more delightful, the grass on the neat front lawns under the rainbow-hued sprinklers greener and more pleasant. 'Now what I want to ask your advice about, Rumpole, is this.' I turned another page; the round, schoolgirlish hand served to make the letter more bulky. 'Ken's got a murder and it's his first and naturally he wants to win, so I feel it's up to us to give him all the help we can. It all happened at Notting Hill Gate tube station (see the enclosed cuttings from *The Times* and the *News of the World* which will give you all the gen). But where you come in is with your marvellous expertise on questions of blood. It seems the client wrote a gruesome sort of letter, probably to the Devil or something equally creepy, in the victim's blood. What we want to know is, is this possible? I mean, wouldn't it congeal or something? And have you ever had a case of blood stains on paper? I don't really want Ken to know that I've asked your advice as he's awfully proud and touchy (like all radical barristers, I suppose) and really wants to feel that he's done it all himself. Claude is really quite well and very proud of Tristan.' Who the hell was Tristan, I wondered? 'As you say, he'll soon be old enough to sit up and draft an affidavit. Tristan, I mean.' Oh, of course, Tristan. The son and heir the Erskine-Browns conceived after one of their nights out at Covent Garden. 'At the moment we've got a most alarming Icelandic au pair and I have to keep out of her way in case she gives in her notice . . .'

'Rumpole!' Hilda was calling to me from the other side of the lawn sprinkler as I stood by the postbox on the road at the end of the garden and read this letter which seemed to smell, even as I held it, comfortingly of fog and damp and old law reports and breakfast in Rex's Café. 'Is there anything in the post?'

'Do write if you can think of any sort of a cunning wheeze for Ken. Hope you're enjoying the sunshine. I do envy you. Phillida (Trant as was) Erskine-Brown.'

'No, nothing really. Just a postcard from my old clerk.' I stuffed Miss Trant's letter into my pocket; for some reason I felt guilty about it, as though I were already plotting the desperate course I was about to take.

'Henry's not wanting you back, is he?' Hilda asked suspiciously about my clerk, at which moment Erica emerged from the house with an ethnic shopping-basket and saw me smiling through the mist of the sprinkler.

'You look much happier today, Dad.'

'Yes. Henry doesn't want me back. There's no mention of that,' I told Hilda more or less truthfully.

'Oh well.' Hilda seemed relieved. 'We're just going down to the drug store.'

'What's the matter? Feeling seedy?'

'Don't be ridiculous, Rumpole. We're going to get Erica's cigarettes.'

As they went off chattering together to Erica's parked station-wagon, I began to wonder at the fact that Hilda, at her time of life, was starting to learn American.

*

The Importance of Blood Stains in Forensic Evidence by Professor Andrew Ackerman, M.R.C.P., F.C. path. The advantage of having a son who has done well in an academic career is that you can have your favourite books about you, even in Miami.

I was in the long, pleasantly cool room of the University library; around me blonde and bronzed young people, dressed in jeans and T-shirts, chewed gum and read the letters of Henry James, or some twelve-volume commentary on the works of Trollope. I leafed rapidly through Ackerman's familiar index. 'Blood stains on clothing . . . On floors . . . On . . . On innocent bystanders . . .' At first I couldn't believe that the Great Ackerman hadn't dealt with the problem, but then I became aware of the fact that Ken Cracknell's murder had, apparently, broken ground untrodden even by the Great Prince of the Mortuaries himself.

> So felt I like some watcher of the skies
> When a new planet swam into his ken . . .

Or a new blood stain I told myself with delight, and I was clutching Andrew Ackerman's weighty volume and crossing the pleasant, tree-lined campus, threading my way among the bicycling and courting couples, when I came up to those former barbecue guests, Professor Blowfield of the Law Department and Paul Gilpin from English, together with that distinguished academic, young Nicholas Rumpole, Head of the Department of Sociology.

'It's the damnedest thing about Tiffany,' Paul was saying as I came up to them. 'She just vanished.'

'Vanished?' Professor Blowfield was saying. 'She can't have *vanished*. Why, here you are, Mr Rumpole. It seems we have a mystery on our hands.'

'Mystery? What mystery?' Fate seemed to have been unusually kind in the matter of handing out mysteries that day.

'Tiffany Jones never showed up at the Department,' Nick said. 'Yet Paul says she left home same time as usual.'

'And there's a young guy on the campus says Tiffany sold him her car yesterday. He picked it up from the street outside our apartment block – with the key on the offside wheel. How the hell's she going to go on living in Miami without a car?'

'She didn't say anything?' Professor Blowfield asked.

'Not that I can remember.'

I spent only a moment lamenting Paul Gilpin's loss of the handsome Tiffany; she had in any event seemed, as far as I clearly remembered, far too good for him, and then I approached Nick with the first stirrings of my Great Plan in mind.

'Nick. I must talk to you.'

'You remember Tiffany Jones, don't you, Dad? The economic statistician. She came to the barbecue.'

'Of course I remember her; but do statisticians ever disappear?'

'She'll call up, I guess. It can't *be* anything.' But Paul Gilpin didn't sound convinced.

'Perhaps she just melted away in the sunshine. Look, Nick. I'll take you out to lunch. Not the canteen. I don't think I could take another three-storey sandwich with a gherkin on a toothpick. Is there a quiet little chop-house somewhere? Where we could talk quietly?'

Chapter Six

We settled on the Magic Bamboo, a Chinese restaurant just off the campus. Clever little people, the Chinese, who would have made splendid Battle of Britain pilots, because they must be expert at seeing in the dark. The room, painted in black lacquer and gold, was plunged into a midnight gloom in which husbands no doubt lunched with their secretaries or other people's wives, or went on what might have been aptly known as blind dates. Faint lights dotted the tables with the effulgence of glow-worms, and pretty young Chinese waitresses passed among them with table-heaters and bowls of oriental delicacies.

'I've got to talk to you seriously, Nick,' I began, and wondered when I had talked to him seriously before.

'Look. If it's about money, there's absolutely no hurry. I know you'll make a contribution when you sell the flat.'

'It's not about money, Nick. Anyway, I may not sell the flat. I've got an idea I may need a pied-à-terre in Froxbury Mansions . . .'

'What are you up to, Dad?' Nick looked at me with some suspicion, and I decided to approach my goal by a circuitous route.

'Look, Nick,' I said. 'When you were a boy, we used to have an oath of secrecy. Remember? If I found you reading comics under the bedclothes or eating gobstoppers? Your mother thought there was something lower class about a gobstopper . . . Anyway, if I discovered any crime of that nature, the motto was N.A.W.T.S.W.M.B.O.'

'What on earth did that mean?' The young have short memories and Nick looked puzzled.

'Not A Word To She Who Must Be Obeyed,' I translated. 'So

you see, if I planned to do the vanishing trick ... like what's her name, the disappearing statistician? Miss Tiffany Jones?'

'Dad. *Is* it about money?' Nick still looked vaguely anxious.

'No, dear boy. My dear Nick,' I set his mind at rest, 'it's about blood.'

'Blood?' Nick seemed not at all reassured.

'Listen, Nick. When I left England, I decided to plonk all my cards face down on the table. When I finally gave match point to His Honour Judge Bullingham and hung up my wig, I thought there were elements in my Chambers, deviously backed by our middle-of-the-road Q.C., M.P. Head of Chambers, who were quite pleased to see the back of old Rumpole. If I'm not mistaken, a certain sigh of relief went up from the clerks' room, where they prefer a barrister who's prepared to kiss his instructing solicitor's backside! But it now seems perfectly clear, Nick. They want me back. They can't do without me!'

'Dad ...' Nick was attempting some sort of interruption, but I was now in full flow.

'I've had a letter from Miss Phillida Trant, a girl whom I brought up in the law. She has written to me by airmail, Nick, sparing no expense. It seems they've got a murder which raises several nice questions of blood. So the cry has gone up from Equity Court in the Temple: Send for Rumpole!'

'Dad, you're not thinking of going back?'

It was a direct question and I decided to put off answering it by swigging the red wine the Chinese waitress had thoughtfully delivered. 'What's this? More Californian claret? Château Deadwood Stage? Not bad, Nick. Not bad at all. Better than Pommeroy's plonk, which in a bad year, if you remember, tasted as if they'd been treading toadstools and paddling in disinfectant.'

'Look. If Erica and I haven't shown we want you ...' Nick was not to be diverted.

'Bless you, Nick,' I hastily reassured him. 'Of course you have! I remember when you were a boy, quite a young boy, you were always about the place. We used to go for walks on Hampstead Heath. We used to track Indian spoor and swear to be blood-brothers. You recall that, don't you, Nick?'

'I don't think so.' For some reason those moments of past, childish excitement seemed to have slipped his memory.

'Well, that's what happened.' I had no doubt about it. 'And then you went off to school and university and forgot about me. I had to let you go and after a while, well, it's quite true, I hardly missed you. You'll have to let me go now, Nick. It won't be a great deprivation.'

It seemed to take a while for him to catch my drift, and when he did he looked puzzled, but not as appalled as a fond father might have hoped. 'I thought,' my son said slowly, 'Erica thought this too, that now we could really get to know one another.'

This did seem to me unnecessary. I mean, when you've seen a man through nappies and paid his school fees, you've really got past the formal introduction stage. 'We knew each other, Nick,' I reminded him. 'You knew me when I sat on the edge of the bath and told you about my murder cases. You don't want to know an old man dying of boredom in the sunshine.'

At which point a waitress passed with a tray loaded with small, steaming, cylindrical, white objects. With the aid of a pair of tongs she deposited one of these on each of our side plates.

'What are you planning?' Nick looked at me with deepening suspicion.

I took another swig of Château Cherokee or whatever it was and told him, 'Going home, Nick. Returning to base. Travel, you see, narrows the mind extraordinarily.' Then I gave him some lines of Ben Jonson that seemed to sum the matter up. They are displayed in all their glory in old Arthur Quiller-Couch's edition of *The Oxford Book of English Verse*, a battered India paper volume which travels always in my suitcase.

> 'No, I do know that I was born
> To age, misfortune, sickness, grief:
> But I will bear these with that scorn
> As shall not need thy false relief.
>
> Nor for my peace will I go far,
> As wanderers do, that still do roam;
> But make my strengths, such as they are,
> Here in my bosom, and at home.'

'Good!' I peered through the blackout at the steaming shape on my side plate. 'They've brought us something to eat at last. I rather like Egg Rolls.' And before Nick could intervene I had seized the imagined delicacy and suddenly filled my mouth with what tasted like a mixture of warm scented soap and cotton fibres. The American passion for hygiene and dark restaurants had made me start my luncheon with an hors d'oeuvre of hot face-towel.

However, I give myself the credit of taking into full account the feelings of She Who Must Be Obeyed. I decided to leave her behind.

My wife Hilda had not, after all, throughout our long lives together, displayed any marked enthusiasm for the company of Rumpole. She frequently resented my presence, as well as my occasional absence at the end of the day in Pommeroy's Wine Bar. She took exception to my old anecdotes and criticized my hat. Hilda, I decided entirely with her best interests at heart, would be far happier if she stayed in America with Nick, Erica and the forthcoming infant Rumpole. I decided, I think wisely, on the selfless course of 'going it alone' as a result of an *ex parte* motion and without notice to the other side. In fact I saw no possible point in an argument with She; her natural desire to win it might force her to come with me, a course which I was convinced was not in the best interests of either of us.

So, with a growing sense of excitement and liberation, I laid my plans. I took time off from our hours at the beach to make a solitary visit to the headquarters of Gaelic Airlines, and secured a seat home in the steerage. As the great day approached I ordered a yellow taxi to call at the house at dawn, with a strict injunction against any sort of toot. When I left She's bedroom she moved uneasily in her sleep and muttered, 'Rumpole'. I was standing with my shoes in one hand and a packed suitcase in the other. I whispered, 'So long, Hilda' with all the cheerfulness of a schoolboy setting out to bicycle to the seaside on the first day of the summer holidays.

Hours later I was hanging in mid air somewhere over the

Atlantic and a stewardess was handing me a miniature bottle of rum with the aloof distaste of a girl who felt her rightful place was with the champagne passengers behind the First Class curtain. I knew how dear old Tolstoy felt when he decided, late in life, to give the joys of matrimony the slip and set out for the railway station. I raised my plastic glass to the memory of the old Russian darling: it's never too late, after all, to strike a blow for freedom.

The machine owned by Gaelic Airlines was a contraption which I suspected was kept together with chewing gum and harp strings. As this unconvincing craft shuddered across the world, the strapping wenches in green kilts slammed trays of inedible food in front of those passengers fortunate enough to have dropped into an uneasy doze, babies screamed and piped music relayed the 'Londonderry Air'. It was a journey no one would be anxious to repeat, having all the glamour of a trip down Charing Cross tube station in the rush hour with the added element of fear.

Why was it that I was so anxious to repeat the miserable experience of being trundled through the stratosphere by courtesy of Gaelic Airlines? Looking back on it I think I must have deceived myself. When I got Miss Trant's letter, it seemed to me that the dull sunshine world of my retirement was suddenly refilled with interest. I convinced myself that I was still needed, that in fact Chambers couldn't do without me. What right had I, I wondered that morning, to deny my undoubted talents and lifetime's experience of blood stains to the British legal system? What was I doing, I asked myself, boring myself to death among a lot of geriatrics and citrus fruits, when the London underground system was still capable of yielding such a fine vintage murder? After only a short while with these thoughts, I came to the clear conclusion that there was only one way for Rumpole to go; sitting on the beach queuing up for death was out; I would meet my end in the full flood of a final speech, and with my wig on.

A confused number of hours, or perhaps days, later Ken Cracknell, the radical lawyer, and his chief fan and most vocal supporter, Miss Phillida Trant, were wending their weary way

back to Chambers from Pommeroy's Wine Bar, where they had
been refreshing themselves after a hard day in their respective
courts. Ever hopeful of prolonging such moments of pleasure
and delight, Cracknell asked his companion if she'd join him for
a hamburger.

'Not tonight.' Miss Trant was genuinely grateful.

'Why not?'

'Claude's getting a baby-sitter. We're going to the Festival
Hall. I promise . . .'

'What?'

'I'll turn you over in my mind, during the Verdi *Requiem*,'
Miss Trant smiled at him.

'Oh, thanks very much.' Cracknell appeared to find the prospect less than satisfying.

'We'll meet tomorrow anyway,' Miss Trant comforted him.
'We're co-defending in that long firm fraud down the Bailey.'

Cracknell sighed and accepted the crumb of comfort. They
had now reached the doorway of our Chambers in Equity Court.
'I suppose I'd better go up and get the brief.'

'I suppose you had.' Looking carefully about her and seeing
no one, in the doorway of our Chambers (so she told me later
over a confessional bottle of claret in Pommeroy's) Mrs Erskine-
Brown, née Trant, kissed Ken Cracknell. It was a moderately
lengthy kiss. Miss Trant at first closed her eyes, the better to
savour the experience, but when she opened them she found
herself looking up at the room occupied by the devoted Ken;
and there she saw an unexpected sight.

'Ken,' she whispered, 'isn't that the window of your room?'

'Yes. Yes, of course it is.' Ken turned and looked up at what
he now regarded as 'his' room. The light was on in the early
evening and on the drawn blind could be seen the silhouette of a
figure who has become, I flatter myself, pretty familiar around
the Temple and the Courts of Law. It was the shape of a man
not tall but comfortably built (Claude Erskine-Brown might say
fat) wearing a bow tie and smoking a small cigar.

'Oh dear,' said Miss Phillida Trant, staring at the clearly
inhabited window, 'what *have* I done? I only wrote him a letter!'

Chapter Seven

I had let myself into Chambers that evening with the key I had never abandoned, and had gone straight up, the clerk's room being empty, to the room which I still considered to be mine. There I at once noted several changes: in place of my old 'Spy' caricatures of forgotten judges, there were posters for the North London Law Centre, for a rock concert in aid of Amnesty International, and for *The Legal Ass*, a new satirical magazine produced by the Hornsey Group of young and radical articled clerks. The space suit and the great globular plastic helmet hung on the back of the door; there were copies both of *Time Out* and of some periodical apparently written in the Welsh language with photographs of old men in dust-sheets singing in the open air. On the mantelpiece there were briefs marked Mr K. Cracknell, and others bearing the inscription Mr Owen Glendour-Owen. Among these pending cases were the papers in R. *v.* Simpson, Cracknell's first murder.

I went over to my old desk. It was covered with an assortment of papers, some unwashed coffee cups with cigarette ends and, in one case, half a ginger biscuit, soaking in the saucers. The eye was immediately assaulted by some luridly covered copies of a magazine entitled *Schoolgirl Capers* in which the schoolgirls in question, none of whom could have been a day under thirty-five, were wearing pigtails and abbreviated gymslips and getting up to no sort of good whatsoever. I lit a small cigar, undid the tape which secured the brief in the Simpson murder and was standing by the window reading contentedly (delightedly conscious of the fact that there was no She Who Must Be Obeyed at home, awaiting my return) when the door burst open and a dark-browed and fiercely scowling young man appeared to make me instantly unwelcome.

'What on earth . . .' the young man started, but I interrupted him.

'I don't think we've met, have we?'

'No, we haven't. I'm Ken Cracknell.'

Of course I should have remembered Miss Trant's letter giving me the low-down on our new 'radical' barrister. I don't know how it was that it slipped my memory, and I was tactless enough to say, 'You're new in the clerk's room, aren't you, Ken? I hope Henry hasn't been caught with his fingers in the coffee money. Oh, by the way, I'm Horace Rumpole.'

'I'm not a clerk!' For an egalitarian barrister with no side Cracknell seemed immoderately outraged. 'I'm a member of the Bar. I was a squatter.'

'Well, I hope you're not going to squat in here.' I looked round my old room, fearful of an invasion of my privacy.

'I was a squatter until they knew you were retiring for good,' Cracknell told me. 'Then they gave me a place in Chambers. Your place, Rumpole. I share this room with Owen Glendour-Owen.'

'They gave you my place?' I couldn't believe it. 'Who gave you my place?'

'The Head of Chambers. It's a squeeze in here for two. We certainly couldn't manage a third.'

'Guthrie Featherstone, Q.C., M.P., gave you my place!' I knew then how Julius Caesar felt when he saw his learned friend Brutus whip out the knife.

'With the full support of a Chambers meeting,' Cracknell added, bringing in the full cast of conspirators. 'That's my brief you're covering with your cigar ash. R. *v.* Simpson. It's a murder.'

'A case where, I gather from Miss Phillida Trant, you are a little out of your depth? I came over to see if I couldn't help out a little, on the question of blood.'

'Thank you.' Cracknell didn't sound particularly grateful. 'It's my first murder, and I intend to cope with it on my own.'

They were brave words, as even I had to recognize. I moved to young Cracknell and gave him an encouraging clap on the shoulder, at which he flinched visibly. 'That's the spirit, Ken! That's the spirit in which I took on the Penge Bungalow Murder.

Of course, in that case I'd also worked out my own line of defence. What's yours?'

When I put the question, he looked at me with continued and blank hostility. The truth of the matter, of course, was that he hadn't worked out a defence at all. I didn't mean to take immediate advantage of this weakness.

'We'll talk about it in the morning, shall we?' I said. 'Two heads are always better than one.' Then I picked up one of the magazines devoted to elderly schoolgirls. 'Oh, I'd be obliged if you'd keep your private reading matter at home. I get some rather sensitive criminals in here for conferences. Safe-blowers are great supporters of Mrs Whitehouse. I must try not to shock them.'

'That's not my private reading matter!' Cracknell appeared to be making an effort to speak and suppressing considerable rage. 'Those are exhibits in an obscene publications case I've got up in the north of England. Grimble Crown Court, as it so happens.'

I put on my hat to leave him then, but I didn't go before I had congratulated him on an excellent start at the Bar. 'Obscenity. Murder. You're leading an exciting life, aren't you, Ken? For one so young.' I moved to the door and smiled. 'I'll speak to our Head of Chambers about you in the morning. See if he can't fix up a little annexe for you somewhere.' And before young Cracknell could explode I was off to savour the pleasures of a solitary evening at Froxbury Mansions, many miles away from She Who Must Be Obeyed.

The next morning, when I presented myself in the clerk's room, my appearance produced what I can only describe as a stunned and embarrassed silence. It was not until I had gone upstairs to announce the glad news of my return to our learned Head of Chambers, Guthrie Featherstone, Q.C., M.P., that Henry recovered himself sufficiently to speak to the assembled company of Miss Trant, Ken Cracknell, Dianne and Uncle Tom.

'I can't believe it!' Henry sounded, according to Miss Trant, as though he'd just witnessed some sort of rising from the dead.

'If he's back already, I don't know why he ever left.' Dianne made her puzzled contribution.

'He left because he lost ten cases in a row before Judge Bullingham. He got terribly depressed about it,' Miss Trant explained to them. 'Oh dear. I only wrote him a letter.' She looked round at their solemn faces and added, as a cheerful afterthought, 'Probably just a visit. He won't be staying long.'

'I gave you good warning.' Uncle Tom nodded wisely. 'He'll always be bobbing back like a bloody opera singer, making his "positively last appearance".'

'Mr Featherstone wants to see him. He'll sort it out, I'm sure.' Henry shelved the problem of Rumpole and then leafed through his diary to check on the future plans of the rest of his stable of hacks and thoroughbreds. He asked Cracknell how long he gave the long firm fraud he was starting that morning, working in double harness with Miss Phillida Trant.

'At least four weeks,' Cracknell said with satisfaction, and Miss Trant nodded; she was also thinking of the fine pile of refreshers.

Henry shook his head doubtfully. 'I'm afraid it's going to clash with your obscenity up north,' he said. 'We'll have to return the brief. And then there's the murder coming up.'

'You'll be getting awfully rich for a radical barrister.' Miss Trant smiled at Cracknell in a proud and almost proprietorial way.

'I can't leave the fraud, Henry.' Ken Cracknell was clear where his duty lay. 'So I may have to give up the dirty books. Come on, Phillida. Time we got down to the Bailey.'

As the growing friendship between Phillida and Ken led them down Fleet Street together, towards the shining dome of the Edwardian *Palais de Justice* and the joint defence of a couple of over-optimistic second-hand car salesmen, I was closeted with our Head of Chambers who rose, on my arrival, with the air of a somewhat more heroic Macbeth who is forcing himself to invite Banquo's ghost to take a seat, and would he care for a cigarette.

'Horace! My dear old Horace. How good of you to look us up while you're in England. We've all missed you terribly. As everyone says, "Chambers just isn't Chambers without old Horace Rumpole."'

'*Is* that what they say?' Personally I had some doubts about it.

'And you look so well!' Featherstone went on, I thought over-eagerly. 'So remarkably well! I've never seen you looking better. Hilda enjoying it out there, is she? I'm sure she is.'

'She Who Must Be Obeyed is perfectly contented. She was never particularly interested in blood.' I sat down and lit a small cigar, apparently to Featherstone's disappointment.

'I'm not quite with you, Horace?'

'I've had quite enough of compassionate leave, Featherstone. I've decided to come back and fight it out down the Old Bailey.'

'Horace,' Featherstone gulped like a man fighting for breath. 'Is that really wise? You were getting dreadfully tired, as I remember.'

I blew out smoke and gave him a sample of Ben Jonson's 'Farewell to the World'.

> 'Nor for my peace will I go far,
> As wanderers do, that still do roam;
> But make my strengths, such as they are,
> Here in my bosom, and at home.'

I wandered to the window and looked out at the green grass, the last damp autumn roses and the familiar grey clouds. 'This is my home, Featherstone. These Chambers have been my home for over forty years. And, as you so eloquently put it, "Chambers just isn't Chambers without old Horace Rumpole."'

'Rumpole . . .' Featherstone, to my annoyance, was doing his best to interrupt my flow.

'I'm glad you said that, Featherstone! Up to now I haven't noticed the red carpet, or the cut flowers on my desk with the compliments of the management. When I put my nose into the clerk's room this morning, they failed to uncork the Moët and Chandon. The champagne was flowing like cement!'

'Well. The fact is . . .' Feather tried to sound confidential. 'You see, Rumpole, your coming back would rather rock the boat of Chambers.'

I wasn't sure I liked the drift of his argument. 'It would?' I said. 'What do you mean, it *would*? I *am* back!'

Featherstone cleared his throat, I'm glad to say in some embarrassment. 'Since your departure we've taken on two new members. We reckoned you were worth at least two other barristers, so we've put two in your room. Glendour-Owen has joined us from Cardiff, and young Ken Cracknell . . .'

'I've met Cracknell,' I assured him. 'He's got himself a nice little murder. I might just be able to help him.'

'Ken's got your room, Rumpole.' Featherstone was becoming more determined, no doubt in desperation.

'My room? Oh yes, I saw him hanging about in my room. Quite welcome, I'm sure. Provided he doesn't litter the place with licentious comics.'

Featherstone went over to the defensive. 'Well, how were we to know you were coming back? It's a *fait accompli*. We've given Ken a seat. And Glendour-Owen, who has a huge practice in motor insurance. "Knock-for-Knock" Owen they call him on the Welsh circuit. We've promised them both seats.'

'Can't you find them seats in some convenient passage?' I didn't see the difficulty.

'We've promised them a *room*.' Featherstone looked pained.

'Then rent some more accommodation. Think big, Featherstone! Expand!'

'We can't afford that, Horace.' Now he looked particularly gloomy. 'We've all got to cut back, reduce our cash flow. England's in for four hard years.'

'Is there no mitigation?' Featherstone said nothing and I gave him a long, accusing look, which I was pleased to see made him squirm visibly. Then I spoke more in sorrow than in anger. 'Are you trying to tell me, Featherstone, in your devious and political kind of way, that there is no room for Rumpole at the Inn?'

'I'm afraid, Horace, that is exactly it!' Featherstone's gloom was impenetrable.

I took a long pause and then said cheerfully, 'I know exactly what I shall do.'

'Go back to Florida?' The good Guthrie seemed to see a glimpse of light at the end of the tunnel. 'Of course you should.

I'm sure we all envy you the sunshine, and wish you many long and happy years in your retirement.'

But I interrupted him in a way that clearly dashed his fragile hopes. 'Go back to Florida? Certainly not. I'm going to give up being an orange.' I moved to the door, and then turned back to smile at Featherstone. 'I shall squat.'

Chapter Eight

It was all very well. I had made my position clear. I was a squatter, and I intended to squat; but as I contemplated empty days ahead, stuck with the *Times* crossword and always in the way, I have to confess that the first fine burst of excitement which had sent me winging over the Atlantic on the Gaelic contraption began to dry to a mere dribble. How foolish should I begin to feel after three weeks of squatting with no work; and should I finally be forced back to the Sunshine State, and She Who Must Be Obeyed, with my tail between my legs? There was nothing I could do about it, of course, except to push open the door of the clerk's room and make it clear that Rumpole was himself again, and available for contested breathalysers. I comforted myself once more with Ben Jonson.

> 'But what we are born for we must bear:
> Our frail condition it is such
> That what to all may happen here,
> If't chance to me, I must not grutch.
>
> Else I my state should much mistake
> To harbour a divided thought
> From all my kind: that for my sake
> There should a miracle be wrought.'

And then a miracle, of a sort, happened. As I pushed open the door of the clerk's room, Henry was on the telephone, and as I loitered, lighting a small cigar, I distinctly heard him say, 'Is that Grimble 43021? Austin, Swink and Pardoner? Oh, could I speak to Mr Handyside please?'

Henry was on the phone to Albert Handyside. Albert had been my old clerk, but had left us after what I felt to be a quite unnecessary inquiry into his management of the petty cash by that infernal busybody Claude Erskine-Brown. Albert had then crossed the Great Divide and gone to work as a solicitor's clerk in a grey and wind-blasted town called Grimble, in the north of England. It was from his firm there that Albert had sent me that unusual little murder in which I had defended the leading lady of the Grimble Rep. with a result which was certainly in her interest, if not in the interest of justice; and I knew that, all else being equal, Albert Handyside might have a leading part to play in the resurrection of Rumpole's practice.

'Oh, Albert.' Henry had got through to his great predecessor whom he was addressing in a somewhat patronizing manner. 'This is Henry. Yes, old boy, Henry. Mr Cracknell's clerk. It's about our obscenity up north, in your neck of the woods. I'm afraid Mr Cracknell's tied up at the Old Bailey for the next two weeks. Miss Trant's in the case with him. Mr Glendour-Owen? He's doing a long rape in Swansea. I'm terribly sorry I can't oblige you. There just isn't anyone in Chambers.'

No one in Chambers! I can only suppose that Henry wasn't aware of the familiar figure standing behind him, smoking a small cigar and ready to fulfil any mission however daring or distant, even in the Grimble Crown Court.

'Henry,' I said loudly, and when he didn't move increased the decibels with, 'A moment of your valuable time, Henry.'

'Yes, Mr Rumpole. What is it?' Henry said testily as he covered the mouthpiece with his hand. 'I'm just on the telephone.'

'On the telephone to old Albert Handyside? Who used to be my head clerk when you didn't know Bloomsbury County Court from London Sessions,' I reminded him. 'Put him through to me, will you, Henry. I'd be glad of a word or two with old Albert. I'll be upstairs,' and I made for the door so that I could speak in private to my old clerk.

'You'll be in Mr Cracknell's room?' Henry asked, and I put him right, quite firmly.

'No, Henry. I'll be in *my* room.'

'Mr Rumpole! Good to hear your voice, sir. I thought you'd retired.'

'Good to hear *your* voice, Albert. Retired? No. Whatever gave you that idea? I just popped over to the States, you know. My wife's gone out there to be with young Nick and his family. But I'm back now, foot-loose, fancy-free and ready for any crime you care to mention.'

'Well, Mr Rumpole. I don't know . . .'

'And I'm delighted,' I cut him off before he could become even more doubtful, 'really delighted we're doing this little obscenity case together in the north of England. Have a bit of fun. Quite like old times, eh, Albert?'

'*You're* doing it, Mr Rumpole?' Albert sounded puzzled, and not quite as overjoyed as I'd anticipated.

'Oh yes. Didn't Henry tell you? I expect it slipped his mind. You see, there's no one else to do it. Ken Cracknell's so terribly busy these days.'

'Perhaps I'd better have a word with your clerk again, sir. I'd be glad to have you up here again.'

'Yes, of course. I'll put you back to Henry. I'm snowed under with work, of course, quite snowed under.' I looked round at the briefs marked Glendour-Owen and K. Cracknell, not one bearing the welcome name of Rumpole. 'But I'll manage to squeeze your little obscenity in. Look forward to it. Give my love to Grimble.'

I then jiggled the instrument and when I heard Henry's distracted voice I told him that Albert Handyside wanted a word with him, and that it was all quite like old times. Then I replaced the receiver and relaxed with a sense of something accomplished, something done.

As I sat back in my old chair (creaking, swivelling and leaking stuffing), I glanced across at that magnet which had drawn me across the Atlantic, the brief in R. *v.* Simpson, the Notting Hill Gate underground stabbing, labelled, by some oversight of fate, Mr K. Cracknell. I heaved myself to my feet, went over to it and slid off the tape.

The first thing I saw was a coloured photostat of the sheet of paper with the letters said to have been scrawled in the victim's blood. The blood itself would no doubt provide infinite opportunities for speculation and debate, and it was the problem of the blood on which I had first been consulted by Miss Phillida Trant. What interested me now was the message. It was the first time I had read it; it was short but somewhat obscure, scrawled but possible to read, and it ran: SUNLIGHT TO CHILDREN OF SUN, BLOOD TO CHILDREN OF DARK.

Well now I realized why fate and Gaelic Airlines and Miss Trant's letter had all combined to bring me winging back to England. I was the only member of Chambers with a chance of helping the unfortunate Simpson. I had the knowledge, and I must be careful how I handled it in acquiring my next Notable British Trial.

'Isn't that Cracknell's brief?'

I turned to find the room inhabited by a small, smiling, grey-haired Celt in a black jacket and pinstripes.

You must be Glendour-Owen by the sound of you, I speculated as the intruder put his briefcase down on *my* desk and started to pollute the area with a number of briefs in trumpery running-down cases. I decided to avoid any immediate confrontation.

'Well, of course you're welcome, Glendour-Jones.'

'Owen.'

'Well, of course you're welcome, Owen. Any time. If you can find yourself a corner. Be a bit of a squash, I'm afraid, until we get things sorted out.'

'Rumpole . . .' The Welsh wizard of the car insurance racket seemed about to protest, but he was interrupted by a knock and the entrance of Henry carrying a brief. It was in the Grimble Crown Court, entitled R. *v.* Meacher, and on it I was satisfied to see that the name 'Cracknell' had been struck out and 'Rumpole' substituted.

'It seems Mr Handyside wants to instruct you in this obscenity, sir,' said Henry, with no particular enthusiasm. 'Mr Cracknell being in a difficulty.'

'Does he really?' I thought it best to affect complete surprise. 'Oh well, I'll do my best to fit it in. I don't mind doing returned briefs, just until things get going again, Henry.' At which point I reached out and grabbed the brief firmly before there was any chance of Henry changing his mind.

'Things, Mr Rumpole?' said Henry looking at me, as I thought, coolly.

'My practice, Henry. Solicitors have been asking for me, have they?' I was undoing the brief, and saw the now familiar covers of *Schoolgirl Capers*.

'No, sir. Not exactly.' Henry spoke without mercy. 'The word seems to have got around, about you losing all those cases down the Bailey.'

'A long run of Judge Bullingham, Glendour-Owen,' I explained my ill fortune to the newcomer. 'That's not going to happen again.'

'How long will you be staying this time, sir?' Henry asked, and the Welshman's little eyes were fixed on me as he chipped in with, 'Yes, Rumpole. How long will you be staying?'

I considered the matter, and gave them the best answer I could. 'Well, I don't know exactly. Nothing wrong with my ticker, thank God, and a good intake of claret keeps me astonishingly regular. I suppose I might be here for another ten, fifteen years.'

At which neither of them looked particularly delighted, and Henry went with a sniff of disapproval. 'Gentlemen in Chambers getting their own work, Mr Rumpole,' he said. 'It's not in the best traditions of the Bar.'

As the door closed I saw the Welsh invader make a beeline for *my* chair. I made a quick dash round the corner of the desk and had got my bottom firmly in it before he could hitch up his trousers. Then I made my comment on our cool clerk. '"Best traditions of the Bar!" He sounds like Judge Bullingham.'

'Rumpole.' The Welshman seemed to be taking in breath for some prolonged protest. As I was in no mood for a lengthy address, I decided that a soft answer would turn away wrath, and that it might be just possible to set this bumptious little person, who was clearly one of nature's Circus Judges, on a road to promotion, which might keep him from hurling himself at my chair every time I felt the need to sit down. Accordingly I looked at him with warmth and admiration.

'Glendour-Owen. You're not *the* Glendour-Owen, are you? Not the one who does all the car insurance?'

'Well, yes. "Knock-for-Knock" Owen is what they call me – on the South Wales Circuit.' He smiled immodestly.

'I was a guest at the Sheridan Club last night,' I lied, I hoped in a good cause. 'The Lord Chancellor was talking about you.'

'The Lord Chancellor?' He breathed the words like a sort of prayer. He was clearly ripe for the Circus.

'"That 'Knock-for-Knock' Owen who does a lot of motor insurance," the Lord Chancellor was saying, "would make a wonderful Circuit Judge. Just the type we need in Wales." He couldn't speak too highly . . .'

'A Judge? I've never even considered . . .' Now the ambitious Celt was lying.

I gave him a beam of encouragement. 'Consider it, Owen. Turn it over in your mind, as you sit in the tube on the way to Uxbridge County Court. The Lord Chancellor's got his eye on you!' I opened my new brief in the obscene publications case and spread it liberally about the surface of the desk, dismissing the embryo Judge with a wave of the small cigar. 'Now, if you don't mind, I've got a practice to look after.'

Chapter Nine

'The expense of spirit in a waste of shame
Is lust in action; and till action, lust
Is perjured, murd'rous, bloody, full of blame,
Savage, extreme, rude, cruel, not to trust;
Enjoyed no sooner but despisèd straight;
Past reason hunted; and no sooner had,
Past reason hated, as a swallowed bait,
On purpose laid to make the taker mad . . .'

I was reciting to myself *con brio* the words of Shakespeare's
most embittered sonnet as some sort of entertainment to keep
me going during the reading of *School Capers* Vol. 1, numbers 1
to 6, which it was my tiresome duty to go through before enjoying the treat of an obscenity trial at the Grimble Crown Court. I
also had to read two remarkably dull works of fiction entitled
Double Dating in the Tower of Terror and *Manacle me, Darling*,
but I kept these back as the main stodge and I was flicking
through *Schoolgirl Capers* Vol. 1, number 4, by way of an hors
d'oeuvre, all the other items of suspect material being in my
briefcase which was open on the floor beside me. Also open on
the floor beside me, as I come to remember it, was a half-full
(you can tell that I was feeling sufficiently comfortable and optimistic not to say half-empty) bottle of Pommeroy's plonk, which
I found left a more pleasant afterglow than the perfectly acceptable Californian Château Wells Fargo, or whatever it was that I
had grown used to drinking. I may say I was on my second
bottle of Pommeroy's Ordinary, and I was full out on the sofa,
cushions under the head, jacket and shoes off, and the open
waistcoat deep in the snow of cigar ash. A saucer of small cigar

ends was also on the floor beside me; in the kitchen, relics of my various meals (I went in for a regular diet of boiled eggs and toast, I don't aspire to *haute cuisine*) covered the table and comfortably filled the sink; among my many talents (blood, typewriters and the art of cross-examination) I do not include bed-making, so the bedroom had what might be charitably described as a 'lived-in' appearance.

Before my eyes the middle-aged schoolgirls capered, lifting their tunics, sticking out their tongues and gyrating in a lethargic, half-gymnastic sort of way, which I found singularly asexual. I turned the page and recited the sonnet to them.

> 'Made in pursuit, and in possession so;
> Had, having, and in quest to have, extreme;
> A bliss in proof, and proved, a very woe;
> Before, a joy proposed; behind, a dream . . .'

Had I not known it to be impossible, I might have thought I heard the sound of a key in the front door of the mansion flat. I went on reciting.

> 'All this the world well knows; yet none knows well
> To shun the heaven that leads men to this hell.'

'Rumpole!'

But this was no dream. I distinctly heard the front door open and a clarion cry with which I was all too familiar. I sprang into activity; my long training in crime stood me in excellent stead, and I started to remove clues and reorganize the scene. The saucer of cigar ends was tipped into the wastepaper basket, the bottles and glass went on the window sill where they might be concealed by the curtain until I got up at dawn, I fastened my briefcase on the sexually explicit material and . . .

'Rumpole! I know perfectly well you're there.' It was a familiar voice.

I looked round for incriminating signs and saw *Schoolgirl Capers* Vol. 1, number 4, on the sofa. It was the work of seconds by a determined man able to keep his head in an emergency to thrust it behind the sofa cushions. I then took in a deep breath, regretted I hadn't finished the second bottle of plonk for courage, and threw open the door that opened into our entrance hall or vestibule.

'What've you been doing, Rumpole? Trying to lie doggo?'

She Who Must Be Obeyed was standing there surrounded by suitcases. Hers, I knew with a sinking heart, was to be no fleeting visit.

After I had left America, it seemed there was a family gathering round the swimming bath. Nick was reading the *New York Review of Books*, Erica was listening to folk music on her cassette machine and knotting string to make hanging plant-pot holders, and Hilda was standing glowering into the water, drawing her cardigan about her as if cold.

'I shall never understand Rumpole, doing a bolt like that!' said She.

'We couldn't keep him here for ever.' Nick did his best to sound reasonable.

'Sneaking out by taxi in the middle of the night. I can't understand how he got back to England.' Hilda's voice, it seems, was full of anger and contempt.

'I think on a cheap standby with Gaelic Airlines.' Nick, of course, knew all about it.

'Back in the flat! We'll never get it sold with Rumpole in it!'

'He wanted you to stay here, you know.' My son Nick was appointed as my advocate.

'Stay here without Rumpole? I've never heard anything like it!' said Hilda, showing a hitherto unknown taste for the presence of Rumpole.

'He thought you'd be happier here.' Erica, give her her due, was doing her best to support Nick's side of the argument.

At this Hilda clicked her tongue, drew her faithful cardigan still more tightly about her and seemed troubled by a new and awful thought. 'You don't think,' she said to Nick, 'you don't think that possibly . . . at his age!'

'What don't I think, Mum?'

After some sort of inner struggle my wife made herself say it. 'Another woman!'

'That's absolutely ridiculous!' Nick told me he laughed in a way which I didn't find altogether flattering.

'Is it?' She was extremely doubtful. 'Men get afflicted by a dreadful Indian summer or something. I'm always reading about it.'

'Not Dad. It's just his endless love affair with the Old Bailey.'

But my wife wouldn't have this. 'He's not in love with the Old Bailey. Judge Bullingham put him off the Old Bailey. It must be . . . *something* else. And I know exactly what I shall do about it.'

'What're you going to do about it, Mum?' Erica was curious.

'You'll see. I shall . . .' For a moment Hilda seemed hesitant, then she said, 'I shall do my duty!' At which she buttoned up her cardigan and went into the house. Forty-eight hours later she was at Heathrow Airport, and so, like a wolf on the fold, she came down by taxi on Froxbury Mansions and shattered the peace of Rumpole.

'Well, Hilda. This is a surprise!' I did my best to smile, but she wasn't smiling.

Instead she asked, 'Why weren't you at the airport?'

'Well, I can't spend my evenings hanging about Heathrow in the vague hope that you'll descend from the skies.' It seemed a reasonable explanation, but it was clearly unacceptable to Hilda.

'I sent you a telegram.'

'You didn't.'

'Of course I did.'

By this time we were both in our living-room and I was eyeing the waste-paper basket with a certain amount of guilt. 'If it had a typed envelope . . .'

'Most telegrams do.'

I picked up the waste-paper basket and found, among ash to equal the destruction of Pompeii, a large number of old cigar butts, a handful of unopened bills and communications from the Inland Revenue (opening such things, I have found, merely causes headaches and other nervous disorders) and an unopened cablegram.

'I must have mistaken it for another *billet doux* from the tax-gatherers,' I said by way of explanation.

At which She made her usual clicking sound and looked desperately round Casa Rumpole. 'It looks like a rubbish tip in here, Rumpole. I suppose the washing-up hasn't been done for a week. And I saw that the "For Sale" sign has been taken down.'

'Well, I could hardly have some . . . some bright young man in the media move in with his extended family. Not while I'm living here, Hilda.' I thought the explanation quite adequate, but her next question took me by surprise.

'Why are you living here, Rumpole?'

'It's . . . it's my home.' It was the best I could do, but meant honestly. However, She Who Must Be Obeyed picked holes in my reply.

'*Our* home was in America, Rumpole,' she said. 'We were perfectly happy. You'd retired and . . .'

'*You* were perfectly happy,' I corrected her.

'Sneaking away like that! Doing a bolt! Leaving that ridiculous note telling me to stay behind and be happy!' She stared at me, the only word is 'implacably'.

'What's at the bottom of this, Rumpole?'

'What's at . . . where?'

'What's at the bottom of your extraordinary behaviour? I shall find out. Don't think I shan't find out. You can't hide anything from me, Rumpole!'

For once I was at a loss for an answer. I shrugged vaguely, having not the faintest idea what she was on about. Then she decided to lift the pressure and rise for a short adjournment.

'In the meantime,' Hilda said, 'you can go and put the kettle on. I think I'll have a cup of instant.'

'She Who Must Be Obeyed,' I murmured as I went obediently to the kitchen door.

'And don't start washing up in there, Rumpole,' Hilda called after me. 'Leave it to me. You'll only break something!'

'I hear, O Master of the Blue Horizons,' I told myself as I went into the kitchen. I looked round the comforting mess and said goodbye to my last meal of boiled eggs and claret. Freedom – I suppose I should have known that it was too good to last.

Chapter Ten

The next day I was standing in front of the desk in what I had been forced to regard as the communal room in Chambers, sorting through the exhibits in my new obscenity case before having a conference with the client Meacher and old Albert Handyside from instructing solicitors in Grimble. As I shuffled through the exhibits I noticed the absence of one item, viz. *Schoolgirl Capers* Vol. 1, number 4. I also became aware of a tall and anxious figure who had percolated into the room. It was our learned Head of Chambers, Guthrie Featherstone, Q.C., M.P., and as I looked up at him I remembered that he might, for once in his distinguished career, come in useful to Rumpole.

'Featherstone,' I said in my most ingratiating manner, 'you play golf with old Keith from the Lord Chancellor's office. Put in a word for that Welsh chap who hangs about in this room.'

'Glendour-Owen?' Featherstone looked puzzled.

'That's the fellow,' I told him. 'He's longing to be a Circuit Judge. Eaten up with ambition for the post. Can't you do something for the poor devil? I mean, there must be vast, lawless stretches of Wales where he could make himself useful.' I was still searching among my papers. *Schoolgirl Capers* Vol. 1, numbers 3 and 5 all present and correct. Number 4 still gone missing. 'Look, Featherstone old darling. I'm just about to have a conference.'

Featherstone looked somewhat taken aback at the news and said, 'I hope this is a one-off, Rumpole.'

'What on earth's happened to *Schoolgirl Capers* number 4?' I demanded of no one in particular. I saw that Featherstone had moved somewhat closer to my deskful of adult reading, sniffing slightly as if he were a dog who had a whiff of a juicy joint cooking. But when he spoke, it was still in a voice full of sadness and disapproval.

'I mean, Henry told me you were taking on this case to help out Ken. I just hope you're not going to make a habit of it. You see, we just haven't got the accommodation.'

'Make a habit of it?' I looked at him, puzzled. 'I've been making a habit of it for the last forty years.'

The phone on the desk rang. It was Henry to say that old Albert Handyside and the client Meacher were awaiting my pleasure. I told him to shoot them up with all convenient speed. As he moved to the door Featherstone said, 'I'll talk to you later. Oh, and Rumpole . . .'

'I seem to have lost . . . half the evidence.' I was still searching, hopelessly, for the missing *Caper*.

Featherstone nerved himself to say, rather too casually, 'I happen to be sitting on the Parliamentary Committee on Pornography. I wonder if you'd let me have a glance at those magazines later? Purely as a public duty, of course.'

'Oh, purely as a public duty? How brave of you, Featherstone!'

The learned Head of Chambers took my tribute with a puzzled frown and vanished, to be quickly replaced by Mr Meacher, Pornographer-in-Chief to the town of Grimble, a large, red-faced man with a bright blue suit, suede shoes, a gold bracelet watch, a North-country accent and an overwhelming smell of after-shave, and Albert Handyside. And so the conference began. Rumpole was in business again.

At which moment the following disastrous event occurred on the home front. She Who Must Be Obeyed paused in the much-needed hoovering of our living-room to plump the sofa cushions. Under one of these cushions she discovered a strange, and to her eye, deeply disturbing object; that is to say, a much-thumbed copy of *Schoolgirl Capers* Vol. 1, number 4. She picked it up as though it were some unmentionable vermin that had crept into the warmth of our sofa and died and, holding it at arm's length, she leafed through the contents. She had got to page 45 when she realized that a desperate remedy was needed. She wrapped the awful exhibit in a sheet of plain brown paper, put on her hat and coat and went straight round to the surgery of our local G.P., a somewhat dour and anxious Scot named Doctor Angus MacClintock.

During the statutory thirty-three and a half minutes for which Hilda was kept sitting in the waiting-room she looked neither to right nor to left; and she read neither last year's *Illustrated London News* nor the June 1976 *Punch*. She held the horrible parcel tightly on her lap, as though it might wriggle in a sensual fashion and slither away. When her turn was called she went straight into the Doctor's consulting room without removing her hat.

'Mrs Rumpole.' Dr MacClintock rose anxiously to greet her. He was a grey man in a grey room and his voice was calculated to produce an instant awareness of death in the healthiest patient. 'I thought you were sunning yourself out in Florida. Nothing serious, I hope?'

'Yes, it is. Very serious.'

'What are the symptoms?'

To which she answered simply, 'The symptoms are Rumpole.'

'Oh dear.'

'I had to come, Doctor.' Hilda spoke in a voice of doom. 'Something terribly strange has happened to my husband.'

'Terribly strange? Oh dear me. Not his back again?'

'*Worse* than his back. I found this. He'd been reading *this*!'

At which Hilda stripped off the discreet brown-paper covering and revealed *Schoolgirl Capers* Vol. 1, number 4, in its full embarrassment to the Doctor's astonished gaze.

'I'm very much afraid, Dr MacClintock,' Hilda told him, 'that Rumpole has *got sex*.'

Meanwhile, up at the mill, I was slogging away and trying to earn an honest bob or two in conference with the bookseller, who was describing the difficulties which face an honest vendor of adult reading material in the town of Grimble. There was, it seemed, a local Savonarola or Calvin who was a particular thorn in Mr Meacher's flesh.

'This Alderman Launcelot Pertwee,' he told me, 'Chairman of the Watch Committee, member of the Festival of Light,

President of the Clean-Up-Grimble Society, walks into my Sowerby Street shop when I'm out at golf.'

'Mr Meacher here owns the Adult Reading Mart with twenty branches in the north of England.' My former clerk Albert Handyside provided the information. Twenty dubious book-shops sounded to me a veritable Eldorado, a promise of briefs beyond price.

'And my damn fool of an assistant, Dobbs,' Meacher went on, 'only sells Pertwee two hundred quid's worth of adult reading, films and visual aids. Of course, Peeping Pertwee's round to the Chief Constable with them in five minutes.'

It was then that I gave Meacher the value of my advice on his particular class of criminal trial. 'Mr Meacher,' I said. 'I have been thinking hard about the nature of your defence. I've read all the numbers of *Schoolgirl Capers* . . . I seem to have lost Vol. 1, number 4 . . . It doesn't matter.'

'Mr Rumpole'll have your defence well worked out, Mr Meacher.' Dear old Albert Handyside was always a great sup-port to me.

'I'd like to go for Prying Pertwee.' Meacher was clearly longing for revenge. 'The man's a hypocrite. There's been some very nasty rumours about the Alderman.'

I lit a small cigar and returned my client to the realm of pure law. 'My first thought was that the prosecution's barking up the wrong tree. They should have done you under the Trade Descriptions Act.'

'What do you mean exactly, Mr Rumpole?' I could see poor old Albert looking puzzled. I did my best to explain.

'Adult reading material, Mr Meacher. Isn't it put forward as something likely to stimulate the senses, to send a young man's fancy wild with unsatisfied desire, to promote venery and to conjure up, for the lonely and unfulfilled citizens of Grimble, all the abandoned delights of the bedchamber?'

'Well, to be quite honest with you, Mr Rumpole,' Meacher admitted, 'yes.'

'Let's be *really* honest,' I replied. 'No! I have looked, swiftly I must confess, through this material. There is only one word for it. "Off-putting".'

'I'm not quite with you.' Meacher's expression was pained.

'I have been thinking to myself . . .' I blew out smoke, enjoying the philosophical argument. 'What are the least aphrodisiac conceptions, the things most deadening to lust? Income Tax? V.A.T.? String vests? Chest protectors? Cardigans? Woollen socks worn with sandals? Fish fingers? Party Political Broadcasts? As deterrents to the tender passion, I would say they all come a bad second to *Schoolgirl Capers* Vols. 1 to 6 and *Double Dating in the Tower of Terror*, and you can throw in *Manacle me, Darling* as an additional extra!'

'Mr Rumpole.' Meacher appeared to be about to protest; but I wasn't accepting questions yet.

'*Schoolgirl Capers!* There can't be a schoolgirl in there under forty!' I paused and relit the wilting cigar. 'However, attractive as it would be to point out that this material is merely a boring waste of money, I shan't in fact take that line.'

'I'm glad to hear it.' Mr Meacher looked distinctly relieved. 'This is a serious case, Mr Rumpole.'

'Yes, of course,' I agreed with him, 'far more serious than the tripe removed by Alderman Pertwee.'

'Stock valued at at least two hundred pounds,' Meacher protested, and I stood to give him what I still believe was one of my finest speeches in the law.

'Stock valued beyond gold, Mr Meacher! Our priceless liberties. Free speech, Mr Meacher! That's how we're going to win this one. The birthright of the Briton, to read and write just as the fancy takes him.' The time had come to call on Wordsworth and I gave Mr Meacher, for the price of his con, a few lines from the old darling.

> 'It is not to be thought of that the flood
> Of British Freedom, which, to the open sea
> Of the world's praise, from dark antiquity
> Hath flowed, with pomp of waters, unwithstood,
> Should perish!'

As I recited I paced, and as I passed the door it opened and there was Ken Cracknell, standing there eagerly, his arms full of papers and other tools of his trade. 'Some other time, Cracknell!' I hissed at him. 'Can't you see I've got a conference?'

'This is my room!' Cracknell sounded outraged.

'Some other time.' And I promised him, by way of compensation, 'I'll want to see you about that little murder of yours. I've had some ideas, as it so happens. Run along now.' At which I shut the door on Cracknell and walked back to my desk, still addressing the North-country bookseller in ringing tones. 'Words, we shall tell the jury, Mr Meacher, must be free, for freedom is indivisible! Man has the right to read the boldest speculations, the most dazzling philosophy, to question God, to explore the universe, to follow poetry into the most exquisite sensuality or the finest religious ecstasy. So he must be granted the freedom to blunt his brains on *Schoolgirl Capers*. I utterly deplore the rubbish you are selling, but I'll defend to the death anyone's right to read it!' I concluded, giving him Voltaire, the Rumpole version.

There was a long pause. My oratory was having an effect; something was stirring in what remained of Mr Meacher's mind after a prolonged course of adult reading. 'Free speech, eh?' he said, blinking.

'In a nutshell,' I told him.

'I like it, Mr Rumpole.' A slow smile spread over Mr Meacher's florid features. 'I really like it. As a defence, I would say, it has a certain amount of class.'

A day or so later I was chewing a piece of breakfast toast and reading the daily paper when up spoke She Who Must Be Obeyed, whom I had noticed eyeing me curiously of late.

'What are you reading *now*, Rumpole?'

'The Obituaries in *The Times*,' I told her.

'Well, that makes a change!' Hilda gave me one of her small, disapproving clicks as she poured the tea.

'I always read the Obituaries in *The Times*,' I explained to her. 'They make me bloody glad to be alive.' I gave her a quotation from a particularly pleasing obituary. ' "Sir Frederick Foxgrove was known and respected as a wise judge and just

sentencer. His behaviour in Court was always a model of dignity."
In other words, old Foxy was Judge Jeffries without the laughs.'

'Is that really *lively* enough reading for you, Rumpole?' I saw
She looking at me with a kind of sadness, and I answered,
puzzled.

'The Obituaries can never be lively reading, exactly. Are you
feeling quite all right, Hilda?'

'I'm not sure, Rumpole,' she sighed. 'Are you?'

'What?'

'Feeling quite all right.' She took a sad swig of tea and then
went on to speak as though there were death in the family.
'Because if you're not, for any reason, I asked Dr MacClintock
to drop in for a glass of sherry this evening. He'll be passing us
on his rounds.'

'Damned expensive sherry, won't it be?' I could see no possible
point in our pouring drink down the medical profession.

'Oh no, Rumpole. He's dropping in purely as a friend. I
thought you could discuss with him any little worries you may
have . . . about anything . . . at all.'

I didn't see how Dr MacClintock could possibly help me to
get hold of the brief in R. *v.* Simpson, or indeed in any important
matter. I rolled up *The Times* and prepared to go off to work.
'I'm catching an early train to Grimble tomorrow,' I warned
Hilda. 'I may have to stay up there for a night or two.'

'Grimble? What on earth are you going to Grimble for?' My
wife looked totally fogged. I suppose the answer I gave her was
somewhat oblique.

'Sex! Some would say sex. Some would say the freedom of
speech.'

And as I left to go about my business, I heard Hilda click her
tongue again, sigh and say, 'Oh dear! I really think you'd better
speak to Dr MacClintock about it.'

When I came, at last, to the end of a not very busy day (briefs
were hardly showering in on Rumpole's return), I decided to
give my favourite watering-hole, Pommeroy's Wine Bar, a miss,
mainly for hard financial reasons, and I went straight back to
Casa Rumpole. There I was sitting with a bottle of take-away
claret (sadly I seemed to be down to the last couple of dozen)

with my shoes and jacket off, reading with envy and disgust the *Evening Standard*'s account of a particularly asinine cross-examination, part of a nice libel action in which Guthrie Featherstone was undeservedly appearing, when She pushed open the door and ushered in the gloomy medico who had us on his panel.

'Here's Dr MacClintock,' she said. 'Come for his sherry.'

Come for *my* sherry might have put it more accurately; but I thought I might as well cheer the old darling up with a glass of the nauseous and liverish brew Hilda's friend Dodo had sent us for Christmas, and which I never drink anyway.

'Sit down, Doctor,' I said. 'We run a little charitable bar here, for depressed quacks.' And added, when I saw the look on Hilda's face, 'Take no notice of me. I was only joking.'

'Well, I'd better leave you two men to get on with it,' said Hilda, about to depart. 'Rumpole, you'd do very well to listen to every word that Dr MacClintock has to say.'

So, as rare things will, she vanished. I looked at the Doctor, who seemed to be going through some kind of terminal embarrassment. I poured him a sherry, for which he seemed unreasonably grateful.

'Excellent sherry, Rumpole. Amontillado?'

'Pommeroy's pale plonk.' It seemed a shame to disillusion him. 'Look, Dr MacClintock. What *are* you doing, dropping in like this? Other than mopping up the Spanish-style gut-rot?'

'Rumpole, your wife Hilda came to see me . . .'

'Feeling seedy, was she? I told her she should never have come back to England. Climate in Florida suited her *far* better.'

The Doctor gulped more sherry, which gave him the strength to murmur, 'She was concerned about *you*, Rumpole.'

'You really like that stuff?' I looked at the iron-stomached Doctor. Then I further cheered him by giving us each a refill of our respective stimulants.

'As I explained to Hilda,' the Doctor spoke in a kind of sepulchral whisper. 'It's nothing for you to be ashamed of.'

'I can't say that I've ever felt *ashamed* of drinking a glass of claret.' The man didn't seem to be making a great deal of sense to me.

'Everyone has their little kinks,' the Doctor suddenly informed me. 'Their little peculiarities. Sometimes a doctor wonders if there's any such thing as a *normal* man.'

'Do you, Doctor?' I sat and lit a small cigar. The medic was failing to hold my attention.

'I have been married to Marcia, as you know, for going on twenty years.' Was this the time for a confession? I didn't want to probe the good Doctor's private grief.

I confined myself to asking politely, 'How is your good lady?'

'And I can't say that I've never been tempted' – the Doctor was now gaining his flow – 'sorely tempted, even to throw it up, well, I won't say for a gymslip and a pair of pigtails . . .'

I looked sadly at the wretched MacClintock. 'You, Doctor?' I didn't, of course, withhold my pity. 'Even *you*? Sometimes I think the whole world's going mad!'

'Hilda told me what you're doing. Try and see it in proportion, Rumpole. It's nothing to be guilty about.' He was now smiling at me in a sickly and reassuring way. I began to wonder if the man had been overworking.

'I don't feel particularly *guilty* about going to the north of England.' I did my best to reassure him.

'Of course not! That's probably a good idea. Bit of a winter break. Marcia and I went to Malta last year.' He then frowned as though an appalling thought had occurred to him. 'I say, Rumpole. You're not going to the north *with* anyone, are you?'

'No, of course not. What do you mean?'

'I shall be able to reassure Hilda. I told her I didn't think there was anyone who'd be interested in going to the north of England with *you*, Rumpole.'

'Is that what you came here to say?' My mind was starting to boggle.

'Yes. Yes, it is. I hope it's made you feel better.'

'As a matter of fact,' I had to be honest with him, 'it's made me feel considerably worse.'

'You're not to *worry*, Rumpole. We all have our own little guilty secret . . .'

Then the Doctor, with the air of a man who has completed a painful duty, leant back and began to discus the plans he had for insulating his loft. I imagine a lifetime of peering down various human orifices does, in the end, soften the brain; but I couldn't really understand why our neighbourhood G.P. had to work out his problems on our sherry.

Chapter Eleven

The next day I travelled up north to put up at the Majestic Hotel, Grimble (how well I remember that icy, marmoreal dining-room, the deaf waiters and the mattresses apparently stuffed with firewood), and to my struggle against censorship in the Grimble Crown Court. And Kenneth Cracknell, Esq., weary after a hard day at the Old Bailey, roared down to Brixton Prison on the Honda and there met his old friend and instructing solicitor Mike Mowbray and his client Percival Simpson, who looked at them, as Mowbray told me later, as if their visit had been a perfectly useless kindness and a complete waste of time.

'I can't fight against them.' Simpson sat at the table in the interview room and looked at them hopelessly. 'Not the miracle workers.'

'Now, Mr Simpson.' Young Mike Mowbray was trying his best. 'You've certainly got a difficult case. But Mr Cracknell's a barrister who's had a lot of success lately.'

'They can change the blood on a piece of paper. How can I fight against that?' Simpson smiled at them gently and then looked out of the window as if the case no longer held his full attention.

'Mr Cracknell has a whole lot of successful defences to his credit,' Mike went on gently.

'I have sinned. I appreciate that. What can I do?' Simpson gave another of his watery smiles.

'Mr Simpson. Who had the knife?' Cracknell felt he had to take some sort of command of this drifting conference, and came out with a pugnacious question.

'He gave me the knife. So I could kill myself. That's the

cunning of *them*, you see,' Simpson said patiently, but apparently without any real hope of being understood.

'You had the knife, Mr Simpson. Now why did you use it? *Why*?' Ken was cross-examining his client, ever an unwise thing to do (you run the extreme risk of the old darling telling you he did the crime, which is hardly welcome information or helpful to the defence). At this point Mowbray was sure that he saw their client casually smother a yawn.

'I'm so *tired*,' Simpson admitted.

'Was it sex, Mr Simpson? Had he come down there to make sexual advances? Were you trying to fight him off?' Cracknell had, in his extreme lack of experience, hit on a somewhat trite defence.

'I must say, that was the line that appealed to me,' Mike Mowbray admitted, showing his prejudices. 'He was that sort of bloke, wasn't he? Eton and the Guards. That sort of character. Your Class A gay.'

'I don't know what sort of person he was, but he was one of *them*,' Simpson agreed.

'Well, exactly!' Mike Mowbray was delighted.

'I can't say any more really.' Simpson stood up to end the meeting. 'I'm tired of fighting . . . Excuse me now, please. I can't say any more . . .'

So it was a despondent Cracknell and Mowbray, counsel and instructing solicitor, who made their way out past the Alsatians and the trusty prisoners weeding the dusty plants in the black flowerbeds under the prison walls. As they approached freedom and the gate, Mike comforted his friend.

'You'll pull off something, Ken,' he said. 'You've always done that up till now.'

'On my own?' Ken sounded unexpectedly incredulous.

Mike was puzzled. He knew his friend was an ambitious young barrister, who wouldn't want to share the limelight which would shine on him in an important murder. 'You don't want a silk, do you?' he asked.

'Not a silk, no.' Ken Cracknell was thoughtful. 'But perhaps . . . a very experienced member of the Junior Bar to lead me. You know, Mike. If you've got to insult an aristocratic corpse, grey hair might be a help.'

'An experienced junior?' Mike thought the suggestion over. 'Like who? You got any ideas?'

'Well, yes,' Ken Cracknell said, and I was amazed when I heard of it. 'I think I have.'

'Alderman Pertwee, did you visit the Adult Book Mart, Sowerby Street, on March 12th last?'

I was at home again, crowned by my old grey horsehair wig (bought second-hand from an ex-Attorney-General of Fiji in the 1930s) with the gown slipping off my shoulders and a collar like a blunt execution. In my sights, just alighted in the witness box, was a plump bird called Alderman Pertwee. He had a large stomach decorated with a gold watch and chain, ginger hair and moustache; he was small of stature and he had a beady and inquisitive eye. Our defence didn't in the least depend on the jury disliking Alderman Pertwee, but I thought that if Rumpole were ever to let him have it with both barrels, they might well be prepared to turn against him. Prosecuting counsel, a tall, skinny, young man named Mackwood, who was clearly horrified by *Schoolgirl Capers*, was leading the Alderman through his evidence-in-chief.

'I did visit the Adult Book Mart, your Honour.' The Alderman gave a small, corpulent and horribly ingratiating bow to the Judge before he answered the question. To his eternal credit the Judge rewarded him with a glassy stare of non-recognition. Pertwee then continued with his so-called evidence. 'I did, your Honour. And I found books and magazines of the most flagrant immorality on display.'

Now was the time to haul myself to my hind legs as in the days of yore. I spoke my first words in Court since my return. 'Your Honour, I object.'

'Yes, Mr Rumpole.' His Honour Judge Matthew was an amazingly civilized character for Grimble, although Albert had warned me that he was a tough sentencer. We had shared coffee and crossword clues the last time I had been up north and when he was still at the Bar, and he gave me a small, but quite charming, smile of welcome.

'If the Alderman could restrain himself from treating us like a

Sunday night gathering at the Baptist Chapel,' I suggested, and his Honour took up the suggestion.

'Just confine yourself to the evidence,' he said courteously to the witness. 'It will be for the jury to decide on the exact nature of the articles for sale in the bookshop. Yes, Mr Mackwood.'

Mackwood asked his final question. 'Did you purchase at that shop the following articles: *Schoolgirl Capers* Volume 1, numbers 1 to 6, *Double Dating in the Tower of Terror, Manacle me, Darling* and the films the jury have already seen?'

'I did, my Lord.'

Mackwood subsided and Rumpole rose to cross-examine, looking hard at the jury and taking his customary ten seconds' pause before firing off the first question. 'Just a few questions, Alderman Launcelot Pertwee. You say this shop, the Adult Book Mart, is a source of corruption to the neighbourhood?'

'I regard it, your Honour' – another small bow, again ignored by the Judge – 'as a terrible source of corruption.'

'Standing as it does,' I put it to him, 'between a betting shop and the off-licence of the Grimble Arms, who's more corruptible, Alderman: the punters or the boozers?'

'I object! How can this witness possibly tell . . . ?' Mackwood rose to his full height to make some alleged objection. I ignored him and he gradually subsided.

'Can't you, Alderman?' I kept my eye on the target witness. 'I thought you came here as an expert on corruption. Does not the Grimble Arms offer "Topless A-Go-Go" on the bar as an attraction on Friday nights?'

'I believe it does. Regrettable . . .' Pertwee sighed in a pained sort of manner. I was delighted to see some of the jury smiling. Laughter is your strongest weapon against prosecutions of pornography. I made a reasonable suggestion to the Alderman.

'You don't think it might be preferable to have sex neatly packaged in books and magazines and not prancing about on the bar, kicking over the pints of Newcastle Brown?' There was laughter in Court, music to Rumpole's ears. 'Tell me, Alderman. There are no kindergartens, no convent schools, no academies for young girls of tender years in Sowerby Street, are there?'

'No, there are not, but . . .'

'But me no buts, Alderman! And does not the Adult Book Mart have written above the door in large letters, "Entry to those under 18 prohibited"?'

'I can think of no sign, Mr Rumpole,' said the Judge with a charming smile, 'that would be more immediately attractive to modern youth.' The jury rewarded him with a little titter. It was undoubtedly his Honour's point. I ignored him also.

'At least there were no kiddiwinks present when you went into the shop, were there, Alderman? No simpering maidens of bashful sixteen? No impressionable young students of theology? Not even the toughest teenager?'

'Not when I was there. No,' the witness admitted reluctantly.

'In fact the clientele consisted of three middle-aged men with suits, umbrellas and brief cases.' I put it to him, 'Perhaps they were all Aldermen of the fair city of Grimble?'

'They were all middle-aged men,' Pertwee admitted.

'Of perfectly respectable appearance?'

'I suppose so.'

'No one was actually slavering at the mouth, or walking with their knuckles brushing the linoleum?' I got home with a reasonable laugh then; the usher called, 'Silence!' and Mackwood looked extremely displeased and got to his hind legs.

'I really don't understand what my learned friend is getting at.' He made a self-consciously languid objection.

'Oh, don't you?' I was anxious to help him out. 'My learned friend says that this rubbish . . .'

'It's not rubbish, Mr Rumpole!' My client Meacher whispered deafeningly from the dock. 'It's adult reading matter of an erotic nature.'

I increased my volume to suppress the sound of my aggrieved client, and turned to the witness box. 'This unmitigated rubbish, Alderman Pertwee, which you encouraged by spending two hundred pounds on assorted magazines and films . . . was it your ratepayers' money?'

'I took a float, yes.' The Alderman sounded defensive. 'When I made this investigation on behalf of my Committee.'

'Do the ratepayers of Grimble know, Alderman, that you're spending their hard-earned pennies on *Schoolgirl Capers*?'

There was another small stir of laughter, which the Judge interrupted. 'Mr Rumpole. If you defer the rest of your cross-examination until tomorrow, we might break off there and the jury will no doubt wish to examine the . . . um . . . literature.'

'If they must, my Lord.' It's no help for the defence in an obscenity case to have anyone actually *read* the works in question. 'I should make it clear that I don't rely on the exact nature of this rubbish. I rely on our historic freedoms. Above all on the freedom of speech.'

'I would like the jury to read every word of these books and magazines,' said the lanky Mackwood, determined to rub their noses in it.

'Very well,' I shrugged at the jury. 'The prosecution is always far more interested in sex than we are.'

So we parted, and I spent the evening drinking claret in the Majestic (it tasted faintly of red ink and was apparently iced) with my old clerk Albert Handyside. When I got to Court the next morning, I was told that the jury were still out 'reading'. (I must say that when they finally returned to Court, some of the young men and women of the twelve seemed to have struck up friendships of a warmth over and above the call of jury service.) I also noticed that Albert and the client Meacher were in close conversation outside the Court with a tall, bony-looking red-haired woman who was wearing a luxurious mink stole and several large diamond rings, court shoes and a small hat with a veil. As he was talking, Albert seemed to be taking notes. Not wishing to interrupt him, and having no doubt that he was at work on another case, I went to a call-box and telephoned the mansion flat and She Who Must Be Obeyed.

'Rumpole, when are you coming home?' The tones were not over-friendly.

'Maybe a day or two. Not that we're *doing* very much. Every-one's sitting around, taking it easy and reading pornography.'

'Reading pornography?' Hilda sounded incredulous.

'Yes, of course. What else would you like us to do?'

'Oh, do be your age, Rumpole!' Whereupon Hilda slammed down the receiver.

Somewhat disconcerted by this I wandered back into Court.

The jury was not yet back and Alderman Pertwee was sitting
alone in a seat near the witness box, waiting to continue his
evidence. He looked an unhealthy colour (bluish, I thought,
around the edges) and was continually wiping his hands on a
large white handkerchief. He also looked at the Court door
from time to time in a nervous manner, and when he saw me his
jaw dropped and his eyes became glassy. Not wishing to distress
the wretched Alderman more than was absolutely necessary, I
left the courtroom again and saw the red-headed woman apparently finishing her conference with Albert.

'Very well, Mr Handyside,' she was saying in a Grimble
accent. 'I want you to handle the divorce. I want the whole
town to know the truth about my husband. And I want them to
know it as soon as possible. Do I make myself clear?'

'Absolutely clear, thank you *very* much,' said Albert and
added, much to my surprise, 'And a very good day to you, Mrs
Pertwee.'

'What?' I asked, coming up to Albert and the beatifically
smiling Meacher. 'What did you call her?'

'He called her Mrs Pertwee,' said Meacher in a voice of un-
mistakable triumph. 'And he called her that because that's who
she bloody is.'

'She came about a divorce. But she wants you to use her
statement to cross-examine her husband this morning. As soon
as Court sits.' Albert's eyes were now shining with a rare excitement. 'She can't wait to read all about it, it's bound to make
front page of the *Grimble Echo*.'

'We've got him.' Meacher was grinning broadly. 'Mr Rumpole, we've got Alderman Purity Pertwee by the short and
curlies!'

Albert leafed through his notebook, in which, it seemed, he
had been taking a statement from the local Savonarola's wife. 'It
does seem to be very valuable material, Mr Rumpole. Mrs Pertwee phoned me and I arranged to meet her here, early this
morning. I'm gratified to say, sir, she gave me all the dirt.'

'She was miffed he wasn't taking her to his Ladies' Night at
the Lodge. He told her she'd let him down. Launcelot Pertwee
told his old woman she always gets pissed on sherry at Masonic

do's, that her face goes red and she's not fit to appear as an Alderman's wife. Silly sod. He's played straight into our hands.' Meacher was elated.

'So she gave me the whole story.' Albert proffered his note-book.

'Read it, Mr Rumpole! It'll make your hair stand on end. Shocked me, it did,' Mr Meacher admitted. 'I'm used to a re-spectable business.'

'He's keeping this young girl at Pond End. That's been going on for years, to her certain knowledge.' Albert was obviously only giving me a taste of the dish he had prepared, a little slice off the end of the joint.

'And Mrs Pertwee had to leave his bed because she failed to agree to certain practices. Have a look, Mr Rumpole.' Mr Meacher sounded pained but enthusiastic. 'And he attended a dubious film show after the annual do of the Management Committee of Grimble United.'

'Mrs Pertwee's found her clothes missing on several occasions. He's actually donned articles of her clothing.'

'He can't be left. Not even with the young girls who man the pumps at the garage he owns. They call him "Forecourt Freddie" because he's always out there chatting them up.'

'Lucky his Honour knocked off when he did. You can use all this stuff on the Alderman when we go back.'

Albert was giving his legal opinion, when I startled them both by saying, 'No!'

'What?' Albert frowned, as though he were hard of hearing.

'No. We can't use it.' I now hoped I had made myself clear.

'What do you mean, Mr Rumpole?' Meacher was deter-minedly reasonable. 'It's all good stuff, what Albert Handyside got you there.'

'Mr Meacher. I explained.' I did so again, quite patiently. 'We're going to win this case on liberty. The freedom of everyone to please themselves. To do as they like – provided they don't do it in the streets and frighten the horses. We are against peeping and prying through bedroom keyholes to censor and condemn our fellow human beings! If we attacked the Alderman for the shortcomings of his private life, we should be selling the pass. Don't you understand that? *We* should be the censors and the hypocrites. We should be selling our liberty!'

Meacher looked stunned, but Albert had the solicitor's immediate reaction: take counsel's advice and then you always have someone to blame if things go wrong. 'Of course, Mr Rumpole,' he said doubtfully. 'You're in charge.'

'Yes, I *am* in charge, aren't I? Don't be a back-seat driver, my dear old Albert, or you, Mr Meacher. Just sit back, relax and try to enjoy the view.'

So when we got back to Court, I told the Judge that I didn't wish to ask Mr Pertwee any further questions. The Alderman looked as though a reprieve had come through, and the sentence of death for which he had been preparing had been altered to a term of office as Mayor of Grimble. He bowed very low to the Judge, he actually contrived to bow to Rumpole, and went triumphantly out of Court.

As I had no intention whatever of putting my client Meacher in the witness box, the evidence was now over. After my learned friend Mr Mackwood had paraded his prejudices in a few ill-chosen words, I rose to make, although I say it myself, one of my very best speeches. I had, of course, had little else to think about and I had rounded the phrases during a long night listening to the central heating (far more noise than heat) in the Majestic Hotel. I won't weary you with the whole oration (the curious may find most of it only slightly misquoted in the *Grimble Echo* of the relevant date), but I will give you the end, the climax, the peroration. I included in it, of course, what is almost my favourite among Wordsworth's poems, dedicated to National Independence and Liberty.

> 'It is not to be thought of that the flood
> Of British Freedom, which, to the open sea
> Of the world's praise, from dark antiquity
> Hath flowed with pomp of waters unwithstood ...
> Should perish!'

I told the Grimble Jury.

I leaned forward then, dropped my voice and addressed them

confidentially. 'Members of the jury. Freedom is not divisible. You cannot pick and choose with freedom, and if we allow liberty for the opinions we hold dear and cherish, we must allow the same privilege to the opinions we detest or even to works of such unadulterated rubbish as *Schoolgirl Capers* Volume 1, numbers 1 to 6. Let those who wish to read it do so; they will soon grow weary of the charms of such elderly schoolgirls. You and I, members of the jury, stand, do we not, for tolerance? We are not intolerant of Alderman Pertwee. He is free to express his opinions. We don't seek to call him a hypocrite, or have him banned.'

Young men and girls in the jury were sitting close together, some may even have been holding hands. I smiled at them. I think they may have smiled back. So I ended my speech.

'Ours is the tolerant approach, and if we are tolerant in great matters, so we must be in the little, trivial matter of these puerile magazines, for once we start in the business of censorship and the banning of books, that is the ending of freedom. Our price-less liberties are in your hands today, members of the jury. There could be no safer place for them!'

In due course the Judge summed up, with devastating fairness, and in due course the jury, having exchanged telephone numbers and arrangements for the weekend, struck their mini blow for respectability and found Mr Meacher guilty on all counts. The Judge dropped about nine pounds of charm and sent him to prison for 'polluting the fair city of Grimble'. It was a disap-pointed Rumpole, feeling every year of his age, who made the unpleasant trip to the cells which every barrister is in honour bound to take after his client has been convicted. And Meacher, I felt sure, wasn't going to prove a good loser; not for him the stiff upper lip of the playing fields of Eton. He was bloody angry, and he had no doubt where the blame was to be laid. As I entered the small cell under Grimble Court with a depressed-looking Albert Handyside, Mr Meacher muttered bitterly, 'Eight-een months!'

'Try and look on the cheerful side, Mr Meacher. You'll be in an open prison, hobnobbing with bent coppers, twisted solicitors and all the toffs.' I saw that I wasn't cheering him up.

'I wouldn't be in no sort of prison if you'd done your job properly.'

'You didn't like the speech?' I was, I must confess, a little disappointed by the client's reaction.

'I told you how to treat that bastard Pertwee. Go for the jugular!'

'It was Mr Rumpole's decision . . .' Albert was going to do his best, but his disappointment was also clear. And he was interrupted by an explosion from Meacher.

'How can pissing Pertwee be on the Council? Lay bloody preacher. Chairman of the Watch Committee. And that Judge gave me eighteen months for polluting the fair city of Grimble.'

'Now that, I grant you, was a bit steep,' I sympathized with him. 'I don't know what he thinks this grimy and draughty northern borough is. I mean, the Station Hotel may have a sort of macabre Gothic charm, but otherwise . . . Well, Grimble's hardly Venice in the springtime.'

'Anyway, I'm going to appeal!' Meacher clenched his fists and looked enormously determined.

'Now that, in my opinion, would be perfectly hopeless,' I told Meacher, and I had no doubt on the subject.

'I don't give a damn for your opinion, Mr Rumpole. You get me a young brief, Mr Handyside. Someone with a bit of guts, who'll tell the truth about Launcelot bloody Pertwee!' From his bench in the cell Meacher looked up at me, I thought malevolently. 'You're just like the old punters we get in our shops, Mr Rumpole, you are. Blokes what is past it.'

So it was in no light-hearted mood that I returned, travel stained, British Railway bashed, and jury battered, to my refuge in Froxbury Mansions. I had expected, on recent form, a cold welcome from She Who Must Be Obeyed. Imagine my surprise therefore, when I let myself in to the flat and found, in my living-room, lights dim, flowers bought and set in a cut-glass vase, and She reclining by the gas fire wearing some sort of dressing-gown. Our old wireless set was on, and from it the disembodied voice of the late Richard Tauber percolated, singing:

> 'Come, come, I love you only
> My heart is true . . .
> Come, come, my heart is lonely
> I long for you . . .'

or words to the like effect.

As I entered the unexpectedly warm gloaming of our living-room She said, 'Rumpole, is that you, dear?'

'*What* did you call me?' I couldn't believe my ears.

'I called you "dear". Can't I call you "dear", Rumpole?' She rose gracefully and actually poured me a glassful of Pommeroy's plonk; and it was a liberal measure.

'I suppose there's no reason why not.' I took a gulp and a sniff round. 'Is there a rather odd sort of smell in here?'

'Is there . . .?'

'Distinctly unusual smell. Mixture of R.C. churches and old flower vases.'

'Well, that's not very romantic.'

'No.'

'I'm wearing lavender water, Rumpole,' Hilda said, almost coyly. 'The lavender water you give me every Christmas.'

'Sorry, I didn't recognize it.' I realized I had said the wrong thing, and returned my nose to my glass.

'Since we met, you have given me thirty-nine bottles of lavender water,' Hilda said without rancour.

'Well, I never knew what else you'd like to smell of.' And then I confessed, 'The case at Grimble was an unmitigated disaster. Very unsatisfied client.' I sat on the sofa and gratefully changed the subject. 'I say, have you got a cold or something? Been in bed, have you, Hilda?'

'What *do* you mean?'

'You're wearing your dressing-gown.' I thought it was about time someone pointed it out.

'It's really more of a négligée . . .' And to my amazement Hilda came and sat down quite uncomfortably close to me. In fact she was squashing up against my knee as I scratched the old sore of my disastrous day in Court.

'I made the mistake of appealing to the old English sense of freedom. Freedom's gone out of fashion in Grimble. That singer appears to be in some pain.' Herr Tauber's voice had risen to a painful squeal. I put him out of his misery and switched him off.

'That was "These We Have Loved".' To my alarm Hilda was squashing up against me even more. 'We're not too old, are we, Rumpole,' she almost whispered, 'to enjoy anything senti-mental?'

'No.' I made a cautious admission. 'But . . .'

And then Hilda said a surprising thing. 'You don't *have* to read those magazines, Rumpole,' she said. 'After all, you are *married*.'

'What magazines?' I wasn't entirely with her.

'A dreadful thing about schoolgirls. I found it behind the sofa cushions.'

I began to get a strange glimmering, a sort of clue to Hilda's incalculable behaviour over the last weeks. 'Good heavens!' I told her. 'I had to read that, yes. It was part of the evidence in my case.'

'Your *what*?' Hilda seemed taken aback.

'The obscenity case. The one I did at Grimble. Good God, Hilda. You don't think I enjoyed reading that rubbish, do you? I've never been so bored in my whole life.'

'Bored?' She sounded curiously disappointed. 'Is *that* what you were?'

'Well, naturally. *You* didn't read it, did you?' My mind began to boggle at the thought of Hilda reading solemnly through 'Changing Room Orgies'.

However, she shook her head vigorously, got up quickly and moved away from me. 'No, of course not,' she said. 'It was your work, was it? That's all it was . . .'

'Absolutely all!' I assured her.

She moved to the door and snapped on the centre light. Then she became brisk and businesslike as she emptied an ashtray and turned down the fire. I was back with the old familiar She Who Must Be Obeyed and it was almost a relief. At least I knew where I was, and she was no longer squashing my knee.

'Well, I've got to get on,' said Hilda. 'No use hanging about in the living-room all night, chattering to you. I've got chops to get under the grill! And you can start laying the table, Rumpole. You really might lend a hand occasionally.'

When she had left the room, I saw that the tide had gone down in the bottle of Pommeroy's claret. I reached up to find a reserve bottle propping up the Criminal Appeal Reports on the top of the shelf. 'That sounds more like your old self, Hilda.'

'What did you say?' Hilda called from the kitchen.

'Just getting another bottle off the shelf, Hilda,' I said, and on that occasion I got away with it.

Chapter Twelve

After the resounding defeat I had suffered in the case of the Grimble Adult Reading Mart, I didn't see young Cracknell for some time; indeed I didn't seek out his company as I thought he was bound to crow a little over my discomfiture, and perhaps suggest that I might vacate 'the room' if all I could do there was to plan the loss of cases. However, I continued to haunt the clerk's room and the library, I called in to Pommeroy's for an evening refresher and I generally planned my days so that I had a credible reason for leaving home at Froxbury Mansions early in the mornings and not returning until nightfall.

One day as I wandered into the clerk's room in a somewhat disconsolate manner and noticed that the mantelpiece was, as usual, bare of briefs marked 'Rumpole', Henry gave me a bit of extremely welcome news.

'Mr Bernard rang of Cripplestone, Bernard & Co. You're wanted for a case at Brixton. Case of Timson.'

Timson! The word was music to my ears. The Timson family were a notable clan of south London villains who had each and every one of them provided work for me over the years. They were a close-knit family who went into crime as other families go into the law. The Timsons thought of spells in the nick as a professional risk, they believed that a woman's place was in the home and they were against the permissive society. There is no greater loyalty than that of one Timson to another, and they had all, when in varied degrees of trouble, relied heavily on the services of Rumpole. It was a tribute to the excellent system of jungle telegraph which existed in the world of crime that Rumpole's return should already have become known to the regular clientele.

'*Bonjour*, Mr Rumpole. *Heureux de vous voir*. Keeping well in yourself, are you?'

Bertie was one of the older members of the Timson family. He was facing a charge of conspiracy to rob the Balham branch of the Steadfast Savings Bank, or, in the alternative, carrying house-breaking implements by night. During a recent spell in the Scrubs he had taken French lessons, and would insist on practising his linguistic skill on his legal advisers.

'It seems you were caught with the following articles in your car, Bertie,' I reminded him. 'One brace and bit, one monkey wrench, two hacksaws, three sticks of dynamite with fuses and four imitation firearms, to wit revolvers.'

'All that in my bleeding *voiture*, Mr Rumpole!' Bertie Timson looked incredulous. 'Never!'

'The jury aren't going to believe you didn't have this stuff in your car. Not if three officers say they saw it there.'

'I do assure you, Mr Rumpole . . .'

'Now it may be that you have an innocent explanation for some of these objects. The carpenter's tools, for instance?'

'An innocent explanation? *Entendu*, Mr Rumpole. I'll think about it.'

'You do that. Oh, and Bertie. *Dépêchez-vous!*'

'Come again, Mr Rumpole?'

'Think as soon as you can. Before your case comes up at London Sessions.'

Meanwhile, back at Chambers, life was filled, as usual, with intrigue and indeed romance. Guthrie Featherstone, who, as I have already indicated, had found the charms of our Portia, Miss Phillida Trant, increasingly irresistible, called on her in her room quite early one morning to find her boning up on the law of evidence preparatory to another day with her fraudsman.

'You're not still in that dreary case down at the Old Bailey, are you?' Featherstone asked gallantly.

'Yes, thank God. With some quite decent refreshers.'

'Pity.' Featherstone moved stealthily nearer to Miss Trant's desk. 'We might have had lunch tomorrow. Taken a trip along to the Trattoria Gallactica in the Fulham Road. You know. That's where all the B.P.s go.'

'The what?' Miss Trant was deep in Phipson's *Law of Evidence*.

'Beautiful People. Like you, Miss Trant. Won't you let me take you to lunch there?'

'I don't think so.' Miss Trant turned a page. 'What would your wife Marigold have to say?'

'I'm not exactly under her eagle eye at lunchtime.' Featherstone sniffed appreciatively. 'What a *super* perfume you're wearing. Do you know "Ma Tendresse"?'

'No. Who's she?'

'Oh, I say. Enormously witty. "Ma Tendresse". It's an absolutely *super* new perfume. Definitely exotic. You should try it.'

'I might ask Claude. But he's not much of a one for buying perfume.'

'No. That's the problem with barristers who get keen on commercial law. They lose the talent for giving perfume.' Featherstone smiled and then allowed his hand to fall casually on Miss Trant's shoulder as he approached the other object of his visit, secondary to the wooing but still of importance. 'Oh, I say, Miss Trant. I think you should know. I thought we might take on a new young member of Chambers. Apparently a brilliant cross-examiner.'

'Oh, really?' Miss Trant was still into Phipson and appeared not to notice Guthrie's hand.

'Yes. I thought you might know her. Her name's Elizabeth Chandler.'

At which Miss Trant shut her book and stood, dislodging Guthrie's grasp and said, with marked disapproval, 'A woman?'

'Probably,' Featherstone conceded. 'If the name's Elizabeth Chandler.'

'Oh, I don't think we want *another* woman in Chambers.' Miss Trant was firm on the subject.

'You don't? How very interesting.'

'Henry has to explain to solicitors about it being a woman he's sending down to the indecent assault. He often gets objections.' Even Featherstone was surprised at the speed at which an ambitious woman can, in the legal profession, show signs of Male Chauvinist Piggery.

'But you, Miss Trant. You're doing so marvellously well!' He smiled at her ingratiatingly.

'Well, I do flatter myself I've been accepted. But I don't think we need another *woman*.'

Featherstone was not displeased with this objection, seeing in it the chance of another meeting. 'Why don't we have a long, long chat, Miss Trant, as to exactly what we *do* need. And I'd like to discuss your life in the law. Old Keith was telling me the Lord Chancellor's office has definitely got its eye on you.'

'On *me*? You must be joking.' Miss Trant looked at her Head of Chambers somewhat more kindly.

'Oh no, Miss Trant,' Featherstone assured her. 'I'm not joking at all. Shall we say next Tuesday? At the Trattoria Gallactica, among the Beautiful People?'

The truth of the matter was that not only did Miss Trant feel that her distinguished position as the only woman in the all-male enclave at Equity Court was threatened; but she was particularly reluctant to admit Miss Elizabeth Chandler, a very warm-hearted blonde who hunted, got sent boxes of chocolates by judges, and conducted her cases with a beguiling mixture of pure law and smouldering sexuality which was quite a match for Miss Trant's courtroom performance. Miss Trant had also, during the time it took him to graduate from squatter to tenant, conceived something of an uncontrollable passion for Ken Cracknell, and she wasn't going to have Miss Chandler luring her impressionable young radical off to Point-to-Points and Hunt Balls and other such sinks of iniquity at the weekends. She raised the matter with Cracknell as they walked together down Fleet Street towards the Old Bailey.

'I don't know what Guthrie Featherstone thinks he's up to. I mean, we're packed like sardines in Chambers as it is.'

'We certainly are.' Ken was sunk in moody and sullen thought. Then he said, 'You did tell me Rumpole left the Bar because he was losing all his cases?'

'In front of Bullingham, yes. It depressed him dreadfully, but I think it was just a run of bad luck. It was bound to end some-time.'

'But he lost his nerve?'

'Yes.'

'And might lose it again. I mean, if he comes any more crop-pers.'

'I know.' Miss Trant looked at him with sympathy. 'He lost your dirty books case in the north. I think that's shaken him too.'

'How much more do you think it'd shake him, if he lost a really big one?' Cracknell asked thoughtfully.

'Well, badly.' They crossed the traffic and walked up to the dome and the lady with the sword, past the Black Marias and taxis loaded with dubious company directors converging on the Old Bailey. 'But about this ridiculous idea of Featherstone's. I really think I'll have lunch and talk him out of it . . .'

So Miss Trant rattled on about her fears and indignation, but Ken Cracknell was hardly listening to her, his mind being on something else entirely.

Not long afterwards I was summoned, together with Bernard, my instructing solicitor, back to Brixton Prison for a second audience with Bertie Timson, whose fertile mind had in the interval provided him with some sort of a defence.

'I've been thinking about that load of stuff in the *voiture*, Mr Rumpole,' Bertie started thoughtfully.

'I'm glad to hear it, Bertie.'

'I've been remembering . . .'

'I had hoped you would.'

'Them things were all to do with members of the family. Know what I mean?' It didn't seem a particularly difficult con-ception and I grasped it. 'Them hacksaws and the brace and bit . . .'

'Not tools for the bank robbery?' I asked.

'D.I.Y.'

I was at sea, in a world of initials. 'Come again?'

'Do It Yourself, Mr Rumpole. Den's Monica was getting married and moving into a mobile home near Harlow. I was going to do up their bathroom.' I wondered what sort of lorry it might have been, off the back of which a mobile home might have dropped as a wedding gift, but I was too polite to interrupt Bertie's flow. 'I was going to give her shelves with concealed lighting and a wooden surround for the bath. *Très élégant.*' Bertie seemed pleased with his explanation and rounded it off in French. 'The toy guns was presents for my sister Vi's kids.'

'I don't want to ask awkward questions . . .'

'Mr Rumpole, I know you don't.'

'But the sticks of dynamite?'

'You want to know the truth?' That was a question I thought it wiser to leave unanswered, so I let Bertie continue. 'My cousin Cyril's got a cottage down in rural Essex. Charming little place. But the fact is . . . I don't want to shock the ladies in the jury.'

'Carry on, Bertie,' I said. 'Have no fear.'

'No main drains, Mr Rumpole. Nothing but a septic affair down the end of the garden. And *malheureusement* this tank gets blocked up . . . it won't seep away, not as it's meant to. And Cyril's old woman Betty, she gets on to him about this. But how do you unblock a septic tank, Mr Rumpole?'

'I can't really say I've given the matter any thought.'

'Dynamite. That's the idea I hit on.'

'Sounds a desperate solution . . .'

'Cyril's Betty was getting desperate, Mr Rumpole. So I happened to meet this Welsh geezer, who works in the quarries . . .'

'A bloke whose name you can't remember, but you happened to meet in a pub?' I suggested, a little wearily.

'How did you know that, Mr Rumpole?' Bertie looked pained.

I might have said, 'From a long experience of Timson family defences.' But I thought it more tactful to keep quiet.

'So this geezer said he had a bit of dynamite to spare, like, and I bought a few sticks off of him. I put them in the car for next time I was going down to Cyril and Betty's for a country weekend. I'd actually forgotten all about them, if you want to know the truth.'

There was a pause as I thought our defence over, then I said, 'Could we call Betty Timson as a witness?'

'Oh no, Mr Rumpole. She wouldn't want to come to Court.'

It was all rather as I had suspected. I sighed and lit a small cigar. 'So that's the story?'

'*Exactement*, Mr Rumpole.'

I blew out smoke and heaved myself to my feet. 'Well, we'll do what we can with it. I can't make any promises. It's a bit more convincing than a complete denial, I suppose.'

I got back from my second conference with Bertie Timson in Brixton Nick, pushed open the door of the common room and found it to be fully inhabited and stinking of some foul tobacco that Ken Cracknell rolled himself to show his solidarity with the working man (who was probably smoking low-tar filter-tip Health Hazards, anyway). Ken was sitting at the desk and Glendour-Owen filled the armchair with himself and a large brief.

I had, as I have said, rather avoided a confrontation with Ken Cracknell since the Grimble débâcle, but now that it could no longer be avoided I decided that the only way was to come clean, confess that I'd been got bang to rights and hope for a conditional discharge.

'Oh, Ken,' I greeted him. 'Do you mind if I call you Cracknell? I'm afraid I didn't do too well up in Grimble.'

'Henry told me.' Cracknell leant back in my swivel-chair and put his feet firmly on my desk.

'A dissatisfied client, I'm sorry to say.'

'Yes.' Cracknell glowered at me and then, quite unexpectedly, he smiled. 'Well. I don't expect it was your fault.'

'It seems Rumpole spouted Wordsworth at the jury. It went down like a lead balloon.' The small Celtic person giggled from my armchair.

'I found the result . . . a little disappointing,' I confessed.

'There'll be other cases.' To my amazement I got the distinct feeling that Ken Cracknell was trying to cheer me up.

'Meacher's got twenty dirty book shops, all coming up for trial.' I didn't want to conceal the extent of the damage. 'I doubt if I'll get a brief in any of them.'

There was a long silence. Cracknell was still smiling, but more to himself, I thought, than to anyone in the outside world.

He took out his cigarette machine and a packet of that tobacco which makes old men cough so terminally on dawn tube trains round the Angel Islington. When he had lit his next offensive cigarette, he said something which made me forgive his roll-ups, his boots on my table, his awful posters on my walls and even made me ready and willing to call him Ken. What he said not only justified my journey across the Atlantic but restored my faith in the law, in human nature, and even made me suspect that some benign Power might be keeping watch over old barristers. As he spoke, it seemed I heard bells ringing and even Owen Glendour-Owen was lapped in a roseate glow.

'I was thinking of asking you to lead me in my murder,' Cracknell said casually, blowing out a cloud of instant bronchitis.

'You . . . ? Me . . . ?' For once in my life I was incoherent.

Cracknell, from now on I shall call him Ken, went to my mantelpiece, took down the coveted brief in R. *v.* Simpson. 'I feel,' said the dear boy, 'that you're absolutely right for this.'

I didn't dispute it. It was a case which I always knew should have been mine.

'I mean, I don't want some smooth leader like Guthrie Featherstone who'll twist Simpson's arm and make him plead guilty.'

'Plead guilty?' I almost exploded. 'I never plead guilty!' At which I grasped the proffered brief before Ken had any chance of changing his mind.

'It's not an easy case, Rumpole.' Ken looked genuinely worried, bless his heart. 'I really don't know what the answer is.'

'Worry not, old darling. My dear Ken, your days of anxiety are over. The answer lies in the blood.'

Chapter Thirteen

I had a murder. I even had a suspected carrying of house-breaking implements by night. It's true that after our singular evening with Richard Tauber a certain amount of cold air had been blowing between myself and She Who Must Be Obeyed. I didn't feel I was forgiven for the sudden dash to freedom, nor was it likely to be forgotten in a hurry. As a consequence, there was a good deal of silence about the matrimonial home, broken, from time to time, only by the clicking of Hilda's tongue.

Once outside the confines of Froxbury Mansions, however, my spirits rose, my step was lighter and I could be heard to hum tunelessly as I emerged from the Temple tube station with the light of approaching battle in my eye. God was in his heaven and I had the brief in R. *v.* Simpson, and so there was nothing much wrong with the world outside Froxbury Mansions.

It was therefore with a feeling of exhilaration and excitement that I returned to that favourite rendezvous of mine, the interview rooms at Brixton Prison. Ken made his own way by bike and young Mowbray had walked down from his nearby office. However, a few minutes with our client Percival Simpson served to lower my spirits. He sat very quiet in his grey clothes, staring through the glass partition at the screws' collection of cactus plants, and he seemed so utterly uninterested in the work at hand, so entirely resigned to his defeat and eventual conviction, that it was, I must confess, a little disappointing.

'It's a miracle,' he said at the outset, and seemed to find the thought depressing.

'Oh, I wouldn't say that, Mr Simpson. It may seem miraculous to you . . .' I started modestly.

'What?' Simpson turned to me then, but without any particular interest.

'My being here!' That, I was sure, was the miracle he meant. 'A gift from heaven! Is that how it strikes you? Rumpole, who many believed was tucked away in some sunshine home, is back in the land of the living.' I lit a small cigar and continued. 'I have news for you, Simpson, old darling. You see, I received a letter about this little murder of yours, which has, I'm bound to admit, some fairly attractive features. And I came back in nothing more miraculous than the cut-price Gaelic Airlines Budget Special, which is a little like being shot across the Atlantic in a rather unclean corner of the tea bar at King's Cross . . .'

'About the blood.' Simpson didn't seem to be following me. 'That must be a miracle.'

'If you have one fault, Mr Simpson,' I told him reluctantly, 'it is that you are a touch too ready to assume the miraculous.'

'I can't fight it.' He shook his head in resignation.

'Oh yes, Mr Simpson, you can fight it and you will fight it.' It was going to be an uphill task putting a little spirit into this Simpson.

'You're going to ask me about what happened in the tube station . . .?' he sounded anxious.

'Am I?'

'I can't tell you about that. They'd never let me go if I told you that. They can work miracles, you see. They always told me they could.'

'They, Mr Simpson?' I was beginning to lose his drift. 'Who are "They"?'

'I can't say. I really . . . can't say.' This time he shook his head and spoke with considerable decision.

'Never mind. All in good time. I'm sure you'll be able to.' I thought it best to gain his confidence by starting as far as possible from the unfortunate incident on the underground station. 'I was going to ask you a little about yourself. You work, don't you, in the office of the Inspector of Taxes, Bayswater Division?'

'Yes.' Simpson seemed this time, perhaps understandably, reluctant to admit it.

'That's not a criminal offence,' I reassured him. 'Although it'll hardly endear you to the jury.'

'I've always been good at figures. Since I was a child. Figures hold no mystery for me.'

'Keen on your work, are you?' As a constant victim of the Revenue's little brown envelopes, I found it hard to restrain a shudder.

'Oh, very keen.' Simpson began to look almost lively. 'Every Thursday evening after work I go to evening classes in Advanced Accountancy.'

I glanced at the brief, checked the day of the murder. 'You went regularly to your evening classes, by tube?'

'Well, I don't run to a car, Mr Rumpole.' Simpson continued to react almost like a living being.

'What about supper?'

'What?'

'What about your supper, when you went to evening classes?'

'I'd always buy a take-away chicken, and then I'd take the tube on to my bed-sit.'

'In Alexander Herzen Road?'

'Yes.'

'And that was your regular routine on Thursdays?'

'Yes, it was.'

It was important information, which I filed away in the back of my mind; but I was getting uncomfortably near the incident which I knew would sting Simpson to silence, so I asked a safer question. 'Who'll talk about your good character? Friends at work?'

'I don't know many people. They call me "The Duchess" in the Inland Revenue.'

'They *what*?'

'It's a bit of a joke on my name, I suppose. Mrs Simpson, you see. The Duchess. I suppose it's a bit of a funny joke . . .'

'I see. Richly entertaining.' I smiled obligingly. 'You've always been in the tax-gathering business?'

'Since I left school at sixteen. I came in as tea boy in the Pay-As-You-Earn. Now I'm Number Two Accountant in the Schedule D.'

'A meteoric rise. And your spare time ... holidays? All that sort of thing?'

'Spare time? Well, it's television. And I bring work home.'

'Speaking as a taxpayer, Mr Simpson ... Duchess. Couldn't you manage to be a little less dedicated to your calling?' I said hopefully, and when he didn't answer I asked, 'What about holidays?'

'Holidays? I used to stay with my mother in Worthing, until she was gathered.' I managed to look suitably sympathetic, and then Simpson said, 'Only this year I managed a holiday abroad. I went to the Sunshine, on a package.'

'Sunshine?' I tried to keep the renewed hope and excitement out of my voice and said, as casually as possible, 'Not the Sunshine State, Duchess? That's not where they sent you on a package?'

'Yes, of course. Florida.' Simpson seemed to be losing interest again.

'Florida! Of course. You took your annual leave in Florida. Just when did it happen? Duchess ... just when and where did it happen?' Simpson didn't answer me, but he shook his head. 'All right. All right. You can tell me later,' I reassured him and then I stubbed out my small cigar and stood. I said the words I remembered. 'We shall meet and talk, friend and brother. As sure as the seed grows in the sunlight. We shall meet and talk.'

The effect was extraordinary. Simpson looked straight at me, his voice seemed forced and his eyes were full of fear. 'They sent you! They sent you ... to betray me!'

'Of course they didn't. Do get your mind off miracles, Mr Simpson. I told you ...' I was tying up my brief with its pink tape. 'I came on a "See the World" Budget Special of Gaelic Airlines. I came entirely of my own accord.'

Simpson didn't look reassured, but I thought there was nothing more I could say to convince him at that moment and that I had learnt all he was prepared to tell me.

Ken and Mowbray and I were sprung from Brixton. As we walked up the long, wet street that leads to the main road, past the little groups of mums and babies and girl-friends come to visit their men in the nick, Ken asked if I thought our client was insane.

'Oh, really, Ken. Who's sane? You or I or the learned judge? Or the screws who've condemned themselves to life imprisonment?'

'All right, then. Is he fit to plead?'

'Of course he is. And he's fit to be acquitted.' I looked at Ken and thought that, in spite of my everlasting gratitude to him for bringing me in as his leader, the time had come for a little gentle criticism. 'I see by your brilliant cross-examination in the Magistrates Court that you were suggesting that Simpson did it while protecting his honour against a homosexual attack.'

'It seemed about the only line.' Ken was unusually modest.

'The Guardsman's Defence, eh? Seems a rather old-fashioned gambit for a bright young radical barrister.'

'You don't think it'll work, sir?' Michael Mowbray was respectful.

'I don't think a Guardsman's Defence works particularly well, if you happen to have a client whose nickname is The Duchess.'

We had reached the car park by the main road, and Ken's Honda was waiting for him. 'Want a lift . . . ?'

'No, thank you. I had enough excitement on Gaelic Airlines.'

Ken armed himself in the huge helmet, strode the motor bicycle and thundered away. Young Mowbray gave me a sympathetic smile. 'Bit of a hopeless case, Mr Rumpole? Beginning to wish you were back across the Atlantic?'

'No, old darling. I don't wish that at all. Oh, you might start making a few tactful inquiries about the Hon. Rory Canter deceased.'

'About his sexual habits?' my young instructing solicitor asked eagerly, and looked quite disappointed when I said, 'Oh, dear boy, no. About his religion.'

There was only one thing to do now in the defence of Percival Simpson, and that was to telephone my son Nick on the other side of the Atlantic. So when I got back to Chambers, I sent instructions down to Henry to place the call, and he received them in a clerk's room crowded with Uncle Tom and Ken and Miss Phillida Trant. According to Miss Trant, this audience received the news from Henry that I was calling my son in America with a good deal of fascination and a certain amount of hope.

'Do you think Rumpole's contemplating doing the vanishing trick again?' Uncle Tom asked. 'Back into the sunset? I wonder if we'll have to give him another clock.'

He was referring, with some bitterness, to the occasion when Chambers had chipped in to buy me a clock against an earlier proposed retirement which never came off. 'Or is this another positively last appearance, like the ageing opera singer?' Uncle Tom went on, talking to no one in particular.

'It's working,' Ken said to Miss Trant, with a good deal of quiet satisfaction.

'What's working?' She wasn't sure if she followed him.

'Just an idea of mine,' said the young radical as he led her down to the Old Bailey and the endless fraud. 'Don't you worry your pretty head about it.'

'Dad. Yes, of course it's me. No . . . I'm not at work. Because it's four o'clock in the morning. Well, no . . . I haven't had your letter.'

I suppose I should have had more consideration for my daughter-in-law Erica, lying in the warm sleep of pregnancy, who was aroused at an ungodly hour to hear her husband Nick talking, in a bewildered sort of way, to the telephone.

'Street corner?' Nick was saying. 'What street? Handing out *leaflets*? And flowers? Yes. Yes, of course I'll try . . . It's all . . . all in your letter, is it? Well, anyway, you sound happy. Yes . . . Yes . . . Love to Mum.'

As Nick put down the phone Erica asked him, in some dread, 'He doesn't want to come back here, does he?'

'No,' said my son, and he sounded puzzled. 'No. He wants me to find Tiffany Jones.'

My Nick is a good lad, and indulgent to the whims of his no doubt trying father. Accordingly he was to be found, when the academic day finally began, in a corner of the tree-lined, bicycle-ridden campus, having a quiet talk with Paul Gilpin from the English Department.

'That last day you saw Tiffany, Paul. Did you notice anything unusual about her?'

'How do you mean, unusual?'

'She wasn't ill or anything?'

'No. She seemed well. Happier than ever. Only one thing. I noticed she'd cut her arm. She was wearing a band-aid. I did ask her about it and she wouldn't tell me.'

'You don't think it was a rusty needle?' Nick had had many unhappy examples of this among his students.

'Oh, come on, Nick. You know Tiffany wasn't like that.'

'And you haven't heard from her since then?'

'Not a single word.' Paul Gilpin was depressed, as anyone would be who is suddenly and mysteriously deprived of a life with a girl like Tiffany Jones.

'She never left a note, no message?'

'Not a thing.'

'It's worrying for you . . .'

'I went mad to start with. Rang round the hospitals and the police, of course. But at least now I know she's alive.'

'How do you know?'

'Someone came round for her things.'

'They did?'

'Didn't I tell you? About three weeks ago, I guess. A guy called and said Tiffany wanted her things.'

'Who was he?'

'The guy who came?'

'Yes.'

'Pretty young. In his twenties, I guess. Nice-looking boy, but nothing you'd notice. Clean jeans and a clean white shirt. That sort of style.'

'He didn't tell you his name?'

'He didn't tell me a damned thing. Said he had strict instructions not to answer questions. Instructions from Tiffany, I guess. I found that very hurtful. Also I thought it was a little strange. The things that she wanted.'

'What did she want?'

'Well, certainly not clothes, make-up, none of the things you'd think a girl might need. He just took her books on math, slide-rule, pocket calculator. Just the things she uses for her work in statistics and economic forecasts.'

'The tools of her trade?'

'Exactly that.'

Chapter Fourteen

Whilst Nick was pursuing his researches into the strange disappearance of Tiffany Jones, and I was hanging round our clerk's room in the hope of picking up any crumbs in the shape of discarded dangerous drivings or superfluous solicitings, Miss Trant kept her luncheon appointment with our somewhat flustered and over-excited Head of Chambers Guthrie Featherstone in the Trattoria Gallactica in the Fulham Road. I owe the following account of this meeting to her subsequent description of it to me over a glass of Pommeroy's plonk.

Featherstone was wearing a new silk tie and had obviously been waiting some considerable time. He was nervously snapping breadsticks between his fingers when Miss Trant arrived the regulation fifteen minutes late. As she sat down, she noticed a brimming campari soda and a gift-wrapped package by her plate. Gulping the one and tearing at the sellotape with inquisitive fingernails at the other, she asked, 'Is this for me?'

'I bought it for you. Yes,' Featherstone admitted.

'What an enormous bottle!' Miss Trant had succeeded in unshrouding what seemed to be a pint or two of 'Ma Tendresse'.

'Well. It's only the toilet water, I'm afraid. I mean, who wants to spend twenty pounds on a bottle of the perfume? I mean, when you get so much more . . . with the toilet water.' Featherstone was struggling, ill-advisedly, with the economics of the situation.

'Exactly. Well, I'll slosh it around,' Miss Trant said cheerfully. 'It'll probably absolutely slay them down at the London Sessions.'

'I bought it for you especially. "Ma Tendresse", from Harrods. Claude won't mind you wearing it?'

'Claude's not terribly into perfume,' Miss Trant admitted, and then went into the subject which was uppermost in her mind. 'Now, about the girl you're thinking of taking into Chambers.'

'Marriage!' Featherstone's mind was on other things. 'It's a funny thing about marriage. Marigold and I, we have our different interests. Marigold's taken up choral singing. They're doing the *Saint Matthew Passion*.'

'Oh yes. And what passion are you doing, Featherstone?' Miss Trant looked at her host with some suspicion.

Featherstone, thinking he was being treated like a dangerous Don Juan, was flattered. 'I say, you *are* sharp, aren't you? But look here, Phyllis. Do call me Guthrie.'

'Phillida.'

'What?'

'My name's Phillida. You see, I've been making inquiries about this Elizabeth Chandler person, and I'm not at all sure she's the type that would really muck in at Chambers. Also, there are only a certain number of matrimonial disputes where solicitors *want* women. I mean, are there enough for two?'

'Matrimonal disputes,' Featherstone said gloomily. 'Well, there are quite enough of those, God knows. But Marigold and I, we just face facts.'

'What facts?' Miss Trant asked without interest.

'Well, we may fancy other people. And well, other people might fancy us.'

'Might they?' Miss Trant's neutral tones didn't betray her incredulity.

'We only stick together, of course, for the sake of the children.'

'Oh. I hadn't heard about the children.'

'Hadn't you really?' Featherstone suddenly became a great deal more relaxed. They had got on to a subject on which he felt thoroughly at home. 'Well, there's Arabella. She goes to this funny little school in Kensington. I mean, she's eight, but she's already got this extraordinary talent for dancing. And little Luke, well, he's only just three, but I've got him down for Marlborough. I imagine he might want to come to the Bar some day.'

'You don't want to fill the Chambers up with Elizabeth Chandler, then?' Miss Trant was quite uncertain as to whether she had scored a victory.

'Look. If you've never actually seen the children, I just happen to have a couple of photographs about me. Only snaps, of course. We took them in Portofino last long vacation. It wasn't frightfully sunny weather. That's Bella on the terrace of our hotel.' Featherstone had produced his wallet, from which he proudly drew a number of creased and faded snaps from the space between his credit cards and his cheque book.

'What's she doing?' said Miss Trant, giving a cursory look. "The Dying Swan"?'

'Oh, yes,' said Featherstone proudly. 'Quite the little Margot Fonteyn, isn't she? And this is old Luke with his fingers in the spaghetti. Oh, my God!' Featherstone's voice had sunk to a hoarse whisper. He was staring across the restaurant at a couple of dark-suited businessmen who were about to settle at a distant table.

'What on earth's the matter?' asked Miss Trant, puzzled.

'My God! My God!' Featherstone moaned gently, his hand on his chest.

'Featherstone. Guthrie! Are you in some sort of pain?' Miss Trant was no Florence Nightingale, and hoped to God she wouldn't be called on to administer the kiss of life.

'Pain? Yes. Pain. That's what I'm in. Of course. I must dash. Immediately! Look, I'll pay the bill.' At which Featherstone stood up suddenly and pushed back his chair.

'Pay the bill? We haven't eaten anything!' Miss Trant pointed out reasonably, but Featherstone was on his way out of the Trattoria Gallactica, waving a limp hand and muttering vaguely, 'Goodbye, Phillida. See you in Chambers. Sometime.'

This highly unsatisfactory luncheon had an immediate effect which unexpectedly involved me, and in a most unwelcome manner. I had just lost a perfectly simple and winnable indecent assault in a cinema at Uxbridge, and was gloomily wondering if I had lost my grip. As I wandered into the clerk's room, Henry told me that there was a lady waiting for me upstairs. As I opened the door, I noticed a welcome absence of Ken and

Glendour-Owen, and the unlikely presence of a handsome woman, about thirty-five years of age with a cashmere twinset, a double row of pearls and an expression of grim determination.

'Mr Rumpole. We have met, over the years. At Chambers parties. I'm Marigold Featherstone.'

I remembered the wife of the Q.C., M.P., our Head of Chambers. 'Of course. Look, I'll just see if Guthrie's in his room.'

'I don't want Guthrie at this particular moment.' I thought the tone was somewhat chilling. 'Thank you very much. It's you I want, Mr Rumpole. Would you mind closing the door?' Hers was a tone of command. I shut the door behind me.

'You want *me*, Mrs Featherstone?'

'Tell me, Mr Rumpole. Do you handle divorce?'

'Only rarely. And then with particularly thick gloves. Why do you ask?' I sat down at my desk.

'I ask, Mr Rumpole, because I have need of your services.'

'Of mine?'

'For a divorce.'

'I mean, who . . .' I thought she perhaps had a lady friend tossed on the rough seas of a stormy marriage, but her answer set me rocking back in the swivel-chair.

'My husband, Mr Rumpole. I'd hardly be bothering to divorce anyone else's husband, would I?' I could see the force of her argument. 'I'm afraid Guthrie's gone completely off the rails.' She sighed, and had she been my Hilda, she would have undoubtedly clicked her tongue. 'He has taken up, Mr Rumpole, with another woman.'

'Oh, well now. Can you be sure about that? I mean, what's the evidence?' I couldn't see a man, even Guthrie Featherstone, suffer such a summary conviction.

'The evidence, Mr Rumpole,' Mrs Featherstone said impassively, 'is the evidence of my own eyes.'

From that moment I began to feel pessimistic about the chances of any sort of defence for our learned Head of Chambers. The eyes of his lady wife were clear and unblinking, the sort of eyes that might well be believed in a court of law. She continued with her evidence.

'I was in the perfume department at Harrods, Mr Rumpole. I

was buying my usual little atomizer. Guthrie never brings *me* perfume home, and I happened to catch sight of him, at the "Ma Tendresse" counter.'

'He was buying perfume?' I hazarded a guess.

'Well, Mr Rumpole. He wasn't buying potatoes.'

I began to see that there was a certain ruthless logic about this woman's mind. I asked the obvious question. 'Did you confront him?'

'I moved towards him, but Harrods was extremely crowded on that day and he escaped. Furtively.'

'Did you ask him about it?'

'No.'

'Why?' Poor old Guthrie had no doubt been condemned without a hearing.

'I didn't want to give him the chance to lie to me.'

A woman of steel, you'd have to agree, this Mrs Marigold Featherstone. However, I did my best to sound unconvinced by the evidence. 'Well, I don't see that adds up to much of a case. He might have been buying scent for anyone, an old aunt perhaps. Has he got an old auntie with a birthday?'

'He was buying it, Mr Rumpole,' said Marigold, driving the final nail into her husband's coffin, 'for the girl he took out to lunch at the Trattoria Gallactica.'

'Oh yes?' I did my best to sound casual. 'And which girl was that?'

'Some little tart. I don't know her name. My brother Tom was lunching his accountant at the Trattoria Gallactica, and he distinctly saw Guthrie at the corner table gazing into the eyes of this King's Road strumpet. And do you know what Tom saw plonked on her plate?'

'Tagliatelle verdi?' I was guessing again, of course.

'A great big bottle of "Ma Tendresse". The toilet water. Of course, as soon as he caught sight of Tom, Guthrie simply got up and legged it. He's a terrible coward, you know.'

The wretched Featherstone clearly needed the assistance of a good lawyer. Always ready to take on a hopeless case, I decided to defend him. 'Mrs Featherstone. If I were to act for you in this dispute with your husband . . .' I started cautiously.

'Yes?' said Marigold eagerly.

'The Head of Chambers! Well, it would cause enormous embarrassment.'

'If I'm divorcing Guthrie, Mr Rumpole, embarrassment is just what I intend to cause!' This was not a woman to be trifled with.

I said, 'Leave it with me, Mrs Featherstone. I'll think it over.' A bit of delay, I had found it an infallible rule, never does any harm to the defence.

'I shall call on you next week,' said Marigold Featherstone coldly. 'Then I shall expect your answer.'

Whilst I set about the unlikely task of finding a defence to the charges brought by this implacable plaintiff against our Head of Chambers, my son Nick, out of the extreme goodness of his heart, was finding out some other answers for me. He climbed into his rather battered Volkswagen (Erica kept the estate car for her use) and drove down to the Miami shopping street where I had been buying small cigars when I first heard about seeds growing in the sunlight.

Nick parked his car and walked up and down the street, but drew a blank. Then he went into a bar and ordered a cold beer and sat staring at the intersection I had recommended to him, but saw nothing unusual. He ordered another beer without incident; but when it came, and he was about to lower his mouth to the tooth-freezing and gaseous liquid, he saw two girls in white dresses come into the bar carrying long-stemmed chrysanthemums. Nick looked, as he told me, and saw the young man in the white shirt and tie standing at the street corner with the flowers which he handed out to the passers-by, all of whom received them and his greetings with politeness and some with interest.

In a moment Nick had abandoned his beer and was standing in front of the young man who had just presented him with a chrysanthemum.

'It's a sunshine day,' said the young man cheerfully.

'Is it? I really hadn't noticed,' Nick said with carefully affected gloom.

'Sunlight to Children of Sun,' said the young man. 'Are you not aware of the sun, our source of strength?'

'I guess I'm only aware of my problems. I've sure got a few of those.' Nick was giving an excellent performance of a young American academic going through a crisis in his personal relationships.

'Meet and talk.' The young man was smiling and interested.

'Pardon me?' said Nick, apparently lost in dejection.

'We shall meet and talk, friend and brother,' the young man repeated, 'as sure as the seed grows in the sunlight.'

'Meet and talk?' Nick looked up gratefully.

'Well, sure thing, friend and brother. You and I have all the time in the world for one-to-one communication. You haven't done much talking lately? Just exchanged words, is that it? Not real talking.' The young man looked at Nick in a kindly and yet penetrating way, and Nick agreed quickly.

'Exchanged words. Yes. That's exactly it!'

'That's all you do on the outside, isn't it?' The young man in the tie nodded understandingly. 'Exchange words in the office, or with your family maybe. But never talk, one heart to another's heart, beating as one. They never know that, the Children of Dark.'

'It's just that I've been feeling terribly lonely lately,' Nick admitted in evident distress.

'Come with me then, friend and brother. The lonely days are over. Come with me, and we'll talk it all through.'

Nick's troubles were apparently serious enough for the young man to shut up the free chrysanthemum service and suggest a walk on Miami beach. He took a lift in that direction in Nick's German antique, and then they walked, two young men in close and confidential conversation, past the bejewelled geriatrics and the golden lads and girls who were presently leaping about at volley ball, or stretched beautifully on towels. In what seems, when you have passed through it, to be a regrettably short period, these golden lads and girls would be in need of hearing aids, bifocals and a cheap blood pressure service.

'What's your name?'

'Nicholas Rumpole.'

'Then you're Nicholas.'

'What's yours?'

'You can just call me William. That's my given name. My family name's forgotten now. A family name's the first thing we give up, we Children of Sun. But then we forget a lot of things.'

'Children of Sun?' Nick sounded puzzled.

'We shall inherit the earth. We Sun Children.' William looked at Nick and he was smiling.

'Sounds interesting. When?'

'In ten years.' William had no doubt about it. 'When the time of Darkness is over, the world shall belong to the Sun's Children.'

'It's a religion?' Nick hazarded a guess.

'It's a whole life.'

'Christian?'

William shook his head. 'Jesus is no use to us. Jesus died. We're not interested in death, Nicholas. Death or sickness. We shall give back health to the world, during the years of Rule.'

'The years of *what*?'

'First we have the years of Preparation,' William explained. 'Then the years of Rule, when the Sun's Children enter into their inheritance. You see, the Master gives us everything. He protects us with his power. His power for the miraculous.'

'Miracles?' Nick inquired simply.

'Oh, sure. *He*'s not bound by the laws of man and nature. *He* gives us perfect freedom, Nick. And in return what do we give him? Well, I guess we just about give him everything. Perfect loyalty. Perfect fidelity. And you know the joy, Nick? He gives us perfect peace.'

A little later they were sitting at a straw-roofed beach bar having a drink. 'Nothing alcoholic,' William had said. 'Just juice, I guess.' So Nick had a beer and William was drinking chemical bottled orange juice (in the State where citrus fruit grows like weeds), sitting on bar stools on the edge of the sand, served by brown-skinned blonde girls in bikini tops and abbreviated shorts.

'It sounds the sort of life I need.' Nick sighed. 'Perfect simplicity.'

'The Dark world's a maze. In the Sunlight all is made clear.

You make your life with us and . . . no more problems. That I guarantee. Will you come to us?' William was still smiling at Nick and looking at him through clear blue eyes with irresistible sincerity.

'If only I could . . .'

'Of course you can. Anyone can. Knock and it shall be opened to you.'

'What shall be opened?'

'Home. Our home and your home. The Sun Valley that's waiting for you.'

'I can't imagine a real home,' Nick said in the most desolate voice he could manage. 'I haven't really had a home life for a hell of a long time.'

'We all make our contribution.' William went on smiling at him. 'All we ask of you is your talent. What's your talent, Nicholas?'

'Me? Oh, I'm a teacher.'

'We need teachers. Teachers will help us educate the world in happiness and positive thinking.'

'What else do you need?'

'All sorts: builders, carpenters, cooks, doctors.'

'Economists?' Nick made an informed guess, based on the letter from me that he had by now received.

'We have the best. We had a bad experience in that department, but now we have the very best. One of our most zealous children.'

'I wonder who . . .' Nick began to ask, but William gave him another welcoming smile and put a hand gently on his arm.

'No more questions, Nicholas. I'm not questioning you about your life or whatever it is that's making you live in Darkness. Come to us in Sunshine. Save the questions until you're safe inside the family.'

'What's *your* work exactly?' Nick asked William.

'My work, Nicholas, is to bring back friends.'

'Bring them back where?'

'Home. You've got your Volks, haven't you. What're we waiting for?'

'I must say, I'm interested.'

'I know you are.'

'I'd like to visit you.'

'To visit with us is to stay with us. You won't want to do anything else. Come and see. Once they're home, no one cares to leave Sun Valley.'

'Well.' Nick finished his drink. 'I don't know what I've got to lose.'

'Only the chains of Darkness.' William smiled at him. 'Shall we go? Oh, and you'll find you won't have a need of that stuff any more.' He nodded towards Nick's beer. 'Only fruit juice and the Word of the Master.'

So eventually they drove off in Nick's old Volkswagen, with William talking soothingly all the time, so that with the heat and the gentle voice repeating encouraging sentiments and messages of hope, Nick said that he felt, in a way, hypnotized and almost fell asleep as he drove along the freeway.

In time they turned off at an exit and were driving past fields and orchards, fruit farms and shacks, low-lying country much afflicted by mosquitoes and hurricanes. They drove on for almost an hour, William giving directions and comfort, and my son Nick saying as little as was needed to keep up the pretence of his disillusionment with a harsh world and of his readiness to put his life at the service of an unknown Master and join the Children of Sun.

'Happiness outside is a thing that has to be forced on you, by money or sex or some other kind of hallucinogenic drug. But flowers don't need money to grow, Nick. They don't need the Big Job of the Wonderful Home. It's because they have the warmth of the Sun *inside* them. You're going to see a whole lot of sights where we're going to, Nicholas, and I sure can't wait to show them to you. But one thing you won't see, and that's an unhappy face.'

'What do I have to do? To get in to your home?' Nick asked innocently.

'Just decide to stay.'

'Is that all?'

'Well. If you do decide to stay with us, Nicholas, there is a contract.'

'A legal document?'

'Scarcely. You have to write out the words of power. And write them in rather a special way.'

'Oh, really? And what sort of a special way is that?'

William turned to Nick for a moment and said quietly, 'You write in your own lifeblood, Nicholas. Everyone does. It doesn't take much to do it.'

At last they came to a high wall, running along the side of a narrow country road. And then there was a wide gate in the wall, painted white and topped with barbed wire. Over the gate there was a high, wooden arch and a sign reading SUN VALLEY and high and triumphant over the sign was a large, glass-covered coloured photograph of a cleric, a man with crinkly white hair, kindly eyes beaming behind rimless spectacles and a deep and healthy suntan. Nick didn't recognize the photograph, but then he had never been in Percival Simpson's bed-sit in Alexander Herzen Road.

William asked Nick to stop in front of the gate, and he clasped his hands and raised them towards the photograph. 'The Master,' he said. Then he asked Nick to honk the horn, and a couple of clean-shirted, large and healthy-looking young men came out of the shed by the gate and looked into the car. William rolled down the window and spoke to them.

'A new friend and brother,' he said. 'His name's Nicholas.'

Nick said that the smiles of the gatekeepers seemed to be suddenly switched on like street lights at twilight.

'Be very welcome, Nicholas.'

'May the Sun shine always on a new friend.'

At which one of them unlocked the huge padlock which held the gate, and the other swung it open.

'We're home, Nicholas,' said William. 'Just drive in slowly.'

Nick, bless his heart, drove in for the sake of the defence of Percival Simpson, and he said it was an extremely unpleasant moment when he heard the gates close and the padlock snap behind him.

There was nothing immediately obvious that could explain the distinct sense of foreboding that my son Nicholas Rumpole felt. What he had driven into was like a spacious and very well-kept farmyard. There was a line of sheds where he guessed animals were kept, and another line of buildings on the other side of the square which might have housed offices and communal rooms. The bottom of the square was also blocked by buildings of some sort, so that the compound was effectively closed in, in a way that made Nick think of a well-run open prison. The inhabitants, however, were all much like William, young men and women, wearing clean jeans and smiling. In a corner of the yard a group were loading boxes and sacks of vegetables onto a new pick-up truck. As they worked they were singing:

> 'Gonna build a kingdom on this sad old ground,
> Gonna build a kingdom all around!
> Gonna call it heaven, cause that's what it'll be,
> A place of beauty, joy and peace for you and me!'

'The Sun's Children,' William said. 'We're always singing.' Strangely enough Nick didn't find even this fact reassuring.

At William's instructions he drove across to the row of communal buildings. He parked and they got out. William led him to what seemed to him to have been a converted cowshed and opened a door.

'This is the reception area, Nicholas. Wait in here. Be at peace, and I'll tell the office you've arrived to make your home with us.'

'Well, I'm not sure . . .' Nick sounded doubtful, but William said firmly, 'Wait here, Nicholas. The Parents in Love will be here to greet a new child. No further decisions are expected of you.'

William left, and Nick found himself in a long room, furnished with sofas and easy chairs. The walls were decorated with a number of bright but amateurish murals of young men and women and some children, walking naked across a primitive landscape hand in hand, or holding up their arms to a round yellow sun surrounded by spiky rays and painted as it would be in a child's painting. The naked figures were so turned that there was no direct display of their private parts, and indeed their sex wasn't always easy to determine. Almost the whole of an end wall was covered with a hugely blown-up photograph of the beaming cleric whose picture hung over the gateway. Hymn tunes of a cheerful nature were being piped into the room by some mechanical musak system. There were long coffee tables on which stood bowls of flowers. There were no newspapers or magazines, no books and no ashtrays.

Nick went to the long windows and stood looking out into the yard. He saw the industrious young people loading the truck; he could see the guardians of the gate talking together by their shed. And then he saw another group of three or four Sun Children come out of what may have been an office and set off towards the building at the end of the square. They were carrying ledgers and files, and walking a little behind them, as though too tired to keep up, he saw Tiffany Jones.

The door was unlocked, either by good luck or by William's forgetfulness. Nick was out of it in a moment and standing in the sunshine calling, 'Tiffany!'

'Nick! It's you. Have you come inside?'

She stood there, a beautiful black girl with her arms full of files, half turned towards him, and he could hear the exhaustion in her voice, although it was denied by the bright and perpetual smile worn by all the Children of Sun.

'Tiffany. What are you doing? We all missed you. Paul's gone crazy looking for you.'

'I'm working, Nick. Working for the Master.' She looked round nervously and lowered her voice. 'We're not supposed to talk . . . Not to Outside People.'

'Working? What the hell are you working at?'

'Oh, the books. Using my skill in figures. I work so hard, Nick.'

'Tiffany. Tell me.' Nick asked what I needed to know.

'I can't tell you. The last guy they had . . . for accounting . . . He was a traitor! He betrayed them, you see? That's why they needed me.'

'Who was he, Tiffany?'

She didn't answer his question and Nick looked round; one of the young men from the gate was coming towards them. 'I can't stop. We'll meet and talk. Not one to one, however. We can only talk together. With all the Children . . .'

On the other side of the square the loading of the pick-up truck was finished, the driver was climbing into his seat and the crowd of loaders was moving away towards the large building at the end. The young man from the gate was moving towards Nick, calling out to him in a voice which had lost some degree of warmth.

'Hey! Hey, you friend. Is that your Volks?'

'Be welcome, Nick. Be very welcome,' Tiffany said faintly.

As she moved away from him, Nick was looking at the cardboard-covered file which was top of those in the black girl's arms. There was a name written on the cover, which had been crossed out, the name 'Percival'.

'Drive that up to the car port with the other gifts.' The young man instructed Nick in a voice that made it clear that it was less a request than an order. Nick looked to the open shed at which the young man was pointing, in which stood a number of new, and not so new, motor cars. Then he pulled his car door open.

'Tiffany.' He spoke to her as calmly as he could. 'Let me take you home.'

'Don't be ridiculous, Nick.' She was smiling at him, and at that moment her smile seemed particularly weary. 'I am home.'

It was the last he saw of her.

'Come on, friend. Move, why don't you?'

The young man from the gatehouse was not to be denied. Nick swung into the driving seat and saw through his dusty windscreen that the gate was open wide to let the truck full of vegetables out. He switch on his engine, put his foot flat on the floor and gripped the steering wheel as his car shot forward. He reached the gate in a cloud of dust just as the truck was moving through it, and, ignoring the shouts of the gatekeepers, he managed to get through in the truck's wake before the gate could close behind it. There was a space in front of the gate in which Nick could pass the truck, and then a long narrow road between banks where he tried to get away from the truck, but it accelerated also and seemed near enough to touch his back bumper.

Then the road twisted and Nick saw the lumbering back of a slow-moving harvester in front of them. He twisted his wheel and, half mounting the bank, managed to squeeze his little Volkswagen past the agricultural implement, leaving the vegetable truck stuck closely behind it. Nick didn't lift his foot from the floor when he reached the freeway, but though he watched his mirror no one seemed to be giving him chase. He didn't feel safe, however, until he had parked in front of his house, got inside and poured himself a long cold glass of Californian white wine in the cause of freedom. He then lifted the telephone and put in a call to Equity Court in the Temple.

Chapter Fifteen

'Splendid, Nick. Absolutely splendid. My dear boy, I'm grate-ful. What a sad loss you are to the law! Well, of course your mother's all right. What on earth's she got not to be all right about? Well, that's very kind ... I miss you too, Nick. Of course I do.'

As I put down the instrument, I became aware of the presence of Guthrie Featherstone lurking by my desk.

'Rumpole! I really think it's time I had a word.'

'That son of mine,' I said in some elation, 'is a chip off the old block, Featherstone. He's just done a splendid job on the Simp-son murder case. An absolutely splendid job.'

'Rumpole. I've been talking things over with Henry and I've come to the conclusion that we've got an overflow problem in Chambers.'

'Then why don't you pull out the plug, my old darling. Do you have to go on finding room for that sinister little Welsh-man?'

'Glendour-Owen has an excellent practice. But you see, we had made our plans on the clear basis of your retirement.'

'Don't tell me you can't find room for me, Featherstone.' I was in no mood to bandy words with my Head of Chambers. 'I hear you were thinking of taking on another lady, some blonde bombshell who hunts and picks up matrimonials.'

'That was rather different. Elizabeth Chandler could have mucked in with Philly. Anyway, I've rather given up on that idea,' said Featherstone, admitting his total defeat at the hands of the redoubtable Miss Trant.

'Well, then. There's absolutely no problem.'

'Oh yes there is, Rumpole. Look, if you *are* coming back to the Bar, which at your time of life I don't honestly advise, I just think you'll have to make other arrangements.'

I looked at Featherstone then with a sort of pity. The poor fellow had no idea of the gaping pit which was about to open at his feet. 'You can't do it, my old darling,' I said. 'You simply can't afford to lose me, Featherstone. You see, you absolutely rely on me to defend you. On a serious charge, before a quite merciless tribunal.'

'Oh really, Rumpole. And what tribunal are you talking about?'

'I am talking, my dear Featherstone, about your wife Marigold.'

And then I told him about the serious charges laid against him, matters which his wife hadn't seen fit to mention in the privacy of their home, and the embarrassing divorce case she was planning. And I was the only advocate with the smallest chance of winning him a verdict of not guilty, I pointed out, and he saw the force of the argument, that continued prattle about there being no room for Rumpole in Chambers was a foolish waste of time.

Featherstone sat with his jaw dropped and a glassy look in his eye. He seemed to see the distant vision of Mr Justice Featherstone in scarlet and ermine vanish before his eyes.

'Marigold *can't* have seen me,' he tried to argue hopelessly, 'in the perfume department.'

'She has the evidence of her own eyes,' I assured him. 'I'm afraid she's prepared to believe them.'

'Or in the restaurant?' he added hopefully.

'There the prosecution relies on her brother's testimony.'

'Tom must have been mistaken.'

'Unlikely. And even if he were . . .'

'Yes?'

'In view of the nature of the tribunal, I think he's likely to be believed.' As with all clients, it was better to point out the worst of the case to Featherstone. Then he would be more grateful for any small success I might achieve.

'Rumpole. I rely on you.' He looked at me in a beseeching sort of way.

'I know.'

'Marigold simply won't discuss the matter with me. She's hardly spoken for the last ten days.'

'So you want me to defend you?' I appeared to be thinking the matter over.

'Please, Rumpole.' His dependence on me was almost endearing. I have always found it hard to actually dislike my clients, so I gave him the benefit of my advice and experience.

'Nothing's so unconvincing as a bare denial. That's what I told Bertie Timson.'

'Who the hell's Bertie Timson?'

'Oh, just one of my other villains,' I told him casually, at which Featherstone protested.

'Rumpole!'

'The old darling stands accused of carrying house-breaking instruments by night. "Come out with a bare denial," I told Bertie, "and no one believes you." Now if the truth of the matter is that you *were* in the perfume department . . .' I brought the general principle back to fit the specific facts in Featherstone *v.* Featherstone.

'But there is some quite innocent explanation!' Featherstone was taking to the life of crime like a duck to water.

'And for you sitting in the restaurant with whoever it was?' I asked.

'Does Marigold *know* who it was?' he asked with terror in his voice, seeing a scandal approaching which would involve the whole of Chambers.

'Not by name. She says she was a floosie. Some little tart from the King's Road,' I reassured him.

'Oh, Rumpole,' Featherstone said in a voice of doom. 'It was Phillida . . .'

'Can you possibly mean Miss Phillida Trant, LL.B. (Hons.) of London University, member of this distinguished Chambers?' I asked incredulously, turning the knife in the self-inflicted wound.

'Yes, Rumpole. I'm afraid that's exactly who it was.'

'Then if there *is* an innocent explanation . . .?' I put the situation before him, in all its seriousness. 'You *must* let me come out with it. Otherwise I don't give a toss for your chances, quite frankly.'

'Of course, Rumpole. An entirely innocent explanation,' Featherstone assured me, somewhat desperately.

'We could call Miss Phillida Trant to give evidence. I imagine she's a witness who would carry a good deal of weight, even with the most obstinate tribunal.'

'Well, no.' Featherstone was doubtful. 'No, I don't think we could really ask Phillida.'

As with Bertie Timson, I saw the red light at once. There is no course more fatal to the defence than calling an unhelpful witness. However, I did my best to fill Featherstone with a sense of urgency. 'Your lady wife says she'll be back to speak to me.'

'Tell her, Rumpole!' He was beseeching me now. 'She'll listen to you. I'm *sure* she'll listen.'

'Tell her? Of course I'll tell her, I'll put your case to her. Fair and square. The only problem is, Featherstone, my old darling defendant . . .'

'Yes?'

'As yet I have absolutely no idea what your case is.'

There was a long pause and then he said, 'I'll think about it.'

'Well, you'd better think quickly,' I warned him. 'Marigold will be here in exactly a week's time.'

In the interim my instructing solicitor, young Michael Mowbray, visited the village near to which the Hon. Rory Canter had farmed almost a thousand acres of rich and productive Hampshire countryside. He drove up to the farmhouse of mature and sunlit Georgian brick, he admired the newly painted white gates and gleaming farm machinery, he saw how sleek and well the black and white cows appeared to be as they were driven to the milking machines, and how neatly and in what good time the fields were ploughed. He also noticed that such farm workers as he saw looked young and intelligent and quite unlike the usual Hampshire labourer.

Having taken a view of the property, Mowbray had a pint of beer and a plate of bread and cheese in the local pub, The

Baptist's Head. There he heard that Fineacre Farm had been taken over by a foreign company, the exact nature of which was unknown to the red-faced, panting landlord, but which seemed to employ a work force of young people who kept themselves a great deal to themselves and were an absolute dead loss as customers. More than that my instructing solicitor could not learn, so he left, having promised to come back at an early date and sample the landlord's Cordon Bleu French dinner, which featured chicken boiled in red wine, frozen vegetables and the Gastronomic Gâteau Trolley – a promise which Mike Mowbray, who despite his deep and long-lasting friendship with Ken Cracknell was a young man of some taste and discernment, had no intention of keeping.

He drove next to the neighbouring town and sought five minutes with the local solicitor, who happened to employ as London agents the firm where Mowbray had served his articles. He said he had a client, and hinted at untold wealth and Arab connections, who was interested in buying the Fineacre property. The elderly partner smiled, shook his head and said he doubted very much if the present owners would sell. He himself had acted in the rather unusual transaction by which they had acquired the farm from Rory Canter. From him Mowbray was able to discover who these owners were, and when he passed the information on to me, I was more eager than ever for the date of the Simpson trial, and to pass on the facts I had collected to an Old Bailey jury.

'In my humble submission to the Court . . . I'm sorry, I mean to you, Mrs Featherstone . . . you have absolutely no reason for a divorce, or indeed to feel any emotion except . . . conjugal love . . . and gratitude towards my client. I mean your husband.'

Before tackling the problems of Percival Simpson, I had Guthrie Featherstone's defence to take care of, and I was engaged on pleading his cause, based on the new and ingenious set of instructions he had given me after our preliminary conference. As I opened the proceedings I saw the tribunal looking distinctly frosty. It was as I had feared all along: Mrs Marigold Feather-stone was going to prove a hard nut to crack, and she was as

unsmiling as a Methodist Magistrate faced with a bad case of
flashing in Chapel.

'What should I say? "Thank you very much, Guthrie, for
messing about with a floosie"?'

'And on that charge I shall be able to demonstrate that Guthrie
Featherstone, Q.C., M.P., is entirely innocent,' I assured the
Court.

'Innocent!' The voice of Marigold Featherstone was the voice
of scorn.

'Oh yes. All men are innocent until they're proven guilty.' I
thought I'd better remind her of the proud principle of British
justice.

'Well, he is "proven guilty", as you call it, by the evidence of
my own eyes. And of Tom's eyes.'

You see what she was like? She was of the stuff of which
Judge Bullingham was made, with his talent for taking every
possible point against the defence.

I came in from another angle and said quietly, 'Mrs Featherstone. When is your wedding anniversary?'

'Next month. The twenty-first. Guthrie always forgets it.'

'Well, this year he didn't forget it. He remembered it, most
devotedly. Tell me, Mrs Featherstone, do you like "Ma Tendresse" perfume?'

I could see the question had surprised her, but she answered
impatiently, 'I have absolutely no idea. I have never tried it.'

'Then it will be a new experience. Your husband hopes you'll
find it enjoyable,' I told her quietly.

'What on earth do you mean?'

'He went into Harrods to buy you a large bottle of "Ma
Tendresse" as a present for your wedding day.'

The Court thought this over, appeared to reflect, but then
said, with a first appearance of doubt, 'But Tom saw him in the
restaurant . . .'

'Purely circumstantial evidence,' I assured her hastily. 'On
which so many people have been wrongly convicted.'

'You're not suggesting Tom was mistaken?' The Court was
still hostile, although perhaps less determined.

'Not in what he saw,' I said reasonably, 'but in the *inter-*

pretation to be placed upon it. You see, Guthrie had just slipped into the Trattoria ... and he happened to see a lady, a member of the Bar as a matter of fact, waiting for a girl-friend.'

'A member of the Bar?' Obviously she hadn't even considered the possibility.

'Oh yes, Mrs Featherstone. A profession open to all sorts and conditions of men and women. He sat down to chat to her, about a case they were involved in, a long firm fraud.'

'Fraud indeed!' Marigold was her old scornful self.

'And then he left her.' I ignored the interruption. 'Her friend never turned up and she went shortly afterwards.'

'But they opened a parcel. A bottle of scent.' I could see that the Court was shaken.

'Of course! He wanted her opinion, as a woman rather than a lawyer, on his choice of a present for you.'

'Oh really? And why did he happen to slip into the Trattoria Gallactica?'

I allowed a long pause and then smiled and said softly, 'Can't you guess?'

'I certainly can't.'

It was time to play my last trump. If this didn't work, then nothing would. 'He went in to book a table, of course. It is there he intends to take you out for a slap-up spread, Mrs Featherstone, with champagne laid on regardless, to celebrate a decade of happy marriage. On the twenty-first of next month!'

After the hard hour with Mrs Featherstone, I went to meet Guthrie, by arrangement, in Pommeroy's Wine Bar where he was waiting for me with considerable anxiety. In fact he could hardly bring himself to ask, 'Rumpole! How did it go?'

'I think I can say, Featherstone, that it was touch and go until my final speech,' I told him, after I had settled down and forced him to buy a bottle of the Pichon Longueville, Pommeroy's best and most costly wine.

'What did you say?'

'I reminded the Court that she enjoyed considerable status as your wife. In the course of time she would almost certainly become Lady Marigold, when you are elevated to the High Court Bench. I think that tipped the scales.'

'And the result was?' Featherstone was looking at me in a hunted fashion. I took a long gulp and reassured the poor blighter.

'I would say, a conditional discharge. "Tell Guthrie I'll forget the divorce," she said, "if he puts his back into being made a judge."'

'Oh, thank God! I say, that's splendid, Rumpole! Of course I owe it to Marigold to get my bottom on the High Court Bench eventually.'

'I think you do.' I regarded him judicially and said, 'I think you've got off extremely lightly, I must say.'

'Well, yes.' At least he admitted it.

'At the mere cost of a bottle of French pong, slap-up do at the Eyetie restaurant, and a dozen of the Pichon Longueville.'

'A dozen?'

'Or should we say two dozen? Twenty-four is a good round number and the advocate, as you always say, my old darling, is worthy of his hire. Oh, by the way, Featherstone. I hear you've been taken in to prosecute Bertie Timson on a quite ridiculous charge of being in possession of house-breaking implements by night, and complicity in the Steadfast Savings Bank robbery. You will remember, won't you, that there may always be an innocent explanation, however unlikely it may sound? Oh, and Guthrie...'

'Yes, Horace?' Featherstone sounded more friendly than at any time since my return.

'About my leaving Chambers . . .'

'Well, that's not necessary, of course. Not,' he added, still a little hopefully, 'until you *really* want to retire.'

I was delighted that I had got the old fathead to see reason at last. 'I mean,' I said, 'I must be here in case you need defending again. I seem to have got the ear of Mrs Marigold Featherstone.'

'Oh, you have, Horace, indeed you have! And I'm most grateful for it.'

I don't know if Guthrie bore my words in mind, but he

prosecuted Bertie Timson like a gentleman. In due course I got my two dozen of Pommeroy's very best and Bertie got acquitted, for which he said a profound and heartfelt *merci beaucoup*. I approached the opening of the Notting Hill Gate Murder at the Old Bailey, therefore, well lubricated with the best stuff, and with a great deal of my early confidence restored.

Chapter Sixteen

By and large I was satisfied with my preparations for my leading role in the case of R *v.* Simpson. I had played my cards pretty close to my chest and I hadn't taken my learned junior, Ken Cracknell, into my confidence about the nature of the defence. I didn't want him dousing my tender schemes in cold water just when they had started to take root, and I wanted to try my ideas out in cross-examination before I paraded them before anyone. When Ken Cracknell asked me about our strategy, I would utter such Sibylline phrases as 'I propose to play it largely by ear', or 'Sufficient unto the day, my dear fellow', or 'Let's just deny everything and then see where we go from there'. I had no real time to wonder why, when I made these hopeless and clearly unprepared pronouncements, my junior counsel looked far from displeased, but instead gave me a small smile of satisfaction.

One front on which I was making absolutely no progress whatever was in my relations with my client. When I went to see Percival Simpson, as I did on a number of occasions, the last one being the afternoon before the trial started, he appeared increasingly lethargic and detached from the reality which faced him.

'Look, Duchess,' I pronounced on that final afternoon, 'you may not give a toss about the outcome of this case, but it's exceedingly important to me. I've come out of my alleged retirement to do this murder, and my whole future, such as it is, depends on it. It may be a matter of complete indifference to you, but I desperately want to win.'

'You want to win?' Simpson looked at me; something seemed to amuse him. 'You want to win my case?'

'That, Duchess, is the general idea. That's why I've been calling on you religiously over the last few months.'

'Win?' He laughed a little contemptuously.

'That's the ticket.'

'You might as well hope to stop the sun rising tomorrow, or put an end to the tides.'

'What *do* you mean? There's no law of nature which says you have to be found guilty.'

'Don't you think there is?'

'When,' I asked him directly for the umpteenth time, 'are you going to tell me exactly what happened when you went for your holiday in Florida?'

'There's absolutely no point in your asking me questions like that.' Simpson shook his head firmly. 'No point whatsoever.'

'But if I don't ask you questions, how do you expect me to win, Duchess?'

'I don't expect you to win. It's only you who keeps talking about winning.'

Discouraging, I'm sure you'll agree. But in spite of the distinct lack of cooperation from the client, I was in a high and even optimistic frame of mind when Henry said, and I thought I detected a new note of respect in his voice, 'Your murder's in tomorrow, Mr Rumpole. You've got a clean start at 10.30. Court Number Two down the Old Bailey.'

Court Number Two wasn't Court Number One. It was not the absolute centre, not quite the *crème de la crème* of Old Bailey Courts. The great classic murders had taken place in Court Number One. But Number Two was a large and impressive arena, one of the Courts in the old block which opened onto the fine marble-tiled hall with its Edwardian civic murals and statues of judges, away from the liverish-looking pale woodwork and concealed lighting of the new Courts. Number Two Court was home.

As, of course, were all the places I visited that morning when I went down to the Old Bailey to do my poor best, in so far as he would allow me, for the accursed Percival Simpson.

'Nor for my peace will I go far,
As wanderers do, that still do roam;
But make my strengths, such as they are,
Here in my bosom, and at home.'

It was ridiculous, but home was walking down to Ludgate
Circus in the rain; home was the admirable scrambled eggs produced by the Italian cook in Rex's Café, eaten among the Fleet
Street printers who had been up all night, and the early working
officers in charge of the case, and a couple of nervous villains,
and some over-eager jurors. Home was the Old Bailey entrance,
with the friends and relations of various villains reading the list
of cases to be tried; home was being greeted by the large officers
inside the swing doors; home was going up to the robing room
and climbing into the fancy dress. In all this excitement, and
drunk with nostalgia, I failed to ask my learned junior, Kenneth
Cracknell, Esq., who appeared wearing a lightish-grey suit under
his gown (no doubt in some radical protest against the regulation
subfusc) with dark hair flowing in some profusion from under
his wig, who was the learned Judge whom Fate had selected to
preside over the trial of the unhappy Revenue official.

When he told me, I felt a sinking stomach and rising nausea.
My hands started to sweat and I was breathing with difficulty.
Home, I discovered with something akin to horror, was his
Honour Judge Bullingham.

This may need a word of explanation, in case it should seem
to the instructed reader that the powers that be, at the Lord
Chancellor's office, had taken complete leave of their senses and
elevated the crazy Bull to the status of High Court or 'Red'
Judges who usually try murders. No such promotion would
have been known to history since the day when the late Emperor
Caligula made his horse a Consul; and Bullingham remained, at
the height of his appalling career, a mere Old Bailey Judge.
However, he was an Old Bailey Judge of such seniority that he
had been empowered to try murders. Of the two High Court
Judges down at the Old Bailey that morning, one was engaged
in trying a well-known politician for forgery, and the other was
doing something mysteriously connected with the three or four
Official Secrets still left to us.

So I drew Judge Bullingham for the eleventh time of asking, and I had the horrible certainty that the old enemy would organize an eleventh crushing defeat, which would make this much sought-after murder the absolute end of the line for Rumpole. If the gods really wish to destroy a person, I remembered, they grant his foolish requests. Had my feverish pursuit of the brief in R. *v*. Simpson been no more than a final act of legal suicide? Filled with such unworthy fears, I kept my eyes to the ground as we all stood and the Bull charged into Court.

But then I remembered that I was an advocate not without experience, that I was doing an important murder that was bound to find its way into the evening papers and would, in all probability, make the *News of the World*, and that the case would not be tried by judge alone, but by a jury of good men, and women and teenagers and true who were even then filing into their box in answer to their names. So I took in several deep breaths and accepted, on behalf of defence counsel, the hard luck of the draw. I force myself to raise my head and look Judge Bullingham in the eye.

Such time as had elapsed since our last encounter had not improved the old devil, and such changes as had taken place might generally be said to have been for the worse. The wig that sat askew his shining bald head seemed even greyer, his yellowing collar and bands looked more grubby and his nose appeared a deeper shade of purple. His eyes had become distinctly more bloodshot, and the lids hung heavily upon them so that they seemed in constant danger of closing, even during the prosecution case when he did his best to appear awake. His teeth, when he opened his mouth to lick the end of his pencil, seemed to be more yellow, and I wondered at what precise moment of the proceedings he would choose to pick his nose, or explore, with an extended little finger, his inner ear.

Our eyes met and he registered, I was pleased to see, the same surprise and dismay that I had felt when I realized that it had been decreed that we should, yet again, work together. Apparently he told his clerk that he thought I'd been put out to grass. He should have known that you can't get rid of Rumpole so easily.

'Mister Rumpole.' The growl came, as usual, somewhere from the depths of the Bull. 'Do *you* appear for the defence?'

When I realized quite clearly that the Judge was just as displeased to see me as I was to be before him, my fear evaporated. I smiled charmingly and gave an inscrutable bow in which I hoped he might have been aware of some small element of mockery.

'Yes, my Lord. I have the honour to represent Mr Percival Simpson. And may I take this opportunity of saying what a pleasure it is to be appearing before your Lordship once again.'

At which the Bull frowned and grunted unhappily. 'Very well,' he said. 'Let's get on with it. Mr Colefax?'

'If your Lordship pleases.' Moreton Colefax, Q.C., leading counsel for the Crown, was a handsome, ex-Guards officer, ex-Eton and New College, member of White's and the Beefsteak Club and a Bencher of his Inn. He was a decent enough prosecutor according to his lights, and I gave him the credit of finding the judicial antics of the Bull, although all meant to assist the prosecution, vulgar and distasteful. I had known Colefax when he was in rompers, doing 'dangerous drivings' in a superior sort of way round the Thames Magistrates Court. He was a man I believed to be totally ignorant on the subject of blood.

'The defence is represented,' Colefax started quietly, 'by my learned friends Mr Horace Rumpole and Mr Kenneth Cracknell. Members of the jury, this case concerns the knifing of a perfectly respectable citizen, a member of a well-known family, late one evening last January in the Notting Hill Gate underground station. It's a somewhat squalid story.'

Oh dear. Poor old Colefax sounded as though the Notting Hill Gate Murder was something he wouldn't wish to touch with a pair of silver sugar-tongs.

'Squalid motives have been suggested for this killing,' Colefax said with some contempt, and I knew that he was referring to the 'Guardsman's Defence' suggested by Ken Cracknell in his cross-examination in the Magistrates Court, which never had a hope. 'Those suggested motives may well be that there was some kind of sexual, or homosexual, reason for this crime. Members of the jury, you will hear that the Honourable

Roderick, known as Rory, Canter was a perfectly normal young man sexually, who had as his fiancée a young lady with good family connections and who was himself a young man of strong religious views.'

I smiled at this and made my first note. Colefax had called the deceased 'religious' and there, I thought, the old darling might be on to something.

My nerves were quite settled before I started to cross-examine the Crown's first witness, Mr Byron MacDonald, the guard of the train that had been standing at the platform of Notting Hill Gate station when the Hon. Rory Canter came down the stairs. His evidence, as elicited in its full details by Moreton Colefax, was in no way helpful to the defence. For a start he made it clear that Canter came down to the platform first and was followed by Simpson, who clearly appeared to be the pursuer, whereas Canter was obviously the victim. He saw, he said, Simpson come down, peer about him and then move towards Canter; they were then locked in the struggle which he saw as his train moved away – a chain of events which, there was no possibility of dispute, ended shortly afterwards with the death of Canter.

Now I rose to question the tall Jamaican guard who stood in the witness box in his London Transport uniform. He had been an excellent witness, and I started with the soft touch, the approach courteous and the questions devious.

'Mr MacDonald,' I began. 'You say you saw the deceased, Mr Canter, come on to the platform first?'

'Yes, Mr Rumpole. He said that,' the Judge growled from his notebook.

'And you saw my client, Mr Simpson, come down afterwards?' I went on, ignoring the Bull for the moment.

'Following him, Rumpole. Your client was clearly the pursuer. Going after his victim.'

'No, my Lord. He didn't say "following".' I sounded patient, as if I only wanted to help the Bull, and I picked up the notebook in which my junior had been writing down the evidence. 'I have my learned friend Mr Cracknell's note. The witness said, "He came down afterwards." '

'Well, if you think it makes the slightest difference . . .' The
Bull snorted and practically winked at the jury as though to say,
'We don't, do we, ladies and gentlemen? We're far too bright to
split hairs with the defending barrister.'

'The difference it makes will become apparent by the end of
this case. Even to your Lordship.' I must say I was starting to
lose my patience with the Bull. He gave a warning growl of 'Mr
Rumpole', but I moved rapidly on to the next question before he
could give voice to his protest.

'For all you knew the Honourable Rory Canter may have
been going down the tube station to *look* for Mr Simpson?'

'I don't know anything about the two gentlemen,' said Mr
MacDonald.

'Exactly!' I did my best to sound satisfied with his answer.
'Or if Canter knew that Mr Simpson was about to make that
journey, he may have deliberately got to the platform first, to lie
in wait for him?'

'That hardly sounds likely, though, does it, Mr MacDonald?'
The Judge, falling into his well-loved role as counsel for the
prosecution, had put the question.

'My Lord, the witness has already said he didn't know anything about the gentlemen,' I reminded him.

'Then it was quite pointless putting the question, wasn't it,
Mr Rumpole?' I got a grin from the yellow teeth, as did the jury.

'I put the question, my Lord, in order that the jury may be
aware of all the possibilities.' I did my best to remain polite.

'All the possibilities, Mr Rumpole? However remote?' The
jury got another sympathetic smile; the Bull was clearly sorry
that they were being troubled by the idiot Rumpole.

'My Lord, indeed yes . . .'

'It's hardly likely, is it, that a man would go down to a station
platform to wait for his murderer. Or go out looking for the
man who's going to attack him?'

'My Lord, I should say that frequently happens.' After all, I
had come half way round the world to find Judge Bullingham.

'Very well. Let's get on with it.' The Judge had decided that
there was nothing to be gained for the moment from bandying
words with Rumpole.

'But you did see the deceased, Canter, waiting in an alcove on the station?' I resumed my dialogue with the witness.

'Yes. He was just standing there,' Mr Byron MacDonald agreed.

'He made no attempt to get on the train?'

'He didn't get on it. No, sir.'

'Although the doors were open, and the train was waiting for him?'

'Yes, it was.'

'So he was clearly waiting for something else.'

'Mr Rumpole. How can the witness tell that?' The Judge came back into the arena.

'He stood there, waiting to accost my client, Mr Simpson, didn't he?' I put the question to the witness, but the Bull growled back.

'I supposed by "accost" you mean "sex", Mr Rumpole.'

'Your Lordship mustn't jump to conclusions, however sensational,' I said politely, although I knew from past experience that the Bull had a resolutely filthy mind.

'Oh, really? I thought we were to be treated to the "Guardsman's Defence".' Bullingham smiled at Colefax this time, with overacted cynicism.

'Your Lordship has the better of me. Is that a legal or a military expression?' I asked innocently, and played straight into the Judge's hands.

'You should know, Mr Rumpole. I've no doubt you've made use of it in a number of cases, when you were practising regularly in this Court.'

When I was practising regularly? What did the old darling think I was doing now? Playing tiddly-winks? I hoped for a normal and uninterrupted cross-examination and turned again to the witness. 'Mr MacDonald, you did see Mr Canter move forward and speak to Mr Simpson, my client?'

'I think I did see that, yes.'

That was something, and at least the Bull was quiet. I had another fact to establish.

'And tell me, Mr MacDonald. How long would it be before the next train arrived?'

'I think about five minutes.'

'My last question. You never saw my client produce any sort of a knife?'

'No.'

'He never saw any knives at all, because his train had left the station!' Bullingham reminded the jury triumphantly.

And then, as I sat down with my work on Mr Byron Mac-Donald completed, the judge sighed with relief and asked Moreton Colefax the name of his next witness.

'Revere, my Lord. Miss Dianna Revere.'

If any members of the jury had found their attention wandering during my cross-examination of Byron MacDonald, they were clearly riveted by Miss Dianna 'Smokey' Revere. She came into the witness box wearing tight black leather with her orange hair stuck out like the quills of a hedgehog, her eyes were shadowed black and her lipstick and fingernails a shade of mauve. She was chewing gum and as she walked she rattled, from the chains she wore round her neck, like a spectre. The Bull looked at her with his eyes bulging, as though years of whisky had finally destroyed the last of his brain cells and he was gently hallucinating.

'Are you Miss Dianna Revere?' Moreton Colefax seemed to have some difficulty in bringing himself to speak to her. She was, in fact, a beautiful although strangely dressed eighteen-year-old girl, who would never have crossed the path of the prosecution Q.C. except in a courtroom.

'They calls me Smokey.' Miss Revere was actually smiling at the Bull, but he looked severely shaken and said, 'Well, never mind about that. Let's get on with it.'

'Miss Revere, were you going down Notting Hill Gate underground station on the night of Thursday, March the 13th?'

'Yeah. With my friends. We were on our way to see the "Public Execution" at Watford.'

'Do they still have those at Watford?' the Bull asked, and the jury laughed obediently.

'No. The "Public Execution". It's a group, innit? Great sound,' Dianna explained patiently, as though to a child.

'Did you notice anything on the platform?'

'Yeah, I saw the two geezers.'

Moreton Colefax, who had noticed that Smokey's evidence seemed to be fighting its way past some impediment, said, 'Miss Revere. Are you eating something?'

'Sorry, my Lord.' Smokey smiled politely, removed her chewing gum with a slender finger and stuck it under the ledge of the witness box.

'What were the two men doing?'

'Well. One was sat on the seat. The other, him what had the bag from the take-away . . .'

'Which one had the bag from the Delectable Drumstick chicken shop?'

'My Lord, there's no dispute that that was my client, Mr Simpson,' I said, I thought helpfully.

'No, Mr Rumpole! I imagine there can be no possible dispute about that.' The Bull growled; he was a person who was incapable of simple gratitude.

'Yes, Miss Revere. We can take it that the man with the bag from the chicken shop was Mr Simpson. What happened then?' Moreton Colefax asked.

'Well, we all got into the train. The boys was kicking a tin and they kicked it into the carriage. We saw the geezer with the carrier bag get in the carriage too.'

'You saw Simpson?'

'He sat down the other end. On his own, like.'

'But it was the same carriage?'

'Yes.'

'Miss Revere. Let me ask you this.' An important question was coming, and Moreton Colefax brought himself to smile at the ornate girl in the witness box. 'Did you notice the man on the seat as your train was pulling out of the station?'

'I saw him, yes. On the platform. I was looking out through the glass of the door, I reckon it was. And I saw him topple over.'

'He toppled over?' Colefax repeated, and the jury were listening interestedly.

'Sort of slid sideways, like. Went all limp and boneless.'

'Why did you think that was?' the Bull asked her.

'I thought maybe he was pissed, or had a bit of the needle. You get a lot of those, round Notting Hill tube.'

'You mean he was drunk?' Moreton Colefax translated.

'How did you guess?' Miss Revere said, and the usher called 'Silence!' before the jury could laugh.

'Did you happen to notice Mr Simpson sitting at the end of your carriage?'

'I just remember him. He was looking in his plastic bag, like. And then I looked away and I think he dropped something into it. I don't know what it was. I heard it drop in. Something heavy, and metal, I think.'

'What did he do then?'

'He closed his eyes and leant back. It looked like he wanted to go to sleep.'

The strange-looking girl and her dramatic evidence had a powerful effect on the jury. I rose to try and neutralize the damage.

'Miss Revere. When you got down to the platform, a train was just coming in?'

'Yes.'

'So that it must have been about five minutes after the previous train left.'

'I don't know about that.'

'How *can* she know?' the Bull grumbled.

'Very well. Miss Revere, I don't suppose you noticed my client particularly at this time?'

'Not particularly, no.'

'So you can't be certain about what you saw him do.'

'I heard about the murder next day. It came on the telly. Then I remembered what I'd seen.'

'You say you saw my client close his eyes, as though he were tired.'

'He looked like it. Yes.'

'You may know that it's a common reaction to be exhausted after you've made a violent attack?' Bullingham asked Smokey. He was absolutely ruthless.

'I suppose so.' Smokey looked suddenly bored, anxious to end her time in the witness box. I had no reason to keep her there except to ask, 'And you may also know that people are frequently exhausted and in a state of violent shock after they've *been* attacked?'

'Yeah. I think so.'

'And you didn't see him writing at all?' I asked very loudly and before the Bull could get a word in edgeways. 'You didn't see my client writing on any sort of scrap of paper?'

'No, I didn't.'

'Thank you, Miss Revere,' I said, and sat down and stared with mysterious triumph at the jury.

After the excitement provided by Dianna Smokey Revere, there came a dullish afternoon of agreed evidence, police photographers, map-drawers, fingerprint experts, ambulance men and the like, and after Court Ken Cracknell met Miss Trant for a drink in Pommeroy's and a discussion of Rumpole's first day on the murder.

'The Judge is firing all his guns at the defence, and the prosecution witnesses are lethal,' Ken told Phillida, and she smiled and said, 'Then Rumpole must be in his element.'

'I'm not so sure. He was looking a bit grey round the edges at the end of the day.'

'No, he's enjoying it,' Miss Trant was certain, and on the whole she was right. 'As for you, Ken' – she looked at her radical admirer with soft-eyed devotion and put her hand on his across their plonk-stained table at Pommeroy's – 'you're angelic to have wangled this brief for Rumpole. It's just what he needs.'

'I hope so,' Ken said and smiled a little. 'I very much hope it'll do the trick.'

'Claude's going away to stay with his parents next week. He's taking the baby. I can't get away with them. It's this long robbery I'm in.'

'What a pity.' Ken was smiling.

'Yes, isn't it. We might have that hamburger you're always on about.'

'And you might see where I live. It's actually perfectly comfortable.'

'I'm sure,' said Miss Trant and her eyes were, I believe, full of promise. 'I'm absolutely sure it is.'

And much later I was in my shirt sleeves working out a way to cross-examine Detective Inspector Wargrave, the officer in charge of the case, and Hilda was knitting some kind of bala-clava helmet or other comfort for the new generation of Rumpoles, when she suddenly asked me, most unusually, how I had got on at Court.

'Bloody badly,' I told her frankly. 'The client won't talk to me and the Bull's madder than ever. I wonder what I'd get, for doing a judge grievous bodily harm?'

Hilda clicked her tongue, worked with her knitting needles and then said, 'That's what you came back to, Rumpole!'

'Don't tell me.'

'I will tell you. I know now. It wasn't even another woman! You came back because you care more for Judge Bullingham than you do for me.' She looked at me in an accusing manner, and I smiled and answered, as I thought, reasonably.

'If you think that, Hilda, wouldn't you really be happier back on the other side of the Atlantic?'

She looked at me in silence for a while, and then she said enigmatically, 'I'm really not sure, Rumpole. But I shall have to think about it.'

I looked at her then, with a sort of vague stirring of hope that perhaps in the not too distant future my freedom would return.

Chapter Seventeen

The first witness the next morning was the Honourable Rory Canter's elder brother, Lord Freith. He was a man in his early forties, quite at his ease in the witness box, and he and Moreton Colefax talked to each other as if they were members of the same club, which indeed they were. The learned judge listened obsequiously, as though he were the slightly comic butler, and the jury and defence counsel were also allowed to overhear.

'Lord Freith,' Moreton Colefax allowed himself to touch an unpleasant subject, 'had your younger brother, to your knowledge, any homosexual tendencies?'

'I can honestly say, my Lord,' Lord Freith included the Bull in the chat, in a truly democratic manner, 'that he had absolutely none.'

'Absolutely none.' Bullingham wrote the words down obediently.

'I think he was of a serious, indeed a religious disposition.'

'He was extremely religious. And, I'm sure, sincerely so.'

'Your brother Roderick, I think,' Colefax continued, 'had a fiancée and was engaged to be married?'

'Oh yes. They'd both dined with me that night at my club. There was absolutely none of the Oscar Wildes about Rory.'

'Thank you, Lord Freith.' Colefax sat down gracefully, with every sign of satisfaction.

I got a dirty look from the judge. 'I suppose you've got some questions Mr Rumpole?' he said.

'Just a few. Lord Freith,' I said, rising to my feet, 'your club is where?'

'In St James's.'

'And after dinner did Rory drive his fiancée home?'

'To her flat in Chelsea,' Lord Freith agreed.

'And *he* lived in Eaton Square?'

'Eaton Place, actually.'

'Another address in south-west London?'

'Yes . . .' Lord Freith frowned as if wondering where these questions were leading.

'Have you any idea what he was doing north-west? In Notting Hill Gate?'

'No. As a matter of fact,' Lord Freith agreed, 'I've wondered about that.'

'So have I. So may the jury. It was nowhere near his route, was it, from St James's to Chelsea?'

'No,' Lord Freith admitted.

'Or from Chelsea to Eaton Place?'

'No . . .'

Things were going too well for the Bull not to intervene. Accordingly he bared his teeth and said menacingly, 'Mr Rumpole. If you're suggesting that this gentleman's brother went to Notting Hill Gate for immoral purposes, I think you should put it fair and square.'

I decided to put an instant stop to this line of judicial offence and I decided to say, 'My Lord, although I'm well aware that a dirty mind is a perpetual feast, I'm making absolutely no such suggestion.'

It was a minor hit. There was laughter in Court, in which Judge Bullingham did not join. He merely grumbled, 'I'm glad to hear it,' being, in fact, quite clearly disappointed.

I turned to Lord Freith and another topic. 'You've told us that your late brother was of a sincerely religious disposition.'

'He's told us that,' the Bull grumbled and only just forgot to add, 'Let's get on with it.'

'And you didn't entirely approve of his religious views, did you, Lord Freith?'

'I didn't approve of all he did, no,' the witness answered carefully.

'Had he made over his farm in Hampshire, by way of a gift, to the particular religious sect he favoured?'

Lord Freith hesitated and then answered frankly, 'He had. He was merely staying on as a manager.'

'Had he also given them a great deal of money?'

'I believe he had.'

'All the money he inherited from your father?'

'I think most of it.'

'And was his fiancée of the same religious persuasion?'

'Yes. They'd met when Rory was in Florida, playing polo. I believe she converted him.'

'So he gave all he had to the poor?'

'We have pretty good authority for *that*, Mr Rumpole.' Bullingham, that great man of religion, was looking wisely at the jury, and some of them even did me the disservice of nodding solemnly and assuming serious and devout expressions.

When I asked my next rude question it was a bit like belching in church. 'Except that you thought he'd given all he had to the rich. You believed it was an extremely rich organization, didn't you, Lord Freith?'

To my great relief the witness seemed to agree with me. 'I thought perhaps they were exploiting Rory,' he said, choosing his words with care.

At the moment when it appeared that I was winning the witness over to my still obscure purposes, Moreton Colefax rose to make a gentlemanly interruption. 'Perhaps my learned friend would be good enough to tell us the name of this alleged organization . . .'

'Oh, doesn't my learned friend know it?' I carefully simulated amazement. 'The name is to be found on that blood-stained scrap of paper, the prosecution's Exhibit One.' I held out my hand and the usher got it for me. 'Thank you, usher. It reads "Sunlight Children of Sun". They call themselves "The Children of Sun", don't they, Lord Freith?'

We had the jury's undoubted interest as he answered, 'I believe that's what they're called.'

'And they offer "Blood to Children of Dark".'

'We've been told that the document was written by your client in the deceased's blood, Mr Rumpole.' Bullingham was beginning to feel out of his depth and so, as usual, he attacked the defence.

'My Lord, there hasn't been a scrap of evidence about it,' I told him, feeling the jury watching me closely.

'Mr Moreton Colefax has told us that he's calling Professor Ackerman. No one knows more about blood stains than Professor Andrew Ackerman.' Bullingham gave the jury a glowing trailer for a prosecution witness.

'I think your Lordship may find that somebody does,' I said, with a certain amount of quiet confidence.

'That would surprise me, Mr Rumpole.'

'Life in your Lordship's Court is full of surprises. I suppose that's why some of us find it so enormously enjoyable.'

Some of the jury appeared to enjoy this, so Bullingham resumed his impatient growl. 'Have you got any more questions for Lord Freith? This must be a painful experience for him.'

It wasn't exactly a Sunday School treat for my client either, I thought. And then I asked the usher for Exhibit Two. I was handed, carefully labelled and wrapped in plastic, the long commando-type sheath knife that had been found inside Simpson's bag of fried chicken. I unwrapped it and examined it carefully in full view of the jury. Then, after a pause long enough to create a suitable tension and feeling of expectancy, I turned to the witness.

'Lord Freith. Your brother went to Sandhurst, I think?'

'Yes, he did.'

'And spent some five years in the army?'

'Yes. Until my father died and left him the farm.'

Lord Freith received the knife from the usher, gave it a cursory glance and put it down on the front of the witness box.

'Do you know that is a regulation army knife, of the sort issued to officers and men undergoing special commando training?'

'I didn't know. But I accept that from you, of course.' Lord Freith was never less than courteous.

'And did your brother, the Honourable Rory Canter, tell you that he had enjoyed such training during his time in the army?'

There was a long pause before the elder brother answered, as casually as possible, 'I believe he told me something of the sort. Yes.'

'Thank you, Lord Freith.' I sat down and glanced at the jury, and I could tell that I hadn't lost their interest.

The learned Judge smiled at Lord Freith with the deepest respect. 'Thank you, Lord Freith. Your ordeal is over,' he said.

The witness left the box, but our ordeal was continuing.

'What are you up to exactly?' Ken Cracknell whispered to his learned leader as we were waiting for the next witness to come into the box. I didn't think he looked particularly elated by my cross-examination of Lord Freith, which, on the whole, I would have marked at least eight out of a possible ten.

'Cracknell, perchance you wonder at our show,' I whispered back at him. 'Then wonder on, till truth makes all things plain. Who's the next witness?'

'D.I. Wargrave. The officer in charge of the case. At least you won't be discussing religion with him.' But there, as a matter of fact, he was mistaken.

After the Detective Inspector had read out, in a monotonous tone of voice and from his notebook, his account of the police interview with Simpson, I rose to cross-examine.

'Mr Wargrave, you say that my client told you that he was guilty?'

'That's what I've got down in my notebook.'

'So, because you've got it down in your notebook, it has the authority of Holy Writ?'

'Mr Rumpole!' As usual I got the warning growl from the Bench.

'I suggest he never used the word "guilty" at all. He said he had "sinned".'

'Doesn't it come to exactly the same thing?' the Judge asked, and I decided it was time to give him a little basic theology.

'Hardly, my Lord. Every clergyman at morning prayers says, "I acknowledge my transgressions and my sin is before me." That can hardly be taken as an admission of stabbing people down the underground.' I picked up the commando knife and weighed it in my hand. 'Officer, this knife, Exhibit Two, would seem to be the fatal weapon.'

'It would seem so, sir.'

'And yet my client possessed a knife, a curved oriental dagger, which you found on his dressing-table.'

'I did, yes.'

'The jury can see that in the police photograph of my client's room, next to the blood-stained letter ... photograph number four in your bundle, members of the jury ...' The twelve old darlings leafed through their bundles of photographs and found the place. 'We know there were no blood stains on that dagger.'

'I believe not,' the Detective conceded.

'So it comes to this, does it? My client's knife had not been used, but what had been used was a commando knife of the sort that Mr Canter might have had?'

'*Might* have had. Yes.' D.I. Wargrave sounded dubious as ever.

'And there were two sets of fingerprints on the handle of *that* knife, Exhibit Two ... somewhat blurred. The fingerprints of my client and those of the deceased gentleman.'

'That is so. Yes.'

'And my client's hands were cut and his clothing cut in some places?'

'Yes, indeed.'

'So what does that indicate to you, Inspector?'

'I suppose it might indicate some sort of struggle for the possession of the knife,' Bullingham said, unable to sit quietly and listen to the evidence. The learned Judge had played straight into my hands.

'If your Lordship pleases!' I gave him a low bow in which there was only the faintest touch of mockery. 'Oh, I am extremely grateful to your Lordship. Your Lordship is always the first to appreciate ... points in favour of the defence.'

For a moment Bullingham was speechless, but then he looked at the clock and was saved by it. 'We'll break off now. Shall we say until five past two, members of the jury?' And he added, in a somewhat desperate bid for their favour, 'It may come as a little relief to you, in your consideration of this rather *sordid* case, to know that England are now eighty-five for two in the Test at Melbourne.'

The Judge smiled at them and withdrew. It was a somewhat desperate gambit on his part, and certainly not cricket.

*

During the luncheon adjournment I took my junior and instructing solicitor down to the cells. There we found the comforting smell of cooking and some screws sitting down to piled plates and great mugs of tea. Our client Simpson came into the little interview room and sat down without a greeting. Young Cracknell, when I looked at him, seemed equally gloomy.

'What's the matter with you all? I get the impression we're doing rather well.' I tried to cheer them up. 'I don't hear anyone say, "The Rumpole hand has lost none of its cunning." I don't hear that exactly.'

'We've still got the letter,' Ken Cracknell sighed. 'You don't write a letter in your victim's blood, not unless it's a deliberate murder. That's what the jury's going to think.'

There was a faint voice: Simpson seemed to be talking to himself. 'The Master is not bound by the laws of man and nature. His is the power of the miraculous.' He then turned to me and said, 'That's what we can't fight. It's no use fighting.'

'You're not going to help me, are you, Duchess? Not until you lose your faith in miracles. Well, that's about to happen,' I told him; it was no use sharing my own doubts and uncertainties with him.

Chapter Eighteen

Professor Andrew Ackerman, that most distinguished pathologist, had been associated with death in its various forms for
so long that he seemed to be ageless. He was a tall, bald man
whose skin had a sort of mortuary pallor and whose voice was
sepulchral and full of respect. He wore small, round, gold-
rimmed spectacles and he gave his evidence impeccably. His
reputation in the Courts was such that he was treated as infallible
by judges and, as the natural successor to the late Sir Bernard
Spilsbury, Ackerman's word on a blood stain, or a bruise, or a
mark of strangulation, was accepted as Holy Writ down the
Bailey. He had only the faintest trace of a Scottish accent from
his distant Edinburgh upbringing and he was in fact, when away
from the courtroom or the morgue, a man of great kindness and
quiet humour who spent his holidays bird-watching and his
evenings listening to Baroque music or re-reading Jane Austen.

'Professor Ackerman. Have you ever tried to write a message
of this sort in blood?'

'For the purposes of this case I did so. It is quite possible, yes.'
The Professor was nothing if not thorough.

'Blood clots in two or three minutes, does it not?' I asked
him.

'Yes, but there would have been continued bleeding from the
deceased in this case.'

'So Mr Simpson would have had to have written this while he
was with the deceased. He couldn't have taken blood home with
him, because it would have clotted?'

'That is so. Yes.'

'The evidence is that he was unobserved on the platform for
about five minutes between the arrival of two trains. He would

have had to write this message during that time, perhaps with the blood on the dagger?'

'It is possible.'

'Just possible, but an extremely strange thing to do?'

'The suggestion is, Mr Rumpole, that you have an extremely strange type of client.' I had left myself wide open to that sort of crack from the Bull.

My mouth was dry and my voice not altogether steady. I took a deep breath, a gulp of water and started a new and entirely friendly dialogue with Professor Ackerman, asking him the questions I had begun to think of, months before, in a Florida library.

'Professor Ackerman, we have known each other for a good many years.'

'Yes, Mr Rumpole, we have.' The mortuary man gave a faint smile.

'And have discussed a good many corpses.'

'Is this to be a time of private reminiscence, Mr Rumpole, or do you intend to cross-examine the Professor?' The Bull was feeling left out of this meeting of old friends. I ignored him.

'And of course the jury may not know as much as you on the subject of blood.' I intended to get down to basics. 'All our red corpuscles are the same.'

'They are. Yes,' Ackerman agreed.

'What varies are the agglutinogens which must fit in with the appropriate agglutinin like a lock fits its own key, and cause the red cells to clump together . . . like bunches of grapes?'

'Mr Rumpole. If you and the Professor understand . . .' The Bull was restive again. I looked him straight in the eye.

'The system can be made clear,' I said, 'even to the simple mind by saying that those varying types of locks can divide human blood into four groups called, for convenience, "O", "A", "B" and "AB".'

Unlike the Bull, the members of the jury were looking interested, and some of them were taking notes.

'That is exactly so,' Ackerman agreed.

'Class "O" blood is rather common and flows in the veins of

forty-five per cent of the population. It flowed in the veins of the Honourable Rory Canter.'

'The deceased was class "O". Yes.'

'Whereas my client, Mr Simpson, is of the forty-one to forty-three per cent whose blood is "A"?'

'He is "A" from the sample I took from him.' The Professor glanced down at his notes.

'And you came to the conclusion that the blood which wrote that letter was class "O" blood, and therefore likely to be Mr Canter's?'

The usher took the exhibit to the Professor, who looked at it again, turning it over with long, surprisingly delicate fingers. 'It responded to the test in that way, yes.'

'You took a minute particle of paper, treated it chemically to detect the antigens and examined it under a microscope?'

'Precisely.'

'Professor Ackerman. When did you think this letter had been written?'

'I assumed, as it was Mr Canter's blood, that it must have been shortly after the murder.'

I gave a small sigh of satisfaction. Ackerman had accepted the instructions given him and, for once, hadn't asked questions.

'But supposing it had been written months before! Suppose my client joined a somewhat dotty religious sect, a sect which required him to write an oath or motto in drops of his *own* blood?'

'But it wasn't his own blood group, Mr Rumpole.' Ackerman smiled patiently.

'But if it *had* been, and had been done months before, wouldn't the antigens have perhaps faded in their strength?'

It was the key question, and the professor considered it. His answer, when it came, was perfectly fair. 'I suppose they might. I hadn't considered that.'

'Consider it now, Professor. I beg of you! The various constituents of blood stains fade in time, don't they?'

'Yes, they do.' He picked up the paper again, with delicate fingers, and looked at it thoughtfully.

'And blood becomes more difficult to classify.'

'I would say, less easy.' Even this caution was good enough for me.

'Less easy! Thank you. But the constituents don't fade evenly, do they? Some factors may vanish before others.'

'It *is* possible.'

'You found my client's blood was "A". Canter's was "O". After that finding you didn't do more tests to break down the classification further?'

'No. The situation seemed perfectly simple.'

'Oh, Professor, let's keep it simple.' I couldn't resist saying, 'For the benefit of the learned Judge.' I went on before there could be any grumbling from the Bench. 'I feel sure the members of the jury will have my point already. Is it not possible that after my client had written this absurd message in his own blood, and kept it, the antigens became less accurately classifiable, and the blood on this paper then gave you an "O" result?'

There was a long pause, during which I hoped I could feel the mystery which surrounded Simpson's defence was beginning to clear. Professor Ackerman picked up the paper again, put it down, smoothed it out and then said, and the words were music to my ears, 'I think the theory you have advanced is a possible one.'

The Bull, of course, was looking disconcerted as he turned to Ackerman. 'Let me get this clear, Professor,' he said, and I hoped he was capable of it. 'Are you saying this letter may have been written by Simpson months before, for some sort of religious reason, in his own blood, and may have nothing to do with this murder?'

'I think now that *may* be so, my Lord.' Ackerman's careful answer was impressive.

'And you can't be sure that it was in fact written in the victim's blood?'

'In view of the possibility that Mr Rumpole has pointed out, no.'

It was then that I silently blessed the good Ackerman and wished him many long and happy years in the morgue.

'Yes, thank you, Professor,' the Bull said, tamed by the Professor's authority. 'I think I understand.'

Wonder of wonders. And I had to hand it to the dear old Bull, I think he did.

'No miracle!' I assured my client when we met in the cells at the end of the day, and he was half smiling when he said, 'No.'

'The universe has recovered its balance. There is a perfectly clear, scientific explanation.'

'I suppose so,' he conceded.

'They can't work miracles, Duchess! You've got nothing to be afraid of.'

'Haven't I?' He still sounded doubtful.

'You can tell the jury the truth now.' There was a long silence and then I pressed him again. 'Tell it! You've got to tell it for the sake of –'

'For *your* sake?' There was no mistake about it, he was smiling now.

I shook my head. 'For the sake of a lot of lonely people,' I told him, 'who go out looking for miracles.'

Chapter Nineteen

In a way, cross-examination is the easiest part of the defending barrister's job. You have the sword, the red cape to swing in the hope of exciting blind and intemperate anger, and, unless you slip on a pile of horse shit and get gored to death, you may hope to be in some sort of control of the situation. When you call your own client to give evidence in his own defence, however, the matter is entirely different. Out there in the witness box he is, for all practical purposes, beyond your help. You can't lead him, or put words into his mouth. For the first time in a trial he must tell his own story and in his own way, and all you can do is guide him towards the main points at issue and then leave him to sink or swim on his own. Calling your own client in a murder case is always an extremely dodgy and nerve-racking business: what made it more alarming in Simpson's case was that I really had no very clear idea of exactly what he was going to say.

After the formalities of getting his name and previous good character were over, I started where I first heard of the Notting Hill Gate Underground Murder, in the Sunshine State.

'Last summer I think you went on a holiday to Florida. Did you meet someone in the street handing out leaflets?'

Once he began to talk, Simpson was articulate, and the old dead look had left him. 'He seemed so clean and respectable. He was wearing a tie and a clean shirt. We started to talk. About loneliness and how to make friends. Oh, and then about all the meanness and cruelty in the world. He took me to meet *his* friends.'

'Where were they?'

'In a sort of farm. It was called the Sun Valley. They were all nice and . . . cheerful. They sang a lot, and they seemed to work

very hard. Later I met a man, he was dressed as a clergyman.
They called him the Master.'

'What did he tell you?'

'My Lord. How can this be relevant?' Moreton Colefax rose
to object, and, wonder of wonders, the Bull, impressed by the
quiet young clerk in the witness box, said, 'I think we must let
Mr Simpson tell his story.'

'What did he tell you?' I repeated the question gratefully.

'He told me I must work for him, in their accounts department. He said that when the Children of Sun took over the
government of the world, I should have some great post . . . in
world economics. I was going to be their Minister of Finance.'

'Did you believe him?'

'Yes, I'm afraid I did.' Simpson smiled, a small apology for a
huge presumption.

'Did you start to work on the books?'

'Almost at once.'

'What did you find?'

'There were hopeless discrepancies.' Simpson looked pained.
'A great deal of money was coming in: the "friends and brothers"
gave all their worldly goods. None of this money was accounted
for. I'm afraid I came to the conclusion that the whole organization of the Children of Sun was a gigantic swindle.'

'Did you tell anyone that?'

'We weren't allowed close friends. They told us that would
destroy our loyalty to the group,' Simpson explained. 'But there
was a young American man I worked with. I told him one night.
He said he'd have to go to the Master and denounce me as a
traitor. That's when I decided to escape. There was a truck
going out of the farm gate with vegetables. I hid in the back of
it.'

'And then?'

'Then I went back to England on the next plane. I'd managed
to keep the ticket.'

'Back to your work in the Inland Revenue?'

'Of course.'

'Were you afraid at all?'

'Yes, I was. I knew I had found out things in Florida that the

Children of Sun wouldn't want to be known. I told myself that I was back in England, and that they'd have no way of finding me, but I often got the feeling that I was being watched when I left home. Once or twice I thought I was being followed, nothing definite you understand, just an uneasy feeling.'

'Yes, I understand. Mr Simpson, will you tell me your routine movements on Thursday evenings?'

'Well, I used to go to my evening class.'

'In advanced accountancy?'

'Yes. And on the way home I would buy my supper at the Delectable Drumstick in Notting Hill Gate and take the train on to Paddington.'

'Anyone who had been watching you over a long period would know that?'

'Yes, I suppose they would.'

'Did you think anyone was following you, or watching you, on that evening of Thursday March the 13th?'

'I had an uneasy feeling. Nothing definite. Not until the man spoke to me on the platform.'

'The man?'

'Mr . . . Canter.'

'Just tell the jury about that, will you, in your own words.'

He was out on his own; but I had no fear for him. The jury were listening attentively, and he told them, quietly and clearly, how that Sun Child, Rory Canter, tried to kill him, and how he fought with an unexpected passion for life, and how the knife was turned on his attacker.

When he had finished, I said, 'Mr Simpson. Why didn't you tell this story to the police when you were arrested?'

'I thought the power of the Master had changed the blood on the letter. I thought it was a miracle.'

'How do you feel, now you know it *wasn't* a miracle?'

'In a way, disappointed.'

'No miracle,' I told the jury in my final speech. 'Perhaps we are a little disappointed also, members of the jury, to discover that this is just another case about human violence and human greed. Or perhaps it is a case in which, after all, the Powers of Darkness had their terrible part to play.'

I was holding the knife, as a prop for the jury's attention, but I didn't need it. The old darlings were all listening intently as I went on. 'Mr Simpson discovered the secrets of a fraud practised upon the gullible and the lonely. Mr Simpson was to be killed, and a faithful servant of the Master, a young fanatic who had been trained in war, named Rory Canter, a man who'd just presented his own large property to this bogus Messiah, was to be the agent of death. What happened? Canter no doubt followed Simpson that night, and waited for him on the platform of the underground station. He accosted him and pulled the knife. He started the attack. You've heard from my client how those two men fought for this knife ... on which were the fingerprints of both of them. You've heard how my client's hands were wounded in the struggle and his clothes cut and, finally, forcing Canter's arm away from him, the point of the knife entered his attacker's body between the third and fourth rib. It was a desperate fight, members of the jury, because Canter was a man more dangerous than any thief or sexual molester; he was a man who believed he had God on his side ...'

The day the trial ended happened to coincide with the visit by Claude Erskine-Brown and young Tristan, attended by the large and glum Miss Reykjavik, to the Erskine-Brown grandparents for the few days' holiday Miss Trant's husband was taking from his never-increasing legal practice. According to plan, Ken Cracknell and Phillida shared their long delayed hamburger together in the All American Bun Fight in Covent Garden, and, although the minced meat was plentiful, the buns huge and the salad crisp, although they drank powerful vodka martinis and pursued them with bottles of icy Löwenbräu, and although Miss Trant held Ken's hand between mouthfuls and her eyes were full of promise, he remained inexplicably glum and apparently much cast-down by the result.

Determined to cheer the handsome radical barrister, Miss Trant returned with him, not without some misgivings, to the 'community' near King's Cross. This proved to be a comfortable and elegant Victorian house in a pleasant square behind the Gray's Inn Road, which young Cracknell shared with a group of friends whose 'communal living' didn't go beyond sharing the kitchen and occasional meetings to 'talk through' problems in the 'interface of domestic group relationships'. In this community Ken Cracknell was undoubtedly the leader: he it was who organized applications to the Rent Tribunal and composed the notices urging consideration for others in the communal loo.

Fortunately most of his cohabitees were out when Ken brought Miss Trant home. She passed the sitting-room door (half-open to emit the sounds of a middle-aged female voice reading some play she had written to an invisible audience) with some trepidation, and she didn't relax until they were in Ken's comfortable and brightly furnished bedroom. He had thoughtfully removed the bedspread and turned back the sheets before he went to Court that morning. She looked at the bed, smiled and kissed him. Then, as he drew the curtains and adjusted the lighting effects she took off her jacket, hung it neatly on the back of a chair and started to undo her shirt.

'Happy?' she asked Ken Cracknell. For an answer he returned to kiss her. '*Are* you happy, Ken?'

'Well ...' She was taking off her shirt and he was offering her, apparently, every assistance. 'Happy about you being here.'

'You should be happy about everything. You had a marvellous win!'

'Did I?' Ken Cracknell paused discontentedly in the act of disrobing Miss Trant.

'Of course Rumpole did it. But I'm sure you were a terrific help.'

'Rumpole!' Ken appeared unexpectedly angry and his fingers stopped working at the clips and buttons. Miss Trant looked up at him in surprise. 'Yes,' he muttered. 'Blast the man! Rumpole pulled it off.'

'What's wrong with that?' Miss Trant looked up at him puzzled.

At which Ken Cracknell burst out with thoughts which he had had to keep to himself for too long. 'What's wrong with it?

Don't you see? It means he'll never go. He'll be round my neck forever! Swamping the desk with his papers and dropping ash like a bloody volcano. That's not why I got him the job!'

'Why? Why did you get him the job, Ken?' She was moving away from him, looking at him with sudden suspicion.

'Well . . .' He seemed, as he looked at her, to have some doubt about answering, but she insisted.

'Why did you get Rumpole to lead you?'

'It . . . it seemed a hopeless case, anyway.' He was almost apologetic, and his apology gave her the answer.

'You wanted him to lose!' Now she was working hard, doing up all the clips and buttons that Ken had so eagerly, if awkwardly, unloosed. 'You thought he'd vanish back into the sunset if he lost another case. That's why you did it, isn't it? *You wanted him to lose!* So you could have him out of your room!'

'Philly . . .' Ken's protest was ineffective. She continued to button, with determination.

'Well, let me tell you something.' Her eyes were no longer soft, but shining with the power of her sudden eloquence. 'You're wrong. Wrong about Rumpole. He's the radical! You're not. You'll grow up to be a prosecutor, or a Circuit Judge! But Rumpole never will, because he says what he thinks, and because he doesn't give a damn what anybody thinks about him. And because he can win the cases you're afraid even to do on your own.'

'Philly! Don't talk to me like that. Don't I mean anything to you?' Ken Cracknell moved towards her, pleading.

She looked at him and said, almost with regret, 'Oh yes. You're a pretty face around Chambers. A little bit of fluff! A reasonably good spot of crumpet. But don't ever get the idea I'd risk a good husband, who knows how to cook, for *you*, Ken Cracknell!'

Christmas came with its usual alarming rapidity. The season of God's birth was celebrated by cards and bits of tinsel appearing in the screws' office in Brixton Prison, and Hilda Rumpole and Marigold Featherstone sang an elaborate version of 'Come All Ye Faithful' with the Bar Choral Society in the Temple Church, to which the faithful, in the shape of their husbands

Guthrie and Horace, dutifully came. I prepared for the occasion by buying what Hilda told me later was her fortieth bottle of lavender water, and she got me the usual gift-wrapped box of small cigars. She posted off innumerable articles of knitwear to Florida in time for Christmas, against the eventual birth of the next generation of Rumpoles. (In due course a boy arrived who was given the name Sam. I laid down a dozen bottles of Pommeroy's best claret for Sam on the top of the bookshelves in Froxbury Mansions. From what I hear the infant, although of tender years, is argumentative by nature and may make something of a career at the Bar.) I sent Nick my old copy of *The Oxford Book of English Verse* (the Sir Arthur Quiller-Couch edition) suitably inscribed. I know the poems I like best in it by heart, and doubt if I shall add many more to my repertoire.

A week or so before Christmas, cases of drink arrived at our Chambers. Dianne helped Henry put up tinsel and paper streamers in Guthrie Featherstone's room. They hung mistletoe from the central light and promptly kissed under it. On the night of our Chambers party, our members arrived with their wives and girl-friends. Henry's wife, a tall schoolmistress, came and put an end to his philandering under the mistletoe. Mr and Mrs Erskine-Brown came together and that small smiling Celt, Owen Glendour-Owen, came with a grey-haired wife who might have been his twin and was also smiling broadly. Uncle Tom brought his sister, who suffered hot flushes after a couple of glasses of sherry. My old friend Judge George Frobisher left his Court to come to our jollification, and Ken Cracknell arrived late by motorbike. The room was crowded when Guthrie Featherstone started to clear his throat, bang his glass against the desk and give every sign of a Head of Chambers who is about to make a ceremonial address.

'Quiet, everyone!' called out Henry, our self-appointed Master of Ceremonies.

'Pray silence' – I added my voice, after I had given myself a generous refill of Château Fleet Street – 'for our learned Head of Chambers.'

'Thank you, Horace.' Guthrie smiled graciously in my direction and then he was off. 'Christmas has put gifts in several of our stockings this year. Horace Rumpole had a very good win in an interesting murder down at the Old Bailey.'

'Did that surprise anybody?' I asked the world at large.

'It surprised Ken,' said Mrs Phillida Erskine-Brown, née Trant. Ken Cracknell glowered at her, whereupon she raised her glass to her husband Claude and said, 'Happy Christmas, darling.'

'And Owen Glendour-Owen,' Featherstone continued with our roll of honour or list of legal triumphs, 'has been appointed by the Lord Chancellor to the Circuit Bench. Our loss is mid-Wales's gain!'

'That's splendid news!' I raised my glass to the small Celtic couple. 'Absolutely splendid!'

I had done nothing but good to 'Knock-for-Knock' Owen, although I meant to take care to avoid Welsh Crown Courts in the future. When the cries of 'Splendid!', 'Yes, of course', 'Well done, Owen' and 'Good show, Judge' had died away, I quickly pointed out the full consequences of the joyful news. 'Which leaves an empty space in my old room,' I said, and looked hard at Featherstone. After all, he had made a private promise, and I wanted it publicly confirmed.

'Yes. Well, we'll consider that, of course. At a Chambers meeting.' It was typical of Featherstone to seek to put off the final, fatal decision. I wasn't letting him get away with it.

'We'll consider it now,' I insisted.

'I'm sure it's a matter you'll want to discuss with your family, Horace.' Featherstone tried to sound conciliatory. 'No one wants to force you back from your retirement, just because we happen to have a gap in Chambers. I'm sure Hilda has views.'

'Views?' No doubt Hilda had, she had about most things, but I didn't think she would feel called upon to speak at what was rapidly becoming a Chambers meeting. I was wrong.

'Yes, as a matter of fact I have,' she said, in a profound and doom-laden voice.

'Mrs Rumpole. Hilda. All in good time.' Featherstone clearly didn't want my wife's views to mar the festivities, but she over-ruled him.

'Since we got back from our holiday in the States . . .' Hilda began.

'Holiday? Did she say holiday?' Uncle Tom was puzzled. 'I thought they'd gone out to grass. For good.'

'With our son, who, as you may know, is now the youngest Professor of Applied Sociology in the history of his university.'

'Oh, I say. Awfully well done him!' Marigold Featherstone gave a half-hearted clap and Guthrie smiled tolerantly.

'Since Rumpole's been back in harness' – Hilda was now in full flow – 'he has, of course, had an enormous success in a most important murder trial, and I am quite convinced that his real love is Judge Bullingham.'

'Really, Hilda!' I didn't know what she'd come out with next, but she looked at me and appeared to be smiling. 'I'm joking, of course,' she said.

'Oh, yes of course.' I was glad to hear it.

'Frightfully funny!' said Marigold Featherstone, and brought her hands together again.

'Most amusing speaker, your wife.' Featherstone's smile was slightly less tolerant.

'And I'm more convinced than ever that my duty is here, at Rumpole's side,' Hilda went on. My heart sank, I must admit it.

'Are you sure?' I asked hopelessly, but it seemed she had come to a firm decision.

'So I shall stay in England,' she said, 'to look after Rumpole.' She Who Must Be Obeyed had spoken and she only had one sentence to add. 'And we are *so* glad to be back in this happy family of Chambers.'

I thought the smiles were a little forced, and Ken Cracknell wasn't smiling at all. Only Mrs Erskine-Brown, our Portia, raised her glass to me, and I thought I noticed a tremor of one eyelid, as though she were about to wink.

'How long will you be staying this time, Rumpole?' Uncle Tom asked, and as I felt an old legal anecdote coming over me, I gave him his answer.

'How long?' I said. 'Who knows how long? I well remember that terrible old Lord Chief when I was first at the Bar. He gave an 86-year-old man fifteen years for persistent theft. At Bodmin

Assizes. "But my Lord," the old man quavered, "I shall never *do* fifteen years." "Well then, my man," the Lord Chief encouraged him, "you must do as much of it as you can." '

I looked round the room at them all. There was a sudden, rather chill silence. And no one laughed.

'That's all I can say,' I told them. 'I shall do as much of it as I can. And a very happy Christmas to you all.'

READ MORE IN PENGUIN

In every corner of the world, on every subject under the sun, Penguin represents quality and variety – the very best in publishing today.

For complete information about books available from Penguin – including Puffins, Penguin Classics and Arkana – and how to order them, write to us at the appropriate address below. Please note that for copyright reasons the selection of books varies from country to country.

In the United Kingdom: Please write to *Dept. JC, Penguin Books Ltd, FREEPOST, West Drayton, Middlesex UB7 0BR*

If you have any difficulty in obtaining a title, please send your order with the correct money, plus ten per cent for postage and packaging, to *PO Box No. 11, West Drayton, Middlesex UB7 0BR*

In the United States: Please write to *Penguin USA Inc., 375 Hudson Street, New York, NY 10014*

In Canada: Please write to *Penguin Books Canada Ltd, 10 Alcorn Avenue, Suite 300, Toronto, Ontario M4V 3B2*

In Australia: Please write to *Penguin Books Australia Ltd, 487 Maroondah Highway, Ringwood, Victoria 3134*

In New Zealand: Please write to *Penguin Books (NZ) Ltd,182–190 Wairau Road, Private Bag, Takapuna, Auckland 9*

In India: Please write to *Penguin Books India Pvt Ltd, 706 Eros Apartments, 56 Nehru Place, New Delhi 110 019*

In the Netherlands: Please write to *Penguin Books Netherlands B.V., Keizersgracht 231 NL–1016 DV Amsterdam*

In Germany: Please write to *Penguin Books Deutschland GmbH, Friedrichstrasse 10–12, W–6000 Frankfurt/Main 1*

In Spain: Please write to *Penguin Books S. A., C. San Bernardo 117–6° E–28015 Madrid*

In Italy: Please write to *Penguin Italia s.r.l., Via Felice Casati 20, I–20124 Milano*

In France: Please write to *Penguin France S. A., 17 rue Lejeune, F–31000 Toulouse*

In Japan: Please write to *Penguin Books Japan, Ishikiribashi Building, 2–5–4, Suido, Tokyo 112*

In Greece: Please write to *Penguin Hellas Ltd, Dimocritou 3, GR–106 71 Athens*

In South Africa: Please write to *Longman Penguin Southern Africa (Pty) Ltd, Private Bag X08, Bertsham 2013*

BY THE SAME AUTHOR

Dunster

Outrageously outspoken and wildly unpredictable, Dick Dunster is the hero – or villain – in a drama of his own making.

'Masterly ... Part thriller, part observer of current mores, realistic yet full of ambiguities, *Dunster* raises every kind of question, moral and psychological, while spinning along at a cracking pace' – *Financial Times*

The Rapstone Chronicles

Two glorious comic novels featuring Leslie Titmuss, *Paradise Postponed* and *Titmuss Regained*, are combined in *The Rapstone Chronicles*, which charts the rise and rise of the odious arch-Tory from his days as an unpopular schoolboy to his success as the pragmatic and self-seeking Secretary of State.

also published:

The Narrowing Stream

'Energy, wit and sheer professionalism' – *Guardian*

Summer's Lease

'Amusing, entertaining ... the writing is smooth, the dialogue splendid and it's a cracking good read' – *Sunday Express*

Charade

'Wonderful comedy ... an almost Firbankian melancholy ... John Mortimer's hero is helplessly English' – *Punch*

and:

Like Men Betrayed

BY THE SAME AUTHOR

THE RUMPOLE BOOKS

The complete Horace Rumpole – irreverent, iconoclastic and as claret-swilling, judge-debunking, impudent, witty and cynical as ever.

'One of the great comic creations of all modern times' – *Evening Standard*

The Second Rumpole Omnibus

Contains *Rumpole for the Defence, Rumpole and the Golden Thread* and *Rumpole's Last Case*.

and:

Rumpole and the Age of Miracles
Rumpole à la Carte
Rumpole on Trial
The Best of Rumpole

PLAYS

A Voyage Round My Father and Other Plays

INTERVIEWS

In Character
Character Parts

AUTOBIOGRAPHY

Clinging to the Wreckage